PINK BEAM:
A Philip K. Dick
Companion

by

Lord RC

ISBN 978-1-4303-2437-9
FIRST EDITION

ACKNOWLEDGMENTS

I could not have written this book without the help of many people and organizations. My thanks equally to the following:

Patrick Clark (*PKD Otaku*), David Keller, Scott Pohlenz, Perry Kinman, Andy Watson and Paul Williams (*The Philip K. Dick Society Newsletter*), Greg Lee (*Radio Free PKD*), Lawrence Sutin, Gregg Rickman, John Fairchild, Orjan Gerhardsson, Simon Russell, Geoff Notkin, Bernie Kling, Barb Mourning-child (*For Dickheads Only*), The Rev. Dr. X *(Ganymedean Slime Mold* Prods), Markus Schurr, Dan Sutherland, Jim Thain, J.R.McHone, Ken Vogel, Pat Decker, Steve Sneyd, Jurgenn Thoman, Linda Pattyn, Rick Calhoun, Gerald Gibson, Benedict Cullum, Jim Steel, Robert Lichtman, Eric Johnson, Dan Bailey, Andy Sawyer, Guy Lillian III, Jim Munroe, Chris Drumm, D.J. Pass, Gordon Benson Jr., Phil Stephenson-Payne, Daniel J. H. Levack, Tony Pfarrer, D. Tibet, Ernest Mann, Sam Umland, Mark Ivins, Allan Kausch, John Boonstra, D.S. Apel, G.W. Thomas, Karen Stern, Kyss Jean-Mary, John Meluch, Joel Margot (Adder's Choice), Mark V. Ziesing, Maestro Takatak, Paul Riddell, John Joyce, Lisa Gemino, E.R. Stewart, Adam Gorightly, F.C. Bertrand, Yael Dragwyla, Ken Lopez, Allen Greenfield, Gretchen Haupert, Stuart Nelson (*King Crab*), E.R. Stewart, Steve Brown (*SF Eye*), Etienne Barillier, Jeff L. Young, Jason Koornick (*Philipkdick.com*) and many more whose names are lost somewhere in my 'files.'

Of course none of these people are responsible for any of the errors in the book. I must take credit for these myself.

This book is dedicated, first of all, to the memory of Philip K. Dick (1928-1982) and further to PKD's fans the world over and lastly to Patti Anderson, my own dark-haired girl.

-- Lord RC

2006

In memory of my brother, Peter Hyde (1949-2006)

CONTENTS

PINK BEAM: A Philip K. Dick Companion

Introduction

This study has two primary audiences: fans and scholars of Philip K. Dick's work who are already familiar with most of his novels and stories, and newcomers who'd like a guide to his opus.

For the first, I have made a survey of most of the principal books, interviews and articles about PKD, as he is known, and have selected and collated these notes into a chronological account by which the fan and student may come to know more about the history of Dick's stories; how he came to write them, when he wrote them and how they came to be published. This present work, then, serves as a basis for further study.

For the general reader who has had his curiosity aroused, perhaps after seeing some of the movies based on Dick's stories, this book may act as a guide to his work. For each of the over 120 short stories and 50 novels that he wrote I have provided, in addition to historical material, a short plot summary and a rating between one and five stars. This is just for fun, of course, as many people will disagree with my ratings.

This book is not intended to be a biography but, rather, a literary chronology. Readers interested in finding out more about the actual life as distinct from the literary record of Philip K. Dick, should read the two biographies written by Gregg Rickman and Lawrence Sutin.[i]

Instead of biography I intend to concentrate on the known details and circumstances that pertain as strictly as possible to the actual stories themselves and their generation, leaving out as much as possible the details of the Philip K. Dick's daily life except where they are relevant to the work at hand. I will also limit any discussion of thematics; many books and essays have already been written which do this very well. However, this restriction in scope, while helpful in curtailing this study has attendant problems: many of PKD's short-stories and even novels have been little commented on by the author or, indeed, by anyone and we are left with only the stories themselves and the bare bones of their publishing history. When that is the case then that is what I present.

A problem of chronology also arises. Before May 1952 Philip K. Dick wrote several short stories that he attempted with some success to market himself without the help of a literary agent. Of these early stories we cannot be certain when exactly they were written or in what order. There have been several published chronologies already, including those in the biographies of Rickman and Sutin already mentioned. But perhaps the definitive one to this time is that by Paul Williams, PKD's friend and the executor of his estate, in his brief study *ONLY APPARENTLY REAL*[ii]. This is the chronology presented in THE COLLECTED STORIES OF PHILIP K. DICK (1987), the indispensable five-volume collection of PKD's short stories.[iii] In this present work, although I have relied heavily on these, I have found it necessary to modify this chronology in some respects, particularly in this first half of 1952. After July 1952, though, it becomes easier to date the stories with more accuracy as that was when PKD secured the services of the Scott Meredith Literary Agency in New York City.[iv] The records of the SMLA show the dates of reception by the Agency of all the short stories PKD wrote from July 1952 to 1980. This is most of them.[v]

Sometimes three or four stories reached the SMLA on the same day in which case I've numbered them in order of publication. Now the order of publication can help us in another way to further narrow down the period when a particular story was written. Back in the 1950s magazine editors typically required a three to six month time lag between reception of a manuscript and final publication in the magazine. So an early short story like "The Gun" which was first published in *Planet Stories* in Sep 1952 can be said to have been written two to four months earlier, around Jun 1952. With most of the later stories, though, we can ascribe their writing to a week or even a few days before the manuscripts arrived at the SMLA.

Besides a literary history and chronological guide I've also tried to make this study of interest to collectors of Philip K. Dick book editions and magazine and anthology appearances. As a collector of twenty years experience myself, I have on occasion hilighted certain editions as being either scarce or common and indicated a reasonable value. Of course, value is a relative thing. Before the advent of the Internet many editions were very hard to find, one searched one's neighborhood and dealt with booksellers as best one could and it was a happy day indeed when one might find a slightly battered Science Fiction Book Club edition of, say, THE THREE STIGMATA OF PALMER ELDRITCH from 1965 or the first edition Ace paperback of EYE IN THE SKY from 1957. Nowadays things are much easier; with an internet connection and a credit card and not much sense one can find just about any book on the internet and purchase it for one's own. I say 'not much sense' because I've done this to my wallet's detriment and caution the reader that its those shipping charges that will get you!

But why did I title this manuscript *PINK BEAM: A Philip K. Dick Reference*? What has any pink beam to do with anything? To explain will require a brief biographical digression:

Philip K. Dick was born in Chicago on Dec 16, 1928, one of a pair of twins. Unfortunately his twin sister, Jane, died shortly after birth and the Dick family moved to Colorado, and then to California.

As he grew up in Berkeley, the young Philip K. Dick became interested in science fiction and fantasy and turned his hand to the writing of it. Shortly we will look at this early period. He actually began writing seriously in about 1950 or 1951 and he made his first professional sale in late 1951. By 1954 PKD was a prolific writer of short fantasy and science fiction stories, appearing in most of the science fiction magazines of the day. In 1954 he wrote his first science fiction novel: SOLAR LOTTERY. Derivative of A.E. Van Vogt's work, this novel stands up well today. In the following years his short story output dropped dramatically and he wrote more novels, both science fiction and mainstream. In 1961 he wrote his Hugo Award-winning novel THE MAN IN THE HIGH CASTLE.

THE MAN IN THE HIGH CASTLE was a turning point in PKD's career. His real ambition was to be a writer of mainstream realist fiction but of all the early mainstream novels he wrote only one was ever published in his lifetime: CONFESSIONS OF A CRAP ARTIST (1975). Discouraged by this he almost gave up writing altogether in 1961. He only started writing THE MAN IN THE HIGH CASTLE because he had nothing else to do at the time except help his then wife work in her jewelry-making business. But with the Hugo Award for Best Novel of 1962 given by the science fiction fans Dick decided to continue writing but in a new way that tried to meld his mainstream aspirations with science fiction and fantasy. But his next novel, WE CAN BUILD YOU, despite mainstream marketing efforts by the SMLA, was seen as only a mediocre science fiction novel. His frustration continued and he was practically forced to write more science fiction novels; nine of them by the end of 1964.

But in 1963 while he was trudging to his little writing shack, PKD saw a vision in the sky that frightened him. A vision of a metallic, slot-eyed face. A visage of perfect evil. This vision lasted through the Summer and became the basis of his most disturbing science fiction novel: THE THREE STIGMATA OF PALMER ELDRITCH which he wrote in 1964. This vision of evil PKD described as 'seeing God backward.'

It would be another ten years before PKD saw God frontward. In early March 1974, after surgery on an impacted wisdom tooth, PKD called the pharmacy for some pain medication to be delivered. When the girl came to the door a flash of pink light reflected from her necklace and into his brain. He asked the girl about the necklace; she explained that it was one of those fish-sign symbols worn by Christians. Immediately PKD experienced what he called 'anamnesis' or 'loss-of-forgetfulness' and he knew himself to be a secret Christian and living back in the apostolic times of the Roman Empire. Ordinary or consensual reality Dick came to see as a false accretion overlaying the true reality of Christian times.

This vision turned into a series of visions that lasted on into 1975 and had a great affect on Philip K. Dick. In trying to explain it to himself he wrote in his journal night after night until his death in 1982. This journal is known as the *EXEGESIS* and runs to a million words of speculation and formed the basis of his last novel, VALIS, in 1978. We will look more closely at all this as we progress through our chronology.

That Dick had the courage to describe these events to all and sundry and even to write about them in fictional form is to be commended, although it has also been condemned. Many of his friends, fellow writers and fans thought Dick had gone crazy, gone over the edge from years of drug abuse and psychological problems. But to refute this perception one has only to point to the novel VALIS which, as we shall see, is a masterpiece that shakes up the field of literature and its conventions.

The visionary experiences of 1974, then, were central to Dick's life. But it is one of the aims of this present study to try and put them into a literary context so we can better understand the work of Philip K. Dick. Hence the 'pink beam' in my title.

But now, to the study!

Early Work

Philip K. Dick began writing as early as 1940 when he was 12 years old and had taught himself to type. Two poems from this time remain, "The Song" and "He's Dead." He also wrote short stories, poems and essays between January 1942 and the Fall of that year. These were published in the *Young Author's Club* column in the *Berkeley Daily Gazette*. His first story to appear in this column (edited by one Aunt Flo or Florita Cook) was "Le Diable" in the Jan 23, 1942 edition of the newspaper. Altogether, he had seven stories published in *The Berkeley Gazette* before he was sent to boarding school in Ojai, California, north of Los Angeles in the fall of 1942.[vi]

He returned to Berkeley in Oct 1943 and promptly had two more stories printed in Aunt Flo's *Young Author's Column*.

In the intervening year he had begun to write his first novel, RETURN TO LILLIPUT, now lost. This novel was not completed – if it ever was – until after PKD returned to Berkeley. In a letter to Philip K. Dick published in her column on Oct 23, 1943, Aunt Flo writes:

{...} 70 type-written pages must have run around 18,000 words – in other words, it's well along the way to becoming a book instead of a story.[vii]

In an interview with Mike Hodel in 1976 PKD says about RETURN TO LILLIPUT:

{...} It was really a bomb. It was terrible. It was the worst novel. I'll sell it some day. I'll find a market for it. It had - it was really neat. They rediscovered Lilliput in the modern world. Like rediscovering Atlantis. These guys report they've discovered Lilliput. But it's only accessible by submarine because it's sunk under the water. You'd think a fourteen year old kid would have a more original idea than that. And I can even tell you the numbers on the submarines. I had, A-101, B-202, C-303 were the numbers and designations of the submarines.

Mike: Makes it a finite number of submarines, then.

Phil: Yeah, well, I realized that when I got halfway through. I wasn't thinking ahead. [viii]

While in Ojai, Dick published with the help of young friends a mimeographed sheet called *The Truth*. According to biographer Gregg Rickman "it survives today in two copies, dated August 30 and October 26, 1943."[ix] *The Truth* sold for 2 cents and the first issue featured the first and only surviving part of a serial called "Stratosphere Betsy."

On his return to Berkeley, PKD again sent stories and poems to *The Berkeley Gazette*. Rickman sees in some of these stories "a substantial advance in quality and substance over what he'd written for her {Aunt Flo} in 1942."[x] As a 'Junior' in Aunt Flo's Young Author's Club, PKD was not allowed to use a pen-name. But after he graduated to 'Senior' status with a story titled "Magician's Box" printed in *The Berkeley Gazette* on Feb 7, 1944, he used the pen-name Mark Van Dyke for his next submission.

It is Rickman's contention that Philip K. Dick also used another pseudonym, that of "Teddy" for many poetic submissions to the Young Author's Club, starting in Jan 1944 and continuing until "Teddy" stopped writing for *The Berkeley Gazette* in July 1945. Altogether there are 17 of these items in Rickman's chronology.

For evidence of this contention, Rickman displays the following points:

"The primary evidence is the work itself. In none of his official contributions, either the material signed "Philip Dick" or in the two stories signed "Mark Van Dyke," do we find anything like this lyrical, quasi-religious nature poem by "Teddy," "Benediction" (July 1944):

> Soft and clear on the still evening air
> Floats from the valley the calm vesper chime
> Soothing the soul as it rests from day's care
> Instilling a peace full of comfort sublime.

Or like November 1944's "Companions":

> I met Him on the mountain top
> And newly confident,
> Together walking side by side
> We faced the steep descent.

Or a number of other contributions by Teddy, the bulk of which are of this inspirational nature.[xi]

In support Rickman also offers that PKD had an imaginary friend as a boy named Teddy; his father's nick-name was Ted; several of his characters are named Ted, and the fact that Philip Dick had wished to use a pseudonym for his Aunt Flo submissions. Add to this fifth wife Tessa's memory of things Phil had said and we have pretty much the whole case.

However, Dick's other biographer, Lawrence Sutin, is not convinced and casts doubt on this contention on these grounds:

(1). PKD consistently described his childhood and adolescence as lacking in Christian (or other religious) convictions {...}

(2). PKD tried to start a Bible Club in junior high school – he was not afraid to show an interest in religious matters, though his friends saw him as an agnostic, not a believer,

(3). Why, in the privacy of his own notebook, did he not paste in the "Teddy" contributions as well?

(4). In the *EXEGESIS*, PKD sometimes looked back on his life in hopes of finding spiritual events precursing (and thus somehow confirming) those of 2-3-74. {...} Why would he have omitted mention of the devout "Teddy" poems?

(5). Finally, the "Teddy" poems don't read like PKD to me.[xii]

We'll let the biographers battle this out; without a close study of PKD's notebooks, the poems and ancillary material I can form no opinion. But I can present another possible item in Sutin's support. In *DIVINE INVASIONS: A Life Of Philip K. Dick*, written by Sutin himself, he, like Rickman in *TO THE HIGH CASTLE*, covers the period when PKD was in school and writing for the Young Author's Club. Dick, it seems, had problems with Aunt Flo's "editorial predilections":

When Aunt Flo termed the piece {"Program Notes On A Great Composer"} a not "strictly creative" factual essay, Phil fumed in his notebook:

"Fooled her completely on this one – knew I would, she doesn't know a satire from a hole in the ground. {...}

last contribution, I think. Have gotten to the point where she doesn't understand my pieces. No point in sending in any more.

Don't think she ever did!"[xiii]

So, perhaps PKD has the last word on this and he never did send in any more stories to Aunt Flo, thus negating the 'Teddy' poems after this time and therefore negating Rickman's whole contention.

The last definite story, then, that can be ascribed to the school boy Phil Dick is "Program Notes on a Great Composer," published on Sep 13, 1944. After that it was only the "Teddy" poems that were printed in the *Gazette*. Eleven of them to July 2, 1945. [xiv]

Between 1945 and 1951 not a lot is known of PKD's literary efforts. One short story, "Stability", has been dated to 1947 when Philip K. Dick was still in high school.[xv] This story, though one of the first written, was one of the last published, appearing first in THE COLLECTED STORIES OF PHILIP K. DICK in 1987. "Stability" is an awkward tale that tries to meld three themes into one: the affect of new ideas on a stagnant society, time-travel and fantasy. It succeeds to a degree but not wholly. "Stability" rates ✳ ✳

In 1948 or 1949, according to PKD's biographers, the young master also began to write a novel titled THE EARTHSHAKER. This now exists as some opening chapters and a detailed outline.[xvi]

Ambitious in scope, THE EARTHSHAKER likely proved too large a task to complete for the young PKD.[xvii]

The curious short story "Of Withered Apples" now comes along. Perhaps it doesn't belong here but Kleo, Phil's wife in 1950, recalls reading some of his stories after they were married:

"Philip was writing wonderful little fantasy stories..." tales of "sad little people," two of which were eventually published, "Of Withered Apples" and "Friday Morning" ("Roog").[xviii]

On the strength of Kleo's memory I have placed "Of Withered Apples" here in the chronology and dated it to circa 1950. Kleo married Phil on Jun 14 1950.[xix]

Obviously, PKD either never sent the story to a publisher or it was rejected if he did because he brushed up the manuscript and sent it of to the Scott Meredith Literary Agency (SMLA) in Jan 1953. It was published eventually in *Cosmos #4* in July 1954, it's only appearance until THE COLLECTED STORIES in 1987.

The story itself is fantasy. A girl is summoned to a distant field by an old and near-dead apple tree. She eats a dried up apple and then dies. But, later, from her grave an apple tree grows, bearing fruit a bit too early.

"Of Withered Apples" rates also ✳ ✳

1951

GATHER YOURSELVES TOGETHER

Another novel, GATHER YOURSELVES TOGETHER was written in this period, likely in 1951. There is some doubt about whether GATHER YOURSELVES TOGETHER was written before VOICES FROM THE STREET. In discussing the book with Kleo, Rickman determines that GATHER YOURSELVES TOGETHER was the first of these to be written. The strong point of Rickman's ascription is that VOICES FROM THE STREET was "set right at that time, {June 1952} and is dedicated to 'S.M.'" {Scott Meredith, PKD's agent}, thus promoting GATHER YOURSELVES TOGETHER to an earlier time.[xx]

Once PKD had signed on with the SMLA in May 1952, he sent them some of his old manuscripts, that for GATHER YOURSELVES TOGETHER was one of them. The Agency did circulate this manuscript in the early 1950s. In a letter from Scott Meredith to PKD dated Jan 17, 1954, Meredith writes that Crown Books – a major mainstream publisher – had not yet reached a decision on publishing GATHER YOURSELVES TOGETHER. However, GATHER was still in circulation in early 1958.[xxi]

This novel was never published until 1994 when Andy Watson of WCS Press published a fine edition. [xxii]

Here Watson describes the novel as

a steamy, claustrophobic tale of two men and a woman isolated by circumstance, and alienated from each other by their pasts. Set in 1949 amongst the evacuation of American businesses from mainland China, middle-age Verne Tilden and half-his-age Barbara Mahler are forced to put aside the lingering resentments and frustrations of a previous, stateside love affair in order to do the job they've been assigned, preparing a factory compound for transfer to the approaching communists. Carl Fitter is the unsuspecting young man who finds himself unknowingly embroiled in their tensions, and around whose sexual awakening with Barbara the novel is structured. Never before published, this is a competent early novel that reveals Philip K. Dick's obvious talent and skill in a manner quite unlike any other book he was ever to produce.[xxiii]

GATHER YOURSELVES TOGETHER rates only ✯✯.

At least one short story was written in 1951, "Roog." PKD wrote the story for a writer's workshop held by Anthony Boucher in his Berkeley, California home in 1951. A series of letters from PKD to Anthony Boucher and Francis J. McComas, editors at *The Magazine Of Fantasy and Science Fiction (F & SF)*, starting in Oct 1951 refer to "Roog."

First, in a letter to McComas, PKD thanks him for his comments and says:

... I went over the story and cut down 19 pages to 9. I think it shines now instead of merely glowing faintly.
And I believe I got the objections out of it, too.
I hope it does. If not, I'm ready to get out the typewriter again.[xxiv]

Evidently this shortened version did do as only a week later we find PKD thanking both editors at *F & SF*:

I'm glad that "Roog" pleased you. Certainly the new title is alright. That's a lot of money for one story. I really feel a little embarrassed...[xxv]
Writing is a major event for me, and I am beginning to find ways of arranging my life around it, rather than squeezing in a few hours after work or on Sunday. Oddly, most of my writing tends to be fantasy of a religious, drifting nature, ill-suited for worldly things or large publications. All I can say to defend it is that people who read it are disturbed, and go off brooding, very puzzled and unhappy.
"Roog", as you slyly guessed, is my first acceptance.[xxvi]

"Roog" was accepted at *F & SF* on Nov 15, 1951. So, then, by November 1951 PKD was a professional science fiction writer, although "Roog" didn't appear in *F & SF* until the Feb 1953 issue. For a living at the time Philip K. Dick was managing a record store part time but he didn't refer to himself as a clerk; when asked what he did he always said

"I'm a writer." This was in Berkeley, in 1951. Everybody was a writer. No one had ever sold anything. In fact most of the people I knew believed it to be crass and undignified to submit a story to a magazine; you wrote it, read it aloud to your friends, and finally it was forgotten. That was Berkeley in those days.

Another problem for me in getting everyone to be awed was that my story was not a literary story in a little magazine, but an sf story. Sf was not read by people in Berkeley in those days (except for a small group of fans who were very strange; they looked like animated vegetables). "But what about your *serious* writing?" People said to me. I was under the impression that *Roog* was quite a serious story. It tells of fear; it tells of loyalty; it tells of obscure menace and a good creature who cannot convey knowledge of that menace to those he loves. What could be more serious a theme than this? What people really meant by "serious" was "important." Sf was, by definition, not important. I cringed over the weeks following my sale of *Roog* as I realised the serious Codes of Behaviour I had broken by selling my story, and an sf story at that.

{...}

The fact that *Roog* sold was due to Tony Boucher outlining to me how the original version should be changed. Without his help I'd still be in the record business. I mean that very seriously. At that time Tony ran a little writing class, working out of the living room in his home in Berkeley. He'd read our stories aloud and we'd see -- not just that they were awful -- but how they could be cured. {...} Tony Boucher is gone. But I am still a writer because of him. Whenever I sit down to start a novel or a story a bit of the memory of that man returns to me. I guess he taught me to write out of love, not out of ambition. It's a good lesson for all activities in this world. [xxvii]

Dick goes on to narrate how the dog in "Roog" is based on an actual dog named 'Snooper' whose job was to make sure nobody stole the food from his owner's garbage can, much like in the story itself.

But, although Tony Boucher and Dick were enamoured of the story such was not the case with everyone:

This notion about each creature viewing the world differently from all other creatures -- not everyone would agree with me. Tony Boucher was very anxious to have a particular major anthologer (whom we will call J.M.) read *Roog* to see if she might use it. Her reaction astounded me. "Garbagemen do not look like that," she wrote me, "They do not have pencil-thin necks and heads that wobble. They do not eat people." I think she listed something like twelve errors in the story all having to do with how I represented the garbagemen. I wrote back, explaining that, yes, she was right, but to a dog -- well, all right, the dog was wrong. Admittedly. The dog was a little crazy on the subject. We're not just dealing with a dog and a dog's view of garbagemen, but a crazy dog -- who has been driven crazy by these weekly raids on the garbage can. The dog has reached a point of desperation. I wanted to convey that. In fact that was the whole point of the story; the dog had run out of options and was demented by this weekly event. And the Roogs knew it. They enjoyed it. They taunted the dog. They pandered to his lunacy.

Ms. J.M. rejected the story from her anthology, but Tony printed it, and it's still in print; in fact it's in a high-school text book, now. I spoke to a high-school class who had been assigned the story, and all of the kids understood it. Interestingly, it was a blind student who seemed to grasp the story best. He knew from the beginning what the word *Roog* meant. He felt the dog's despair, the dog's frustrated fury and the bitter sense of defeat over and over again. Maybe somewhere between 1951 and 1971 we all grew up to dangers and transformations of the ordinary which we had never recognized before, I don't know. But anyhow, *Roog*, my first sale, is biographical; I watched the dog suffer, and I understood a little (not much, maybe, but a little) of what was destroying him, and I wanted to speak for him. That's the whole of it right there. Snooper couldn't talk. I could. In fact I could write it down, and someone could publish it and many people could read it. Writing fiction has to do with this: becoming the voice for those without voices, if you see what I mean. It's not your own voice, you the author; it is all those other voices which normally go unheard.

The dog Snooper is dead, but the dog in the story, Boris, is alive. Tony Boucher is dead, and one day I will be, and, alas, so will you. But when I was with that high-school class and we were discussing *Roog*, in 1971, exactly twenty years after I sold the story originally -- Snooper's barking and his anguish, his noble efforts, were still alive, which he deserved. My story is my gift to an animal, to a creature who neither sees nor hears, now, who no longer barks. But goddamn it, he was doing the right thing. Even if Ms. J.M. didn't understand. [xxviii]

PKD further expounds on this argument with Judith Merrill in an interview with Dick Lupoff:

I remember that Judith Merrill saw the story and refused to anthologize it because she said that garbage men don't have thin necks, and wobbly heads, and so on. It's not true. So I wrote her a long letter explaining to her that that's the way the dog saw it and she would have to accept the dog's viewpoint. But she still wouldn't accept the story for anthologizing because she said it just wasn't true. Garbage men aren't that way.

So I said to her, "It's a fantasy, Judy. A fantasy. Do you understand what is meant by a fantasy?" But she said, "No, a fantasy is a story with a fantasy premise, and then it's realistic from then on."

So I said that in this story the fantasy premise is that the dog has a different point of view from us and that everything is predicated on that. But I couldn't convince her. The story is still in print. Bob Silverberg reprinted it recently in one of his collections, *Science Fiction Bestiary*, so it's still in print. [xxix]

"Roog" rates ✳ ✳ ✳ ✳

Although the sale of "Roog" was a high-point in PKD's early career, it had not been easy for him. Gregg Rickman refers to some friends of PKD who remember his "remarkable collection of rejection slips," and to Dick's second wife, Kleo, who recalls

"There were fifteen or twenty (short stories) out before we sold one. {...} One morning we went out, and seventeen of his manuscripts had been returned in one day. They were spilling out all over the front porch. I think it was one of the worst days of our lives, but we just went in and addressed new envelopes, and sent them out again."[xxx]

What these seventeen or so short stories are we can only partially ascertain. Most likely included in this pile of rejection slips were the manuscripts for most of the pre-SMLA stories like "The Gun," "The Skull" and "Mr. Spaceship;" perhaps most of the stories that were not published in *F & SF*. Sutin thinks that most of these early stories have been lost.[xxxi]

"Roog" may have been Philip K. Dick's first short story sale but it wasn't the first of his stories published, that honor goes to "Beyond Lies The Wub" which appeared in *Planet Stories* in July 1952 and is our next story in this chronology.

"Beyond Lies The Wub" was written no later than Dec 1951 and was published in, as PKD himself called it, "the most lurid of all pulp magazines on the stands at the time, *Planet Stories.*"[xxxii]

The evidence for placing "Beyond Lies The Wub" in late 1951 is found in PKD's 1968 'Self Portrait.'

I began to mail off stories to other sf magazines, and lo and behold, *Planet Stories* bought a short story of mine. In a blaze of Faust-like fire I abruptly quit my job at the record shop, forgot my career in records, and began to write all the time (how I did it I don't yet know; I worked until four each morning). Within the month after quitting my job I made a sale to *Astounding* (now called *Analog*) and *Galaxy*. They paid very well, and I knew then that I would never give up trying to build my life around a science fiction career. [xxxiii]

This informative passage dates the time it refers to as Jan 1952 (PKD having quit his job at the record store in December 1951). The sale to *Planet Stories* would be "Beyond Lies The Wub", placing the writing of this story perhaps as early as November 1951.

The story itself, the tale of a piggish Captain Franco (named after the Spanish dictator) who gets his just desserts at the hands of the gentle Wub, was one of PKD's first efforts at defining what is human:

"The idea I wanted to get down on paper had to do with the definition of "human." The dramatic way I trapped the idea was to present ourselves, the literal humans, and then an alien lifeform that exhibits the deeper traits that I associate with humanity: not a biped with an enlarged cortex -- a forked radish that thinks, to paraphrase the old saying -- but an organism that is human in terms of its soul.
{... ...}
I liked the blurbs that *Planet Stories* printed for "Beyond Lies The Wub." On the title page of the magazine they wrote:
Many men talk like philosophers and live like fools, proclaimed the slovenly wub, after death.
And ahead of the story proper they wrote: *The slovenly wub might well have said: Many men talk like philosophers and live like fools.*
Reader reaction to the story was excellent, and Jack O'Sullivan, editor of *Planet*, wrote to tell me that in his opinion it was a very fine little story -- whereupon he paid me something like fifteen dollars. It was my introduction to pulp payment rates.[xxxiv]

PKD was perhaps not too surprised at the reaction "Beyond Lies The Wub" got from his peers in Berkeley:

As I carried four copies into the record store where I worked, a customer gazed at me and them, with dismay, and said, "Phil, you read *that* kind of stuff?" I had to admit I not only read it, I wrote it.[xxxv]

Over the years this story has proven to be a popular one, appearing in two of Dick's major collections, THE PRESERVING MACHINE and Other Stories (1969) and THE BEST OF PHILIP K. DICK (1977) as well as giving its name to the title of the first volume of THE COLLECTED STORIES OF PHILIP K. DICK (1987).

Beyond Lies The Wub" rates ✻ ✻ ✻ ✻ ✻

After "Beyond Lies The Wub" we enter into 1952 proper.

1952

Next in the chronology is "The Little Movement." Records at *F & SF* state that this story was accepted at the magazine on Feb 15, 1952. But although accepted earlier, Dick was still working on the story on March 5, 1952 and still at it by March 19, 1952 when he wrote again to the editors at *F & SF*:

"The Little Movement" -- a brand new pretty typed-up version with a few minor changes only, all for the good, I think. It's much smoother.
{...}
(If "Little Movement" comes back with a rejection slip, I'll have a stroke)[xxxvi]

Philip K. Dick was proud of this short story and in 1958, six years after the initial correspondence between Dick and Boucher, "The Little Movement" figured again. Boucher was looking for a short story for an anthology he was working on and Dick suggested "The Little Movement (along with "Foster, You're Dead!" and "Beyond Lies The Wub"):"

What about some of those short fantasies that you printed of mine? Or is this a strictly s-f collection? If I live to be 100 I'll never write anything as good as those, again. Especially LITTLE MOVEMENT. When I read that, I marvel that I could have written it. Ah, the inspiration of youth ...[xxxvii]

Boucher took no heed of PKD's suggestions selecting instead "The Father-Thing" for his anthology, *A TREASURY OF GREAT SCIENCE FICTION, Vol. 1*, Doubleday, 1959.

"The Little Movement" was published in *F & SF* in the Nov 1952 issue and was selected for PKD's first major collection, A HANDFUL OF DARKNESS published in Great Britain by Rich & Cowan in 1955. Since then it has appeared in a couple of anthologies.[xxxviii]

In this story tiny aliens in the shape of toy soldiers infiltrate a family household with plans to take over the world. Unfortunately for them, though, the toys that are already there don't take kindly to aliens and Teddo the teddy bear leads the fight to oust them.

"The Little Movement" rates ✻ ✻ ✻ ✻

It is hard to set specific dates for many of PKD's early short stories; we have acceptance dates of those published in *F & SF* but not for stories published in the other sf magazines of the time. So, on meager evidence we place "The Skull" at this point in our chronology.

Although "The Skull" was published first in *Worlds Of If* in the Sep 1952 issue, it was accepted as early as Mar 5, 1952. [xxxix]

After its initial appearance in *If* the story never reappeared until THE COLLECTED STORIES in 1987.

"The Skull" concerns a future society threatened by a religious cult. The government sends a man back in time to kill the religion's founder. Unfortunately, this very act brings about the problem it is designed to solve. A time-travel paradox that cannot be resolved.

"The Skull" rates ✳ ✳

The next story PKD wrote was likely "Project: Earth" – although there is uncertainty about this as "Project: Earth" may have been in PKD's rejection pile in 1951. The evidence for "Project: Earth's" status is slim. Paul Williams, Editor of *The Philip K. Dick Society Newsletter (PKDS)* and executor of PKD's estate notes that Underwood-Miller editor, Don Herron, has acquired:

> a sheaf of previously unknown PKD letters written to J. Francis McComas and Anthony Boucher between 1951 and 1967. {...} As for the newly discovered letters: the first batch is from '51 – '53 and primarily focuses on the submitting and rewriting of short stories.
>
> {...} we learn that "Project: Earth" was submitted to *F & SF* in March of 1952 (and presumably rejected).[xl]

However, in PKD's "Self Portrait" of 1968, quoted above, he writes:

> Within the month after quitting my job I made a sale to *Astounding* (now called *Analog*) and *Galaxy*. They paid very well, and I knew then that I would never give up trying to build my life around a science fiction career.[xli]

There is a bit of a problem with this statement, though. To ascertain which stories he sold to *Astounding* and *Galaxy* should be a simple matter but Phil only had one story ever published in *Astounding* and that was "Impostor" in Jun 1953. Also, the manuscript for "Impostor" reached the SMLA on Feb 24, 1953, precluding any previous sale. My conclusion from this is that PKD, in 1968, was remembering incorrectly. The sale was not to *Astounding* but possibly to *Imagination* and the story was "Project: Earth."

His first published story in *Galaxy* was "The Defenders" in the Jan 1953 issue. It is possible that it was written in Jan 1952.[xlii]

Such are the problems trying to sort out PKD's early stories. Certainly included in these pre-SMLA days are rejected stories later sent to the SMLA. Only one of these can be nailed down with reasonable certainty, "Of Withered Apples," already mentioned. But it's likely that some of the other stories sent to the SMLA early in 1953 also qualify.[xliii]

"Project: Earth" was one of these. Under the manuscript title of "One Who Stole", the short story "Project: Earth" was sent to *F & SF* in March 1952, as mentioned above. Later, presumably after rejection by *F & SF*, PKD sent the story off to the SMLA where it arrived on Jan 6, 1953. The story was first published in *Imagination* in Dec 1953.

Small boys figure again in this story of a quiet man who is compiling a great book about a secret project. Curious, one of the boys investigate and finds a box of miniature aliens which he frees with unhappy consequences for the man and his project.

"Project: Earth" rates ✳ ✳ ✳

In early 1952 Philip K. Dick was sending stories off to mainstream publishers such as *The Saturday Evening Post*. On asking Anthony Boucher's advice on finding a literary agent, he was directed to Willis Wing who turned him down. Later he would hook up with Scott Meredith.[xliv] But before finding an agent Dick sent his stories not only to mainstream magazines but also to the science fiction pulps, primarily Boucher's own *Magazine Of Fantasy & Science Fiction.*

One of the first sold to *F & SF* after their acceptance of "Roog" and "The Little Movement" was "He Who Waits," later retitled "Expendable." It may not have been written directly after "Roog" but certainly by March 1952 it was under consideration by Boucher as in a letter at that time PKD explicitly refers to "He Who Waits:"

> Here is a new page 11 for "He Who Waits." I hope it does...
> {...} As to the title: how about "Protection." Or: "The Protectors." Or: "Protection Agency." Etc., etc. I like the last. We seem to have plenty of time to decide, if the first "Dick" is coming out in August. I wonder if perhaps this yarn wouldn't be the best "first." "Roog" is more ordinary; its kind is common. This one (and "Little Movement") is more my own kind of story. I'll leave it to you.[xlv]

"He Who Waits" was accepted at *F & SF* on Apr 7, 1952. The title decided on was "Expendable" although Dick apparently had nothing to do with it. In a letter to Boucher dated May 18, 1953 Dick wonders:

> One more item. I have received a check from your NY office for foreign rights to "Left Shoe, My Foot." I am pleased-surprised-thankful. But I am puzzled by the new title "Expendable." What does it mean? How does it fit the story? Who put it on? And -- is there any way I can get hold of the foreign edition it appears in? I've never had this experience, and would like to see how I look in non-American format (Herr Philip K. Dick, etc.) If you know where or how I can get the foreign edition copy, I'd appreciate it.[xlvi]

Dick is confusing two stories here: "Expendable" and "Left Shoe, My Foot." We can conclude from this letter that, first, "Left Shoe, My Foot" – published as "The Short, Happy Life Of The Brown Oxford" – had just been sold to *F & SF* and, second, that "He Who Waits" under the title "Expendable" had been accepted at *F & SF* earlier than "Brown Oxford" else why the notification of foreign rights which typically are negotiated after a domestic sale? And on this I have confirmation from Gordon van Gelder, current editor at *F & SF*, that "He Who Waits" (later titled "Expendable") was accepted at *F & SF* on Apr 7, 1952 while "Brown Oxford" was accepted exactly a month later on May 7, 1952.[xlvii]

Philip K. Dick said of "Expendable":

> I loved to write short fantasy stories in my early days -- for Anthony Boucher -- of which this is my favorite. I got the idea when a fly buzzed my head one day and I imagined (paranoia indeed!) that it was laughing at me.[xlviii]

"Expendable" was published in *F & SF* in the July 1953 issue. It has proved a popular little fantasy over the years, appearing in two of the major PKD collections: A HANDFUL OF DARKNESS (1955) and THE BEST OF PHILIP K. DICK (1977)

This is another fantasy story wherein a conspiracy of insects sets out to destroy a man in his home. But the man has friends among the spiders, at least, and they might win the war but as for this particular battle... well, some things are expendable.

"Expendable" rates ✳ ✳ ✳ ✳

The next two short stories PKD wrote are closely intertwined. These are "The Short, Happy Life Of The Brown Oxford" and "The Preserving Machine." The records at *F & SF* show that "Brown Oxford" was accepted there on May 7, 1952 and "The Preserving Machine" a week later on May 15, 1952. Dick wrote to the editors at *F & SF* in February and discussed the two stories:

Dear Sirs,

Please pardon me all to hell, but I am sending you this story while you still have the previous one. The reason: both stories are related, and I feel sure you will want to see them together.

Now, "The Preserving Machine" is long, contemplative, and philosophical. "Left Shoe, My Foot" is short, descriptive, and hard. In the back of my mind is the idea that they form a kind of series with maybe more to follow. Their theme is the same, the characters are the same, etc. But you may feel that one or both should be given up; maybe the idea of the series.

Of the two, I like "Left Foot" better. That it may survive and "Machine" fail wouldn't surprise me. {...}[xlix]

"Left Shoe, My Foot" is, of course, "The Short, Happy Life Of The Brown Oxford." PKD worked on both stories over the months February to April, 1952:

I understand about the Labyrinth stories. I've already reworked them, cut the "Machine" from 23 pages to 10; the other from 29 to 15, made strong the end, made smooth the style, but I'm content to bask and sun myself and hold them up indefinitely. But they *are* ready, if you suddenly run out of short stories. I won't send them off anywhere else.[l]

But by the middle of April he was still not done with "Left Shoe, My Foot," writing to Boucher again, sounding a little discouraged and trying to talk him into acceptance:

Well, here is the other one, "Left Shoe, My Foot." It has really been worked over, from start to finish. I sat up with it all over the weekend.

I have used your suggestions regarding the ending. Also I have reorganized it so that the dead part in the center is gone.

Also I have made the tone of it conform more with the other, "Preserving Machine." Doc Labyrinth figures much more in it, etc.

I hope you like it, and it will do, but if it will not do, then I'm happy to rework it again.

Thank you very much for the help, especially the suggestions. I consider them apt, valid, useful, and the very kind of thing that is good to hear.[li]

Having suitably squeezed their young writer enough, Boucher and McComas accepted both stories, this acceptance acknowledged by Dick in a letter dated May 7, 1952:

I received word about PM & LSMF and I rejoice mightily.
{...}

Well, thank you all very much for your kindness and patience with PM & LSMF. I'm glad they finally went. {...}[lii]

"The Short, Happy Life of The Brown Oxford" was published in *F & SF* in the Jan 1954 issue. The story was collected in I HOPE I SHALL ARRIVE SOON (1985) and later formed the title of the first volume of THE COLLECTED STORIES OF PHIIP K. DICK (1987).

Another fantasy in which Doc Labyrinth, using the 'principle of sufficient irritation', animates a shoe, only to see it run off into the bushes with a lady's slipper.

"The Short, Happy Life of The Brown Oxford" rates ✳ ✳ ✳

As for "The Preserving Machine" which PKD worked on simultaneously with "Brown Oxford," the correspondence is practically the same. Dick was revising this story by March 19, 1952 and still at it to April 12, 1952 when he pushed for "The Preserving Machine"s' acceptance regardless of the decision on "Brown Oxford." In this series of letters PKD is either trying to push one or the other of the two stories while at the same time putting them forward as the beginning of a series:

I hope you won't be too disconcerted to see this epic coming right back, so soon. "Preserving Machine" has been carefully worked over, so here it is. The other one will take a little longer. Maybe quite a bit longer. It needs more.

I agree that the second version of P.M. was too short. It read like a synopsis, and in some respects was not as good as the first. Therefore I have done a completely new version which is SENSATIONAL, and that is what you will find just below this letter. Below *that* are the previous versions, the too-long and the too-short, just for any value they might have for comparison purposes.

Now, I wonder if it would be alright with you that P.M. might be considered intrinsically, not waiting for the other to follow? I would be much happier having this one out of the way. {...} [liii]

As noted above, "The Preserving Machine" was accepted by *F& SF* by May 15, 1952. It was published a year later in the June 1953 issue of *F & SF*. PKD acknowledged its publication in a letter to Boucher dated May 18, 1953:

Thank you very much for the very nice things you said in the printing of "The Preserving Machine." I was overcome with delight.[liv]

Later, the story would give its name to the 1969 Ace Books collection of his stories, THE PRESERVING MACHINE And Other Stories.

"The Preserving Machine" is another invention of Doc Labyrinth's. Thinking to preserve great music in animate form, the good doctor feeds sheet music into his machine and creatures attuned to the musical scores come out the other end. So, music is saved for the ages, right? Not quite because Doc Labyrinth forgot to factor in evolution and the survival of the fittest.

An amusing fantasy, "The Preserving Machine" deserves ✳ ✳ ✳.

In our chronology we are still in the period before Philip K. Dick signed on with the SMLA (which happened in May 1952). "The Gun" and the next few stories fall into that nebulous time.

"The Gun", about a sketchy interstellar survey team that is shot down by a gun firing from the surface of an uninhabited planet, is a story about which very little has been written. It dates, most likely, from early 1952 and was first published in *Planet Stories* in Sep 1952. It's only other appearance besides THE COLLECTED STORIES in 1987 was in a rare Australian magazine, *SF Monthly #12* published in Aug 1956.

"The Gun" rates ✳ ✳

"The Gun" is followed by "Mr. Spaceship," likely written in early 1952. In this story we're at war with the 'Yucs' from Proxima Centauri – and losing. Our automatic warships cannot compete with the intelligent craft of the Yucs. We need manned ships but the human body cannot take the stress of space battle. The human brain can, though, and one is extracted from a volunteer and installed in the latest ship. Unfortunately, the brain has a mind of its own and prefers a new life to an old war.

Other than its initial publication in the Jan 1953 *Imagination*, "Mr. Spaceship" was lost until inclusion in THE COLLECTED STORIES in 1987.

"Mr. Spaceship" rates ✳ ✳

The next story, "Piper In The Woods", is fantasy masquerading as science fiction and tells the tale of a survey crew on an uninhabited planetoid who, for some unknown reason, start thinking they're plants. Other than its publication in *Imagination* in the Feb 1953 issue, its only other appearance was in THE COLLECTED STORIES. However, in the issue of *Imagination* in which "Piper In The Woods" appeared, Philip K. Dick had a self-written autobiographical blurb printed on the inside of the front cover, one of *Imagination*'s ongoing "Introducing The Author" profiles. The profile is accompanied by a small photo of PKD. Here's what Dick had to say about science fiction and his life at that time:

Once when I was very young, I came across a magazine directly below the comic books called *Stirring Science Stories*. I bought it, finally, and carried it home, reading it along the way. Here were ideas, vital and imaginative. Men moving across the universe, down into sub-atomic particles, into time; there was no limit. One society, one given environment was transcended. Stf was Faustian: it carried a person up and beyond.

I was twelve years old, then. But I saw in stf the same thing I see now: a medium in which the full play of human imagination can operate, ordered, of course, by reason and consistent development. Over the years stf has grown, matured toward greater social awareness and responsibility.

I became interested in writing stf when I saw it emerge from the ray gun stage into studies of man in various types and complexities of society.

I enjoy writing stf: it is essentially communication between myself and others as interested as I in knowing where present forces are taking us. My wife and my cat *Magnificat*, are a little worried about my preoccupation with stf. Like most stf readers I have files and stacks of magazines, boxes of notes and data, parts of unfinished stories, a huge desk full of related material in various stages. The neighbors say I seem to "read and write a lot." But I think we will see our devotion pay off. We may yet live to be present when the public libraries begin to carry the stf magazines, and someday, perhaps, even the school libraries. -- *Philip K. Dick*

"Piper In The Woods" gets ✳ ✳

"The Infinites" is a memorable story of evolution. In this tale evolution is a relative thing. Sometimes a few hours head start is all that's necessary to win the battle of survival.

Historian Thomas Clareson sees "The Infinites" as a significant story, together with "James P. Crow", for its presaging of the direction science fiction would take in the 60s and 70s regarding social criticism.[lv]

Other than the desirable for collectors editions of *Planet Stories* (May 1953) and the rare Australian magazine *SF Monthly # 18* (Feb 1957), "The Infinites" was not seen again until THE COLLECTED STORIES.

"The Infinites" rates ✳ ✳ ✳ ✳

PKD's first appearance in *Fantastic Story Magazine* was "The Indefatigable Frog." In this one Zeno's paradox is put to the test – with uncertain results. It is akin to the two 'Doc Labyrinth' stories ("The Short, Happy Life of The Brown Oxford" and "The Preserving Machine") and with just a slight rechanging of character names one can see it fitting in well with those two stories.

Published in *Fantastic Story Magazine* in the July 1953 issue, "The Indefatigable Frog" was collected into PKD's first anthology, the English A HANDFUL OF DARKNESS in 1955. Beyond its inclusion in THE COLLECTED STORIES, it appeared in THE ASCENT OF WONDER (Ed. David Hartwell and Kathryn Kramer) from Tor Books in 1994. In this anthology PKD has written an introduction to the story.

"The Indefatigable Frog" rates ✳ ✳ ✳

Another first for PKD was the printing of his story "The Variable Man" in the British magazine *Space Science Fiction* in Sep 1953. How it ended up there I do not know. This is a long story about a man dredged from the past into the future of an interstellar war. Government computers predict the odds of Terra's winning the war at any particular moment. About to go on the offensive, Terra is stymied when this variable man is factored into the calculations.

The story lent its name to an early PKD collection: THE VARIABLE MAN And Other Stories, Ace Books, 1957. It also figures in his 1963 short story, "Waterspider," wherein PKD refers to himself and several of his contemporary science fiction writers as well as some other short stories. "The Variable Man" is mentioned:

"I got going the article in *Space Science Fiction*," Nils said thoughtfully, "called *The Variable Man*. It tells about faster-than-light transmission. You disappear and then reappear.

Some guy named Cole is going to perfect it, according to the old-time precog who wrote it." He brooded about that. "If we could build a faster-than-light ship we could return to Earth. We could take over."

"The Variable Man" rates ✳ ✳ ✳ ✳

"The Crystal Crypt" is another story of little note; this one tells the story of the start of war between Terra and Mars. Three terran agents destroy a major Martian city – supposedly – and are hunted by the Martian police. But the city is not destroyed only miniaturized into a paperweight.

As in "Stability" and "Project: Earth" (and RETURN TO LILLIPUT), Dick writes of the large and the small, a theme he will return to again in several different ways throughout his writing career.

"The Crystal Crypt" never saw republication after its initial showing in *Planet Stories* in Jan 1954 until volume one of THE COLLECTED STORIES.

"The Crystal Crypt" rates ✷ ✷ ✷

A popular story, "The Defenders" was written in 1952 before PKD signed on with the SMLA. He submitted it directly to H. L. Gold at *Galaxy* himself. Gold thought the story such a fine one that he had top sf artist Ed Emshwiller illustrate it for the cover as well as internally. PKD's first cover illustration for one of his short stories when it was published in the Jan 1953 issue of *Galaxy*.[lvi]

The story itself is about deluded people living underground, fighting an awful war – or so they think – while above the surface robots prepare the ground for a peaceful world. Later, this idea was expanded by PKD into his 1964 novel THE PENULTIMATE TRUTH.

"The Defenders" has been well-anthologized, appearing in THE BOOK OF PHILIP K. DICK (1973) as well as several other anthologies. It can be found in THE COLLECTED STORIES OF PHILIP K. DICK, Vol. 1. (1987)

"The Defenders", together with "Colony", was adapted; not by PKD, for the radio series "X Minus One" in 1956.[lvii]

In his short story "Waterspider" (1963) Philip K. Dick mentions "The Defenders":

Fermeti stared at Anderson a long time. "Take the first article in the January 1953 *Galaxy*," he said quietly. "*The Defenders*… about the people living beneath the surface and the robots up above, pretending to fight the war but actually not, actually faking the reports so interestingly that the people –"

"I read that," Poul Anderson agreed. "Very good, I thought, except for the ending. I didn't care too much for the ending."

Fermeti said, "You understand, don't you, that those exact conditions came to pass in 1996, during World War Three? That by means of the article we were able to penetrate the deception carried on by our surface robots? That virtually every word of that article was exactly prophetic –"

"Phil Dick wrote that," Anderson said, "*The Defenders*."

"Do you know him?" Tozzo inquired.

"Met him yesterday at the Convention," Anderson said. "For the first time. Very nervous fellow, was almost afraid to come in."[lviii]

"The Defenders" rates ✷ ✷ ✷ ✷ ✷

The stories listed above were all likely written before May 1952. Early in that month or in April, Philip K. Dick contacted the Scott Meredith Literary Agency in New York.[lix] Already by then and thanks to his own efforts, PKD had sold a number of stories to the sf magazines of the day – the ones listed above with the exception of "Stability" which was never sold.[lx]

Dick felt competent to market his short stories himself and was primarily interested in having the Agency handle his mainstream novels. A look at the calendar of PKD's work in 1952 shows that the last two stories we can date with reasonable certainty ("The Short, Happy Life of The Brown Oxford" and "The Preserving Machine") were accepted at *F & SF* on May 7 and May 15, 1952. After that there is a gap of almost three months before the next short story, "The

Builder" arrived at the SMLA. During this period PKD sent the long manuscript for GATHER YOURSELVES TOGETHER to the SMLA and, shortly after in early June 1952, sent off the manuscript for VOICES FROM THE STREET.[lxi]

But Scott Meredith wanted to be the agent for all of Philip K. Dick's writing, not just these long and (I must admit in the case of GATHER at least) boring novels.[lxii] Meredith knew the market for science fiction was about to explode and was building his clientele. Dick agreed to this finally although he insisted the Agency try to sell his two mainstream novels; which they did with no success. It was different, though, with his short stories, for all of which the SMLA was able to find a market. It may have taken a few years with some of them but eventually all of PKD's short fiction was sold by the Agency.

So, then, in April through June of 1952 PKD was preparing GATHER YOURSELVES TOGETHER for submission to the SMLA and writing VOICES FROM THE STREET. Both of these are long novels, GATHER coming in at 481 manuscript pages and VOICES FROM THE STREET at 652 pages.[lxiii]

VOICES FROM THE STREET has been found! The novel will be published by Tor Books in January 2007.

But, no money was coming in while he worked on VOICES FROM THE STREET and after he sent that off to the SMLA Dick returned to writing short stories. The first to reach the SMLA was "The Builder" on July 23, 1952, followed a day later by "Meddler."

Although PKD had sold 15 short stories it wasn't until July 1952 that the first of these was actually published; "Beyond Lies The Wub" in *Planet Stories*. No doubt seeing his work on the newsstands and in the bookstores encouraged Dick to continue.

"The Builder" isn't much of a story: a man and his son, under some personal sense of doom, construct a vast ark in their back yard. The ending is inevitable and obvious. Still, the sub-agent at the SMLA liked it well enough, writing on the Agency's 'green card' (their file of index cards that recorded information on stories sent to them): "IT ISN'T SCIENCE FICTION" but still he rated it a "G plus." The Agency sent it off first to *Atlantic Monthly* and then *Harper's* before foisting it off where it belonged at *Amazing*.[lxiv]

Altogether "The Builder" was published in *Amazing* three times; first in the Dec 1953/Jan 1954 issue, then in the British edition in April 1954 and finally, twelve years later, in the June 1967 issue. It was also selected for PKD's first hardcover collection A HANDFUL OF DARKNESS published by Rich & Cowan in the UK in 1955. From there oblivion until THE COLLECTED STORIES.

"The Builder" rates ✳

"The Builder" was followed by "Meddler" which reached the Agency on July 24, 1952. It's a much better story; a sorry tale of time-travel wherein each time a man goes into the future he finds things there progressively worse. Is it his fault? Well, probably. It reminds me of another old sf story the name and author of which I forget but which concerns a man travelling into the past where he steps on a butterfly, thus changing things. In Dick's story, too, the butterflies are best to be avoided.

"Meddler" was first published in *Future Science Fiction* in Oct 1954. Later in 1980 Mark Hurst would select it for his Philip K. Dick collection, THE GOLDEN MAN. In the 'Story Notes' to this collection PKD writes of "Meddler":

Within the beautiful lurks the ugly; you can see in this rather crude story the germ of my whole theme that nothing is what it seems. This story should be read as a trial run on my part; I was just beginning to grasp that obvious form and latent form are not the same thing. As Heraclitus said in fragment 54: "Latent structure is master of obvious structure," and out of this comes the later more sophisticated Platonic dualism between the phenomenal world and the real but invisible realm of forms lying behind it. I may be reading too much into this simple-minded early story, but at least I was beginning to see in a dim way what I later saw so clearly; in fragment 123 Heraclitus said, "The nature of things is in the habit of concealing itself," and therein lies it all.[lxv]

"Meddler" rates ✳ ✳ ✳ ✳

One week after these two stories reached the SMLA, three more rolled in all on the same day: "Paycheck," "Out In The Garden" and "The Great C." As "Paycheck" was the first of these to be published we'll look at it first.

July 31, 1952 was the day these stories arrived. "Paycheck" at 13,000 words was the longest of them. It's another time-travel story which, like "Meddler" is well-handled. A repairman for a mysterious company is sent to the past and when he returns he's snatched up by the police. But with the help of his paycheck for two years of unconscious work – a handful of common objects with little intrinsic value – he escapes and succeeds to his hidden goal. This story reminds me of the much later "We Can Remember It For You Wholesale" for some reason.

"Paycheck" found its way to *Imagination* and was printed in the June 1953 issue. It was selected for the Ballantine collection of PKD stories THE BEST OF PHILIP K. DICK in 1977. Dick himself had this to say about "Paycheck":

How much is a key to a bus locker worth? One day it's worth 25 cents, the next day thousands of dollars. In this story I got to thinking that there are times in our lives when having a dime to make a phone call spells the difference between life and death. Keys, small change, maybe a theater ticket -- how about a parking receipt for a Jaguar? All I had to do was link this idea up with time travel to see how the small and useless, under the wise eyes of a time traveler, might signify a great deal more. He would know when that dime might save your life. And, back in the past again, he might prefer that dime to any amount of money, no matter how large. [lxvi]

"Paycheck" rates ✳ ✳ ✳ ✳ ✳

"Out In The Garden" is pure fantasy. The fable of Leda and the Swan retold but with a duck this time. July 31, 1952 is the date the story arrived at the SMLA. It was sold to *Fantasy Fiction* magazine and printed for the first time in the Aug 1953 issue. No one seems to have commented on it that I can find and other than a brief appearance in the anthology *SATAN'S PETS* in 1972 it was not brought back into print until THE COLLECTED STORIES OF PKD in 1987. Due to its style and the slight nature of the story it is possible that "Out In The Garden" was one of those short fantasies that Kleo refers to as having been written before she met Phil; perhaps written in 1950 or 1951.

"Out In The Garden" rates ✳

"The Great C" is the first of PKD's stories set in a post-apocalypse world. Survivors of 'The Great Smash' must sacrifice one of their tribe each year to the Great C, a computer that has also survived. Of course, the sacrificial lamb has a chance to avoid his fate if only he can stump the Great C with one of his three questions. But civilization has fallen far and, anyway, how exactly did the world begin?

The manuscript for "The Great C" arrived at the Agency the same day as the two previous stories above, July 31 1952. It was first published in *Cosmos Science Fiction #1* in the debut issue of Sep 1953. It also made an appearance in PKD's staunch Australian ally, *SF Monthly* in their seventh issue in March 1956. Later, PKD and his one-time collaborator, Roger Zelazny would incorporate the story into their novel DEUS IRAE (1976).

"The Great C" rates ✳ ✳ ✳

Less than a week after sending in the previous batch of three stories to the SMLA, Philip K. Dick mailed in the manuscript for "Shadrach Jones And The Elves." It arrived on Aug 4, 1952. Somehow, between the time of its reception and its publication in *Beyond Fantasy Fiction* in Sep 1953, the title was changed to "The King of The Elves."

This story, another pure fantasy of a lonely gas-station attendant chosen by the elves to replace their dying king and fight the trolls, has proven popular over the years, particularly since its publication in THE COLLECTED STORIES.

After initial publication in *Beyond* it was selected for Mark Hurst's THE GOLDEN MAN collection in 1980. After THE COLLECTED STORIES in 1987, though, "The King Of The Elves", perhaps due to the widespread reception of THE COLLECTED STORIES, appeared in six more anthologies between 1987 and 1997.

Philip K. Dick wrote this about "The King Of The Elves":

This story, of course, is fantasy, not sf. Originally it had a downbeat ending on it, but Horace Gold, the editor who bought it, carefully explained to me that prophecy always came true; if it didn't ipso facto it wasn't prophecy. I guess, then, there can be no such thing as a false prophet; "false prophet" is an oxymoron.[lxvii]

"The King Of The Elves" rates ✳ ✳ ✳ ✳

A week after sending off the manuscript for "Shadrach Jones And The Elves," PKD mailed in the one for "Colony." It reached the SMLA on Aug 11, 1952 and, as would happen fairly often, the Agency landed it a spot in *Galaxy*. It showed up in their June, 1953 issue.

This is one of my favorite of PKD's short stories and reminds me of the old *Dan Dare* comics strips of the 1960s, one of the first sci-fi things I read as a child.

"Colony" has had a wider audience than many of PKD's short stories (perhaps that's because it's better than most). After publication in the USA edition of *Galaxy* and, a few months later in the UK version, it was included in PKD's first collection: A HANDFUL OF DARKNESS (1955).

From there it appeared in a Book Of The Month Club selection from Doubleday (*SPACE OPERA*, ed. Brian Aldiss, 1974) and Ballantine's collection THE BEST OF PHILIP K. DICK in 1977. Even since publication of THE COLLECTED STORIES in 1987, "Colony" has been in Robert Silverberg's *WORLDS OF WONDER* anthology (1987).

"Colony" together with "The Defenders" was adapted into a radio play for the *X-Minus One* radio series in 1956.[lxviii]

In conversation with Mike Hodel of radio station KPFK-FM in 1976 Dick talks about the X-1 radio series and "Colony":

The novel of ideas is still the cardinal thing in science fiction. All we've got now is tedious sermonettes masquerading as literature, Adventure, Space Opera. I had a strange experience. I played over a X-1 cassette that somebody sent me for one of my X-1 shows that NBC did in 1954. 1954. And it was indistinguishable from the latest science fiction like Space 1999, is that what it's called? And Star Trek. Mine was as modern in 1954 as what they're doing now.

{...}the one I played over was "Colony." Remember, we listened to that tape? And we marveled that in 1954, I didn't do - I don't take credit for the radio treatment of it. Somebody else did it. But what he was doing in '54, treating my story, was as modern as what they're doing now.

{...}You wouldn't know it was done in '54. There was nothing to give it away.

{...}there were two of mine, "Colony" and "The Defenders." And it was just scary to listen to it and look on the date, you know, '54, and realize here we are in 1976 and we've made no steps forward. You know we're still, it's still as follows - Captain, there's something hideous on the viewscreen. Captain says, turn on the laserbeams. And then a voice comes out of no where, all looking under the seat cushions to see where the voice comes from and it's talking through an echo chamber and it says, I can read your thoughts. I need your assistance. And they say, it's a ruse. Get the eagles going. Zzzt zzzt zzzt. The eagles take off. We know this is a ruse. This is the Captain talking from the control room. We know it's all a ruse. You don't need our help. You're going to zap us as soon as we take off to zap you first. And, you know, nothing has progressed. I am a superior being. I am a kindly old fellow. You can believe everything I'm telling you because I'm really a computer and would a computer lie. And I thought, oh my god I just saw that on the air Saturday night and I says that's HAL talking again. That's ol' HAL, you know, shining everybody on. My name is HAL. Would I lie? Would a computer lie? [lxix]

One wonders when Hollywood will turn this story into a blockbuster movie.
PKD in his 'Story Notes' says this about "Colony:"

'The ultimate in paranoia is not when everyone is against you but when every*thing* is against you. Instead of "My boss is plotting against me," it would be "My boss's phone is plotting against me." Objects sometimes seem to possess a will of their own anyhow, to the normal mind; they don't do what they're supposed to do, they get in the way, they show an unnatural resistance to change. In this story I tried to figure out a situation which would rationally explain the dire plotting of objects against humans, without reference to any deranged state on the part of the humans. I guess you'd have to go to another planet. The ending of this story is the ultimate victory of a plotting object over innocent people. [lxx]

Interstellar explorers find a virgin planet and can't wait to get home to tell everyone about it – at first. But when towels start wrapping themselves around people's necks and razors take on a life of their own, well, the explorers can't wait to get out of there! Strange, though, how their spaceship is parked a lot closer than they'd thought.

"Colony" gets the highest rating of ✳ ✳ ✳ ✳ ✳

"Prize Ship" was titled by PKD "Globe From Ganymede" when he sent it off to the Agency. It arrived there three days after "Colony" on Aug 14 1952. The story is an overt homage to Jonathon Swift's Brobdignagian and Lilliputian tales. For a melding of fantasy and science fiction it comes off well, bringing in a relativistic explanation for everything at the end.

As in "Stability," "Project: Earth," "The Little Movement" and "The Crystal Crypt," Philip K. Dick works with themes of scale: the big and the small.

After its first printing in *Thrilling Wonder Stories* in the Winter of 1954, the story lay idle until THE COLLECTED STORIES. It has been little commented on.

Terra is at war with Ganymede again and its looking pretty grim as Earth's outlying colonies on Proxima start running out of supplies. Things pick up though when Terra captures the latest Ganymedean spaceship. Using the ship a squad of Terrans takes off for they know not where. When they finally land and encounter miniature men who immediately attack them, the commander realises that they are in Lilliputia.

Twisting the unfamiliar dials of their ship in the opposite direction the intrepid Terrans determine to go and find Brobdignag. In the end, though, is the ship really a spaceship – or something else?

A confusing homage to Jonathon Swift, "Prize Ship" rates ✻ ✻ ✻

In the middle of August 1952 Dick wrote and submitted another group of three stories to the SMLA. About the time he sent them in he must've seen copies of *Planet Stories* and *Worlds Of If* on the newsstands. Inside his stories "The Skull" and "The Gun."

The first story dropping in the slot at the SMLA from this batch was "Nanny" on Aug 26 1952. In the thematic chronology of PKD's short stories this was something new: Robot nannies that go out at night when the kids are asleep and prowl their territory. Very territorial these nannies, fighting any other nanny they see no matter how advanced. Of course, the manufacturers are behind it as each family tries to keep up with the Joneses by buying at great cost the latest model. Similar to the later "Foster, You're Dead!" in intent and reminiscent of the stories of Frederik Pohl, "Nanny" comes off well. What I like is the fact that the nanny never speaks.

The story was first published in *Startling Stories* in the Spring of 1955 and was selected for Don Wollheim's collection THE BOOK OF PHILIP K. DICK in 1973.

"Nanny" rates ✻ ✻ ✻ ✻

The day after reception of "Nanny," the manuscript for "The Cookie Lady" arrived at the SMLA on Aug 27 1952.

This little tale of a psychic vampire who trades cookies for children's life force is effective, even memorable when one thinks about it. I think it would've made a good script for Rod Serling's *Night Gallery* or *The Twilight Zone*. In fact, "The Cookie Lady" was turned into a teleplay which was aired on Metromedia TV sometime in the 1970's.[lxxi]

Published first in *Fantasy Fiction* in June 1953, "The Cookie Lady" was selected for PKD's first collection, A HANDFUL OF DARKNESS in 1955. It has been intermittently anthologized since then, notably in *ALFRED HITCHCOCK PRESENTS: THE MASTER'S CHOICE* published by Doubleday in 1979. It is the first story in the second volume of THE COLLECTED STORIES.

"The Cookie Lady" gets ✻ ✻ ✻ ✻

The manuscript for "The Cuckoo Clock" reached the SMLA on Aug 29, 1952, the last of six short stories PKD mailed to the Agency in August. In fact, the last story he submitted for a month as in September, 1952 he either did no writing or was working on something else as the records at the SMLA show no other manuscripts between "Beyond The Door" and "Second Variety" in early October. Indeed, September was an idle month for PKD throughout his life as the calendar of submissions to the SMLA shows.

Philip K. Dick Biographer Gregg Rickman says that the SMLA "made more than one attempt to break their author through into the non-sf market. "The Cuckoo Clock" was submitted to *Esquire* and *Today's Woman*, among others, before winding up at *Fantastic Universe* as "Beyond The Door" in January 1954.[lxxii]

Other than its original appearance in *Fantastic Universe*, "Beyond The Door" was not available in English until the publication of the second volume of THE COLLECTED STORIES in 1987. The story did, however, appear in foreign-language collections and gave its name, in French, to the 1988 Denoel collection DERRIERE LA PORTE.

For the first time infidelity enters into one of PKD's stories and a cheap cuckoo clock has a mind of its own. Another fantasy tale.

"Beyond The Door" rates ✳ ✳

After the hiatus in September 1952, Dick sent off the manuscript for "Second Variety." It arrived at the Agency on Oct 3 1952. At 16,000 words this is a long short story and perhaps explains the seeming period of inactivity in September.

With "Second Variety" PKD arrived with a vengeance. Arguably this is one of his best short stories ever. In a future post-apocalyptic world man has turned the manufacture of weapons over to machines. Machines that kill and evolve to one purpose only: the destruction of mankind. This is such a good story that Hollywood thought it suitable to turn into a movie. In 1995, *SCREAMERS* starring Peter Weller was released to worldwide non-acclaim although some fans consider this film to be the most faithful to the original story than any of the PKD-based movies. In this story, as in "The Little Movement", a teddy bear figures; but not so benevolently this time.

"Second Variety" was first published in *Space Science Fiction* in May 1953. It was selected for the PKD collections THE VARIABLE MAN in 1957 and THE BEST OF PHILIP K. DICK in 1977 as well as lending its name to the title of the third volume of THE COLLECTED STORIES.

Popular over the years with editors, "Second Variety" has one of the best records for anthology appearances of all Dick's stories; having at least 16 such between 1954 and 2001. Notable among these is the Australian *SELECTED SCIENCE FICTION #1* in May 1955 for which this story provides the cover. Also, Kingsley Amis and Robert Conquest's anthology *SPECTRUM II* of 1963 should be mentioned and Fred Saberhagen's *MACHINES THAT KILL* in 1984. Most recently the story can be read in Harry Turtledove and Martin Greenburg's *THE BEST MILITARY SCIENCE FICTION OF THE 20TH CENTURY* published by Del Rey in May 2001.

Philip K. Dick had this to say about "Second Variety":

My grand theme -- who is human and who only appears (masquerades) as a human? -- emerges most fully. Unless we can individually and collectively be certain of the answer to this question, we face what is, in my view, the most serious problem possible. Without answering it adequately, we cannot even be certain of our own selves. I cannot even know myself, let alone you. So I keep working on this theme; to me nothing is as important a question. And the answer comes very hard.[lxxiii]

He also talks about *SCREAMERS* in an interview with John Boonstra:

"I have been up there to another film project, the little Capitol Pictures one, called *Claw*. (Based on his short story "Second Variety," with a screenplay by Dan O'Bannon, and subsequently retitled *Screamers*(1995)) They're very nice. I really like them. Every change that's made, they send me a copy to get my opinion. They just treat me like a human being. In other words, I am able to discriminate between essentially reputable people up there, and these high-pressure types.[lxxiv]

"Second Variety" rates ✳ ✳ ✳ ✳ ✳

Arriving at the SMLA on Oct 21, 1952, the manuscript for "Jon's World" (originally titled simply "Jon") somehow ended up in August Derleth's collection *TIME TO COME* in 1954. *TIME TO COME* had at least four separate editions between 1954 and 1965. But other than that the story never again saw the light of day until the second volume of THE COLLECTED STORIES in 1987. There have been no comments on it that I can find. This is surprising as "Jon's World" is a sequel to "Second Variety" set on Earth after the Claws have destroyed each other. Going back in time to retrieve the papers of the scientist who invented the Claw brains, the time-travelers get the papers but kill the scientist in the process. This naturally changes things in the future and, for once, it's to the good.

"Jon's World" rates ✳ ✳ ✳ ✳

Originally titled "Burglar," the ms for "The Cosmic Poachers" reached the SMLA on Oct 22, 1952, a day after that for "Jon's World." Other than its first appearance in *Imagination* in July of 1953 and in Roger Elwood's *ALIEN WORLDS* in 1964, the story can only be found in the second volume of THE COLLECTED STORIES OF PKD (1987). Little comment has been made about it other than the brief comment by the sub-agent at the SMLA who said of "Burglar": 'Huh, ho hum.'[lxxv]

"The Cosmic Poachers" is almost as bad a title for this story as "Burglar." Neither seems to really apply. Perhaps a better one would be "The Cosmic Poached Eggs"… It's a kind of trick story where Dick shows his ability to keep the reader wondering until he's ready to reveal the trick at the end. If the reader would pause for a moment while reading this and similar tales he'd realize what was going on. But then, it's the writer's job to keep you reading and PKD was very good at it. Like "Beyond Lies The Wub" and "Meddler", "The Cosmic Poachers" can be construed as a backwards-sort of alien invasion tale.

"The Cosmic Poachers" rates ✳ ✳ ✳

In November 1952 PKD was writing and submitting his stories at a steady pace. Six in all reached the SMLA in this month and as he was writing these stories, he was able to see the Nov issue of *F & SF* on the stands with his story "The Little Movement" in its pages.

The first to arrive in November was the manuscript for "Some Kinds Of Life" (originally titled "The Beleagured") which reached the SMLA the same day as that for "Progeny" on Nov 3, 1952. It was published under a pseudonym – 'Richard Phillips' – in *Fantastic Universe* in the Oct-Nov issue in 1953. The reason for the pseudonym seems to be that the same issue of *Fantastic Universe* also carried the short story "Planet For Transients" by Philip K. Dick. I guess it wasn't done to have two stories by the same writer in the same magazine at the same time. [lxxvi]

But other than this appearance, "Some Kinds Of Life" lay dormant for 34 years until the second volume of THE COLLECTED STORIES in 1987.

This again is surprising to me as this story hits pretty hard at rampant consumerism. Perhaps PKD overdoes the ridiculous inevitability of the disaster if things are taken to their ultimate conclusion but in "Some Kinds Of Life" that's where they end up. This story is something like one of Fred Pohl's anti-commercialism stories but on a cramped scale.

"Some Kinds Of Life" rates ✳ ✳ ✳ ✳

"Progeny" arrived manuscript-wise at the SMLA on Nov 3, 1952, the same day as the ms for "Some Kinds Of Life." It was published in *If* in the Nov 1954 issue.

After its initial showing in *If*, "Progeny" was selected for Rich & Cowan's UK collection, A HANDFUL OF DARKNESS, published in 1955; PKD's first collection. It seems to have been a popular story for editors of the burgeoning academic science fiction market in the mid 1970s, being selected for two anthologies aimed at this audience. And after this nothing until inclusion in the second volume of THE COLLECTED STORIES.

Philip Dick must've been in a bad mood when he wrote these last two stories. "Some Kinds Of Life" is a nasty sideswipe at the car of capitalism while "Progeny" is a vicious slap at 'family values' and what we today call political correctness. This is a different tone from anything he has expressed before in his previous short stories. Even with "Nanny," where he'd come close to hitting both targets: family values and consumerism, he'd held back a bit. But in these stories he doesn't hold back.

"Progeny" rates ✳ ✳ ✳ ✳ ✳

Another practically forgotten story, "Martians Come In Clouds" arrived two days later on Nov 5, 1952. This story was originally titled "The Buggies" but by the time of publication in the June-July 1953 issue of *Fantastic Universe* the title had changed to "Martians Come In Clouds."

After its initial printing the story was not seen again until THE COLLECTED STORIES in 1987.

In the subtle kind of fear that PKD evokes in this tale – call it xenophobia – we see echoes of "Beyond Lies The Wub," and also, more explicitly, the novel THE WORLD JONES MADE(1954).[lxxvii] The fear that Jones stirs up at the sight of the *drifters* in THE WORLD JONES MADE and uses to his political benefit, is in "Martians Come In Clouds" only just beginning to be realised. It's as if the Martians in "Martians Come In Clouds" were the very first *drifters* to appear in Jones' World.

"Martians Come In Clouds" rates ✳ ✳ ✳ ✳ ✳

Two weeks later "The Commuter" dropped in the mail slot at the SMLA on Nov 19, 1952. The Agency, prompt as always, sent it off to the magazines where it was snapped up by *Amazing Stories* for their Aug-Sep 1953 issue.

It was selected for Don Wollheim's collection THE BOOK OF PKD in 1973. After that Lee Harding selected it for his Australian anthology *BEYOND TOMORROW* in 1976. The next year this anthology was published in England by The New English Library (NEL), then, as was the fate of many of these early stories, "The Commuter" was not seen again until the pages of THE COLLECTED STORIES.

"The Commuter" tells of a town that isn't there; and then it is. But when one town seeps into existence does another one fade away? And what about the wife and kids? Wait, does Bob *have* a wife and kids?

"The Commuter" rates ✳ ✳ ✳ ✳

Another story practically forgotten until the publication of THE COLLECTED STORIES, the manuscript for "The World She Wanted" reached the SMLA on Nov 24, 1952, a few days after that of "The Commuter." It was published in *Science Fiction Quarterly* in May 1953. The cover and interior illustrate PKD's story and are by Milton Luros.

"The World She Wanted" is a spiritual cousin to Jerome Bixby's "It's A *Good* Life." A man is swept off his feet by a girl who insists that this is *her* world and in her world things are the way she wants them to be. But he disagrees; this is *his* world. A story you don't want to think about too much lest you start thinking about the real world.

"The World She Wanted" gets ✳ ✳ ✳ ✳

After arriving at the SMLA on Dec 2, 1952 – the last submission of the year -- "A Surface Raid" apparently went round and round in the offices of the sf magazines of the day, landing at *Fantastic Universe* on its twelfth trip. After initial publication in July 1955 the story dropped from sight until the second volume of THE COLLECTED STORIES in 1987. No commentary on it has been found other than the opinion of the agents at the SMLA. For "A Surface Raid" the comment was 'Another of Dick's Weirdies." [lxxviii]

Human is as human does, the saying goes. But what is human? That depends on who's doing the defining. In this post-apocalypse tale underground dwellers raid the surface for slaves and a youth cons his way along for the trip. He sees a beautiful girl but she sees him too and what she sees is not attractive.

"A Surface Raid" rates ✳ ✳ ✳

So ends the year 1952. A busy and promising year for our 24 year-old author. He'd sent out about thirty short stories and seen four of them published. He'd also worked on two long novels, GATHER YOURSELVES TOGETHER and VOICES FROM THE STREET. And, importantly, he'd found an agent with whom he'd stay, except for a minor squabble later in his career, for the rest of his life. He became in this year an established writer of short science fiction stories.

Of the thirty-seven short stories we've looked at so far, nine of them are outright fantasies and there are several fantasy/sf hybrids like "Piper In The Woods" and "The Indefatigable Frog." Many, too, are straight science fiction.

On reading the stories, we can pick out a few themes and commonalities. The fantasies deal with themes such as imputing life and consciousness to inanimate objects and diverse creatures. For example, the dog in "Roog" and the toys in "The Little Movement." As the year progresses, the stories change from fantasy to science fiction. One of the first of these, "Beyond Lies The Wub," deals with PKD's prototypical theme, what is human? A theme that is continued in "Second Variety".

Questions of scale also appear, marking the influence of Jonathon Swift on PKD's work. These stories all involve differences in physical size in one way or another: "Project: Earth", "The Indefatigable Frog", "The Crystal Crypt" and "Prize Ship".

With "The Short, Happy Life Of The Brown Oxford" and "The Preserving Machine", Dick had ventured a series that ultimately came to nothing, due probably to the lack of enthusiasm on the part of the editors at *F & SF*. But, interestingly, there is another possible series of stories began in this year, although PKD himself never said that they formed a series. These are the what I call 'up-from-under' stories. Post-apocalypse tales about people living underground and conditions on the surface of a war-ravaged Earth. The first of these is "The Defenders" followed by "The Great C" and then "Second Variety" and "Jon's World." Lastly, "A Surface Raid" falls in this category. The culmination of this thematic line of thinking is, of course, THE PENULTIMATE TRUTH (1964).

Built around standard sf themes, other stories like "The Gun", "The Skull", and "Mr. Spaceship" are in the main unremarkable. "Paycheck" is a strange but effective take on Van Vogt.

But, again starting with "Beyond Lies The Wub", and continuing through "Colony", "The Cosmic Poachers" and "Martians Come In Clouds", we can detect a similarity in that these stories subtly imply a sort of backwards alien invasion. This xenophobic theme continues throughout PKD's short stories and is best expressed in his 1954 novel THE WORLD JONES MADE.[lxxix]

Towards the end of the year we can see the affect of Frederik Pohl's anti-social science fiction on PKD. Stories like "Nanny", "Some Kinds Of Life" and "Progeny", all take a swipe to some degree or other at the commercialism of 1950s' America. He would continue this theme into 1953.

PKD's other main theme, what is real?, shows up first in stories like "Paycheck", "Colony", "The Commuter" and "The World She Wanted." A direct descendent of "The Commuter" is THE COSMIC PUPPETS (1954) wherein Phil first struggles with reality in an extended way. TIME OUT OF JOINT (1959) and UBIK (1969) also come to mind as fine examples of this theme.

So much for the stories. But what else was going on in Philip K. Dick's life during the fine Year of Our Lord 1952?

He was still married to his second wife, Kleo, and was living in Berkeley, California and buying a house. Of course he was still poor and, literally, living on dog food.[lxxx] Writing short science fiction didn't pay much and even though Kleo worked part-time it was hard making ends meet.

At some time in 1952 the FBI came knocking on the couple's door. Kleo, a typical Berkeley student, was peripherally involved in left-wing politics; nothing rabid but she had been photographed by the FBI at rallies and the like often enough for them to pay a visit. But the FBI agents weren't too bad and after offering them jobs as informers at the University of Mexico in Mexico City (which they declined) they lost interest although one of them helped teach Phil how to drive.

Family life occupied much of their time: visiting Kleo's parents and Phil's mom, Dorothy and sometimes his dad, Edgar.

On the downside, though, Phil's mom married her sister Marion's widower, of which marriage Phil disapproved. Also, this loss of Aunt Marion in November 1952 was a sore blow to PKD and affected his relations with his mother, Dorothy.

Life goes on. If you were to ask me, even though I didn't know him, I'd say two things drove Philip K. Dick on in 1952: The pressure of money and the determination not only to succeed but to never have to go back to the workaday world again.

1953

1953 started off promisingly enough for Philip K. Dick's writing career. Fresh on the stands was the January *Galaxy* featuring a cover painting by Ed Emshwiller, one of the top sf artists of the time, illustrating his short story "The Defenders." This was PKD's first cover illustration and his first appearance in the science fiction field's top magazine, *Galaxy*. He would appear there again several times but I bet this first was the most satisfying. And sitting beside this *Galaxy*, or close nearby, was the Jan issue of *Imagination* including his story "Mr. Spaceship."

PKD had been seemingly idle over the holidays. A look at the calendar shows that nothing dropped in the slot at the SMLA until the manuscript for "One Who Stole" ("Project: Earth") arrived on Jan 6, 1953.

Now, it might be recalled that PKD had *already* sent this manuscript to the editors at *F & SF* in March 1952 (and they'd presumably rejected it). I think what happened is that Dick went through his old manuscripts over Christmas and discovered one, at least, that had not been sold – "One Who Stole" – and sent it off to the SMLA while he geared himself up for more writing after a break. "Project: Earth" was published in the Dec 1953 *Imagination*.

The first new story to arrive, then, was "The Trouble With Bubbles" on January 13, 1953. The trouble with "The Trouble With Bubbles" was that after its initial appearance in *Worlds Of If* in Sep 1953 and the UK edition of *If* in Feb 1954, the story was never seen again until THE COLLECTED STORIES in 1987.

"The Trouble With Bubbles" is a story about a future world of jaded idleness where the population – barred from space because of the lack of inhabitable planets – spends their time building fancy world-bubbles in competition with each other and then destroying them. A moral question arises about the doomed inhabitants of the bubbles and when new planets are discovered things start going wrong with the real world. This is another of PKD's stories where physical size becomes relative and man plays at being God.

"The Trouble With Bubbles" rates ✳ ✳

On Jan 17 1953 two manuscripts arrived at the SMLA; that for "A Present For Pat" and that for "Breakfast At Twilight."

"A Present For Pat" was published in *Startling Stories* in Jan 1954. After that it was published in the UK version of the magazine in March 1954. Then, almost twenty years later, Donald Wollheim selected it for his PKD collection, THE BOOK OF PHILIP K. DICK (1973). A few years later it appeared in THE TURNING WHEEL (1977) from Coronet publishers in the UK.

"A Present For Pat" is a story where a minor deity from Ganymede is sold to a Terran and brought back to Earth, where it immediately starts causing trouble. A would-be funny story that sometimes is and at others is simply obvious.

"A Present For Pat" rates ✳ ✳

Arriving at the SMLA on the same day as "A Present For Pat" -- Jan 17, 1953 -- "Breakfast At Twilight" found a home at *Amazing Stories* magazine and was published in July 1954.

Apparently, while making its rounds, the story was *not* sent to *Galaxy* as in a note by Scott Meredith's sub-agent at the SMLA on the story file it is noted: "Don't try Gold, as he doesn't like this kind of yarn, Dick sez" [lxxxi]

Fairly popular over the years it was selected by both Don Wollheim and Betty Ballantine for their respective PKD collections: THE BOOK OF PKD (1973) and THE BEST OF PKD (1977).

Philip K. Dick himself describes the story:

There you are in your home, and the soldiers smash down the door and tell you you're in the middle of World War III. Something's gone wrong with time. I like to fiddle with the idea of basic categories of reality, such as space and time, breaking down. It's my love of chaos, I suppose.[lxxxii]

"Breakfast At Twilight" rates ✳ ✳ ✳ ✳

On Jan 26, 1953 the manuscript for "Of Withered Apples" together with that for "The Hood Maker" reached the SMLA. A discussion biographer Rickman had with PKD's second wife, Kleo, implies that "Of Withered Apples" was one of the earliest stories PKD wrote, perhaps even before they were married in 1950, as discussed above.

If this is so and the story was written early then Dick almost certainly revised it before he sent it off to the SMLA. His writing habits at the time, wife Kleo says,

involved doing several drafts "he'd make a lot of changes even to the last copy – he might change words or phrases because they felt right. He had a very strong aesthetic sense, at that time anyway. What might appear to be very small things were quite important." [lxxxiii]

Perhaps, then, this story, like "Project: Earth" was one Dick selected from his pile of old manuscripts, brushed up a bit over the holidays and sent off to the SMLA for them to sell where earlier he had failed.

"Of Withered Apples" was published in *Cosmos #4* in July 1954, it's only appearance until THE COLLECTED STORIES.

"The Hood Maker" arrived at the SMLA on Jan 26, 1953 – the same day as "Of Withered Apples." The story was originally titled "Immunity" and was published in *Imagination* in the Jun 1955 issue. After that it didn't reappear until THE COLLECTED STORIES in 1987.

Again with this story, PKD presents us with something new: telepaths. As might be expected from PKD's rather sour outlook at this time his telepaths are not a boon to mankind, even though *they* might think so! Sallow and callous youths; the offspring of the survivors of a nuclear bomb in Madagascar, think they'll take over the world. After all, they're more advanced than the rest of us: genetic mutants, the next stage in evolution, *homo superior*. And they don't like the metallic' hoods' that thwart their mind-reading abilities so a power struggle results in which the teeps powers are ultimately used against them. An engaging and thought-provoking story.

"The Hood Maker" rates ✳ ✳ ✳ ✳ ✳

As PKD was mailing off his next story, "Human Is," he could see copies of *F & SF* on the stands with his story "Roog." It had taken a while but his first professional story had finally made it to the science-fiction reading public. It was accompanied by the Feb issue of *Imagination* with his story "Piper In The Woods."

After January's two offerings of "Mr. Spaceship" and "The Defenders" in the magazines I wonder what the fans thought of this tricky science fiction writer who was now, all of a sudden, cranking out fantasy?

"Human Is" reached the SMLA on Feb 2, 1953. It was published in *Startling Stories* in the Winter 1955 issue and selected for Ballantine Books' THE BEST OF PHILIP K. DICK in 1977.

In a letter to editor Terry Carr in 1964 thanking him for his comments on his novel collaboration with Ray Nelson (THE GANYMEDE TAKEOVER), PKD mentions "Human Is" in passing:

{…} by the way: as to my story "Human Is". If you prefer not to include it, by all means don't. The judgement is up to you fellas at Ace, not me; I was merely hoping. Assemble, from all that I sent, what *you* consider the best; okay? I'm sure I'll be pleased, even if it's the same story twelve times.[lxxxiv]

Of the story Phil Dick had this to say:

To me, this story states my early conclusions as to what is human. I have not really changed my view since I wrote this story, back in the Fifties. It's not what you look like, or what planet you were born on. It's how kind you are. The quality of kindness, to me, distinguishes us from rocks and sticks and metal, and will forever, whatever shape we take, wherever we go, whatever we become. For me, "Human Is" is my credo. May it be yours.[lxxxv]

The story is similar to "Beyond Lies The Wub" in that a human is 'possessed' by an alien in a beneficial way. When Lester comes home from Rexor IV he's a changed man alright, but his wife and nephew don't seem to mind; in fact he's much better now than what he was.

"Human Is" rates four stars but loses one for obviousness ✳ ✳ ✳

About a week later, on Feb 11, 1953, two more stories rolled into the SMLA. These were "The Impossible Planet" and "Adjustment Team." As "The Impossible Planet" was published first we'll look at it first.

"The Impossible Planet" was originally title "Legend" by PKD and was first printed in *Imagination* in the Oct 1953 issue. It was selected for Rich & Cowan's UK collection A HANDFUL OF DARKNESS in 1955. Twenty years later Brian Aldiss picked the story for his anthology *SPACE ODYSSEYS* in 1974.

It tells the story of a little old rich lady who wishes to see Earth before she dies. An unscrupulous spaceship captain agrees to take her there even though the planet Earth is now only a legend. So he searches his computers for the most likely place and takes her there. But is it Earth? Or is he just taking her money and running? Well, that's why Phil wrote the story.

Once again Philip K. Dick comes up with a new angle on the old science fiction idea of the lost planet of origin of a future galactic empire. This is a great little story because it shows clearly how Dick creates his characters to perfectly fit the story. In "The Impossible Planet" there are four main characters: the opportunistic captain, his partner with moral qualms, the little old lady so wasted that she has to lean on her 'robant' servant, the fourth of the group. With these characters PKD, in a few thousand words, manages to create the image of a galactic empire in its totality.

Perhaps the ending is a bit convenient but "The Impossible Planet" rates ✳ ✳ ✳ ✳

"Adjustment Team" is a longer story than "The Impossible Planet" but it's not necessarily a better one. After its reception at the SMLA on Feb 11, 1953 it was first published in *Orbit Science Fiction #4* in the Oct-Nov 1954 issue. It was selected for THE BOOK OF PHILIP K. DICK in 1973. There is a literary curiosity out there somewhere; the Australian book *THE SANDS OF MARS And Other Stories* published by a company called 'Jubilee' in 1958 which contains this story.[lxxxvi] There is also a Hungarian appearance from 1983.[lxxxvii]

As for the story, a late-rising businessman was where he shouldn't have been when the Adjustment Team come along to shore up reality. He sees what lies beneath and doesn't like it wanting only to return to his normal life. In the end he knows he's going to be adjusted but is glad and not too concerned with the question of ultimate reality.

"Adjustment Team" rates ✳ ✳ ✳

One of Philip K. Dick's best-known stories, "Impostor", was next to arrive at the Agency on Feb 24, 1953. It was published for the first time in *Astounding Science Fiction*, June 1953 and was selected by Rich & Cowan for their PKD collection, A HANDFUL OF DARKNESS (1955) and by Ballantine for their THE BEST OF PHILIP K. DICK (1977). Also, it was published several times in every decade up to the new century, over twenty anthology appearances altogether.

Sometime circa 1967 or 1968 the story was sold, apparently, to the BBC for "something like $443." This would most likely have been for a radio adaptation and not a teleplay if it was ever produced.[lxxxviii]

In 2002 it was made into a Hollywood movie staring Gary Sinise and Madeleine Stowe. Although not bad, *IMPOSTOR* wasn't that good either and it quickly disappeared from the theatres after the initial run in February.

From the Introduction to the story in *GREAT SCIENCE FICTION OF THE 20TH CENTURY*, here's what the tale is about:

"Aliens come in all shapes, sizes and intentions in science fiction, but what if they looked like us? The shape-changer is a particularly frightening and dangerous creature because when he is present it becomes impossible to trust anyone, even friends or members of the family. It is this sense of increased vulnerability that makes Mr. Dick's story so terrifying. It is worth noting that he wrote it at the height of the "McCarthyist" period in the United States" [lxxxix]

Philip K. Dick wrote about "Impostor":

Here was my first story on the topic of: Am I a human? Or am I just programmed to believe I am human? When you consider that I wrote this back in 1953, it was, if I may say so, a pretty damn good new idea in sf. Of course, by now I've done it to death. But the theme still preoccupies me. It's an important theme because it forces us to ask: What *is* a human? And -- what isn't.[xc]

This science fiction story about a man who thinks he's a man but who may not actually be a man but instead an alien bomb awaiting only the trigger before blowing up, is an early definer of PKD's theme of what is human? But what is the trigger that will send Spence Olham off?

"Impostor" rates ✳ ✳ ✳ ✳ ✳

Over three weeks passed before the next story reached the SMLA. This was "James P. Crow" on Mar 17, 1953. It found a home in *Planet Stories* in May 1954. This story was little known as it appeared nowhere else until THE COLLECTED STORIES in 1987.

It's unpopularity was too bad as this is an excellent satire on racism wherein humans are now become the slaves of robots. Cowed by impossible tests and grumbling about it, humanity can't quite figure out what to do with themselves until one of their kind, Jim Crow, starts passing the robots' tests and is put in a position of power. Besides its ironic reversal of roles, the story is fast-paced and well told.

This is one of the stories historian Thomas Clareson sees as significant for its foreshadowing of "the direction science fiction was to take in social criticism in the 1960s and 1970s. [xci]

"James P. Crow" rates ✳ ✳ ✳ ✳ ✳

One more week went by before two more short stories reached the SMLA. These were "Planet For Transients" and "Small Town" on Mar 23, 1953.

Under the manuscript title of "The Itinerants," "Planet For Transients" was published in the Oct-Nov issue of *Fantastic Universe* magazine and was selected for A HANDFUL OF DARKNESS in 1955. Later the story was incorporated into the novel DEUS IRAE which PKD (and Roger Zelazny) spent a long time writing and which was finally published in 1976.

It amazes me sometimes to see the publication history of some of these short stories. For instance, "Planet For Transients" is as good a short story as Phil ever wrote, why it was never snapped up by a half-century's worth of anthologizers is beyond me.

In a future, nuclear-war ravaged Earth, a dwindling group of humans sends out scouts to try and find more of their kind. To the radiation-adapted quasi-humans that they encounter they are a curiosity – and good luck to find one. In the end the humans escape to space and realise that they cannot return to Earth except as visitors.

"Planet For Transients" rates ✳ ✳ ✳ ✳ ✳

"Small Town" arrived the same day as "Planet For Transients" on Mar 23, 1953 and was published in the May 1954 issue of *Amazing Stories*. Dick had titled the manuscript "Engineer" but that was changed by the time of publication.

Other than *Amazing*, it was selected for Dick's THE GOLDEN MAN collection in 1980. Then, as usual, it disappeared until THE COLLECTED STORIES.

PKD wrote this about "Small Town":

Here the frustrations of a defeated small person -- small in terms of power, in particular power over others -- gradually become transformed into something sinister: the force of death. In rereading this story (which is of course a fantasy, not science fiction) I am impressed by the subtle change which takes place in the protagonist from Trod Upon to Treader. Verne Haskel initially appears as the prototype of the impotent human being, but this conceals a drive at his core self which is anything but weak. It is as if I am saying, The put-upon person may be very dangerous. Be careful as to how you misuse him; he may be a mask for thanatos: the antagonist of life; he may not secretly wish to rule; he may wish to *destroy*.[xcii]

Have you ever wondered about those people who build and run huge train-sets layouts in their basements? Well, wonder no more. Here PKD explains all that's going on. In the small town of Woodland everything is just super but in the larger world outside things are not so good.
"Small Town" rates ✷ ✷ ✷

The last manuscript to arrive at the SMLA in March 1953 was that for "Souvenir," which showed up on the 26th. The Agency found the story a spot in *Fantastic Universe* magazine of Oct 1954. And that's it until THE COLLECTED STORIES.
The title says it all. You'll have to read the story to realise it, though, but sometimes a souvenir is all that ever remains. A wooden cup from a lost civilization kindles a fire in a young boy's eyes.
"Souvenir" rates ✷ ✷ ✷ ✷ ✷

PKD followed "Souvenir" a week later with "Survey Team" on Apr 3, 1953. The agency placed the story at *Fantastic Universe* where it was included in the May 1954 issue. Then, again, it was not reprinted until THE COLLECTED STORIES.
This is another of Dick's up from under the surface of the Earth stories, but once on top the explorers find devastation and determine to escape to Mars, even though it doesn't appear too promising to the survey team sent to scope out the red planet. In fact its already been used up by the Martians before they left. But where did they go? Well, you can guess this one, suffice to say that even though it's hopeless the survey team decides to go onwards to find an unspoiled world.
"Survey Team" rates ✷ ✷ ✷

Two weeks passed before the manuscript for "Vulcan's Hammer" reached the SMLA on Apr 16, 1953. On this dating, though, Rickman has an alternative date of exactly one year later on Apr 16, 1954, for reception of "Vulcan's Hammer."[xciii] A look at the calendar for these two years shows that in both PKD was not so busy as to preclude the writing of the story in either year. [xciv] But, if it was written in 1954 then it would have been done directly after SOLAR LOTTERY. On the subjective grounds that the story is vastly inferior to SOLAR LOTTERY and also not in the vein of his other short-story submissions in early1954, which are mostly stories about psionics, I'd place "Vulcan's Hammer" in 1953. PKD scholar Frank Hollander agrees with me on this.
The story was published in 1956 in *Future Science Fiction #29,* with a fine cover illustrating the story. Later, in 1960, Dick would expand the story into a novel of the same name for Don Wollheim at Ace Books. At the appropriate time we'll look at the expansion. In a letter to his agent, Scott Meredith, in 1960, when PKD was considering the expansion, he mentions the short-story somewhat disparagingly:

"Vulcan's Hammer" is a botched job, in the printed version. I botched it myself. I consider it one of the worst of my efforts. However, parts are good, even superb. If I am to expand it, I must do more than literally put in two words where one now stands throughout...

I would build up the best parts, and eliminate or lessen the weaker parts. I believe that the true body of good ideas lies in the first portion of the story -- in about the first third. The ending is terrible...[xcv]

At almost 23,000 words this long story tells of a future in which mankind has turned governmental rule over to a computer, Vulcan 3. In the stagnation that follows various groups wish to take back control but Vulcan 3 does not wish to relinquish its power and a mighty struggle results.

"Vulcan's Hammer" rates ✳ ✳ ✳

"Prominent Author" was received at the SMLA on Apr 20, 1953. The Agency placed it at *If* and it was published for the first time in the May 1954 issue. After that the story was selected for PKD's first collection, A HANDFUL OF DARKNESS in 1955. Then, 32 years later, its final appearance in THE COLLECTED STORIES.

The story itself is a precursor to THE CRACK IN SPACE (1965) in that a businessman takes the 'jiffi-scuttler' short-cut through space to his office and finds a thin spot in the wall of the tunnel itself. On the other side of the wall little people run around and send miniature messages to him. He translates these and sends messages back. Soon he realizes that these people are starting to worship him and in the end, when he's caught by his boss and fired, he receives one last missive from the little people and discovers, with satisfaction, that he is the author of a famous book: *The Holy Bible.*

PKD in this story once again deals with the theme of scale.

Similar in feeling to "The Builder", "Prominent Author" rates ✳ ✳ ✳

The manuscript for "Fair Game" reached the SMLA one day after that for "Prominent Author" on the 21st Apr, 1953. The Agency must've had some difficulty placing the story as it was not published until Sep 1959 in *If.* After that, the fate of "Fair Game" was that of many of PKD's early short stories: oblivion until volume three of THE COLLECTED STORIES in 1987. Comments on the story are non-existent.

As for the story: Professor Douglas is the top physicist in the world, not worried by the young upstarts. But when a giant eyeball peers in his window and bars of gold and pretty girls appear from nowhere he succumbs to his fate as mankind's top representative to an alien civilization. Or, at least, that's what *he* thinks. To the aliens, though, he's another kind of catch.

"Fair Game" rates ✳ ✳ ✳

May 1953 saw three more stories published in the sf magazines: "The Infinites," "Second Variety" and "The World She Wanted." In almost every one of the next 28 months PKD had at least one short story published.

"The Hanging Stranger" reached the SMLA on May 4, 1953. It was published in the Dec 1953 issue of *Science Fiction Adventures* – the only one of PKD's stories to ever appear in that magazine. After that, the tale is the familiar one of nothing until volume 3 of THE COLLECTED STORIES in 1987.

In a variation of Dick's up-from-under plot, a man surfaces from his basement to find flying insect-like aliens changing into human semblance and trying to take over the town. He flees and is caught and, in the end, is there any need to ask who the hanging stranger is?

Similar to "Adjustment Team", "The Hanging Stranger" rates ✱ ✱ ✱

May 13, 1953 marks the arrival of the manuscript for "The Eyes Have It" at the SMLA. The Agency sold the story to *Science Fiction Stories* and it was printed in the late 1953 issue. Two anthology appearances 30 years later and then THE COLLECTED STORIES is about it for "The Eyes Have It."[xcvi]

That any anthologizer, let alone two, should have picked up "The Eyes Have It" and have ignored "Jon's World" is incredible. This is possibly one of the worst short stories Dick ever wrote. Really, at 1300 words, it's just a throwaway.

A man takes literally what is obviously metaphorical and imagines an alien invasion. And like the man, even though my eyes also roam around the room, I have no stomach for this story either. A joke.

"The Eyes Have It' gets ✱

June 1953 was one of the best months ever for PKD's short story publications. Six stories appeared in the June science fiction magazines: "Colony", "Impostor", "Martians Come in Clouds", "Paycheck", "The Cookie Lady" and "The Preserving Machine." With the three stories published in May these six make up probably the strongest set of his short work ever laid before the avid science fiction public in the 1950s. Of these nine stories, I have rated eight at four stars or better, only "The Preserving Machine" falters a bit, dropping to three stars.

When we look to the short stories that PKD wrote in June we note that "The Eyes Have It" must've been something that he had to get out of his system. His next stories were long and complex in plot: "Time Pawn", "The Golden Man", "The Turning Wheel" and "The Last Of The Masters."

These were all good stories, but some were better than others...

Unfortunately, "Time Pawn" wasn't one of the best. Ambitious at over 22,000 words and, besides "A Glass Of Darkness", the longest of all his short stories, the ms clunked to the floor at the SMLA on Jun 5, 1953. The Agency quickly found it a home in the 25th anniversary issue of *Thrilling Wonder Stories* in the Summer of 1954, illustrated by Virgil Finlay. After that it was never republished – not even in THE COLLECTED STORIES. This exclusion would also occur with a couple of other novelettes, "Vulcan's Hammer" and "A Glass Of Darkness." I suppose that the editors of THE COLLECTED STORIES thought it best to leave these long stories out since they would later be expanded into novels.[xcvii] "Time Pawn" involves a future American Indian society wherein sterilization and euthanasia are the norm; a doctor is sucked from the past into this society where he actually saves someone's life thus contravening every law imaginable. In the end, after much involvement with a revolutionary clan within this society, the doctor is returned to his own time.[xcviii]

Even though the sub-agent at the SMLA thought "Time pawn" gave its reader "high hopes for abt 1/3rd of the way" in the end he found it "very disappointing."[xcix]

In 1959 Don Wollheim of Ace Books would approach PKD with the notion of expanding "Time Pawn" into a novel. This Dick did with the unhappy result of DR. FUTURITY. Later we will examine this expansion.

As a novelette "Time Pawn" rates ✷ ✷

Three weeks after mailing in the ms for "Time Pawn", PKD sent off another long story, "The God Who Runs." This reached the SMLA on Jun 24, 1953. It was published in the Apr 1954 issue of *If* under the title "The Golden Man." The story illustration was by Kelly Freas.

Sporadically anthologized over the last 50 years, "The Golden Man", by lending its name to the 1980 collection THE GOLDEN MAN, marks a focal point in the parade of Philip K. Dick's short stories. This was the last of the story collections published before his death and it gave PKD the opportunity to comment on the stories selected by the editor, Mark Hurst. In many cases, these comments are the only thing we have by PKD on these stories. For "The Golden Man" Dick had much to say:

In the early Fifties much American science fiction dealt with human mutants and their glorious super-powers and super-faculties by which they would presently lead mankind to a higher state of existence, a sort of promised land. John W. Campbell. Jr., editor at *Analog*, demanded that the stories he bought dealt with such wonderful mutants, and he also insisted that the mutants always be shown as (1) good; and (2) firmly in charge. When I wrote "The Golden Man" I intended to show that (1) the mutant might not be good, at least good for the rest of mankind, for us ordinaries; and (2) not in charge but sniping at us as a bandit would, a feral mutant who potentially would do us more harm than good. This was specifically the view of psionic mutants that Campbell loathed, and the theme in fiction that he refused to publish… so my story appeared in *If*.

We sf writers of the Fifties liked *If* because it had high quality paper and illustrations; it was a classy magazine. And, more important, it would take a chance with unknown authors. A fairly large number of my early stories appeared in *If*; for me it was a major market. The editor of *If* at the beginning was Paul W. Fairman. He would take a badly-written story by you and rework it until it was okay – which I appreciated. Later James L. Quinn the publisher became himself the editor, and then Frederik Pohl. I sold to all three of them.[c]

In the issue of *If* that followed the publishing of "The Golden Man" appeared a two-page editorial consisting of a letter by a lady school teacher complaining about "The Golden Man". Her complaints consisted of John W. Campbell, Jr.'s complaint: she upbraided me for presenting mutants in a negative light and she offered the notion that certainly we could expect mutants to be (1) good; and (2) firmly in charge. So I was back to square one.

My theory as to why people took this view is this: I think these people secretly imagined they were themselves early manifestations of these kindly, wise, super-intelligent *Ubermenschen* who would guide the stupid – i.e. the rest of us – to the Promised Land. A power phantasy was involved here, in my opinion. The idea of the psionic superman taking over was a role that appeared originally in Stapleton's *ODD JOHN* and A.E.Van Vogt's *SLAN*. "We are persecuted now," the message ran, "and despised and rejected. But later on, boy oh boy, we will show them!"

As far as I was concerned, for psionic mutants to rule us would be to put the fox in charge of the hen house. I was reacting to what I considered a dangerous hunger for power on the part of neurotic people, a hunger which I felt John W. Campbell, Jr. was pandering to – and deliberately so. *If,* on the other hand, was not committed to selling any one particular idea; it was a magazine devoted to genuinely new ideas, willing to take any side of an issue. Its several editors should be commended, inasmuch as they understood the real task of science fiction: to look in *all* directions without restraint. (1979)

Here I am also saying that mutants are dangerous to us ordinaries, a view which John W. Campbell, Jr. deplored. We were supposed to view them as our leaders. But I always felt uneasy as to how they would view us. I mean, maybe they wouldn't want to lead us. Maybe from their superevolved lofty level we wouldn't seem worth leading. Anyhow, even if they agreed to lead us, I felt uneasy as to where we would wind up going. It might have something to do with buildings marked SHOWERS but which really weren't.(1978)[ci]

As for the story itself, in a post-apocalypse world a fearful government sends out agents to hunt down mutants and kill them. Always afraid of finding the one that will undo *Homo Sapiens* status in the world they finally find him. But can they destroy him? Or will he escape to breed?

"The Golden Man" earns ✭ ✭ ✭ ✭ ✭

In 2007 "The Golden Man" will appear as a movie under the title 'Next.' It will star Nicolas Cage.

July 1953 saw three more stories on the stands: "The Indefatigable Frog", "Expendable" and "The Cosmic Poachers." During the month Dick sent three more stories in to the SMLA.

The first of these to arrive was "The Turning Wheel" on July 8. It was published in *Science Fiction Stories #2* in 1954 and was first collected in A HANDFUL OF DARKNESS in 1955 and then, in 1973, in THE BOOK OF PHILIP K. DICK (published by Coronet in the UK in 1977 as THE TURNING WHEEL And Other Stories).

The story concerns a far-future society in which the artistic class called the Bards are at the top and the Technos at the bottom. The Bards believe in reincarnation and act accordingly so that in their next birth they will move up on the wheel of life and not down. For the protagonist, though, who has seen his death from the plague and a future incarnation as a blue-assed fly on another planet, things don't look too good. Even when he meets the Tinkerist clan of the Technos and is given some pills to forestall the plague he doesn't have the wit to use them. On the turning wheel of life it is obvious that soon the Bards will fall while the Technos will rise.

An interesting thing about this story is that the future deity is named Elron Hu. The whole story, in fact, is a snide commentary on L. Ron Hubbard's quasi-religion called Dianetics. John W. Campbell, editor of *Astounding* had championed this movement in the pages of his science fiction magazine. Hubbard, after all, was a science fiction writer and A.E.Van Vogt himself had aligned himself with Dianetics. But even when Dick's mother, Dorothy, joined up, Dick was not impressed. He'd been reading Hubbard's lousy science fiction stories for some time. As Dick's wife, Kleo at the time, said:

When Dorothy was interested in Dianetics, {...} she tried to get us interested too. The main problem was that Philip had been familiar with the writing of L. Ron Hubbard when he was a lousy science fiction writer, and it was pretty hard to take seriously anything that he was doing.[cii]

Dianetics evolved into the world-wide religion called Scientology. It has many adherents even today. One wonders whether they have read much of Hubbard's science fiction... But, as a story, "The Turning Wheel" gets ✭ ✭ ✭ ✭

A week after sending in "The Turning Wheel" Dick sent off the manuscript for "Protection Agency." This arrived at the SMLA on July 15 and was first published on *Orbit Science Fiction* in Nov 1954 under the title "The Last Of The Masters."

Surprisingly enough for such a good story, it was scarcely anthologized although Mark Hurst included it in his 1980 collection, THE GOLDEN MAN. About the story, PKD wrote this:

Now I show trust of a robot as leader, a robot who is the suffering servant, which is to say a form of Christ. Leader as servant of man; leader who should be dispensed with -- perhaps. An ambiguity hangs over the morality of this story. Should we have a leader or should we think for ourselves? Obviously the latter, in principle. But -- sometimes there lies a gulf between what is theoretically right and that which is practical. It's interesting that I would trust a robot and not an android. Perhaps it's because a robot does not try to deceive you as to what it is.[ciii]

Here's a good description of the story courtesy of Hazel Pierce:

In "The Last Of The Masters" Dick continues to make us aware of the paradoxical cast of human existence. Even as the Anarchist League glories in its two-hundred-year-old success at destroying all government, it hears a rumour of a remnant of the old order that is still flourishing. The League goes on a search and destroy mission, an unnecessary move. The small anachronistic society is gradually breaking down of its own entropy. Complete with a disciplined economic organization (but no market to supply) and a well-trained military (but no enemy to fight), the group exists at the will of a deteriorating pre-war robot master. Even as the Anarchists break the robot up beyond all salvage, one of the service men pockets a memory chip "just in case the times change." [civ]

"The Last Of The Masters" gets ✶ ✶ ✶ ✶

A week later on July 21, 1953, the manuscript for "The Father-Thing" reached the SMLA. It was first published in *F & SF* in Dec 1954 and was selected for Ballantine's THE BEST OF PHILIP K. DICK collection in 1977.

If anthology appearances are anything to go by, "The Father-Thing" is one of Dick's most popular – and well-read – short stories. Since 1959 to the end of the 20th century the story was chosen by such editors as Anthony Boucher, Martin Greenburg and Isaac Asimov for different anthologies.

In a brief flurry of letters to the editors of *F & SF* in September 1953, Dick wrote about "The Father-Thing.":

Here is the rewrite on "The Father-Thing." Eleven new pages. A new ending, as you suggested, and reworked material throughout: pages I thought could be improved. The new ending adds one page to the yarn; I tried to keep the length down as much as possible. I agree the old ending cut off too soon, didn't really resolve the situation. Seems to me the main fault lay in the sudden defection of Daniels and Peretti. I built up a picture of their realism, their loyalty, their organization -- and then had them flee in the moment of crisis, to leave Charles alone. An insult to kids! I think this will do it, but if it doesn't, I'm always glad to rewrite a rewrite, as I did on the two Doc Labyrinth yarns. I wonder if you would mind letting me know how this goes, in either case. Okay? And meanwhile, I'll keep rustling around, trying to dig up transportation, so we can get together and talk about the ways of fiends.[cv]

Four days later he wrote again to *F & SF*:

I hope this won't foul everything up, but here is *another* ending for "The Father-Thing." A shorter version: knocks off four pages. Eliminates considerable material, and the ending is more powerful (I think).

In connecting the enclosed with what you have, join these pages (12 through 18) with 1 through 11 of the *second* version. In other words, this third version makes use of the new pages that preceed page 12.

What a mess. But I wanted you to see both endings together. Okay? [cvi]

"The Father –Thing" was accepted at *F & SF* on Sep 25, 1953, a few weeks after this letter.

Of "The Father-Thing", PKD had this to say:

I always had the impression, when I was very small, that my father was two people, one good, one bad. The good father goes away and the bad father replaces him. I guess many kids have this feeling. What if it were so? This story is another instance of a normal feeling, which is in fact incorrect, somehow becoming correct ... with the added misery that one cannot communicate it to others. Fortunately, there are other kids to tell it to. Kids understand: they are wiser than adults -- hmmm, I almost said, "Wiser than humans." [cvii]

In 1972, a science fiction anthology, *THEMES IN SCIENCE FICTION* was published. In it was PKD's "The Father-Thing". This anthology was intended as a text for High School students and over the next few years Dick received letters from several kids asking about the story. Usually he responded with the same reply:

... The idea really came to me when I was a kid. My parents were divorced, and I sometimes didn't see my father for as long as five years at a time. When I did see him, he was always a stranger to me, different from what I remembered. I always remembered him as a kind man, but when I saw him again, he always seemed harsh and cruel. It was if {sic} there were two fathers: the real one whom I remembered, and the "other" father who looked like mine, but was really inhuman and a stranger. [cviii]

The story itself is similar to the famous movie, *The Invasion Of The Body Snatchers* (1956) but Dick's story was published a year before Jack Finney's novel *THE BODY SNATCHERS* on which the movie was based. [cix]

"The Father-Thing" is a fantasy. In the story a young boy sees *two* fathers in his garage. One comes into the house – the wrong one – and the scared child climbs out the window and runs away. But he's an intrepid kid and he rounds up his friends who unearth the pods in which the mother-thing and the kid-thing are about to hatch. After a struggle they set fire to the alien usurpers and there the story ends.

"The Father-Thing" deserves ✮ ✮ ✮ ✮ ✮

After "The Father-Thing" PKD sent off the short story "Immolation." It reached the SMLA on Aug 4 1953 and was published in *Imagination* in Dec 1954 under the title "Strange Eden."

"Strange Eden" was never anthologized and only resurfaced in volume 3 of THE COLLECTED STORIES in 1987. Comments on it are non-existent.

In the story a two-man survey team discovers an unspoiled world. They land and one man, despite his captain's qualms, goes off to explore. He spots a large cat-like creature and decides to do some big-game hunting. But his attention is distracted by a beautiful girl and he thinks she would be a better trophy. She's willing, but her pet cats are about to increase in number by one…

"Strange Eden" doesn't really work that well and only rates ✶ ✶

The next story PKD sent in to the SMLA was one of his longest. "A Glass Of Darkness" reached the Agency on Aug 19 1953. At about 40,000 words it was practically a novel. The story was first published in the Dec 1956 issue of *Satellite Science Fiction*. The cover illustrates the story and is by Kelly Freas. Internal art is by Arnold Arlow. Later the story would be revised and retitled as THE COSMIC PUPPETS and published by Ace Books as one half of an Ace Double in 1957. Later we will look at this revision. "A Glass Of Darkness" was inspired by Dick's love for the magazine *Unknown*. In 1981 he told interviewer Gregg Rickman that "one day he decided to try and write an *Unknown*-style fantasy, 'a fantasy novel for a publication which I loved, which no longer existed.'" *Unknown* hadn't existed since 1943.[cx]

The title for the story was taken from *1 Corinthians 13*, the paragraph that goes:

"For now we see through a glass, darkly; but then face to face; now I know in part; but then shall I know even as also I am known. And now abideth faith, hope, charity, these three: but the greatest of these is charity."

Which is a part of a lecture on the supreme virtue of charity.

The story should've shown up in one of the science fiction magazines in late 1953 or early 1954. That it didn't Rickman attributes to the fact that this story is a fantasy, not science fiction, and the market for fantasy tales in the mid Fifties was practically non-existent.

However, it finally landed in the second issue of *Satellite Science Fiction* (1956-1959) in December of 1956.

The story, at 92 pages, filled the bulk of the magazine, pushing much shorter efforts by Arthur C. Clarke, Frank Bryning, Michael Shaara, Dal Stevens, Algys Budrys and Gordon R. Dickson into the last thirty pages. Dick was paid $400.[cxi]

In 1954 Dick referred to "A Glass of Darkness" in a letter:

{…}I have a ms of a fantasy novel which I wrote two years ago. It runs about 80,000 words. My agent won't handle it because there is no market... I've thought about printing it privately. The only catch is this -- its not exactly the kind of fantasy one reads in fantasy magazines. It's a psychological fantasy of the dream type, more like Kafka I suppose, or like "The Man Who Was Thursday." There is no fantasy premise: that is, a fantastic postulate from which things proceed logically; the beginning is natural, factual, normal, as in Hubbard's "Fear;" the ordinary world, in fact. From there, the book "degenerates into sheer fantasy," as my agent puts it. It progresses, I would say, into greater and deeper levels of fantasy; a trip into the dream regions of symbolism, the unconscious, etc. as one finds in "Alice in Wonderland," where the work ends with a final cataclysm of dream-fantasy.[cxii]

If, indeed, PKD was referring to "A Glass Of Darkness" in this letter (and he could've been referring to nothing else; his only novels written in or before 1953: GATHER YOURSELVES TOGETHER and VOICES FROM THE STREET are much longer works and not fantasies) then he has the word-count wrong. "A Glass Of Darkness" comes in at about 40,000 words not 80,000. But perhaps he reduced the length of the story before its publication.

The story concerns a man who returns to his home town after a long absence only to find everything subtly changed. Strange beings called 'Wanderers' walk through walls and appear to be counting their steps as if trying to find paths that are now lost to them. Two children, Mary and Peter, the offspring of the ancient Zoroastrian deities, Ormazd and Ahriman, conduct a vicious war while their deity parents are locked in a frozen struggle in the sky above the town.

In essence, "A Glass Of Darkness" is the result of PKD's interest in dualistic religions. He told Rickman:

Although I researched Zoroastrianism simply to write a novel, I found that once I had studied a dualistic, bitheistic religion, it was very hard for me to go back to monotheism after that.... Once I got the hang of bitheism it was hard to drop it.[cxiii]

"A Glass Of Darkness", even before its revision into the novel THE COSMIC PUPPETS rates ★ ★ ★ ★ ★

At the end of August two more stories arrived at the SMLA on the same day, Aug 31, 1953. These were "Tony And The Beetles" and "Null-O."

"Tony And The Beetles" was published in *Orbit Science Fiction #2* in Dec 1953. After that, apart from an obscure appearance in the Australian anthology *PLANET OF DOOM and Other Stories* (1958) under the title "Retreat From Rigel", the story was not seen until the third volume of THE COLLECTED STORIES in 1987.

Not much has been said about "Tony And The Beetles." The agent at the SMLA who reviewed the story called it "pedestrian… Rather corny stuff pretending to be impressive." Accordingly, according to Rickman, it was sent not to one of the larger sf magazines, like *Galaxy, If* or *F & SF*, but to the "lower markets", namely, *Orbit SF*.[cxiv]

"Tony And The Beetles" is a study of racism in a colony world. Terra has been beating the Beetles of Orion for many years and has even set up colonies in their home system. But things are about to change when Earth suffers a major defeat. From the point of view of Tony, a small boy born on one of the colony worlds and knowing no other life, this change in Terra's fortunes has unfortunate consequences: his friends, the Beetle children, turn out to be not so friendly after all. In fact, they turn against him just as one imagines the children of crumbling empires in India, Africa and South America turned against the colonists in 20th century earth.

"Tony And The Beetles" gets ★ ★ ★

"Null-O", which arrived at the SMLA on Aug 31 1953, the same day as "Tony And The Beetles", was originally titled "Loony Lemuel." The story was published in the Dec 1958 issue of *If*. Again, after initial publication, the story dropped from sight only to reappear in THE COLLECTED STORIES OF PKD (1987).

Why it took five years to find publication is not known although biographer Gregg Rickman suggests it may have been due to the story's message:

"In "Null-O" a motley crew of the ordinary people he favors rises up and destroys the rationalist scientists who have wrecked the earth's surface; an overtly radical message that may explain the five year delay in the story's publication (1953 to 1958).[cxv]

"Null-O", in fact, is a jaundiced look at A.E.Van Vogt's concept of 'Null-A' (*THE WORLD OF NULL-A* and its successors). Lemuel is a boy with a super-logical mind, incapable of feeling normal human emotions like compassion, sorrow or pity. Lemuel hooks up with others of his kind; paranoids who believe that the universe must be homogenized into an undifferentiated state. Of course, the Null-O's are just the ones to do this, designing a C-bomb to render down the cities of Earth and then an E-bomb to detonate the Earth itself, and then an S-bomb for the sun and so on up to the U-bomb to take care of the universe. But their plans come to a screeching halt when thousands of ordinary men who have been living underground surface and wreck all the Null-O plans and equipment and kill most of the Null-O's. Some escape on a rocket-ship, though, and Lemuel is heartened by their fading message that they will continue their plans – right before he, himself, is captured by the ordinaries.

This story is a bit unfair, perhaps, to Van Vogt's original conception. Just because a thalamic pause and a logical mind figure in his novels doesn't mean that his characters are paranoid, just, well, *logical*.

The name 'Loony Lemuel' recurs in PKD's later novel THE SIMULACRA but belongs to a different character altogether.

"Null-O" rates ✶✶✶

September 1953 was another bumper month for Dick's short stories on the newsstands. Five more stories appearing then: "The Trouble With Bubbles", "The Variable Man", "The Skull", "The King Of The Elves" and "The Great C."

But this month, September, was typical in that PKD submitted no short stories to the SMLA. However, there is evidence that he was working on the short story, "Explorers We" during the month, writing to Tony Boucher to discuss a rewrite of that story. However, "Explorers We" was not published until 1959. We will look at the story when we reach that year in our chronology.[cxvi]

The next story to reach the SMLA was "To Serve The Master" on Oct 21, 1953. Originally titled "Be As Gods" the story was first published in *Imagination* in the Feb 1956 issue. With the exception of Patricia Warrick's *ROBOTS, ANDROIDS AND MECHANICAL ODDITIES* (1984), "To Serve The Master" was not reprinted until the third volume of THE COLLECTED STORIES.

The story has aroused little comment. The sub-agent at the SMLA wrote on the story's file card: "Just another happy ending as far as I'm concerned."[cxvii]

In a future society a mailman finds a decrepit robot and helps it to repair itself. But, he should have left well enough alone as this sole survivor of an ancient war between man and machines threatens the stability of this future world. And, besides, for the mailman himself, once he lets the cat out of the bag, his life becomes worthless – and short.

"To Serve The Master" rates ✶✶

The manuscript for "Exhibit Piece" was received at the SMLA on the same day as that for "To Serve The Master", Oct, 21 1953. It found first publication in *If* in Aug 1954 and was selected for PKD's first UK collection, A HANDFUL OF DARKNESS in 1955. Then… THE COLLECTED STORIES in 1987.

This is a good story. A museum curator in the future becomes so involved in his specialty – the 20th century – that he decides to move into his faithfully reproduced exhibit. He's comfortable for a while until he reads the newspaper and discovers he's living on the eve of a nuclear war.

"Exhibit Piece" rates ✷ ✷ ✷

"Foundling Home" was the next story to arrive at the SMLA on 29th Oct 1953. It was published in *Imagination* in July 1954 under the title "The Crawlers." After selection by Ace books for their 1969 PKD collection THE PRESERVING MACHINE, it went mostly unnoticed until THE COLLECTED STORIES.

In this story pitiful human mutant children who look like grubs with human faces are rounded up by the authorities and transported to a distant island where it is hoped they will live out their lives in peace and away from normal human habitations. Somewhat like groundhogs, the mutants delve deep under the island and expand their territory to the mainland. That's when the *real* building will begin. But... some of the Crawler offspring just don't look normal to their mutated parents.

"The Crawlers" rates ✷ ✷ ✷

Oct 1953 had seen three more Philip K. Dick stories on the newsstands: "Planet For Transients", "The Impossible Planet" and "Some Kinds Of Life." Add to that the one story published in November – "The Eyes Have It" – and we can see that PKD's publication pace had not slackened.

Only one short story was sent to the SMLA in November and this was "Sales Pitch" which arrived on the 19th. The Agency knew right where to send it and it was published in *Future Science Fiction* in the Jan 1954 issue. Later Mark Hurst selected the story for inclusion in his PKD collection, THE GOLDEN MAN (1980) and Patricia Warrick chose it for her 1984 collection *ROBOTS, ANDROIDS AND MECHANICAL ODDITIES*.

This story is another slap at rampant consumerism with a domestic robot that refuses to take no for an answer as it foists itself on an unsuspecting family. Sure, the fasrad can do just about anything around the house but its all too much for the harried and harassed homeowner who determines to escape the non-stop intrusive advertisements that dog him on his long commute from Earth to Ganymede. In a desperate attempt to reach the colony worlds on Proxima Centaurus, the businessman takes the fasrad along (he had no choice; it came). But his ship is a family model unsuited for the long trip to Proxima and breaks down before reaching its goal. The fasrad does its best to keep the ship going but ultimately fails. In the end the businessman is left with only the broken fasrad for company. And to make matters worse, it delivers its sales pitch *ad nauseum*.

"Sales Pitch" is one of my favorite PKD stories. The opening section dealing with the long commute to Earth from Ganymede is pretty funny and reminiscent of the beginning of THE UNTELEPORTED MAN.

PKD wrote this about "Sales Pitch":

When this story first appeared, the fans detested it. I read it over, perplexed by their hostility, and could see why: it is a superdowner story, and relentlessly so. Could I rewrite it, I would have it end differently. I would have the man and the robot, i.e. the fasrad, form a partnership at the end and become friends. The logic of paranoia of this story should be deconstructed into its opposite; Y, the human-against-robot theme, should have been resolved into null-Y, human-and-robot-against-the-universe. I really deplore the ending. So when you read the story, try to imagine it as it ought to have been written. The fasrad says, "Sir, I am here to help you. The hell with my sales pitch. Let's be together forever." Yes, but then I would have been criticized for a false upbeat ending, I guess. Still, the ending is not good. The fans were right.[cxviii]

"Sales Pitch" rates ✯ ✯ ✯ ✯ ✯

December 1953 was another good month for PKD's short story publication with four more stories available to the science fiction consuming public: "Tony And The Beetles", "Project: Earth", "The Hanging Stranger" and "The Builder." In the month Dick sent in three more stories.

The first to reach the SMLA was "Shell Game" just before Christmas on Dec 22, 1953. The Agency placed it at *Galaxy* and it was first published there in the Sep 1954 issue. In 1973 Don Wollheim selected the story for his collection THE BOOK OF PHILIP K. DICK. In 1964 Dick would incorporate the story into his novel THE CLANS OF THE ALPHANE MOON.

Survivors of an interstellar spaceship crash fight against mysterious unseen foes. Tension is high amongst the ruling council and everyone suspects everyone else of being in league with the attackers. But when they find out that they are the remnants of a hospital ship full of paranoid psychotics on the way to Betelgeuse and a mental asylum, they don't really believe it and determine to raise their battered ship and drop nuclear bombs on their probably non-existent attackers.

PKD would revisit this idea again with the 'Pares' (paranoids) and 'Manses' (maniacs) in CLANS OF THE ALPHANE MOON.

"Shell Game" is worth ✯ ✯ ✯ ✯

Arriving at the SMLA just before the new year on Dec 30, 1953, "Upon The Dull Earth" was first published in *Beyond #9* in 1954. Later, it was selected by Rich & Cowan for their 1955 collection A HANDFUL OF DARKNESS and was also included in the 1969 Ace collection, THE PRESERVING MACHINE.

This is a fantasy story and one of PKD's best. A witchy girl, Sylvia, invites alien 'angels' into her life using animal blood as an attractant. But when she inadvertently cuts herself one day she cannot stop the 'angels' from taking her with them. Her boyfriend doesn't like it and decides to try and bring her back. This he does but things don't turn out the way he hoped as now all the world seems to be nothing but Sylvia. And when he looks in the mirror...

PKD's biographer, Greg Rickman, in a fan poll run by the fanzine *For Dickheads Only* sees "Upon The Dull Earth" as PKD's "most important story... More for its importance for Phil's future work and for understanding him, than in objective quality (though it's damn good)

If Phil ever wrote a horror story, this must be it. Outré and unsettling "Upon The Dull Earth" rates ✯ ✯ ✯ ✯ ✯

PKD followed "Upon The Dull Earth" a day later with "Foster, You're Dead!" This story was first published in Fred Pohl's *Star Science Fiction Stories #3* in 1955. Then in 1977 it was chosen for Ballantine's THE BEST OF PHILIP K. DICK collection.

From there it was picked up (illegally) by the Russian tabloid *Ogonek* (1958). On this appropriation by the Russians, Philip K. Dick's friend, Betty Jo Robirds, recalls

him telling her that he was listening to KPFA one night, heard a discussion of the lead story in the Russian magazine that was equivalent to *Life* and that he recognized it as his own work. 'Phil thought he was having an hallucination!'[cxix]

PKD's bibliographer notes that

The author's complimentary copy was destroyed by the U.S. Post Office as Communist propaganda.[cxx]

But with this Rickman disagrees, resurrecting one of PKD's relations, Neil Hudner, who remembers being shown the story in Russian.[cxxi]

In a 1958 letter to his friend, Walt Lanferman, Dick wrote of the situation with *Ogonek*:

But, more interesting, the Soviet Union has taken an interest in my stuff (so long, Walt. Nice having known you). Their largest circulation weekly, *Ogonek*, printed in a Russian translation, with illustrations, a story of mine, *Foster, You're Dead*, an anti-war story; it took up five of the *Look*-size glossy pages, five out of about 32.
Ogonek is printed by *Pravda*, and this particular week's edition had a circulation of one and a half million. So a fair amount of royalty money was due me. I wrote the Soviet Union and got no answer. But recently, apparently due to the fact that Stevenson went there this summer represented various US authors such as myself (in fact he was given my name by the American Authors' League) there's been a change of policy, and now *Ogonek* writes me to say they've sent a royalty check. I'm told that it should run about 4,000 rubles -- about $1000. Also, *Ogonek* wants me to submit material to them direct -- the story they used was reprinted from a US Ballantine anthology which caused quite a stir here; was written up in a *Harper's* editorial and in an article in the Bulletin of the Atomic Scientists (the latter unfavorably) {...}[cxxii]

When Tony Boucher was preparing his anthology, *A TREASURY OF GREAT SCIENCE FICTION* (published in 1959), PKD wrote to him and suggested that "Foster, You're Dead!" was 'about my best' and thought that it might fit well in Boucher's anthology. (In the end, Boucher selected "The Father-Thing" for this anthology)

In this letter Dick refers again to his *Ogonek* dealings:

By the way -- the above mentioned story was picked up by *Ogonek*, the largest circulation Soviet weekly (1,500,00). They even drew a number of archaic, foul illustrations for it ... so I have more readers in the USSR than in this country. An odd situation. I never got a cent for the reprint; I wrote to *Ogonek*, asking for a copy of the magazine, but they didn't answer the letter. [cxxiii]

Of the story itself, PKD had this to say:

One day I saw a newspaper headline reporting that the President suggested that if Americans had to *buy* their bomb shelters, rather than being provided with them by the government, they'd take better care of them, an idea which made me furious. Logically, each of us should own a submarine, a jet fighter, and so forth. Here I just wanted to show how cruel the authorities can be when it comes to human life, how they can think in terms of dollars, not people.[cxxiv]

It is fitting that "Foster, You're Dead!" was first published by Fred Pohl as the story is similar in intent to several of Pohl's own science fiction tales dealing with runaway consumerism (see his *THE SPACE MERCHANTS*, for example).

In Dick's tale a young boy is completely demoralized by his family's lack of a nuclear bomb shelter. He faces ridicule at school and hostility at home when he tries to talk his dad into buying the latest model. His father finally gives in and buys the shelter only to find a few days later that it is useless against the Soviet's new bore-pellets weapon. To make the shelter worthwhile will take an expensive adapter… which dad can't afford and he sends the shelter back to the shop. In the end, the boy sneaks into the dealer's showroom and attempts to move into his repossessed shelter. But he's ejected and we find him aimlessly walking the streets perhaps with the fifty cents fee in his pocket for entrance to the public shelter, perhaps not.

"Foster, You're Dead" rates ★ ★ ★ ★ ★

So, then, Philip K. Dick ended the year 1953 with a bang. And it gives us the opportunity to draw a breath in this chronicle of PKD's short stories and look back to see what we have covered.

Dick had had published 31 short stories in 1953 and he had written at least 35. This would be the most he ever wrote in a single year and even though he continued the pace into 1954 one can sense, just from reading this exhausting survey presented here, that burn-out could not be too far off.

At the end of 1952 we categorized somewhat the stories Dick wrote in that year. Let's look beyond the numbers in 1953 and see what PKD had accomplished with his tales in that year.

Three of the stories PKD wrote in 1953 were outright fantasies – and some of his best: "Small Town", "A Glass Of Darkness" and "Upon The Dull Earth."

If a fantasy is a story that lacks a logical or scientific explanation for its premises like in The Little Movement" where no reason is given for the intelligence of the toys, then these 1953 fantasies differ from those he wrote in 1952 in that here he does not impute consciousness to animals and inanimate objects, as in "Roog", "The Short, Happy Life Of The Brown Oxford" and "The Little Movement" but rather sets up more complicated premises: analogy of scale in "Small Town" with the train set directly equated with the town at large; the town of Milford itself being false without explanation in "A Glass Of Darkness"; and the vampiric nature of the alien 'angels' in "Upon The Dull Earth." In Dick's fantasies things are just the way they are because that's the way they are. His two main themes: what is human? And what is real? find further expression in several stories. The stories "Human Is", "Impostor" and "The Father-Thing" all involve humans possessed by aliens who then masquerade as humans. In other, subtle ways too Dick wonders about humanity, developing a social conscience with his tales of mutants who are hunted and killed as in "The Golden Man" or rounded up and segregated as in "The Crawlers."

The nature of reality itself Dick questions in his stories "Adjustment Team", "A Glass Of Darkness" and "Exhibit Piece."

Another theme he continues from 1952 are his stories of people living underground who surface only to find living conditions strange and difficult. In "Planet For Transients" his underground humans arise only to find a world completely unsuitable for them, so much so that they must leave the planet altogether. In "Survey Team" underground dwellers surface in the middle of a war-torn world and flee to a desolate Mars where they delude themselves into thinking that other worlds hold promise for their unmutated kind. And in "Null-O", the masses living underground arise to thwart the plans of the paranoids who rule above.

Mutants as such, too, figure in several stories: ""The Hood Maker", "The Golden Man", Null-O" and "The Crawlers." These stories, including, "The Turning Wheel", can be seen as Philip K. Dick's response to John W. Campbell Jr.'s notion – pandering to the neurotic science fiction audience – that mutants would be benign and superior and lead the human masses to a better future.

One wonders why Dick felt this animosity towards Campbell; perhaps because he rejected dogma of any kind? Or because he thought Campbell was antipathetic to the sort of science fiction Dick was writing? Campbell published only one of PKD's stories in *Astounding* and that was "Impostor" in June 1953.

Beginning in 1952 with "The Great C" and continuing through "Nanny", "Second Variety" and "Jon's World" Philip Dick wrote of the battle between Man and Machine. He continued this in 1953 with "James P. Crow", "Vulcan's Hammer", "The Last Of The Masters", "To Serve The Master" and "Sales Pitch."

In these stories Man in general and in particular is usually the worse off from his mechanical interactions as Dick underscores the folly of war and the idiocy of consumerism.

World War 3 also figures in two stories, "Breakfast At Twilight" and "Exhibit Piece." While social criticism can be found in many stories notably "James P. Crow", "The Chromium Fence", "Tony And The Beetles", "The Crawlers", and perhaps the finest of them all, "Foster, You're Dead."

Continuing his stories from 1952 which were influenced by Jonathon Swift, Philip K. Dick wrote three more stories in 1953 that had to do with matters of scale: "The Trouble With Bubbles", "Small Town" and "Prominent Author."

In some stories PKD uses what might be called a stock character: the space explorer with the bad attitude, like Captain Franco in "Beyond Lies The Wub." He resurfaces again in 1953 as Captain Andrews in "The Impossible Planet" and Brent in "Strange Eden."

God or at least religion also figures in several of Dick's stories in 1953. Man-as-God can be found in "The Trouble With Bubbles" and "Prominent Author" although the most subtle expression of this idea is found in "A Glass Of Darkness." God, or at least a god, pops up in "A Present For Pat" but in an offhand sort of way as in PKD's later novel OUR FRIENDS FROM FROLIX 8 in which God, or at least *a* god, is found floating dead in space.

But there is much that the fertile mind can find and cogitate about in the short stories of Philip K. Dick. Here I've touched on a few of the themes and notions that Dick wrote about in1953. Much of his writing is on typical science fiction themes of the day and reflects the emerging social conscience of science fiction writers, editors and fans who had finally seen the dark side of the Cold War and the injustices and inequalities of capitalism. What lay beneath this social criticism one finds in Dick's stories was, from the evidence of the stories themselves, the realisation that Government itself was at fault and why this was so is the nature of the capitalist technological drive to pervert science for base and ignoble ends. This does not make Dick a communist any more so than it makes George Orwell, say, or Fred Pohl a communist. It was merely a sign of the times.

This period, the early to late Fifties was a golden age for science fiction. Many magazines were published – PKD himself had stories in eighteen sf magazines in the Fifties. It would come to an end after 1959 and the launching of *Sputnik* by the Russians.

Now we must turn our attention to the year 1954. The year when Philip K. Dick, while still writing short stories, made the decision to write his first science fiction novel, SOLAR LOTTERY.

1954

January 1954 saw four more of Philip K. Dick's short stories on the newsstands; "The Short, Happy Life Of The Brown Oxford", "The Crystal Crypt", "Beyond The Door" and "A Present For Pat."

During this month Dick's novel GATHER YOURSELVES TOGETHER was under consideration for publication by Crown Books and Dick sent in one story to the SMLA. This was "Pay For The Printer."

Under the manuscript title "Printer's Pay", this story arrived at the SMLA on Jan 28, 1954. It was published in *Satellite Science Fiction* as "Pay For The Printer" in the Oct 1956 issue. It was selected for the Ace Books 1969 PKD collection THE PRESERVING MACHINE and was not seen again in English until THE COLLECTED STORIES in 1987.

"Pay For The Printer" is a clever story that gently chides consumer culture by positing a post-nuclear culture in which alien 'Biltongs' duplicate things that mankind cannot now manufacture. Things like watches, Scotch whisky and cigarette lighters. Unfortunately, the Biltongs are getting worn out and expiring leaving the dependent survivors to fend for themselves. But this they are mostly incapable of doing. One enterprising craftsman, though, is proud of his little wooden cup.

"Pay For The Printer" rates ✶ ✶ ✶ ✶

February 1954 saw only one new PKD story published. This was "Jon's World" in August Derleth's anthology *TIME TO COME*. In this month PKD also sent only one story off to the SMLA, "War Veteran" arriving at the Agency on Feb 17.

"War Veteran", at almost 17,000 words was a long short story and it found publication as the feature story in the Mar 1955 issue of *If*. The story is illustrated by Kelly Freas. Like "Pay For The Printer", "War Veteran" was selected for the Ace Books PKD collection THE PRESERVING MACHINE in 1969 but was not seen again until THE COLLECTED STORIES in 1987. No comments have been made on this story.

"War Veteran" is an excellent story and ranks with Dick's best. A mercantile dispute between Earth and a Venus-Mars coalition threatens to bring all out war. But an old soldier from the future remembers fighting in the coming war and remembers the utter defeat of the Earth forces. But is he for real? The Earth authorities determine to find out before any war declaration is made.

"War Veteran" is awarded ✶ ✶ ✶ ✶ ✶

"War Veteran" in mid-Feb 1954 was Philip K. Dick's last short story for a while as he turned his attention now to writing his first science fiction novel, SOLAR LOTTERY.

But although his short-story output dropped drastically in 1954 – he sent in no stories to the SMLA in March and only one in April and one in May and altogether submitted only ten all year – the publication time-lag made it appear that PKD was as prolific as ever.

March saw publication of "The Turning Wheel" and April publication of "The Golden Man." But the early part of the year was mostly spent by Dick in the writing of SOLAR LOTTERY.

SOLAR LOTTERY

PKD's first true science fiction novel has a complicated publishing history, appearing in two versions; one called SOLAR LOTTERY in the United States and one called WORLD OF CHANCE in the United Kingdom. Originally Dick had named the novel QUIZMASTER TAKE ALL but this was changed by Ace Books... Well, let's trace the history out.[cxxv]

The manuscript of QUIZMASTER TAKE ALL reached the Scott Meredith Literary Agency on March 23, 1954. An employee of SMLA wrote on the Agency's record card that "I had the author do some rewriting to give it depth."[cxxvi]

The original manuscript, at 63,000 words, was then revised by Dick: "...I had about 45 characters in the original version. My agent made me throw most of them out."[cxxvii]

On its return to the SMLA the revised manuscript was sent to Ballantine Books, the top-of-the-line sf paperback publishing house, where it was rejected, as it was at two other publishers before the Agency sent it to Ace Books. Don Wollheim, editor at Ace, liked it. But he wanted some changes and sent it back to Dick for what PKD called "major revisions." Dick told Rickman that "Ace Doubles were very, very precise as to how long these books were ... It had to be exactly 6,000 lines long. That was a marketing thing and I understood that."[cxxviii]

But, in the same passage in which this quote was found in Greg Rickman's *To The High Castle*, Wollheim says to that: "Bullshit! Baloney. That was never true of us. We had a certain page-range -- 320 pages to begin with. You knew lengths by rule of thumb." [cxxix]

According to the SMLA's file the revision that was sent to Ace in December 1954 was "cut to 60,000 words." But whether this revision was the first one requested by the Agency employee or that by Wollheim is not clear. Wollheim himself doesn't remember asking for a rewrite.[cxxx]

Nevertheless, Ace published the newly retitled SOLAR LOTTERY in May 1955 as one half of an Ace Double. Presumably the decision to change the title from Dick's original QUIZMASTER TAKE ALL was made sometime after Jan 10, 1955 when the *Oakland Tribune* noted that PKD had a "forthcoming pocket book novel, QUIZMASTER TAKE ALL, readied for Fall, U.S. publication."[cxxxi]

The decision to change the title was made by A.A.Wyn, publisher of Ace Books. Wollheim: "Wyn insisted on doing the titling. He had a pulp mind, so I gave him a whole long list of titles and he picked that one (SOLAR LOTTERY)."[cxxxii]

Wollheim says he himself wrote "most all" of Ace's ad copy. 'First Prize Was Earth Itself!' was the line used for SOLAR LOTTERY. He also instructed the art director in the matter of cover art: "The covers are definitely supposed to illustrate the book. Wyn personally supervised them." [cxxxiii]

Dick was promptly paid by Ace, Wollheim: "We paid $1500 for a Double, split in half. The author got $750 and half of the royalties..."[cxxxiv]

Dick was grateful for this, crediting Wollheim with his continuing as a sf novelist after Wollheim's acceptance of SOLAR LOTTERY:

Don was the only editor who risked buying SOLAR LOTTERY; no one else would take it, and if Don hadn't, you wouldn't have been able to identify me as a novelist at all. Had SOLAR LOTTERY not sold, I would have abandoned attempts to write novels, and would have gone back to the stories. [cxxxv]

And now this publishing saga gets even more complicated. During the SMLA's dealings with Ballantine, the other publisher's, and Ace, a copy of the original manuscript was sent to England where it was picked up by Rich & Cowan, a hardcover sf publisher. But before Rich & Cowan were ready to publish it they wrote to the SMLA asking for a rewrite. But Dick, having gone over the manuscript twice already and not wanting to do it again, wrote to Scott Meredith on May 16, 1955 that "they can have a copy of the Ace edition, which will be out in a day or so. They can print from that."[cxxxvi]

Apparently though, from Rickman's research, they didn't. Rickman believes that they edited down the original first manuscript of QUIZMASTER TAKE ALL themselves, butchering it in the process.[cxxxvii]

But this may not be correct. In an interview with Richard Lupoff Dick says,

They bought SOLAR LOTTERY, my first novel, and brought it out as WORLD OF CHANCE. But they brought it out in a truncated form. They insisted that a great deal be deleted from it. I did, in fact, make a different version of SOLAR LOTTERY for them. It's quite different from the U.S. version. [cxxxviii]

So anyway you look at it we cannot be sure at the moment which draft was used for WORLD OF CHANCE and who, if anyone other than Dick, did the butchering. As to exactly how this was done we must refer the reader to *PKDS#21*: "What The Quizmaster Took," by Gregg Rickman. In this special issue of the *Philip K. Dick Society Newsletter* Rickman does an involved study of the differences between the British WORLD OF CHANCE -- for such did Rich & Cowan title it on its publication in 1956 -- and the Ace SOLAR LOTTERY. These differences are sometimes extensive as well as significant.

The question yet remains, Why did Philip K. Dick write SOLAR LOTTERY? Why all of a sudden after more than two years of writing short stories, did he decide to write a novel? And why SOLAR LOTTERY?

The two factors which bear most directly on Dick's deciding to write an sf novel were his own dissatisfaction with the quality of his short stories and a dawning awareness of the economics of the sf field: short stories, no matter how many he cranked out, just didn't pay enough. Couple this all together with his sense of finding "something mysterious" in science fiction and we have pretty much the whole story. PKD tells it in his 1968 *Self Portrait*:

In 1953 I sold stories to fifteen different magazines; in one month, June, I had stories in seven magazines on the stands at once. I turned out story after story, and they all were bought. And yet -- with only a few exceptions, my magazine-length stories were second rate. Standards were low in the early 50s. I did not know many technical skills in writing which are essential ... the viewpoint problem, for example. Yet, I was selling; I was making a good living, and at the 1954 Science Fiction World Convention I was very readily recognized and singled out...I recall someone taking a photograph of A. E. Van Vogt and me and someone saying, "The old and the new." But what a miserable excuse for the "new"! And how much the field was losing by Van Vogt's leaving it! I knew that I was in serious trouble. For example, Van Vogt in such works as *The World Of Null-A*, wrote novels; I did not. Maybe that was it; maybe I should try an sf novel.[cxxxix]

This passage, besides telling the main story, also brings up a sometime habit of PKD's: the telling of his personal history in a way that makes the best story. This occasionally results in a little bending of what actually happened. In this case his attributing the decision to write a science fiction novel to his meeting with A.E.Van Vogt at the 1954 World Con in San

Francisco. But as both Paul Williams and Lawrence Sutin point out, Dick had written SOLAR LOTTERY before he attended the 1954 World Con in San Francisco: as evidenced by the files of the Scott Meredith Literary Agency in New York which lists the manuscript for SOLAR LOTTERY as having arrived in March 1954 while the Worldcon was held in August.

But irregardless of whether he met Van Vogt at the Worldcon, Van Vogt's writing was a heavy influence on SOLAR LOTTERY. In conversation with Arthur Byron Cover, PKD mentions the early influence of Van Vogt:

I started reading sf when I was about twelve and I real all I could, so any author who was writing about that time, I read. But there's no doubt who got me off originally and that was A.E. van Vogt. There was in van Vogt's writing a mysterious quality, and this was especially true in *The World of Null A*. All the parts of that book did not add up; all the ingredients did not make a coherency. Now some people are put off by that. They think that's sloppy and wrong, but the thing that fascinated me so much was that this resembled reality more than anybody else's writing inside or outside science fiction.[cxl]

And talking with Greg Rickman:

When I wrote SOLAR LOTTERY I modeled it on A.E.Van Vogt, and I modeled it deliberately on Van Vogt, and I have no shame, because he was my hero as a writer and as a person. I wrote a Van Vogtian novel. I was not an original writer at that time. I was a very derivative type of writer. I had heroes and I tried to write like they wrote. He was my *idée fixe* as far as a writer. So it does resemble a Van Vogt novel, which Damon Knight pointed out. When you read it now -- when Tom Disch did the Gregg Press novel, he really couldn't see anything good in this novel. But Tom is forgetting the time in which it was written... 1954. Well, shit! There was nothing good then. There was one novel, one science fiction novel that had been written that was good. And that was Bester's *THE DEMOLISHED MAN* (1952). And I cribbed from that, the Telepathic Corps. [cxli]

Which seems clear enough, as well as introducing another influence on SOLAR LOTTERY, Bester's *THE DEMOLISHED MAN*.

As for the mysterious quality he'd discovered in science fiction Dick had more to say; in conversation with Charles Platt:

A point came when I began to feel that science fiction was very important. Van Vogt's *THE WORLD OF NULL-A*-- there was something about that which absolutely fascinated me. It had a mysterious quality, it alluded to things unseen, there were puzzles presented which were never adequately explained. I found in it a numinous quality; I began to get an idea of a mysterious quality in the universe which could be dealt with in science fiction. I realize now that what I was sensing was a kind of metaphysical world, an invisible realm of things half seen, essentially what medieval people sensed as the transcendent world, the next world. [cxlii]

And at this point a brief look at A. E. Van Vogt's *THE WORLD OF NULL-A* would be appropriate. In this fascinating novel, not one of Van Vogt's first, the never-say-die hero, Gilbert Gosseyn, dies a series of deaths only to reawaken in a different body each time. This is driving him nuts as he has no idea of what's going on. But he's determined to find out. The problem with *THE WORLD OF NULL-A* is that nothing seems to really resolve but in its very irresolution the story hints at something mysterious that can perhaps be grasped by utilizing a non-Aristotelian approach. This 'null-A' logic Van Vogt relies on is based on the Theory of

General Semantics by Alfred Korzybski. This theory today forms much of the underpinning of modern Semantics. PKD used a similar notion of 'minimax' to underlie SOLAR LOTTERY.

Perhaps the affect of *THE WORLD OF NULL-A* on PKD was similar to mine. A sense of discovery of something new in science fiction, something that could be *used.* For, to someone unfamiliar with General Semantics its appearance in a science fiction novel would surely be intriguing. In a way Van Vogt's novel was doing science-fiction's essential task: that of advancing the knowledge and field of Science. *THE WORLD OF NULL-A* was not just about science, it was science. As any young science fiction fan knows, this is why we read science fiction. We are doing science.

The writing mechanics of *THE WORLD OF NULL-A* also affected SOLAR LOTTERY. Dick says he wrote "a Van Vogtian novel", but what does that mean? Commonly it is understood as referring to the convoluted plotting of *The World Of Null-A*. And this is so, but critic John Huntington refers to a writing 'rule' that Van Vogt used while writing his stories[cxliii]:

{of} writing a story in scenes of about 800 words, and each scene has five steps in it. If all those steps aren't there in their proper way, then there's something wrong with that scene. First, you let the reader know where this is taking place. Then you establish the purpose of the main character or the purpose of that scene. Then you have the interaction of his trying to accomplish that purpose. The fourth step is, make it clear: did he or did he not accomplish that purpose? Then the fifth step is that, in all the early scenes, no matter whether he achieves that purpose or not, things are going to get worse.[cxliv]

While noting that there is no direct acknowledgement by PKD of his use of Van Vogt's idea -- borrowed from John Gallishaw's *THE ONLY TWO WAYS TO WRITE A SHORT STORY*, Huntington goes on to assume the application of this 800-word rule in Dick's work, notably DO ANDROIDS DREAM OF ELECTRIC SHEEP?, THE THREE STIGMATA OF PALMER ELDRITCH, UBIK and VALIS.

Huntington makes interesting use of this assumption when discussing Dick's writings, we might even agree that it is valid but, without direct acknowledgement by PKD to Van Vogt's 800-word rule or a complete mechanical analysis of these novels, we can only say that SOLAR LOTTERY does reflect this intricacy. Our opinion -- in agreement with Huntington -- is that Dick was influenced by the effects of Van Vogt's method without realizing its mechanical nature.

But despite all this Van Vogtian influence, there are several other things impinging on Dick's mind as he prepared to write SOLAR LOTTERY.

In addition to Van Vogt, Bester and Vonnegut, PKD was also influenced by the French Realist writers:

I wasn't writing novels when I started out. I was writing stories. But the second I switched to novels, this inner template based on the French realistic novels just turned on like a circuit board. You can see that SOLAR LOTTERY, my first novel, is literally like the French novels in that respect: all manner of people in all walks of life... portrayed as best I could.[cxlv]

Not knowing much about French Realism, I cannot comment on this. However, PKD still had to face the problem of how to write the story on more than instinct and a broad reading in the Classics.

In conversation with Rickman, PKD addresses this:

They're really very early novels, and I had no control over viewpoint then. I only got control over viewpoint because of a chance remark, a friend of mine, a Western writer named
WillCook...

But he found out that I varied my viewpoint, and I didn't even know of the concept "viewpoint". I was so naive and so amateurish. So I asked him what my viewpoint was, he says, sometimes its third-person interior, something like that. It's like suddenly being equipped for the first time with such concepts as ontology. And I said, "Gollee!" I just fathomed what he was saying. So I said, well, are there any other kinds of viewpoints? He said, Oh, yeah! there's first-person, you know, and he explained to me all about viewpoint.

And I really just memorized everything he said. I thought "Goddamn! This is really great! I can do all kinds of things I didn't know." In SOLAR LOTTERY, there's a scene in the first chapter, where I could not fathom how to handle the viewpoint. I literally did not know about interior third person versus omniscience. So I was having a hell of a time. So he clued me in to all that stuff.

So once I got into the viewpoint problem as a problem, I decided to explore all the possible viewpoints that might exist, not just the ones that were conventionally used. Like he said, there's just three viewpoints, really. There's third-person omniscient, there's first person -- there's actually first person interior, like James Joyce did in *ULYSSES*. I knew that. Like you're almost getting down in the unconscious. And then there's third person interior, versus third-person external. And he explained the difference to me... ...[cxlvi]

So, with the help of Will Cook and the Realists and his science fiction contemporaries, Dick sat down and wrote SOLAR LOTTERY.

For months I prepared carefully. I assembled characters and plots, several plots all woven together, and then wrote everything into the book that I could think of. It was bought by Don Wollheim at ACE Books and titled SOLAR LOTTERY... Standing there at that point I did some deep thinking. It seemed to me that magazine-length writing was going downhill -- and not paying very much. You might get $20 for a story and $4000 for a novel. So I decided to bet everything on the novel..." [cxlvii]

Dick wrote the story in February and March 1954 and was paid $1000 by Ace Books, as mentioned above.

On its publication in May 1955, Dick liked the reception it got from the science fiction magazine editors and critics, as well as its circulation.

Ah, 1954. I wrote my first novel, SOLAR LOTTERY; it sold 150,000 copies of itself and then vanished, only to reappear a few years ago. It was reviewed well, except in *Galaxy*. Tony Boucher liked it; so did Damon Knight. But I wonder why I wrote it -- it and the 24 novels since. Out of love, I suppose; I love science fiction both to read it and to write it. We who write it do not get paid very much...[cxlviii]

There was some negative criticism, or what could be construed as such. In 1958 he told James Blish that his next novel THE MAN WHO JAPED was written partly to dispel the notion that SOLAR LOTTERY was written from "an extreme left position."[cxlix] This idea was still current twenty years later when Tom Disch noted that:

"SOLAR LOTTERY, along with most of its successors (in Dick's oeuvre) may be read as self-contained social allegories of a more-or-less Marxist bent."[cl]

58

Dick responded to this, saying,

anyone who understands... MAN WHO JAPED would never make the error of thinking that I was a communist or Marxist. Because there is a very, very sincere attempt to show the very dangerous trends in Communism, the communist state.[cli]

But later, in 1978, PKD returns to Disch's essay and this time agrees with him:

Glanced over SOLAR LOTTERY & Tom Disch's intro; he's right. I was/am the sole Marxist S-F writer. I may not have been/am CP, but the basic Marxist sociological view of capitalism -- negative -- is there. Good. But after glancing at it I feel the old fear -- like c. 1971/73. When the blow fell. Glancing at SOLAR LOTTERY I can see that it had to, eventually & that I knew it. If I just hadn't passed over into the dope stuff I'd have ceased to be relevant, & been safe but nooo. I got caught up in the 60s, & stayed on to 74 and TEARS. [clii]

In another conversation with Rickman he further elaborates on his Marxist bent:

In many ways I was an anti-capitalist, but that doesn't make me a Marxist. I was very, very suspicious, terribly suspicious of totalitarian states, whether right or left wing. I would say the real enemy, the enemy which to me is the paradigm of evil, is the totalitarian state... My real stance was opposing authority. And I opposed the Communist authorities as much as I opposed the American authorities. [cliii]

Other critics have also noted this Marxist angle in SOLAR LOTTERY.[cliv] Dick was pleased with the sales of his first novel. His friend, Paul Williams, recalls that "Phil used to say it had sold over 150,000 copies, which then allowed him to say that his first book was his most successful and it had been downhill from there." [clv]

Also, in an interview with John Boonstra, PKD brought up SOLAR LOTTERY's sales:

By the year 1959 the sf had totally collapsed. The readership had shrunk down to 100,000 *total*. Now, to show you how few readers that is, SOLAR LOTTERY alone had sold 300,000 copies in 1955.[clvi]

Some reviewers also thought highly of the novel; Anthony Boucher in *F & SF*, Aug 1955:

Philip K. Dick's SOLAR LOTTERY (Ace, 35 cents) is kept from a Grade A rating only by a tendency, in both its nicely contrasted plots, to dwindle away at the end. This first novel by one of the most interesting new magazine writers (one of *F & SF*'s discoveries, I may add proudly) creates a strange and highly convincing and self-consistent future society, peculiarly governed by Games Theory and the principle of randomness; against this background, built up with the detail of a Heinlein and the satire of a Kornbluth, it relates a taut melodrama of political conflict and a stirring space-quest to rediscover a lost tenth planet.[clvii]

Some didn't; here's Floyd C. Gale in *Galaxy*, Nov 1955:

SOLAR LOTTERY is something else again. It's a longer story and has ten times as much plot, so I guess it should be ten times better than its companion story [Leigh Brackett's *THE BIG JUMP*] but ...

Anyhow, it concerns a society that is founded on the monstrous descendents of our present industrial giants; a governmental setup that uses "teeps" – telepathic agents; rule-by chance succession that is determined by lottery and lots, lots more. Too much if you ask me. There's a limit to how many ideas a writer can compress into a story. After that, it's profitless squandering.[clviii]

As Mr. Gale intimates, there is a lot going on in SOLAR LOTTERY. Ted Benteley, the protagonist, has been fired from his job with one of the industrial giants and he signs on with the present quizmaster not knowing that the 'bottle' is about to twitch another man into power. But the quizmaster doesn't wish to be deposed and by invoking the legalized principle of assassination he attempts to kill his successor. But how does he get around the Telepathic Corps whose job it is to protect any quizmaster? Add in a sub-plot wherein a group of ordinary workers seek the mysterious tenth planet called the Flame Disc and much palace intrigue and we do, indeed, have a novel in which PKD threw in everything he could think of.

All in all, SOLAR LOTTERY was a very successful first science fiction novel for PKD.[clix]

It's also one of my favorites and I give it ✵ ✵ ✵ ✵ ✵

While wrestling all year long with rewrites of SOLAR LOTTERY, Dick continued sending in short stories to the SMLA and continued seeing his stories in print in the science fiction magazines on the newsstands. In April 1954, one more of his stories was available to the fans – "The Golden Man" -- and he was writing his first short story after sending in the manuscript for SOLAR LOTTERY in March. This was "The Chromium Fence."

"The Chromium Fence" reached the SMLA on April 9, 1954 and was first published in *Imagination* in July 1955. The story never resurfaced until THE COLLECTED STORIES in 1987.

As for comments, we have those of the reader at the SMLA who thought "The Chromium Fence" was 'a fine story that never quite attains any stature.' The file card at the Agency also notes that Dick himself characterized "The Chromium Fence" as 'a *New Yorker* story set in the future' so the Agency suggested trying to sell the story to the *New Yorker*, then *Esquire* then Fred Pohl who was then preparing an anthology, then Horace Gold. The story ended up at *Imagination* and PKD was paid $50.[clx]

The story is a strange one of a man living in a future society where two factions, the Naturalists and the Purists vie for supremacy at the polls. The Naturalists believe in letting mankind be, well, natural, whereas the Purists cannot stand things like bad breath and sweat and wish to mandate that everyone have their sweat glands removed and other bodily functions sanitized. The Purists win the election and Don Walsh, the protagonist, who just wants to be left alone is turned in to the authorities by his own son and even though Walsh wants simply to live his life in peace, he cannot opt out of his society. In the end, despite being given an out by a state psychiatric robot, Walsh is rounded up by the police and eliminated.

Perhaps this story is a comment by PKD on fascism or nazism. Later in several stories the character of the 'Hitler youth' will recur.

"The Chromium Fence" rates ✶ ✶ ✶

In April 1954 Philip K. Dick wrote to Anthony Boucher inquiring about his short story, "Explorer's We", and wondering if Boucher wanted a rewrite. We will look at this situation when we reach the year 1958 in this chronology.[clxi]

There is also the case of "Vulcan's Hammer" to consider here. Although we have earlier ascribed the writing of "Vulcan's Hammer" to 1953, Rickman gives an alternative date of April 1954 for the reception of the manuscript of "Vulcan's Hammer" at the SMLA. See above for discussion of this matter.

After sending in "The Chromium Fence" in April, the next story to arrive with any certainty at the SMLA was "Misadjustment" in May.

May 1954 was a good month for PKD's short story publications. On the newsstands five stories were available: "Survey Team", "Time Pawn", "James P. Crow", "Prominent Author" and "Small Town."

The manuscript for "Misadjustment" arrived at the SMLA on May 14, 1954. The story was published in *Science Fiction Quarterly* in Feb 1957 and is illustrated by Ed Emshwiller. After this initial publication it was not reprinted until volume 3 of THE COLLECTED STORIES.

"Misadjustment" is another story about mutants. A powerful industrialist is detected as a mutant by the government's security arm and despite his efforts to flee he eventually gives himself up at a party. The occasion for the party is to reveal a fine jet transport craft that another man has grown in his back yard… Unfortunately, that makes him a mutant too and he is killed by the industrialist as the party-goers flee in panic. But, what exactly *is* this industrialist's mutation?

This is a powerful story if you stop and think about it because it treats 'mutation' as somehow subjective – delusional – as well as objective – real. If a man can grow a rocket-ship and another can walk through walls then what does that say about reality? No wonder the Government in the story is scared; if this is allowed to continue then pretty soon there will be no consensus to which society can adhere.

"Misadjustment" is similar to "The Golden Man" and gets ★ ★ ★ ★

Two more stories were published in June: "Martians Come In Clouds" and "Sales Pitch."

Almost a month passed before Dick's next story dropped in the slot at the SMLA. This was "A World Of Talent" on June 4, 1954.

"A World Of Talent", originally titled "Two Steps Right" by Dick, was published in *Galaxy* in the Oct 1954 issue and was selected for Ace Books' PKD collection THE VARIABLE MAN in 1957. Little comment has been made on the story.

The story itself tells of a mixed bag of mutants on the Proxima colony planets who are at war with Terra as they fight for independence. They're also at war with themselves as one faction of psis – the telepaths – try to take over rule of the colony. The protagonist discovers a new kind of mutant; an anti-psi whose powers cancel out that of her opposite type. For telepaths there are anti-telepaths, and so on. In the end after the girl is killed the hero searches for a way to bring her back to life.

Interestingly enough, the girl's name is Pat Connley. PKD would resurrect this name and character as Pat Conley in UBIK (1968). In UBIK, too, Pat is an anti-psi but her character is much darker: PKD's typical dark-haired girl but with a nasty edge. Before reading UBIK I'd recommend that one read "A World Of Talent" first as the story is in some ways a preview of the novel and explains the psi talent that the girl in UBIK exhibits.

Perhaps, as Gregg Rickman says, the story was a response to *Galaxy* editor John W. Campbell's "dogmatic insistence in the early 50s that a positively portrayed 'psionics' (such extrasensory powers as telepathy, telekinesis, and precognition) 'was the necessary premise for science fiction stories.'[clxii]

"A World Of Talent" rates ✭ ✭ ✭ ✭

PKD followed "A World of Talent" a few days later with his story "Outside Consultant" the manuscript arriving at the SMLA on June 8, 1954. The title was changed to "Psi-Man, Heal My Child!" by the time of publication in *Imaginative Tales* in Nov 1955. The story was selected by Don Wollheim for his 1973 collection THE BOOK OF PHILIP K. DICK and then nothing until THE COLLECTED STORIES. Comments on it are non-existent. In a post-nuclear future survivors spurn the scientific offerings of their communes in favor of the mutant psi-talents of those living outside. In effect they reject science for magic. The psis themselves display many talents, one of them can travel through time and does so in an effort to prevent the war that has brought the world to its sorry state. But this effort fails and in the end the psis decide to help the present populace with their powers.

"Psi-Man, Heal My Child!" deserves ✭ ✭ ✭

July 1954 saw three more short stories published: "Breakfast At Twilight", "Of Withered Apples" and "The Crawlers." And in August there were two more: "Exhibit Piece" and "Upon The Dull Earth." Also in September there were another two: "Shell Game" and "Adjustment Team."

Looking at the calendar in mid 1954 shows that from mid-June to mid-October little in the way of writing was done by PKD. In August he attended science-fiction fandom's greatest event, the Worldcon, which was held in San Francisco that year. As we've noted above, the Worldcon had an affect on PKD. Meeting the great writers of his time: Poul Anderson, A. E. Van Vogt, and the up-and-coming like Harlan Ellison, and talking business with the old pros and editors and the like confirmed Dick's decision to concentrate on writing science fiction novels. Of course, he still wanted to write mainstream novels but was realistic enough to realise that money could be made by selling science fiction novels. The first one he would attempt after attending the Worldcon was THE WORLD JONES MADE which was completed by the end of the year.

But before turning to THE WORLD JONES MADE, we will look at five more short stories that Dick sent to the SMLA in late 1954.

The first two to arrive – on the same day – were "Service Call" and "Autofac" in mid-October 1954.

"Service Call" reached the SMLA on Oct 11, 1954 and was first published in the July 1955 issue of *Science Fiction Stories*. The story was anthologized three times before publication of THE COLLECTED STORIES. First in the Belmont paperback *MASTERS OF SCIENCE FICTION* in 1964. Then it was selected for Ballantine's THE BEST OF PKD in 1977 and, lastly, in Patricia Warrick's *ROBOTS, ANDROIDS AND MECHANICAL ODDITIES* in 1984.

The story concerns a research engineer who is visited at home by a swibble repairman. But he has no swibble and doesn't know what one is and he irritably dismisses the repairman. Later he discovers that the repairman is from the future and when he returns again, certain that he has the correct address, the engineer and his associates try to find out what exactly a swibble is. Turns out it's some sort of bionic-mechanical device for ensuring loyalty in the survivors of a nuclear war. If one doesn't adhere to the dominant ideology then the swibble will eat you up.

The swibble will return in Dick's 1966 story "Your Appointment Will Be Yesterday" on which the novel COUNTER-CLOCK WORLD is based. But there it is merely a name for something that no one now recalls.

Of the story PKD had this to say:

When this story appeared many fans objected to it because of the negative attitude I expressed in it. But I was already beginning to suppose in my head the growing domination of machines over man, especially the machines we voluntarily surround ourselves with, which should, by logic, be the most harmless. I never assumed that some huge clanking monster would stride down Fifth Avenue, devouring New York; I always feared that my own TV set or iron or toaster would, in the privacy of my apartment, when no one else was around to help me, announce to me that they had taken over, and here was a list of rules I was to obey. I never like the idea of doing what a machine says. I hate having to salute something built in a factory. (Do you suppose all those White House tapes came out of the back of the President's head? And programmed him as to what he was to say and do?)[clxiii]

"Service Call" rates ★ ★ ★

The manuscript for "Autofac" showed up at the SMLA on the same day as that for "Service Call" – Oct 11, 1954. The story was sold to *Galaxy* and was printed in the Nov 1955 issue of that magazine.

A popular story over the years, "Autofac" was selected for five anthologies including THE BEST OF PHILIP K. DICK, before publication of THE COLLECTED STORIES in 1987.

This story caused strife between PKD and Horace Gold, editor of *Galaxy*. Gold's custom was to alter facets of stories accepted by *Galaxy*, a practice which did not sit well with the authors. Philip K. Dick was annoyed at this meddling with "Autofac" and wrote, "Despite the fact that *Galaxy* was my main source of income I told Gold that I would not sell to him unless he stopped altering my stories -- after which he bought nothing from me at all."[clxiv]

Later, though, Philip K. Dick did sell stories to *Galaxy* but no earlier than "War Game" in 1959.

Here's a precis of the story courtesy of Hazel Pierce:

To sustain the population during a war, far-sighted engineers built completely automated underground factories. Sophisticated in design, each one seeks its raw materials, manufactures and delivers the goods, and *in extremis* repairs or rebuilds itself elsewhere. To the survivors struggling to establish the necessary agrarian economy, the glut of manufactured stuff proves burden, not boon; the men cannot win. The autofacs outwit all efforts toward their destruction by the sheer complexity of their own survival programming.[clxv]

Of "Autofac" Dick wrote in 1976:

Tom Disch said of this story that it was one of the earliest ecology warnings in sf. What I had in mind in writing it, however, was the thought that if factories became fully automated, they might begin to show the instinct for survival which organic living entities have... and perhaps develop similar solutions.[clxvi]

"Autofac" is akin to "Pay For The Printer" and rates ✶ ✶ ✶ ✶

Only a week passed before two more stories arrived at the SMLA. These were "Captive Market" and "The Mold Of Yancy" on Oct 18, 1954.

"Captive Market" was first published in *If* in Apr 1955. Fairly popular with editors, the story was anthologized first in 1957 in *THE FIRST WORLD OF IF*, then collected in THE PRESERVING MACHINE (1969) and in 1988 included in Isaac Asimov and Martin Greenburg's prestigious anthology *THE GREAT SF STORIES 17*.

"Captive Market" is a grim little story in which a precognitive old lady who owns a country store finds a future where survivors of a nuclear war need provisions to escape Earth for Venus. Greedily she sells them whatever they need but with her precog powers she can always find a future where they do not escape and keep on coming back for more. This is another of Dick's unique takes on psionics as he invests the powers into a small-minded old lady with nothing but money and profit on her mind. Certainly she's no super-human mutant ready and able to lead humanity to a better future.

"Captive Market" earns ✶ ✶ ✶ ✶ ✶

Accompanying "Captive Market" in the mail delivery to the SMLA on Oct 18, 1954 was the manuscript for "The Mold Of Yancy." The story found its way to *If* and after slight revision was published in the Aug 1955 issue. Later, it was selected for Mark Hurst's PKD collection THE GOLDEN MAN (1980). The idea of the story was adapted into Dick's 1964 novel THE PENULTIMATE TRUTH and the story's title, in a slightly amended form as "In The Mold Of Yancy" was intended as the original title for THE PENULTIMATE TRUTH.[clxvii]

According to the Agency's records, "The Mold Of Yancy" was rewritten for *If* and reduced from 9,500 words to 7,000 words.[clxviii]

Of the story PKD had this to say:

Obviously, Yancy is based on President Eisenhower. During his reign we all were worrying about the man-in-the-grey-flannel-suit problem; we feared that the entire country was turning into one person and a whole lot of clones. (Although in those days the word "clone" was unknown to us.) I liked this story enough to use it as the basis for my novel THE PENULTIMATE TRUTH; in particular the part where everything the government tells you is a lie. I still like that part; I mean, I still believe it's so. Watergate, of course, bore the basic idea of this story out.[clxix]

As to the story; sophisticated computer analysts on Earth detect totalitarian leanings in Callisto government. But when Earth spies go to Callisto they can find nothing wrong. The society is open and not repressive, the people enjoying life, reading, listening to music, watching TV, even complaining about the Government. The only problem is that they're all reading, listening and watching the same thing: whatever the ubiquitous John Edward Yancy gently suggests they be interested in. But, as for real opinions on real subjects like war, the Callistotes have no opinion at all, they just think they do. Earth realises what's going on and with the help of a disgruntled Callistote programmer they reprogram the Yancy simulacrum to encourage diversity in the populace.

Even though Philip K. Dick wrote "The Mold Of Yancy" and based Yancy himself on President Eisenhower, as mentioned above, to a later reader the story and Yancy in particular remind one of President Ronald Reagan. In this story Dick makes the important connection between conformity and totalitarianism.

"The Mold Of Yancy" deserves ✮ ✮ ✮ ✮ ✮

October 1954 had seen four more of Dick's short stories published: "A World Of Talent", "Adjustment Team", "Meddler" and "Souvenir." November saw two more: "Progeny" and "The Last Of The Masters." But after the flurry of submissions in October, it was not until late December that another story reached the SMLA. This was "The Minority Report" on Dec 22nd. During the interim, Dick was working on his novel THE WORLD JONES MADE, the manuscript for which was completed by mid-December.[clxx]

The manuscript for "The Minority Report" reached the SMLA on Dec 22, 1954. This was a week before the Agency received the manuscript for THE WORLD JONES MADE. At almost 17,000 words "The Minority Report" can be considered a novelette rather than a short story. It was first published in *Fantastic Universe* in Jan 1956.

The story was selected for PKD's first USA collection THE VARIABLE MAN in 1957. It would be another thirty years before it reappeared in THE COLLECTED STORIES where it gave its name to the title of the fourth volume. After that, when interest in the Stephen Spielberg movie began to grow, "The Minority Report" was republished in 2000 in the UK and in 2002 a small hardback edition of the story alone was issued by Pantheon at a price of $12.95! Almost as much as PKD got paid for the first publication.

The movie, *THE MINORITY REPORT*, directed by Spielberg and starring Tom Cruise and Sean O'Farrell, was released in May 2002 to worldwide acclaim and box-office bonanza (the movie was the largest grossing movie on its premiere weekend, bringing in over $36 million).

Little early comment was made on the story although, since the release of the movie in 2002, both the story and the movie have been voluminously written about. A visit to www.philipkdick.com reveals several reviews of the movie which can be found in such publications as *The New York Times*.

This story set in the near future revolves around the establishment of the new government entity called Precrime. By using mutant precogs the police authorities can preview who will commit future crimes; the suspects, guilty before they act, can then be arrested and their crimes prevented. Trouble is, John Anderton, the director of the new agency, is himself pre-fingered for murder, and either way you look at it the status of the Precrime Agency itself is in jeopardy. But is Anderton being set up? And if so by whom?

A particularly relevant story in post-9 11 America, "The Minority Report" earns ✮ ✮ ✮ ✮ ✮

"The Minority Report" was the last story sent to the SMLA in 1954, and one of only eleven submitted during the year. However, Dick had had published 29 stories. The last of these appeared in December: "Prize Ship", "Strange Eden" and "The Father-Thing."

All-in-all 1954 was a good year for Philip K. Dick. His short-story output had dropped but, on the other hand, he had sold his first science fiction novel, SOLAR LOTTERY and written another, THE WORLD JONES MADE.

The short stories themselves continued on from those he wrote in 1953. Many of them dealt with mutants and their shortcomings: "Misadjustment", "A World of Talent", "Psi-Man, Heal My Child!", "Captive Market" and "The Minority Report." Others are set in a post-atomic world and illustrate some pitfalls of capitalism: "Pay For The Printer" and "Autofac", while others yet, particularly, "War Veteran", "Service Call" and "The Mold Of Yancy" are not so easily classifiable but all alluding in some degree to the folly of war.

THE WORLD JONES MADE

Philip K. Dick's second science-fiction novel, written in late 1954 after SOLAR LOTTERY and a handful of short stories, was originally titled WOMB FOR ANOTHER. The manuscript arrived at the SMLA on Dec 28, 1954 and even the sub-agent at the Agency liked it and recommended it for "hardcovers, Ballantine, *Astounding*, etc." As critic Gregg Rickman says, this list reflected the pecking order of book publication in the mid-50s.[clxxi]

The story was purchased by Ace Books in 1955 and, as usual, they immediately changed the title. In March 1956 THE WORLD JONES MADE came out as one half of an Ace Double, backed with Margaret StClair's *AGENT OF THE UNKNOWN*.[clxxii]

THE WORLD JONES MADE is a story of a precog – Jones – and the traps that precognition can bring.

PKD sees precognition as a mixed blessing:

"In my stories, and especially in the novel {JONES}, it placed the character in a closed loop, a victim of his own determinism; he was compelled … to enact later what he foresaw earlier, as if by previewing it he was destined to fall victim to it, rather than obtaining the capacity to escape it. Precognition did not lead to freedom but rather to a macabre fatalism…"[clxxiii]

Dick has similar thoughts in other places.[clxxiv]

In responding to a bad review of the novel by James Blish, PKD writes that the idea for the book was:

a sort of transformation of the situation in Germany after World War One. A liberal government, democratic in nature, is in power. It fights against absolutist extremist elements growing from within; it tries to use its military and police power against them, and fails. Jones, as a person, is based on what I've read about Adolf Hitler. The drifters, of course, are the Jews (Damon Knight, I believe, noticed this). I tried to catch what I imagined was the zeitgeist of Weimar and translate it into sf terms. God knows what the mutants would be. Here the analogy breaks down.[clxxv]

In this same letter he refers to James Joyce for his writing technique in THE WORLD JONES MADE;

The "Jones" book was a failure. Let's face it. But the desire behind it was not base or ignoble. I've always been interested in the Joyce technique of starting with more than one thread and drawing these threads together at some nexus later in the book. {...} However, in my "Jones" book the threads don't come together; specifically, there is no relationship between the mutant group who open the book and the Jones political movement. Those two threads have no nexus. A is related to B, and B to C, and C to D, but A has no relationship to D. And it should have had. I think, had there been a relationship between those two particular threads, the book would have come off. Originally, the MS was much longer. ACE agreed to publish it if I'd cut it. I cut out the mutant-thread entirely (which would have left a more unified book). But ACE demanded that I restore that thread. Without it the book was thin. This showed me that I had got off in the wrong direction in my novel writing, and the next books were based on a more unified approach. [clxxvi]

The plot of THE WORLD JONES MADE revolves around Floyd Jones, a precog who can see exactly one year into the future. When giant seed-like things start floating to Earth from outer space Jones rouses the population against these *drifters* and they are burnt as soon as they land. This arouses the ire of the government who see the *drifters* as harmless and a power struggle starts between Jones and the laissez-faire government.

An excellent follow-up to SOLAR LOTTERY this is a novel which many readers do not see as a failure. In fact, its as good as his first and THE WORLD JONES MADE rates ✴✴✴✴✴.

1955 EYE IN THE SKY

The next book was not long in coming. In a blaze of energy in early Feb 1955, Philip K. Dick wrote EYE IN THE SKY in two weeks. Under the manuscript title of WITH OPENED MIND, it reached the SMLA in New York on February 15, 1955. Two years before it would see publication in 1957 (indeed, THE MAN WHO JAPED, written shortly after EYE IN THE SKY, saw publication first in 1956). What took so long?

The manuscript was apparently welcome at SMLA where

the Agency reader thought it "'Very odd... Off trail but good of its kind.' He suggested trying Ballantine Books first, but they and several other publishing houses passed on it; it didn't sell until its eleventh go-round and second try at ACE -- after some extensive rewriting." [clxxvii]

On this rewriting, PKD in a 1957 letter to Tony Boucher commented:

To tell you the truth EYE IN THE SKY is not a terribly recent novel of mine; in fact it was written before THE MAN WHO JAPED. And the reason that it did not appear until now is that nobody wanted to touch it because of the various "controversial" ideas. Donald Wollheim at ACE had it a long time ago and returned it with regrets. But evidently after they had put so much into my stuff (after they had bought three) they felt they could go ahead and take a chance. Even so I had to rewrite large portions of it. But I had new ideas to put in, so I didn't mind; in fact, I think it came out better -- which is an anomaly...[clxxviii]

So, then, why did Wollheim at Ace Books send the novel back with regrets?

"'I was very reluctant to do it. I enjoyed it immensely. But paperbacks were in a young state, and we didn't want to offend anybody. Here was a book that would offend religious people -- God enters it, the Eye of God.' He feared that the American Legion might object, and other groups. 'Wyn read EYE before we published it, and we talked a lot about it. He'd been a Socialist in his youth so he took a chance -- if they argue, they argue. No one complained.'" clxxix

Nevertheless some changes had to be made. Wyn insisted on it:

"What did A.A.Wyn object to in all this? Sylvester's fanatical universe, in which engineers work on the problem of 'maintaining a constant supply of untainted grace for all major population centers', was just the sort of thing that could piss off the American Legion and fundamentalist Christians. And so Wyn insisted that Sylvester's God be called "(Tetragrammaton)" and that his "Babiist" cult be designated Moslem in origin -- how many outraged Islamic sf readers could there be?" clxxx

"'Yes, it was safer that way,' says Wollheim. 'God is God, but we weren't going to step on somebody's toes.'" clxxxi

The happy result of all this was the publication of EYE IN THE SKY in 1957 as a full-size ACE novel which meant Dick was paid the full price of $1500. Not bad for two weeks work.

But even with this, only his fourth novel sale, Dick was starting to realise that novels may well pay better than short stories but they still don't pay enough. Dick complained to Boucher in the Jun 1957 letter mentioned above that,

Where the real crying on the shoulder comes in is at the money point... on a book like EYE IN THE SKY which you seem to feel is a worthy contribution to the field (and thanks for that) I get so little return that financially it isn't really worth it on a strictly cold-blooded basis. Figuring work-hours versus pay, its a losing struggle at this pay rate, not to mention the holy anger that a writer feels to see his stuff go for peanuts when he knows -- he just plain knows --that his stuff is worth far more. Yet again I say, thank God for ACE; they've kept me alive. If it hadn't been for them I'd no longer be in the writing business. As Scott points out, it's one thousand from ACE compared with nothing but talk from the other publishers. And here, of course, is the tragedy; no hardcover house was even remotely interested in, say, EYE IN THE SKY. (I did get a letter from the editor-in-chief at Putnam, as I recall, saying that they had read it but that it was simply not well enough done to go into their list). Beyond that no hardcover house said anything at all, but I know Scott tried it around -- for a couple of years.... ... clxxxii

Money grumbles aside, we can sense from his comments that Philip K. Dick was well-satisfied with EYE IN THE SKY: "I enjoyed writing all of them. But I think that if I could only choose a few, which, for example might escape World War III, I would choose, first, EYE IN THE SKY..." And, "I really like... EYE IN THE SKY."clxxxiii

Plus the feedback he was getting was positive: "Tony Boucher gave it the best novel of the year rating, and in another magazine *Venture* Ted Sturgeon called it, 'the kind of a small trickle of good sf which justifies reading all the worthless stuff.'" clxxxiv And a letter from Don Wollheim at ACE Books further testifies to everyone's satisfaction with EYE: "... Glad you liked the cover, and especially the presentation of EYE IN THE SKY. We can't keep a copy in the office; visiting fans keep carrying them off..." clxxxv

That cover of the first ACE edition, D-211, published in 1957, is of course one of the most memorable in the annals of science fiction cover art. The huge eyeball pinning the mortals in its penetrating glare. The painting is by Valigursky. To top Dick's satisfaction, EYE

IN THE SKY was published as a full-size ACE Double, the pages not shared with another writer turned upside-down. In a sense, then, this was PKD's first full published novel. SOLAR LOTTERY, THE WORLD JONES MADE and THE MAN WHO JAPED were all half of ACE Doubles.

But, as might be expected with PKD, getting the novel on the newsstands was no simple thing. Apparently he wrote the book quickly enough: "EYE IN THE SKY... I wrote in two weeks..."[clxxxvi] and: "I don't know where I got the dialogue from, it just rolled out of me ... It took only two weeks to write the first draft. Ah, but could I do it now! I'm far too tired."[clxxxvii]

But one wonders if he told Ms. Meisal that he wrote it under the influence of amphetamines? PKD began using amphetamines in the 50s:

[Paul Williams]: When did you start taking them? {amphetamines} [PKD]:Well, in the... Fifties.
[Williams] So really early on in your writing career?
[PKD] Yeah. Um, by the time I wrote EYE IN THE SKY. And I attributed my speed of writing, my rapidity, and my high productivity and my pushing myself, to the amphetamines. And then I find now I do exactly the same without."[clxxxviii]

Philip K. Dick uses EYE IN THE SKY as an example to refute claims that he was a Communist or Marxist writer:

That's another thing that indicates that I can't really be said honestly to be a Communist. I parodied and savagely attacked them in EYE IN THE SKY. And Poul Anderson noticed that. Poul said he thought that part where the Communist slogans fall out of the sky, fiery symbols fall from the heavens, and set fire to somebody's house was one of the funniest things he had ever read.
EYE IN THE SKY was not only openly attacking the McCarthy witch-hunts, because that was written during the McCarthy witch-hunt period, but I was also attacking communism too. I was attacking them both. So I don't *understand* this business [of saying I'm a Marxist].[clxxxix]

After his religious experiences and mystical visions of 2-3-74, Philip K. Dick saw EYE IN THE SKY as significant to his inspired world-view:

My writing deals with hallucinated worlds, intoxicating and deluding drugs, & psychosis. But my writing acts as an *antidote* -- a detoxifying -- not intoxicating -- antidote. {...} It's like EYE when actual rescue is right at hand but they can't wake up. Yes, we are asleep like they are in EYE & we must wake up & see past (through) the dream -- the spurious world with its own time -- to the rescue *outside* -- outside *now*, not later.[cxc]

And:

So JOINT, EYE, STIGMATA, UBIK, MAZE & TEARS are progressive parts of one unfolding true narrative, in which the genuine Hermetic macro-microcosmology is put forth.[cxci]

As for the plot of EYE IN THE SKY, after an accident at a Bevatron a group of tourists is dosed with radiation. When they awake they find themselves in a reality which they slowly discover reflects the inner religious world of one of their members. But which one? Eventually they kill the suspect and return to the real reality only to find that this one, too, is false and another subjective world has taken over. In progressively shorter terms they live through more subjective worlds. But will they ever return to the objective world to which they all agree is the true one?

In many ways EYE IN THE SKY is the ultimate 'what is reality?' novel. One can see it's descendence in a direct line from THE COSMIC PUPPETS and going on to TIME OUT OF JOINT, THE MAN IN THE HIGH CASTLE, THE THREE STIGMATA OF PALMER ELDRITCH, A MAZE OF DEATH and so on.

It's also a funny book that well deserves ✳ ✳ ✳ ✳ ✳

As Dick was writing EYE IN THE SKY and working on the revision of WORLD OF CHANCE in early 1955, his short story output had dropped to zero. The last short story he had submitted was "The Minority Report" in Dec 1954. It would be six months before the next story came in to the SMLA. This was "The Unreconstructed M" in Jun 1955.

But, still, his stories were appearing at the rate of one a month in the sf magazines on the stands. "Nanny" in Feb 1955, "War Veteran" in March, "Captive Market" in April and "Foster, You're Dead!' in May. And, of course, the first edition Ace paperback of SOLAR LOTTERY came out in May 1955.

Apart from "The Unreconstructed M", Dick gave up writing short fiction in May 1955. It would be three years before he wrote another short story. He determined now to turn his undivided attention to his real goal: that of getting a mainstream novel published.

The first of these to reach the SMLA was MARY AND THE GIANT, although this story was probably begun earlier than mid-1955.[cxcii]

MARY AND THE GIANT

MARY AND THE GIANT is another early PKD mainstream novel about which little of its history is known. On the basis of textual clues, Sutin estimates it as being written between 1953 and 1955.[cxciii] Certainly, by May 1955 it was under consideration at Julian Messner Publishers as an editor there wrote a letter to PKD which discusses MARY and suggests a rewrite.[cxciv]

A look at the calendar in 1955 shows a three month gap between mid-Feb and the end of April during which Dick was working on a revision of WORLD OF CHANCE for Rich & Cowan publishers. To me, this is the likeliest time for Dick to have been working on a final draft of MARY AND THE GIANT.

In a 1957 letter to Anthony Boucher, Dick mentions having nearly sold MARY AND THE GIANT:

{...} In fact we had an oral okay over the phone from the editor-in-chief of a reputable hardcover house. They held the MS for six months and then -- as I stood waiting for the contracts, still keeping faith at my end -- they returned the MS with a short note. Personally, I believe they couldn't get a pre-publication softcover house to go along with the book to underwrite their costs. {... ...}[cxcv]

No luck, then, for MARY at Julian Messner's. By Jan 1956 the story was being rejected again at Crown Publishers; the excuse being that it lacked "sales potential."[cxcvi]

All in all, according to Rickman, MARY AND THE GIANT was rejected by twenty-five publishing houses.[cxcvii] The novel would not be published until David Hartwell at Arbor House decided to publish it in 1987.[cxcviii]

The story about a good-looking young girl in over her head in the nighttime world of Jazz was daring for its time, dealing as it did with interracial relationships and sex between the generations.

MARY rates ✳ ✳ ✳

"The Unreconstructed M" was received by the SMLA on Jun 2, 1955, PKD's first and only short-story submission of the year. It was published in *Original Science Fiction Stories* in Jan 1957 and selected by Mark Hurst for his PKD collection THE GOLDEN MAN in 1980. Finally it reappeared in THE COLLECTED STORIES in 1987.

"The Unreconstructed M" is a science fiction detective story. A murder occurs and machine-faked evidence leads to complications in its solution. The name if not the character of David Lantano recurs in PKD's 1964 novel THE PENULTIMATE TRUTH. Reminiscent of "Paycheck" in its use of small 'tokens'.

Here's what PKD said about the story:

"If my main theme throughout my writing is, "Can we consider the universe real, and if so, in what way?" my secondary theme would be, "Are we all humans?" Here a machine does not imitate a human being, but instead fakes evidence *of* a human being, a given human being. Fakery is a topic which absolutely fascinates me; I am convinced that anything can be faked, or anyhow evidence pointing to any given thing. Spurious clues can lead us to believe anything *they* want us to believe. There is really no theoretical upper limit to this. Once you have mentally opened the door to reception of the notion of *fake*, you are ready to think yourself into another kind of reality entirely. It's a trip from which you never return. And, I think, a healthy trip... unless you take it too seriously."[cxcix]

"The Unreconstructed M" rates ✳ ✳ ✳ ✳

After the Jun 2 1955 letter from Julian Messner's suggesting a rewrite of MARY AND THE GIANT, Dick most likely worked on that chore through June and into July. June had seen publication of "The Hood Maker" in *Imagination* and July saw three more stories on the stands: "A Surface Raid," "The Chromium Fence" and "Service Call."

A HANDFUL OF DARKNESS

The calendar of events after June is fairly empty. In August "The Mold Of Yancy" was published in *Worlds of If*. But the highlight of this period was publication in England of Dick's first collection, A HANDFUL OF DARKNESS by Rich & Cowan in Aug 1955.

This edition is now a sought-after collector's item and demands high prices. A second edition printed by Rich & Cowan in Jun 1957 is only slightly less desireable. The collection was never published in the United States until the Gregg Press edition in 1978.[cc] Other editions came later, particularly in England from Panther/Granada/Grafton. In foreign languages, editions have been done in Dutch, German, Danish and Swedish.

It had taken quite a while to get this collection together. Rich & Cowan had approached Dick with the idea of a collection in late 1953, contacting Dick through the Agency.[cci] I imagine it took so long to publish due to transatlantic communications delays. Looking over the contents, we see some of PKD's best stories and a couple of his worst. The cutoff date appears to be the end of 1953, with "Upon The Dull Earth" the last written story included in the collection, and that was written in Dec 1953. [ccii]

Anthony Boucher, editor of *F & SF*, reviewed the volume well:

In short stories, I discover belatedly that one of 1955's best science fantasy volumes by an American appeared only in England: Philip K. Dick's A HANDFUL OF DARKNESS (Rich & Cowan, 10s. 6d.). Readers of *F & SF*, which enjoyed the honor of discovering Dick, know the freshness of his concepts, his sharp sense of unfamiliar terrors, the easy naturalism of his everyday people against strange and imaginative backgrounds. Here are 15 of his stories (3 from these pages), almost all of them ranging from good to excellent and only one previously reprinted. (I don't understand why Dick has been so neglected by anthologists ... including, I must confess, me.) I urge readers to order the volume through book-importers – and urge American publishers to correct the local absence of a Dick collection.[cciii]

As a collection of PKD stories, the selection in A HANDFUL OF DARKNESS rates ✳ ✳ ✳ ✳

As the year 1955 wound on, PKD saw publication of his short stories dwindle. There were none in Sep and Oct. In Oct he also had the discouraging news that VOICES FROM THE STREET, his 1952 mainstream novel which had been making the rounds of the publishers, was being withdrawn from consideration by the SMLA.

So after working on rewrites of MARY AND THE GIANT in the summer, Dick began his next science fiction novel, THE MAN WHO JAPED.[cciv]

THE MAN WHO JAPED

The manuscript for THE MAN WHO JAPED reached the SMLA on Oct 17, 1955. After revision it was published by Ace Books as one half of an Ace Double in Dec 1956. It was the only one of his early novels published by Ace that retained Dick's original title.[ccv]

Between reception and publication Dick revised the manuscript, telling Tony Boucher,

In my own opinion THE MAN WHO JAPED is a far better book than any of the others. I had to cut 75 typescript pages from it, though. To fit into the ACE Double edition. But I would be the last to complain about ACE, since they've kept me alive these several years. And on a personal level Don Wollheim has given me extraordinary encouragement and attention -- as have you, as you well know. {...}[ccvi]

The subject of THE MAN WHO JAPED is explained by PKD in a letter to James Blish. In this letter Dick responds again to interpretation of SOLAR LOTTERY in leftist political terms:

As to JAPED: I have to, in all fairness, say this: the topic is not American culture but the society coming into existence in Mainland China. The Puritanical left-society with its emphasis on confession, fear, guilt, omphalos: which is the critical concept: *the idea of center*. In really authoritative CP writings, you get this again and again: "Center says... it's the policy at center." This is the nature of totalitarianism, this facing toward the center. The hub. You see, I wanted to show that as dreadful as commercial bourgeois US culture could be, there are things that pose a greater danger, go further in destroying the integrity of the individual. Block committees are worse than TV. And -- I was motivated by the acclaim in some circles toward my first book, SOLAR LOTTERY; they seemed to feel that I was bitterly attacking *democrat* society! That I was taking an extreme left position. They saw more in my book than I meant... and I wanted to take the "other side", then, and have a go at the left. And by golly, those same reviewers denounced JAPED. Evidently they grasped that I was getting at their sacred cow. {...}[ccvii]

Later, responding to Tom Disch's 'Marxist bent' comment, Dick referred to THE MAN WHO JAPED to refute it:

anyone who understands...THE MAN WHO JAPED would never make the error of thinking that I was a communist or Marxist. Because this is a very, very sincere attempt to show the very dangerous trends in Communism, the Communist state.[ccviii]

Several influences on THE MAN WHO JAPED have been noted. Lawrence Sutin sees Allen Purcell's big jape in the novel as a rip-off of Jonathon Swift's *A Modest Proposal*. Damon Knight sees the novel as echoing Cyril Kornbluth and Fred Pohl's *THE SPACE MERCHANTS* and also sees the effect of Alfred Bester's *THE DEMOLISHED MAN* on the plot.[ccix]

As for the plot. In an extremely moral and uptight society Allen Purcell, the man in charge, finds that he has for some reason snuck into the park in the middle of the night and sawn off the head of the statue of Major Streiter, the founder of 'Moral Reclamation.' This sacrilegious act throws the government into a tizzy because, despite the omnipresent 'juveniles'-- scurrying robots with video cameras -- and the dreaded 'block meetings', people are actually laughing in the streets! In the end before he is found out Purcell conspires to completely unbalance this stagnant society by going on TV and propounding the principle of 'active assimilation' – the eating of one's enemies. Undoubtedly, as Sutin notes, this is borrowed from Swift's *A Modest Proposal*.

This novel is difficult to rate but THE MAN WHO JAPED is worth at least ✳ ✳ ✳ ✳

In Oct 1955, after sending the manuscript for JAPED to the SMLA, PKD re-concentrated on writing and selling his mainstream fiction, indicating this redirection of his energies in the letter to Blish above:

Now, to your review of JAPED, which you liked. I appreciated your statements, esp. your saying that you enjoyed the choice of words. This was my last s-f novel -- came later than EYE IN THE SKY. Here, I think I got onto a much higher level of style. Anyhow, I tried to. JAPED is my favorite of my books; I feel it has genuine literary worth. The sentences are built better. The language itself is of a higher character. And here, I made my departure from s-f to straight novel-writing, which I've done ever since. I'm determined to do a good solid contemporary novel. Maybe someday I'll sell one of them; I have five or six that Scott is submitting to hardcover houses.[ccx]

And, earlier, in 1957 he had said the same thing to Anthony Boucher:

Tiresome as all this is, there's worse to come. I have ceased to write either s.f. or fantasy, Tony; I stopped writing short stuff for magazine publication back in May of '55; since then I've done only novels, both s.f. and what I call straight contemporary serious quality fiction about non-myth type people, and in the last year its been just the latter, the non-s.f. I have five of these novels in circulation (...) We damn near sold one of them (called MARY AND THE GIANT). [ccxi]

So, between June 1957 and Feb 1958, almost a whole year, Dick was waiting on good news about his mainstream novels.[ccxii]

But we're jumping ahead. For Philip K. Dick in late1955, his decision to write mainstream novels henceforth must have felt like a liberating one. He reasoned that as he'd already achieved some name recognition as a novelist, albeit in science fiction, he would not have too much trouble finding a publisher for his next novel which he began working on after writing THE MAN WHO JAPED.

A TIME FOR GEORGE STAVROS

When the manuscript for A TIME FOR GEORGE STAVROS bounced through the mail slot it was not a happy day at the Scott Meredith Literary Agency. There is no record of this date, most likely in late 1955 or early 1956, but the Agency reviewer had this to say:

Didn't like this before, & still don't. Long, rambling, glum novel about 65 yr old Greek immigrant who has a weakling son, a second son about whom he's indifferent, a wife who doesn't love him (she's being unfaithful to him). Nothing much happens. Guy, selling garage and retiring, tires{sic} to buy another garage in new development, has a couple of falls, dies at end. Point is murky but seems to be that world is disintegrating, Stavros is supposed to be symbol of vigorous individuality, now a lost commodity.[ccxiii]

This implies that the Agency reviewer had already seen the ms for STAVROS before and Dick had sent in a rewrite. I don't know. The Agency duly sent it off on its rounds to the publishers where STAVROS was rejected 23 times. Don Wickenden, an editor at Harcourt, Brace rejected it with regrets in Feb 1956.[ccxiv]

In a reply to a letter from Eleanor Dimoff on February 1st, 1960, PKD went on at some length about the mainstream novels he had written thus far. Dimoff had made some solid criticisms of A TIME FOR GEORGE STAVROS to which Dick agreed; but he liked the character of George Stavros himself and felt that

George Stavros is as good a character as any I have produced. There is as much chance that he could be the basis of a successful book as any character, so I would be willing -- even pleased -- to start with him as a premise in this work. [ccxv]

Now whether Dimoff, an editor at the Harcourt Brace publishing house, had suggested that her publishing house would welcome another rewrite of STAVROS, or Dick had determinedly talked himself into using Stavros as a character on whom to base another novel, is unclear. Rickman's research implies that A TIME FOR GEORGE STAVROS had already had one rewrite between the time of its submission in 1956 to the time of Dimoff's letter in 1960. And now here was Dimoff asking for another. From this slim evidence I feel that Dick, hope springing eternal for mainstream publication, tried to salvage something from A TIME FOR GEORGE STAVROS – it's main character – and grasped at Dimoff's implied straw of better consideration for any new Philip K. Dick novel. But he definitely, in this letter, would

...scrap the book called A TIME FOR GEORGE STAVROS, withdraw it, and take it apart. I'll save the theme that here is an old man with enormous appetite, wit, and tenacity, a kind of genius -- and yet hopelessly ignorant of the contemporary ways by which men rise to economic and social success. I'll saddle him with the physical defect of a failing heart, and equip him with an animal-like cunning, an ability to spar, fight, scrap and wrassle. And -- an ability to see through humbug, the pretensions of others.[ccxvi]

The result, as Rickman said, was "one of his gloomiest books, HUMPTY DUMPTY IN OAKLAND, a book with no readily "identifiable" characters at all."

HUMPTY DUMPTY IN OAKLAND reached Harcourt, Brace in October 1960. Anne Dick, having read both novels, believes that HUMPTY DUMPTY IN OAKLAND was "probably 95% the earlier novel."[ccxvii]

Here's what Philip K. Dick had to say about A TIME FOR GEORGE STAVROS in his 1960 letter to Eleanor Dimoff:

Here, a man arises who denies the above. Contact with vile persons does not blight or contaminate or doom the really superior; a man can go on and be successful, if he just keeps struggling. There is no trick that the wicked can play on the good that will ultimately be successful; the good are protected by God, or at least by their virtue. The good have better luck than the bad; otherwise they could not afford to be good in the first place. It is the weak who are vicious, not the strong. And the weak, although very dangerous, have no stamina; they can be outlasted. And they are terribly gullible; they can be misled by a good man who is astute enough to put up a good line. In fact, the weak -- e.g. Andrew -- will mislead themselves with their own silly stories, their vain and pompous plans. Stavros is an aristocrat. He would have been able to manage Hig; he would have slighted him, sent him packing, humiliated him. Being able to see through pretensions, Stavros would have not even been worried by Hig. But he would have had trouble with Milt Lumky, whom he would have identified as a good man, a fine fellow. It would have baffled him that Lumky, in the end, did a bad thing. Lumky's bitterness would've made Stavros bitter, too. They probably would've stepped out and taken a couple of swings at each other. There would have been bad feeling between them. And Bruce's wife -- Stavros simply would have avoided her without even trying to understand her. Likewise Fay, in CONFESSIONS OF A CRAP ARTIST. Stavros would have avoided her by instinct, not insight. He would have liked Charley Hume, but shaken his head sadly at the man's stupidity. He would have kicked Nat in the ass for ever getting mixed up with her. Reform her? Hell -- dunk her head in a bucket. Without having read *TAMING OF THE SHREW*, Stavros would have known what to do. And yet the contemporary institutions would have defeated Stavros as they defeated the two kids in THISBE. Or so I believe.[ccxviii]

The end of 1955 went out in a blaze of glory for PKD's short stories. He had had no stories on the stands since August but in November, three more caught the public's eye. These were "Human Is", "Psi-Man, Heal My Child!" and "Autofac."

In December, while he was revising THE MAN WHO JAPED for Ace Books, he had no new short stories in print.

1956 "To Jones The Future Was An Open Book!"

The calendar of PKD's publications and manuscripts in 1956 is rather bare. The year started off with two more short story appearances, "Minority Report" in January and "To Serve

The Master" in February. An early highlight for the year was the first Ace publication of THE WORLD JONES MADE in March.[ccxix]

But, after THE WORLD JONES MADE saw the light of day, it would be six more months before "Pay For The Printer" showed up in the Oct *Satellite*.

What was Philip K. Dick doing in 1956?

For most of the year he must have been writing the next two novels, PILGRIM ON THE HILL and THE BROKEN BUBBLE OF THISBE HOLT.

PILGRIM ON THE HILL

The manuscript for PILGRIM ON THE HILL arrived at the SMLA on Nov 8, 1956, followed a few days later by that of THE BROKEN BUBBLE OF THISBE HOLT on Nov 13.

Not much is known about PILGRIM ON THE HILL and, unfortunately, the manuscript has been lost. About all we have are the comments of the reviewer at the SMLA, one "jb":

Another rambling, uneven totally murky novel. Man with psychosis brought on by war thinks he's murdered his wife, flees. Meets 3 eccentrics: an impotent man who refuses to have sex with his wife, the wife – a beautiful woman who's going to a quack doctor for treatment, an animalistic writer with ambition but no talent. Man has affair with wife, is kicked out by husband, tries to help slob. Finally collapses, is sent to hospital, recovers, returns to home. BUT WHAT DOES IT ALL MEAN? Try Miss Pat Schartle at Appleton. [ccxx]

Other than that, the records at the SMLA show that PILGRIM was rejected 15 times by the publishers of the day.[ccxxi]

THE BROKEN BUBBLE

The situation is better with THE BROKEN BUBBLE OF THISBE HOLT. The novel survives and was published by David Hartwell at Arbor House in 1988 under the title THE BROKEN BUBBLE. A year later, Gollancz in England put out an edition.[ccxxii]

As we have seen, the manuscript for THE BROKEN BUBBLE OF THISBE HOLT, reached the SMLA on Nov 13 1956. The reviewer at the SMLA saw it as a

Typical Dick novel, desperately needs cutting, reorganizing, clarifying.[ccxxiii]

And he commented further:

Too complicated to synopsize, but gen. Has to do w/sterility of modern life (displaced people, vacuity of advertising, lack of standards). Disc jockey divorced fr wife because he was sterile "adopts" yg married teen-age couple. Ex-wife has affair w/ young hubby, yg wife wants to share her strength & coming child w/ d.j. At end both couples inextricably bound up w/ ea other.**[ccxxiv]**

The names of two of the main characters in the story– Jim Briskin and Thisbe Holt—are used in other PKD stories (earlier: "Stand-By" and "What'll We Do With Ragland Park?" and later: THE CRACK IN SPACE)

Well received by reviewers in 1988, BUBBLE is now a favorite – together with MARY AND THE GIANT and CONFESSIONS OF A CRAP ARTIST – with fans of PKD's straight writing. Andy Watson, publisher of GATHER YOURSELVES TOGETHER, has this to say about BUBBLE in a fan poll run by the zine *For Dickheads Only* in 1994:

The best of the straight novels, this one serves up more tension and anxiety than any of the others, while still managing to be playful in the manner PKD virtually trademarked. The parody of the sci-fi "fans" and the short story written by one of them, embedded in the story somewhat gratuitously, are nearly unique in all of PKD's writings, and are entirely welcome as a diversion, as a time-marking device, in order to pace the rest of the book to best advantage. This is PKD's "coming of age" novel, and as with everything else he wrote, his take on this form is utterly unique.[ccxxv]

When published in 1988 at the peak of PKD's posthumous popularity, THE BROKEN BUBBLE received mixed reviews. The New York Times Book Review didn't care for it but John Clute writing in the Times Literary Supplement liked it. [ccxxvi]

Here's a fine synopsis of the story courtesy of Andrew M. Butler:

San Francisco. Jim Briskin is suspended from his radio programme for refusing to read an advert over the air. He meets Art and Rachael Emmanuel, a teenaged married couple, and is so taken by them that he introduces his ex-wife Pat to them. Pat gets Art to take her for a drive and they have sex at Twin Peaks. Jim, concerned that Rachael will go after Pat, starts having his meals with Rachael and avoids being seduced by her. Pat, alternating between leading Art on and rejecting him, decides that she does want to be with Jim after all. Art, who has narrowly avoided arrest for an action by a group of sf fan revolutionaries, is wrongly arrested for vandalism involving a plastic bubble full of rubbish which has been dropped from a hotel. Jim stands him bail, and later takes Rachael to have her baby.[ccxxvii]

PKD had this to say about BUBBLE in his 1960 letter to Eleanor Dimoff:

I estimate this to be a marred work -- marred by a romantic sentimentality. It is a Quixotic novel; not the protagonist but the author was the tilter at windmills. But it has style, some good characters, good scenes. It is not funny. It is full of fear, apprehension, and hate. I identify with the most helpless, the most defenseless and weak persons in society -- the kids. Pathetic idealism, plus an almost morbid imagination, are the keys in this book. It is a bad dream, but possibly true. As Mailer says, "The shits are killing us." The institutions of society are cruel; it is Kafka's law courts without the religion and mysticism.[ccxxviii]

BUBBLE is a lot of fun to read, with the sub-text of the crazed science fiction fans (including a short story written by one of the fans) and the naked Thisbe Holt being rolled around a hotel room to the delight of drunken conventioneers. I'd give it ✳ ✳ ✳ ✳

After sending THE BROKEN BUBBLE OF THISBE HOLT off to the SMLA in Nov 1956, Dick began working on his next novel, PUTTERING ABOUT IN A SMALL LAND.

Dec 1956 saw publication of "A Glass Of Darkness" in Satellite and the first Ace edition of THE MAN WHO JAPED.[ccxxix]

Dick's first full year as a straight novel writer had not been a lucrative one; four short stories and two science fiction novels published were just enough to keep him going. 1957 would be a little better.

1957 "Something had upset the natural laws of the universe"

The year 1957 began with the first publication of PKD's story "The Unreconstructed M" in Original Science Fiction Stories in January, followed by "Misadjustment" in Science Fiction Quarterly in February. The big event early in the year, though, was undoubtedly publication of the first Ace edition of EYE IN THE SKY in March. This was not an Ace Double but a full-size novel; in a sense his first solo novel.[ccxxx]

THE COSMIC PUPPETS

While PKD was writing PUTTERING ABOUT IN A SMALL LAND in early 1957, an opportunity arose that he could not turn down – an opportunity to make some money.

Recall that in Dec 1956, Satellite had published PKD's 1953 novelette "A Glass Of Darkness." Don Wollheim, editor at Ace Books, had evidently seen the cover of the magazine because in Mar 1957 he wrote to Dick:

Scott hasn't yet shown us anything of yours in that non-stf category, probably he's trying them out on hardcover markets first. But please remind him that ACE Books might be especially suggestive to your work – if you think any of it would fit the paperback market (...). We've done quite a range of original and reprint modern novels... You mention having written but 4 sf novels. What then was that one you had in the second issue of Satellite? I haven't seen it, but why not have Scott submit that one too? Then we could have five Dick fantasies...[ccxxxi]

On being informed of this the SMLA immediately sold the story to Ace for an advance, presumably, of $1000.[ccxxxii]

And just in the nick of time, too, as Ballantine Press, in the person of Tony Boucher, also showed interest. In a letter dated June 5, 1957, Boucher wrote:

...& why, I wonder, haven't I seen any of the long Dicks in MS? If I'd liked A GLASS OF DARKNESS we'd've paid exactly twice Satellite's $400. I'd certainly have bought EYE & probably SOLAR LOTTERY – either (depending on our publishers variable policy at the moment) as a serial or to be condensed into a one-shot – wh wd've meant anywhere fr $600 to $1600 according to the length used .[ccxxxiii]

But... too late for Ballantine. "A Glass Of Darkness", revised and newly titled THE COSMIC PUPPETS by Ace, was published in late 1957 as one half of an Ace Double backed with SARGASSO OF SPACE by Andrew North (Andre Norton).[ccxxxiv]

Dick presumably expanded "A Glass of Darkness" into what would become THE COSMIC PUPPETS in between the time he got Wollheim's letter (late March 1957) and the time the SMLA has noted down for the reception of the manuscript on May 1, 1957. In other words, Dick rewrote the story in a month -- I'd guess in one sitting.

By June 3, 1957 PKD was writing to Anthony Boucher regarding the sale to Ace:

... ACE has one more book of mine, but this one has already appeared in a magazine (Satellite); the title for that printing was A GLASS OF DARKNESS; and it runs about 40,000 words. You can see that it is slight compared with the others, but again I personally like it; its pure fantasy, which as you know has always been my favorite.[ccxxxv]

And there the story lies for the next 22 years until January 1979 when Russ Galen at Berkley Books purchased THE COSMIC PUPPETS together with DR. FUTURITY and THE UNTELEPORTED MAN as part of a package deal that paid Dick $14,000. The novel was reissued by Berkley in October 1983 as a paperback after they had canned plans to issue an illustrated version.[ccxxxvi]

Asked by Rickman why it had fallen out of print for twenty-two years, Wollheim of Ace said, "I don't even recall the story. It was not reprinted because I forgot it."

But a curious thing happened on the way from 1953 novelette to 1957 novel. The present author did a comparison of the two versions, "A Glass Of Darkness" and THE COSMIC PUPPETS.[ccxxxvii]

Without a doubt, PKD totally rewrote the whole story, clipping and changing most paragraphs, eliminating words, tightening the prose... There are many textual changes throughout and also a repositioning of the opening chapters. Originally the novelette begins with Ted Barton and his wife driving through Virginia and continues up to Ted's discovery that his lucky compass has been changed into a piece of dry bread, followed by the scene of the children playing with the clay in its entirety.

In the novel this is rearranged. First comes one half of the children playing scene, then the material on Barton and his wife driving, and then the remainder of the children's scene. After this initial repositioning the chapters, despite different breaks, follow each other in tandem.

Overall, the changes between novelette and novel do make a difference to the story. But, with all this clipping, eliminating and tightening going on, it is hard to see where the novel is an expansion of the story. And, indeed, it's not. An average word count for the Berkley COSMIC PUPPETS comes out at 44,030 while "A Glass Of Darkness" comes in at 44,770. A difference of a mere 740 words but nevertheless a definite contraction (which might make it rather awkward for future bibliographers: "A Glass Of Darkness", 1953, published 1956, novelette. Contracted to THE COSMIC PUPPETS, published 1957, novel...)[ccxxxviii]

The story itself concerns a man who returns to his childhood home only to see it all changed in obscure ways. As he tries to figure out what's going on with the help of the town drunk he encounters weird things and when he tries to leave town he finds he can't, becoming mixed up in a maze of time. Another main thread of the story revolves around two children, Peter and Mary, who each possess strange powers. Over the whole thing hangs the presence of two ancient Zoroastrian deities locked in a frozen struggle in the sky.

Critic Barb Morning Child sees THE COSMIC PUPPETS as a novel conducted on three levels akin to the Marxist concepts of false consciousness, class consciousness and true consciousness. Add in the Phildickian idea borrowed from Gnosticism of the world as the product of an evil demi-urge (later much-worried upon in VALIS) and we have a complex short novel that is in many ways definitive PKD. [ccxxxix]

THE COSMIC PUPPETS has been under-rated, but not anymore. It rates ✳ ✳ ✳ ✳ ✳

After dropping everything to do the expansion of "A Glass of Darkness", Dick returned to work on PUTTERING ABOUT IN A SMALL LAND.

PUTTERING ABOUT IN A SMALL LAND

The manuscript for PUTTERING ABOUT IN A SMALL LAND arrived at the SMLA on May 15, 1957. The agent who read it commented that PUTTERING was the

Usual serious Dick novel, less murky than others but overlong, confused... is basically ironic comedy, but overwritten, distasteful.[ccxl]

It also got the usual reception for PKD mainstream novels at the publishing houses to which the SMLA submitted the novel in the late 1950s: rejection, eight times in all.[ccxli]

PKD's one-time collaborator, Ray Nelson (THE GANYMEDE TAKEOVER), believes that Dick pandered to the market by changing his story lines. For instance,

PUTTERING ABOUT IN A SMALL LAND gets a new ending. The original ended at the end of Chapter 20 with the words, 'It would bother me,' plus a little 'moving vehicle' coda, now lost. Now the hero's mean wife demands the hero's store -- and gets it. Two new chapters give the hero a new lease on life and a car load of TV sets to sell.[ccxlii]

On notice of the sale of the novel to Academy Chicago Publishers in 1984, Paul Williams, publisher of *The Philip K. Dick Society Newsletter*, waxed enthusiastic while summarizing the plot:

Publication of this novel (tentatively scheduled for Spring '85) may well provide the springboard for a reappraisal and discovery of PKD as an important American novelist by the Literary Establishment in the U.S.. I also believe PUTTERING will be very enthusiastically received in Europe. It is a novel of the human condition -- cruder, lacking the subtle ironies and textured writing of CRAP ARTIST, but more passionate, more joyous and more despairing, full of empathy, very alive. The characters are Roger, cautious, tenacious, owner of a store that sells and repairs TVs, his wife Virginia, intellectual, nervous (at least partially based on PKD's mother Dorothy), their son, Chic, a businessman with plans for Roger's store, and Chic's wife Liz, a vivacious woman who says whatever comes into her head, one of PKD's most memorable characters and, mysteriously, one who does not seem to recur in his later work. Roger and Liz, against all reason, have a passionate affair and their little worlds start to fall apart. But not necessarily for the worst. Publication of PUTTERING will provide a new perspective on much of PKD's later work. In fact, perhaps Liz Bonner is in some sense a forerunner (in heart, not in intellect) of Zina in THE DIVINE INVASION... The setting is Los Angeles in the early 1950s; PUTTERING was probably completed in early 1957. After 28 years it will be published at last.[ccxliii]

PUTTERING ABOUT IN A SMALL LAND was published in hardback by Academy Chicago in Oct 1985.[ccxliv]

Ediciones Alcor, the Spanish publisher, won a special award for its 1988 edition of PUTTERING ABOUT IN A SMALL LAND at the 1989 Gigamesh Awards for works first appearing in Spanish in 1988.[ccxlv]

As for rating PUTTERING, it's difficult. I'd say ✳ ✳ ✳

May 1957 saw the publication of the second English edition of WORLD OF CHANCE from Rich & Cowan and in June, PKD's first USA collection, THE VARIABLE MAN, was published by Ace.

THE VARIABLE MAN contains five stories from 1953 to 1956. Although small in number these stories are mostly long and are some of PKD's best.[ccxlvi]

Tony Boucher reviewed THE VARIABLE MAN in *F & SF* in the Jan 1958 issue:

... The Dick book contains the title novella and 5 novelets (one previously anthologized). It seems probable that the medium length is least suited to Dick's talents: both his short stories (which have been collected in England but not here) and his full length novels are more individual and impressive. But though there are awkwardnesses and confusions in these fairly long stories, you'll also find fertile ingenuity and a striking power in the use of evocative symbols.[ccxlvii]

As a collection, THE VARIABLE MAN rates ✳ ✳ ✳ ✳ ✳

Good news as it was to see the editions of WORLD OF CHANCE and THE VARIABLE MAN, in the matter of his mainstream novels it was not so good. With five straight novels in circulation, PKD was still not getting any solid bites from the publishers. But he soldiered on quietly through the year, seemingly doing not much of anything. October saw publication of THE COSMIC PUPPETS from Ace and, basically, that was it for the year.

But PKD had not been idle in the latter half of the year, working on another mainstream novel, NICHOLAS AND THE HIGS.

NICHOLAS AND THE HIGS

NICHOLAS AND THE HIGS is now a lost novel and there's not much information to be found about it. The manuscript was apparently completed by Jan 3, 1958 and rewritten (reduced to half its size) by Apr 30, 1958.[ccxlviii]

The manuscript of NICHOLAS AND THE HIGS reached SMLA at the same time as the manuscript for TIME OUT OF JOINT.[ccxlix]

The editor at the SMLA tells us a bit about the story:

Very long, complex story, usual Dick genius for setting. Future society wherein trading stamps have replaced currency and people live hundreds of miles from work (drive at 190 mph), have set up living tracts. Cars often break down, so they have tract mechanic on full-time basis. Mechanic old, has bad liver, seems to be dying. People of tract use general fund to buy pseudo-organ but man is dead for a few days and 'comes back' a bit touched. Sub plot concerns man from whom tract got organ (which is illegal), and how his presence causes moral breakdown of people in tract.[ccl]

PKD briefly mentions this novel in his 1960 letter to Eleanor Dimoff:

This is an odd one, half 'straight', half science fiction. An inferior man can destroy a superior one; a Robert Hig can move in and oust Nicholas because he, Hig, has no morals {...} Only by relying on base techniques can Nicholas survive; {...} Awareness of this is enough to drive Nicholas out; he must give up because to win is to lose; he is involved in a terrible paradox as soon as Hig puts in his appearance. In other words, you can't really best the Adolf Hitlers; you can only limit their success. {...} Stavros is an aristocrat. He would have been able to manage Hig; he would have slighted him, sent him packing, humiliated him. Being able to see through pretensions, Stavros would have not even been worried by Hig.[ccli]

NICHOLAS AND THE HIGS was rejected by four publishers at its original length of 128,000 words and even when PKD cut it down to 75,000 it was rejected by nine more.[cclii]

It's unfortunate that this novel is lost, as NICHOLAS AND THE HIGS may well have been on a par with TIME OUT OF JOINT – one of Dick's best early novels and itself a hybrid 'straight'/science fiction novel. The character of the sick mechanic needing an organ transplant reoccurs in PKD's 1964 novel THE PENULTIMATE TRUTH.

But it's to 1958 and TIME OUT OF JOINT that we now turn our attention.

1958 "In his mind he chronicled all the lights he could think of."

1958 was a slow year for Dick as far as new publications are concerned. Only one short story hit the newsstands and that was "Null-O" in the Dec *If*. But, again, Dick was not idle. He started the year working on a major rewrite of NICHOLAS AND THE HIGS, which was completed by the end of April and, perhaps simultaneously with this, was writing TIME OUT OF JOINT. He also submitted three more short stories in this year, "Recall Mechanism," "Explorers We," and "War Game." And to top it all off, he was writing IN MILT LUMKY TERRITORY in the Summer and Fall.

But, first, to TIME OUT OF JOINT.

TIME OUT OF JOINT

The manuscript for TIME OUT OF JOINT arrived at the SMLA on Apr 7, 1958. As usual it was sent off to Ace Books where editor Don Wollheim said that they accepted it but publisher Wyn wanted a rewrite, objecting to "things like the 'soft drink stand' that disappears." But before Dick could respond to Ace's suggestions, hardcover publisher Lippincott contacted Scott Meredith and said they were going to start a science-fiction line. And with the manuscript for TIME OUT OF JOINT at hand, Meredith sent it off to Lippincott and they accepted it as was, requiring no changes.[ccliii] Dick's fee was $750.[ccliv]

On the sale to Lippincott, PKD wrote:

I remember how Don Wollheim, back in the Fifties, viewed the MS of TIME OUT OF JOINT; if he were to publish it, substantial revisions (on the order of those you propose for SCANNER) would have had to take place. However, while Don was stating these proposals, Lippincott was purchasing it as it stood for their hardback market. It was my first hardback sale. True, Lippincott did not pay me as much as Ace Books would have, but in my opinion, I was right to leave TIME OUT OF JOINT as it stood, which was exactly the way Lippincott wanted it (except they did want the ending beefed up, which I agreed with, and did).[cclv]

But it looks like Lippincott backed away from beginning a science-fiction line with TIME OUT OF JOINT as they published it instead as "A Novel of Menace" in 1959. Later, the story was abridged and serialized in the British science-fiction magazine *New Worlds*, #89, 90, 91 in Dec 1959 and Jan/Feb 1960

Philip K. Dick wrote the story quickly. In the 1960 letter to Dimoff, an editor at Harcourt, Brace publishers at the time, Dick says

... Under certain conditions... I can write very fast, even without notes. The Lippincott book [TIME OUT OF JOINT] was written in two weeks, proof read and then retyped in two more. But it took me years to work out the basic idea of the book...[cclvi]

An episode included in TIME OUT OF JOINT was, according to Dick himself, the reason he wrote this novel. The episode is, of course, the famous one of the missing light cord. In an interview with Charles Platt PKD describes it this way

I wrote TIME OUT OF JOINT in the 1950s, before I had even heard of LSD. In that book a guy walks up to a lemonade stand in the park, and it turns into a slip of paper marked Soft Drink Stand, and he puts the slip of paper in his pocket. Far-fucking-out, spacey, that's an 'acid experience'. If I didn't know better I'd say that this author had turned on many times, and his universe was coming unglued -- he's obviously living in a *fake universe.*

What I was trying to do in that book was account for the diversity of worlds that people live in. I had not read Heraclitus then, I didn't know his concept of *idios kosmos,* the private world, versus *koinos kosmos,* which we all share. I didn't know that the pre-Socratics had begun to discern these things. There's a scene in the book where the protagonist goes into the bathroom, reaches in the dark for a pull-cord, and suddenly realizes there is no cord, there's a switch on the wall, and he can't remember when he ever had a bathroom when there was a cord hanging down. Now, that actually happened to me, and it was what caused me to write the book. It reminded me of the idea that Van Vogt had dealt with, of artificial memory, as occurs in *THE WORLD OF NULL-A* where a person has false memories implanted. A lot of what I wrote, which looks like the result of taking acid, is really the result of taking Van Vogt seriously! I *believed* Van Vogt, I mean, *he wrote it,* you know, he was an authority figure. He said, people can be other than whom they remember themselves to be, and I found this fascinating. You have a massive suspension of belief on my part.[cclvii]

Dick speaks further on TIME OUT OF JOINT with Rickman:

Now that was a really perilous gamble on my part to write because there was no chance that Donald Wollheim would buy TIME OUT OF JOINT. That meant that I could not possibly sell it as a science fiction novel. It was bought by Lippincott as a "novel of menace." I only got 750 bucks for it. It was really a risky thing to do. But there again we are dealing with fake reality and I had become obsessed with the idea of fake reality. I was just fascinated with the idea. So that's a pivotal book in terms of my career. It was my first hardcover sale, and it was the first novel in which the entire world is fake. You find yourself in it when you pick up the book and turn to page one. The world that you are reading about does not exist. And this was to be essentially the premise of my entire corpus of writing, really.[cclviii]

He says more of Don Wollheim's reaction to TIME OUT OF JOINT in a 1981 interview with Gregg Rickman:

And Donald Wollheim read that – it got submitted to Ace by mistake – and Wollheim – I've never read such a long, angry letter from an editor in my life. He was incredibly threatened by that novel. He saw everything that he construed as science fiction as going down the tubes with what that novel did. If it ever got into print, which he doubted it ever would, he said the only thing salvageable was the last chapter, where there was the war on the moon. And I should build back from the last chapter. And the style was wrong, because it was essentially pedestrian, he said...[cclix]

Bruce Gillespie sees TIME OUT OF JOINT as a critical novel in Dick's oeuvre, one in which he was first able to incorporate minimal science fiction elements into a mainstream novel and avoid the strictures of his realist novels, the very strictures that make them 'fail.'

What we find in TIME OUT OF JOINT is that the bits and pieces of a science fiction superstructure, which gradually invade Ragle Gumm's consciousness, are actually more autobiographical, more real to the author, than the accurately drawn worlds he presents in the non-sf novels. It is for this reason that the non-sf novels fail, not because of any intrinsic demerits. In TIME OUT OF JOINT Dick finds metaphors for the very real paranoia which afflicted him from time to time. The miracle is that he finds coherent metaphors that he can use to construct an exciting story... The non-sf novels have to take the ordinary world as a given. In the end, Dick felt this was untrue, and he was untrue to himself by portraying the world thus.[cclx]

This failure of the mainstream novels has bothered lots of fans and critics over the years. Gillespie, here, puts his finger on it: The non-sf novels have to take the ordinary world as given. Dick has to deal with 'reality' as it has been dealt with by generations of traditional realist writers; in a sense Dick has to deal with Literary History itself in his straight novels. Fantasy elements such as disappearing soft-drink stands cannot be snuck into, say, MADAME BOVARY because it just isn't done. It's ironic that Don Wollheim, a traditionalist of the science fiction sort, was so upset at the injection of fantasy into TIME OUT OF JOINT when science fiction itself is so anti-realist.

To my mind the published straight novels lack the very thing that distinguishes PKD's science fiction writing, that is, imagination. But not just ordinary imagination along conventional realist lines – he had that aplenty, but science fiction imagination. The unexpected, the unknown, the artifact from left field and the collapse of reality so common to Dick's science fiction writing are just missing in his mainstream novels. As the frustrated hints of the agents at the SMLA and the editors at the publishing houses reveal, the straight novels are boring because nothing ever happens. People go through their little lives fornicating, fighting and fixing things but it all has a certain inevitability to it that makes the effort of reading it unfulfilling. Like Chinese food or something, you know the minute you finish the meal you're going to want to go out and get something that leaves a warmer glow in your belly. But, instead, Dick's mainstream novels, with a couple of exceptions, leave you feeling empty.

To Philip K. Dick reality wasn't solid, wasn't accepted as, in some way, Real, as Gillespie notes above. But something, perhaps the rewrite of "A Glass Of Darkness" into THE COSMIC PUPPETS in 1957, prompted PKD to look at reality a bit differently in 1958.

THE COSMIC PUPPETS is a novel very similar to TIME OUT OF JOINT. They both take place in a false town, the heroes cannot escape, reality breaks down in similar ways, etc. They are both fantasies, really, not science fiction despite the ending of TIME OUT OF JOINT. Throughout his life and, especially early on in his career, PKD was possessed of a strong tilt towards fantasy. This had been squashed by the early editors he dealt with when he first started writing tales of "sad little people." The public, the editors and Don Wollheim at Ace Books wanted science fiction, not fantasy. But, flattened as it was, PKD's fantastic yen returned in 1958 with TIME OUT OF JOINT.

In this novel one can almost see a light bulb go off in Dick's head as he sees the possibilities of incorporating fantasy ideas – not science fiction ideas – into his rapidly going nowhere straight novels. TIME OUT OF JOINT is the first of these to be fully realised.

For collectors of Philip K. Dick editions, the first edition Lippincott hard-cover of TIME OUT OF JOINT is a prize indeed. Copies in near fine condition with dust-jacket intact command up to $1000. Even a good specimen of the first UK Science Fiction Book Club edition of 1961 can go for two or three hundred dollars.

P. Schuyler Miller reviewed TIME OUT OF JOINT in the Jan 1960 issue of *Astounding*:

I shouldn't have to tell any "faithful reader" of today's science fiction that Philip K. Dick is developing into one of the most original talents in our field. He may not be in it long: this first hard-cover book is jacketed as "a novel of menace" – which it is. It also happens to be good, hard-shell science fiction, handled with consummate skill, so that an unsuspecting mystery reader may just find himself trapped before he realizes he is reading "that stuff."

You are introduced to Ragle Gumm, living with his sister and brother-in-law in a smallish town, and living off his winnings in an interminable newspaper contest, in which he is the invariable winner. This odd pattern of life grows a little odder; the reader begins to spot small contradictions and discrepancies that the characters seem to miss; and finally Ragle develops the growing conviction that he is somehow the center and raison d'être of a colossal piece of play-acting – as though the entire cast of De Mille's "Ten Commandments" has been rehearsed to convince one insignificant extra that he is an Egyptian laborer.

Now Ragle Gumm tries to break out of his barless cage, only to be deftly turned back again and again. Of course he does get out, and he does find out what is happening, but not until the beginning of the last chapter, when he sits down to read his own biography in Time. It's a grand job of writing. [cclxi]

And with that TIME OUT OF JOINT rates ✳ ✳ ✳ ✳ ✳

On May 2, 1958 the short story "Recall Mechanism" was received at the SMLA. The story was published in *If* in July 1959. But the story was not originally written in 1958 but most likely in late 1954. The only evidence we have for this earlier ascription is a letter from PKD to Bill Hamlin at *Imagination* in Sep 1955:

Dear Bill:
My agent Scott Meredith has relayed to me your request for a rewrite on my story RECALL MECHANISM.
The story is a good one, and I am proud of it. When a rewrite improves the story I'm glad to perform it. I welcome suggestions that help a story. In this case, however, the rewrite would turn a good yarn into a cornball nothing.
With great pride, and a sense of my responsibility to writers in general, to my own ethics, and to science-fiction readers, I refuse.
I have informed Scott, and I assume he'll be looking for the MS back.
Cordially,
Philip K. Dick[cclxii]

It's possible the story was written in early 1955 but a peek at the calendar for that year shows PKD writing EYE IN THE SKY and revising WORLD OF CHANCE. Dick himself said that in May 1955 he stopped writing short stories altogether so "Recall Mechanism" was almost certainly written before then.

The story itself has to do with a reclamation engineer in the future of a post-atomic world. He suffers from a nightmarish fear of falling. He visits a psychiatrist who discovers that the man is a weak precog and is previewing his own violent death by being thrown down a dark hole. At the end, another man exhibits a fascination with heights from which he likes to push people off...

Not really much of a story, despite PKD's letter to Bill Hamlin, "Recall Mechanism" gets only ✳ ✳

"Explorers We" is another difficult story to date with any accuracy. The manuscript arrived at the SMLA a few days after that for "Recall Mechanism" on May 6, 1958. But, again, earlier correspondence between PKD and Anthony Boucher at *F & SF* shows that the story was written much earlier. In a 1954 letter to Boucher, Phil wrote:

I'm sorry to keep bothering you with phone call and letter, but I understand that Scott Meredith is going to write to you about "Explorers We" and I wanted to get hold of you first.

As you recall, late in September of last year you wrote to me, expressing an interest in that story, and suggesting changes. I made changes and mailed them back within the week; during the first part of October. Since then I haven't heard hide nor hair from you, but I understand that you are officially away, these days, so I have been happy to wait. However, now I'm getting worried. Maybe there was a slip-up and you didn't receive my rewrite. Or something.

In any case, if you want another rewrite, etc, etc. let me know and I will produce. It may be that the time travel angle didn't convince you, in which case I'm sure another resolution can be found. Okay? Thanks a lot ... and maybe we could get together one of these days, as both of us repeatedly suggest.[cclxiii]

This letter mentions Boucher's interest in the story as early as September 1953. A possible resolution of this is that PKD wrote a version of the story in 1953. Then, prompted by Boucher, he rewrote the story in Oct 1953 and sent it back to Boucher who, apparently, never after contacted Dick or the Agency about the story. What happened after this 1954 letter until early 1958 – four years delay – is not known. I think, because Dick mentions another rewrite removing the time-travel angle, that he inventoried his pile of unsold manuscripts in 1958 and recalled that the time-travel angle was unsuitable to Boucher and rewrote the story again at that time, removing this angle, and sent it to the SMLA who then zipped it off once again to *F & SF* where it was accepted finally on June 2, 1958.[cclxiv]

"Explorers We" was published in the Jan 1959 *F &SF*. Much later, in 1985, it was selected for PKD's collection I HOPE I SHALL ARRIVE SOON. In Sep 1977 the story was reprinted as a limited-edition booklet to commemorate PKD's visit to the Second International Festival of Science Fiction at Metz in France.[cclxv]

"Explorers We" is another of Dick's backwards alien invasion tales with a happy crew of Terran explorers returning to Earth after a long stint in space. The excited crew emerges from their spaceship only to be gunned down by the FBI. Can't blame the FBI for ruining a happy homecoming, though, as this was the twenty-first time the explorers had returned...

Reminiscent of "Impostor" and "Human Is", "Explorers We" gets ✳ ✳ ✳ ✳ ✳

Besides the strange cases of "Recall Mechanism" and "Explorers We", Philip K. Dick was working on another straight novel in the Summer of 1958. This was IN MILT LUMKY TERRITORY.

IN MILT LUMKY TERRITORY

The manuscript for IN MILT LUMKY TERRITORY reached the SMLA on Oct 8, 1958. One cannot say that the Agency was pleased to see it although the reader there found it "real and warm, if not inspired." But once again despite Herculean efforts by the Agency this novel was rejected twelve times over the next few years before the SMLA returned it with regrets to PKD in 1963 as unsaleable.[cclxvi]

Undoubtedly this continuing rejection was incomprehensible to PKD. In this novel he had tried to address some of the complaints against his straight stories saying in the Author's Foreword

This is actually a very funny book, and a good one, too, in that the funny things that happen happen to real people who come alive. The ending is a happy one. What more can an author say? What more can he give?

Well, it wasn't enough. The publishers could find little humour in MILT LUMKY; an editor at Crown Publishing, Arthur C. Fields, wrote the Agency in 1959 when they rejected the story:

I don't know what to say about Philip Dick. He has extraordinary talent, tremendous facility, and acute penetration. He is able to lay bare the essential core of a situation in a few deft strokes. He has a flamboyance and an extraordinary eye for detail. The problem: His outlook on life, which is bleak and as chilling as any it has been my misfortune to come across.... What he does is to write in flat understatement a detailed analysis of the emptiness of everything so that the writing takes on an emptiness itself... We have seen three of these now, and they all have the same vacuum-like outlook.[cclxvii]

Of the story itself, Philip K. Dick had this to say in a letter to Eleanor Dimoff in 1960:

Virtue fails. Ambition, without experience, falls to dust. The clever and neurotic win -- a woman who is unable to trust anyone else, another person's judgment, and a bitter salesman, Lumky, who begrudges a younger man his success in marrying a woman that he himself wanted. The heavenly city of the rational man, the optimistic man, falls down, leaving the real world exposed. No one can be trusted, because everyone is too fearful to behave honestly; no one is disinterested. Only in fantasy -- in Bruce's dreams -- is there a little white cottage with roses twining up it. Once a boob, always a boob. Once burned, twice burned; if you make a mistake it is a sign that you are one of the doomed. Better give up; leave the gaming table. Gambling is for professionals; the sucker will be taken to the cleaners. And it is your wife and your best friend who will do the fleecing, not some con man you never saw before; the enemy is right at hand.[cclxviii]

IN MILT LUMKY TERRITORY wasn't published until June1985 when David Hartwell at Dragon Press in New York published a limited edition. Gollancz in England soon followed with an edition in October and a trade paperback edition from Paladin Press came out in 1987. The novel also has editions in France, Italy and Germany.

IN MILT LUMKY TERRITORY rates ✳ ✳ ✳

PKD sent one more short story to the SMLA in 1958, the manuscript for "Diversion" reaching them on Oct 31, 1958. Even though the sub-agent didn't think much of it, rating it as "better than G but not much," it was eventually accepted by *Galaxy* and published in the Dec 1959 issue as "War Game". [cclxix]

After that, it was chosen for THE PRESERVING MACHINE (1969) and two anthologies before finding its final resting place in THE COLLECTED STORIES OF PHILIP K. DICK (1987).

War Game" tells the tale of an uneasy economic battle between Earth and the Jupiter moons. Earth suspects the Ganymedeans of trying to infiltrate weapons into Terra in the guise of toys so every Ganymedean import must be tested by the Bureau of Standards. One game in particular causes concern: a war game in which miniature soldiers attack a miniature citadel. But while the Bureau of Standards is concentrating on this what else is slipping by?

"War Game" rates ✳ ✳ ✳ ✳

1958 cannot be said to have been a good year for Dick. Three short stories sold and one novel, TIME OUT OF JOINT, was it for the year. Domestic publication had also fallen to two short stories: "Jon's World" in a reprint of *TIME TO COME* from Berkley Books and "The Mold Of Yancy" in *THE 2ND WORLD OF IF* from Quinn Publishers.

But the situation was a little better in the foreign markets with Jubilee Publishers in Australia printing three of his stories in separate anthologies ("Adjustment Team", "The last Of The Masters" and "Tony And The Beetles")[cclxx]

Also, THE WORLD JONES MADE saw publication of its first German edition from 'Abenteur im Weltenraum' as GEHEIM PROJEKT VENUS.

In the bleak future of the next few years, re-editions of his novels and foreign editions would help sustain PKD as he continued determinedly on with his desire to write a saleable mainstream novel.

One of these foreign appearances of his story "Foster, You're Dead!" in 1958 was startling to PKD. He heard about it by listening to discussion of a story in a Russian magazine on the radio and recognised it as his own. The magazine was *Ogonek*, the Russian equivalent of *Life*. This was an unauthorized printing but PKD did eventually receive his royalties by complaining to a friend of his who worked for the FBI.[cclxxi]

In his life, besides the all-important writing, PKD continued to be happily married to Kleo through 1958. But he was a bit of a recluse and didn't like to go visiting family and friends too much. Perhaps the amphetamines he used to help him write (the use of which he seems to have hidden from his wife) made him withdrawn and edgy. But from all outward appearances they were a happily married couple. Even a brief affair Phil had at the end of 1957 did not destroy the marriage. That would occur in 1959 after the couple moved to Point Reyes Station in Marin County, California and Phil met Anne Rubinstein.

But perhaps the worst blow for PKD during the year was the death of his beloved grandma, Meemaw, in the Summer. With this death Phil and Kleo's ties to Berkeley were loosened and the couple made the move to Point Reyes Station in September, buying a small house there.

All was happy for a while until word of the science fiction writer who had just moved into town got around. One of Phil and Kleo's neighbors was Anne Rubinstein, a young widow who's husband had just died. She introduced herself one day and the three soon became friends, visiting back and forth. And then Phil started visiting Anne alone while Kleo commuted three days a week to her job in Berkeley. By the end of 1958 Phil and Anne were in love and the marriage to Kleo on the rocks.[cclxxii]

1959 "You have a massive suspension of belief on my part."

1959 started off well for Dick, his short story "Explorers We" was published in the Jan *F & SF* and in England the paperback edition of WORLD OF CHANCE was published by Panther in February. In April, as we've seen, IN MILT LUMKY TERRITORY was rejected by Crown Publishers and the news must've reached PKD by the end of the month.

But what was he working on? IN MILT LUMKY TERRITORY had been sent to the Agency in October the year before and a look at the calendar shows him working on nothing new until the expansion of "Time Pawn" into DR. FUTURITY in the middle of 1959.

No doubt the breakup of his marriage to Kleo and his subsequent moving in with Anne and her three children in February had an effect on his writing. We know that after the marriage to Anne on April 1st, Phil switched his writing time from the nighttime to the daytime so he could spend his evenings with the family.

DR. FUTURITY

The question is, did PKD write CONFESSIONS OF A CRAP ARTIST before the "Time Pawn" expansion?

PKD gives us one clue. In an interview with Richard Lupoff he speaks of CRAP ARTIST:

That's really the bridge between my Ace Double science fiction type of writing and MAN IN THE HIGH CASTLE. Actually, if you read what I wrote for Ace prior to Putnam's buying MAN IN THE HIGH CASTLE, you cannot account MAN IN THE HIGH CASTLE. It doesn't seem to come out of Ace Books. But if you read CONFESSIONS OF A CRAP ARTIST and date it as 1959 and 1961 for MAN IN THE HIGH CASTLE, you can bridge the gap between the two.[cclxxiii]

This implies, perhaps, that CRAP ARTIST was done second after DR. FUTURITY. The manuscript for DR. FUTURITY reached the SMLA on July 28 1959.

But why bother with the expansion in the first place? Most readers and critics see DR. FUTURITY as Phil's worst science fiction novel. Certainly, his heart doesn't seem to have been in it.

The most likely reason was financial. Plus, Don Wollheim his editor at Ace Books was probably intent on hanging onto his promising science fiction author as much as he could. Ace had published nothing new by PKD in 1958 and had had TIME OUT OF JOINT snatched from under their noses by Lippincott. So, perhaps in late 1958 or early 1959 Wollheim contacted PKD and urged the "Time Pawn" expansion. Reluctantly, one senses, PKD agreed.

"Time Pawn", as we have seen, was a novelette that Dick wrote in 1953. At 22,000 plus words it was well along towards being a novel already. Patrick Clark has made a detailed study of the two versions and notes:

When it came time to expand "Time Pawn" into a novel, Phil recycled a great deal of his original work. The first five chapters of DR. FUTURITY are essentially the same as the short story. The future is better defined, there is more detail about the society and the narrative is more logical. There are certain changes in the basic structure. Parsons is now in California rather than New York. He is only 400 years in the future instead of 700. Males are sterilized at the onset of puberty instead of at birth – someone must have pointed out the flaw in Phil's earlier scheme. Gametes are still harvested based on success in the Lists – and the fact that the participants are pre-pubescent children continues to be ignored. To further the expanded plot the nature of the Cube government is changed. In "Time Pawn" it is essentially decent, even humane. In the novel it is much less so. It is now something of a police state using specially trained juveniles called "shupos" as vicious storm troopers. The woman, Icara, is shot not by a companion but by the shupos during a raid on a clandestine political meeting. The title "Stenog" is now a name, Al Stenog, and he is depicted as vaguely sinister and decadent, rather like an SS official. And the Cube government is aware of time travel. They initiated the experiments but abandoned it as unproductive.

Most of the key elements of the short story – the culture of death, the operation of the Cube, Parsons' "crime" of restoring the injured and his sentence to exile on Mars – remain intact in the novel, sometimes uncomfortably so. It would appear that Phil had no desire to begin his novel from scratch and by using most of "Time Pawn" he had nearly a third of the novel written before he started.[cclxxiv]

By the time DR. FUTURITY got to Don Wollheim Dick was probably glad to get it out of the way and on with what he really wanted to write, which was CONFESSIONS OF A CRAP ARTIST. And even though he wondered at Wollheim's reaction to the rewrite, saying:

I admire and like Don, and he and I have had a rather long and happy business relationship, but his statements about my rewrite of TIME PAWN make me uneasy -- and well they might. You know that I worked hard on the TIME PAWN rewrite, and I did what I believed to be a good job, one that would please Don. If I went haywire, its news to me. Also, I got it in very early, far in advance of the deadline. I did everything I could to rebuild the story in the best possible way, and the letter that I sent outlining my intentions was a fair and accurate statement by me of what I intended to do, and what I actually did do. He was not stuck or stung. He had the legal right to reject my work entirely, to request any amount of changes he wished. Now, I say this only because his odd way of reacting -- both in terms of what he said and when he said it -- makes me fear on this VULCAN'S HAMMER job. From my standpoint, Don is an enigma. I honestly can't tell what will please him, obviously.[cclxxv]

One can sympathize with Don Wollheim in this case, even though it appears Wollheim himself rewrote some of it. Asked by Lupoff if Wollheim ever messed with his copy, Dick replied:

Never. Oh, once with DR. FUTURITY. He made a lot of cuts in DR. FUTURITY, but outside of that he never messed with them.
Lupoff: He didn't monkey with any of your other stuff, why did he cut DR. FUTURITY?

Because in DR. FUTURITY I had Christianity dying out and interracial marriages. Don disapproved of Christianity dying out or talk of it dying out. And he definitely disapproved of the interracial marriages.[cclxxvi]

But despite grumblings on both sides, DR. FUTURITY, backed with *SLAVERS OF SPACE* by John Brunner, was published in February 1960 by Ace Books as one half of an Ace Double. In England, the novel was published in A PKD OMNIBUS from Sidgwick & Jackson in 1970 (now a rarity) and two more editions came from Methuen (1976) and Magnum (1979).

Ace backed DR. FUTURITY with THE UNTELEPORTED MAN and issued them as an Ace Double in 1977. And there the novel sat until Mark Hurst at Berkley Books acquired reprint rights in 1979 and planned a "heavily revised DR. FUTURITY (changing title to TIME PAWN and adding some sex)."[cclxxvii] But this didn't happen (one can imagine PKD not wanting to work on Dr.F again!) and Berkley produced a new edition with the same old text in Aug 1984.[cclxxviii]

The plot of DR. FUTURITY is too convoluted to explain shortly. Suffice to say that it involves excessive time travel and Sir Francis Drake. It rates ✳

So, with that chore out of the way, PKD turned now to his new love, Anne, and the novel he would write which included her as a character. For PKD has said that Fay was based on Anne, he told her so during their honeymoon period.[cclxxix]

CONFESSIONS OF A CRAP ARTIST

If PKD followed Sutin's observation that Dick

As a good provider, {...} would keep a pace of two novels per year – each novel taking six weeks for the first draft and another six weeks for the second (retyping and minor copy editing). Between each novel would be six months devoted to thinking out the next plot.[cclxxx]

Then we have PKD thinking about CRAP ARTIST in the late Spring of 1959 and actually writing the novel in late 1959; probably in the period between July and October. We know from a copy of a letter in the SMLA's files that Don Wickenden, then an editor at Harcourt, Brace Publishers, had turned down CRAP ARTIST by Oct 29, 1959 and, therefore, that the novel was done by then. [cclxxxi]

With CRAP ARTIST the Agency tried a new tack; sending the novel to the publishers as if it was written by Jack Isidore and not Philip K. Dick – presumably this was done on PKD's suggestion. But the publishers were not fooled for long. In his letter commenting on CRAP ARTIST Wickenden wrote:

How many pages of CONFESSIONS OF A CRAP ARTIST had I read before I began to suspect that the actual author was Philip K. Dick? Five, perhaps. By the time I'd read ten I was sure.[cclxxxii]

Another publisher, Knopf, almost bought the novel in 1960 but asked for a rewrite. But PKD couldn't do it, despite Scott Meredith's urging that this was his big chance. He told wife Anne:

It's not that I don't want to, it's that I'm not able to. [cclxxxiii]

Lawrence Sutin thinks that Dick was not able to because the story didn't need it. Perhaps, also, this is a novel that Dick wrote in the full flush of love with Anne and, though he still loved her, he could not be in that same circumstance again.

Grove Press was also interested in CRAP ARTIST but decided not to go with it because "there was no sex in it." [cclxxxiv]

As we have noted above, PKD saw CRAP ARTIST as a bridge between his Ace Double type of science fiction and THE MAN IN THE HIGH CASTLE. Later, in 1980 toward the end of his life, PKD dismissed his straight fiction including CRAP ARTIST:

I really liked that one, myself, {...} But I've lost interest in writing non-sf. Their time has passed. They're essentially fossils. When I'm dead and lying in the marble orchards, I won't stop my heirs from digging them up and publishing them. But I don't want to flood the market with a bunch of my old non-sf now. [cclxxxv]

The plot of CRAP ARTIST is complicated, having to do with Jack Isidore – the crap artist of the title – and his relationship with his sister Fay and her husband Charley Hume. Dick employs several viewpoints as he writes of Fay's affair with Nat Anteil, the young husband of Gwen. Charley decides to murder his bitch wife, Fay, but in the end instead kills all his pet sheep and then himself. Hilarious at times and shocking at others, CRAP ARTIST is the best of PKD's straight novels and the only one to see publication in his lifetime. PKD himself said that it was "about one-half fiction and one-half the truth." A limited edition, now valuable, was published by Paul Williams' Entwhistle Press in 1975.

CONFESSIONS OF A CRAP ARTIST (subtitled 'A Chronicle of Verified Scientific Fact') rates ✳✳✳✳✳

By the Summer of 1959 all news was not bad for PKD's career. Lippincott published his first ever hard-cover novel, TIME OUT OF JOINT in June and his short stories, "Recall Mechanism", "Fair Game" and "War Game" appeared in the sf magazines by the end of the year. Finally, in December, *New Worlds* in England, began to serialize TIME OUT OF JOINT. It would run in three consecutive issues of *New Worlds* to Feb 1960. A couple of anthology appearances filled out the year: "Expendable" in *SF SHOWCASE* -- which was a memorial edition for C.M. Kornbluth containing stories by his friends -- from Doubleday, and "The Father-Thing" in Anthony Boucher's *A TREASURY OF GREAT SF* also from Doubleday. Foreign editions continued to appear: EYE IN THE SKY from Mondadori in Italy and *Satellite* in France. Then TIME OUT OF JOINT also in Italy.

The most encouraging news, though, came from Harcourt, Brace Publishers in December. Even though they'd rejected everything the Agency had sent them they sent Dick $500 as half payment for a new novel he was to write. Harcourt, Brace also wanted Dick to go to New York to work with their editor there, but Dick's agoraphobia precluded him from making the trip. Instead he worked through the mail with Harcourt. Brace editor, Eleanor Dimoff. And this is where the important correspondence between the two concerning PKD's straight novels began.

Dimoff constructively criticized five of Dick's novels and offered suggestions about how PKD should build his next novel.

This next novel was THE MAN WHOSE TEETH WERE ALL EXACTLY ALIKE.

1960

THE MAN WHOSE TEETH WERE ALL EXACTLY ALIKE

While Dick was wrestling with THE MAN WHOSE TEETH in early 1960, he was no doubt also looking over copies of the Ace Books first edition of DR. FUTURITY which hit the bookstores in February. But the biggest news of the year was certainly the birth of his and Anne's daughter, Laura, on Feb 25.

The genesis of THE MAN WHOSE TEETH WERE ALL EXACTLY ALIKE was an argument PKD had with wife Anne about whether Neanderthal Man was a vegetarian or a meat eater. Anne rounded up the facts and presented them to Phil who became furious and vowed to write a novel refuting the facts.

This he did and, surprisingly enough despite the bad science, wrote one of his better novels – also one of his bitterest.

THE MAN WHOSE TEETH WERE ALL EXACTLY ALIKE is a story of small town hatred and revenge. Due to a misunderstanding between Walt Dombrosio, a craftsman, and Leo Runcible, a real estate agent, a nasty feud is begun. Dombrosio makes a fool of Runcible by manufacturing and then planting fake fossil evidence showing that Neanderthal man was, indeed, a vegetarian. Runcible falls for it hook, line and sinker and is eventually humiliated. The setting is in the area of Phil and Anne's home town of Pt. Reyes Station.

Evidently PKD had not taken Eleanor Dimoff's criticism to heart. For some reason he just couldn't write what other people wanted him to. When TEETH reached Harcourt, Brace in June it didn't take Dimoff long to reject it with comments:

> At some point, the relationships between Phil's couples become so crystallized into a nasty, inhuman quarreling (or such a dead end) that somehow the characters become interesting only in a clinical way.[cclxxxvi]

Dick, later in life, saw TEETH as "a fusion of Nathaniel West and F. Scott Fitzgerald" and he likened Leo Runcible to Gatsby. The character of Leo Runcible was actually based on a man Phil and Anne knew in Point Reyes Station: a civic-minded man who, at great cost to himself, organized the clean-up of the water supply in Point Reyes Station.[cclxxxvii]

THE MAN WHOSE TEETH WERE ALL EXACTLY ALIKE was PKD's second favorite of his straight novels and the first published after his death. Mark Ziesing Publishers producing a trade paperback edition and a limited hardback edition in June 1984.

The novel is not nearly as grim as it sounds and rates ✳ ✳ ✳ ✳

Okay, so Harcourt, Brace rejected TEETH but did they want their $500 back? Not yet. As we've seen above Dick latched onto Dimoff's positive comments about A TIME FOR GEORGE STAVROS and proposed to rewrite that novel, salvaging the main character. But, despite Dimoff's urging to make his characters more likeable and engaging, Dick could not compromise his writing to the extent of pandering to Dimoff's view of the market and, again, he wrote what Rickman has called one of his "gloomiest books", HUMPTY DUMPTY IN OAKLAND.

We will turn our attention to HUMPTY DUMPTY IN OAKLAND in a moment but, first, there is the expansion of the short story "Vulcan's Hammer" into the novel VULCAN'S HAMMER to consider.

VULCAN'S HAMMER

The manuscript for "Vulcan's Hammer" was received at the SMLA on April 16, 1953 and the story was published in 1956 in *Future Science Fiction #29*, as noted above.

In early January 1960 Scott Meredith forwarded a letter to Philip K. Dick from Don Wollheim at Ace Books. This letter referred to Wollheim's interest in having Dick do an expansion of "Vulcan's Hammer" into a 40,000-word novel. In his reply Dick expresses concern about writing the expansion on spec for Don Wollheim, particularly after Wollheim's negative attitude towards Dick's earlier expansion of "Time Pawn" into DR. FUTURITY.[cclxxxviii]

In his letter to Scott Meredith replying to the notice that Don Wollheim of Ace Books wanted him to expand "Vulcan's Hammer", PKD wrote:

The letter from Don Wollheim about a rewrite of VULCAN'S HAMMER to expand it to 40,000 words has reached me. In some ways the situation looks good, but its a complex situation and I want to discuss it with you point by point, if you will bear with me.

(one) Risk. Since this expanded version would be dead on the magazine market, we would have to sell it to Don or have it not sell at all, I presume. This gives Don all the cards in a spec rewrite. I admire and like Don, and he and I have had a rather long and happy business relationship, but his statements about my rewrite of TIME PAWN make me uneasy -- and well they might. {...}

Now, I say this only because his odd way of reacting -- both in terms of what he said and when he said it -- makes me fear on this VULCAN'S HAMMER job. From my standpoint, Don is an enigma. I honestly can't tell what will please him, obviously. It would take me several months of intensive work to get a rewrite of this story to him and I can't absorb all the risk. Therefore, to go ahead, I must discuss in detail, as I go along, what I am doing. I see no other way out, If ACE can't put up any money in advance.

(two) Defects in the story. VULCAN'S HAMMER is a botched job, in the printed version. I botched it myself. I consider it one of the worst of my efforts. However, parts are good, even superb. If I am to expand it, I must do more than literally put in two words where one now stands throughout. This may bring about another TIME PAWN situation, right? However, it would not be my intention to put in ideas not already there, as I did in TIME PAWN. I would build up the best parts, and eliminate or lessen the weaker parts. I believe that the true body of good ideas lies in the first portion of the story -- in about the first third. The ending is terrible. For three days I have studied the story, made elaborate notes. I want you to pass on to Don these notions regarding the rewrite {...} Here are the notions, expressed informally:

{There follows a page and a half of material on VULCAN'S HAMMER. See: SL-38, p51ff}

(three) If I go ahead and do this on spec, I would like Don and you to permit me to send in, not a finished draft at first, but a carbon -- or my original, if you want -- of my first rough draft. {...}

(four) Other pressing work. {...} Shouldn't I be a little wary of getting too much in VULCAN'S HAMMER and this Don Wollheim s-f notion of "Phil Dick's true vocation"? It might throw me off my real work. which is of course the straight-novel contract.[cclxxxix]

(c) If I am to do any s-f, any bread-and-butter work, since VULCAN'S HAMMER can only be marketed to ACE, wouldn't it be more practical {...} for me to go and do a wholly new s-f novel, based on new ideas, which, if ACE doesn't buy, would be marketable to other houses? I want to do a psychological s-f book in the tradition of my TIME OUT OF JOINT. {...} In other words, it seems to me that I must have some stronger assurance that when I get the VULCAN'S HAMMER work done, I *will* get a sale from ACE on it. I want to do it -- that is, the job. I'd enjoy it. But it would be real work for me (that TIME PAWN rework almost killed me; it was the hardest job I've done to date). I know VULCAN'S HAMMER would turn out really swell. {...}

I'll hold off further work on VULCAN'S HAMMER, hoping that you can go to Don with portions of this letter, and get from him a more complete acceptance of what I propose to do than obtains at present. I would not mind dealing with him direct, if you want me to. But only if you want it. Okay? And thanks for your willingness to read this long rather rambling letter.[ccxc]

In the event, he did expand the short story into the novel VULCAN'S HAMMER in March and April 1960, after sending in the manuscript for CONFESSIONS OF A CRAP ARTIST. It was sold to Ace and published by them in September 1960 as one half of an Ace Double, backed with *THE SKYNAPPERS* by John Brunner.[ccxci]

The plot of VULCAN'S HAMMER pretty much follows the short story: Government is in the hands of a computer, Vulcan 3, and when the people try to take it back a struggle ensues. A good premise but indifferently handled by Dick.

VULCAN'S HAMMER, the novel, still rates ✳✳

After taking time out to do the VULCAN'S HAMMER expansion, Dick finished up THE MAN WHOSE TEETH WERE ALL EXACTLY ALIKE, the manuscript for which reached the SMLA in May. It was rejected by Harcourt, Brace publishers in July.

Now even though Harcourt, Brace didn't want their money back right away, with the rejection of TEETH Dick had to quickly begin another novel perhaps more suited to Harcourt, Brace's sensibilities. As we have seen above, Dick latched onto Dimoff's positive comments about A TIME FOR GEORGE STAVROS and proposed to rewrite that novel, salvaging the main character. But what resulted, as Rickman noted, was HUMPTY DUMPTY IN OAKLAND, one of Dick's "gloomiest books."[ccxcii]

HUMPTY DUMPTY IN OAKLAND

HUMPTY DUMPTY IN OAKLAND, arrived, manuscript-wise, at the Scott Meredith Literary Agency in October 1960.[ccxciii]

It took three months for Harcourt, Brace to reject it. In a letter to the SMLA, editor Don Wickenden said

One is left asking, at the end, what the book has really been about, what the author is trying to do and say in it. As with earlier Dick novels, it simply doesn't add up to enough.[ccxciv]

Dick was given eighteen months to return the $500 advance.[ccxcv]

HUMPTY DUMPTY IN OAKLAND was first published in England by Gollancz in Oct 1986 and later a trade paperback edition came from Paladin Press in 1988. There has been no USA edition.[ccxcvi]

The novel itself is a harsh one about a used-car salesman and his neighbor, the owner of a service garage. Life is hard for them and even when Jim Fergesson, the owner of the garage, retires and invests in real estate things don't improve. In the end he has a heart attack and dies. Philip K. Dick himself said of the novel:

HUMPTY DUMPTY IN OAKLAND is a novel about the proletarian world from the inside. Most books about the proletarian world are written by middle-class writers.[ccxcvii]

HUMPTY DUMPTY IN OAKLAND rates ✳ ✳ ✳

With some fast correspondence and some fast writing, Dick had written two novels for Harcourt, Brace and $500. Unfortunately, as we have seen, neither one was acceptable to this publisher and even though PKD kept the money when he looked back on the year 1960 from the point of view of his career, he had only two things to show for it: publication by Ace Books of his two worst science fiction novels, DR. FUTURITY and VULCAN'S HAMMER. No wonder that in 1961 he practically gave up writing altogether.

On the bright side, though, he and his wife did have a bouncing baby girl, Laura, and Anne was pregnant again in the Fall.

We now come to perhaps the gloomiest time of Dick's writing career: 1961.

1961. It Is The Morning After Doomsday. America Has Been Attacked And Overcome.

A look at the calendar of submissions and publications in 1961 shows a sorry state of affairs. In January, *Galaxy* in the UK printed his short story "War Game" and in October the UK Science Fiction Book Club edition of TIME OUT OF JOINT was published. And that's about it other than a Spanish edition of THE VARIABLE MAN from Cenit.

In January PKD learned that his last mainstream effort, HUMPTY DUMPTY IN OAKLAND had been rejected by Harcourt, Brace and this seems to have been the last straw as far as his mainstream career. He would write no more mainstream novels until, perhaps, his last, THE TRANSMIGRATION OF TIMOTHY ARCHER.

THE MAN IN THE HIGH CASTLE

So, then, a glum PKD skulking around the house with Anne and the kids, somewhat at a loss and not knowing what to do. Hiding out in his $25 a month rented hut up the road which he called the Hovel, and reading Carl Jung and Taoist texts. Becoming interested in the ancient Chinese oracle, the *I Ching*, and consulting it with Anne on many occasions in the summer of 1961, asking questions about life, the universe and whether or not they should sell their old car. And though Anne got bored with it, Phil continued to use the *I Ching* daily. Finally, through lack of anything better to do, he started helping Anne with her jewelry making business:

I did the seven stages of silver polishing for a while, and I built her bench, mounted motors for her, etc., and even made the first important sales of her wares.[ccxcviii]

But Phil was not happy:

I didn't enjoy making jewelry. I had no talent whatsoever. She had the talent. She is still a jeweler and a very fine one, making gorgeous stuff which she sells to places like Neiman-Marcus. It's great art. But I couldn't do anything except polish what she made.

I decided that I'd better tell her I was working on a book so I wouldn't have to polish her jewelry all day long. We had a little cabin, and I went over there with a sixty-five-dollar portable typewriter made in Hong Kong -- the "e" key was stuck on it. I started with nothing but the name "Mister Tagomi" written on a scrap of paper, no other notes. I had been reading a lot of Oriental philosophy, reading a lot of Zen Buddhism, reading the *I Ching*. That was the Marin County zeitgeist at that point, Zen Buddhism and the *I Ching*. I just started right out and kept on trucking. It was either that or go back to polishing jewelry. [ccxcix]

Mr. Tagomi is, of course, the hero of THE MAN IN THE HIGH CASTLE. PKD speaks of his origins further in a 1970 letter:

I had gotten involved with my quondam wife's jewelry business: polishing silver and the like, as depicted in the novel. As far as I was concerned the period in my life in which I was a sf writer had ended, not with a bang and not even a whimper. But then one day as I was driving to my cabin in Inverness, Calif., a thought entered my mind. Mr. Tagomi. I got to the cabin, wrote down his name, and then I saw him seated in his office, keeping the ultimate of evil at bay in his own small fashion. And, with no further planning or notes, I wrote the book. [ccc]

The *I Ching* was involved from the beginning. In 1961 Phil's friend, Iskandar Guy – also a devotee of the *I Ching* – in conversation with Lawrence Sutin remembers hearing

Phil complain that the oracle could speak with a forked tongue. Guy recalls: "I told him, 'It goes back at least to 1165 BC. Who are we to question an entity functioning at that level all this time?' He said, 'Fuck it, I'll fix it – I'll write a novel based on it." ...[ccci]

But he was not writing it yet. The situation re the jewelry business had to be resolved. In 1976 Dick told Daniel DePrez:

MAN IN THE HIGH CASTLE was an anomaly in my writing. I had given up writing. I had actually decided to give up writing, and was helping my wife in her jewelry business. And I wasn't happy. She was giving me all the shit part to do, and I decided to pretend I was writing a book. And I said, "Well, I'm writing a very important book. And to make the fabrication convincing, I actually had to start typing. And I had no notes, I had nothing in mind, except for years I had wanted to write that idea, about Germany and Japan actually having beaten the United States. And without any notes, I simply sat down and began to write, simply to get out of the jewelry business. [cccii]

Anne disagrees that it was all her fault. Phil, she says, became so enthusiastic that he threatened to take over the jewelry making as his own:

I think he saw it as a way for him to have a normal business. He found himself trapped in writing at the time because he couldn't really make enough money to raise a family on it – I think he was real sensitive about that. He was a great jewelry maker, he had talent. I think he was so mad I pushed him out – that's why he talked so badly about it.[ccciii]

Not only did Anne push Phil out of her jewelry business, she pushed him out of the house altogether. Earlier Phil had rented a hut (the 'Hovel') up the road which he next determined to move into so he could write and leave Anne in peace to her creations. He moved his typewriter, stereo and books into the Hovel and despite Anne's pleas and his own desires stuck to his guns and worked there from then on.[ccciv]

His first novel written there was THE MAN IN THE HIGH CASTLE. With the *I Ching* to hand and the name 'Mr. Tagomi' written on a scrap of paper PKD sat down to write.

But, of course, it was not as simple as that. Even though he began the novel with only a name, PKD had been thinking about it for a long time:

I did seven years of research for THE MAN IN THE HIGH CASTLE. Seven years of research: it took me seven years to amass the material on the Nazis and the Japanese. Especially on the Nazis. And that's probably the reason why it's a better novel than most of my novels: I knew what I was talking about. I had prime-source material at the Berkeley-Cal library right from the Gestapo's mouth--stuff that had been seized after World War II. Stuff that was marked for the eyes of "the higher police" only. I had to read what those guys wrote in their private journals in order to write THE MAN IN THE HIGH CASTLE.[cccv]

How Dick approached the underpinnings of the story also took some thought:

I had to structure out the decisions that the Nazis would have had to make, the changes in history that would have permitted them to win that war. It would be a very long list of things that would have had to happen, and they're not all in MAN IN THE HIGH CASTLE. Just for example, Spain would've had to grant them the right to go through, you know, from France to take Gibraltar and close off the Mediterranean. That war was not really as close a call as we thought it was. I mean, it is just not that easy to defeat Russia -- as certain people in history have found out. I hope we're not about to find that out ourselves.[cccvi]

The *I Ching* was also a great help. Asked by interviewer Arthur Byron Cover whether he used the *I Ching* as a plotting device, PKD responded:

Once. I used it in THE MAN IN THE HIGH CASTLE because a number of characters used it. In each case when they asked a question, I threw the coins and wrote the hexagram lines they got. That governed the direction of the book. Like in the end when Juliana Frink is deciding whether or not to tell Hawthorne Abendsen that he is the target of assassins, the answer indicated that she should. Now if it had said not to tell him, I would have had her not go there. But I would not do that in any other book.[cccvii]

Of the writing of the novel itself, PKD said that this one was done differently from his normal approach:

{...} mostly I wrote for the editor. To me it wasn't the reader who bought it, it was the editor who bought it; it was as simple as that. The big change came when I wrote THE MAN IN THE HIGH CASTLE, because the book was *not* written for Donald Wollheim. I had sold TIME OUT OF JOINT, and had gotten the idea of selling a hardcover novel. With MAN IN THE HIGH CASTLE, I had no concept of an audience at all. I had no concept even of an editor. It was a pure relationship between me and the characters in the novel, and it stayed pretty much that way. [cccviii]

And speaking of these characters, PKD when asked why he loved writing and creating characters, said:

It's not generally recognized that the author is lonely. Writing is a solitary occupation. When you start your novel you seal yourself off from your family and friends. But in this there's a paradox, because you then create new companions. I would say I write because there are not enough people in the world who can give me enough companionship. To me the great joy in writing a book is showing some small person, some ordinary person doing something in a moment of great valor, for which he would get nothing and which would be unsung in the real world. The book, then, is the song about his valor. You know, people think that the author wants to be immortal, to be remembered through his work. No. I want Mr. Tagomi from THE MAN IN THE HIGH CASTLE always to be remembered. My characters are composites of what I've actually seen people do, and the only way for them to be remembered is through my books. [cccix]

Mr. Tagomi was a favorite character of Dick's and when the novel was finished he had a difficult time separating himself from him. In a late night soliloquy in 1968 Phil wrote of the heartbreak of the writer:

What matters to me is the *writing*, the act of manufacturing the novel, because while I am doing it, at that particular moment, I am in the world I am writing about. It is real to me, completely and utterly. Then, when I'm finished, and have to stop, withdraw from that world *forever* -- that destroys me. The men and women have ceased talking. They no longer move. I'm alone, without much money, and, as I said before, nearly 40. Where is Mr. Tagomi, the protagonist in MAN IN THE HIGH CASTLE? He has left me; we are cut off from each other. To read the novel does not restore Mr. Tagomi, place him once again where I can hear him talk. Once written, the novel speaks generally to everyone, not specifically to me. When a novel of mine comes out I have no more relationship to it than has anyone who reads it -- far less, in fact, because I have the memory of Mr. Tagomi and all the others... Gino Molinari, for example, in NOW WAIT FOR LAST YEAR, or Leo Bulero in 3 STIGMATA. My friends are dead, and as much as I love my wife, daughter, cat -- none of these nor all of these is enough. The vacuum is terrible. Don't write for a living; sell shoelaces. Don't let it happen to you.
I promise myself: I will never write another novel. I will never again imagine people from whom I will eventually be cut off. I tell myself this... and, secretly and cautiously, I begin another book. [cccx]

But to backtrack for a moment, let's take a look at the publication chronology of THE MAN IN THE HIGH CASTLE.

In the summer and Fall of 1961 PKD was in his hovel banging out HIGH CASTLE on his old Japanese typewriter with the missing "e" key. By 29 Nov 1961 the novel was completed. [cccxi]

When he was done with the writing he proudly showed the manuscript to his wife, Anne. But she was not impressed, saying

"It's all right, but you'll never make more than $750 off of it. I don't even see where it's worth your while to submit it to your agent."   I said, "What the hell!" And THE

MAN IN THE HIGH CASTLE was bought by Putnam's for $1500, which isn't a great deal more than she had prophesied.[cccxii]

Acceptance by Putnam's came quickly. By Dec 10, 1961 PKD was informed of the sale. He was soon doing a rewrite for his editor at Putnam's, Pete Israel.[cccxiii]

Dick, of course, was wondering whether Putnam's – a mainstream publisher – would market HIGH CASTLE as science fiction or mainstream. In a letter to Tony Boucher PKD expanded on this:

I called Pete Israel, my editor at Putnam's, after talking to you, and he assured me that they "could have it both ways": market their printing of MAN IN THE HIGH CASTLE in a mainstream type way as well as a way that would appeal to the s-f reader, especially in terms of my name. Pete said, "Of course, I guess you're not as well-known as Heinlein, are you?" In a rather hopeful tone, as if he were wondering if maybe I *was* as well-known, and how nice that would be, like Pooh wondering if there was another jar of honey, or had he eaten the last, etc. "Pete," I said, "I may not be as well-known as Heinlein, but Tony Boucher says --" and here, I admit I attributed to you certain favorable statements as to me & my work, which, I could tell, did not fall on deaf ears. As they are now just copy-editing the MS, this is my last time to make any pitch to them ... so forgive me if I used you as a totem god mask of Power and Magic by which to make effective my wish...[cccxiv]

In the event, Putnam's published THE MAN IN THE HIGH CASTLE as sort of both mainstream and science fiction, calling it "An electrifying novel of our world as it might have been" on the cover of their edition which came out at the end of October 1962.[cccxv]

But despite this have-their-cake-and-eat-it-too decisiveness on the part of Putnam's, Doubleday selected the novel for their Science Fiction Book Club in late 1962 and the SFBC edition came out in early December.[cccxvi] PKD acknowledged this, saying

It did get tremendous reviews. Part of that was due to the good fortune that it was picked up by the Science Fiction Book Club. Had it not been picked up by them, it would not have won the Hugo Award, because the edition would have been too small.[cccxvii]

The SFBC edition was published only a couple of months after the Putnam first edition and is practically identical to it in looks, even down to having Putnam's and not Doubleday as the publisher. However, for collector's, the first edition is scarce and can cost from $300 to over $1000 depending on condition. The SFBC edition on the other hand can be had for around $50.[cccxviii]

As to the reviews of THE MAN IN THE HIGH CASTLE, Dick was generally happy, thanking Avram Davidson at *F & SF* for promoting it. But Tony Boucher, Davidson's ex-stablemate at *F & SF*, who you'd think would be most enthusiastically behind it, didn't care for it too much. While listening to the radio one day, PKD heard Boucher pan the novel:

Tony Boucher called it a failure; I heard him review it on the radio, and he said that it was not a science-fiction novel, it was actually just a mainstream novel, once you got past the alternate-world premise. Later he came up to me and said that he now felt that it was a breakthrough novel. Donald Wollheim said, "It is sick, dated, and not science fiction." But most of the criticism was very positive.[cccxix]

What Wollheim actually said on one occasion if not this one was:

And of course I read Philip K. Dick with bemused interest. Essentially most of what he says is true, and curiously enough much of what is said in opposition is also true. To attempt to go through it and pick nits in disagreement would take more pages and more documentation than it could be worth, and everything said could in turn be rebutted. The way I feel about it now is that having lived in the USA of 1945-1964, none of us are in a position to criticize where the question of individual guilt is concerned.

However, personally I am numbered among those who found MAN IN THE HIGH CASTLE irritating, outmoded, and sick. Whatever its merits as literature, it was a totally wrong choice for a Hugo. It is questionable by what definition or standard it could be called science-fiction. Dick has written some <u>great</u> science fiction stories, but this wasn't among them.[cccxx]

Don Wollheim, though, no matter what he thought of HIGH CASTLE as science fiction, was not about to let his old stalwart go without at least complaining. Ed Meskys recalls PKD telling him that

Don Wollheim kept writing him complaining now that he had a major success with CASTLE he would be abandoning Don and Ace.[cccxxi]

Of course this didn't happen. In fact, PKD's next novel, WE CAN BUILD YOU, written in 1962, was published by Wollheim in 1972 when he was editing his own line of paperbacks, DAW Books, and THE GAME-PLAYERS OF TITAN (written late 1962/early 1963) was published by Ace Books in 1963. Dick would have several more paperback originals published by Ace over the next 20 years. But... the stranglehold was broken. With the success of HIGH CASTLE and its subsequent winning of the Hugo Award for best science fiction novel of 1962, PKD was now able to attract the attention of other publishers, notably Ballantine Books where Tony Boucher was now an editor. MARTIAN TIME SLIP, which PKD wrote in late 1962, was sold to Ballantine and published by them in 1964. With the success of the SFBC edition of HIGH CASTLE, hardback sf publisher Doubleday also got into the act, snapping up several of PKD's novels in the coming years.

When HIGH CASTLE won the Hugo Award, it made a difference to PKD's life and writing. Commenting on this later in his life PKD wrote:

Now, most readers do not know how little SF writers were paid. I had been earning about $6000 a year. In the year following the Hugo Award, I earned $12000, and close to that in the subsequent years (1965-68). And I wrote at a fantastic speed; I produced twelve novels in two years... which must be a record of some sort. I could never do this again -- the physical stress was enormous... but the Hugo was there to tell me that what I wanted to write was what a good number of readers wanted to read. Amazing as it seems!
[cccxxii]

As to how his writing changed with and after HIGH CASTLE, Dick explains:

{...} all of a sudden something happened. I know it happened to me, because one day I was writing VULCAN'S HAMMER for an Ace double and the next day I was writing, without even notes, MAN IN THE HIGH CASTLE. I say <<next day,>> but actually almost two years passed in which I wrote nothing at all. And then when I did go back I was different and what I wrote was different. In the old days I wrote s-f, and then put what literary mini ability I had into mainstream and experimental literary-type novels -- which never sold, bringing about a situation in which what I wrote that was marketable was separated from what I wrote that had literary value -- and only the first category ever saw print. I saved my best for mainstream writing... and now, since MAN IN THE HIGH CASTLE, I put all the literary skill I have into my s-f, my marketable work. The field gains when its writers do this, and when they do not -- when they do what I formerly did -- the field loses.{... ...} cccxxiii

Dick also saw THE MAN IN THE HIGH CASTLE as a turning point in his career. He felt he'd found a new way of merging his mainstream-type writing with his science fiction to create a successful blend of literature. Unfortunately, his vision was dashed with the reception of WE CAN BUILD YOU which he wrote in mid 1962 after acceptance of HIGH CASTLE by Putnam's:

With HIGH CASTLE and MARTIAN TIME SLIP, I thought I had bridged the gap between the experimental mainstream novel and science fiction. Suddenly I'd found a way to do everything I wanted to do as a writer. I had in mind a whole series of books, a vision of a new kind of science fiction progressing from those two novels. Then TIME SLIP was rejected by Putnam, and every other hardcover publisher we sent it to.

My vision collapsed. I was crushed. I had made a mis-calculation somewhere, and I didn't know where. The evaluation I had made of myself, of the marketplace, went poof! I reverted to a more primitive concept of my writing. The books that might have followed TIME SLIP were gone. cccxxiv

This account is, as Paul Williams noted, incorrect. The novel that Dick meant to refer to was WE CAN BUILD YOU and not MARTIAN TIME-SLIP:

I came across very convincing evidence that the above quoted account is incorrect in some key details. MARTIAN TIME SLIP was never submitted to Putnam. There was another novel that Phil's agent, if not Phil, saw as the appropriate work to follow in the footsteps of HIGH CASTLE. It was called THE FIRST IN YOUR FAMILY.

...

These cards {in the SMLA file} clearly indicate that the first recorded receipt by the Agency of a manuscript from Phil following HIGH CASTLE was a novel called THE FIRST IN YOUR FAMILY (finally published ten years later as WE CAN BUILD YOU), received Oct 4, 1962. cccxxv

The manuscript for MARTIAN TIME SLIP arrived at the end of the month on Oct 31, 1962 and the SMLA had no difficulty selling it first to *Worlds Of Tomorrow* for serialization in Aug, Oct and Dec 1963 and then to Ballantine Books for publication in Apr 1964. So, in the above account by PKD substitute WE CAN BUILD YOU for MARTIAN TIME SLIP and it will be correct.

But before all that, PKD was obviously gratified with the reception that HIGH CASTLE had with the science fiction reading public and the critics. The Hugo Award was indeed a milestone in his career and also a determinant of his future. Suddenly he was in demand, particularly in the science fiction magazines for which he again started writing short stories in 1963 after notification of the Hugo Award reached him. But we will turn to the year 1963 shortly. Before that we must round out this section on THE MAN IN THE HIGH CASTLE.

An interesting sidelight to HIGH CASTLE's publishing history is what happened to the novel when it was published in Japan and Germany. In a 1968 letter PKD wrote to the Japanese translator of HIGH CASTLE. No doubt he had been told about the Hayakawa Shobo edition of 1965. Here's the contents of this letter:

Dear Mr. Kawaguchi,

I am told by Mr. Fukushima of Hayakawa Shobo & Company that you translated my novel, MAN IN THE HIGH CASTLE. I wonder if I could ask you several questions about the Japanese edition. Viz.:

Did the novel sell well in Japan?

Were the reviews of the novel favorable? If so, what did the reviewers like, and if not, what did they dislike?

I like Japanese people and Japan (which I would very much like to visit). In the novel did I manage to convey my positive feelings toward Japan and the Japanese? I felt that the Japanese occupation of the USA, described in the novel, would be stern but fair -- unlike the German. A major aspect of the novel was my desire to contrast the two, German and Japanese occupation. Did this contrast get across? I would be very distressed if it turned out that my favorable feelings toward Japan did not come across in the novel, as seen from your standpoint. After all, the basis of the novel was Mr. Tagomi's thwarting of German designs, his deep humanitarian quality which defied the German authorities. Of all the fiction I have written, nothing has meant more to me than the scene in which Mr. Tagomi confronts the German authorities and wins out against them, in the name of humanity.

Did the special speech of the Japanese living in the USA West Coast seem convincing to you? Or did I misrepresent the Japanese manner of speaking English? I would be very upset if, in your opinion, this special speech was not convincing.

Did you yourself personally like the novel?

I am sorry to be putting so many questions to you, but all this is very important to me. I am sorry for causing you any inconvenience, and any and all answers you might give me to the above questions would be quite valuable to me. Thank you very much for your trouble and time, and I will hope to hear from you.[cccxxvi]

Mr. Kawaguchi replied to this letter and PKD commented on it in his essay "The Mainstream That Through The Ghetto Flows":

First of all, he said, "Your book wasn't any good to start with." Secondly, he said, "You've also confused Chinese culture and Japanese culture. The Chinese are inferior people, and the *I Ching's* Chinese and not Japanese. No Japanese would ever use some Confucian classic. Only foreigners use those." I was quite amazed at how up-front he was in his contempt for the book, but it's still in print in Japan. It's sold very well, and I've made almost thirty-five dollars off of it. Over a ten-year period.[cccxxvii]

In this same interview, PKD talks about the German edition of THE MAN IN THE HIGH CASTLE:

They didn't know that I could read German. A publisher bought it in Germany and began to translate it, and when I learned that they'd bought it, I said, "Oh, no, you're not going to put that book out in Germany without letting me see the German translation." I said, "Listen, Scott, we're not going to let them publish that book lest I read the galleys. It's gotta be *sine qua non*. It's gotta be a condition." Well, they didn't have galleys. They just had the typescript, so they had to send that to us. When I started reading that thing, I could see that they had destroyed the book. They'd turned it into a travesty of itself. I actually burst into tears when I finished reading it. Here was my best novel, right, and they said, "We didn't know you could read German." They actually said that in their letter. They gave me five days to read it, and my German got very fluent. I stayed up night and day with my Cassell's German-English Dictionary and I read every single word, comparing the German line by line with the English. They hadn't changed any of the political parts-- all the anti-Nazi stuff was still there. They'd just turned it into a cheap adventure novel. I remember one part where it read: Tagomi stolzierte einher wie Wyatt Earp." Now, I never mentioned Wyatt Earp in my book. "Tagomi swaggered like Wyatt Earp"! "Tagomi swaggered like Vyatt Oorp"! [cccxxviii]

THE MAN IN THE HIGH CASTLE, as we've noted above, was written with the aid of the *I Ching*. Several critics, including PKD himself, have noted that the *I Ching* failed at the end of the story to fully resolve the plot. This, perhaps, has to do with the nature of the oracle itself; it provides answers to questions but always refers to itself again, it is circular in nature. When Juliana at the end of the book asks the *I Ching* why it wrote *The Grasshopper Lies Heavy* (the novel within THE MAN IN THE HIGH CASTLE written by Hawthorne Abendsen in which the Nazis and Japanese *lost* the War), the oracle returns the hexagram, Inner Truth. That is, in the fictional reality of the novel we won the war and the Axis powers lost it. Abendsen's book is true.

But, and this is where I do not see the failure of resolution in HIGH CASTLE, in *The Grasshopper Lies Heavy*, a work of fiction within a fictional reality, the truth is that we won the war. But, one can see THE MAN IN THE HIGH CASTLE itself as strictly analogous to *The Grasshopper Lies Heavy*: It is a fictional work in *our* reality, therefore HIGH CASTLE too is the truth. We really did lose World War 2 and the Nazis and Japs won and we are living – apparently unknowingly – under fascist rule. Now whether this is really true or not I'll let the reader decide…

Critic Patricia Warrick also notes this theme but considers it in the context that our reality is the true reality and not some 'occlusion' as PKD would later term it after his 1974 Pink Beam experiences:

And what is the inner truth? That Germany and Japan lost the war, just as Abendsen's book describes. The winner of the war is really the loser. Dick here asks the reader to follow him through a series of reflections in the artifices mirroring reality. In the world of TMITHC, the Nazis really won the war, but in the SF world of *The Grasshopper Lies Heavy* (representing inner truth), they really lost it. If the reader moves back a step, he realises that in the real world of human construct, the US and its allies won the war, so the inner truth, contained in Dick's SF, is that they really lost it. An equation is established in which Dick's novel is to the real world what Abendsen's novel is to Dick's fictional reality. The winner of any war is locked into the necessity of continuing to fight to maintain his superior power position. The effort eventually destroys him. On a moral level, he has already been destroyed because of the horrendous acts he committed to win. The winner paradoxically is the loser. The reader's eyes meet Dick's in the hall of mirrors the fiction builds when he understands this meaning.[cccxxix]

Dick presages this concept in another way within HIGH CASTLE. When Mr. Tagomi sits in the park contemplating the silver triangle of jewelry given to him by Robert Childan, he is somehow translated to another reality from his own. Perhaps this is our reality – the reality of San Francisco in the early 1960s. And perhaps its not. It's close but not quite the same and thus Dick again brings into doubt the nature of the alternate reality referred to in HIGH CASTLE; that is our reality.

THE MAN IN THE HIGH CASTLE is the *I Ching* and Dick playing with reality in a way that adds powerfully to the tradition of the alternate-universe story. Many novels have been written in which the Nazis and Japs won the war but in none of them does the author imply that this is actually the truth!

PKD had worked this theme of irreality before, most notably in EYE IN THE SKY where that whole novel can be seen in its consecutive realities to bring into question the nature of *any* reality. The characters in EYE IN THE SKY believe – hope – that each subsequent reality is the real one and, of course, it's not. Even when the reader is done with the novel and he sets the book down and looks about him at his surroundings, are these not then, too, brought into question?

On the question of reality in THE MAN IN THE HIGH CASTLE, PKD said this himself:

As a science fiction writer I gravitate towards such ideas as this; we in the field, of course, know this idea as the "alternate universe" theme. Some of you I am sure, know that my novel THE MAN IN THE HIGH CASTLE utilized this theme. There was in it an alternate world in which Germany and Japan and Italy won World War 2. At one point in the novel Mr. Tagomi, the protagonist, somehow is carried over to *our* world, in which the Axis powers lost. He remained in our world only a short time, and scuttled in fright back to his own universe as soon as he glimpsed or understood what had happened -- and thought no more of it after that; it had been for him a thoroughly unpleasant experience, since, being Japanese, it was for him a *worse* universe than his customary one. For a Jew, however, it would have been infinitely better -- for obvious reasons.

In THE MAN IN THE HIGH CASTLE I give no real explanation as to why or how Mr. Tagomi slid across into our universe; he simply sat in the park and scrutinized a piece of modern abstract handmade jewelry -- sat and studied it on and on -- and when he looked up, he was in another universe. I didn't explain how or why this happened because I don't know.{...}[cccxxx]

And further, after his visionary experiences in 1974, PKD incorporates HIGH CASTLE into his post Pink Beam world view:

The irony of this ending -- Abendsen finding out that what he had supposed to be pure fiction spun out of his imagination was in fact true -- the irony is this: that my own supposed imaginative work THE MAN IN THE HIGH CASTLE is not fiction -- or rather is fiction only *now*, thank God. But there was an alternate world, a previous present, in which that particular time track actualized -- actualized and then was abolished due to intervention at some prior date. I am sure, as you hear me say this, you do not really believe me, or even believe that I believe it myself. but nevertheless it is true. I retain memories of that other world. That is why you will find it again described in the later novel FLOW MY TEARS, THE POLICEMAN SAID. The world of FLOW MY TEARS is an actual (or rather once actual) alternate world, and I remember it in detail. I do not know who else does. Maybe no one else does. Perhaps all of you were always – have always been – here. But I was not. In March 1974 I began to remember consciously, rather than merely subconsciously, that black iron prison police state world. Upon consciously remembering it I did not need to write about it because I have always been writing about it.[cccxxxi]

Indeed. No doubt our Marxist critics will have a field day over this one!

In 1974 Philip K. Dick was contemplating writing a sequel to THE MAN IN THE HIGH CASTLE. This novel was to be titled RING OF FIRE – referring to the ring of volcanic islands in the Pacific which delimited the Japanese Empire at the end of HIGH CASTLE. He actually started this sequel; two chapters survive. [cccxxxii] But, ultimately, he was unable to write the book, saying:

I had to read what those guys wrote in their private journals in order to write THE MAN IN THE HIGH CASTLE. That's also why I've never written a sequel to it: it's too horrible, too awful. I started several times to write a sequel, but I had to go back and read about Nazis again, so I couldn't do it. Somebody would have to come in and help me--someone who had the stomach for it, the stamina, to think along those lines, to get into the head of the right character. Now, Richard Condon, who wrote *The Manchurian Candidate*, also wrote a thing called *An Infinity of Mirrors*, which is about Reichsfuhrer Himmler and Condon knew everything there was to know about Himmler. He got into Himmler's head; he had the guts to do that. I don't, and that's why my book, THE MAN IN THE HIGH CASTLE, is set in the Japanese part. I just have little glimpses of the Nazi part. [cccxxxiii]

As to the meaning of THE MAN IN THE HIGH CASTLE, Dick mostly left it to the critics to figure out, saying only:

...Dick Lupoff put it very well: In 1964 he was at this party, and was discussing with somebody the meaning of the ending of THE MAN IN THE HIGH CASTLE. And (he said) there was this guy, smoking a cigar, who kept trying to butt into the conversation and say what the ending meant. Finally, Lupoff turned to the guy and said, "Will you *please* not bother us; we're discussing the ending of THE MAN IN THE HIGH CASTLE." And the guy says, "Well, I'm Philip K. Dick, and I wrote it." (*laughter*) I can see myself standing at the periphery of a circle of my own fans, and they're all discussing some book of mine, and I'm saying, "Um...um...What *I* think he meant was..." and they turn to me and say, "Butt out, joker." It would either go that way, or they'd want to know what I thought, and that would be a drag...[cccxxxiv]

Considered by many to be a masterpiece, THE MAN IN THE HIGH CASTLE would, in the alternate universe where I might rate PKD's novels, deserve ✵✵✵✵✵

1962

The early part of 1962, as we have just seen, was occupied by PKD in preparing THE MAN IN THE HIGH CASTLE for publication by Putnam's. This was most likely finished by May and HIGH CASTLE, of course, was published in October.

With this acceptance, finally, of one of his hybrid sf-mainstream novels by Putnam, PKD turned eagerly to his next novel which, as previously noted, was WE CAN BUILD YOU.[cccxxxv]

WE CAN BUILD YOU

The manuscript for WE CAN BUILD YOU, titled THE FIRST IN YOUR FAMILY, reached the SMLA on Oct 4, 1962. It was sent to Putnam's on the same day but was inexplicably rejected by them, as it would be at Doubleday, Simon & Schuster, Ballantine and Crown Publishers over the next four months. It was finally bought by Ted White at *Amazing Stories* magazine in 1969 and serialized there in Nov 1969 and Jan 1970 as "A. Lincoln, Simulacrum." In 1972 Don Wollheim of DAW Books acquired the story and published it as WE CAN BUILD YOU in July of that year.[cccxxxvi] Again, why did it take so long to find publication? Certainly the novel is inferior to THE MAN IN THE HIGH CASTLE but one might think that Putnam's would've taken a chance even though news of HIGH CASTLE's success and Hugo Award would not happen until early 1963. Perhaps if the Agency had waited a few months before sending the manuscript out WE CAN BUILD YOU would have sold sooner than 1969, six years later. But… we really do not know why it took so long to publish. Ted White thinks it was because the story didn't resolve (see below). It's possible that many of the publishers it was sent to (Putnam's, Crown and Simon & Schuster, for example) had seen too many of PKD's mainstream novels and rejected them that they saw this new one as more of the same, not noting the new way Dick was melding his science fiction writing with his mainstream writing.

Of the novel's publication history Dick said:

I wrote that novel before Disney even proposed to build the Lincoln simulacrum. I couldn't sell it for years and years and years and years. I wrote it while I was trying to fuse my mainstream stuff with my science fiction stuff, so its not *quite* science fiction, in the usual sense of the word. Finally Ted White, who knew of the existence of the manuscript, asked for it so he could publish it in a magazine. Ted added a final chapter to it, because -- as is well known -- writers are incapable of writing their own books. (…) If it wasn't for kindly editors, who are your best friends, who'll help you out by adding another chapter, or removing one here or there, or turning one inside out, or changing all the names, or whatever, you'd never have gotten off the ground. Naturally I was very indebted to Ted White, and I let him know. The way I let him know was that when Wollheim published the book, I told Wollheim to remove the final chapter. So one day I ran into Ted White, and he said, "Do you know what they did to *our book*?" I says, "I know exactly what they did to '*our book*', Ted. They took the '*our*' out of '*our book*'!"

I have seen the Lincoln simulacrum down there. I cut out the notice in the newspaper that Disney planned to build the Lincoln simulacrum and pasted it up on the wall of my study. I remember doing that because the novel had already been written. So he built it and I went to Disneyland and looked at the goddam thing…[cccxxxvii]

To this, Ted White responded in a letter to *PKDS*:

I'd been wondering when the Apel/Briggs interview with Phil Dick would crop up in the Newsletter. I was shown a copy of this interview in ms. form in 1979 or 1980 and I was disturbed at the time by the wholly erroneous description of the events surrounding the publication of WE CAN BUILD YOU in *Amazing* as "A. Lincoln, Simulacrum." I write now in an effort to set the record straight, although my disappointment with Phil has worn off since his death.

The original title of the novel was THE FIRST IN YOUR FAMILY {…} It was the only first-person-narrated novel, and it had one rather major problem, a problem which had kept it from selling for ten years before I bought it: it had no ending. It didn't resolve.

{…}

I'd heard about the novel, as he says, from someone at Scott Meredith -- maybe from when I worked there (1963), or perhaps later, I no longer recall -- and when I became editor of *Amazing* I asked for it. Scott was glad to send it out; it had been unsold for ten years by then, perhaps the only remaining unsold sf property of Phil's. I read it and realised what the problem was, and I asked Phil about two things: changing the title (to "A. Lincoln, Simulacrum," my choice) and adding an ending. Now to put this into context I must point out that I had met Phil in 1964, lived in his house, had him read the *I Ching* for me (a startling experience, the validity of which I believe to this day), and had been publicly described by Phil as the man who knew his work and understood it best. In 1965 or 1966 he had given me the first fifty pages and the synoptic essay for DEUS IRAE and asked me to finish it for him. In other words, this was a man who professed admiration and respect for me and wanted me to collaborate with him. (As a jape, he gave Penguin a photo of me and it was printed [as a photo of the author] on the back cover of the British THE MAN IN THE HIGH CASTLE.)

So I called Phil up; he had no objection to my proposed title change and he suggested I write the ending to the novel. I counter-suggested that I write a first draft and send it to him for him to rewrite, and he agreed. So I wrote a somewhat off-the-wall final chapter in skeletal form. I expected Phil to either reject it out of hand or rewrite it and flesh it out. He did neither. He returned it to me with three words changed and praised its economy.

As far as I knew when I ran "A. Lincoln, Simulacrum" it was in a form satisfactory to Phil. Because I considered myself a friend of Phil's, I tried to do more for him. I knew the novel had been rejected by every market that had seen it, and that undoubtedly included Ace (his original publisher), but ten years had passed and now it had an ending, so I gave a copy to Terry Carr, who was then editor of the Ace Specials. He didn't like it, but passed it on to Don Wollheim -- who had rejected the original version -- who also refused it. However, after Don went to DAW he must have had second thoughts, because he bought it for DAW and published it under a third title, WE CAN BUILD YOU --sans my ending.[cccxxxviii]

When Don Wollheim bought "A. Lincoln, Simulacrum" for publication as WE CAN BUILD YOU in his new DAW Books imprint in 1972, Philip K. Dick had occasion to again comment about one of his editors:

Oh, I'll tell you another {Wollheim} story. He was late in paying me for WE CAN BUILD YOU. I was really broke; matter of fact, I was starving to death. My wife and I were living in Southern California, sharing one can of Chunky Chicken soup a day; that was all we could afford. So I wrote Wollheim this piteous letter: "Dear Don: I must tell you that I have been forced to give up writing science fiction and am going to work at Disneyland as one of the janitors who sweeps things up. The reason is because you have not sent me the money due me on WE CAN BUILD YOU. And you know what his answer was? "Why don't you come to New York and go on Welfare?" (...) He said that! Talk about your heart of stone! Shit![cccxxxix]

As we've seen above while looking at THE MAN IN THE HIGH CASTLE, Dick saw the rejection of THE FIRST IN YOUR FAMILY as ruining his hopes for a new kind of science fiction/mainstream style of writing that would be successful for him:

My vision collapsed. I was crushed. I had made a mis-calculation somewhere, and I didn't know where. The evaluation I had made of myself, of the marketplace, went poof! I reverted to a more primitive concept of my writing. The books that might have followed TIME SLIP {that is, THE FIRST IN YOUR FAMILY} were gone.[cccxl]

One can only wonder what PKD had in mind concerning his future books. Certainly, the next novel that he wrote after WE CAN BUILD YOU -- MARTIAN TIME-SLIP -- must've included some of his intentions. Thanks to Patrick Clark digging them out of the magazines we have a fine review of WE CAN BUILD YOU by Theodore Sturgeon from the Jan 1973 issue of *Galaxy*:

WE CAN BUILD YOU proves for all time that: 1) Philip K. Dick is overwhelmingly competent and capable and might – probably will –produce a major novel and that: 2) this isn't it. I base the first on his handling of his characters, who are consistently and warmly recognizable even in their stubborn irrationalities, on the boldness and provocation of his themes and his side remarks, on the richness of his auctorial background and the sparkles of laughter finger-flicked all over his work. I base the second on his willingness to pursue some collateral and fascinating line at the expense – and even the abandonment – of his central theme, which was (or so in the book he told me) the manufacture of exact simulacra of any human being and the impact of this development on humanity. The pursuit, in and out of the fringes of insanity, of an obsessive love-affair had me laughing and crying, but Dick and I were both conned, weakwilled as dieter gobbling hot fudge sundaes, into this delight instead of going about our business.[cccxli]

WE CAN BUILD YOU tells of the machinations of the small firm MASA Associates as they build two simulacra, one of Edwin M. Stanton and one of Abraham Lincoln. Stanton was Lincoln's Secretary of War. Their scheme is to build a swath of Civil War simulacra so that they can stage a full-scale recreation of the Civil War. This is all sidetracked, though, when magnate Sam Barrows wants the company to make simulacra for use as companions to the colonists on the moon. Emigration isn't going too good and Barrows figures the simulacra will spur the colonization effort.

But this is all secondary to the relations between the characters. These are dominated by that of Louis Rosen, a partner in the firm, and Pris Frauenzimmer, a psychotic girl who helped design the simulacra and who has a fixation on Sam Barrows.

Against all sense and reason, Louis falls in love with Pris and their relationship comes to dominate the novel. Pris is absolutely the worst kind of individual it would be the misfortune for anyone to meet, let alone fall in love with. She's a schizophrenic who has just been released from a Federal mental health clinic; supposedly cured. She has, basically, no emotional components other than a biting, vicious repartee, which she uses to keep people away from her. Louis Rosen falls in love with this thing of a person – the two simulacra have more feelings than her – but he's just hapless and borderline crazy himself. As one reads the novel, following Louis along as he tries to contact and win Pris's affections, one hopes that she will turn her favors upon him but… she doesn't. In the end Louis goes into a fugue state where he imagines that Pris does return his affections. Even when he himself is carted off to the mental clinic he's unable to snap out of his imagined world. Finally released, Louis prepares to face reality.

Whoof! This is some novel! And one can see to some degree what PKD was trying to do as he explicated his own vision of a novel to follow THE MAN IN THE HIGH CASTLE in which he put in all his literary ability to forge a successful mainstream/science fiction novel.

But one gets the sense that he rushed into WE CAN BUILD YOU without fully thinking it out. It starts off as science fiction with the expected plot of the conflict between MASA Associates and Barrows being developed with Louis and Pris's relationship percolating away in the background. Then the Barrows plot sort of falls apart and everything starts to revolve around Louis and Pris. But as the story is written in the first person from the view of Louis perhaps it's to be expected that the plot would turn to him and his concerns.

The obvious contrast between the 'humanness' of the two simulacra and the 'machine-like' nature of Pris underscores the plot. The two main characters, Louis and Pris, are well developed and evoke a response in the reader. Louis' wretched attraction to Pris perhaps foreshadows the attraction that Rick Deckard has to the android Rachel in DO ANDROIDS DREAM OF ELECTRIC SHEEP? For Pris is practically an android herself.

Overall, though, it seems PKD's mainstream yen won out over the science fiction and about half way through the novel it takes over and, as Ted White suggested, the plot in its science fictional aspect doesn't really resolve. But the relationship between Louis and Pris, excruciating as it is, does come to a resolution. This relationship is much like those PKD writes in his straight novels (which had failed, as Eleanor Dimoff said, due to the characters being of interest in only a clinical way).

WE CAN BUILD YOU, then, cannot be said to be a successful melding of science fiction and mainstream writing. In this novel PKD scrambles through the science fiction aspects in his rush to explore the relationship between Louis and Pris. And this relationship is, like many in his mainstream novels, about as gloomy as you can get.

As for rating WE CAN BUILD YOU, I waver between ✻✻ and ✻✻✻✻. Give it, then, ✻✻✻.

MARTIAN TIME-SLIP

MARTIAN TIME-SLIP started life as GOODMEMBER ARNIE KOTT OF MARS. The manuscript reached the SMLA on Oct 31, 1962 – less than a month after the Agency received the manuscript for WE CAN BUILD YOU -- and the story was first serialized as "All We Marsmen" in *Worlds Of Tomorrow*, Aug, Oct, Dec 1963. Prior to serialization the manuscript was sold to Ballantine in June 1963 after being rejected by Ace, Berkley and Pyramid publishers, and the first paperback edition under the title MARTIAN TIME-SLIP came from Ballantine in April 1964.[cccxlii]

Despite the PKD-induced confusion concerning whether WE CAN BUILD YOU preceded MARTIAN TIME-SLIP cleared up by Paul Williams and discussed above, biographer Lawrence Sutin sees the fact that MARTIAN TIME-SLIP was accepted as science fiction and not as a mainstream or hybrid-mainstream novel like THE MAN IN THE HIGH CASTLE as a 'defeat' for Philip K. Dick. Sutin notes that the novel's reception as science fiction was itself problematical: Don Wollheim at Ace Books turned down MARTIAN TIME-SLIP because it took place in 1994. Wollheim says:

"It offended my science fiction sense. {...} There couldn't have been a Mars colony when he put it -- if he'd thrown it ahead a hundred years, I would have liked it."[cccxliii]

MARTIAN TIME-SLIP is a favorite of PKD fans and even of PKD himself:

I enjoyed writing all of them, but I think that if I could only choose a few, which for example might escape WW3, I would choose ... MARTIAN TIME SLIP...[cccxliv]

And although he said on another occasion that

I don't care for MARTIAN TIME-SLIP ... I think it's a very dull book.[cccxlv]

it is generally agreed by fans and critics alike that he was not serious with this comment. Greg Lee, for instance, publisher of *Radio Free PKD*, sees in the fan poll run by the zine *For Dickheads Only* that:

I think this is the closest Dick came to melding his SF sensibility with his growing "mainstream" (whatever that means, I hate the word) skills. Real people with real problems; the exploitation theme is highly relevant to today's age.[cccxlvi]

Paul Williams, publisher of *The Philip K. Dick Society Newsletter* sees the themes in MARTIAN TIME-SLIP as anticipating "R.D.Laing and many other gurus of the 60s and 70s." [cccxlvii]

But it must be noted that not everyone was content with MARTIAN TIME-SLIP. His wife, as PKD recalls, once said to him:

"I'd rather be a whore and walk the streets than live off money earned by stuff like this."[cccxlviii]

In a 1976 letter to his mother, Dorothy, Dick commented on MARTIAN TIME-SLIP:

In the hospital I had the occasion to reread my '64 novel MARTIAN TIME SLIP. I found it weak dramatically (weak in plot) but extraordinary in its ideas. I stripped the universe down to its basic structure. I guess I always do that when I write: analyze the universe to see what it's made over. The floor joists (sp?) of the universe are visible in my novels.[cccxlix]

The story of a hard-scrabble colonial society on Mars revolves around a small boy, Manfred Steiner, who is autistic. The character of Manfred is, according to Rickman,

drawn from Bruno Bettelheim's 1958 *Scientific American* article "Joey The Mechanical Boy," later incorporated into his *The Empty Fortress.*[cccl]

And Sutin says that Dick was influenced in the depiction of Manfred by the autistic son of his old friend, Vince Lusby. Phil and Kleo had babysat the boy. [cccli]

As for the psychological theory behind Dick's description of autism and schizophrenia, Sutin writes:

The key source for Phil's ideas on schizophrenia -- in TIME SLIP and throughout his last two decades -- was Swiss analyst Ludwig Binswanger, whose study of a schizophrenic, "*The Case of Ellen West*", terrified Phil when he read it in the early 60s. Phil used Binswanger's term *tomb world* (schizophrenic self-entrapment) in several 60s sf works...[ccclii]

Sutin also notes the influence of Durkheim's sociological interpretation of Kant's theories on Dick's depiction of the Bleekmen in MARTIAN TIME-SLIP.[cccliii]

The Binswanger concept of the 'tomb world' finds expression here as the *gubble, gubble* world of Manfred (and also in Mary Ann Reynold's personal hell in MARY AND THE GIANT and the post-atomic urban wastelands of DO ANDROIDS DREAM OF ELECTRIC SHEEP?).[cccliv]

And on the 'gubble, gubble' world PKD had this to say in a letter to Australian critic Bruce Gillespie:

I'm glad you liked *All We Marsmen* (also called MARTIAN TIME-SLIP). Remember the part near the end when the man is reading the newspaper and the gubble-gubble words appear. It is entropy at work, decay of the meaningful (form) into the meaningless (entropic formlessness). This force, intruding itself, is objectively real; *this* is not the hallucination – and much of what in my books are regarded as hallucinations are actually aspects of the entropy-laden *koinos* world breaking through into the little warm living room with the dog sleeping before the fire, the wife sewing, the husband reading the newspaper – which begins to say, "Gubble, gubble", all at once. Kant's space-time-etc structuring mechanism of the psyche has begun to fail.[ccclv]

After publication of MARTIAN TIME-SLIP, the story was proffered to the British Broadcasting Company (BBC) by Brian Aldiss for consideration as a five-part television mini-series. The adaptation to be written by Aldiss himself. I'm not sure whether this was done but I think it was and was produced circa 1985.[ccclvi]

The novel also influenced editor Mark Hurst to write to PKD in 1974, thus starting a correspondence which lasted until Dick's death in 1982. In 1974 Hurst also wrote to Judy-Lyn Del Rey to ask Ballantine, where Del Rey was editor, to reissue MARTIAN TIME-SLIP. This was done in 1976 and a new dedication to Hurst was included at that time.[ccclvii]

After his visionary experiences in 1974, Dick considered many of his novels and stories as supportive of his changed world-view. MARTIAN TIME-SLIP was one of these:

In fact, schizophrenia could be considered evidence for my system; it is an instance of the malfunction of that system, & with my system in mind, can be readily understood (in MARTIAN TIME SLIP I saw it as a breakdown of proper time functioning, which was close)...[ccclviii]

He also commented on this breakdown of time in other places:

For absolute reality to reveal itself, our categories of space-time experiences, our basic matrix through which we encounter the universe, must break down and then utterly collapse. I dealt with this breakdown in MARTIAN TIME SLIP in terms of time...[ccclix]

And, when talking about orthogonal time:

The idea of dysfunctions such as bounce back and bounce forward are possible, here, but these would serve no teleological purpose; they would be time-slips, as in my novel MARTIAN TIME SLIP. Yet, if they were to occur, they would serve a purpose for us, the observer or listener; we would suddenly learn a great deal more about our universe. I believe these ontological dysfunctions in time do occur, but that our brains automatically generate false memory-systems to obscure them, at once. The reason for this carries back to my premise: the veil or *dokos* is there to deceive us for a good reason, and such disclosures as these time dysfunctions make are to be obliterated that this benign purpose be maintained.[ccclx]

These brief excerpts from several of Dick's essays and his *Exegesis* that I've included haphazardly throughout this dissertation may not make a lot of sense at this point. However, when we examine Dick's novel VALIS I'll attempt a more coherent explanation of Dick's notions of time, space, God and the universe. Please bear with me until that point. But one last comment from PKD concerning the writing of MARTIAN TIME-SLIP before closing out the year 1962:

I myself have derived much of the material for my writing from dreams... In MARTIAN TIME-SLIP I've written in so many dream experiences that I can't separate them, now, when I read the novel.[ccclxi]

Here's a good description of MARTIAN TIME-SLIP courtesy of Steven Owen Godersky:

The unions control Mars, the colonial world of speculation, and Arnie Kott the plumber is at the top of the heap. Arnie wants to use the time-warping abilities of Manfred, a schizophrenic child, to control Martian real estate. Kott sets Jack Bohlen the task of building a machine to communicate with Manfred. Instead, Manfred catches them up in a degenerating time-loop, fearing the vision of his own future. Only the Martians can communicate telepathically with Manfred and aid him in escaping from a future that is gradually spreading back to obliterate the past.[ccclxii]

MARTIAN TIME-SLIP is indeed an exceptional science fiction novel and down in the hovels they give it ★ ★ ★ ★ ★

1963

Going into 1963, then, Philip K. Dick had achieved one of his goals: publication of a second hybrid mainstream/science fiction novel in hardcover: THE MAN IN THE HIGH CASTLE from Putnam's. This followed TIME OUT OF JOINT from Lippincott in 1959. It would be 1965 before he would have another hardcover edition with Doubleday's SFBC edition of THE THREE STIGMATA OF PALMER ELDRITCH.

But this year, the most productive in Philip K. Dick's career, started out badly. The Scott Meredith Literary Agency realised that after publication of THE MAN IN THE HIGH CASTLE and acceptance of "All We Marsmen" for serialization now would be a good time to return all of PKD's mainstream novel manuscripts to him, these having failed to sell after numerous attempts.

Yet despite this Dick did not seem too disheartened; rumblings were about that THE MAN IN THE HIGH CASTLE would be nominated for the Hugo Award as best science fiction novel of 1962. And while he was anticipating this he must've felt his name was in demand again and by the end of February he was once more sending short stories to the SMLA. But before turning to short stories again, Dick was working on his next science fiction novel which would eventually be published as DR. BLOODMONEY: Or How We Got Along After The Bomb.

DR.BLOODMONEY: Or How We Got Along After The Bomb

Under the working title of 'IN EARTH'S DIURNAL COURSE: A Terran Odyssey', the manuscript for what would become 'DR. BLOODMONEY: Or How We Got Along After The Bomb' reached the SMLA on Feb 11, 1963. Under this new title the novel was published by Ace Books as a paperback original on Jun 11, 1965. Publication in the United Kingdom would not occur until Oct 1977 when Arrow Books published a paperback edition.[ccclxiii] DR. BLOODMONEY was nominated for the Nebula Award by the Science Fiction Writers of America (SFWA) for the best novel of 1965.

On March 17, 1964 the SMLA received a manuscript titled "A Terran Odyssey". This was a short story that PKD put together from sections of DR. BLOODMONEY. This story was published for the first time in Volume 5 of THE COLLECTED STORIES OF PKD.[ccclxiv]

Dick was unhappy with the new title for his novel. In a 1965 letter to Scott Meredith complaining about Don Wollheim's reaction to the expansion of THE UNTELEPORTED MAN to novel length, Dick wrote:

{...} Anyhow, be this as it may, we are stuck with the fact of Don's reaction; but, if you will recall my fears, you will see at once that basically I anticipated this. I did so on the basis of two events; one {...} and two: the absurd title which I am informed he has tormented me with on my Ace novel to be released next month, something on the order of DOCTOR BLOODMONEY OR HOW WE LEARNED TO LIVE AFTER THE BOMB, a title which will ring down the chambers of time as long as I am so unfortunate as to exist.[ccclxv]

Don Wollheim probably renamed the novel after seeing the success of the movie *DR. STRANGELOVE* for, certainly, Dick's novel preceded the film.

The title IN EARTH'S DIURNAL COURSE occasions some confusion. Apparently Ray Nelson, Dick's collaborator on the novel THE GANYMEDE TAKEOVER, had said that the original title for THE GANYMEDE TAKEOVER was THE EARTH'S DIURNAL COURSE. To this, Terry Carr, an editor at Ace Books at the time DR. BLOODMONEY was published, responds:

Ray's mentioning that THE GANYMEDE TAKEOVER was originally titled THE EARTH'S DIURNAL COURSE is a bit confusing to me. Probably Ray is right in saying so -- though the title would have been IN EARTH'S DIURNAL COURSE, a line from a Romantic poet, well-known, but I forget which one. The apparent fact that Phil's and Ray's THE GANYMEDE TAKEOVER originally had this title, till Scott Meredith changed it, surprises me because Phil had earlier put that title on some other novel published by Ace Books and it was Don Wollheim who changed it -- I think it was DR. BLOODMONEY, OR HOW WE GOT ALONG AFTER THE BOMB, though I can't swear to that. (90% chance I'm right, no more). Since DR. BLOODMONEY was published in 1965 and THE GANYMEDE TAKEOVER in 1967, its quite possible that after Don Wollheim had changed that title once, Scott Meredith may have felt it would be fruitless to submit another even partly PKD novel to Don under the original title.[ccclxvi]

Philip K. Dick was proud of this novel, mentioning it in correspondence on several occasions. In his 1968 'Self Portrait' he singles the novel out as one of his personal favorites, DR. BLOODMONEY coming in fourth of his selections.[ccclxvii]

And in conversation with Apel & Briggs he said:

... I *do* like DR. BLOODMONEY; I reread that recently, and I really thought that part where Bill is swallowed by the owl and the owl barfs him up, and he's shouting, y'know, "Write letters of protest to President Johnson!" was one of the best scenes in science fiction I've ever read. I like the whole book.[ccclxviii]

And again in a letter to Sandra Miesel:

Your husband comments favorably on DOCTOR BLOODMONEY. I do not consider this a minor work of mine (although God knows I've written many minor works). It's a long novel and very complex, and is a s-f version of a straight literary novel I long ago wrote. Do you want the truth? I like DOCTOR BLOODMONEY better than anything else I've written. Roger Zelazny said that he thought it equal to ANNA KARENINA{...}[ccclxix]

And, lastly, in the Anton & Fuchs interview conducted at Metz, France in 1977, when asked what he thought of Norman Spinrad's 'Introduction' to DR. BLOODMONEY, Dick replied:

It just simply astounded me. I was astounded that anyone would think so highly of my writing and also he understood it so well. It wasn't simply complimentary, like saying that I wrote very well, it was his analysis of me as a metaphysical writer, something that I'm just becoming aware of myself, that my writing is progressively assuming more and more metaphysical implications. I got up in the middle of the night and reread it, I found it so interesting, because the book that I'm working on now, my Bantam novel in progress, is extraordinarily metaphysical.[ccclxx]

The Bantam novel in progress is, of course VALIS.

In 1979 Dick himself wrote an introduction to DR. BLOODMONEY this introduction appearing for the first time in the 1985 edition of the novel from Bluejay Books. As he goes on at length about DR. BLOODMONEY in this I have taken the liberty of reproducing his introduction in full here:

Well, I predicted wrong when I wrote DR.BLOODMONEY back in 1964. Events that I foresaw never came about, and as you read this novel you will see what I mean. But it is not the job, really, of science fiction to predict. Science Fiction only *seems* to predict. It's like the aliens on *STAR TREK*, all of whom speak English. A literary convention is involved, here. Nothing more.

I am amused, however, to see what specifically I got wrong. Worst of all, I totally misread the future of the manned space program. But this only shows how rapidly history unfolds. In DR.BLOODMONEY I have one American circling the world forever. This is obvious nonsense, either there would be many Americans -- and many Russians, for that matter -- or none at all.

Of course, the major item that I got wrong is the End of the World. Back in 1964 I was expecting it at anytime; I kept checking my watch. Horace Gold, who edited *Galaxy* magazine, once chided me for anticipating global wipe-out within the next week. That was back around 1954; I anticipated it by 1964. Well, such were the fears of the times. Right now we have other worries. Our problem seems to be paying our debts with incredibly inflated dollars, finding gas for our cars -- much more mundane worries. Less cosmic.

Oddly, these are the sort of worries that assail the characters in DR.BLOODMONEY in their post-World War Three world. There are horses pulling cars. Eyeglasses are rare and treasured. A man who manufactures cigarettes is honored wherever he goes. Of supreme value is someone who can fix things. Society has reverted, but not to the brutal level that we might expect. Rather, it has become rural in nature. The vast cities are gone, and, in their place, a sort of countryside exists that is not awful at all. I must add, however, that in no sense does it resemble any world that we actually have.

But then, of course, we haven't had World War Three.

In my opinion, this is an extremely hopeful novel. It does not posit the end of human civilization as a result of the next war. People are still around and they are still coping. Those who survive, anyhow, are fairly lucky in their new lives. What is interesting is the subtle change in the relative power status of the survivors. Take Hoppy Harrington, who has no arms or legs. Before the bomb hits, Hoppy is marginal in terms of power. He is fortunate if he can get any kind of job at all. But in the postwar world this is not the case. Hoppy is elevated by stealthy increments until, at last, he is a menace to a man not even on the planet's surface; Hoppy has become a demigod, and a complex one at that. He is not really evil but that his *power* is evil.

In the satellite, Walt Dangerfield is transformed from a man assisting the fragmented postwar society, giving it unity and strength, raising its morale, to a man desperate for help from it, a man who is becoming weaker day by day. He signifies isolation, which is the horror of the many down below; isolation and a loss of the objects and values that comprised their original world. As time passes, Walt Dangerfield must gain strength from those on the planet's surface, rather than giving strength to them. And into the vacuum created comes Hoppy Harrington, who epitomizes the monster in us: the person who is hungry. Not hungry for food but hungry for coercive control over others. This drive in Hoppy stems from a physical deprivation. It is a compensation for what he lacked from birth. Hoppy is incomplete, and he will complete himself at the expense of the entire world; he will psychologically devour it.

You will note in DR.BLOODMONEY an account of a test conducted in 1972 that turned out to be a catastrophe, and, of course, there was in fact no such test and no such catastrophe. But then, there was no such person as Dr. Bluthgeld. This is a work of fiction. And yet at a certain level it is not. The West Marin County area where much of the novel is set is an area that I knew well. When I wrote the novel I lived in that area. Many of the features that I describe are real. So a great deal of the veridical is blended in with the fiction. As do some of the characters, I searched for wild mushrooms in West Marin, and I found the varieties they find (and avoided the varieties they avoid). It is one of the most beautiful areas in the United States, and is called by the Sierra Club "The Island in Time." When I lived there in the late 50s and early 60s it was set apart from the rest of California and therefore seemed to me a natural locus for a postwar microcosm of society. Already, in fact, West Marin was a little world. When I read over DR.BLOODMONEY I discover, to my pleasure, that I have captured in words much of that little world that I so loved -- a little world from which I am now separated by time and distance.

My favorite character in the novel is the TV salesman Stuart McConchie, who happens to be black. In 1964, when I wrote DR.BLOODMONEY, it was daring to have a major character be a black man. My God, how much change has taken place in these recent years! But what an excellent change, one we can be proud of. In my first novel, SOLAR LOTTERY, I had a black man as captain of a spaceship -- daring, indeed, for a novel published in 1955. Stuart is in my opinion the focus of the novel, and he appears first. It is through his eyes that we initially see Dr. Bluthgeld, which is to say, Dr. Bloodmoney. Stuart's reaction is simple; he is seeing a lunatic, and that is that. Bonny Keller, however, knowing Dr. Bluthgeld more intimately, holds a more complex view of the man. Frankly, I tend to see Bluthgeld as Stuart McConchie sees him. I am, so to speak, Stuart McConchie, and at one time *I* was a TV salesman at a store on Shattuck Avenue in Berkeley. Like Stuart, I used to sweep the sidewalk in front of the store in the early morning, noticing the cute girls on their way to work. So I do have to confess to an overly simple view of Dr. Bluthgeld: I hate him and I hate everything he stands for. He is the alien and the enemy. I cannot fathom his mind; I cannot understand his hates. It is not the Russians I fear; it is the Dr. Bluthgeld's, the Dr. Bloodmoney's in our own society that terrify me. I am sure that to the extent that they know me, or would know me, they hate me back and would do exactly to me what I would do to them.

"And, sure enough as Stuart watched, leaning on his broom, the first furtive nut of the day sidled guiltily toward the psychiatrist's office."

This is our initial glimpse of Dr. Bloodmoney: through the eyes of a man pushing a broom. I am with the man pushing the broom, here at the beginning of the novel and all the way to the end. Stuart McConchie is an astute man, and in seeing Dr. Bloodmoney he has experienced a moment of instant insight that Bonny Keller in her years of personal, intimate knowledge lacks. I admit to prejudice, here. I think the first response by the man pushing the broom can be trusted. Dr. Bloodmoney is sick, and sick in a way that is dangerous to the rest of us. And much of the evil in our world now emanates from such men, because such men do exist.

So in writing DR. BLOODMONEY in 1964 I may have erred in many of my predictions. But upon rereading the novel recently I sensed a basic accuracy in it -- an accuracy about human beings and their power to survive. Not survive as beasts, either, but as genuine humans doing genuinely human things. There are no supermen in this novel. There are no heroic deeds. There are some very poor predictions on my part, I must admit; but about the people themselves and their strength and tenacity and vitality... there I think I foresaw accurately. Because, of course, I was not predicting; I was only describing what I saw around me, the men and women and children and animals, the life of this planet that has been, is, and will be, no matter what happens.

I am proud of the people in this novel. And, as I say. I would like to number myself as one of them. I once pushed a broom on the sidewalk of Shattuck Avenue in Berkeley and I felt the joy and sense of busy activity and industry that Stuart feels, the excitement, the sense of the future.

And, as the novel depicts, despite the war -- the war that did not in fact happen -- it is a good future. I would have enjoyed being there with them in their microcosm, their postwar West Marin world.[ccclxxi]

The novel is set in Marin County, California after nuclear bombs have devastated the world. In this milieu a depleted micro-society goes about its daily living, adapting to a life of sudden deprivation. But there's some mighty strange characters gathered here. For instance, Dr. Bruno Bluthgeld, the man who is blamed for starting the whole shooting match. Then there's Hoppy Harrington a 'phocomelus' who wields obscure powers as he rolls around in his little cart. Over this little world a satellite looks down, inhabited by a stranded disc jockey who dispenses news and music and who is slowly going insane. Toss in Bill, an embedded and hidden twin who is telepathic and inevitably we have a plot that defies description. All the commingling is great fun, though, and DR. BLOODMONEY: Or How We Got Along After The Bomb gets ✳ ✳ ✳ ✳

After completing DR. BLOODMONEY in early Feb 1963 Dick turned his hand once again to the writing of short stories. The first of these to arrive on Feb 27, 1963 was "If There Had Never Been A Benny Cemoli."

"If There Had Never Been A Benny Cemoli" was sold to *Galaxy* and published under the grammatically modified title "If There Were No Benny Cemoli" in the Dec 1963 issue.

This story has been fairly anthologized over the years, first in *THE EIGTH GALAXY READER* (1965) then in Ace Books' 1969 PKD collection THE PRESERVING MACHINE. It was also included in the PKD collection THE BEST OF PHILIP K. DICK in 1977. There are other anthology appearances before publication in volume 4 of THE COLLECTED STORIES in 1987 and one more in 1992: *THE GREAT SF STORIES 25*, edited by Isaac Asimov and Martin Greenburg.

The name and perhaps some of the character of George Stavros appears in this story. Here, although his first name is not specified, Stavros is a Greek chef and covert government hero.

Of the story PKD wrote in 1976:

I have always believed that at least half the famous people in history never existed. You invent what you need to invent. Perhaps even Karl Marx was invented, the product of some hack writer. In which case -- [ccclxxii]

"If There Were No Benny Cemoli" is a story of a devastated Earth trying to rebuild but invaded by the ex-colony of Proxima Centaurus who, United Nations-like, think they can do a better job of reconstruction. The Centaurans are also interested in war crimes and wish to locate the people who started the war that ruined Earth. But, those once in power are usually always in power – and they don't wish to be discovered.

"If There Were No Benny Cemoli" earns ✮ ✮ ✮ ✮ ✮

Almost a month after mailing in the manuscript for "If There Had Never Been A Benny Cemoli" Dick sent in the Novelette "At Second Jug." This arrived at the SMLA on Mar 23, 1963 and it was sold to *Fantastic* where it appeared under the title "Novelty Act" in the Feb 1964 issue. The back cover illustration by Lutjens complements the story.

Between the time of its initial publication and 1987, the story was anthologized twice, in William F. Nolan's *THE HUMAN EQUATION* in 1971 and in Martin Greenburg's selection from the annals of *Fantastic: FANTASTIC STORIES: Tales Of The Weird And Wonderful*, in 1987.

In mid 1963 PKD would expand "Novelty Act" into the novel FIRST LADY OF EARTH (published as THE SIMULACRA).

At almost 13,000 words "Novelty Act" is a long story and the length is necessary to tell the tale. In a crowded future people live in huge communal apartment buildings where rules of conduct are strict and rigidly enforced by councils made up of the tenants. The main goal of the tenants is to produce entertainers who will be spotted by White House talent agents and who will then go on to entertain the First Lady, Nicole Thibodeaux, at the White House in person. Nicole, adored by the Nation, is not quite what she seems and when two brothers who play classical jug music use a copy of a telepathic Martian papoola – a lifeform now extinct – to win one of the coveted spots on the program, things start to go wrong. Loony Luke, the owner of a string of fly-by-night jalopy lots (guaranteed to get you to Mars if you're lucky), who is about to be put out of business by Nicole's police, takes control of the fake papoola and has it bite Nicole during the jug act. The jug artists escape and in the end are on their way, jalopy-wise, to Mars.

"Novelty Act" is a good story – funny too -- and may be even better than THE SIMULACRA. It rates ✮ ✮ ✮ ✮ ✮

The next story to reach the SMLA was "Waterspider" this arrived almost a month after "Novelty Act" on Apr 10, 1963. It was published in *If* in the Jan 1964 issue. After inclusion in THE COLLECTED STORIES in 1987, the story was chosen by Mike Resnick for his anthology *INSIDE THE FUNHOUSE: 17 SF Stories About SF* (1992).

As "Waterspider" included some prominent science fiction writers of the day and mention of some of their works – including Philip K. Dick himself, the editor at *If*, Fred Pohl, thought it necessary to get releases from some of Dick's fellow writers before publishing the story. In regards to this, PKD wrote to Pohl on June 23, 1963

In answer to your letter of June 14, I talked to Poul Anderson and he will send a release to you regarding his part in my story WATERSPIDER. As to Kris Neville ... I think the solution there is for you to do this (and I'm not joking; please believe me). Remove the word "Kris" in the sentence "Kris is stoned again" and put in "Phil" so it reads "Phil is stoned again." Okay? It could be thought to refer either to me or to Philip Jose Farmer.

I think we can take a chance on the others, although if you are further worried you could delete the statements made by Ray Bradbury; that's all I'm at all concerned about, myself.[ccclxxiii]

"Waterspider" is a fascinating story including as it does mention of many science fiction writers and editors who attended the Science Fiction Worldcon in San Francisco in 1954. Besides Philip K. Dick himself and his stories "The Variable Man", "The Defenders" and "The Mold Of Yancy," it also mentions about twenty of his contemporaries in 1954.[ccclxxiv]

Of the stories mentioned in "Waterspider", there is one anomaly at least. This is mention of a story by Poul Anderson titled "The Fisher Of Men" which supposedly was published in the May 1971 edition of *If*. Well, as PKD wrote "Waterspider" in 1963 how could he know that Anderson's story appeared in the May 1971 issue of *If*? If it ever did? On this point I have been unable to check the details not having a copy of this issue of *If* or even knowing whether Poul Anderson ever wrote a story titled "The Fisher Of Men."

Another interesting point is that in the same issue of *If* in which "Waterspider" first appeared, the cover story is "Three Worlds To Conquer" by Poul Anderson. And the cover illustration is by Virgil Finlay. A strange coincidence...

As to the letter from PKD to Fred Pohl quoted immediately above, on reading the story one notes that Kris Neville is mentioned only once and only by his first name and there is no mention of either he or PKD being stoned. Philip Jose Farmer is not mentioned at all. So, by the time of publication either PKD or Fred Pohl had edited some of the story out.

The story itself takes place in the future as well as in the past of 1954 and the Worldcon held in San Francisco that year. In the future, a society is trying to perfect interstellar travel but is having problems and even though it's only convicts who are the dying guinea pigs – and there are plenty of those to spare – they wish to solve the problem. To do this they turn to the Library of Congress which has complete files of all the science fiction magazines published in the Twentieth Century. But to these futurians these magazines contain not fiction but the views of precogs living at that time. What in 1954 was considered fiction is in the future considered fact.

To cut a long summary short, the futurians decide that Poul Anderson in his precog story "Night Flight" has the solution to their space travel needs. They send a time dredge back to the days of the Worldcon in 1954 and kidnap Anderson and bring him to the future. There they make him write "Night Flight" including their desired solution. But, when they send him back to 1954 they must wipe his brain clean of all memories of the future and by doing so they also remove their own memories of ever having brought him forward in the first place. The problem of interstellar flight remains unsolved.

As a fun sort of story full of inside jokes and real-life science fiction characters "Waterspider" rates ✩ ✩ ✩ ✩

Five days after they got the manuscript for "Waterspider", the SMLA received the next PKD manuscript. This was the 17,000-word novelette "Man With A Broken Match" which arrived at the Agency on Apr 15, 1963. It was published under the title "What The Dead Men Say" in the June 1964 issue of *Worlds Of Tomorrow*.

This story was selected for Ace Books' 1969 PKD collection THE PRESERVING MACHINE and was excerpted and adapted into the first chapter of PKD's novel UBIK in 1969.

A notable fact about "What The Dead Men Say" is that, as has been noted by several readers, PKD predicted the comeback of Richard Nixon and his election to the Presidency in 1968.[ccclxxv] Here's the passage from the story:

"Do you think Gam has a chance this time?" Kathy asked.
"No, not really. But miracles in politics do happen; look at Richard Nixon's incredible comeback in 1968."

Here's what PKD had to say in RADIO FREE ALBEMUTH about Richard Nixon (Ferris Fremont):

The purpose of killing the leading political figures in the United States by violent assassination, allegedly by screwed-up loners, was to get Ferris F. Fremont elected. It was the only way. He could not effectively compete. Despite his aggressive campaigns, he bordered on the worthless. Some time ago one of his aides must have pointed that out to him. "If you're going to get into the White House, Ferris," the aide must have said, "you've got to kill everyone else first." Taking him literally, Ferris Fremont did so, starting in 1963 and working his way forward during the administration of Lyndon Johnson. By the time Lyndon Johnson had retired, the field was clear. The man who could not compete did not have to.
{...} When he took office, it was on the wave of a huge mandate. Who else could they vote for? When you consider that in effect Fremont was running against no one else, that the Democratic Party had been infiltrated by his people, spied on, wiretapped, reduced to shambles, it makes more sense. Fremont had the backing of the U.S. intelligence community, as they like to call themselves, and ex-agents played an effective role in decimating political opposition. In a one party system there is always a landslide.[ccclxxvi]

"What The Dead Men Say" is similar to the start of UBIK as far as people being frozen in cold-pac, Resurrection Day, and Herbert Schoenheit von Vogelsang are concerned. But it goes off on its own track fairly quickly.

In the story a powerful magnate has died and he's put into cold-pac. But efforts to revive him fail and a multi-media empire is about to fall apart. The wolves move in but are thwarted by the rambling voice of the dead man which comes through on every outlet: TV, radio, print, telephone. These ramblings tell his survivors and subordinates how to run the business and also to support a mysterious also-ran in the upcoming Presidential election. And when the daughter of the dead magnate shows up watch out!

At the end of the story, though, it begins to fall apart. Read it and you'll see. I get the impression that Dick brought it to a hurried end – or was unwilling at that time to continue it to novel length. It would have been fascinating if he had went on with "What The Dead Men Say" instead of bringing it to an unsatisfactory halt.

This is a story reminiscent of "Upon The Dull Earth" and one that deserves some thought, especially for a fuller understanding of UBIK.

"What The Dead Men Say" is that this story gets ✫ ✫ ✫

On Apr 16, 1963 only a day after "Man With A Broken Match" arrived at the SMLA the Agency noted the reception of another short story, "Orpheus With Clay Feet." But this one was written by someone named Jack Dowland. After scratching their heads a bit and reading the story they realised that this story was indeed by Philip K. Dick but pretending to be Jack Dowland!

Was this shades of CONFESSIONS OF A CRAP ARTIST??? No, it's Philip K. Dick having fun with the science fiction format, bleeding his fiction into reality by writing a story in which a crucial point is that the story be written by a fictional character!

So, "Orpheus With Clay Feet" was first published in *Escapade* in 1964 as by 'Jack Dowland.' This was PKD's first appearance in a so-called 'Men's Magazine' and perhaps he wasn't too unhappy to pose under a pseudonym. At least it wouldn't be a complete copout; those who read the story could find his name therein! But… I wonder how many men actually read the texts in *Escapade*… Of course the situation was different in 1980 when "I Hope I Shall Arrive Soon" was published in *Playboy*. By then it had become prestigious to appear in men's magazines! As a collector's item I imagine that this *Escapade* would now be quite valuable.

After its initial publication the story was lost until THE COLLECTED STORIES were published in 1987.

The story told in "Orpheus With Clay Feet" is really a mini-masterpiece. A loser of a man pays to take a trip back in time to inspire some historic genius in his or her art or science. His first choice (to inspire Beethoven to write his Choral Symphony) is already taken and he decides instead to go back and inspire one of the greats of Literature: the famous science fiction author Jack Dowland. Unfortunately he fails at this and actually *uninspires* the famous author so much that he gives up writing science fiction altogether. And in the histories of the future the name of Jack Dowland shrinks to a footnote and the once-great author dies an anonymous hack.

But, undeterred, and espying a new angle for their business, the time-travel agency decides to add a new category to its offerings: uninspiration. They decide to send the loser back to uninspire Adolf Hitler, that is, if he pays first…

A playful, loosely written story, "Orpheus With Clay Feet" got ✫ ✫ ✫ ✫ ✫ and won the Nebula Award back at the same 1956 convention in which Jack Dowland won Best Novel of The Year for his masterpiece of future history *THE FATHER ON THE WALL*.

Two days after "Orpheus With Clay Feet" reached the SMLA the agents at the agency recorded the reception of two more Dick manuscripts. These were "Stand By" and "The Days Of Perky Pat" and the date was Apr 18, 1963.

Originally titled "Top Stand-By Job" the story that would become "Stand-By" on publication in the Oct 1963 *Amazing* plopped in the mail slot at the SMLA on Apr 18, 1963. The back cover of this *Amazing* illustrates Dick's story and has a short quote. In 1966 the story was adapted into Dick's novel THE CRACK IN SPACE. It has been occasionally anthologized since and was selected for the PKD collection THE PRESERVING MACHINE (1969) under the title "Top Stand-By Job."

"Stand-By" can be read in conjunction with PKD's story "What'll We Do With Ragland Park?" which has many of the same characters in a later situation.

In "Stand-By" Earth is being invaded by unknown beings from outer space and the United States – still the top military power – is being governed by a giant computer in Washington D.C. Of course, there's a human stand-by president who has just died and is to be replaced by Max Fischer, the selection of the Union boys in Chicago. Unfortunately, just as Max assumes his do- nothing stand-by job the aliens knock out the computer and Max has to assume office for real. But no sooner is he installed than he faces political opposition in the form of Jim-Jam Briskin, the system's top news-clown. With thousands of TV outlets and billions of faithful viewers Briskin calls for an election which he knows he will win. But Max Fischer isn't about to go down without fighting; he's had a taste of *real* power and he's not going to give up his presidency lightly, alien invasion or no.

A pointed little story, "Stand-By" rates ✶ ✶ ✶

The ms for "In The Days Of Perky Pat" arrived at the SMLA on Apr 18, 1963, the same day as "Stand-By". With the title changed slightly, "The Days Of Perky Pat" was published in *Amazing* in the Dec 1963 issue. The back cover of the magazine has a drawing and short quote from the story.

"The Days Of Perky Pat" was selected for THE BEST OF PHILIP K. DICK in 1977 and for the 60th anniversary issue of *Amazing Stories* in 1985.

Of the story, PKD had this to say:

It was the Barbie-Doll craze which induced this story, needless to say. Barbie always seemed unnecessarily real to me. Years later I had a girl friend whose ambition was to be a Barbie-doll. I hope she made it.[ccclxxvii]

Later on he had much more to say:

"The Days Of Perky Pat" came to me in one lightning-swift flash when I saw my children playing with Barbie dolls. Obviously these anatomically super-developed dolls were not intended for the use of children, or, more accurately, should not have been. Barbie and Ken consisted of two adults in miniature. The idea was that the purchase of countless new clothes for these dolls was necessary if Barbie and Ken were to live in the style to which they were accustomed. I had visions of Barbie coming into my bedroom at night and saying, "I need a mink coat." Or, even worse, "Hey, big fellow... want to take a drive to Vegas in my Jaguar XKE?" I was afraid my wife would find me and Barbie together and my wife would shoot me.

The sale of "The Days Of Perky Pat" to *Amazing* was a good one because in those days Cele Goldsmith edited *Amazing* and she was one of the best editors in the field. Avram Davidson of *Fantasy & Science Fiction* had turned it down, but later he told me that had he known about Barbie dolls he probably would have bought it. I could not imagine anyone not knowing about Barbie. I had to deal with her and her expensive purchases constantly. It was as bad as keeping my TV set working; the TV set always needed something and so did Barbie. I always felt that Ken should buy his own clothes.

In those days -- the early Sixties -- I wrote a great deal, and some of my best stories and novels emanated from that period. My wife wouldn't let me work in the house, so I rented a little shack for $15 a month and walked over to it each morning. This was out in the country. All I saw on my walk to my shack were a few cows in their pastures and my own flock of sheep who never did anything but trudge along after the bell-sheep. I was terribly lonely, shut up by myself in my shack all day. Maybe I missed Barbie, who was back at the big house with the children. So perhaps "The Days Of Perky Pat" is a wishful fantasy on my part; I would have loved to see Barbie -- or Perky Pat or Connie Companion -- show up at the door of my shack.

What did show up was something awful: my vision of the face of Palmer Eldritch which became the basis of the novel THE THREE STIGMATA OF PALMER ELDRITCH, which the Perky Pat story generated." {...} I found in the story "The Days Of Perky Pat" a vehicle that I could translate into a thematic basis for the novel I wanted to write. Now, you see, Perky Pat is the eternally beckoning fair one, *das ewige Weiblichkeit* -- "the eternally feminine," as Goethe put it. Isolation generated the novel and yearning generated the story; so the novel is a mixture of the fear of being abandoned and the fantasy of the beautiful woman who waits for you -- somewhere, but God only knows where; I have still to figure it out. But if you are sitting alone day after day at your typewriter, turning out one story after another and having no one to talk to, no one to be with, and yet pro forma having a wife and four daughters from whose house you have been expelled, banished to a little single-walled shack that is so cold in winter that, literally the ink would freeze in my typewriter ribbon, well, you are going to write about iron slot-eyed faces and warm young women. And thus I did. And thus I still do. [ccclxxviii]

The story is a cruder, early version of the Perky Pat layouts used by the hovelists on Mars in THE THREE STIGMATA OF PALMER ELDRITCH. Instead of the sophisticated 'translation' drugs used by the hovelists to inhabit Perky Pat and her boyfriend Walt in the novel, the Perky Pat layout and Pat herself are simple carved and molded figures and the game is played not on Mars but on post-apocalypse Earth by the survivors – called 'flukers' as by some fluke they survived the holocaust. The game is played without drugs in a fashion similar to Monopoly.

The flukers of the Pinole fluke hear of a rival to Perky Pat called Conny Companion doll which is part of a game played down in the Oakland fluke pit. The Pinole flukers determine to find out about this new doll and lug their layout to Berkeley where they play against the Oakland flukers, the stakes being the respective dolls. The Pinole flukers win the game and bring home Conny Companion but when their fellow flukers find out that Conny is pregnant, well, the morals of this survivalist society are greatly offended and the winning players are ousted from their pit.

Included in the story as counterpoint to the adults preoccupation with the game are the thoughts and doings of their children who, born after the war, are not concerned with trying to relive the pre-war life but to get on with living in this their only known world.

"The Days of Perky Pat" is similar in feel to three of Dick's earlier stories: "Souvenir", "Pay For The Printer" and "Tony And The Beetles." It rates ✯ ✯ ✯

The manuscript for "No Ordinary Guy" reached the SMLA on Apr 29, 1963. The story was published under the new title, "What'll We Do With Ragland Park?" in the Nov 1963 issue of *Amazing Stories*. Later, it was selected for inclusion in another pulp collection: *The Most Thrilling Science Fiction Ever Told, #13* in 1969. Then, two years before it inclusion in THE COLLECTED STORIES OF PKD, editor Mark Hurst included it in the PKD collection, I HOPE I SHALL ARRIVE SOON (1985).

This story is a sequel to "Stand-By" which has the same characters in an earlier situation.

"What'll We Do With Ragland Park?" starts where "Stand-By" leaves off. President Max Fischer has managed to permanently disable the governmental computer Unicephalon 40-D and has slapped rival Jim Jam Briskin in jail. But a new rival to Fischer's power arises: Sebastian Hada, the owner of another system-wide television empire. Hada wants Briskin released from jail so he can broadcast for his network and help pick up sagging ratings. But how to get him out of jail? Well, along comes folk balladeer Ragland Park with a curious ability to be able to write songs that somehow come true… So Rags writes a ballad depicting Briskin's release and it comes true! President Fischer realises his danger and, almost too late, decides what to do with Ragland Park.

Like "Stand-By" , "What'll We Do With Ragland Park?" deserves ✯ ✯ ✯

With "Stand-By" and "What'll We Do With Ragland Park?" Philip Dick had made a stab at what looked like a promising series. In retrospect one may wish he had continued with it. Max

Fischer's political machinations and his on again, off again relationship with Jim Briskin had the potential for a fascinating series of stories. But, after completing 'What'll We Do With Ragland Park?" the next story he sent into the Agency was completely different.

The manuscript for what would become "Oh, To Be A Blobel!" reached the SMLA on May 6, 1963. It was published in *Galaxy* in Feb 1964. Philip K. Dick didn't like the new title, preferring his own: "Well, See, There Were These Blobels." [ccclxxix]

The story was first anthologized in 1965 in Ace Books' *WORLD'S BEST SCIENCE FICTION: 1965*. This was a sale that PKD needed at the time as he was again financially strapped, writing to Scott Meredith at the Agency in 1965:

"Thank you very much for your letter notifying me of the anthology sale of OH TO BE A BLOBEL to Ace. Yes, things are rather rough here financially. I wasn't able to pay my rent last time; {...}" [ccclxxx]

Unfortunately for Phil's pocket; at least as far as sales of this story were concerned, "Oh, To Be A Blobel!" didn't reappear until his THE PRESERVING MACHINE collection in 1969. But, overall, though "Oh, To Be A Blobel!" has been successful. It was collected again in THE BEST OF PHILIP K. DICK in 1977 and the 1980 Playboy Press retrospective: *GALAXY: Thirty Years of Innovative Science Fiction*. Altogether this story has had nine printings including THE COLLECTED STORIES in 1987.

Of the story PKD had quite a bit to say:

Here I nailed down the ultimate meaningless irony of war; the human turns into a Blobel, and the Blobel, his enemy, turns into a human, and there it all is, the futility, the black humour, the stupidity. And in the story they all wind up happy. [ccclxxxi]

This short story also enables us to see some of the problems Dick had to handle facing different magazine editors:

At the beginning of my writing career in the early Fifties, *Galaxy* was my economic mainstay. Horace Gold at *Galaxy* liked my writing whereas John W. Campbell, Jr. at *Astounding* considered my writing not only worthless but as he put it, "Nuts." By and large I liked reading *Galaxy* because it had the broadest range of ideas, venturing into the soft sciences such as sociology and psychology, at a time when Campbell (as he once wrote me!) considered psionics a *necessary* premise for science fiction. Also, Campbell said, the psionic character in the story had to be in charge of what was going on. So *Galaxy* provided a latitude which *Astounding* did not. However, I was to get into an awful quarrel with Horace Gold; he had the habit of changing your stories without telling you: adding scenes, adding characters, removing downbeat endings in favor of upbeat endings. Many writers resented this. I did more than resent this; despite the fact that *Galaxy* was my main source of income I told Gold that I would not sell to him unless he stopped altering my stories -- after which he bought nothing from me at all.

It was not, then, until Fred Pohl became editor of *Galaxy* that I began to appear there again. "Oh, To Be A Blobel!" is a story which Fred Pohl bought. In this story my enormous anti-war bias is evident, a bias which had, ironically, pleased Gold. I wasn't thinking of the Vietnam War but war in general; in particular, how a war forces you to become like your enemy. Hitler had once said that the true victory of the Nazis would be to force its enemies, the United States in particular, to become like the Third Reich -- i.e. a totalitarian society -- in order to win. Hitler, then, expected to win even in losing. As I watched the American military-industrial complex grow after World War Two I kept remembering Hitler's analysis, and I kept thinking how right the son of a bitch was. We had beaten Germany, but both the U.S. and the U.S.S.R were getting more and more like the Nazis with their huge police systems every day. Well, it seemed to me there was a little wry humour in this (but not much). Maybe I could write about it without getting too deep into polemics. But the issue presented in this story is real. Look what we had to become in Viet Nam just to lose, let alone to win; can you imagine what we'd have had to become to win? Hitler would have gotten a lot of laughs out of it, and the laughs would have been on us... and to a very great extent in fact were. And they were hollow and grim laughs, without humour of any kind." [ccclxxxii]

"Oh, To Be A Blobel" is indeed a grim comment on the aftermath of war. PKD makes literal Hitler's comment that to win a war one must become like one's enemy. George Munster, a Terran spy on Titan in the Earth-Blobel war, was transformed into an amoebic blob to infiltrate the Blobel society. But after the war his government informed him that they could not completely turn him back into human form; half of the time he would revert to his Blobel shape. Naturally this causes him psychological problems and he visits a homeostatic psychiatrist who is actually of some help, fixing George up with a Blobel spy who is, part of the time, stuck in human form. It helps that this human form is that of a beautiful young woman. Eventually the two get married and have children. But this causes further problems as two of the children are hybrid Terran-Blobels while one is a full-blooded Terran and the other a perfect Blobel. Marital problems ensue and in an ironic ending George, now a successful businessman, moves to Io and becomes fixed in Blobel form while his wife, Vivian, remains on Earth now fixed into human form.

A sardonic anti-war story, "Oh, To Be A Blobel" rates ✶✶✶.

"The Little Black Box" arrived at the SMLA on the same day as "Oh, To Be A Blobel!", May 6, 1963. It was first published in *Worlds Of Tomorrow* in Aug 1964, shortly after "Cantata 140."

Sutin says that the story was originally included in THE GANYMEDE TAKEOVER but was excised from the final version of that novel. The name and character of Joan Hiashi appear in the story and the novel. [ccclxxxiii]

By 1968 PKD had expanded and incorporated the religion of 'Mercerism' as found in "The Little Black Box" into his novel DO ANDROIDS DREAM OF ELECTRIC SHEEP? In 1980 the story was chosen for PKD's collection THE GOLDEN MAN.

PKD had this to say of "The Little Black Box":

I made use of this story when I wrote my novel DO ANDROIDS DREAM OF ELECTRIC SHEEP? Actually, the idea is better put forth in the story. Here, a religion is regarded as a menace to all political systems; therefore it, too, is a kind of political system, perhaps even an ultimate one. The concept of *caritas* (or *agape*) shows up in my writing as the key to the authentic human. The android, which is the unauthentic human, the mere reflex machine, is unable to experience empathy. In this story it is never clear whether Mercer is an invader from some other world. But he must be; in a sense all religious leaders are... but not from another planet as such. [ccclxxxiv]

In his Afterword to THE GOLDEN MAN collection, Dick refers again to "The Little Black Box":

... I would ask you to read "The Little Black Box" last of all the stories, because it is closer to being my credo than any of the other stories here. As with "Precious Artifact" I asked that it be included. It is a story about trust. Caritas in the final analysis is emotional trust. I trust, then, that you will not misread me and see dislike and anger only; please reach out to me at the core below that, the core of love.[ccclxxxv]

Here, from the Starmont Reader's Guide is a brief description of the story:

"The Little Black Box" looks at spiritual superiority. When the time has come for a superior idea to sweep through human brains, can it be destroyed at the source? Even if eradicated, that source lives on stronger in martyrdom than in life. All differences, physical, mental or spiritual, feed the flame of fear in the limited mind. It is that very limitation, not the difference, which destroys.[ccclxxxvi]

"The Little Black Box" is like several others of PKD's short stories; the action is just developing into a nicely built-up plot when he curtails everything and brings it to an abrupt end. Still, this one deserves ✶ ✶ ✶ ✶

There is no reception date for "The War With The Fnools" at the SMLA and it's possible that it may have been written later in 1963 or early 1964. But it falls in this period. The story was published in *Galactic Outpost #2* in Spring 1964. In 1980 mark Hurst selected the story for inclusion in THE GOLDEN MAN.
PKD said this of "The War With The Fnools":

Well, once again we are invaded. And, humiliatingly, by a lifeform which is absurd. My colleague Tim Powers once said that Martians could invade us simply by putting on funny hats, and we'd never notice. It's a sort of low-budget invasion. I guess we're at the point where we can be amused by the idea of Earth being invaded. (And this is when they really zap you.)[ccclxxxvii]

In "The War With The Fnools" Terra is invaded by aliens who take on the guise of real estate salesmen, Volkswagen mechanics and the like as they try to fool supposedly unwitting humans into believing that they too are human. The problem is that the Fnools don't understand the concept of 'size' and appear ridiculous as they are only one-and-a-half feet tall! But they're still deadly, though, and must be fought. But once the protagonist gives a captured Fnool a puff on a cigarette; explaining that that is what makes humans so tall, the Fnool – in fact, all of them at once – immediately double in size to three feet tall. Disconcerted, the protagonist gives the Fnool a drink of whisky, only to see them all double in size again! The Fnools are happy with this growth in stature and are relishing the future success of their invasion as they are now indistinguishable from true humans (well, of certain types anyway). But, fortunately for mankind the Fnools soon experience sex with more surprising results.
Drugs booze and sex: the initiatory rites to manhood for human children are paralleled in this story onto an alien race as PKD writes one of his funniest short stories. A little contrived, perhaps, but "The War With The Fnools" rates ✶ ✶ ✶ ✶.

After sending off these last short stories in the Spring, Dick learned of the acceptance of MARTIAN TIME-SLIP from Ballantine in June. In August the serialization of "All We Marsmen" began in *Worlds Of Tomorrow*. The biggest news of the year, though, came in

September when the science fiction fans awarded Dick the Hugo for the best science fiction novel of 1962: THE MAN IN THE HIGH CASTLE. October saw first publication of "Stand-By" in *Amazing*.

On retrospect this outburst of short stories by PKD in early 1963 was an astute move for his career. With the publication of the SFBC edition of THE MAN IN THE HIGH CASTLE in Dec 1962 and the consequent rumblings about the Hugo Award, Dick must've looked to the future and anticipated success. With the time-lag between writing and publication of short stories, early 1963 would've been the right time to crank out some stories for publication in the Fall and Winter magazines. Thus, if he did win the Hugo for HIGH CASTLE his name would be featured in the magazines and remain in the public eye. Perhaps, too, Dick reasoned his stories would carry him into 1964 and by that time the novels he was going to write would be in the publication mill.

And this is exactly what happened. As the voting for the Hugo Awards was winding up in Sep 1963 Dick's "All We Marsmen" was in the middle of its serialization in *Worlds Of Tomorrow* and then "Stand-By" appeared in the Oct *Amazing* with the back cover illustrating PKD's story. In all, of the eleven short stories Dick wrote in the Spring of 1963, five of then saw publication with his name on the front and/or back covers. Then, by Dec 1963, of course, Ace published the first edition of THE GAME-PLAYERS OF TITAN.

This was an exciting time for Dick's career. Going into 1964 he would see the first paperback edition of THE MAN IN THE HIGH CASTLE from Popular Library and several short stories on into April when the first paperback edition of MARTIAN TIME-SLIP was trotted out by Ballantine. More short story publications followed into August when THE SIMULACRA saw the light of day from Ace Books and September followed with THE PENULTIMATE TRUTH. Rounding out the year was "Precious Artifact" in October and then two blockbuster novels: CLANS OF THE ALPHANE MOON and THE THREE STIGMATA OF PALMER ELDRITCH both in November. And finally December 1964 saw "The Unteleported Man" blazoned on the cover of that month's *Fantastic Stories*.

All in all the period from mid-1963 to the end of 1964 was one of the most intense of Dick's career and the stories he wrote in 1963 helped bridge an important gap between winning the Hugo for HIGH CASTLE and his transition once again to novels in 1964.

So, with a bundle of short stories completed by the Spring of 1963 Dick again turned to the novel, writing what would become in many reader's eyes his follow-up to the fame of the Hugo Award: THE GAME-PLAYERS OF TITAN.

THE GAME-PLAYERS OF TITAN

This novel was written, most likely, in May of 1963 and the manuscript reached the Agency on Jun 4, 1963. The story was published by Ace Books as a full-size paperback novel on Dec 12, 1963. This publishing date thus preceding that of the paperback edition of THE MAN IN THE HIGH CASTLE in Jan 1964.[ccclxxxviii]

It is unfortunate that there are so few public records on THE GAME-PLAYERS OF TITAN; we have from Dick himself only the following: In a 1965 letter to Scott Meredith in which PKD complains about Don Wollheim and the expansion of THE UNTELEPORTED MAN he mentions THE GAME-PLAYERS OF TITAN in passing:

And the "far-out" elements which I added {to THE UNTELEPORTED MAN}, which were not there in the original, i.e., all which Don objects to, were necessary if the piece became a true novel and not merely a longer story. There is a real irony here, too, because a much better case could be made against my additions than the one Don chose to make; fundamentally, the additions follow the lines laid down in my Ace novel THE GAME PLAYERS OF TITAN, which Don nominated for the Hugo.... [ccclxxxix]

Alas, that's all we have. No one seems to have commented on THE GAME-PLAYERS OF TITAN. And I cannot confirm that Don Wollheim nominated the novel for the Hugo.

The novel itself is set on Earth after a war with the Titanian 'Vugs'. A greatly reduced population plays formalized Monopoly-like territorial games designed to increase the population. But when the Vugs horn in on the action and a group of Terrans find themselves playing for ultimate survival, things get interesting. A bit confusing, perhaps, but THE GAME-PLAYERS OF TITAN is worth ✳ ✳ ✳ ✳

Once he had completed the manuscript for THE GAME-PLAYERS OF TITAN in early June, Dick took three months to send in his next novel. This was THE SIMULACRA.

THE SIMULACRA

Written in the summer of 1963 THE SIMULACRA was originally titled FIRST LADY OF EARTH and is an expansion of the novelette "Novelty Act" which PKD had written in March 1963 and which was published in *Fantastic* in Feb 1964. The expansion and reworking of "Novelty Act" was finished by 28 Aug 1963 when the longer manuscript dropped in the mail slot at the SMLA. THE SIMULACRA was published by Ace Books as a paperback original in Aug 1964. [cccxc]

In August and October 1964 Dick had corresponded with Terry Carr, then an editor at Ace Books, on at least three occasions. In these letters he covers the title change and publication of THE SIMULACRA:

... However, what is "THE SIMULACRA"? Is that what I called "FIRST LADY OF EARTH"? I mean, have I forgotten an entire novel? Wire instructions. Wire diagrams as to how to reassemble memory of forgotten novel. Or *something*. [cccxci]

And:

I know now that THE SIMULACRA is (one) out and (two) FIRST LADY OF EARTH because my lawyer one night, while drunk, called me from his mistresse's apartment to say, "Yr logich inna buk wunt so shitty damn smart, an no wunner your so fucked up in yr life, cuz ya cant think fuckin straight and wanna meet Jean, here? Here's Jean, baby." Etc. [cccxcii]

And:

{...} even my wife, whom I hate so, and who I guess hates me or some such fool thing, remarked that in reading THE SIMULACRA she saw, for the first time in my work, what she called "signs of true genius." For her that is a rather strong statement. So I guess I can take pride in my work. {...} [cccxciii]

Philip Dick himself was fond of THE SIMULACRA. In his 1968 survey of his work till then (his 'Self Portrait') he selects THE SIMULACRA as the last favorite of his books right after THE PENULTIMATE TRUTH. And in his interview with Apel & Briggs he says:

... I like THE SIMULACRA; I think its a very fine book in some ways. It's incredibly complex. There's an incredible number of characters...[cccxciv]

And in another interview when asked what he thought were some of his best novels, PKD selected THE SIMULACRA:

Well, the novel that I like the most is THE SIMULACRA, because there are more characters in it and it is more of the slice of life thing where you have all kinds of things and it culminates in what I regard as one of the funniest scenes of human disaster that is imaginable.

We have two characters who are equivalent to used-car salesmen, and their great hope is to perform before the first lady of the White House. When they finally get their chance, their little animal, the Papoola, bites somebody and they're ruined. Their whole career has worked up to this point and this loveable little animal, the Papoola, who does it bite? The first lady?

(A & F:) I think so, I can't remember.

(PKD:) It does something dreadful. To me it's a funny matter, because it's a comic tragedy and a tragic comedy. That they have pinned all their hopes on this moment and then this little animal, which normally is completely benign, suddenly takes it into its head to bite the first lady.

What I like best in my own writing is blending humor and tragedy together, to show that they are inseparable, like yin and yang. They are the two forces of the universe, the dark and the white. At any moment some grand, tragic situation is susceptible to being suddenly comic.

{...}

But that's why I like THE SIMULACRA because we have the desperate ambitions of two human beings. This ambition first culminates in a titanically unexpected invitation to the White House and then it's all ruined by this little animal biting the first lady. And the first lady doesn't exist anyway. She's just an actress who is playing the role of the first lady. And so the whole thing is a comedy of tragedy and a tragedy of comedy.

{...} There is a tremendous opportunity for humour within this context, which all goes back to what started this diatribe, my book THE SIMULACRA. That is why I like it so much, because these men have devoted their entire lives, to aspire, to perform before the first lady. That is the highest joy this society offers. You can go to perform before the first lady. And she's a complete fake, she's an actress, and when they do perform their little animal screws it all up for them. And yet they go on living. And all the other characters go on living too. [cccxcv]

In another interview conducted when PKD went to Metz, France for a science fiction convention in 1977, he commented on his relationship with the French science fiction readers:

And in a sense, I was learning about the novel not from English prose models but from French prose models. So it makes sense, perhaps, that my writings would be well received in France. A novel of mine, such as THE SIMULACRA, for example, which contains maybe 15 or 16 major characters, is definitely derived from such French writers as Balzac...[cccxcvi]

But THE SIMULACRA is not a favorite of everyone; in the fan poll ran by the zine *For Dickheads Only* one respondent thought:

The only PKD novel I've found less than fascinating is THE SIMULACRA. Don't ask me why, but it just fails to take off -- everything in it seems cribbed from other PKD novels, there's too much intrigue and not enough plot, there's precious little of PKD's dark humour, and it just gives the impression of being a piece of hack-work.[cccxcvii]

The story THE SIMULACRA incorporates almost wholesale Dick's 1963 novelette "Novelty Act."

"Novelty Act" becomes a subplot in THE SIMULACRA around which Dick builds a story of political intrigue and technological machinations. The President's wife, Nicole, still persists eternally but the President himself, Rudy Kalbfleisch, is a simulacrum that is breaking down. Society is divided into those who know the truth about the Government and those who don't. Add in the character of Richard Kongrosian, an unbalanced and psychic pianist, and the 'Chuppers'; a small society of Neanderthal-like throwbacks, and its no wonder that the plot is practically indescribable – and why it all falls apart in the end. A nice try from a good idea that was stretched too much.

THE SIMULACRA (even though Nicole will kill me) rates ✷ ✷ ✷

There is one more short story that needs consideration here in Sep 1963. This is "Cantata 140." I have no record of a reception date at the SMLA for this story but two authorities, Andy Butler and Perry Kinman, date the 'first part' of THE CRACK IN SPACE to Sep 9, 1963. And as "Cantata 140" forms the first part of the novel then "Cantata 140" must be what is being referred to.[cccxcviii]

But, certainly, "Cantata 140" was accepted at *F & SF* on Jan 13, 1964 and was first published there in the July 1964 issue. The cover illustrating PKD's story is by Ed Emshwiller.

At 22,000 words "Cantata 140" is already half a novel and, indeed, that's what it proved to be when THE CRACK IN SPACE was published in Feb 1966. PKD said

'"Cantata 140" is a cut-down version of a 60,000 novel, hence somewhat aborted. Oh well. So geht das Leben.'[cccxcix]

Of the story itself, Steven Owen Godersky gives an excellent description:

Frozen sleep seems like a humane way to end unemployment and overpopulation pressures: Send the excess citizens to the future. Government warehouses are filled with bibs and a political fight erupts over whether or not to dispose of them through a space-warp. Then an unknown agency begins to help the sleepers to awake.[cd]

"Cantata 140" rates about ✷ ✷ ✷.

In Oct 1963 Philip K. Dick received a letter from his agent, Scott Meredith, detailing news of a novel assignment from Pyramid Books. This was to be called THE ZAP GUN on the publisher's directive. But before we look at THE ZAP GUN, we must first address NOW WAIT FOR LAST YEAR for, certainly, this was written before THE ZAP GUN and most likely written in the last few months of 1963.

NOW WAIT FOR LAST YEAR

The manuscript for NOW WAIT FOR LAST YEAR reached the SMLA on Dec 4, 1963.[cdi] The novel was sold to Doubleday and was published in hardback in May 1966.[cdii]

Apparently the novel did not make Dick too much money as a 1968 letter from Doubleday gives royalty statements for a six-month period in early 1968. The amount is a trifling $6.32 for NOW WAIT FOR LAST YEAR. This compares to $671.38 for DO ANDROIDS DREAM OF ELECTRIC SHEEP? [cdiii]

In 1988 NOW WAIT FOR LAST YEAR shared the Gilgamesh Award for Best SF Novel (for works first appearing in Spanish in 1988) with George R.R. Martin's *TUF VOYAGING* and Jack Vance's *DEMON PRINCES.*[cdiv]

The situation with NOW WAIT FOR LAST YEAR is similar to that of THE GAME-PLAYERS OF TITAN – not much has been said about the novel other than occasional critical comments. PKD himself refers to it on a couple of occasions, as follows:

Yes, well, we touched on another topic in the interview I had with those people and that was my attitude toward drugs. They said, isn't there an affinity between you and Timothy Leary's attitude toward drugs? And I said, well, actually a scrupulous reading of my novels that deal with drugs such as 3 STIGMATA OF PALMER ELDRITCH, NOW WAIT FOR LAST YEAR, "Faith Of Our Fathers", and A MAZE OF DEATH show the possibility -- again we get into the area of possibility, not certitude -- that there are really just a whole number of things happening in 3 STIGMATA and in NOW WAIT FOR LAST YEAR, The drug is destructive, it's addictive, it's used as a government weapon as a matter of fact.[cdv]

And:

When a novel of mine comes out I have no more relationship to it than has anyone who reads it -- far less, in fact, because I have the memory of Mr. Tagomi and all the others... Gino Molinari, for example, in NOW WAIT FOR LAST YEAR, or Leo Bulero in 3 STIGMATA. My friends are dead, and as much as I love my wife, daughter, cat -- none of these nor all of these is enough. The vacuum is terrible. Don't write for a living; sell shoelaces. Don't let it happen to you.[cdvi]

That's about it for comments on NOW WAIT FOR LAST YEAR. As for the critics, they were amazed as usual by Dick's daring inventiveness. Bruce Gillespie, for instance, commented:

The occurrences in Philip Dick's novels are impossible. In what future will you find (a) one man who may exhibit all the signs of an illness of a man in the next room, (b) a process by which time devolves around a modern man without him going mad, or the whole chemistry of his body collapsing, or (c) a drug (JJ-180, the star of NOW WAIT FOR LAST YEAR) that literally, magically, turns back the tides of time, wipes out memory or transfers people between different time zones, all in the space of one second? More importantly, how often would you find people who would know what was going on when these things happened? Yet try to invent a science that will explain all the elements in NOW WAIT FOR LAST YEAR, for instance.[cdvii]

In the story, Earth is in an uneasy alliance with the alien but human-looking supermen from Lillistar and are fighting a war against the insect-like Reegs. The war is not going well and the 'Starmen want Earth to put more effort into it. But Terra's leader, Gino Molinari, manages to forestall extra conscripts by having a series of near-fatal illnesses at the last minute thus frustrating the 'Starmen. How can Molinari die and then reappear again better than ever? Well, he's got secret access to a series of para-worlds where younger versions of himself reside. And then there's the time-shifting drug JJ-180 to consider...

NOW WAIT FOR LAST YEAR should deserve ✶ ✶ ✶ ✶

THE ZAP GUN (part 1)

As we briefly noted above, Dick was contacted in October 1963 by his agent concerning a novel assignment from Pyramid Books. This was for a novel to be named THE ZAP GUN. Here's the letter:

> I'm happy to report that we have a novel assignment for you from Pyramid Books. We had a meeting with Don Benson, the editor over there, and he has an idea for a science fiction novel entitled THE ZAP GUN.
> Of course, you'll recognize the zap gun as the old Buck Rogers standby. Don wants to do a book that would be somewhat tongue-in-cheek, but about the serious possibility of a real "blaster". The blaster seems much more a possibility today because of the experiments with the laser beam.
> Don has agreed to contract on the basis of a detailed outline from you and will pay an advance of $1500: $500 on signature of contract, $500 on completion, and $500 on publication.
> I hope this idea interests you, and I'll look forward to an outline from you shortly.[cdviii]

The idea certainly did interest Dick. $500 right away was good money. So by Dec 5, 1963 the Agency was in proud possession of an outline for THE ZAP GUN. This outline was published in *PKDS-16* and consists of nine double-spaced typed pages. And the manuscript for THE ZAP GUN, which, as Paul Williams noted, had nothing to do with the earlier outline, was received by the SMLA on April 15, 1964. The novel was published by Pyramid Books in Jan 1967.[cdix]

But before paperback publication the story was sold to *Worlds Of Tomorrow* and serialized in the Nov 1965 and Jan 1966 issues of that magazine as "Project Plowshare".

Between the time of the outline for THE ZAP GUN (Dec 1963) and the time the manuscript was finished on Apr 15, 1964 Dick wrote three more short stories and almost certainly wrote his novel CLANS OF THE ALPHANE MOON the manuscript for which arrived at the SMLA on Jan 16, 1964. First we'll look at these stories and then CLANS and after that we'll return to THE ZAP GUN.

"A Game Of Unchance" reached the SMLA on Dec 9, 1963.[cdx] It was published in *Amazing* in Jul 1964. Occasionally anthologized, notably in THE GOLDEN MAN in 1980, "A Game Of Unchance" is now easiest to find in Volume 5 of THE COLLECTED STORIES OF PKD (1987) and later reprints of these volumes.

Of the story, PKD had this to say:

> I feel the same way about this little story as I do about Harlan Ellison: I love the little bastard. It's a well-constructed story, with what for me (in rereading it) is a totally unexpected ending. A carnival is feral; another carnival shows up and is pitted against the

first one; and the antithetical interaction is preplanned in such a way that the first carnival wins. It's as if the two opposing forces that underlie all change in the universe are rigged; in favor of thanatos, the dark force, yin or strife, which is to say, the force of destruction.[cdxi]

In this story hicks on a backwards planet are visited by an itinerant carnival, but not the same one as *last* year when they were taken for all their goods. This is a different carnival and this year the rubes have something up their sleeve: a telekinetic boy who they think will enable them to win. So, the colony gathers together all its produce and goes off to the fair. They win, alright, but what good are these little dolls they've won? After accidentally turning one of the dolls on the colonists are infested with little killer dolls. Even the U.N. can't do much to stop them. But then *another* carnival shows up with a possible solution – if the hicks can win again.

"A Game Of Unchance" is an amusing cautionary tale that rates ✮ ✮ ✮ ✮.

"Precious Artifact" reached the SMLA on the same day as "A Game Of Unchance" – Dec 9, 1963 -- and was published in *Galaxy* in Oct 1964.[cdxii]
On Philip K. Dick's insistence it was included in his collection, THE GOLDEN MAN in 1980.
As he himself said:

I insisted that this story be included in this collection. It utilized a peculiar logic which I generally employ, which Professor Patricia Warrick pointed out to me. First you have Y. Y. Then you do a cybernetics flipflop and you have null-Y. Okay, now you reverse it again and have null-null-Y. Okay, the question is: Does null-null-Y equal Y^3? Or is it a deepening of null-Y? In this story, what appears to be the case is Y but we find out the opposite is true (null-Y). But then *that* turns out not to be true, so are we back to Y? Professor Warrick says that my logic winds up with Y equals null-Y. I don't agree, but I am not sure what I do wind up with. Whatever it is, in terms of logic, it is contained in this particular story. Either I've invented a whole new logic or, ahem, I'm not playing with a full deck.[cdxiii]

"Precious Artifact" tells the tale of Milt Biskle, a terraforming engineer who has just turned his section of Mars into habitable land for human occupation. But something is nagging him in the back of his mind and he has doubts about the recent war in which Terra defeated the invading Proxmen. On his return to Earth his doubts are confirmed and he finds that beneath the surface of the seemingly normal world there is complete destruction. The Proxmen won the war, not the Terrans. Despite the presence of the nubile Mary Ableseth – a Proxman in disguise – Milt wishes to return to Mars for a rest before taking on the job of terraforming Earth to the Proxmen's designs. His one wish is that he be allowed to take a kitten back with him. This is granted and with the hope that he may talk the Proxmen into letting cats exist in the future he returns to his (fake) wife and children on Mars. But in the Proxmen's worlds there isn't much room for anything but Proxmen…
A bittersweet story into which PKD weaves his love of cats, "Precious Artifact" gets ✮ ✮ ✮ ✮ ✮.

A couple of weeks after sending off these last two short stories, PKD sent in the manuscript for "Retreat Syndrome". It arrived at the SMLA on Dec 23, 1963.[cdxiv] The story was first published in *Worlds Of Tomorrow* in Jan 1965. No comments on the story have been found.

A fairly complicated story, "Retreat Syndrome" is about a man who believes the world around him is not real and despite the efforts of his psychiatrist he continues to believe that he killed his wife on Ganymede for betraying the Revolution. He tries to kill his wife again but are his delusions real, or is he only imagining things?

"Retreat Syndrome" is worth ✰ ✰ ✰ ✰.

At the end of 1963, then, Dick could look back on the year with some satisfaction: about fifteen short stories written; sale and serialization of MARTIAN TIME-SLIP; winner of the Hugo Award for THE MAN IN THE HIGH CASTLE and publication of THE GAME-PLAYERS OF TITAN. Plus completion of another novel, NOW WAIT FOR LAST YEAR and the prospect of some easy money from Pyramid Books for writing THE ZAP GUN. Admittedly, he'd had all his unsold mainstream manuscripts sent back to him by the Agency but things were looking up.

Also in 1963 PKD had had four short stories published. These were: "Stand By" in Oct, "What'll We Do With Ragland Park?" in Nov, and "If There Were No Benny Cemoli" and "The Days Of Perky Pat" in December.

But, even though I haven't mentioned it until now, another significant event happened to Philip K. Dick in the summer of 1963. We've already mentioned this in connection with the story "The Days of Perky Pat" but we'll repeat it here. This was... Well, we'll let PKD say it in his own words:

In those days -- the early Sixties -- I wrote a great deal, and some of my best stories and novels emanated from that period. My wife wouldn't let me work in the house, so I rented a little shack for $15 a month and walked over to it each morning. This was out in the country. All I saw on my walk to my shack were a few cows in their pastures and my own flock of sheep who never did anything but trudge along after the bell-sheep. I was terribly lonely, shut up by myself in my shack all day. Maybe I missed Barbie, who was back at the big house with the children. So perhaps "The Days Of Perky Pat" is a wishful fantasy on my part; I would have loved to see Barbie -- or Perky Pat or Connie Companion -- show up at the door of my shack.

What did show up was something awful: my vision of the face of Palmer Eldritch which became the basis of the novel THE THREE STIGMATA OF PALMER ELDRITCH. which the Perky Pat story generated.

There I went, one day, walking down the country road to my shack, looking forward to 8 hours of writing, in total isolation from all other humans, and I looked up at the sky and saw a face. I didn't really see it, but the face was there, and it was not a human face; it was a vast visage of perfect evil. I realize now (and I think I dimly realised at the time) what caused me to see it: the months of isolation, of deprivation of human contact, in fact sensory deprivation as such... anyhow the visage could not be denied. It was immense; it filled a quarter of the sky. It had empty slots for eyes -- it was metal and cruel and, worst of all, it was God.[cdxv]

This vision persisted through the summer months and one can imagine PKD trudging to his shack, head bowed under the awful gaze of Palmer Eldritch in the sky. This vision would have a great affect on Dick and in 1964 he would write it into his novel THE THREE STIGMATA OF PALMER ELDRITCH. We will turn to that masterpiece shortly but first we must note that the assassination of President John F. Kennedy occurred in Dallas in November of 1963. This assassination following the Cuban missile-crisis had a great effect on many people throughout the world, including Philip K. Dick, and no-doubt colored his stories henceforth (not that the threat of the Bomb hadn't already influenced his stories…).

1964

January 1964 saw publication of the first paperback edition of THE MAN IN THE HIGH CASTLE from Popular Library and also publication of the short story "Waterspider" in *If*. February saw three more short stories on the stands: "Novelty Act", "Oh, To Be A Blobel!" and "Orpheus With Clay Feet". In April "The War With The Fnools" saw the light of day and the first edition MARTIAN TIME-SLIP was published by Ballantine. The first novel of the year to be completed was THE CLANS OF THE ALPHANE MOON.

While he was writing the next several books Philip Dick's marriage to Anne was falling apart. Phil was spending more time at his mother's in Berkeley than at home. He filed for divorce on Mar 9, 1964 and it became final in Oct 1965. [cdxvi]

CLANS OF THE ALPHANE MOON

Andrew Butler and Perry Kinman have this novel completed by Jan 16, 1964. As yet I am unable to confirm this date.[cdxvii] We only know for sure that Ace Books first published it as a full-size novel on Nov 12, 1964.[cdxviii]

PKD's 1954 short story "Shell Game" is similar to CLANS OF THE ALPHANE MOON in that it too deals with a group of stranded mental patients on their way to a hospital planet.

Surprisingly for such a popular novel there has not been much in the way of solid comments on it. Philip K. Dick had only a few occasions to mention the novel. For instance, in conversation with Briggs & Apel:

(PKD:) I love CLANS OF THE ALPHANE MOON, because the whole entire thing works up to this one funny scene where they call off the attack on the rocket ship and the robot hasn't been told and he goes and hammers on the door.
(DSA:) I really love that book too, for a number of reasons, not the least of which is the scene near the end where the relations among all the characters get so complex that the main character has to just sit down for about 3 pages and try and untangle who is on who's side. He finally realises that its an impossible equation to solve; there is just too many people doing too many illogical things, some entirely on their own!
(PKD:) That's a funny book in many ways…[cdxix]

Dick, in the same conversation, mentioned CLANS OF THE ALPHANE MOON in connection with his French publishers and editions:

(PKD:) In comparison to, like ACE books… I used to hold the French edition in one hand and an ACE edition in the other… CLANS OF THE ALPHANE MOON is the one I used…
(DSA:)(sarcastically) Yeah… Great cover for that book… The guy with the gun…
(PKD:) (also sarcastically) Yeah, right. It's a book about guns (laughter). So I said, "Holy smoke! I can see a tremendous difference in the physical qualities of the two books. And they say they're gonna publish all of my novels." Well they didn't publish all of my novels because other French publishers bid on them and outbid them for a large number of novels. So Opta just published the ones they had acquired title to. Someone told me I have like 26 to 29 novels in print in France.[cdxx]

After PKD's death some of his friends got together to talk about their departed companion. Parts of this were selected for print in the *Philip K. Dick Society Newsletter* in 1985. They weren't too happy with Barry Malzberg's 'Afterword' to the Bluejay edition of CLANS:

(TP:) It's easy to do, as Barry Malzberg did in his really surprisingly misinformed and error-filled essay in whichever Bluejay book that was (CLANS OF THE ALPHANE MOON), to jump to the conclusion that Phil was nuts. I think Malzberg says that Phil was living at some focus of God's attention and couldn't leave his shabby apartment because that's where God's speakers were. (Laughter) (a). it wasn't a shabby apartment; and (b). God talked to him all over the place -- in Fullerton, several addresses in Fullerton. Everything Malzberg says is wrong! He's got wrong Phil's age at death, by I think more than one year. He's got wrong the number of days Phil was in a coma. He's got wrong -- everything! Details that a newspaper could have cleared up.

(JBR:) Or maybe that the newspaper got wrong.

(TP:) Well, it's really shockingly careless from a writer of Malzberg's stature. He was just shooting for cheap, quick, uninformed color. Which may be fine in fiction, but if you write about a guy who actually lived, it's...

(AW:) Glib?

(JBR:) And disappointing?

(TP:) Glib, disappointing and very unprofessional.

(AW:) I think a lot of people had that same reaction. A lot of informed people anyway. I'm surprised that it was accepted for publication. Just because it was solicited and then written doesn't mean that it had to end up between covers.

(TP:) I really expected better

(JBR:) I don't know. Maybe because its an Afterword, it is sort of quick editorialism, and should be taken in that light.

(TP:) If you simply want to dismiss the subject and move on to something else, that's a good way to go, but if you really want to understand what propelled Phil, and what was the fuel that kept him moving, it was a whole lot more subtle than that. And more rational than that. It's the same way with saying he's paranoid: superficially that sounds correct and can cover most of the facts, but it won't really work in the long run. Too many screwy things really did happen to him, and too many of his outlandish dreads turned out to be all too well-founded.[cdxxi]

And that's all as far as comments go. Of course, there's lots of criticism of this novel but that will not concern us here. The story takes place on Terra and the third moon of the Alphane System. A group of metal patients on their way to a hospital planet have diverted to the Alphane System and have been forgotten by Earth authorities. When they are rediscovered many years later, the nuts have established a viable society that is separated into 'clans'. These clans fall along the lines of psychiatric classification: 'Manses' (manics), 'Pares" (paranoids), 'Heebs' (Hebephrenics), 'Ob-Coms' (Obsessive-Compulsive), 'Deps' (Depressives), and so on. Feeling the threat from Earth the clans organize for defense, led by the Manses and Pares. But Chuck Rittersdorf and his wife Mary, sent to investigate and vet this crazy society, have problems of their own. Mary is PKD's prototypical 'bitch wife' always egging her husband on and no matter what he does it doesn't satisfy her. Chuck himself feels he's going crazy but with the help of a friendly telepathic slime mold from Ganymede named Lord Running Clam, he finally realises that he's not nuts; it's his wife who's crazy. He is 'normal' and in the end he moves to the Alphane moon and establishes his own clan, that of the 'Norms.'

From this description we can sense that this is indeed a crazy novel. Dick, familiar with psychiatrists from his own life, smacks the 'profession' in the face with a cold, wet haddock. It should be mandatory reading in the 'colleges' where they teach such pseudo-scientific nonsense.

As a novel CLANS OF THE ALPHANE MOON gets different ratings depending on which clan you talk to. In Da Vinci Heights it gets zero stars from the Manses who don't read fiction. The Pares, of course, give it ✫ ✫ ✫ ✫ ✫ because they know the truth when they see it. The Ob-Coms dither between ✫ ✫ and ✫ ✫ ✫ while the Heebs and Deps couldn't be bothered to vote. In the normal world it gets ✫ ✫ ✫ ✫.

With CLANS OF THE ALPHANE MOON out of the way Philip K. Dick got very busy and even before completing THE ZAP GUN in April 1964 he worked on the expansion of "Cantata 140" into THE CRACK IN SPACE and then wrote the novel THE THREE STIGMATA OF PALMER ELDRITCH. But that's not all! He also found time to prepare outlines for THE PENULTIMATE TRUTH and DEUS IRAE before April. For the historiographer this is indeed a difficult time to sort out.

THE CRACK IN SPACE

Just above we looked at PKD's novelette "Cantata 140". This novelette formed the first half of what would become the novel THE CRACK IN SPACE. The manuscript for "Cantata 140", as we've noted, reached the SMLA on Sep 9, 1963 and that for the finished novel, THE CRACK IN SPACE, on Mar 17, 1964. THE CRACK IN SPACE was first published by Ace Books in Feb 1966. [cdxxii]

Unfortunately, this novel fell through the cracks as far as commentary by PKD and almost anyone else. In a Jun 1964 letter to James Blish, PKD refers to "Cantata 140" which had just been published as "a cut down version of a 60,000 word novel, hence somewhat aborted..."[cdxxiii]

Terry Carr, an editor at Ace Books at the time, talks of the title change:

My favorite story about Ace's title-changes has to do with another Phil Dick book which he called *Cantata 140*. It concerned, among other things, a whorehouse in orbit around Earth. When I saw the memo that said the title had been changed to THE CRACK IN SPACE, I rushed into Don's office and explained the double entendre to him (he'd intended the title to refer to a leakage between dimensions in the novel). Don said, "Oh, well. No one will notice."[cdxxiv]

And that is all I have found comments-wise on THE CRACK IN SPACE. However, PKD's biographer Gregg Rickman selected this as PKD's worst novel in the *FDO* fan poll, saying:

Worst novel, at least unique, is THE CRACK IN SPACE.[cdxxv]

The story itself incorporates almost wholesale the short story "Cantata 140". In an overpopulated world people are coerced into being frozen with the promise that they will be awoken at a later date when conditions improve. But do they merely become the supply of organ parts for the ruling geriatric generation?

Against this backdrop Jim Briskin is running for president, using a satellite whorehouse run by two-headed George Walt as his whipping boy. But when a crack is found in space that leads to a parallel world, Briskin finds a solution to overpopulation as well as his failing opinion polls.

A fun novel that occasionally falls apart, THE CRACK IN SPACE deserves ✳ ✳ ✳.

THE THREE STIGMATA OF PALMER ELDRITCH

THE THREE STIGMATA OF PALMER ELDRITCH was written in early1964, though it could date back to 1963. Andrew Butler sets a specific date for the novel's completion: Mar 18, 1964.[cdxxvi]

Whether it was revised, how it was done or anything else about the novels' publishing history we do not know. Only the publication date of the first edition. This was from Doubleday publishers on Nov 17, 1964. The Science Fiction Book Club Edition (SFBC), also from Doubleday, came out in Jan 1965.[cdxxvii]

The first UK edition was from Cape publishers in 1966.[cdxxviii]

In 1965 THE THREE STIGMATA OF PALMER ELDRITCH was nominated by Dick's science fiction-writing peers for the Nebula Award for Best Novel of 1964.

THE THREE STIGMATA OF PALMER ELDRITCH was Dick's first novel sale to Doubleday (one recalls the success they'd had with the SFBC edition of THE MAN IN THE HIGH CASTLE) and, as Sutin notes, they didn't pay much more than Ace Books – an advance of $2000 on average. But at least it was in hardcover with a dustjacket.[cdxxix]

In 1976 Mark Hurst acquired the rights to PALMER ELDRITCH for Bantam Books.[cdxxx]

Dick, in one of his usual hard-luck modes in 1965 writes of PALMER ELDRITCH in an undated letter to his agent:

{...} I wasn't able to register my car for '65, and the Highway Patrol gave me two citations, which, if I can't pay -- as well as registering my car and fixing the muffler -- I'm going to be jailed on April 7th {...} But I can't see borrowing any more, even though the advance from you is down now to $750. What I'm holding out for is the Jonathan Cape money from the U.K. Do you think it'll be coming through soon? I think that good news about that would really cheer me up. That is really quite a lot of money, when you think about it.

I guess if the J.C. money won't be in for a while I'll have to consider trying to borrow some more. Keerist. How dismal.

If something extremely good happens you can reach me by phone again: not my own, since the Bell people took it away, but my girl's phone: {...-..._....} That's a bit less dismal.

I'll hope, then, to hear from you as to the U.K. sum.[cdxxxi]

The "Jonathan Cape money" he writes about almost certainly refers to the UK sale of PALMER ELDRITCH to Cape publishers. And as PKD mentions the upcoming date of April 7th we can assume this letter was written before then and the sale to Cape also occurring before this date.

As we have already said above, one day in the summer of 1963 Phil was walking down the path past the cows and his sheep on the way to his hovel, looking forward to another day of writing when:

... I looked up at the sky and saw a face. I didn't really see it, but the face was there, and it was not a human face; it was a vast visage of perfect evil. I realize now (and I think I dimly realised at the time) what caused me to see it: the months of isolation, of deprivation of human contact, in fact sensory deprivation as such... anyhow the visage could not be denied. It was immense; it filled a quarter of the sky. It had empty slots for eyes -- it was metal and cruel and, worst of all, it was God.

{... ...}

... Isolation generated the novel and yearning generated the story {"The Days Of Perky Pat"}; in the novel a mixture of the fear of being abandoned and the fantasy of the beautiful woman who waits for you – somewhere, but God only knows where; I have still to figure it out. But if you are sitting alone day after day at your typewriter, turning out one story after another and having no one to talk to, no one to be with, and yet pro forma having a wife and four daughters from whose house you have been expelled, banished to a little single-walled shack that is so cold in winter that, literally, the ink would freeze in my typewriter ribbon, well, you are going to write about iron slot-eyed faces and warm young women...[cdxxxii]

The short story "The Days Of Perky Pat" which Dick wrote in 1963 is the one he mentions here. Like THE THREE STIGMATA this story is about Martian colonists in their hovels playing with Barbie Dolls.

Dick refers to this 1963 vision on another occasion:

... The Palmer Eldritch novel came out of an actual mystical experience, lasting almost a month, in which I *saw* the face of evil hovering over the landscape, and the three stigmata were aspects of him that I saw – I mean, objectively, literally – in particular the slotted, empty eyes. It was a true trip before I had seen any LSD, much less taken any. In an effort to help myself I became a convert to the Anglo-Catholic church, but their teachings do not include that of a real, active, evil power who has control – or near control – of the earth we live on. I even took the rite of unction, but it didn't help, and I wandered away from the church. The point is this: if a person's *idios kosmos* begins to break down, he is exposed to the archetypal or transcendental forces of the *koinos kosmos*, and if the time comes that he lives *only* in the *koinos kosmos* he is exposed to powers too great for him to handle (this part of the theory is *opposite* to Jung's theory that each of us needs subjective constructs – such as space and time – as a framework structuring "reality"). In other words, we must have our *idios kosmos* to stay sane; reality has to filter through, carefully controlled by the mechanisms by which our brains operate. We can't handle it directly, and I think that this was what was occurring when I saw Palmer Eldritch lingering, day after day, over the horizon. Something should have stood between me and it – and the Anglo-Catholic Church wasn't enough (neither was psychiatry, needless to say). My first LSD experience, by the way, confirmed my vision of Palmer Eldritch; I found myself in the hell-world, and it took almost two thousand (subjective) years for me to crawl up out of it.[cdxxxiii]

This passage reminds one of the plot notion of the two Zoroastrian deities facing off in the sky above the town of Millville in THE COSMIC PUPPETS (1957).

Dick's mention of LSD brings up another matter: that due to the nature of the novel many fans and others have wondered if Dick wrote THE THREE STIGMATA after taking the psychedelic drug LSD. Dick denies this several times:

(Vertex): You are known as one of the first authors to experiment with LSD. What effect has it had on your writing?

(PKD): I don't know of any. It's always possible that it's had an effect I don't know about. Take my novel THE THREE STIGMATA OF PALMER ELDRITCH, which deals with a tremendous bad acid trip, so to speak. I wrote that before I had ever seen LSD. I wrote that from just reading a description of the discovery of it and the kind of effect it had. So if that, which is my major novel of a hallucinogenic kind, came without my ever having taken LSD, then I would say even my work following LSD which had hallucinations in it could easily have been written without taking acid.

{...}

(Vertex): In the light of your own experiences with acid, how accurate do you think THE THREE STIGMATA OF PALMER ELDRITCH is as far as drugs are concerned?

(PKD): You remember what happened when they got on that drug? It was bad, wasn't it? It was so bad it taxed my ability to imagine bad. And it didn't do them any good to stop taking the drug because they had flashbacks. And nobody at the time knew LSD was going to produce flashbacks. I had it in mind that the ultimate horror would be to get an addictive, hallucinogenic drug out of your system and you would say, "Well, I'm back in the real world now." And suddenly a monstrous object from the hallucinogenic world would cross the floor and you would realize that you were not back. And this is what has happened to many people who have dropped acid. It was just an accidental prophecy on my part.[cdxxxiv]

And again:

... My drug experiences have not manifested themselves in my work. Many critics have said that THE 3 STIGMATA OF PALMER ELDRITCH was the first "LSD novel." I wrote that after reading a magazine article on hallucinogenics by Aldous Huxley.

Drugs have taken the lives of some very, very dear friends of mine.[cdxxxv]

And once more:

(PKD:) I took amphetamines for years in order to get energy to write. I had to write so much in order to make a living because our pay rates were so low. In five years I wrote sixteen novels, which is incredible. I mean, nobody, I don't think anybody's ever done it before. And without amphetamines I couldn't have written that much. But as soon as I began to earn enough money so I didn't have to write so many books, I stopped taking amphetamines. So now I don't take anything like that. And I never wrote anything under the influence of psychedelics. For instance, PALMER ELDRITCH I wrote without ever having even seen psychedelic drugs.

(A & F:) In Germany the book was titled LSD ASTRONAUTEN.

(PKD:) I know, Franz Rottensteiner did that.[cdxxxvi]

With that out of the way let's turn our attention to what Philip K. Dick himself said about his infamous novel. Leo Runcible, the irascible hero of THE THREE STIGMATA, has a little preface to the novel all his own. It's his credo – and also Dick's – and shows PKD's faith in the common man:

In my novel THE THREE STIGMATA OF PALMER ELDRITCH, which is a study of absolute evil, the protagonist, after his encounter with Eldritch, returns to Earth and dictates a memo. This little section appears ahead of the text of the novel. It *is* the novel, actually, this paragraph; the rest is a sort of post mortem, or rather, a flashback in which all that came to produce the one-paragraph book is presented. Seventy-five thousand words, which I labored over many months, merely explains, is merely there to provide background to the one small statement in the book that matters. (It is, by the way, missing from the

German edition.) This statement is for me my credo -- not so much in God, either a good god or a bad god or both -- but in ourselves. It goes as follows and this is all I actually have to say or want ever to say:

I mean, after all; you have to consider, we're only made out of dust. That's admittedly not much to go on and we shouldn't forget that. But even considering, I mean it's a sort of bad beginning, we're not doing too bad. So I personally have faith that even in this lousy situation we're faced with we can make it. You get me?

This tosses a bizarre thought into my mind: Perhaps someday a giant automated machine will roar and clank out, "From rust we are come." And another machine, sick and dying, cradled in the arms of its woman, may sigh back, "And to rust we are returned." And peace will fall over the barren, anxiety-stricken landscape.[cdxxxvii]

He refers to the character of Leo Runcible again, obviously proud of his creation:

There is in THE THREE STIGMATA and MARTIAN TIME-SLIP something that I regard as funny, which nobody else apparently thinks is funny.

Let's say that Palmer Eldritch is evil to the extent of being an evil deity. He is not just an evil man, an evil human being. He is like a deity; he is the evil being. And he is defeated by a very ordinary, somewhat vulgar human being. He is not defeated by some noble human superman. I regard this as a very pleasant thing, as a very enjoyable thing, that the evil deity is not defeated by man's finest examples; human beings rising. The standard way that this would be handled would be if an evil being invades the earth and some kind of Flash Gordon-like personage emerges who is the embodiment of all that is noble in human beings. But in my book what emerges to defeat this is some kind of bumbling, coarse, garrulous, low-class person who you would expect to be a loan-shark or something like that; some disreputable, virtually disreputable person.[cdxxxviii]

By the time of the writing of THE THREE STIGMATA Dick had the confidence to revert to the type of writing he had done in the beginning of his career: fantasies wherein his characters' thoughts are actualized into the real world. In this regard the short stories "The World She Wanted", "Upon The Dull Earth" and even "A Glass Of Darkness" come to mind. But in regard to THE THREE STIGMATA as a fantasy he said:

I remember I had a term I used to defend this kind of internal projection stories. Stories where internal psychological elements were projected onto the outer world and became three dimensional and real and concrete. Scott, my agent, wrote me incredibly long letters saying that there was no such thing. There was the inner world of dreams and fantasies and the unconscious and then there was the objective outer world, and the two never mixed. So I gave up. Later, when I'd established myself more securely in the field, I began to go and do it in such books as THE THREE STIGMATA OF PALMER ELDRITCH. I reverted to what I wanted to do and had the nightmare inner content objectified in the outer world. So I slowly began to reintroduce those elements into my writing.

LUPOFF: Do you do any fantasy now?

DICK: No. No I don't. It pretty much cured me of trying any fantasy.[cdxxxix]

Dick thought highly of THE THREE STIGMATA OF PALMER ELDRITCH saying,

An interesting one is THE 3 STIGMATA OF PALMER ELDRITCH, as far as I'm concerned. I have read that and have the distinct impression that it was an extraordinary book -- so extraordinary that it may have no peer. It may be a unique book in the history of *writing --nothing* was ever done like this. And then I've read it over and thought it was completely crazy, just insane; not *about* insanity, it *is* insanity. God, it's a weird book.

(Briggs:) If I were to pick a favorite of mine from among your books, that would be it.

(Apel:) Right, same here. It is certainly in a class by itself. That's the book that should probably be pointed to as your major work.

(PKD:) I think if anything I write is to be retained within the cultural flow that THE 3 STIGMATA OF PALMER ELDRITCH stands a very good chance. Either it will eventually be consigned to oblivion as a bizarre excersize in madness, or it will be considered a breakthrough book. I have a very strong feeling that UBIK, too, contains some important ideas.[cdxl]

But, much as he liked his own novel he didn't like all of it:

Religion ought never to show up in SF except from a sociological standpoint, as in *Gather Darkness* [a novel by Fritz Leiber]. God per se, as a character, ruins a good SF story; and this is as true of my own stuff as anyone else's. Therefore I deplore my PALMER ELDRITCH book in that regard. But people who are a bit mystically inclined like it. I don't. I wish I had never written it; there are too many horrid forces loose in it. When I wrote it I had been taking certain chemicals and I could see the awful landscape that I depicted. But not now. Thank God. *Agnus Dei qui tollis peccata mundi* [Lamb of God who lifts the sins of the world]. [cdxli]

One wonders what these 'certain chemicals' were in light of Dick's denying that he had taken LSD prior to writing THE THREE STIGMATA? Certainly he was ambivalent if not downright apprehensive about THE THREE STIGMATA:

Reaction to THE THREE STIGMATA was mixed. In England some reviewers described it as blasphemy. Terry Carr, who was my agent at Scott Meredith at the time, told me later, "That novel is crazy," although subsequent to that he reversed his opinion. Some reviewers found it a profound novel. I only find it frightening. I was unable to proofread the galleys because the novel frightened me so. It is a dark journey into the mystical and the supernatural and the absolutely evil as I understood it at the time. Let us say, I would like Perky Pat to show up at my door, but I dread the possibility that, when I hear the knock, it will be Palmer Eldritch waiting outside and not Perky Pat. Actually, to be honest, neither has shown up in the seventeen or so years since I wrote the novel. I guess that is the story of life: what you most fear never happens, but what you most yearn for never happens either. This is the difference between life and fiction. I suppose it's a good trade-off. But I'm not sure.[cdxlii]

And again in his 1968 'Self Portrait':

I enjoyed writing all of them...

But this leaves out the most vital of them all: THE 3 STIGMATA OF PALMER ELDRITCH. I am afraid of that book; it deals with absolute evil, and I wrote it during a great crisis in my religious beliefs. I decided to write a novel dealing with absolute evil as personified in the form of a "human". When the galleys came from Doubleday I couldn't correct them because I could not bear to read the text, and this is still true.[cdxliii]

One recalls PKD's difficulty writing RING OF FIRE, the proposed sequel to THE MAN IN THE HIGH CASTLE because he could not face the reality of the Nazi evil.

THE THREE STIGMATA OF PALMER ELDRITCH figures in another way. Lawrence Sutin, the author of the fine biography of PKD: *DIVINE INVASIONS: A Life Of Philip K. Dick* which we have heavily referenced in this present study, has said that he decided to write this biography after reading THE THREE STIGMATA in 1976.[cdxliv]

And, of course, this novel of ultimate evil concerned Dick greatly after his 'pink beam' experiences in 1974.

But most of all I recall what I saw when I awakened: I saw God, smiling in the sunlight of day. Once, during the years of the Terrible Separation,[cdxlv] I saw Palmer Eldritch in the Sun -- I saw God backward, but sure enough, in the daytime sun; at high noon, and knew him to be a god. THE 3 STIGMATA if read properly (i.e. reversed) contains many clues as to the nature of God and to our relationship with him. I was motivated to flee, then, fearing what I saw, so vast was the breach then. it was definitely a true vision of God, but grown (to my blind sight) terrible; still, it was the beginning of my seeing: that I could see God at all, in the sun, showed that I was not entirely blind, but rather deranged. My 3-74 experiences are an outgrowth of my Palmer Eldritch experience of over ten years earlier.[cdxlvi]

He sees in THE THREE STIGMATA evidence that this world that we all live in is fake:

The Gnostic message in my writing can be seen when we realise that it is a Gnostic revelation that this world is a *bungled counterfeit* of the celestial world, esp. *time* as a poor counterfeit of eternity. & Palmer Eldritch equals (is) the Gnostic demiurge creator, spinning out evil & false worlds to feed his drive for power. In STIGMATA the evil quality of the creator is expressed, & man (Leo Bulero) pitted against the False evil cosmos & its evil creator -- a *very* acosmic novel...[cdxlvii]

Judith Merrill reviewed THE THREE STIGMATA OF PALMER ELDRITCH for *F & SF* in 1965. Here's what she had to say about the novel:

Philip K. Dick did it better three years ago in THE MAN IN THE HIGH CASTLE.
I don't mean, this time, that his new book is similar in theme or treatment. Rather, that I wish it were more so, at least in characterization and structure.
Phil Dick is, one might say, the best writer s-f has produced, on every third Tuesday. In between times, he ranges wildly from unforgivable carelessness to craftsmanlike high competence. In the case of PALMER ELDRITCH, I would guess he did his thinking on those odd Tuesdays, or rather on *one* of them, and the actual writing in every possible minute before another Good Tuesday came on him. Here is a riotous confusion of ideas, enough for a dozen novels, or one really good one; but the stuff is unsorted, frequently incompleted, seldom even clearly stated. The style is alternately dream-slow-surreal and fast-action pulp. Thematically, he at least approaches, and sometimes stops to consider, virtually every current crucial issue: drug addiction, sexual mores, over-population, the economic structure of society, the nature of religious experience, parapsychology, the evolution of man – you name it, you'll find it.
The book, with all this, is inevitably colorful, provocative and (frustratingly) readable. I wish I thought it possible that Dick might sometime go back to this one, publication not withstanding, and finish writing it.[cdxlviii]

THE THREE STIGMATA OF PALMER ELDRITCH is a novel of alien invasion but an alien invasion unlike any other ever written. Usually, no matter how weird or horrifying a writer may try to make his aliens, their motives and actions can be directly related to human motivations: conquest, *lebensraum*, hatred and fear; but in PALMER ELDRITCH Philip. K. Dick describes an alien presence with an unknown purpose that can only be described as pure evil. On reading the novel there comes a point when one realises that Palmer Eldritch is not human and his – its – motives are completely alien and incomprehensible and one's skin crawls in sympathy with Runcible and his predicament. Even at the end of the novel one cannot be sure that Runcible ever returns to 'reality' after he has taken the drug Chew-Z. And even though no time passes in the real world Runcible's subjective hell goes on forever. THE THREE STIGMATA OF PALMER ELDRITCH is truly a horror story that puts to shame a vast swath of what passes for such today.

Down in the hovels of Mars the hovelists, in fear and loathing, rate the novel with minus ✶ ✶ ✶ ✶ ✶.

DEUS IRAE (Part 1)

The next thing up for Dick in early 1964 was a signed a contract for a novel or, possibly a series of novels, with Doubleday publishers. In a May 1968 letter Dick refers to this contract:

Roger Zelazny & I are going to collaborate on a novel. The basis of it is an outline I did back in 1964 which Doubleday bought. I was never able to actually write the actual damn book, and had Ted White take a look at the outline. He in turn, having decided (I guess) that he couldn't do it either, or didn't want to, gave it to Zelazny, with whom I was already discussing a possible collaboration. I did not remember the outline, however (it's called DEUS IRAE and deals with a future religion).[cdxlix]

And again in 1976:

A novel that Roger Zelazny and I wrote, DEUS IRAE, took twelve years to write. I signed a contract with Doubleday in 1964, and this is 1976, right?[cdl]

According to Andrew M. Butler, the outline was completed by March 27, 1964.[cdli]

In a letter to James Blish in May PKD mentions the outline and having sent it to his agent.[cdlii]

And of the outline itself, Roger Zelazny, Dick's ultimate collaborator on DEUS IRAE, said in a 1978 speech after DEUS IRAE was published:

Some years ago, Phil Dick, who is a very hot writer when he is on top of things, had agreed to write twelve books in a years time -- a book a month. Apparently he delivered 11 of the books. It got to be December, and the book was a thing called DEUS IRAE, for which he'd written an outline, I thought my outlines were pretty good when it came to faking the action and taking the publisher completely, but this was a masterpiece. It was much longer than those I usually manage, but it said less even. It was basically a philosophical essay, quite lovely, and then there were fifty pages of copy. At that point Phil Dick stopped. He was blocked.[cdliii]

I have been unable to confirm that the contract with Doubleday involved the writing of twelve novels in twelve months.

But, after writing this outline for Doubleday in 1964 for a novel with the working title of THE KNEELING, LEGLESS MAN – which would turn into DEUS IRAE, Dick, as he says

144

above, "was never able to actually write the actual damn book" and the outline was set aside for another year. We will look at DEUS IRAE when we arrive at the year 1976 when the actual damn book was published. However, between 1964 and 1976 spurts of activity on this novel occurred and I will mention them as we progress through the years to 1976.[cdliv]

About the same time that he worked on this first outline for DEUS IRAE Dick was working on two other novels simultaneously, these were THE ZAP GUN and THE PENULTIMATE TRUTH.

Evidence for stating that PKD wrote these novels simultaneously comes from PKD himself when he said in his 1968 'Self Portrait'

...Then THE ZAP GUN and THE PENULTIMATE TRUTH, both of which I wrote at the same time.[cdlv]

And is supported by Thomas M. Disch in his 'Afterword' to the Bluejay edition of THE PENULTIMATE TRUTH (reprinted in the Carroll & Graf editions):

According to the records of the Scott Meredith Literary Agency, the outline for THE PENULTIMATE TRUTH was received in March 1964, and the completed manuscript in May.[cdlvi]

And recall that the outline for THE ZAP GUN was written in Nov 1963, sent to the Agency on 5 Dec and the manuscript completed by 15 Apr 1964, then it definitely looks like PKD wrote the two novels at the same time.

As the first of these two novels to be completed was THE ZAP GUN we will take another look at that novel at this time.

THE ZAP GUN (Part 2)

Once THE ZAP GUN was published in Jan 1967 – and presumably Dick had collected the full $1500 due – PKD was disparaging about his novel on a couple of occasions, saying to Sandra Miesel in 1970:

(I sort of hate GALACTIC POT-HEALER, as well as ZAP GUN plus a few more. Wrrgh.)[cdlvii]

And to interviewers Apel & Briggs in 1977:

The intent is not sufficient to guarantee a good result. Some of the worst books I've written -- like THE ZAP GUN-- are books I've labored over...[cdlviii]

When Bluejay Books published their edition of THE ZAP GUN in 1985 a new Afterword by Maxim Jakubowski went so far as to quote PKD as saying:

A lot of them (...) are pot-boilers. Well, they weren't intentionally, they worked out that way. I always write it as well as I can. But sometimes I just don't have the sacred fire to enflame my talent into, you know, a level of genius and what I wind up with is some turkey like ZAP GUN... The first half is totally unreadable, I don't know where or what... I can hardly reconstruct the thinking that underlay the first half of that book. Just totally unintelligible.[cdlix]

In regard to these negative comments by PKD on his books, Paul Williams notes that readers and future scholars should not pay too much attention to Dick's evaluations of his own work; in some interviews he is swayed by the seeming attitude of the interviewers and in others he's just in a strange mood. [cdlx]

As far as THE ZAP GUN goes though he wrote in his 1968 'Self Portrait' that

I enjoyed writing all of them. But I think that if I could only choose a few, which, for example, might escape World War Three, I would choose ... Then THE ZAP GUN and THE PENULTIMATE TRUTH, both of which I wrote at the same time...[cdlxi]

Thus he belays a little bit his other comments.

On reading THE ZAP GUN one finds it amusing and flashy. Lars Powderdry, Wes-Bloc's resident weapons designer in the struggle with Peep-East takes drugs to help him in his work which mostly involves turning weapon designs into toys. That is, until the aliens invade and he is forced in concert with his Peep-East counterpart to design actual real weapons. He fails miserably at this but Earth is saved at the last minute by a disheveled side-character who also sells toys.

I don't think THE ZAP GUN is that bad, in fact I read it occasionally because it's so much fun. I'd give it ★ ★ ★

THE PENULTIMATE TRUTH

As we've noted THE PENULTIMATE TRUTH was written concurrently with THE ZAP GUN in early 1964. It's possible the outline for THE PENULTIMATE TRUTH was written by March 1964 as stated by Thomas M. Disch, and the completed manuscript by May 12,1964. The novel was first published by Belmont Books in paperback form in Sep 1964.[cdlxii]

Disch in his 'Afterword' to the Bluejay edition of THE PENULTIMATE TRUTH goes on to say:

Conceptually it represented the splicing together of two short stories Philip K. Dick had written in the earliest years of his apprenticeship. The first of these, "The Defenders," appeared in the January 1953 issue of *Galaxy*. It duplicates, in miniature, the Nicholas St. James portion of the plot...
{...}
The second source for the novel was published in *If* (August 1955), and its title, "The Mold Of Yancy," was intended, in a slightly emended form, "In The Mold Of Yancy", as the original title of the book...[cdlxiii]

In 1968 Dick himself commented on the connection between "The Mold Of Yancy" and THE PENULTIMATE TRUTH:

I liked this story ("The Mold Of Yancy") enough to use it as the basis for my novel THE PENULTIMATE TRUTH; in particular the part where everything the government tells you is a lie. I still like that part; I mean, I still believe it's so. Watergate, of course, bore the basic idea of this story out. [cdlxiv]

Dick also liked the story. In his 1968 'Self Portrait' when he surveyed some of his novels, he said:

I enjoyed writing all of them. But I think that if I could only choose a few, which for example might escape World War 3, I would choose ... THE PENULTIMATE TRUTH...[cdlxv]

Interestingly enough, THE PENULTIMATE TRUTH was the *penultimate* selection on his list of favorites followed, lastly, by THE SIMULACRA.

Another note of interest, as Disch records in his 'Afterword', is that Dick gave the name of the Agency that controlled the situation in THE PENULTIMATE TRUTH the same address as that of his literary agent, Scott Meredith. This address was then 580 Fifth Avenue, New York City.

Later in an interesting interview with Joe Vitale in 1978, Dick was asked whether visits by the 'Red Squad' (FBI agents) had anything to do with the break-in of his home in 1971. He replied:

I really don't know. In the early 60s I *did* write a novel about a phony war between the United States and Russia that's carried out with the sole purpose of keeping the citizens of those countries underground while the leaders lived in palatial splendour above ground. In the novel, some Americans and some Russians are able to get above ground and find out what's really going on and they become friends.

Now maybe certain people thought this was too close to the truth and that I had some kind of information. Maybe that's why they wanted to get my files. I don't know.[cdlxvi]

That's about it for comments. In Sep 1964 Belmont Books published the first edition of THE PENULTIMATE TRUTH in paperback. The first UK edition followed three years later with the hardback from Cape Publishers in Jun 1967. The novel has English-language editions – many of them – in every decade from the 60s to the end of the century as well as many foreign-language editions.

The plot of THE PENULTIMATE TRUTH is based on the simple premise that things are not quite what they seem in the world. The majority of mankind is repressed and coerced by means both subtle and overt into believing that their condition is a natural and right one. They do not know the truth. Dick, in his typical paranoid way, extrapolates – and I use the word carefully – from this notion a world which explains the falsehood of life under a mendacious government rule. He explains, in effect, the political tactic of 'the big lie': tell the people often and loudly enough what you want them to believe and eventually they will believe it unquestioningly. And even though THE PENULTIMATE TRUTH is not a parable or an analogy, after reading the novel one cannot help but turn a jaundiced eye towards our own system of government.

In the story Dick creates a world where men are forced to live underground and to manufacture robots ('leadies') which they are told will be used to fight an above-ground war but which, in actuality, are used to tend the palatial demesnes of the rich. Once the underground dwellers surface they discover that they have been living a lie but are prevented from returning below to inform their fellows of this truth. Instead, the government, uncharacteristically benign, informs them that it has only been living off the fat of the land for the benefit of the underground 'tankers'. In fact, they've been preparing the surface world for that – not so long off – day when all the underground dwellers can be brought up to a world of peace, harmony and good living...

I wonder that PKD titled the novel THE PENULTIMATE TRUTH; he could have easily titled it THE TRUTH.

Anyway, this novel would rate ✶ ✶ ✶ ✶ down in the 'ant-tanks.'

In June 1964 Dick had another short story published, this was "What The Dead Men Say", and in July he had two more: "A Game Of Unchance" and "Cantata 140". Then in August, "The Little Black Box" appeared and Ace Books published the first paperback edition of THE SIMULACRA. September, of course, saw the first paperback edition of THE PENULTIMATE TRUTH, also from Ace Books. And in October "Precious Artifact" was published for the first time. But the biggest month of the year was undoubtedly November when Ace Books published CLANS OF THE ALPHANE MOON in paperback and Doubleday put out the first edition hardback of THE THREE STIGMATA OF PALMER ELDRITCH.[cdlxvii]

The final PKD publication for 1964 came at the end of the year. This was the December issue of *Fantastic Stories* with "The Unteleported Man" blazoned on the cover.

In other ways, though, things happened to PKD in 1964 that affected his writing. In the summer of the year he took his first trip on LSD with friend Jack Newkom and then others including Ray Nelson. And in July he rolled his girlfriend Grania's Volkswagen and ended up in hospital in a body cast and arm sling. This effectively halted his writing work for two months. However, he was able to attend the 1964 SF Worldcon in Oakland with Grania. But that was about the end of the road for this relationship as Grania Davidson left PKD around Halloween. It was not until October that Dick could turn serious attention to the expansion of "The Unteleported Man."[cdlxviii]

THE UNTELEPORTED MAN

Philip K. Dick's novelette "The Unteleported Man" and subsequent expansion into the novel THE UNTELEPORTED MAN is the most complicated of all PKD's stories from a historical point of view. Like Dr. Bloode's book within the story

There were several editions of the Text. And evidently not all were accurate. Like the range of paraworlds, the texts were mutually exclusive; one replaced the other, supplanted and abolished earlier versions.[cdlxix]

For, see, the UNTELEPORTED MAN itself went through several versions and even today there is no real definitive text. It all started in the summer of 1964 when *Fantastic Stories* commissioned PKD to write "The Unteleported Man". By the end of August Dick had finished the story – a novelette at 32,000 words – and the story wound its way to *Fantastic Stories* where it appeared with full-cover illustration by Lloyd Birmingham in the December issue.

Between the time the novelette manuscript was done (26 Aug 1964) and its publication in December, Don Wollheim at Ace Books requested that the story be expanded. Terry Carr, an editor at Ace at the time, was instrumental in the expansion. In a letter to PKDS Carr expounds on this:

But while I'm writing about what happened sometimes between PKD and ACE, allow me to address the question of the supposedly censored text of THE UNTELEPORTED MAN that Ace published. The story originally appeared in *Fantastic*, December 1964, and when I read it there I thought it was excellent: I gave a copy to senior Ace editor Don Wollheim and urged him to buy it. But it was just 32,000 words, pretty short for a novel, so though Don liked it too he wanted to know if Phil could expand it to book-length. Phil said sure, no problem, and signed a contract to produce an expanded version -- which he did within a few months, and it was given to me to read first.[cdlxx]

Carr probably read the story in early November when the issue of *Fantastic Stories* hit the stands a month ahead of the publication date as usual. As for the expansion, Dick was interested in having his future collaborator Ray Nelson (THE GANYMEDE TAKEOVER) work on it with him. The idea to include Ray Nelson as a collaborator probably occurred in mid-1964 when PKD hosted science fiction writers at his home in Oakland. Among these was Ray Nelson and the group would brainstorm ideas and plots. An idea for a novel to be called *THE WHALEMOUTH COLONY* turned into THE UNTELEPORTED MAN.[cdlxxi]

In a series of letters to Terry and Carol Carr and his agent, Scott Meredith, in late 1964 and early 1965, PKD wrote of THE UNTELEPORTED MAN expansion. First to the Carr's in November:

What would (again I'm asking off the cuff) Ace's reaction be? For instance, in the expansion of THE UNTELEPORTED MAN, what if Ray was brought in? And his name -- despite the contract being in my name only -- appeared with mine? (this would not apply to CANTATA 140, which is written already.) After all, I am dividing, as in the case of THE UNTELEPORTED MAN, the sum with someone else, cutting my earnings in half; obviously I must believe in Ray's intrinsic contribution to the piece, since as you know; I write fast, and escalating the piece from 20 thousand to 50 thousand would be easy for me... but would it be as good if Ray worked on it too? {...}

Let's put it this way. Ace let the contract for THE UNTELEPORTED MAN to me, and if they want only my byline on it, etc., naturally they are entitled, legally and morally, to that; no question there. I'm just arguing that it would be to their advantage to have both bylines. And both of us at work on the piece. Ray sees so many things that I don't; I picked him because of a comment he sent in to *Fantastic* about a short story of mine; I knew at once that I had hold of someone who "fused" with my mind -- and then some. For instance, I have let him read the gallies of the *Fantastic* novelette THE UNTELEPORTED MAN, and he has already made several terrific suggestions -- informally -- as to how best it could be made into 50,000 words -- and his basic suggestion would never have occurred to me. I can tell you this, for what its worth: doing it along Ray's suggestion, there would not be a mere padding of the magazine novelette, no overwriting which really added nothing to the 20,000 piece; the additional 25,000 words would be new, original, and in my mind beyond dispute exceptionally good. (I don't mean that Ray would write the needed 25,000 additional words; I mean that he would, in plot sessions, mostly orally done, would interact with me -- you know; what they call brainstorming. Then each of us, using the notes he had made, or perhaps a tape of the session or sessions, would repair to his study and conscientiously do an outline of the 25,000 word additional material. Then we would go over carbons of each other's outline and, from the two, find the best part and finalize on *one* joint outline; then this would be written, with me doing the final, so that style, pace, etc., would coincide with the already written 20,000 words. Now, who is being gypped by this? Ace? Hardly As I say, it's me that pays out the money to Ray, not them. {...}

So, please, Terry, old U-No bar comrade, answer me informally, in confidence (like the confessional) which I ought to do:

(1) Expand THE UNTELEPORTED MAN solo.

(2) Expand it in collaboration with Ray, but under my byline, and give him no credit (though he deserves it, and will let it be known anyhow, as I said before; and I see lots of trouble there)

(3) Expand it in open collaboration with Ace's official approval, in that I would serve formal notification to Don, via Scott, etc. {...}{...}[cdlxxii]

Philip Dick, then, was thinking about the expansion in Nov 1964 and was still working on it in Jan 1965. Whether Ace later approved of a collaboration with Ray Nelson is not known but Nelson was in at the start of things as we've seen. However, Dick was certainly writing the expansion in Jan 1965:

After New Year's I went back to the expansion of THE UNTELEPORTED MAN and so, except for my relationship with Nancy, there isn't much action in progress, here in East Gakville ... except of course for the Mormon Temple turning on and off all night. {...} Anyhow, it seems almost certain that she and I will be leaving here, probably for the East Coast, most likely as soon as I finish the work on THE UNTELEPORTED MAN for Ace.[cdlxxiii]

Nancy here refers to Dick's girlfriend, Nancy Hackett whom he had fallen in love with by Dec 1964 after Grania had left him and who would become his fourth wife in July 1966.

As for the nature of the expansion itself we must return to Terry Carr's explanatory letter to *PKDS* in 1985:

I discovered that what Phil had done was break into the narrative at its crucial point by having someone shoot the narrator with what amounted to an LSD dart, and then he spent 25,000 or 30,000 words telling us about the "acid trip" the protagonist had, after which Phil returned to the original text which had wrapped up the story. The material Phil wrote in the "acid trip" section had nothing to do with anything (it was a great description of an acid trip but honestly, all of it was quite irrelevant to the story), so I told Don that I thought Phil had "expanded" the story by adding a bunch of irrelevant bullshit. Don then read the ms., and he agreed with me, so he made an arrangement with Phil whereby Ace would publish only the original novella as half of an Ace Double, though as I recall Phil got paid as much money as he would have if he'd expanded his novella to a novel that Ace would have published with pride. [cdlxxiv]

Perhaps this 'acid-effect' was the result of PKD's taking LSD for the first time that summer of 1964. Evidently Don Wollheim must've contacted Dick or his agent and commented negatively on Dick's expanded THE UNTELEPORTED MAN when he read it before May 1965 as PKD wrote an injured letter to Scott Meredith at that time:

Don's reaction to the expanded UNTELEPORTED MAN must have been as great a surprise to you as to me, in view of your earlier remark to me that I had nothing to fear; in fact, "that my fears were unfounded," a rather ironic statement in that my fears were justified. {...}
{...} And it has been some time since I was capable of turning space opera out; THE UNTELEPORTED MAN, in its original form in *Fantastic*, was just about it; the end of the line for me in that direction. However, when I went to expand it for Ace, I did not pad it -- a suggestion which is, at best, an insult as to my integrity -- but to transform it from what was actually not a novel at all but a long story into a true novel -- which I did. And the "far-out" elements which I added, which were not there in the original, i.e., all which Don objects to, were necessary if the piece became a true novel and not merely a longer story. There is a real irony here, too, because a much better case could be made against my additions than the one Don chose to make; fundamentally, the additions follow the lines laid down in my Ace novel THE GAME PLAYERS OF TITAN, which Don nominated for the Hugo.
I wish, too, to complain of something else: Don's tying in the purchase of my story collection with the completion of the contract for THE UNTELEPORTED MAN. This is a club held over my head, entirely unnecessary, since I frankly worked my goddam ass off over the expansion -- as everyone who knows me is aware of. If Don sees fit, in view of his

rejection of the completed -- and to my mind satisfactory -- UNTELEPORTED MAN, to reject the story collection as further punishment, then I will insist that the Agency take note of this violation of what Rick Prindle called a "quasi-contract", by that meaning that Ace's statement that they wished to buy a story collection of mine did in no way originally hang on the purchase of THE UNTELEPORTED MAN as a separate expansion; nor, in fact, did such a separate expansion even exist. What has happened here is that by failing to satisfy Don on THE UNTELEPORTED MAN I may find myself facing the loss of other sales *which have absolutely no connection with it.* In professions other than fiction writing a good strong union generally can take care of fink tactics like this; unfortunately we s-f writers do not have a union {...}[cdlxxv]

The collection Dick refers to in this letter is probably THE PRESERVING MACHINE which Ace Books published in 1969 and which Terry Carr (probably having read Dick's complaining letter about Don Wollheim) was instrumental in publishing.

For the last word on the expansion we return to Terry Carr and his 1985 letter to PKDS:

THE UNTELEPORTED MAN has recently been published in its "full" version, each time with Introductions that castigated the Ace editors for "censoring" the longer text that included Phil's cop-out insertion. I will agree that the irrelevant material Phil added was enjoyable, but I still claim it shouldn't have been there: it's worth reading now solely because Phil wrote it. So what if it showed Phil, uncharacteristically, as essentially a hack writer? PKD had had enough of that characterization by then, and he was beginning to write the novels -- some dreadful, some adventurous and wonderful -- that established and confirmed his reputation.[cdlxxvi]

And there THE UNTELEPORTED MAN lies for the next 22 years, until January 1979 when Russ Galen at Berkley Books purchased THE COSMIC PUPPETS together with DR. FUTURITY and THE UNTELEPORTED MAN as part of a package deal that paid Dick $14,000.[cdlxxvii]

Now we must look at the different editions of THE UNTELEPORTED MAN for, like Dr. Bloode's text, they are all different.

First is the original novelette, "The Unteleported Man" written by Dick in 1964 and published in *Fantastic Stories* in December of that year. This first version was expanded by Dick in early 1965 but the expansion was rejected by Ace Books and the story was published in its original version as one half of an Ace Double in Nov 1966.[cdlxxviii]

In England, Sidgwick & Jackson included the original text in A PHILIP K. DICK OMNIBUS in 1970.[cdlxxix]

Then in 1972 Ace paired THE UNTELEPORTED MAN with DR. FUTURITY and issued them together as an Ace Double. Next, in England, Methuen brought out a paperback edition in 1976 followed by Magnum in 1979. These editions all consisted of the original novelette text.

The big change came in 1983 with the Berkley Books paperback edition. As just noted, Russ Galen had acquired the rights to THE UNTELEPORTED MAN in 1979 and, for whatever reason, thought to include the expansion text rejected by Don Wollheim in 1965. But... there was a slight problem with this. Some of the pages in the expansion section had been lost in the meantime. So Berkley published the novel with three gaps indicated in the text and on the front cover they splashed the blurb: 'The World Famous Classic Now Uncensored For The First Time!' and below that 'With The Author's Previously Unpublished Original Ending.' No doubt this was what upset Terry Carr as he was one of PKD's editors castigated in the Berkley edition.

When Gollancz publishers in England picked up the novel and published their edition in 1984, they retitled the novel LIES, INC. and once again the text was changed. Apparently PKD had revised the text in 1979 but these changes were not discovered until after the Berkley edition was published in 1983. So Gollancz incorporated these 1979 changes in the rejected expansion text into their edition of LIES, INC. What Dick's revision amounted to was elimination of the third gap. So in the Gollancz edition of LIES, INC. the third gap is eliminated by PKD's changes but the first two gaps (which at this time were still there) were smoothed over by science fiction writer John Sladek who was asked by Gollancz to write some short bridging material. This is indicated in the Introduction.[cdlxxx]

The 1985 paperback edition of LIES, INC. from Granada in the United Kingdom duplicates the Gollancz text.

But, and as if that wasn't enough, after all these editions were published Paul Williams, executor of PKD's estate, found the missing pages of Dick's expansion text and published them in *The Philip K. Dick Society Newsletter* in 1985. But, so far though, no publisher has yet reincorporated these missing pages into either the 1983 Berkley text or the 1984 Gollancz text[cdlxxxi]

With all this confusion one can only sympathize with serious PKD collectors trying to determine which of THE UNTELEPORTED MAN texts is definitive, hence most valuable. Here one describes the situation:

The really collectable items are seldom the true first editions, and that the first editions themselves may not necessarily be the only first edition. Take the case of "The Unteleported Man", for instance, which was first published in book form by Ace Books as part of an Ace Double in 1966, and reprinted in Britain by Methuen ten years later. Neither of these were the full version since the second half of the book, amounting to some 30,000 words, had been omitted due to space restrictions. The first printing of the complete issue was issued under the original title by Berkeley Books as a paperback in 1983, but even this edition was full of printing errors and there was no attempt to bridge the gaps left by missing pages in the manuscript. Gollancz eventually published the only really complete and definitive edition in 1984, the only version to be published in hardback, with a new title, "Lies, Inc.". Ironically, this edition was eventually remaindered. So which is the real first edition, and which version will ultimately prove to be the most collectable?[cdlxxxii]

Thus Kruse Demon reiterates what we've expressed above. But this still leaves us with the question, which is the definitive text for THE UNTELEPORTED MAN?

Well, from our research there is no one definitive text. The closest we can come is to combine the 1983 Berkley text with the missing pages published in 1985 in the eighth issue of the *PKDS Newsletter*. But that combination doesn't cover the discovery of the revisions made by PKD in 1979 and which are incorporated into the 1984 Gollancz edition of LIES, INC. So, really, for a comprehensive reading of THE UNTELEPORTED MAN, one would have to have both the Berkley and Gollancz editions as well as *PKDSN#8* to hand and flip back and forth at the appropriate times...

This novel is certainly indeterminate and I'm not even sure if I've got it right. But the story, in its two parts, is a good one. Here's a brief description courtesy of Lawrence Sutin:

A fascistic megacorporation lures colonists to a mysterious far-off planet named Whales' Mouth through a one-way-only teleportation system. Protagonist Rachmael ben Applebaum decides to investigate by illicitly commandeering an interstellar spaceship. After numerous twisted drug trips, Rachmael alerts Earth to the Nazi-like terrors on Whale's Mouth.[cdlxxxiii]

This is a personal favorite of mine and in the fan poll run in *For Dickheads Only* I selected it as my #1 fave:

I know you all'll think I'm being contrary by picking THE UNTELEPORTED MAN as my #1 Fave of all PKD novels. But it's not so. I've thought a lot about it and I love this book. First because it has the funniest opening of any of his novels with Rachmael Ben Applebaum being hounded by the creditor-jet balloon. And the story really grips you. What the hell is going on at Whale's Mouth? And the sub-plots all work in perfectly. Then, at the end -- which is what a lot of fans have bitched about -- you have that great bit where reality breaks down and the worst thing that could happen is that any two of the characters can agree on it![cdlxxxiv]

And with that I give THE UNTELEPORTED MAN in its longer versions ★ ★ ★ ★ ★

One last note for 1964. Late in the year Dick wrote an essay for Terry Carr titled "Drugs, Hallucinations, and the Quest for Reality." It was published in Carr's fanzine *Lighthouse* #11, in November 1964. This essay takes a look at mental illness as it has been described from Freud through Jung and on to modern ideas. As it was written around the time that PKD wrote CLANS OF THE ALPHANE MOON this essay can be taken as showing some of Dick's thoughts as he composed that novel.[cdlxxxv]

1965

January 1965 saw publication of the SFBC edition of THE THREE STIGMATA OF PALMER ELDRITCH and the short story "Retreat Syndrome". In February the first paperback edition of TIME OUT OF JOINT came out from Belmont. Then in June paperback originals of DR. BLOODMONEY and THE CRACK IN SPACE were published by Ace. Finally in November THE ZAP GUN began serialization in *Worlds Of Tomorrow* as "Project Plowshare".

DEUS IRAE (Part 2)

One thing about THE UNTELEPORTED MAN we can pin down is its status as the last novel PKD worked on in 1964. And he worked on it into 1965. But other than that the calendar for 1965 is surprisingly blank. But likely sometime during the year PKD sent off some sample pages for DEUS IRAE to Ted White to have him finish that manuscript for him. White notes:

In 1965 or 1966 he had given me the first 50 pages and the synoptic essay for DEUS IRAE and asked me to finish it for him. In other words, this was a man who professed admiration and respect for me and wanted me to collaborate with him.[cdlxxxvi]

Dick also refers to this:

One other item of interest. Roger Zelazny & I are going to collaborate on a novel. The basis of it is an outline I did back in 1964 which Doubleday bought. I was never able to actually write the actual damn book, and had Ted White take a look at the outline. He in turn, having decided (I guess) that he couldn't do it either, or didn't want to, gave it to Zelazny, with whom I was already discussing a possible collaboration. I did not remember the outline, however (it's called DEUS IRAE and deals with a future religion). But when Zelazny wrote to say he had possession of the outline and LIKED IT, I went mad with joy. You see, I think very highly of his work and evidently he thinks the same about mine. {...}[cdlxxxvii]

So, DEUS IRAE wends its slow way towards completion in 1976.

But, at least, we can now take a breather as Dick worked on only four major things in 1965. These were the essay "Schizophrenia and the Book of Changes" written early that year and first published in *Niekas* in March.[cdlxxxviii] Then the short story "Your Appointment Will Be Yesterday" which he expanded into the novel COUNTER-CLOCK WORLD begun late in the year. Possibly, too, he continued his collaboration with Ray Nelson that would end up being THE GANYMEDE TAKEOVER. And, of course, he was still worrying over the expansion of THE UNTELEPORTED MAN into the summer months.[cdlxxxix]

In the short, casual essay "Schizophrenia and the Book of Changes" PKD writes of the onset of schizophrenia as due to the wider world of reality (the *Koinos Kosmos*) breaking in and taking over the *Idios Kosmos* of young people as they reach maturity. As PKD writes:

What distinguishes schizophrenic existence from that which the rest of us like to imagine we enjoy is the element of time. The schizophrenic is having it all *now*, whether he wants it or not; the whole can of film has descended on him, whereas we watch it progress frame by frame. So for him, causality does not exist. Instead, the acausal connective principle that Wolfgang Pauli called synchronicity is operating in all situations – not merely as only one factor at work, as with us. Like a person under LSD, the schizophrenic is engulfed in an endless now. It's not too much fun.[cdxc]

The *I Ching* comes into it since it is based on synchronicity -- events occurring outside of time -- and by its use synchronicity can be dealt with. The *I Ching* then is a useful tool for schizophrenics, helping them cope with reality. Dick suggests using the *I Ching* sparingly and only for the big questions like 'Should I marry this girl?' But above all, he cautions, don't, like him, become dependent on it.

"Your Appointment Will Be Yesterday" is another of PKD's short stories that not much has been written about. The manuscript arrived at the SMLA on Aug 27, 1965 and the story was first published in *Amazing Stories* in Aug 1966 where it was the feature story. Later in 1965 PKD would expand this story into the novel COUNTER-CLOCK WORLD.

The story was never reprinted until THE COLLECTED STORIES in 1987.

As in COUNTER-CLOCK WORLD, the Hobart Phase – a reversal of time – causes things to run backwards. People rise from the grave, food is thrown up to uncongeal on plates and eventually return to the earth. A government agency has the impossible task of 'uninventing' things so history has no loose ends as it progresses backwards. The problem is that the 'swabble' must be uninvented but as the time nears for the inventor's first manuscript to be destroyed the world is thrown into an infinite regression and its destruction cannot be accomplished without also destroying the Hobart Phase. This plot device is similar to PKD's handling of Zeno's paradox in "The Indefatigable Frog."

The character 'Bard Chai' from PKD's 1953 short story "The Turning Wheel" makes a reappearance here but although he is still of the Bard class the setting of the story is completely different in "Your Appointment Will Be Yesterday."

An interesting but awkwardly handled plot means that "Your Appointment Will Be Yesterday" gets only ★★★.

COUNTER-CLOCK WORLD

Information on the genesis of COUNTER-CLOCK WORLD is sketchy. The novel is based on PKD's short story "Your Appointment Will Be Yesterday". Originally the novel manuscript was titled THE DEAD GROW YOUNG and/or THE DEAD ARE YOUNG. Lawrence Sutin says that the novel was written in 1965. But he is the only source for this that I can find.[cdxci]

The novel was first published by Berkley Books as a paperback original in Feb 1967. A UK edition from Sphere Books followed in 1968. It has seen many editions both in the English language and in other languages. Perhaps the most valuable edition for collectors is not the paperback from Berkley but the first hardback from White Lion Press in England which came out in 1977.[cdxcii]

Philip Dick in a 1967 letter comments on the Berkley edition:

Meanwhile, my writing career creaks on. My Berkley book, COUNTERCLOCK WORLD, just came out, with a very nice cover -- which shows a girl who looks exactly like Nancy. What is more, the girl in the story, Lotta, is based on Nancy. I keep wondering if by any chance Terry and/or Carol Carr gave Damon Knight (the editor at Berkley Books) a picture of Nancy (they have several which I sent them). Otherwise it must be chalked up to psi, I suppose.[cdxciii]

Sutin notes that other characters in the novel are also based on real people: Anne McGuire on PKD's third wife Anne, and the Anarch Peak on Bishop James A. Pike who would also figure in PKD's last novel THE TRANSMIGRATION OF TIMOTHY ARCHER.[cdxciv]

Unfortunately Dick had little occasion to comment on this novel. He mentions it while discussing foreign editions of his books:

It wasn't until 1964, when Editions Opta of Paris approached me with the extraordinary proposition that they would publish every novel that I had written. They have a fancy bookclub edition that they put out, and for this they got a picture of me for the back cover, and an article about me by John Brunner. They sent me a copy of the first book -- THE MAN IN THE HIGH CASTLE and COUNTERCLOCK WORLD -- and they had a complete bibliography of my stuff. They had everything and it was beautiful. In comparison to, like ACE books...[cdxcv]

And, as might be expected, COUNTER-CLOCK WORLD with its backwards time or retrograde time figures minimally in PKD's *EXEGESIS*:

Time is about to end (lineal time) as a factor of life; it won't reverse, as in COUNTERCLOCK WORLD, but our present will dissolve as all the accretions of the last 3500 years will vanish, as if dreamlike. They never took place...[cdxcvi]

That is all we can find comments-wise by Dick himself. The novel has been reviewed and commented upon by many others (mostly negatively) and is not highly rated by fans and critics.

We will now take a quick look at the plot.

As in "Your Appointment Will Be Yesterday" time is flowing backwards due to the Hobart Phase. The protagonist, Sebastian Hermes is the proprietor of The Flask of Hermes Vitarium, which helps the newly risen dead get back on their feet again as they progress towards their youth and eventual oblivion in their mother's wombs. Sebastian knows the location of the grave of the Anarch Peak, a famous black religious leader who is about to be reborn. The Anarch Peak is a controversial figure and many people wish to see him dead for good. Peak is eventually captured and after machinations and murders he contacts Sebastian telepathically and declares himself the Redeemer.

A nice try at handling a difficult plot, COUNTER-CLOCK WORLD rates ✶ ✶ ✶.

THE GANYMEDE TAKEOVER

This novel was slow in development and dates to the summer of 1964. When Philip K. Dick lived in Oakland he was part of a circle of science fiction writers and their families. While sitting around partying they'd toss around ideas. Ray Nelson, Dick's collaborator on the novel, recalls the good old days:

> In the dream I remembered the brainstorming sessions I had had with Phil and the many other members of the San Francisco Bay Area science fiction community on those long lazy Sunday afternoons in East Oakland. Three outlines for novels had been developed during these sessions during which everyone threw ideas into the common pool, and I had gone home to put the resulting chaos into some sort of order. Only the first, THE GANYMEDE TAKEOVER, was actually written and published.[cdxcvii]

Nelson goes on to talk about how the book was written:

> The fact is, we wanted to write RING OF FIRE, but we had to write something, so we wrote TAKEOVER
> Since we were "only practicing" for "the big one", we wrote the book we did in a spirit of almost hysterical hilarity, enclosing weird newspaper clippings and Beatle bubblegum cards in the installments of the ongoing story we mailed back and forth. When we met --first at his place in East Oakland and later at his other place in Marin County near the water, we often spent more time smoking grass, dropping acid and flirting with each others' wives than working. Not for nothing is TAKEOVER dedicated to both Kirsten and Nancy. Joan Hiashi is a composite in many ways of these two remarkable women, and many of the concepts and plot twists were contributed by them in the nonstop brainstorming that always formed a part of our relationship. We never actually "swapped wives" or "swung", yet the emotional involvement of this foursome went far beyond what normally passes for friendship between two married couples.[cdxcviii]

This fragment of conversation from Ray Nelson helps us date the genesis of THE GANYMEDE TAKEOVER (as well as THE UNTELEPORTED MAN) to between mid 1964 and late 1965 when Phil and Nancy moved to San Rafael, California.[cdxcix]

There is some confusion as to the original title that the two authors gave to the story – for once not occasioned by PKD himself. In a letter to his agent, Scott Meredith, in 1968, PKD wrote:

I am very anxious to get back from Ace the outline for THE STONES REJECTED (retitled by Ace, THE GANYMEDE TAKEOVER). Could you get the outline for me? [d]

But responding via *PKDS* to Ray Nelson's remarks in Apel & Briggs' *THE DREAM CONNECTION*, Terry Carr wrote:

Ray's mentioning that THE GANYMEDE TAKEOVER was originally titled THE EARTH'S DIURNAL COURSE is a bit confusing to me. Probably Ray is right in saying so -- though the title would have been IN EARTH'S DIURNAL COURSE, a line from a Romantic poet, well-known, but I forget which one. The apparent fact that Phil's and Ray's THE GANYMEDE TAKEOVER originally had this title, till Scott Meredith changed it, surprises me because Phil had earlier put that title on some other novel published by Ace Books and it was Don Wollheim who changed it -- I think it was DR. BLOODMONEY, OR HOW WE GOT ALONG AFTER THE BOMB, though I can't swear to that. (90% chance I'm right, no more). Since DR. BLOODMONEY was published in 1965 and THE GANYMEDE TAKEOVER in 1967, its quite possible that after Don Wollheim had changed that title once, Scott Meredith may have felt it would be fruitless to submit another even partly PKD novel to Don under the original title.[di]

And with that covered we find that there is no more information worth noting about THE GANYMEDE TAKEOVER.

The novel was published by Ace Books under their title of THE GANYMEDE TAKEOVER in June 1967. The first UK edition did not appear until 1971. Of all editions the British hardcover from Severn House in 1988 seems to be the most valuable for collectors.[dii]

Earth is occupied by telepathic slug-like Ganymedeans who with the help of their terran stooges attempt to consolidate their power. But in Tennessee the black guerilla leader, Percy X, and his cohorts still fight on employing a variety of horrific weapons. But Percy's distrust of his white allies leads to complications.

THE GANYMEDE TAKEOVER is worth ✳ ✳ ✳

Philip K. Dick wrote several more short stories in late 1965 and into 1966. After completing "Your Appointment Will Be Yesterday" in August the next two stories reached the SMLA on the same day: "We Can Remember It For You Wholesale" and "Holy Quarrel." These stories arrived on Sep 13, 1965.

"We Can Remember It For You Wholesale" was first published in *F & SF* in Apr 1966. It reappeared in the 30th anniversary issue of *F & SF* in Oct 1979. This story has been anthologized many times – it may be the most popular story of all of them in this respect. But, although it was selected for *NEBULA AWARD STORIES 1967* by Brian Aldiss and Harry Harrison, and also in *WORLD'S BEST SCIENCE FICTION 1967* by Don Wollheim and Terry Carr, the story was never selected for one of PKD's own collections until publication of THE COLLECTED STORIES in 1987. It's most recent appearance was in *Rosebud Magazine* in 2002.

In 1990 the story formed the basis of the Hollywood movie, TOTAL RECALL, starring Arnold Schwarznegger and Sharon Stone.

The movie pretty much recapitulates the story with Doug Quail purchasing a 'memory' of a life as a secret agent on Mars. Turns out, though, that he really was a secret agent on Mars and is now the key to stopping an alien invasion.

"We Can Remember It For You Wholesale" rates ✳ ✳ ✳

As just noted, the manuscript for "Holy Quarrel" arrived at the SMLA on Sep 13, 1965. In May 1966 the story was published in *Worlds Of Tomorrow*. It was never anthologized or collected until publication of the fifth volume of THE COLLECTED STORIES OF PHILIP K. DICK in 1987.

Paul Williams, executor of the Philip K. Dick Estate and publisher of *The Philip K. Dick Society Newsletter*, sees the story as "one of those fascinating mid-1960s PKD stories that seem to be trial balloons -- I'll start writing this and see if there's enough going on for it to become a novel..."[diii]

In his bibliography Levack includes a good description of "Holy Quarrel":

The Genux-B computer has declared a state of red alert and plans to obliterate Northern California. Frantic repairmen learn only that the computer wishes to destroy one Herb Sousa and his chain of gum-ball machines. Genux-B believes the gum-balls are alive and that Herb Sousa is the devil incarnate.[div]

"Holy Quarrel" is an amusing story with humans trying to reason with a computer like in Stanley Kubrick's movie *2001: A Space Odyssey* and the more obscure movie *Dark Star*. I waver on this one but think it deserves ✳ ✳ ✳ ✳ ✳.

A week after the previous two stories were sent off the next one, "Not By Its Cover" arrived at the SMLA on Sep21, 1965. The story was first published in *Famous Science Fiction* in the Summer of 1968 and it was collected in Berkley's 1980 PKD collection THE GOLDEN MAN. After an obligatory appearance in THE COLLECTED STORIES in 1987, Peter Haining chose "Not By Its Cover" for his 1997 anthology, *WIZARDS OF ODD*, reprinted in 1999.

In his GOLDEN MAN notes PKD wrote this of the story:

Here I presented what used to be a wish on my part that the Bible was true. Obviously, I was at a sort of halfway point between doubt and faith. Years later I'm still in that position; I'd *like* the Bible to be true, but -- well, maybe if it isn't we can make it so. But, alas, it's going to take plenty of work to do it.[dv]

In this story wubs make a reappearance; or at least their skins. A publisher produces an expensive edition of Lucretius' *De Rerum Natura* bound in Martian wub-fur. But once the book hits the market experts start to complain that the text is not true to the original and on examination the publisher discovers that the Wub-fur bound editions have been subtly changed to a text that teaches a message diametrically opposed to that of the original. Instead of promoting a philosophy of resignation to mortality the book now propounds one of immortality. The publisher finds that all its editions bound in Wub-fur indicate the same philosophy. What's going on? Is it a property of the Wub-fur itself, which never dies? In the end the publisher finds another use for the mysterious Wub-fur.

An imaginative story that is perhaps not fully thought out, "Not By Its Cover" rates ✳ ✳ ✳.

The last short story to reach the SMLA in 1965 was "Return Match" which was received at the SMLA on Oct 14, 1965. It was first published in *Galaxy* in Feb 1967 and was selected by editor Mark Hurst for his 1980 PKD collection THE GOLDEN MAN.

In the Story Notes to THE GOLDEN MAN, PKD says this about "Return Match":

> The theme of dangerous toys runs like a tattered thread throughout my writing. The dangerous disguised as the innocent...and what could be more innocent than a toy? This story makes me think of a set of huge speakers I looked at last week; they cost six thousand dollars and were larger than refrigerators. Our joke about them was that if you didn't go to the audio store to see them, they'd come to see *you*.[dvi]

An engaging story, "Return Match" tells of illegal outspacer gambling operations on Earth. The fly-by-night casino operators land in remote locations and when they are discovered by the police they quickly disappear into space as their rockets burn up all the evidence, including all the people unlucky enough to be gambling at the time. Through much effort officer Joe Tinbane (reprising his role to some degree from COUNTER-CLOCK WORLD) and his police cohorts manage to salvage one of the outspacer gaming machines: a pinball machine, in fact.

But this is no ordinary pinball machine and once Tinbane plays it he discovers to his consternation that while he is trying to beat the machine the machine is trying to beat him! The stakes are life and death for Tinbane as the machine is encephalotropic and has his brain-pattern in its circuitry. Is he doomed or can he beat the alien machine in the return match?

Having spent much of my misspent youth plying the silver balls (and an acknowledged pinball wizard at the time) I must say that this story struck a responsive chord in me and therefore I give "Return Match" ✳ ✳ ✳ ✳ ✳.

So with the year 1965 behind us – a successful one for Dick with four novels published in the U.S., one serialization begun and one short story published – we turn to 1966, another good year.

1966

The year begins with publication of the second part of "Project Plowshare" in *Worlds Of Tomorrow* in January and the first paperback edition of THE CRACK IN SPACE from Ace in February. April saw "We Can Remember It For You Wholesale" for sale and in May "Holy Quarrel" saw its first printing. Also in May the first edition hardcover of NOW WAIT FOR LAST YEAR came out from Doubleday. To finish of the year for publications, August had "Your Appointment Will Be Yesterday" and in November THE UNTELEPORTED MAN came out as half of an Ace Double backed with *THE MIND MONSTERS* by Howard Cory.

While puttering around, perhaps swapping correspondence with Ray Nelson on THE GANYMEDE TAKEOVER, Dick started the year with a short story. This was "Faith Of Our Fathers."

"Faith Of Our Fathers"

"Faith Of Our Fathers" was the result of Harlan Ellison's one-man crusade to inject some life into the, as he thought, moribund science fiction scene in the 1960s. Championing a 'New Wave' in sf Ellison after great effort edited a collection of short stories and novelettes from the cream of science fictiondom. Established writers and up-and-comers were solicited for their most dangerous visions in story form. Philip K. Dick was one of these approached by Ellison.

The manuscript for "Faith Of Our Fathers" reached the SMLA on Jan 17, 1966. It was first published in Harlan Ellison's *DANGEROUS VISIONS* in 1967 from Doubleday via their Science Fiction Book Club. Lawrence Ashmead was Doubleday's supervising editor on this one. In 1969 *DANGEROUS VISIONS* was published by Berkley in paperback. "Faith Of Our Fathers" was selected for the PKD collection, THE BEST OF PHILIP K. DICK in 1977. It has also been occasionally anthologized.

Ellison's hype of his 'dangerous visions' included drug-influenced writing; anything to project a sense of danger into his anthology. PKD went along with this at first acceding, at least on paper, to Ellison's request that he write something under the influence of LSD. Whether PKD actually did so or not is still under debate. Nevertheless, after the contretemps described below PKD attempted to annul the *DANGEROUS VISIONS* perception by modifying his Afterword to the story. This new Afterword appeared in all editions of *DANGEROUS VISIONS* from 1975 onwards.[dvii]

Let's look at the controversy.

In his introduction to "Faith Of Our Fathers" in *DANGEROUS VISIONS* (1967) Ellison writes of Dick:

I asked for Phil Dick and got him. A story to be written about, and under the influence of (if possible), LSD. What follows, like his excellent offbeat novel THE THREE STIGMATA OF PALMER ELDRITCH, is the result of such a hallucinogenic journey.
{...}
My theory, developed over years of seeing people deluding themselves for the bounce they got, was that the creative process is at its most lively when it merges clean and unfogged from whatever wells exist within the minds of the creators. Philip K. Dick puts the lie to that theory.

His experiments with LSD and other hallucinogens, plus stimulants of the amphetamine class, have borne such fruit as the story you are about to read, in every way a "dangerous" vision.
{...}
He is with us today in his capacity of shaker-upper of theories. And if he doesn't nibble away at your sense of "reality" just a little bit in "Faith Of Our Fathers," check your pulse. You may be dead. [dviii]

Naturally, after *DANGEROUS VISIONS* was published in 1967, PKD gained the reputation as an 'acid' writer. It took many years of questions and interviews to dispel this notion. Here's one such:

VERTEX: Isn't "Faith of Our Father's," from Harlan Ellison's *DANGEROUS VISIONS*, supposed to have been inspired by or written under the influence of acid?
DICK: That really is not true. First of all, you can't write anything when you're on acid. I did one page once while on an acid trip, but it was in Latin. Whole damn thing was in Latin and a little tiny bit in Sanskrit, and there's not much market for that. The page does not fall in with my published work. The other book which suggests it might have been written with acid is MARTIAN TIME-SLIP. That too was written before I had taken any acid.
VERTEX: How much acid did you take anyway?
DICK: Not that much. I wasn't getting up in the morning and dropping acid. I'm amazed when I read the things I used to say about it on the blurbs of my books. I wrote this myself: "He has been experimenting with hallucinogenic drugs to find the unchanging

reality beneath our delusions." And now I say, "Good Christ!" All I ever found out about acid was that I was where I wanted to get out of fast. It didn't seem more real than anything else; it just seemed more awful.[dix]

Of the story Philip K. Dick wrote:

The title is that of an old hymn. I think, with this story, I managed to offend everybody, which seemed at the time to be a good idea, but which I've regretted since. Communism, drugs, sex, God -- I put it all together, and it's been my impression since that when the roof fell in on me years later, this story was in some eerie way involved.[dx]

And in his first Afterword to the story in *DANGEROUS VISIONS* he expounds further on the ideas in his story:

I don't advocate any of the ideas in "Faith Of Our Fathers"; I don't, for example, claim that the Iron Curtain countries will win the cold war – or morally ought to. One theme in the story, however, seems compelling to me, in view of recent experiments with hallucinogenic drugs: the theological experience, which so many who have taken LSD have reported. This appears to me to be a true new frontier; to a certain extent the religious experience can now be scientifically studied … and, what is more, may be viewed as part hallucination but containing other, real components. God, as a topic in science fiction, when it appeared at all, used to be treated polemically, as in *"Out Of The Silent Planet."* But I prefer to treat it as intellectually exciting. What if, through psychedelic drugs, the religious experience becomes commonplace in the life of intellectuals? The old atheism, which seemed to many of us – including me – valid in terms of our experiences, or rather lack of experiences, would have to step momentarily aside. Science fiction, always probing what is about to be thought, become, must eventually tackle without preconceptions a future neo-mystical society in which theology constitutes a major force as in the medieval period. This is not necessarily a backward step, because now these beliefs can be tested – forced to put up or shut up. I, myself, have no real beliefs about God; only my experience that He is present … subjectively, of course; but the inner realm is real too. And in a science fiction story one projects what has been a personal inner experience into a milieu; it becomes socially shared, hence discussible. The last word, however, on the subject of God may have already been said: in AD 840 by John Scotus Erigena at the court of the Frankish king Charles the Bald. "We do not know what God is. God himself does not know what He is because He is not anything. Literally God *is not*, because He transcends being." Such a penetrating – and Zen – mystical view, arrived at so long ago, will be hard to top; in my own experiences with psychedelic drugs I have had precious tiny illumination compared with Erigena. [dxi]

To this Afterword PKD wished to add the following:

In his Introduction to "Faith of Our Fathers" Harlan gives the misleading impression that my story was written under the influence of LSD. This is not so. About all a person can write while on LSD, I have found, is his own short and involuntary obituary. What *did* influence this story was my desire to produce the most frightening vision I could imagine. Sometimes I think I did too well. I'm just glad this vision isn't true.[dxii]

"Faith Of Our Fathers" also figures into Philip K. Dick's 'pink-beam' inspired cosmology. He categorizes the story in with THE 3 STIGMATA OF PALMER ELDRITCH, UBIK and A MAZE OF DEATH as crucial to his new religious apprehension.[dxiii]

PKD scholar Sam Umland had the opportunity to examine an original manuscript of "Faith Of Our Fathers":

The manuscript that I have examined was given to Anne Dick by Ray Nelson in 1986; Dick presumably had given it to Nelson several decades earlier. The manuscript consists of 41 double-spaced typed pages. 39 of the pages are typed on inexpensive onion-skin "erasable" typewriter paper; these 39 pages represent what I believe to be the first, or rough, draft. The 40th page is numbered "43" and was typed on somewhat better quality paper (the watermark reads "Millers Falls EZERASE). I believe this to be the final page of Dick's second draft; the number 43 indicates the length of the ms. after Dick retyped the first draft with his additions, emendations and corrections. The 41st page of the ms, I examined is a carbon copy of the same page 43. this suggests to me that Dick, having revised the story once, still was not happy with the ending -- he pulled the last page along with its carbon, and rewrote the ending into the final version as published in *DANGEROUS VISIONS*.[dxiv]

One last note: "Faith Of Our Fathers" is not to be confused with "The Story To End All Stories For Harlan Ellison' *DANGEROUS VISIONS*." This was a brief satire that PKD wrote for Ed Meskys and his zine *Bumbejimas* in 1968.

Hazel Pierce has a good description of "Faith Of Our Fathers":

The most sensitive and serious probe of alternate realities in the Dickian short stories tests meta-reality. "Faith Of Our Fathers" challenges both the concept of the charismatic leader and that of the spiritual fountainhead. In this multi-racially governed world, a group of undercover dissidents work assiduously to separate the real Supreme Benefactor from the public facade. If indeed there is a difference. After using anti-hallucinatory drugs, they descry a variety of decadent and evil non-human forms. While these individual visions shatter the earlier beneficent image, they also pose a third and more disturbing alternative reality -- good and evil fused inescapably together. If this is the ultimate reality, then all our cultural beliefs in a saving Good are false. The human mind balks at this loss of innocence. One character openly muses on the strong possibility that men *need* mass hallucination for sheer psychic survival. Philip Dick offers an even more frightening alternative in "The Electric Ant".[dxv]

The story reminds one of the second, formerly suppressed half, of THE UNTELEPORTED MAN. And with that said "Faith Of Our Fathers" receives ★ ★ ★ ★ ★.

DO ANDROIDS DREAM OF ELECTRIC SHEEP?

Now we come to one of Dick's most famous novels: DO ANDROIDS DREAM OF ELECTRIC SHEEP? For a novel that has been much commented upon, mostly because of its adaptation into the film *BLADE RUNNER*, it is difficult to determine when it first started. Sutin says that the novel was completed in 1966 and Perry Kinman and Andrew Butler have it completed by Jun 20, 1966. Presumably this is the date the manuscript reached the SMLA.

Sutin notes that the novel had several original titles: THE ELECTRIC TOAD; DO ANDROIDS DREAM?; THE ELECTRIC SHEEP and THE KILLERS ARE AMONG US! CRIED RICK DECKARD TO THE SPECIAL MAN. It's a wonder Doubleday didn't go with that last one... certain to grab the browser's attention at the newsstand. The one they did decide on, DO ANDROID DREAM OF ELECTRIC SHEEP? was almost as bad. I remember seeing this title on the bookshelves and after an idle glance passing it by in favor of something like Fritz Lieber's *THE SILVER EGGHEADS*.

ANDROIDS was first published by Doubleday in March 1968 in an edition that is now so scarce that a copy commands into the thousands of dollars. [dxvi]

The novel takes off from Dick's short story "The Little Black Box" written in 1964 in that the 'empathy boxes' and the religion of Mercerism from the story return in a different context in the novel.

This was another novel about which PKD made contrary comments in his interview with Apel & Briggs:

> (PKD:) Somebody has told me that I have to see that film (*Last Year At Marienbad*). Anyway... I don't like DO ANDROIDS DREAM at all; I really loathe that book.
> (Briggs:) Oh good. I have to tell you I detest it.
> (PKD:) Yeah, there are certain books of mine I wish I could shovel under, and that's one of them. [dxvii]

But... no one takes Dick seriously on this.

Perhaps it's to be expected but there is much more known about the transition from the novel DO ANDROIDS DREAM OF ELECTRIC SHEEP? to the movie *BLADE RUNNER* than is known about when, where, how or why Dick wrote the story in the first place. Perhaps the idea had been in his mind as early as 1964 and "The Little Black Box"?

Still, if completed in June 1966 it took almost two years to see publication in 1968. During this period nothing is known about ANDROIDS. In 1968, however, things begin to pick up after Doubleday published the first edition.

At this time we will not concern ourselves with the transition from novel to movie but will defer that to 1968. Instead we will note only the effect this had on his sales.

In May 1968 Phil Dick was hard up as usual and glad to receive a letter from his agent, Sidney Meredith, telling him of the sale of the German rights to ANDROIDS for $375 and enclosing German tax forms. [dxviii]

Dick replied a few days later:

> Here are the German tax forms back for DO ANDROIDS DREAM. Thank you very much for the sale; I can use it. [dxix]

But only three days after thanking his agent for this German sale, Philip Dick must've been much gratified to receive a congratulatory letter from Lawrence Ashmead at Doubleday on the sale of the movie rights to DO ANDROIDS DREAM OF ELECTRIC SHEEP?

This first Doubleday edition of ANDROIDS was a successful one as shown by the letter to Dick from Marcia Howell of Doubleday at the end of August which announced royalties for a six month period in 1968. The amount for ANDROIDS was $671.38. This compares with $6.32 for NOW WAIT FOR LAST YEAR.[dxx]

In November PKD was happier yet. Writing to his friend and collaborator Roger Zelazny whom he'd finally met at the Baycon science fiction convention held in San Francisco in August:

I've been thinking about the Convention and you, wondering how you are and how you're busy schedule of work is ~~ioi~~ going. (Please forgive the bad typing; I just finished an outline and some sample chapters for Ace, and my fingers are tired.) Anyhow, I wanted to tell you my reaction to *LORD OF LIGHT*, with its beautiful cover -- plus what you wrote in my copy. {...} I think I'll simply type my notes, taken as i read it, onto this sheet of paper. here goes.

(...)

(eight) How did you do on paperback resale? I got $9,000 for ELECTRIC SHEEP. I hope you got more -- the novel deserves it.[dxxi]

One can imagine that even this amount paled beside the first paperback edition of *BLADE RUNNER* that followed the movie release in 1982. As Paul Williams notes:

BLADE RUNNER / ANDROIDS is by far PKD's best seller (in the US anyway) with 325,000 copies sold.[dxxii]

Judy-Lyn Del Rey was the editor responsible for publishing this first edition of *BLADE RUNNER* from Del Rey Books in May 1982.[dxxiii]

As regards this first edition of *BLADE RUNNER*, On the cover under the large *BLADE RUNNER* title logo is found, in parentheses, in miniature, DO ANDROIDS DREAM OF ELECTRIC SHEEP? The story of how Philip K. Dick got even that concession from the movie producers will have to wait until we look at the year 1968. But the financial result was that Dick got $12,500 for reissuing ANDROIDS whereas if he'd've suppressed the original novel and written a 'quickie' movie novelization he'd've accrued something like $400,000.

Again, despite PKD's bad-mouthing his own work, we can tell that he was fond of DO ANDROIDS DREAM OF ELECTRIC SHEEP?:

DO ANDROIDS DREAM? has sold very well and has been eyed intently by a film company who have in fact purchased an option on it. My wife thinks its a good book. I like it for one thing: it deals with a society in which animals are adored and rare, and a man who owns a real sheep is Somebody... and feels for that sheep a vast bond of love and empathy. Willis my tomcat strides silently over the pages of that book, being important as he is, with his long golden twitching tail. Make them understand, he says to me, that animals are really that important right now. He says this, and then eats up all the food we have been warming for our baby. Some cats are far too pushy. The next thing he'll want to do is write sf novels. I hope he does. None of them will sell.[dxxiv]

And it is also a favorite among fans:

Fan Fave: DO ANDROIDS DREAM OF ELECTRIC SHEEP? Just what is it that makes a true human? I think he hit it right on the nail -- empathy, or compassion, as the Buddhists would have it.[dxxv]

The story centers around Rick Deckard, android bounty hunter, and his desire to own a real sheep instead of the electric one on the roof of his conapt. But real sheep are rare and expensive and Deckard will have to eliminate the group of Nexus-6 androids that have returned to Earth illegally. One by one he goes about his business even though it getting increasingly difficult to distinguish between androids and humans. And when he falls in love with Rachael, herself an advanced android, Deckard begins to lose sight of his goal. In the end Rachael kills his new pet goat and Deckard finds a toad in the desert. But toads are supposedly extinct and Deckard's salvific find turns out to be a fake.

DO ANDROIDS DREAM OF ELECTRIC SHEEP? deserves ✳ ✳ ✳ ✳ ✳

With DO ANDROIDS DREAM OF ELECTRIC SHEEP? done – we will look at its transition into *BLADE RUNNER* shortly -- Phil Dick and Nancy Hackett decided to get married, and this they did in July. As a wedding present PKD learned of the sale of THE GANYMEDE TAKEOVER to Ace on Aug 16, 1966.

The next novel Dick wrote in 1966 was UBIK although a case could be made that his children's story NICK AND THE GLIMMUNG was written before UBIK as both manuscripts reached the SMLA on the same day, Dec 7, 1966. But as this novel was obviously done to commemorate the upcoming birth of his and Nancy's daughter, Isolde – born on Mar 15, 1967 – the couple could have hardly been aware of the pregnancy until at the earliest about September 1966. And ANDROIDS was finished in June. So Dick more than likely started on UBIK shortly thereafter.

UBIK

The manuscript for DEATH OF AN ANTI-WATCHER reached the SMLA on Dec 7,1966. The story under the title UBIK was first published by Doubleday in May 1969.[dxxvi] Why it took so long to publish is again a mystery. As we've noted earlier UBIK relies on PKD's earlier story "What The Dead Men Say" written in 1963.

The Philip K. Dick papers discovered by Patrick Clark at the Bowling Green State University in Ohio reveal that the novel was in the publication mill at Doubleday by Jan 1968. A letter to PKD from Doubleday found in the BGSU Papers included the cover artwork for UBIK at that time.[dxxvii]

Further correspondence in March from Larry Ashmead at Doubleday informs PKD that UBIK will be a Science Fiction Book Club selection with a $1,000 advance against royalties of 6 cents per copy sold.[dxxviii]

And into May the letters continued with some questions about the UBIK cover art.[dxxix]

It would be a year before any more documented comments were made on UBIK. Dick himself in a letter to critic Peter Fitting circa early May 1969 mentions his new novel:

My most recent novel will be out May 9th, published by Doubleday, called, UBIK. It is a very strange one.[dxxx]

And after the first edition and the SFBC edition were published the paperback from Dell Books came out in May 1970.[dxxxi] On this edition Dick said in an interview that

...for Ubik, I got ten thousand dollars for the paperback of which I got five thousand and Doubleday got the other five.[dxxxii]

Many editions followed these first three. A now valuable hardback came from Rapp & Whiting publishers in the UK in June 1970 and another in paperback from Panther in May 1970. Once Mark Hurst had acquired the rights to UBIK in 1976 for Bantam Books their edition followed in Jan 1977. This is the one with the naked woman partially hidden in the spray can of Ubik on the front cover.[dxxxiii] More editions followed including the first USA hardback of UBIK from The Gregg Press in 1979. Foreign editions, too, are numerous. For collectors the first non-SFBC edition from Doubleday is the prize, followed by the Rapp & Whiting edition from 1970. The Gregg Press edition also is of good value.

One need not be surprised that Dick saw UBIK as an important work in his oeuvre. In conversation with Apel & Briggs he said, " I have a very strong feeling that UBIK, too, contains some important ideas."[dxxxiv]

And in another interview the questioner got onto the subject of his favorite Dick novels:

(Mike Hodel:) Of all the novels you've written, I guess my own particular favorites are The Man in the High Castle, of course, and Ubik.
(Dick:) *You*-bick?
(Hodel:) *You*-bick.
(Dick:) *You*-bick. The French call it *Ooh*-bick. Deek's *Ooh*-bick. It's called *Ubick, Mia Signore* in Italian. I guess that means *Ubick, My Dear Sir* or something like that. Well, it *does*--I looked it up.
{...}
You don't just write whatever comes into your head while you're sitting there in front of the typewriter. When I wrote UBIK, I got about twelve pages done and couldn't think of anything else, so I just wrote whatever came into my mind. I wrote it from my unconscious: I let the right hemisphere of my brain do all the thinking, and I was as surprised as anybody as to what came out. In France, of course, it's considered a great novel because it doesn't make any sense; in France, it's a roman de pataphysique. Ever since Alfred Jarry hit town, they've loved stuff that doesn't make any sense. Maybe it does make sense when you translate it into French. Maybe I'm a great writer in France because I've got good translators.
(Hodel:) You are better known, I think, in France than you are here.
(Dick:) Germany, France--England, too. [dxxxv]

As to his own foreign relations PKD tells a funny story about the Russians;

"I got this letter, direct from Moscow," he told us, "signed by some fairly important scientists, who invited me to visit Russia so they could talk to me."
"What on Earth for?" I asked.
"Well, it seems they had read UBIK, and had already formulated theories that the afterlife was remarkably close to what I had theorized in that novel," he explained. "They wanted me to come over so they could find out what I knew -- and probably experiment on me to find out *how* I knew," he chuckled. "You didn't go," I stated, prompting.
"I actually considered going for a while {...}

And so, instead, one day a few months later, this black limousine, with the shaded glass windows and so on. And three men in trench coats got out and came to the door. I was watching this from the window, and I was thinking, *oh shit. They've finally caught up with me.* I had, at that time, no idea about who 'They' were; I was just convinced that *someone* had caught up with me for whatever sins I might have committed. Or they thought I had committed.

At any rate, it turns out they were from the Russian Embassy. The scientists in Moscow had received my letter, in which I had fabricated some excuse for not visiting, and they had requested that the Embassy send a delegation to interview me in my own home. They were very nice and polite, and once they explained who they were and what they wanted, I let them in and we talked about UBIK for an hour or so. I didn't tell them nothin'. Just played stupid. Then they left, and I've never heard from them since.[dxxxvi]

Perhaps Dick was too close to the thoughts of Dr. Kozyrev...:

Within a system which must generate an enormous amount of veiling, it would be vain-glorious to expostulate on what actuality is, when my premise declares that were we to penetrate to it for any reason this strange veil-like dream would reinstate itself retroactively, in terms of our perceptions and in terms of our memories. The mutual dreaming would resume as before, because, I think, we are like the characters in my novel UBIK; we are in a state of half-life. We are neither dead nor alive, but preserved in cold storage, waiting to be thawed out. Expressed in the perhaps startlingly familiar terms of the procession of the seasons, this is winter of which I speak; it is winter for our race, and it is winter in UBIK for those in half-life. Ice and snow cover them; ice and snow cover our world in layers of accretions, which we call dokos or Maya. What melts away the rind or layer of frozen ice over the world each year is of course the reappearance of the sun. What melts the ice and snow covering the characters in UBIK, and which halts the cooling-off of their lives, the entropy which they feel, is the voice of Mr. Runciter, their former employer, calling to them. The voice of Mr. Runciter is none other than the same voice which each bulb and seed and root in the ground, our ground, in our winter-time, hears. It hears: "Wake up! Sleepers awake!" Now I have told you who Runciter is, and I have told you our condition and what UBIK is really about. What I have said, too, is that time is actually as Dr. Kozyrev in the Soviet Union supposes it to be, and in UBIK time has been nullified and no longer moves forward in the lineal fashion which we experience. As this has happened, due to the deaths of the characters, we the readers and they the personæ see the world as it is without the veil of Maya, without the obscuring mists of lineal time. It is that very energy, Time, postulated by Dr. Kozyrev as binding together all phenomena and maintaining all life, which by its activity hides the ontological reality beneath its flow.

The orthogonal time axis may have been represented in my novel UBIK without my understanding what I was depicting; i.e. the form regression of objects along an entirely different line from that out of which they, in lineal time, were built. This reversion is that of the Platonic Ideas or archetypes; a rocket-ship reverts to a Boeing 747, then back to a World War I "Jenny" biplane. While I may indeed have expressed a dramatic view of orthogonal time, it is less certain that this is orthogonal time undergoing an unnatural reversion; i.e. moving backwards. What the characters in UBIK see may be orthogonal time moving along its normal axis; if we ourselves somehow see the universe reversed the "reversions" of form which objects in UBIK undergo may be momentum towards perfection. This would imply that our world as extensive in time (rather than extensive in space) is like an onion, an almost infinite number of successive layers. If lineal time seems to add layers, then perhaps orthogonal time peels these off, exposing layers of progressively greater Being. One is reminded here of Plotinus's view of the universe as consisting of concentric rings of emanation, each one possessing more Being -- or reality -- than the next.[dxxxvii]

This fascination with time and UBIK would further occupy Dick's mind:

In UBIK the forward moving force of time (or timeforce expressed as an ergic field) has ceased. All changes result from that. Forms regress. The substrate is revealed. Cooling (entropy) is allowed to set in unimpeded. Equilibrium is affected by the vanishing of the forward-moving time force-field. The bare bones, so to speak, of the world, our world, are revealed. We see the *Logos* addressing the many living entities.. Assisting and advising them. We are now aware of the *Atman* everywhere. The press of time on everything, having been abolished, reveals many elements underlying our phenomena.
If time stops, this is what takes place, these changes.
Not frozen-ness but revelation.
There are still the retrograde forces remaining, at work. And also underlying positive forces other than time. The disappearance of the force-field we call time reveals both good and bad things; which is to say, coaching entities (Runciter who is the *Logos*), the *Atman*, Ella; it isn't a static world, but it begins to *cool*. What is missing is a form of heat; the *Aten*. The *Logos* (Runciter) can tell you *what* to do, but you lack the energy -- heat, force -- to do it. (i.e. time).[dxxxviii]

And further:

In my novel UBIK I present a motion along a retrograde entropic axis, in terms of Platonic forms rather than any decay or reversion we normally conceive. Perhaps the normal forward motion along this axis, away from entropy, accruing rather than divesting, is identical with the axis line that I characterize as lateral, which is to say, in orthogonal rather than linear time. If this is so, the novel UBIK inadvertently contains what could be called a scientific rather than a philosophical idea. But here I am only guessing. Still, the fiction writer may have written more than he consciously knew.[dxxxix]

And finally:

UBIK was primarily a dream, or series of dreams. In my opinion it contains strong themes of pre-Socratic philosophical views of the world, unfamiliar to me when I wrote it (to name just one, the views of Empedocles)[dxl]

But maybe the last word on this should go to George Melrod:

What may be most ironic about Dick is that, over time, he came to believe in these possibilities as viable models of reality. As he wrote later, "All I know today that I didn't know when I wrote UBIK is that UBIK isn't fiction."[dxli]

Several years after first publication of UBIK Dick in 1974 decided to write a screenplay for UBIK. This he did in short order but it was not published until after Dick's death when Corroboree Press produced a beautiful illustrated edition in 1985. We will look at UBIK: THE SCREENPLAY when we come to 1985 in our chronology.

UBIK, although a progression from "What The Dead Men Say" is completely different in its plot… The novel starts with Joe Chip arguing with the door of his apartment. Without the five cents to trigger its mechanism it won't let him out. But with a promise of later payment Chip emerges only to find himself and his job as telepathic scout in urgent demand. His boss, Glen Runciter, runs a service that supplies a corps of anti-psis to other businesses to counteract the effects of telepaths, precogs and other psis. But the main psi Runciter Associates has been keeping its eye on has disappeared. When the cream of Runciter's organization is lured to the Moon and there blown up by a homeostatic bomb things get decidedly strange.

Runciter, now dead, survives on in cold-pac from where he communicates with his family and associates as he organizes the continuing struggle against Stanton Mick and his organization of psis. In this war of psi and anti-psi Joe Chip finds himself in the lead. But when personal messages appear on bathroom walls and Runciter's head appears on coins Chip gets mightily confused. His situation isn't helped when his cigarettes go stale and his car devolves back to a Model A Ford. And when he tries to fly to Cheyenne and the plane he is in turns into a Curtiss 'Jenny' he knows he's in trouble.

Pat Conley, an anti-psi who Joe Chip discovered, works with Joe even though he is not sure of exactly what her talent is. And when he himself starts to devolve on the stairs leading to his hotel room while Pat looks on and laughs he about gives up the struggle. But at the last moment he acquires a spray can of Ubik which halts and reverses the process of decay. And even when his spray can devolves into a tin of quack patent medicine it still works. But his supply is running short and, anyway, what really is this ubiquitous Ubik?

In the end Joe is startled to see his own face appearing on a coin.

UBIK is a shimmering story of irreality and definitely one of PKD's best. It deserves ✵ ✵ ✵ ✵ ✵

With UBIK written and a baby on the way Philip Dick veered away from the weird and sometimes scary world of UBIK to the gentle climes of children's fiction. In honor of his soon to be born baby he decided to write a children's story.

NICK AND THE GLIMMUNG

The manuscript for THE GLIMMUNG OF PLOWMAN'S PLANET reached the SMLA on Dec 7, 1966 – the same day as the ms for UBIK. The story was not sold until 1987 (after numerous rejections) and was first published by Gollancz in the UK in 1988 as NICK AND THE GLIMMUNG. There has never been an American edition. Paul Williams says of the manuscript:

The original ms of GLIMMUNG is 96 pages, about a third of the length of Dick's regular novels. It was rejected by 15 publishers in 1967-68. The Agency then put it aside as a manuscript "awaiting new markets" (...) In late '67 or early '68 Dick wrote an adult sf novel called GALACTIC POT-HEALER, in which the Glimmung of Plowman's Planet is a major character. No part of the story or text of GALACTIC POT-HEALER is taken from the earlier book, however.[dxlii]

PKD himself refers to the story only once in an undated letter to Tony Boucher; probably written in Dec 1966:

I hope you're feeling better. I just sold another book to Doubleday & I'm feeling very good. And I sent off my first children's novel, with many high hopes. {...}
May the Blessings of Christmas be with you through all the New Year.[dxliii]

As for the rest of its publishing history, The Philip K. Dick Society Newsletter relates the tale starting in 1987:

Victor Gollancz, Ltd. of London has announced plans to publish Philip K. Dick's novel THE GLIMMUNG OF PLOWMAN'S PLANET perhaps as soon as Summer 1988. It will be issued as a children's book; Paul Demeyer has been commissioned to illustrate the novel, which will then be retitled, NICK AND THE GLIMMUNG.

NICK AND THE GLIMMUNG will be the last of PKD's science fiction novels to be published...[dxliv]

And a few months later in 1988:

NICK AND THE GLIMMUNG, Philip K. Dick's first last best and only children's sf novel, has been published in the UK by Victor Gollancz Ltd. for L7.95. A charming tale written in the late 60s, it includes a great many elements recapitulating the whole canvas of Dickian sf constructs, including wubs, werjes, klakes, printers, trobes, nunks, father-things and a number of other items familiar from the settings of GALACTIC POT-HEALER and A MAZE OF DEATH. The story stands well on its own, though, and has the trans-generational appeal of a Heinlein juvenile (but without the libertarian proselytizing). More than many other Dick novels, this one seems intentionally funny, a tone which is echoed in Paul Demeyer's excellent cartoon-style illustrations. The main character is Nick Graham, a small boy who's family emigrates off-planet in order to allow him to keep his pet cat, Horace, who otherwise would be confiscated (pets are illegal on Earth because they consume food needed by the ever-growing population of humans). Their adventures upon arriving are classic PKD investigations into the nature of reality and fate, the qualities of humanity versus simulacra, and the necessity for doing the right thing even when it requires personal risk. A fun book, nicely packaged, this is another delightful posthumous surprise for Philip K. Dick readers everywhere -- and their kids, as well! [dxlv]

And in 1989:

Incidentally, I believe the (rather large) first printing of NICK AND THE GLIMMUNG is almost exhausted, so if you don't have a copy I'd grab one quick. Apparently it did well in the children's book market in England, which is good news indeed. Still no glimmering of an American publisher for the book.[dxlvi]

NICK AND THE GLIMMUNG has never been published in the United States. But in 1990 Piper publishers in the UK issued a paperback edition.[dxlvii]

The story is, as Andy Watson expresses in his capsule review above, a charming and sometimes funny story about a boy and his cat forced to leave earth and take up life on Plowman's Planet where strange and wonderful aliens help and hinder the family as they find lose and regain a book belonging to the Glimmung. In the end Horace the cat chooses his right master over a Nick-thing. The story borrows several lifeforms from Dick's earlier short stories: wubs, printers and father-things, for example.

Meant for children but eminently readable by adults, NICK AND THE GLIMMUNG gets ✭ ✭ ✭ ✭

1967

We now cast our attention on the year 1967. This was not a good year for PKD overall. Despite the joy of a new baby, Isolde born on Mar 15, Phil and Nancy were rocked in June by the death of Maren Hackett, Nancy's stepmom, by suicide. This following the death of PKD's two cats. Then in July PKD suffered a nervous breakdown occasioned by Maren's death and the fact that he was being hounded by the IRS for back taxes for his best years yet, 1964 and 1965. For these two years PKD had stated incomes of $12,000 and $5,000 respectively. Add to all this Phil's drug problems; mostly with pills of one sort or the other and its no wonder that he had that nervous breakdown.[dxlviii]

But as far as his writing career was going, the year started well with publication of THE ZAP GUN from Pyramid Books in January, followed by his short story "Return Match" in February's *Galaxy*. Also in February came the first paperback original of COUNTER-CLOCK WORLD from Berkley Books. In June "Faith Of Our Fathers" came out in *DANGEROUS VISIONS* and the first paperback of THE GANYMEDE TAKEOVER was out from Ace Books.

Before Isa was born, Dick wrote a treatment for the TV series called *The Invaders*. I'm not certain but I think this treatment is the one published in the SHIFTING REALITIES OF PHILIP K. DICK (TSR) by Lawrence Sutin as "TV Series Idea" (1967) -- even though it really doesn't fit in with the idiom of that TV show...[dxlix]

Phil's "TV Series Idea" concerns and old but small and outmoded firm of Guardian Angels in heaven who intercede for clients who are in trouble on Earth. The main character would be Herb DeWinter, a bumbling parody of James Bond with his magical attaché case. Full of characters with names like Anastasia Kelp and Theola Feather it's no wonder that this idea was not taken seriously by the TV agencies.

In April 1967, replying to a letter from Avram Davidson, Dick sent him an outline for a novel. The outline was titled 'Joe Protagoras Is Alive And Living On Earth' and it seems PKD's intent was to lend this outline to Davidson so that he, a fellow sci-fi writer experiencing writer's block, could use Dick's outline to gain an advance from some publisher. But Davidson sent it back as something he couldn't use. Dick acknowledged this in a letter to Davidson on Apr 27, 1967:

I'm awfully sorry that my outline wasn't anything you could use. I sort of had it in mind that maybe you could send it off *qua* outline, more or less as it was, and maybe land an advance thereby. This is what I've done, now, by the way – sent it off as it stood, with that hope in mind. {...}[dl]

This outline reached the SMLA on May 1, 1967. Paul Williams notes that the 'Joe Protagoras' outline was submitted to Doubleday and Avon, who rejected it, and then to Berkeley Books who hung onto it for a year and a half before giving PKD a contract and advance on Jan 31, 1969. But PKD never wrote this novel and Berkeley settled for a collection of his short stories. This was to become THE GOLDEN MAN in 1980. Even though it is sad that Dick never wrote this novel in one way it's good because the 'Story Notes' Dick wrote for THE GOLDEN MAN collection are often the only comments by him that we have on these short stories.

The outline 'Joe Protagoras Is Alive And Living On Earth' was published in *New Worlds #2* in 1992.

On May 4, 1967, three days after receiving the 'Joe Protagoras' outline, the SMLA found another one lying on their doorstep. This was an outline for a novel to be titled THE NAME OF THE GAME IS DEATH. Two weeks later more material for THE NAME OF THE GAME IS DEATH arrived, perhaps sample pages. The outline was sent to Terry Carr at Ace Books. Five months later he sent it back. Avon and Lancer also got a look at it before the Agency sent it to Doubleday in May 1968.

In September 1968, as we shall see shortly when we look at A MAZE OF DEATH, Scott Meredith wrote to PKD mentioning Doubleday's interest in obtaining a contract for THE NAME OF THE GAME IS DEATH. Philip K. Dick eventually wrote a novel that had no relationship to this outline and Doubleday published it as A MAZE OF DEATH in 1970.[dli]

However, from his research into the BGSU Papers, Patrick Clark concludes that THE NAME OF THE GAME IS DEATH was not a working title for A MAZE OF DEATH nor a source of ideas for the plot.

The outline itself was published along with the 'Joe Protagoras' outline in *New Worlds #2.*

DEUS IRAE (Part 3)

In October PKD had agreed with Roger Zelazny that they should collaborate on a novel. Details of this are minimal but it seems DEUS IRAE was not initially what the two had in mind. Paul Williams in his *New Worlds* Introduction references a letter from PKD to Zelazny dated Oct 26, 1967 in which he expands on this:

Larry Ashmead at Doubleday saw 'a brief outline of the work' (this would have been the 'Joe Protagoras' outline), 'and he said he'd sign a contract on the basis of the outline except that they signed a contract on a previous outline of mine, a novel from which never emerged (*true*).' This is a reference to DEUS IRAE, which Dick sold in chapter and outline form in 1964, which did in time become the project that Dick and Zelazny wrote together. At this point, however, Dick is not suggesting DEUS IRAE as their joint project.[dlii]

Williams goes on to explain that what PKD had in mind was a lamination of the two outlines of 'Joe Protagoras Is Alive And Living On Earth' and THE NAME OF THE GAME IS DEATH. In the end, though, nothing came from these suggestions except the decision to work on DEUS IRAE. Perhaps Zelazny, his interest piqued about PKD's mention of the forlorn 1964 outline, inquired about that and PKD started telling him and... before you know it DEUS IRAE is revived from the dead with Ted White passing on the sample pages of DEUS IRAE to Zelazny at his or PKD's request. This most likely occurred in early 1968.[dliii]

So the saga of DEUS IRAE lurches on.[dliv]

Dick did pull himself together enough by the end of the year to work on an outline for his next novel, GALACTIC POT-HEALER. He was also working with Ace editor Terry Carr on the preparation of his collection THE PRESERVING MACHINE And Other Stories, this would come to fruition in 1969.

GALACTIC POT-HEALER

The early days of this novel are fairly well documented. The earliest reference we have to an outline for GALACTIC POT-HEALER is a letter from PKD to his agent, Scott Meredith, dated Nov 3, 1967:

Here are the three signed contracts back, to be given to Berkley Books for their signatures. (The contracts are for the outline called THE GALACTIC POT-HEALER.) Now, I notice that the contracts specify "sample chapter and outline form." They do have the outline, of course, but no sample chapter. Therefore I have written a sample chapter, plus excerpts from other chapters, which you will find included. They total thirty pages and should give Tom Dardis all that he needs.

However, if Mr. Dardis will sign the contracts *without* seeing these thirty pages, then let him do so; i.e. you might merely send the contracts back to him, retaining the thirty pages in your own office. Then, if he asks for the sample chapter, send him the thirty pages. My reasoning is as follows: he might not like the thirty pages, so if we can get a signature without them then by all means let's do so. Would you not agree?

By the way -- thanks from the bottom of my heart for this sale. We are almost out of money and couldn't have made it another month. God bless you. You are the best agent in the world.[dlv]

Whether Mr. Dardis requested the sample pages I do not know. However, early the next year Dick again contacted his agent:

I have finished the novel for Berkley Books, the outline for which is called , THE GALACTIC POT-HEALER. All that is left is doing the final draft, which usually takes me no more than ten days to two weeks. I can't find my copy of the contract with Berkley Books, and I am not sure whether the novel is due on the first of March or the fifteenth or the thirty-first; all I remember is that its due in March. Could you check over your copy of the contract of Berkley's and then let me know. If its due on the first, then ask them for two more weeks or until the end of the month. The novel came out quite well, I think. If Berkley doesn't buy it I'm sure Doubleday would...[dlvi]

GALACTIC POT-HEALER was basically finished then by the end of February 1968. It was published by Berkley Books in June 1969 and a hardback edition came from the SFBC in April 1970.[dlvii] UK publication followed in July1971 with the Gollancz hardback edition.[dlviii]

Perhaps PKD's letter to his agent mentioning Doubleday spurred the SFBC edition. Or, perhaps it was Doubleday's policy to scour recently released paperbacks and buy the best for their book club? Anyway, after these three editions several more came out through the 70s and 80s from Pan and Grafton in England and Berkley and Vintage in the USA. Blackstone Audio Books produced a cassette version of the novel in 1989.[dlix]

GALACTIC POT-HEALER is another novel about which PKD has expressed negative thoughts:

One that I vacillate about is GALACTIC POTHEALER. Sometimes it seems funny to me, sometimes it seems...stupid. Stupid. Nothing can be said for it.[dlx]

And again in a 1970 letter to Sandra Miesel:

GALACTIC POT-HEALER is minor, very minor; in fact I wish I hadn't written it. I think, though, it has one good part: the section in which -- aw the hell with it. No part of it is any good (I was going to say the part where the protagonist is reached by telephone while crouched in a packing crate). (I sort of hate GALACTIC POT-HEALER, as well as ZAP GUN plus a few more. Wrrgh.)[dlxi]

To which PKD's friend and fellow writer, Tim Powers replies:

Oh, he says about, for example GALACTIC POTHEALER, that he "just winged it", and didn't think about it twice. Wrote it out fast and was never in control. But in some ways that is one of his very best books.[dlxii]

And science fiction writer James Tiptree Jr. must've agreed with Powers:

On one occasion she describes taking GALACTIC POTHEALER and mailing it to herself after reading the opening pages, as the only way to force herself to meet a writing deadline (if the book was in the house she would have to go on reading it).[dlxiii]

Although the Glimmung of Plowman's Planet is a major character in GALACTIC POT-HEALER and first occurred in NICK AND THE GLIMMUNG, the two stories have very little in common. Certainly plot-wise they are far apart.

No edition of GALACTIC POT-HEALER is especially valuable. The SFBC edition from 1970 would be desirable (and easily found) as would the Gollancz edition from 1971.

P. Schuyler Miller reviewed GALACTIC POT-HEALER in *Analog* in 1970:

No, Waldo… Mr. Dick is not urging a "pot" centered society upon us. The pots that Joe Fernwright "heals" are the things that grandma used to call "crocks" when she made pickle in them, and Aunt Sophie called "vahses" when she used them for bouquets, and archeologists use to support vast hypotheses of human and cultural flux. Joe just fixes pots – better than new – in a crazy future Welfare State. Then a vastly ancient shape-changing monster from far, far, far beyond anywhere hires him and a shipload of other specialists to raise a pagan temple out of the sea on a bizarre world.

The whole thing is fascinating in a surrealistic sort of way, but never as believable as -- for instance – Samuel Delaney or Avram Davidson would make it. The pot healer and other technicians never get a chance to do their stuff, so there is never any logic to their having been selected. They do serve another purpose, but that seems to be pure luck. If there is deep significance anywhere, I missed it.[dlxiv]

For once we can agree with Mr. P. Schuyler Miller and rate GALACTIC POT-HEALER with ✮ ✮ ✮

1968

After a bad and somewhat slow year in 1967 Philip K. Dick started the year 1968 by looking over the cover artwork for his forthcoming novel UBIK, as stated above. He was also in the process of getting his Ace collection THE PRESERVING MACHINE ready to go and by the end of February had written the first draft of GALACTIC POT-HEALER.

In February the popular SFBC edition of THE THREE STIGMATA OF PALMER ELDRITCH was published by Doubleday.[dlxv] And something that worried PKD for some time to come was published in *Ramparts* magazine. This was an anti-Vietnam War statement that he had signed together with many other artists and writers in 1967. The consequences of this, Dick thought, were continued hassles with the IRS and seizure of his car in 1969.[dlxvi]

Good news came in February and March, though, when Dick learned first of the sale of foreign rights for SOLAR LOTTERY to the Dutch publisher Born Pockets for $207, half going to Dick, half going to Ace Books.[dlxvii] And then in March of the sale of UBIK to the SFBC with a $1000 advance. This month, too, the first edition of DO ANDROIDS DREAM OF ELECTRIC SHEEP? came out from Doubleday.[dlxviii]

All in all things looked promising for PKD at that time. But tragedy would strike again soon. Anthony Boucher, PKD's first editor and mentor, died in April 1968. After the death of Maren Hackett in the previous year this loss must've been hard on our anxious author. Yet, even with this loss, Dick soldiered on, learning of the German foreign rights sale of ANDROIDS in May and the film option taken out on ANDROIDS the same month.

In June, with the help of his mother Phil, Nancy and Isa moved to a new house in San Rafael. And while he was taking care of the moving chore he could see on the newsstands another of his short stories for sale: "Not By Its Cover" in the Summer issue of *Famous SF*.

In the Fall, though it went mostly unnoticed at the time, came his scrap of a story "The Story To End All Stories For Harlan Ellison's *DANGEROUS VISIONS*" which was printed in the fanzine *Niekas #20* in the Fall of 1968. This is not really a story, coming in at only 117 words, but more a story summary; something PKD tossed off for no apparent reason. It is not worth rating although is, perhaps, a 'dangerous vision.'

In August Dick received royalty statements from Doubleday for his novels NOW WAIT FOR LAST YEAR and DO ANDROIDS DREAM OF ELECTRIC SHEEP?, as we discussed above. August also allowed for a little excitement in his life as the Baycon Science Fiction convention was held in San Francisco in that month. This convention, known as the 'Drugcon' because of all the drugs floating around and of which PKD partook, was where he met his correspondent and collaborator Roger Zelazny for the first time. Once again the subject of DEUS IRAE comes up...

DEUS IRAE (Part 4)

Of the meeting with Zelazny at the Baycon SF convention in August, PKD wrote to Lawrence Ashmead his editor at Doubleday:

I attended the Baycon and met Roger Zelazny. He and I got together in an abandoned room and talked business for many hours -- e.g. our collaboration on DEUS IRAE, which he has told me he likes very much. I am reading *LORD OF LIGHT* by the way, and find ample reason for it winning the Hugo; it is a superb book, and the religious elements convince me -- if I wasn't already convinced -- that he can do quite right on DEUS IRAE...^{dlxix}

Recall that Dick had signed a contract with Doubleday in 1964 for DEUS IRAE and had sent 50 sample pages to Ted White in 1965 or 1966 but White had been unable to progress with the novel and had given the sample pages to Zelazny in 1967 or 1968. Sporadic correspondence between Dick and Zelazny in the next few years had resulted in little progress. But, now, in 1968, the two actually met at the Baycon in San Francisco and a new spirit of commitment to the collaboration was kindled. In the letter to Ashmead just quoted PKD goes on to talk about this:

As to DEUS IRAE, which I know you want to know about, Roger wants to do the next fifty or so pages, and I agreed, because as you know I myself am stopped dead. However, contractual obligations have him tied up until January, but at that time he will begin on it; he will carry on where my initial fifty pages left off. I am sorry that we can't do it sooner, but I can't do it at all and Roger is committed for the remainder of the year. But consider: a novel by me and Roger Zelazny. Shouldn't that be quite something? God help us if it isn't. I know it will be good. I think that ultimately everyone will be glad that I pooped out after the first fifty pages because that gave Roger a chance to enter (I typed "end" a Freudian slip!).^{dlxx}

On this meeting Dick remarks further:

I got maybe a third of it done and discovered that I didn't know anything about the subject matter, which is Christianity. I could sing a few hymns, you know, and I could cross myself, but that was about all. Anyway, I had embarked on a theological novel without knowing anything about theology. So when I ran across Zelazny in 1968, I'd been working for four years on the novel, and I said, "Zelazny, do you know anything about theology?" He said, "You better believe it, Jack," and I said, "How would you like to collaborate with me? I got one-third of this thing done, and it's all about Christianity." So he took it.^{dlxxi}

At the end of September Dick's agent wrote to him concerning DEUS IRAE. This letter was mentioned above in the section on THE NAME OF THE GAME IS DEATH:

{Doubleday} very anxious about DEUS IRAE, mostly because they'd like to contract for THE NAME OF THE GAME IS DEATH as soon as possible, but cannot until they have something more on DEUS IRAE.^{dlxxii}

This letter also refers to a sum of money from Doubleday to the amount of $4500. Scott Meredith enclosed a check for $1350 ($1500 minus his commission) as part of this, explaining that the full amount had not yet come to Doubleday from NAL. What this money was payment for I do not know. I have never seen a NAL edition of any of PKD's books, although NEL brought out several editions of MARTIAN TIME-SLIP in the 70s. Also in this letter Meredith mentions the interest of Essex House in any of PKD's old unpublished sf novels, and of Collier Books interest in doing a collection of Dick's stories based on one underlying theme of Dick's choosing.

In November PKD wrote to Zelazny commenting on DEUS IRAE:

After reading *LORD OF LIGHT* I can see that you will have no trouble with our collaboration, DEUS IRAE. By the way -- an idea came to me about that ({...}). Maybe the viewpoint -- and locale -- could shift, at about page 55, to the God of Wrath himself. That's something that didn't occur to me until today ... and it's been four and a half years! Shifting viewpoint is a method I always use... but for some reason this never occurred to me. Any good? Yes? No? In-between?[dlxxiii]

What Zelazny thought about this suggestion is not known. But presumably he started working on DEUS IRAE in January 1969. And there, once again, we must let the novel sit until 1976 when Doubleday once again pressed for their long-contracted-for novel.

THE PRESERVING MACHINE And Other Stories

This prestigious collection of Philip K. Dick's short stories goes back to 1965. As we've related above, Dick wrote a bruised letter to his agent (copies to Don Wollheim) complaining about Wollheim's reaction to his expansion of THE UNTELEPORTED MAN. In this May 1965 letter he is particularly irked that Wollheim wishes to tie the purchase of Dick's story collection to the satisfactory -- to Wollheim -- completion of the expansion of THE UNTELEPORTED MAN. Dick feels "this is a club over my head…" and quasi-illegal.[dlxxiv]

I imagine it took most of the rest of 1965 to work this one out between Dick, the Agency and Wollheim. At any rate, this proposed collection didn't resurface until early 1968, although it is obvious that by then the collection was well along its way to publication. First mention then of THE PRESERVING MACHINE by name is in a letter from Terry Carr in February summarized here by Patrick Clark:

Cover letter accompanying proofs for THE PRESERVING MACHINE and photocopy of the book jacket artwork. Problems with the typesetter precludes copies for advance reviews but Carr will solicit input of Brunner, Boucher and Ellison by phone.[dlxxv]

It would be another eight months before we hear mention of THE PRESERVING MACHINE again. This time in a letter from Marcia Howell in October that accompanied the contracts for THE PRESERVING MACHINE.[dlxxvi]

Shortly after this Terry Carr wrote to Dick about copyrights for the stories in THE PRESERVING MACHINE and offers to

consider any new novel Phil might want to write for Carr's Ace Specials at $2500, against 6% - 8% royalties.[dlxxvii]

A week later Carr was writing to Dick telling him that copies of the stories in THE PRESERVING MACHINE were being sent to him separately and again renewing his offer to consider any new Dick novel for Carr's Ace Specials.[dlxxviii]

To these missives PKD replied in short order:

Thank you for the memo of November 6 in which you thank me for the copyrights on THE PRESERVING MACHINE. I am glad -- god, how I am glad -- that you can finish the matter, because it's items like that that destroy my will and curdle my brain tissue.
{...}
As to famous persons seeing the proofs of THE PRESERVING MACHINE, in the fashion that I saw John Brunner's proofs for *THE JAGGED ORBIT*. I think Bob Silverberg would be a good one to send it to, and possibly Harlan (although he might excoriate it), and

then Phil Farmer. Also, I have written to Roger Zelazny (with whom I am doing a collaboration for Doubleday) asking him if he has time -- he is very busy -- to read my collection. I should know very soon if he can do this. Maybe you can think up someone else. I'd trust your instincts in this matter far more than I would mine.

Nice to hear from you, and give my love to Carol. I hope you'll keep me informed as to the progress of THE PRESERVING MACHINE. I'd like very much, for example, to see a Xerox copy of the cover, when it's ready, and see the blurbs, too.[dlxxix]

Dick was glad to finalize the contracts on THE PRESERVING MACHINE and he was indeed chuffed in a Dec letter to sf writer John Brunner:

As far as my own work goes, I have sold a story collection to Ace for a special, then an outline and 3 sample chapters at $2500, then my newest novel to Doubleday... so I have made three book-length sales in less than a month. Now I can pay off all my enormous debts.[dlxxx]

One last letter from this period from Terry Carr asks if Dick wants to write an introduction to THE PRESERVING MACHINE and mentions A.E.Van Vogt's interest in reading it once it is published.[dlxxxi]

Moving into 1969 activity on THE PRESERVING MACHINE continued with Dick announcing to Peter Fitting:

a full and successful collection of my stories, ranging from those written in 1951 up to the present, is being brought out by Ace in a week or so; I'm very proud of it (It's called THE PRESERVING MACHINE, and the editor has so carefully combed my 150 odd stories so as to make it appear that I'm a good short story writer, which I am not).[dlxxxii]

Once the collection came out from Ace in April 1969, Dick in a letter to fellow writer, John Jakes, remarks again on his editor at Ace:

A good deal of credit for PRESERVING MACHINE should go to Terry Carr, who rounded up all my stories (about 150), read all of them and then made what I regard as a superior choice as to what ought to go in the volume. He makes me look better than I am.[dlxxxiii]

The Ace paperback of THE PRESERVING MACHINE was published in April 1969 and the SFBC hardback followed in Jan 1970. The first edition in the United Kingdom was a hardback from Gollancz in Feb 1971.[dlxxxiv]

Many editions have followed through the years. In the UK many of the earlier editions dropped the story "What The Dead Men Say" (perhaps it was too long?) but this was restored to the collection with the 1987 Grafton edition. Foreign editions are also numerous with interesting titles like LA MAQUINA PRESERVADORA, LA TIERRA SOMBRIA and LA VOCI DI DOPO.

With fourteen short stories one might think that there would be a few bad ones in this collection but they are all excellent stories, ones I've rated with four or five stars with the single exception of the title story itself, "The Preserving Machine."!

As a collection, then, THE PRESERVING MACHINE certainly deserves ✭✭✭✭✭. Terry Carr did, indeed, do a good job.

After Phil and Nancy and baby Isolde had moved to their new house in San Rafael in June 1968, Dick was either in the middle of or just about to begin another novel. This he would title THE HOUR OF THE T.E.N.C.H. It would be published by Doubleday in July 1970 as A MAZE OF DEATH.

A MAZE OF DEATH

Among the papers at the Bowling Green State University in Ohio Patrick Clark discovered several manuscript sections and one manuscript for a novel with the working title of THE HOUR OF THE T.E.N.C.H. This would become A MAZE OF DEATH on publication. These manuscripts date to some time in 1968. The longest of them is a 422 page typewritten draft of the novel with ink corrections throughout. The fragments consist of some handwritten notes and a 16 page section titled "Notes on the Tench Novel." In *PKD Otaku #7* Clark writes further on these notes and reprints parts of them in the zine.[dlxxxv]

And in RFPKD #7 he describes the establishment of this hithertofore unknown cache of Dick papers:

In his many years as a writer Philip K. Dick left a paper trail of massive proportions. Much of his later output is in private hands, either with his literary estate or various collectors and booksellers. The largest collection open to the public is at the University of California-Fullerton Library holding materials from Phil's teenage notebooks through 1975. There is at least one other depository as well. A small collection of PKD's papers is housed in the Popular Culture Library at Bowling Green State University in Northern Ohio. This library was established in 1969 under the direction of Raymond Browne and contains primary research material of the study of 19th and 20th Century American culture.

On Feb 27 1969, Browne wrote to Phil asking him to donate some of his papers to the project. Phil was enthusiastic and replied on Mar 6, asking for more details. On Mar 21 he sent Browne "a mass of materials including the rough draft of a novel (which, by the way Doubleday has bought), typed notes, holographic notes, letters to me and from me." All of this material seems to have remained untouched for the most part since it arrived at Bowling Green.[dlxxxvi]

About the 422 page manuscript titled THE HOUR OF THE T.E.N.C.H. Clark goes into some detail:

This seems to be a copy of the draft received by the SMLA on Oct 31, 1968 and published in 1970 by Doubleday. The draft and the published novel are virtually the same. The draft itself has numerous, minor changes. None of these are significant. In most cases the changes are single-word substitutions or deletions...

Phil's major edit on the draft is the deletion of one paragraph in Chapter One (page 17 of the Doubleday edition). Ben Tallchief, upon learning that his prayer for a transfer has been answered by the Manufacturer, muses about A. J. Specktowsky's *How I Rose From The Dead In My Spare Time and So Can You*:

"Strange, he thought, that a Communist theologian put it all down first, before anyone else. God is not supernatural. The premise of the most important book ever written. And we have forty god-worlds to prove it. They have let us study them and we have verified, by the mot scientific means, our religious presumptions – or anyhow many of them. Though admittedly there remains errors of detail." Specktowsky's book had been introduced two pages previously and this paragraph would have better fit there. But in any event, Phil chose to cut it. Phil always said he didn't do multiple drafts until FLOW MY TEARS and the BGSU manuscript certainly bears this out. [dlxxxvii]

When Dick sent the manuscript for THE HOUR OF THE T.E.N.C.H. to the SMLA where it arrived on Oct, 31 1968 it was titled as such. But in a letter to Don Wollheim dated Oct 22, 1968 -- a week earlier -- he refers to the novel as A MAZE WITH DEATH:

Yesterday I sent off a new novel. A MAZE WITH DEATH, to Scott. It is an s-f mystery, and Larry Ashmead is interested in it for a series of <<future mystery, novels>> as they'll be called. I mention this only to indicate that I am actively writing, these days...which is not always so -- I go in cycles of creativity and sloth, as you may know. Anyhow, I have this one new novel in the works and intend to start on another as soon as possible. {...}
{...} do you want me to handle any particular theme? Do you want me to avoid any particular theme (such as reality-versus-illusion, for example)? {...}
PS. Another thought just struck me. If Doubleday turns down A MAZE WITH DEATH, perhaps you would like to see it. Do you think so?[dlxxxviii]

This would indicate that the T.E.N.C.H. manuscript was a draft written before Oct 22, 1968 although it is the one he sent to the SMLA... This is all very confusing and maybe what happened is that PKD intended A MAZE OF DEATH to be the title all along but, on a whim, knowing his titles always got changed anyway, he slapped THE HOUR OF THE T.E.N.C.H. on the manuscript and sent it off.[dlxxxix]

Certainly on the same day he wrote to Wollheim he is also wrote to his agent, Scott Meredith, and talked more of these matters:

I just now received a very nice letter from Don Wollheim, in which he picks up where he and I left off at the convention. At that time I told Don I wanted to do another novel for Ace, and in his letter he asks if I meant that and still mean it. He says: <<... I would like to see you keep on with us, even though report has it you have made pots of money with Doubleday. I don't know about pots of money, but I think we can come to some reasonable accommodation financially if given a reasonable chance.>> I have no new novel in the works, however, because I have been working on A MAZE WITH DEATH, but it occurs to me that if Larry Ashmead doesn't want it, maybe Don might. I am writing Don, and I'm mentioning A MAZE WITH DEATH. Could we try him if Doubleday turns the novel down? (By the way -- Don wants my material presented directly to him and not through Terry Carr. He says, <<... this is for me and would be published under my editorship.>>
Because of Don's interest I will start as soon as possible on another new novel... but it will take a while. Would he buy an outline and sample chapter? Or does he want the whole thing? [dxc]

A few weeks later on Nov 13, 1968 we find that this is all resolved; PKD wrote a letter to Ace editor Terry Carr telling him that Doubleday had bought A MAZE WITH DEATH but that he is working on a new novel for Ace and has already sent three and a half chapters and an outline to Don Wollheim. This new novel would eventually become OUR FRIENDS FROM FROLIX 8.[dxci]

The title of A MAZE OF DEATH was still not decided as late as January 1970 when Dick wrote:

I, too, prefer MAZE OF DEATH, but I think a THE should start it; i.e., THE MAZE OF DEATH (or possibly A MAZE OF DEATH). So go ahead.[dxcii]

Doubleday published the newly title A MAZE OF DEATH in July 1970 in what is now a very scarce edition. Daniel Levack, PKD's bibliographer, relates that David Hartwell said that this first edition was "accidentally pulped, leaving only library and review copies actually distributed." [dxciii]

That may be so, I have never seen a copy even in a library. But an ex-library copy in merely 'good' condition was for sale by one bookseller for $699! And another for $400. As this Doubleday edition is the only USA hardcover and it was mostly destroyed one can see that these prices are really quite fair. The only other hardcover in English came from Gollancz in England in 1972. This edition too would have some value to the PKD collector.[dxciv]

In 1976 Mark Hurst acquired the reprint rights to A MAZE OF DEATH – along with several other PKD novels – for Bantam Books. Accordingly, in Sep 1977 Bantam produced their paperback edition.[dxcv]

More editions followed from DAW Books and Vintage Books in the USA and from Grafton and Voyager in the UK.

As usual when PKD discussed his books with interviewers Apel & Briggs in 1977, he was less than totally positive about A MAZE OF DEATH:

Another one I'm not sure of is A MAZE OF DEATH. I get different reactions when I read different parts. There's a part in there where the same whole conversation is repeated twice. It's long, and everybody's babbling away. But it's different -- it's carefully rewoven so that the second time around it's not the same; it has a different meaning.[dxcvi]

A MAZE OF DEATH also contributed to PKD's post-Pink Beam world view:

My 3-74 experiences are an outgrowth of my Palmer Eldritch experience of over ten years earlier. "Faith Of Our Fathers" shows this, too; I knew Him to be real ...but only in UBIK does he begin to appear as benign, especially then in A MAZE OF DEATH.[dxcvii]

And:

in MAZE OF DEATH there are endless parallel realities arranged spatially.[dxcviii]

Hopefully these cryptic remarks will make sense later when we reach 1974…

In the story Ben Tallchief, Seth Morley and others are enticed to the planet Delmak-O. Once there they can find no reason for their existence and as they muddle their way around, they die one by one, either by murder, accident or reasons unknown. At last they wake up to find themselves in a doomed spaceship the computer of which has generated a series of virtual worlds to occupy the crew while they wait to die. But once awake the crew debate the situation on virtual world Delmak-O and despite the violence decide to return there – its better than all the other worlds they've tried so far.

A MAZE OF DEATH gets ✳ ✳ ✳ ✳

OUR FRIENDS FROM FROLIX 8

We've just seen that during the time Philip K. Dick and his agent were selling publication rights for A MAZE OF DEATH to Doubleday, they were also preparing the ground for writing a new novel for Don Wollheim at Ace Books. This novel would eventually be published by Ace in June 1970 as OUR FRIENDS FROM FROLIX 8.

It all started, as we have seen, at the Baycon Science Fiction Convention held in San Francisco in August 1968. At this convention Dick had met his long-time Ace editor, Don Wollheim and they'd discussed Dick's writing something new for Ace. In a letter to Scott Meredith in October, Dick mentions this and informs Meredith that he will start a new novel for Ace:

I just now received a very nice letter from Don Wollheim, in which he picks up where he and I left off at the convention. At that time I told Don I wanted to do another novel for Ace, and in his letter he asks if I meant that and still mean it...

{...}(By the way -- Don wants my material presented directly to him and not through Terry Carr. He says, <<... this is for me and would be published under my editorship.>>

Because of Don's interest I will start as soon as possible on another new novel... but it will take a while. Would he buy an outline and sample chapter? Or does he want the whole thing?[dxcix]

Some early notes for FROLIX 8 were found in the BGSU Papers; these consisted of:

Handwritten notes for another novel, OUR FRIENDS FROM FROLIX 9. Five sheets of typing paper, folded in half, with writing on the recto and verso, and one sheet of unfolded lined notebook paper numbered 1-9. Ideas, characters and plot lines.[dc]

Note that at this time our friends were from Frolix 9, not Frolix 8. For the next step in the progression of this novel we turn to Paul Williams who notes:

On November 6, 1968, the Scott Meredith Literary Agency received from Philip K. Dick an outline and four sample chapters (40 manuscript pages) for a novel to be called OUR FRIENDS FROM FROLIX 8. This was only a week after he'd sent them the finished manuscript for A MAZE OF DEATH, written under contract to Doubleday. (October-November was typically the most productive time of year for Dick). The Agency immediately sent the FROLIX material to Donald A. Wollheim at Ace Books, who purchased the unfinished book for $2500 (half on signing of the contract, half on delivery and acceptance of the finished manuscript)...[dci]

To get a feeling of what Dick's outlines were like we've included the first part of the one he wrote for FROLIX 8, courtesy of *The Philip K. Dick Society*:

Outline for science fiction novel called: OUR FRIENDS FROM FROLIX 5̶ 8

Theme: Earth is invaded by aliens whom the great majority of people welcome.

Locus of action: Earth in 2190

Situation: Within the last century two new types of human beings have arisen as sport-mutations desired and preserved until by 2085 they fill the top levels of business organizations -- and, in the planet-wide federal government, <u>all</u> persons who pass the Civil Service tests must be either a New Man or an Unusual. The New Men possess magnified cerebral cortexes, the so-called Nodes of Rogers. Their I.Q. is twice that of a brilliant Old Man -- as the unevolved are called. (Most people are Old Men, so this makes the New Men an elite -- along with the Unusuals.)

The Unusuals are mutants who have freak abilities; i.e. all the familiar psionic gifts having to do with reading minds, knowing the future, moving objects at a distance, etc. They, too, can pass the Civil Service tests and obtain G ratings. And hence rule, along with the New Men.

Neither group likes the other very much. In particular, the New Men look down on the Unusuals as being merely odd.

The highest official on Earth is the Council Chairman of the Extraordinary Committee For Public Safety. He, too, must hold a Civil Service rating. This office, over the years, has passed back and forth between New Men and Unusuals. At this moment the council Chairman is an Unusual named Willis Gramm.

In addition one further group exists. An illegal organization by Old Men calling themselves -- not Old Men -- but <u>Under</u> Men. There is no way they can rule legally, but at least they can fight. But up to now they have done nothing but print tracts and hang up lurid posters in the dead of night.

Their paralysis is understandable; they are waiting for their hope, their saviour. Led by their pro tem spokesman, Eric Cordon, who is in prison, they are standing firm until the day that Thors Provoni returns from the distant star-system which he is visiting. "Provoni will come back with help," the Under Men say, but, as they wait, the police (the PSS: Public Security Service) get them one by one; the police have successfully infiltrated the ranks of the Under Men and are destroying them from within.

Plot: The novel opens in on Bobby and his father Nick Appleton. Along the crowded sidewalk, at a snail's pace, they are making -- or trying to make -- their way to the Federal Bureau of Personnel Standards; there, Bobby (who is twelve) will try to score highly enough on his first Civil Service test to give the Appleton family some hope for the future... since Nick himself has never been able to obtain even a G-one rating, the lowest there is.
{... ...}^{dcii}

Although PKD wrote the outline and sample pages quickly enough, he took a little longer to finish the novel manuscript. But he tried to keep Don Wollheim happy as he went along slowly falling behind the deadline:

Great news. Although I am a little late, I have finished the novel, OUR FRIENDS FROM FROLIX 8, which, as you will recall, I am under contract for (sometime last month it was due). All I need do now is simply type up the final draft; there will be no further revision, that having already been done.

The novel runs longer than my others. They all came out at about 215 typescript pages; this comes out to 268, which I would estimate as between 70,000 and 80,000 words. I hope that the length is satisfactory to you; i.e. the contract called for 70,000, rather than the usual 60,000, so I assumed you wanted a longer novel; hence this length, which was most carefully planned on my part; it didn't just happen that way.

Not since EYE IN THE SKY have I so much enjoyed working on a novel. Usually I get up at noon; while writing this I got up at seven a.m. and tottered my way to the typewriter, my mind filled with dialog. There is nothing about reality-versus-illusion in it, no hallucinations, etc. I did depart from the latter part of the outline, but the book remains as the outline described it; I think it is fair to say that it is true to the outline.

Please write me and let me know if the length is okay. But I really don't want to trim it; I would appreciate it very, very much if you let me leave it at its present length. Okay? [dciii]

This letter from April 1969 was not the end of it as a month later PKD still wasn't done. In this next letter to Wollheim he is heartily sorry:

I have been stewing and fretting about completing the final copy of OUR FRIENDS. First, when I began typing the final version, I discovered that I had to change some of the material. Then I came down with Hong Kong flu, with complications. And as the coup de grace, my Olympia typewriter broke down and had to go to the shop for repairs {...} typing 80,000 words on this damn {loaner} thing is next to impossible (it's a 1941 Royal). I have to have my own machine, and when I get it back I'll resume the typing of the final draft (which I had gotten well into before the troubles began). I am very sorry and I know the novel is overdue, but the revisions have been made {...}[dciv]

Whether that was the final excuse or his dog later ate the manuscript, I don't know. But I think Dick was glad to get FROLIX 8 finished. It would be the only novel he completed in 1969.

In any case, Ace Books published OUR FRIENDS FROM FROLIX 8 in a fine paperback edition in June 1970.[dcv] A hardback from the SFBC followed in Feb 1971.[dcvi] First English publication came from Panther in Jan 1976.[dcvii] The novel has seen many editions but perhaps the most valuable to collectors is the 1989 hardback edition from Kinnell Publishers which has a great wraparound cover from Keith Roberts.[dcviii]

For the ultimate collector the following edition was offered for sale on the internet via book-seller *Phildickian.com*:

OUR FRIENDS FROM FROLIX 8, Kinnell, hb, 08-2, 1989 (1st UK hb). UNIQUE "founder's copy" of first trade hardcover edition (preceded in hardcover only by an American book club edition). Bound-up from the first sheets supplied to the publisher by the printer. This copy was specially bound for the founder of Kinnell Publications Limited, in three-quarter brown Morocco (goat skin) with gold lettering on a maroon Morocco lettering-piece, gold stamping, raised bands, and with top and fore-edge gilt. This copy, and this copy only, has a colophon. This copy, then, is the first copy of the first trade hardcover edition, in a unique and handsome binding. FINE. With a signed letter of provenance from Kinnell's founder, A. E. Cunningham. WITH an unfolded copy of the dust jacket. $3,000.00.

With PKD's outline of FROLIX 8 describing the plot and main characters, partially included above, it remains only for me to rate the novel with ★★★★.

One last item came up for PKD at the end of 1968. This was a request from Edward L. Ferman at *F & SF* requesting a short story from Phil for the upcoming 20th anniversary issue of the magazine. This request would result in "The Electric Ant".

"The Electric Ant" was written after Nov 15, 1968 and the manuscript reached the SMLA on Dec 4, 1968. The story was accepted at *F & SF* on Jan 4, 1969. It all started with a Nov 2, 1968 letter from Edward L. Ferman, editor at *F & SF*, requesting from PKD a short story for the upcoming 20th anniversary issue of *F& SF*. [dcix] PKD replied to Marcia M. Howell at the SMLA on Nov 15, 1968:

This letter is in answer to Ed Ferman's request that I do a short story for the twentieth anniversary issue of *F&SF*. I would very much like to, and I hope you will tell Mr. Ferman this. However, I won't be able to get to it right away ... but I am sure it will be done by the April first deadline.

F&SF is a fine magazine and published some of my best stories. Also, it was the first magazine to buy a story from me; *F&SF* launched me on my career as a professional writer. So I very much want to do this... despite the fact that I have not done any magazine-length material for several years.

Thank Mr. Ferman for his request, and thank you, too, for passing it along to me. I'm sure the issue will be excellent. [dcx]

"The Electric Ant' was published in Oct 1969 in *F & SF*.

The story is a popular one, with many anthology appearances, including Harry Harrison and Brian Aldiss' *BEST SF: 1969* published in 1970. It was also selected for Ballantine's PKD collection THE BEST OF PHILIP K. DICK in 1977. More anthologies followed before it was published for the last time in THE COLLECTED STORIES.

It is also a favorite of many fans; in the poll run by *FDO*, Gregg Rickman selects "The Electric Ant" as his fave short story:

Best Story (for its formal perfection, and in so well displaying Phil's characteristic themes and strengths): "The Electric Ant." -- Gregg Rickman, CA

Of the story PKD said this:

Again the theme: How much of what we call 'reality' is actually out there or rather within our own head? The ending of this story has always frightened me ... the image of the rushing wind, the sound of emptiness. As if the character hears the final fate of the world itself" [dcxi]

"The Electric Ant" is a good story and thought-provoking as well. It tells the tale of Garson Poole who after a squib crash discovers he is not a man but an android; an electric ant as they're called. Determined to free himself from his programming he opens his chest compartment and examines his 'reality tape'. This is a micro-punched tape that slowly unreels beneath a miniature scanner. Poole experiments with the tape, blocking holes, cutting strips out, turning bits around. In the end he decides to remove a strip altogether and let total reality into his perceptions. Though technicians warn him not to do this he goes ahead and is burned out by the multi-sensory totality of perceptions that now flood him. The question is, if Poole's reality is changed does everyone else's stay the same?

This is another example of PKD's fake reality stories, and one of the best. "The Electric Ant" has ✭ ✭ ✭ ✭ ✭ on my reality tape.

Before we leave 1968 we will take a slight step backwards and note that DO ANDROIDS DREAM OF ELECTRIC SHEEP? was first optioned for film in this year.

BLADE RUNNER (Part 1)

Philip K. Dick first learned that a film option was taken out on DO ANDROIDS DREAM OF ELECTRIC SHEEP? sometime in May 1968. A letter from his Doubleday editor, Lawrence Ashmead, on the 29th congratulates him on the sale of the movie rights.[dcxii]

In his 'Self Portrait' written soon after he learned of the sale, PKD refers to this possible filming of his novel:

DO ANDROIDS DREAM? has sold very well and has been eyed intently by a film company who have in fact purchased an option on it....[dcxiii]

The producer who had optioned ANDROIDS was Bertram Berman. However, Berman had nothing to do with the final movie. Apparently, Herb Jaffe later picked up the option, probably around 1973.[dcxiv] Philip Dick talks of those early days:

It all began years ago", he explains, "Martin Scorsese and Jay Cocks were both interested in ANDROIDS but they didn't option it. That was the first movie interest in any property of mine. Then later Herb Jaffe optioned it and Robert Jaffe did a screenplay back about 1973. The screenplay was sent to me and it was so crude that I didn't understand that it was actually the shooting script; I thought it was the rough. I wrote to them and asked if they would like me to do the shooting script, at which point Robert Jaffe, the one who wrote the screenplay, flew down here to Orange County and confessed that he had written it under a nom de plume. I said to him then that it was so bad that I wanted to know if he wanted me to beat him up there at the airport or wait till we got to my apartment."

Robert Jaffe was very straightforward and asked Dick if he really thought it was that bad, whereupon Dick responded candidly. "I said, 'All I ask is that you do not drag me down to ruin with you.'" I said that I'd honestly prefer to buy back the property than let them make a film based on that screenplay and he was real nice about it. I gave him suggestions and he took notes and then I noticed that he wasn't actually writing, but rather he was just moving the pen about a quarter of an inch from a piece of paper that already had printing on it so that he was only pretending to take notes. I realized then that there was a gulf between me and Hollywood.{...}" [dcxv]

And in another interview he talks about it again:

A producer by the name of Herb Jaffe has an option on DO ANDROIDS DREAM OF ELECTRIC SHEEP? I don't dare bad-mouth his silly movies, but if You're listening, Herb Jaffe, I love your money, but you sure write lousy scripts. You're a Neanderthal Man. You're back with George pal, and I don't want you to make a movie out of my book. The screenplay that they wrote for ANDROIDS was a combination of Steve Reeves and Maxwell Smart. Robert Jaffe, Herb Jaffe's son, flew down to Fullerton to talk with me about it because I didn't think it was a final shooting script; I thought it was just a rough draft. I told him, "I'm going to beat you up right here in the airport, because you're going to drag me down with you guys and ruin my career if you make a movie out of my book." He said, "You mean it's that bad?" and I said, "Yeah." Finally, he said, "You mean you wrote that book *seriously*? You science fiction writers take your work *seriously*?" I said, "Seriously enough to throw you right out of this moving car." I said, "I'm going to buy it back from you and give you the two-thousand-dollar option money back." Then we had a four-hour rap session which was very productive: they didn't make the movie. They just continued to hold the option, and I'm hoping they *don't* make the movie unless they write a decent script.[dcxvi]

At this point we will defer further exploration of *BLADE RUNNER* until 1981 when things heated up on the movie and it actually went into production. So ends 1968 then. A good year for Dick's career but a sad one personally with the loss of Anthony Boucher, to whom he dedicated his novel UBIK. 1969 would not be an improvement.

1969

Due to the publication time lag, 1969 doesn't look as empty as it really was for PKD's writing career. In January Roger Zelazny was supposedly tackling the arduous task of writing the next stage of DEUS IRAE and February saw "The War With The Fnools" reprinted in *Galaxy*. Then in March the first paperback edition of DO ANDROIDS DREAM OF ELECTRIC SHEEP? came out from Signet Books.[dcxvii] And, in the UK, Rapp & Whiting brought out their hardcover edition.[dcxviii] In April Ace Books published the paperback original of PKD's collection, THE PRESERVING MACHINE.[dcxix] In May the first UK edition of THE GAME-PLAYERS OF TITAN was published by Sphere.[dcxx] And Doubleday released the first edition of UBIK.[dcxxi]

So far, so good. But there was more to follow. In June 1969 Berkley published the first paperback original of GALACTIC POT-HEALER.[dcxxii] Then July saw the SFBC edition of UBIK for sale.[dcxxiii] The short story "The Electric Ant" came out in the twentieth anniversary edition of *F & SF* in October and, to round out the year, NOW WAIT FOR LAST YEAR began serialization in *Amazing* as "A. Lincoln, Simulacrum."[dcxxiv]

But, as we've already noted, the only novel PKD completed in 1969 was OUR FRIENDS FROM FROLIX 8. That and "The Electric Ant" were the only two items he finished in that year. Phil was in a slump. In a May letter he explained his inactivity:

I have a theory: I can't sit and write one novel following another; between each I have to emerge from my shell and be with people; otherwise my novels resemble each other too much.[dcxxv]

Dick at this time was taking too much speed. This would be disastrous in August when, after taking some bad street-speed, he developed pancreatitis and this put him in hospital, effectively stopping his writing until well into 1970.[dcxxvi]

This continuing use of amphetamines was also affecting his marriage to Nancy who was afraid that it would kill him. Then, in September, Dick's friend Bishop James A. Pike wandered into the Israeli desert with a only a bottle of Coca Cola and died while in search of evidence for the historical Jesus. This was too much and Phil's writing slump deepened.[dcxxvii]

1969 then was a good year for publication of Dick's work but a bad one for his writing. The effect, although delayed, would show up in 1971.

1970

Jan 1970 saw the second part of "A. Lincoln, Simulacrum" in *Amazing* and publication of the SFBC edition of THE PRESERVING MACHINE. In England Panther published a paperback edition of THE WORLD JONES MADE that month. That was it until April when the SFBC edition of GALACTIC POT-HEALER became available to the club members. In May Dell published a paperback edition of UBIK and Penguin a paperback of THE PENULTIMATE TRUTH in the UK. In June Ace released the first edition paperback of OUR FRIENDS FROM FROLIX 8.[dcxxviii] Also in June Rapp & Whiting issued their hardcover edition of UBIK – the first UK edition of this novel.[dcxxix] In July Doubleday issued the first edition hardback of A MAZE OF DEATH, as we've noted above.

Other English language editions of Dick's novels appeared during the year: SOLAR LOTTERY and EYE IN THE SKY from Ace Books and, again in the UK, Sidgwick & Jackson brought forth A PKD OMNIBUS in October which contained three Dick novels: DR. FUTURITY, THE CRACK IN SPACE and THE UNTELEPORTED MAN.[dcxxx] A curiosity for this year was another book from Sidgwick & Jackson: THE WORLD JONES MADE in *SCIENCE FICTION SPECIAL #1*. This edition may be a phantom.

I've listed these various editions and reprints of PKD's stories in 1970 to show that, while he wasn't too active writing that year, he was still being published – and no doubt eventually received royalties for these various editions. But we cannot be too sure on this as Dick complained through the years that he never did receive proper royalties from some publishers, notably Ace Books and Doubleday. In connection with Doubleday he had this to say:

(Mike Hodel:) All right. You do writing which is excellent. It's labeled science fiction, and therefore it doesn't sell much. It winds up next to the bra and panty ads.

(Dick:) Wrong. Doubleday gets to market it through their el-cheapo book club. They get to sell it for a dollar, and the author gets to make a penny. Robert Heinlein explained this to me one time. You sell a book to a hardcover publisher and the Doubleday Book Club snatches it right up and markets it for a dollar no matter how many pages it's got. Naturally, we're speaking in hyperbole here, but nevertheless your royalties immediately descend to the level of the miniscule again: the more copies your book sells, the less money you make. Heinlein says that he was financially ruined when they picked up *STRANGER IN A STRANGE LAND* because they made him market this giant thing for a dollar and destroyed the trade edition. I always thought it was *good* when I had a book picked up by the Doubleday Book Club, but I found out that I made no money. I looked at my royalty receipts. That's where the money is, though, marketing it through a book club: the *publisher* makes the money and the author doesn't. He makes his ten percent of the flat price on the trade edition only. What they do is this: they print up about two thousand copies of the trade edition, sell five hundred of them, and pulp the rest the next day. So the author looks at his royalty sheet and says, "that's really strange." [dcxxxi]

Similar grumbles can be found in other interviews late in PKD's life.

The one major thing that Philip K. Dick began in 1970 was his famous novel FLOW MY TEARS, THE POLICEMAN SAID.

FLOW MY TEARS, THE POLICEMAN SAID

FLOW MY TEARS, THE POLICEMAN SAID is a pivotal, even crucial novel in Dick's career. Soon we shall see why but first we'll look at the origins of the novel.

It all started in May of 1970 when PKD took some mescaline. This trip had a powerful affect on him. In a letter to Sandra Meisel in August he explains:

I have just finished the rough draft of a new, long, s-f novel, FLOW MY TEARS, THE POLICEMAN SAID. {...} I've reworked it and reworked it; I rewrote the final section seven times, plus holographic changes. At one point in the writing I wrote 140 pages in 48 hours. I have high hopes for this. It is the first really new thing I've done since EYE IN THE SKY. The change is due to a change that overtook me from having taken mescalin, a very large dose that completely unhinged me. I had enormous insights behind the drug, all having to do with those whom I loved. Love. Will love.[dcxxxii]

And in another letter about the same time he again refers to this mescaline trip and his insights:

With acid I never had any genuine insights, but on mescalin I was overwhelmed by terribly powerful feelings – emotions, I guess. I felt an overpowering love for other people, and this is what I put into the novel: it studies different kinds of love and at last ends with the appearance of an ultimate kind of love which I had never known of. I am saying, "In answer to the question, 'What is real?' the answer is: this kind of overpowering love.["][dcxxxiii]

But, as referred to in this last letter, Dick was also in FLOW MY TEARS, THE POLICEMAN SAID trying to answer the question, What is real? This question having been brought up by Terry Carr. We'll let PKD explain:

(PKD:) *They* say I have to say what reality is, and I never had any intention of doing that. And the reason that I never had any intention of doing that is that *I don't know* -- I have no knowledge at all of what reality is. All I can do is plaintively inquire "Hey, gang, what is really real?" And then here is Terry Carr -- the great anthologizer -- and a major figure in the field -- and he says "All right!" and he blows on his little whistle, like the Recreation Director at camp has. . ."All right! Time to write about what reality is!"
{...}
So I discovered -- as amazing as it may sound -- that it was a lot harder to *say* what it was than to ask what it was.
(DSA:) What was it?
(PKD:) Damned if I know! {(...)} But I thought: *I'll fake it.* So in 1970 I started working on FLOW MY TEARS, THE POLICEMAN SAID. And it was my intention to resolve the problem by the discovery of what reality really was. So that meant there was a three year ellipsis in my writing...
(DSA:) When you had to go out and find out what it was?
(PKD:) Yeah. Well, I just sort of sat there at the typewriter. I did eleven drafts of that novel. I mean literally; I'm not using that as hyperbole. I had a complicated code system worked out so I wouldn't start feeding old drafts back in, in which case I guess I'd still be there today.
I decided the thing that was really real was *love*. Then I thought, *Y'know, somebody else said this; now who the hell was it that said this?* Well, actually, a lot of people have

said it. My revelation which I'm about to lay on the world is not going to come as a complete surprise.

(DSA:) St. Augustine said it, and Aleister Crowley...

(PKD:) St. Paul said, "If I have not love then I am jack shit"... or something like that. So anyway, I worked for three years on FLOW MY TEARS, then when Terry Carr wasn't looking, I began to go back to the question of what is real.[dcxxxiv]

This, then, is how the novel began. To Dick himself the novel was essentially finished by Aug 2, 1970. In a letter to his agent, Scott Meredith dated then he rhapsodizes about FLOW MY TEARS:

I want to give you a progress report on my new novel, FLOW MY TEARS, THE POLICEMAN SAID. I have now read over the rough draft, revised several scenes, added more material and built up the ending so that it is more effective. And then I have read the novel once again with all these changes. I think it is the best s-f novel ever written. Certainly it is the best thing I have ever done, and I have no idea as to how I managed to do it. At one point in 48 hours I wrote 140 pages. At other times I revised one sole passage again and again -- in one case 7 times -- until I had what I wanted. There will be no further changes in the novel when I go to do the final draft; the novel is done.

{... there follows a brief description of the plot by PKD...}

I only wish I could go on writing this novel forever, because it has given me intense joy in the writing of it. But, as I said, it is finished.[dcxxxv]

But even though PKD wrote to Meredith that the novel was done by the beginning of August, this was not really true. Dick acknowledges this in an October letter to correspondent Valerie McMillan:

News about the novel I'm working on, FLOW MY TEARS, THE POLICEMAN SAID. Although I have not finished it, and they have not read it, Doubleday (the hard-cover house) has bought it! And for an *extra* thousand dollars!, on the strength of what I've told them about it. The novel is a good one -- I think one of the best science fiction novels written -- and a long one. It deals with a variety of forms of love, about ten kinds in all, ending with a form of love which I can't explain but which has to do with strangers. (It's explained in the novel, but it took me 320 pages, so obviously I can't do it here in one paragraph -- thank god ... because if I could, then there would have been no reason to write a 320 page novel about it.) At the end of the novel the protagonist lands at night at a 24-hour gas station in Los Angeles and hugs a big, well-dressed black man who is waiting for his car to be gassed and ready. At first the black man is puzzled, and not pleased, but then he understands the kind of love the protagonist is feeling and he expresses something back, a kind of understanding. He invites the protagonist to visit him at home and meet his wife and children. They talk, and then the protagonist flies off. The novel is over. After I wrote the ending -- ninth in a series of endings -- I said to myself, "Maybe people who read it will think it's a plea for homosexuality." {...}

Don't you agree that it seems like a vote of confidence by Doubleday toward me that they bought my novel without having read it? I told them, "Look, I've written this novel and it's the best I've ever done, and one of the best in the field, and it's long, and multifaceted, funny and sad -- sad as in the two pages I sent you -- and dramatic and meaningful, with a new kind of love to offer." And they said fine. They wrote me, "If anybody on the Doubleday book list can do it, you can." It made me very happy.

I love my work; I mean, I don't love what I write but the act of writing it, rereading it, altering, selecting, cutting, revising, adding to it, shaping it again and again until, at last, it's what I want. Before this I have never really been satisfied with any novel I wrote; I could sense the shortcomings but couldn't see how to change or improve it.[dcxxxvi]

With Doubleday saying, 'if anyone one our list can do it, you can', we get a sense of how powerful a writer Dick was in the eyes of the professionals of the day. Here's someone proposing to write about love, ten different kinds of love. One can imagine that any other writer making this proposition would be greeted with high skepticism. But Dick... a writer who's been all over the map, who's plumbed the depths of fear and horror and explored the commonplace of everyday life and scathingly revealed the machinations of politics; if anyone can do it he can. And throw in another thousand dollars just for the sheer nerve of it!

But FLOW MY TEARS, THE POLICEMAN SAID was not to be finished for several more years. With all the turmoil of life and the stress on Nancy, Phil and baby Isa of drug abuse, lack of money, sickness and death, something broke and Nancy left Phil in September 1970, taking along the baby. This was devastating for Dick. His fourth marriage: collapsed. Alone again with one foot in the streets. To continue writing FLOW MY TEARS was impossible for him following Nancy's exit. How can one write about love when one's life is a total disaster?[dcxxxvii]

As Dick recalled this period to Paul Williams in 1974:

... there really was no point in writing. As a matter of fact, when you conceive of how you write – one writes by going off into privacy, alone – one hour of solitude would have meant my demise, after Nancy left with my little girl, it was too risky. I had to be with people. I flooded the house with people. Anybody was welcome. Because the sound of their voices, the sound of their activity, the din in the hall, anything, it kept me alive. I literally was unable to kill myself then, 'cause there was too much going on.[dcxxxviii]

Drugs, particularly amphetamines – white cross speed – became an even larger part of Dick's life. But the side-effects of too much speed are edginess and paranoia. And loss of financial control. This last resulted in failed mortgage payments and news that his house was being foreclosed in early 1971. Two brief visits to psychiatrists followed and the second one in August resulted in Dick giving his attorney the manuscript for FLOW MY TEARS, THE POLICEMAN SAID.[dcxxxix]

This was a fortunate happenstance as only a few months later, while Phil was enduring the mandatory waiting period before he could pick up his new gun, his house in San Rafael was broken into and smashed, trashed and ripped-off. Particularly noticeable among the wreckage was his fireproof file cabinet which had been blown open by what looked like plastic explosives. All his papers were gone. Among them would have been the manuscript for FLOW MY TEARS, THE POLICEMAN SAID. Of the break-in PKD wrote in 1975:

My most recent novel, FLOW MY TEARS, THE POLICEMAN SAID, deals with the USA as a total police state (as you may know). What most readers of s-f do not know is that it was actually written back in 1970 (not in 1972 or 1973 as generally believed); I wrote the novel and then placed the manuscript -- the sole copy -- in my lawyer's safe to protect it. In 1971 my house was broken into and my files blown open and most of my business documents, records and written notes were stolen. I remain convinced to this day that it was an agency of the US federal government which did this; we have just learned, for example, that the FBI alone conducted 1,500 such illegal burglaries. What most frightens me is to think what might have happened had they found the manuscript of FLOW MY TEARS, a book which so well depicts their own activities and nature. I am sure it would not ever have been published, and it is even possible that it was this particular manuscript which they were seeking. Ah, that such events could have happened here! [dcxl]

To pick up on the progress of FLOW MY TEARS then we must move forward to the end of 1972 when Dick, now living in Fullerton with Tessa, his soon-to-be fifth wife, wrote to his attorney requesting his manuscript back.[dcxli] This was duly returned to him. Paul Williams explicates:

It arrived January 6, 1973, and Dick retyped it over the next four weeks and mailed it to his agent in New York. The agent received the completed manuscript on February 7, 1973. On April 6, 1973 Dick learned that Doubleday had accepted the novel, and a few days later he received a letter from his editor at Doubleday, Diane Cleaver, telling him how much she liked the book and offering a few editorial suggestions.[dcxlii]

These suggestions and Dick's replies, Williams goes on to relate, were contained in a series of letters between Dick and Cleaver in April 1973 with a few follow-ups later in the year. Here are a few excerpts, courtesy of PKDS:

Cleaver to Dick (Apr 5, 1973): "The only other thing is something I think you'll feel strongly about -- Ruth Rae. Her long discussion with Taverner really is too long and I think destroys the movement of the story and it could be cut somewhat without ruining the point you're making about Taverner {...}"

Dick to Cleaver (Apr 9, 1973): "Re: paragraph three of your letter, the Ruth Rae section, which I regard as the mid-section of the novel. Here is my feeling about that. I will cut this section. I will go over it entirely and tighten. {... ...}

Cleaver to Dick (Apr 24, 1973): "Thank you for taking so generously to my suggestions on FLOW MY TEARS, THE POLICEMAN SAID." {...}[dcxliii]

The cuts suggested by Cleaver in the discussion between Ruth Rae and Jason Taverner in the novel would eventually take on a life of their own, particularly in the French editions of the novel. And under the title "The Different Stages Of Love" they were published in *The Philip K. Dick Society Newsletter* in 1992. This is an interesting sidelight and we'll go into it soon. But first, we'll continue with the main line of progression for FLOW MY TEARS.

On April 6, 1973, the day he learnt of Doubleday's acceptance of the novel, PKD wrote to Charles Brown, editor of *Locus Magazine*, and talked more of the situation anent FLOW MY TEARS at that time:

I thought I'd give you a piece of news that for me, anyhow, is exciting: I have just now sold my new large sf novel, FLOW MY TEARS, THE POLICEMAN SAID, to Doubleday. I've been working on this novel since mid-1970 and finished it in January of this year.

In the novel I try to say what I believe is real – rather than ask, What is reality? What is illusion? As I tended to do in previous novels.

Doubleday was the first publisher to see the ms; in fact Larry Ashmead tied it up in late 1970 without having seen it – he had only my description of it in a letter from me to him.

Ashmead suggested I continue to work on the novel until I was thoroughly satisfied with it – no contract deadline. This is exactly what I did. Two complete revisions, before I at last sent it off.[dcxliv]

One more letter followed shortly in May, this one to his Swedish translator, Goran Bengtson:

For me the big news (besides me and Tessa getting married) is that I have sold *two* new novels to Doubleday, the first of which is FLOW MY TEARS. I have said to you that I considered it perfect and finished; it was neither -- I had to do a total rewrite before sending it off at last. Ten rewrites, the last of which was monumental! Anyhow now it is bought and will be coming out. But for me the later one, A SCANNER DARKLY, which is only finished in rough, is the one now. TEARS, when I reread it early this year before typing it up, turned out to be sentimental; so much for what I called 'the perfect' novel.. Only in the final draft did I get any bite into it, any grit.[dcxlv]

Tessa gave birth to baby Christopher on July 25, 1973, and in another letter to Diane Cleaver two days later Dick proudly announced the birth of their son. He also used the occasion to excuse his tardiness in completing the rewrite of FLOW MY TEARS.[dcxlvi] But by November the novel was truly done and PKD was editing the galleys that month. In a letter to Patrice Duvic, PKD's editor at the French publisher Editions Opta, Dick mentions this:

Because of my flu I couldn't complete my editing of the galleys on FLOW MY TEARS. I hope it makes sense. It seems to me that my agent is supposed to send you a copy of the MS; did he do so? [dcxlvii]

This letter to Duvic was probably the start of the divergent French editions of FLOW MY TEARS.

The novel was finally published by Doubleday at the beginning of 1974 and Dick wrote to Lawrence Ashmead, his editor at Doubleday, thanking him:

The book came out looking wonderful -- in my opinion by far the best so far. I wanted to tell you, too that the cuts which Diane suggested, and which I made, greatly improve the novel, as she thought they would. Also, I want to thank and commend your copy editors who built the missing bridge across one of the cuts; they did a superb job. I could only have done worse.[dcxlviii]

This first Doubleday edition of FLOW MY TEARS, THE POLICEMAN SAID exists in three states, each valuable to collectors. These states are:

1). The true first edition, described by bibliographer Levack: 'Bound in rust-colored cloth with silver lettering on the spine. Date code '050' [50th week of 1973] at lower left margin of page 231. States 'First edition' on the copyright page... '1974' on the title page of the first printing only. According to the author there were about 7500 copies of the first printing

2). The first edition, according to Levack: 'was reprinted with a date code of 'P7' [7th week of 1974] on page 231 and this printing was remaindered. The later printing leaves out the statement 'First edition' on the copyright page -- normal practice for Doubleday'. The remaindered copies can be told by the purple splotches on the bottom edges of the book; the normal way to mark remainders used by Doubleday.

3). Remaindered copies of the true first edition. Levack: 'Among the remaindered copies... were some first printings'. These remainders also had the Doubleday purple splotches.[dcxlix]

Copies of the true first edition in near-fine condition sell for over $500 and even an ex-library copy can fetch $100. The remaindered second printing, too, is valuable, and sells for about $100. One can assume that a remaindered true first edition would be very expensive indeed.

The English first edition came from Gollancz in October 1974.[dcl] And a UK SFBC edition followed in 1975 from Reader's Union publishers. Both of these British editions can be found for less than $100 in reasonable shape.

FLOW MY TEARS, THE POLICEMAN SAID was nominated by the fans as the Best Novel of the year and Dick's fellow writers nominated it for the Nebula Award for Best Novel of 1974. The novel actually won the John W. Campbell Memorial Award or Best Novel in 1975.

Now it's time to look at the excerpt from FLOW MY TEARS known as "The Different Stages of Love" and its connection with the French editions of the novel.

The name, "The Different Stages of Love" was applied to the excerpt by Paul Williams, as we've noted. The excerpt can be found in the 28th issue of *The Philip K. Dick Society Newsletter*. It was cut from the published edition of FLOW MY TEARS starting less than one page into chapter 11.[dcli]

But what has this to do with the French? Well, Gerard Klein, an editor at the French publisher 'Editions Laffont', read a copy of FLOW MY TEARS in 1974 but decided not to publish it in his line of science fiction books known as 'Ailleurs et Demain'. The novel ended up at a less-prestigious publishing house, 'Le Masque Science Fiction', who published the novel under the title LE PRISM DU NEANT in 1975. Years later, Klein had the opportunity to read the novel again and recognized along with other critics that the translation was not the best:

Indeed, it was said in many places that the translation was not what it should have been. I reread the available American edition, I read the French translation, done by a translator usually faithful, in fact excellent, and a friend of long standing, Michel Deutsch; and I did notice some singularities, not to say anything worse, for which he was certainly not responsible. And I finished by being in a position to repair my error, to give the French reader, at last, a version of FLOW MY TEARS that was reasonably close to the original.[dclii]

Klein asked translator Isabelle Delord to do a comparison of the Le Masque edition and the original English-language edition. Delord found seventeen cuts in Chapter 12. Klein notes:

These cuts were certainly not the doing of Michel Deutsch but were without the least doubt the work of an editor frightened by the description in the mutilated chapter of a homosexual episode, a description that stopped far short of anything pornographic.[dcliii]

He goes on to note further:

But what was much more surprising was that the French text also contained eight interpolations, that is to say, eight passages, often quite substantial, that were not in the text of the DAW Books edition which had served as our reference.[dcliv]

Mr. Klein goes on to suggest that the original translator, Michel Deutsch, made his translation from a *manuscript* that differed from the published Doubleday (and DAW) editions. After much research, Philip K. Dick's literary executor, Paul Williams, discovered a 1970 draft of FLOW MY TEARS in the Fullerton Archives. It is not known if this is the same manuscript that went to France. It does contain, however, the material cut from the English language version of the published novel. It may well be, too, that the copy of the manuscript sent to Dick's French agent, Patrice Duvic, in 1973 by the SMLA was an uncut version. Or, as Williams said,

> This suggests that a manuscript did go from the American agent to the French agent, and thence to French publishers; another possibility is that the American agent sent an uncorrected set of galleys to his French counterpart.[dclv]

At any rate, Klein went on to publish a new French edition of FLOW MY TEARS in 1985. I'm not certain but I think he asked the original translator, Michel Deutsch, to write the new version from Editions Laffont titled COULEZ MES LARMES, DIT LE POLICIER.[dclvi]

So for the reader to get a fuller – or at least slightly different – version of the novel, he or she must needs combine the text of "The Different Stages of Love" as found in *PKDS-28* with the existing text starting in Chapter 11 of the American editions.

Seeing FLOW MY TEARS through to publication was a triumph for Dick over many obstacles. And it was important to him:

> It was a struggle taking place in the arena of human history and I was a Son of Light who had come here, forgotten his origin, identity and purpose, but regained memory and understanding of all this after I had done my work -- which was done when FLOW MY TEARS was published.
>
> Close of 1973 and opening of 1974: realization that I could not regain what I had lost, for several reasons, but still professional pursuit of my work; i.e. seeing TEARS through to its publishing in Feb of 1974 and awareness of a mysterious importance of this, as well as a mysterious threat or danger to me and the book, stemming from the same forces which had assaulted me at the close of 1971.[dclvii]

He speaks further of the mysterious, precognitive nature of FLOW MY TEARS to interviewers Apel & Briggs in 1977:

> That precognitive thing in my novels has really spooked me. It's really there. You can see how I would become aware of it in direct proportion to the number of books I wrote: if there was such a factor, the more I wrote, the more I'd begin to notice this.
>
> Let's establish just for the record examples thereof. In the rough draft of FLOW MY TEARS, THE POLICEMAN SAID, there's a girl named Kathy. Her husband's name is Jack. She is nineteen years old. She appears to be working for the criminal underground, the anti-establishment thing, but actually -- because she hopes to get her husband out of a forced labour camp through cooperation -- she is working for the police. The policeman she is working with is on the Inspector level, which is unusual.
>
> Now, that was written in 1970 and the first draft put aside. In December of 1970 I met a girl whose name was Kathy, who was nineteen years old, who appeared to be a dope dealer, who, it turned out much later -- I didn't know this for *one year* -- had been arrested and had made a deal to inform to the police if they'd drop the charges. Her boyfriend was named Jack, and the policeman she worked with was an Inspector. That's when the precognitive thing in my books really hit me. My novel was so close it was damn near actionable. I could just see an attorney listing all this stuff, you know. Precise details.

{...} I really had to ask myself about this. And what I began to notice was that the precognitive material was coming to me in my sleep, in dream form. That was in 1972, and I began to pay real attention to my dreams from that standpoint. The more time passed the more I was forced to face the actuality of the precognitive elements.

{...}

By the time I read over the final draft of FLOW MY TEARS and realised that I had shown real precognitive elements, I had to accept something which I'm not really interested in, which is the ESP stuff. Its not really something which I particularly like. I mean, I don't get off on it. I've written books and stories where parapsychological talents were employed, you know, but I can't honestly say I've ever believed in them as real things.

But there was something about that book that really freaked me. There's a dream sequence... General Buckman's sister is dead, and he's flying home, and he's really grief-stricken. And he has this dream. His main feeling is hatred... the desire to kill Jason Taverner. Buckman has set up Jason Taverner to be busted. Taverner has actually committed no crime. And Buckman in his psychotic grief at the death of his sister -- which was purely accidental -- has lost touch with reality. He's forgotten he's setting up an innocent man. He was looking for a collar on Taverner, then his sister dies in Taverner's proximity, and Buckman begins to talk about shooting Taverner, just as if he thought that Taverner had actually done it. So he makes this complete psychotic break. He's on his way home, and he's all screwed up about this. And he goes to sleep and has this dream. It's set in a rustic background, where Buckman lived as a child. He dreams of a posse of men on horseback, wearing helmets and multi-colored robes. There's one who looks like a wise old king... he has a snow white beard, like wool. And there's a man whom the posse is going to kill, sealed up in a nearby building. The man cannot see them coming, but he hears them coming and lets out a great shriek of fear. At which point Buckman's psychotic rage -- his desire to kill Taverner-- is completely transmuted into grief for this man hiding in the building in the darkness; grief for this man who is going to be killed.

Buckman is brought back to sanity by this dream. He's brought out of psychotic anger at an innocent man -- previously Buckman's been talking about taking a piss on Taverner's shoe; he takes it *that personally* -- to an appropriate affect, which is grief. He comes out of the dream and he lands his vehicle at an all-night gas station and he embraces the first human being he sees. It happens to be some black guy standing there while his tires are being rotated. He embraces a complete stranger.

So the dream brought Buckman back to sanity. That's the part that I rewrote very carefully. That's also the part -- I've been told -- for which the John W. Campbell Committee presented me with their award for that book; mainly for that specific episode.

I actually had that dream. There was a case where I consciously wrote something that I dreamt in my writing. But when the book came out, I had the curious feeling that I wrote more than I realised. I couldn't put my finger on exactly what it was. You know, you hear the phrase, "the author wrote more than he knew"... well, I had this feeling. Very, very strong feeling. I was waiting for feedback from my readers. I'm very, very responsive to reader criticism. Not so much professional critic criticism, but reader criticism. I thought someone might let me know what was going on.

FLOW MY TEARS came out in 1974. Now this is where my head was at in February 1974. This was a very stressful period for me. I was having wisdom teeth removed and receiving regular injections of sodium pentathol. Meanwhile I was experimenting with Linus Pauling's orthomolecular vitamin program, and my thoughts began to go very fast. I had read that orthomolecular vitamins, used with schizophrenics, produced more synchronous neural firing, but that it also speeded up neural firing. What occurred to me was, "Well, it can't hurt." (*laughter*) Evidently. That's the thing about water-soluble vitamins, y'know; they're not gonna leave traces of heavy metals in the neuroreceptor sites...[dclviii]

All this is, of course, was preparatory to PKD's notorious 'pink beam' experiences of Feb-Mar 1974, about more which later.

Surrounding FLOW MY TEARS, then, we can discern two perhaps ancillary tracks: the, for want of a better word, metaphysical or parapsychological, and the paranoid. Although, as one later troubadour sung: 'Just because you're paranoid don't mean they're not after you.'

In this connection we've already seen Dick's concern about the manuscript for FLOW MY TEARS in 1971; his giving it to his attorney for safe keeping just before his apartment was raided by persons unknown and his papers stolen. But what is it in the novel that PKD thought might arouse the attention if not the ire of the authorities?

Perhaps it's the notion that police officials can be human, can experience love and be changed by it? In the dialectic of the 1970s political world such a notion was anathema to those on the left wing who considered political agents like the police to be the henchmen of established capitalist institutions and to be despised. And on the other hand, in the violent decade of the 1960s and its aftermath in the 70s, paranoid authorities would certainly not look kindly on a writer who actually proposes a hazy solution to the problem of police and, hence, state or corporate sponsored violence. A solution in favor of the ordinary man and not in favor of the authorities. For, surely, like Ghandi, PKD had seen the power of non-violence to curb the excesses of the police state. The hippies had found this answer too and it nearly toppled the American government of the time. Even Nixon's downfall can be attributed to this insight into the nature of revolutionary thought. The answer to authoritarian violence was put simply and best by John Lennon: All you need is love. On this Dick had this to say:

… what I'd hope to show was the vulnerability of this type of apparatus. That within this apparatus there are individuals who are capable of mitigating the tyrannical rule of which they are a spokesman. Now, Buckman has already been presented as making attempts to diminish the effect of the concentration camps. He has sought ways of assisting the persecuted and what we have seen here is the fact that these are all innocent human beings.

I guess if you read about a totalitarian government and you read about one of the police officials as being human at all, you are liable to the accusation that you are somehow defaming the apparatus or not defaming the apparatus. I'm simply saying that within the apparatus there must exist individuals who come to doubt the moral mandate through which they govern. In fact it's specifically stated that Buckman had been reduced in rank from, I believe, a commission as Marshall to a commission as General, because of his humane attitude.

In England, a review came out that this was the first book I'd ever written in which the establishment spokesman is created sympathetically. This then gave rise to the mistaken idea that I had mellowed out in my attitude toward the tyrannical, totalitarian police state. But of course I haven't mellowed out toward that. What's happened is that in the book one of the spokesmen of the police state has begun to mellow out in terms of his relationship, vis-à-vis those who he normally persecutes. And what I was trying to do was anticipate - and, I think, successfully - the collapse of the tyrannical American State, because that tyrannical apparatus did disintegrate in America.[dclix]

And again in the same interview:

… Felix Buckman, who is the embodiment of the police establishment, is treated sympathetically. But he's treated sympathetically because he undergoes a conversion at the end to a feeling of love for the very kind of person who he has systematically persecuted, that is, a stranger. And the essence of police persecution, of course, is that all citizens are strangers and somehow to be suspected of evil intent. And he undergoes an almost religious conversion and instead of treating the black man at the gas station as a hostile stranger about who he, the policeman should be suspicious, Buckman actually embraces him and with a feeling of love.

What I was trying to show very simply was the possibility of the police apparatus undergoing a turning point in its attitude. {...}

In his *EXEGESIS* written after his experiences of 2-3-74, PKD combines his mysticism with his anti-authoritarianism:

The idea that seized me twenty-seven years ago and never let go is this: Any society in which people meddle in other people's business is not a good society, and a state in which the government "knows more about you than you know about yourself," as it is expressed in FLOW MY TEARS, is a state that must be overthrown. It may be a theocracy, a fascist corporate state, or reactionary monopolistic capitalism or centralistic socialism -- that aspect does not matter. And I am saying not merely," It can happen here," meaning the United States, but rather, "It *did* happen here. I remember. I was one of the secret Christians who fought it and to at least some extent helped overthrow it. [dclx]

The mystical apprehension that Dick refers to here and, generally, in many of his post-Pink Beam writings is that the common world we live in is in some way an illusion. The *true* reality is that we are still living in Christian times and are still under Roman rule. And Dick, as he said, was one of the secret Christians dedicated to the overthrow of the Roman empire. In the short excerpt from his *EXEGESIS* quoted immediately above he even says that he helped overthrow the empire in some small way. His novel FLOW MY TEARS is critical to Dick's new world view after March 1974. Within the pages of the novel, hidden from the eyes of the Roman authorities, was embedded a secret cypher. Dick's friend and fellow science fiction writer Tim Powers refers to this:

On p151 0f VALIS, Fat tells his friends "The two-word cypher signal KING FELIX" was sent out in Feb '74, and that "the United States Army cryptographers studied it, but couldn't discern who it was intended for or what it meant." Fat's friends ask him how he knows that, but he won't say; nor does he explain in what form it appeared.

Phil himself, though, was less reticent, and once pointed out that on p218 of the first edition of FLOW MY TEARS the last paragraph break juxtaposes the word "king" directly over the name "Felix". The novel was published in Feb 1974, and Phil said Doubleday told him that the Army did buy -- as I recall -- more than 400 copies of it.[dclxi]

But to explain this complex world-view further we must wait until we reach the year 1974 in our chronology and also until we study Dick's novel VALIS; for as Paul Williams notes, much of Dick's *EXEGESIS* is taken up with interpretations of his earlier novels, particularly UBIK and FLOW MY TEARS "in terms of the VALIS universe." [dclxii]

Before we move on though, here's another teaser in which FLOW MY TEARS, THE POLICEMAN SAID figures:

(PKD:) And I remembered an existence in which the world described was the same as the world in FLOW MY TEARS

(DSA:) So... it wasn't a previous existence, but an *alternate* existence...

(PKD:) You got it. You got it. Exactly right. Only it took me three years to figure it out. For three years, I spent between four and eight hours a day doing research and trying to understand how I could have a previous existence in the *present.*

If I were to detail that world, it would be completely congruent with the world in FLOW MY TEARS. Then I asked myself, *Does this explain where the corpus of my writing comes from?* And the answer is *Yes.* The entire corpus of my writing deals with *a landscape...* a kind of world which is somewhat like ours and somewhat different. And all my books interrelate. Ursula LeGuin pointed that out -- that all my books seemed to take place on a particular alternate world. And in 1974, I actually remembered being in that world. Some of the technology was more advanced than ours, like in my books. They made great use of advanced hydraulics, for instance. But it was a ghastly garrison state, with forced

labor camps. And in that other world, I was an active political revolutionary. I was not just a passive opponent of the Establishment. I remember we blew up a big fortress, a big prison. Actually blew it open, like you'd blow open a safe. I remember being pursued by that authorities.

The Establishment was just like it was shown to me in FLOW MY TEARS. In that world, all civil rights movements had failed. Most amazing of all, Christianity was outlawed.

(DSA:) Had it always been outlawed?

(PKD:) That I don't know. I inferred that what happened was that in the world, Christianity had been completely absorbed by the Roman Empire and a Romanesque civilization, along those lines.

Apparently I got zapped in that other world. We were Christians, but more in the political revolutionary sense; you know, blowing up prisons. Anarchistic. A lot of people were in prisons or forced labor camps.[dclxiii]

FLOW MY TEARS, THE POLICEMAN SAID is a favorite of Dick's fans. Here's comments from two of them:

Quite simply the ultimate expression of everything PKD's genre novels were about: identity, paranoia, redemption, shifting worlds...[dclxiv]

FLOW MY TEARS has the most touching, beautiful, needy, human, crazy kind of scene where Felix hugs a hapless stranger under the fluorescent lights of a gas station. Aren't we (really) all desperate to one degree or another for human connections? [dclxv]

The novel has been turned into theatre form by Linda Hartinian and the script published in 1990. The play has been performed by various theatre groups in Boston, New York and Chicago. In the 1990s a teleplay was shot of a performance at the Propp Theatre in Chicago and made available on videotape.[dclxvi]

As for the plot of FLOW MY TEARS, THE POLICEMAN SAID, there is no better brief description than that of Philip K. Dick:

This is the whole basic plot of the novel: One morning Jason Taverner, popular TV and recording star, wakes up in a fleabag dingy hotel room to find all his identification papers gone, and, worse yet, finds that no one has ever heard of him -- the basic plot is that for some arcane reason the entire population of the United States has in one instant of linear time completely and collectively forgotten a man whose face on the cover of *Time* magazine should be a face virtually every reader would identify without effort. In this novel I am saying, "The entire population of a large country, a continent-sized country, can wake up one morning having entirely forgotten something they all previously knew, and none of them is the wiser." In the novel it is a popular TV and recording star whom they have forgotten, which is of importance, really, only to that particular star or former star. But my hypothesis is presented here nonetheless in a disguised form, because (I am saying) if an entire country can overnight forget *one* thing they all know, they can forget *other things*, more important things; in fact, overwhelmingly important things. I am writing about amnesia on the part of millions of people, of, so to speak, fake memories laid down. This theme of faked memories is a constant thread in my writing over the years. It was also Van Vogt's. And yet, can one contemplate this as a serious possibility, something that could actually happen? Who of us has asked himself that? I did not ask myself that prior to 1974; I include myself.[dclxvii]

This concept of fake memories is a main reason why FLOW MY TEARS, THE POLICEMAN SAID figures in PKD's post-Pink Beam ontology.

FLOW MY TEARS is certainly a turning-point in Dick's career. The novel is longer than usual for PKD and took longer to write. And after FLOW MY TEARS Dick took much more time to write his novels. No more one draft, retype then mail it off to the SMLA. The novel wins ✶ ✶ ✶ ✶ ✶ in at least one alternate world.

1971

Like 1970, 1971 was a dry year of writing for Philip K. Dick. No new novels and only one story were attempted that year. As we have seen, Dick, with Nancy and Isa gone, sort of fell apart and surrounded himself with street people and hangers-on all doing a cornucopia of drugs. His house was broken into and his files blown open in November. But even though he was idle his books continued to be published in new editions. In Feb 1971 OUR FRIENDS FROM FROLIX 8 had its first SFBC appearance and THE THREE STIGMATA OF PALMER ELDRITCH saw its first paperback publication from MacFadden. Two other novels also had their first paperback editions that year: A MAZE OF DEATH from Popular Library, and DO ANDROIDS DREAM OF ELECTRIC SHEEP? from Signet. In the United Kingdom, Gollancz published the first UK edition of THE PRESERVING MACHINE and Arrow the first UK edition of EYE IN THE SKY. And there are two more first UK editions, those for GALACTIC POT-HEALER from Gollancz in July and THE GANYMEDE TAKEOVER from Arrow.

As this was a quiet year for writing we'll take a swift look to see what was going on as far as PKD editions in other countries.

DO ANDROIDS DREAM OF ELECTRIC SHEEP? saw two foreign editions, one from Heyne in Germany and one from La Tribuna in Italy. NOW WAIT FOR LAST YEAR also had an Italian edition from Editions Nord, SOLAR LOTTERY came from Goldmann in Germany and THE PENULTIMATE TRUTH from Meulenhoff in Holland. THE WORLD JONES MADE had two editions, one from Prisma in Holland and one from Goldmann in Germany. THE ZAP GUN was also printed in Holland by Born Publishers. Some of these books had interesting titles in translation. See if you can guess what novels these titles refer to:

ILLUSIONE DI POTERE, IL DISCO DI FIAMMA, HAUPTGEWINN DIE ERDE, UUR DER WAARHEID, VLUCHT NAAR VENUS, IN DE BAN VAN DE BOM.[dclxviii]

No doubt these reprints, paperback editions, UK editions and other foreign editions enabled PKD to maintain his lifestyle through the year. But, for the literary chronicler there's little more to say for 1971.

However, Dick did write one short story in 1971. This was "Cadbury, The Beaver That Lacked." Little is known of the genesis of this story. Rickman refers to it in a footnote only as a 'privately circulated story from 1970, first printed in THE COLLECTED STORIES.'[dclxix]

"Cadbury, The Beaver That lacked" is a short-short story that is rather strange. Cadbury is a beaver who is viciously hen-pecked by his wife as he strives and fails to earn enough 'blue chips' to satisfy her. He longs for escape and sends a message sealed in an empty tin of snuff down the river. He receives a reply and after many message-bearing tins of snuff float back and forth on the river Cadbury decides he's in love with his unknown correspondent. He builds a secret hide and then follows a snuff-tin down the river and meets his love, Carol Stickyfoot. After declaring his love and it being accepted by Carol she changes into *three* women: each in her own fashion manipulative and wanting Cadbury only for what he can do for them. In the end as Cadbury fades into non-existence he sees one of the girls lingering and looking back. "I love you" she says. But Cadbury is unable to hear her.

In this story, despite the fact that Cadbury is a beaver and the Carol Stickyfoot's are human, PKD seems to be writing of the yearning for 'the beautiful woman who waits for you -- somewhere, but God only knows where' as he mentioned in connection with his story "The Days Of Perky Pat" as noted above.

A mixed-up fantasy "Cadbury The Beaver That Lacked" rates about ✳ ✳ ✳.

1972

Philip Dick started out the year on a good note with a quick visit to Canada in February. Here PKD was the guest of honor at a large science fiction convention in Vancouver. And mightily honored was he indeed: Dinner in his honor, his speech "The Android and the Human" delivered to a packed house, girls vying for the attention of this famous weird sf writer. Yes, Dick was in a positive place and he decided to stay in Vancouver. It helped that he had met another girl with whom he promptly fell in love. But, shortly, she left and Phil ended up crashing on the couch of two people he'd just met. But Phil was soon too much for his hosts and he moved into his own apartment in Vancouver.

The next thing you know he's had a two-week blackout and was trying to commit suicide. Fortunately he was able to dial for help at the last minute and was saved from death only to be placed in a drug-rehabilitation center called X-Kalay where he underwent 'group therapy' with the mostly heroin-addicted residents. Memories of this place would recur to him when he wrote his next novel A SCANNER DARKLY. And his time at X-Kalay at least wised him up to his amphetamine abuse and after he left he never took the drug regularly again.[dclxx]

Before entering the clinic PKD had written to Professor Willis McNelly at the California State University extension in Fullerton, California. The professor read PKD's letter in which he expressed his wish for a new home to his students, and two young female students wrote to PKD offering space in their apartment to the hapless and exiled writer. McNelly also offered his university's library as a good place for Dick to house his papers.

This was a godsend for Phil who promptly flew down to Fullerton in April. He was met at the airport by the two girls and another, dark-haired girl, Linda Levy, with whom PKD immediately fell in love, and a young man, Tim Powers, who would become Dick's friend and a science fiction writer in his own right. Dick didn't stay long with the two girls but soon moved in with a more congenial young man with whom he made new friends and resumed some sort of life in Orange county. But, despite his declarations and best efforts, Phil was never able to attain a stable relationship with the young Linda Levy. It wasn't until July that PKD met his next love, Tessa Busby, at a party. She was eighteen and would become his fifth and final wife.[dclxxi]

Sometime around the Summer of 1972 Doubleday was bugging Dick about the incomplete collaboration with Roger Zelazny, DEUS IRAE. But it would be a few more years yet before the two writers would actually finish this novel.[dclxxii]

In September the couple attended the 1972 Los Angeles Worldcon science fiction convention at which Phil sat on some discussion panels. Then in October they traveled to San Francisco to finalize Phil's divorce from Nancy.

On the literary front, Dick's novels continued to be reprinted both in the United States and abroad. Ace Books republished CLANS OF THE ALPHANE MOON, THE GAME-PLAYERS OF TITAN, VULCAN'S HAMMER and, in a unique Ace Double, THE UNTELEPORTED MAN backed with DR. FUTURITY. Don Wollheim's new line of paperback science fiction, DAW Books, published the first edition of WE CAN BUILD YOU in paperback this year.[dclxxiii]

UK editions, too, were plentiful: A MAZE OF DEATH from Gollancz, THE PRESERVING MACHINE from the UKSFBC (Reader's Union publishers), SOLAR LOTTERY from Arrow, DO ANDROIDS DREAM OF ELECTRIC SHEEP? from Panther and two from Pan: GALACTIC POT-HEALER and THE PRESERVING MACHINE collection of short stories.

But for PKD the big news was publication in Poland of UBIK. This had been accomplished by the famous Polish writer Stanislas Lem.[dclxxiv] Also, as we've noted above, PKD's French editor, Patrice Duvic, visited him late in the year and discussed the possibility of writing a screenplay based on UBIK.

As the year waned and Phil's relationship with Tessa blossomed, he felt the urge to write again and sent for the manuscript of FLOW MY TEARS from his attorney and on its reception he turned to finishing that novel in 1973 as we've seen above.

In 1972, though, the one notable thing PKD wrote was his Vancouver speech, "The Android and the Human." We'll cast a glance at this before moving on to 1973.

In the *Vertex* interview conducted by Arthur Byron Cover PKD goes on at length about his Vancouver Speech:

(Vertex): You've stated privately that your Vancouver speech is the most important thing you've ever written. Would you care to elaborate on that statement?

(PKD): I worked on it for three months and I was very low in those days. I had thought that I would never write again. I had actually gone for two and a half years without writing anything. I decided that I should take all the ideas I had in my head that were worth anything and put them in the speech. It was finished in January 1972 and it said that the totalitarian state Orwell had predicted was already with us and that rebellion against this evil and corrupt state was already with us. The title of this speech was "The Human and the Android," subtitled "The Authentic Person Vs. the Reflex Machine."

(Vertex): What did you try to accomplish in this speech?

(PKD): I tried to define the real person, because there are people among us who are biologically human but who are androids in the metaphoric sense. I wanted to draw the line so I could define the positive primary goal of stipulating what was human. Computers are becoming more and more like sensitive cogitative creatures, but at the same time human beings are becoming dehumanized. As I wrote the speech I sensed in it the need for people who were human to reinforce other people's humanness. And because of this it would be necessary to rebel against an inhuman or android society.

(Vertex): What do you believe defines a human being?

(PKD): For example, the capacity to say no when what one was told to do was wrong. Someone saying, "No, I won't kill. I won't bomb." A balking. And this balking I saw in the teenagers, in the so-called "punks." A non-political rebellion of the youth which in the long run, without their realizing it, had very great political significance. Not in terms of elections and parties, but with the emergence of kids who could not be bribed, who could not be intimidated, who would not listen to propaganda. I saw the need of an illegal rebellion against what was basically an illegal system. In other words, you can't say to a kid, "Don't break the law. Always obey the law," because the law was in itself unjust.

(Vertex): Do you feel that recent events such as the Watergate hearings have supported the ideas expressed in the speech?

(PKD): I think -- and this is perhaps a strange thing to say -- that those people in the Administration who broke the law should be forgiven, also, for breaking the law, just as those I feel should rebel should be forgiven. Everybody on both sides is sort of saying that the law is no longer meaningful, that it is no longer equated with justice. I think it was Jeb Magruder who said, "We found it frustrating to have to operate within the law." Perhaps that is just an indication that a vast revision of our legal system is in order. Nevertheless, my speech did advocate rebellion and breaking the law in the name of morality. And like the *I Ching* said, if practicality and morality are polarized and you must choose, you must do what you think is right, rather than what you think is practical.[dclxxv]

And it is now to 1973 that we turn our attention.

1973

As we've discussed above, Dick spent much of 1973 revising and rewriting FLOW MY TEARS, THE POLICEMAN SAID. However, he did manage to write two short stories, "A Little Something For Us Tempunauts" and "The Pre-Persons."

"A Little Something For Us Tempunauts" was written by special request; as Tessa Dick said:

Even then I wanted to get a job, and Phil said, "No way." So he started more writing. While he was somewhere in between finishing FLOW MY TEARS for Doubleday and beginning SCANNER, Ed Ferman wrote from *F&SF* and said they were doing an anniversary issue and they would like a story. So Phil wrote the story of the Tempunauts.[dclxxvi]

Phil, too, writes of this time:

In August 1970 I stopped writing, mid-point through FLOW MY TEARS, THE POLICEMAN SAID, and almost never wrote again. I had never in my life gone two whole years without being able to work, and I became more and more convinced with each passing month that I would never find my way back to writing – various editors asked me for stuff, I tried to write, I could not; I had to say sorry I have ceased writing, probably forever. Around December of 1972 I got a letter from Ed Ferman requesting a story and I sure wanted to write it; Tessa and I needed the money and I yearned to get back to writing... if I did not, and soon, then we could not marry, I was doomed forever in my sole career... I thought and thought but couldn't get the handle on any idea worth anything – I was going to write to Ed and say what I had been saying to everyone else: "Sorry, but I can't do it."

Then a friend came by with the story *The Poets of Millgrove, Iowa*, and I read the first sf story in years that galvanized me into new life – like Kant reading Hume.

That story, by John T. Sladek, can stand in the ranks of the all-time great short stories in the English language. Not with sf stories but with all, The masterpieces.

Perhaps the first sf story to do so. Let's face it – could any before that really do that?

The Poets of Millgrove, Iowa changed in a flash my entire conception of what a good sf story is.

So then I wrote "A Little Something For Us Tempunauts" for Ed Ferman because I had a new mind, a whole mind again, a writer's mind, and it was set facing the future once more. Not miserably back in the direction of the past.[dclxxvii]

Strangely enough, though, "A Little Something For Us Tempunauts" didn't get published in *F & SF* but first saw publication in *FINAL STAGE* in 1974. Although Tessa Dick refers to the story as being written for *F & SF*, it was actually requested by Ed Ferman for *FINAL STAGE*. PKD clears this up in a letter to Charles Brown:[dclxxviii]

P.S. Also, Charlie, I wrote and sold a 5,500 word story, the first story-length piece I've done in years. To Ed Ferman and Barry Malzberg for their new anthology, *FINAL STAGE*. They commissioned it. On the topic of time travel.

It's a downer, too. I consider time-travel a distinct downer. As bad as dope.[dclxxix]

"A Little Something For Us Tempunauts" was selected for the 1977 Ballantine collection, THE BEST OF PHILIP K. DICK and has other anthology appearances also.

Philip Dick said of this story:

In this story I felt a vast weariness over the space program, which had thrilled us so at the start -- especially the first lunar landing -- and then had been forgotten and virtually shut down, a relic of history. I wondered, if time-travel became a 'program', would it suffer the same fate? Or was there an even worse possibility latent in it, within the very nature of the paradoxes of time-travel? [dclxxx]

In this story tired chrononauts crash and die when their time machine returns from a trip to the future. But they're still alive… and participate in their own funeral. Are they in a closed time-loop – and can they get out of it? Only time will tell…

"A Little Something For Us Tempunauts" rates ✳ ✳ ✳

The only new USA first edition to appear in 1973 was THE BOOK OF PHILIP K. DICK from DAW in paperback. This came out in February. This collection contained nine of PKD's short stories dating back to the Fifties. In July 1977 this collection was published in England by Coronet publishers as THE TURNING WHEEL And Other Stories.[dclxxxi]

Not much has been said about this collection as a collection, only one comment by PKD can be found and that is, rather, in connection with his other short story collection, THE BEST OF PHILIP K. DICK which came out from Ballantine in 1977. Asked by interviewer Kevin Briggs if PKD had a Don Wollheim story, PKD replied:

Matter of fact. I have. When I was preparing the Ballantine collection {THE BEST OF PKD}, Donald Wollheim wrote to me and said, "I'd like to do a collection of your stories." I said, "I'm sorry, Don, but I'm going through my stories to sell to Ballantine right now." He wrote back and said, "Well, Betty" -- Betty Ballantine was still editor --"Betty and I have different tastes. Give me what Betty doesn't want." And that's exactly what he got. Wollheim read them over and became hysterical. He said, "These are Betty Ballantine rejects!" I says, "Don, that's what we contracted for." He says, "Well, the stories aren't very good." And I said, "Yeah, and the price ain't very good, either." He published them, but he was grumpy about it. That's my Wollheim story.[dclxxxii]

But looking over the contents of THE BOOK OF PKD we can really find only one clunker, "A Present For Pat", the rest of the stories I've rated at 3 or 4 stars with one story, "The Defenders" having 5 stars. As a collection, then, THE BOOK OF PKD rates between ✶✶✶ and ✶✶✶✶.[dclxxxiii]

The other short story that Dick completed in 1973 was "The Pre-Persons." This manuscript arrived at the SMLA on Dec 20, 1973 and was then forwarded to *F & SF* where it was accepted on Feb 13, 1974 for inclusion in the 25th anniversary edition of the magazine which appeared in Oct 1974. It was also selected for the PKD collection THE GOLDEN MAN in 1980.

PKD's anti-abortion story caused a slight flurry on its publication. As PKD wrote:

In this, the most recent of the stories in this collection, I incurred the absolute hate of Joanna Russ who wrote me the nastiest letter I've ever received; at one point she said she usually offered to beat up people (she didn't use the word "people") who expressed opinions such as this. I admit that this story amounts to special pleading, and I'm sorry to offend those who disagree with me about abortion on demand. I also got some unsigned hate mail, some of it not from individuals but from organizations promoting abortion on demand. Well, I have always managed to offend people by what I write. Drugs, communism, and now an anti-abortion stand; I really know how to get myself in hot water. Sorry, people. But for the pre-persons' sake I am not sorry. I stand where I stand: "Hier steh' Ich; Ich kann nicht anders," as Martin Luther is supposed to have said." [dclxxxiv]

And in his Afterword written for the stories in THE GOLDEN MAN collection, Dick expands on his earlier comments:

Throughout this volume of short stories the theme of fakes, of deception, the theme of guile and cunning, are evident, but I would also like to have a theme of human trust noted, even though it may be submerged at times under the ominous. In "The Pre-Persons" it is love for the children that I feel, not anger toward those who would destroy them. My anger is generated out of love; it is love baffled. I hope you can see this in even this story. If not, then I've failed...[dclxxxv]

Given the nature of the abortion controversy in the USA at the time – and still percolating as I write – one can accord with Hazel Pierce's description of the story:

But even wry smiles fade with "The Pre-Persons" and its futuristic comment on abortion laws. The title hints at the core question: when does a human organism attain true identity? Hyperbole dramatizes the issue as Dick's future society names age twelve as the time when a human being acquires soul and thus is rendered inviolate. Whatever one's predisposition toward this touchy and eminently contemporary issue, Dick does force renewed attention to the deep conflict of ethics and law.[dclxxxvi]

"The Pre-Persons" rates ✶✶✶✶

Reprints of Dick's books continued to be published in 1973, particularly in England where THE GAME-PLAYERS OF TITAN had an edition from Sphere Books and the first UK paperback of UBIK was printed by Panther in May. Another first UK paperback edition came from Penguin in October; this was THE THREE STIGMATA OF PALMER ELDRITCH and to round out the year, Pan produced an edition of A MAZE OF DEATH in November.

But while Dick was mostly revising FLOW MY TEARS, he was anxious to get on with his next novel, A SCANNER DARKLY.

A SCANNER DARKLY

The idea for A SCANNER DARKLY occurred to PKD in 1972 and, like FLOW MY TEARS, THE POLICEMAN SAID, this novel took him a long time to write. In the Apel & Briggs interview he explains:

> working all those years on FLOW MY TEARS, doing all those drafts, changed my work habits. I'd never done more than a rough draft and a final on a novel before. And there was eleven drafts. God, I was reshaping it word-by-word. Once in, never out; I couldn't go back to doing a rough draft and a final draft, just like that. So the next novel was A SCANNER DARKLY and it took *years* to write SCANNER; it just took *years*. The idea came to me in the early part of 1972, and it wasn't until 1976 that I sent the manuscript off to Doubleday. And I wasn't trying to say what was real; I was just no longer able to dash off the stuff at the rate that I had before...[dclxxxvii]

Perhaps the idea for A SCANNER DARKLY occurred to PKD in 1972 but it was in 1973 that PKD really formed the novel in his mind and actually wrote the first draft. He describes this period in a letter to his former wife Nancy and daughter Isa in April:

> After sending the novel [FLOW] to my agent [...] I started another one [SCANNER] [...] (a) a 62-page outline; (b) 82 final pages to mail to accompany the outline for submissions; (c) 240 pages more in rough. Add that up, for a period from February 20 to April 2, and how many pages of writing do you get? A fatal stoke, that's what.[dclxxxviii]

And in an open letter to fellow science fiction writer John Sladek, also in April, Dick again covers this:

> The reason why I've failed until now to answer your good letter of March 1 is that after writing nothing at all during 1971 and 1972 (except my Vancouver speech) I finished up a novel I began in 1970 and sent it off to Doubleday, and while I was waiting to hear from Doubleday I got a really good idea for a new novel and wrote that, too. So now Doubleday has bought two novels from me.[dclxxxix]

So these two letters indicate that Doubleday had accepted, if not a draft, at least a 62-page outline and 82 final pages of A SCANNER DARKLY sometime around April 1973. In another letter in May 1973 PKD again refers to this Doubleday sale:

> For me the big news (besides me and Tessa getting married) is that I have sold two new novels to Doubleday, the first of which is FLOW MY TEARS...
> But with SCANNER -- it is all bite, all grit; it is a great tragic anti-dope novel, an autobiographical account, set as science fiction, of what I saw in the dope world, the

counterculture, during the two years after my wife and daughter left me. I believe nothing in fiction matches it in the hell it portrays...[dcxc]

As we've seen and as Phil has said, A SCANNER DARKLY came out of PKD's collapsed marriage to Nancy and the aftermath where to retain his sanity he surrounded himself with street people. As he notes:

But on the drug thing, what happened was that after my wife Nancy left me in 1970, I was in a state of complete desolation and despair, and suicidally depressed because I really loved her. She took my little girl with her, who I really loved, and I didn't see my little girl for - I saw her only once in a whole year, just for a few minutes. I got mixed up with a lot of street people, just to have somebody to fill the house. She left me with a four bedroom, two-bathroom house and nobody living in it but me. So I just filled it with street people and I got mixed up with a lot of people who were into drugs. But that was for a period of just about a year. And then I just took amphetamines. I have never ever taken hard drugs. But I was in a position to see what hard drugs did to people, what drugs did to my friends...

Everything in A SCANNER DARKLY I actually saw. I mean I saw even worse things than I put in A SCANNER DARKLY. I saw people who were reduced to a point where they couldn't complete a sentence, they really couldn't state a sentence. And this was permanent, this was for the rest of their lives. Young people. These were people maybe 18 and 19, and I just saw, you know, it was like a vision of Hell. And I vowed to write a novel about it sometime, and I was just...I'm just...it's just...well, I was in love with a girl who was an addict and I didn't know she was an addict and it was just pathetic. So I wrote A SCANNER DARKLY.[dcxci]

In the April letter to Sladek already mentioned PKD refers more to SCANNER's genesis:

In my second-sale-to-Doubleday-this-month novel, A SCANNER DARKLY, I have gone into new depths of What is reality? That no one ever before imagined could be posed as a question, let alone answered. It is a furiously anti-dope novel, and I spent all of 1971 doing first-hand research for it... although I did not know this at the time. I just thought I was turning on with all my friends. But toward the start of 1972 I woke up one day and noticed that all my friends either were dead, had burned-out brains, were psychotic, or all of the above. Then I fled to Canada, then later on here to Fullerton, which is close to Disneyland. You won't believe how screwed-up reality is actually, John, until you read SCANNER; I had no idea myself. Anyhow, writing the novel almost killed me, and reading it almost killed little Tessa, my wife; it is a very sad novel and very sad things happen to very good people.[dcxcii]

But the manuscript path of A SCANNER DARKLY is not as simple as that. Paul Williams includes in his description of a package of SCANNER-related documents he was offering for auction a:

Xerox copy of the original rough draft of A SCANNER DARKLY written in 1973 and never submitted to Doubleday. This Xerox circulated to other publishers when Phil was trying to get out of the Doubleday contract. "This rough draft differs enormously from later versions".[dcxciii]

This rough draft may be the 240 pages PKD wrote between Feb and April and which he mentions in his letter to Nancy and daughter Isa quoted above.

In regards to PKD's disaffection with Doubleday perhaps we can refer to his remarks following their publication of A SCANNER DARKLY:

…it started to bother me, finally, when I wrote my anti-dope book, A SCANNER DARKLY. And I realized I had written a really great novel. Actually I had finally written a true masterpiece, after 25 years of writing, and my agent wrote back when he read the first part, and he said, "You're absolutely right, this is exceptional material." And then he went out and sold it to Doubleday for the same old goddamn two thou -- by that time they were up to $2500 -- still Mickey Mouse money. "Here is this masterpiece, and we are going to pay you $2500 for it." And I fired my agent, and I prepared to buy the manuscript back from Doubleday, and I could never raise the money to buy it back from Doubleday. I couldn't get enough cash to buy it back. And Simon & Schuster offered to buy it from Doubleday for $4000, so I would get a little more money (Larry Ashmead having then gone to Simon & Schuster). But Doubleday refused to relinquish it. They said $3000 was their limit for science fiction, and then they admitted $4000 was their limit, and then they turned around with A SCANNER DARKLY, and turned it over to their trade department, to sell it as a trade book, and there is no limit in the advance to a trade book. So they weren't limited to $3000. And they've got a masterpiece, and they put out almost no money at all.

So the next book then, I sold to Bantam for $12,000, and Doubleday was just out of luck. Doubleday said on the phone, very bitterly, "You're mercenary." And I said, "No, I have to eat. I have to live. That's what we have here. I owe the IRS $4,700. I can't afford to sell you a novel for $3000." And, of course, I especially couldn't if I could sell it to Bantam for $12,000.

I never really got angry until this book, A SCANNER DARKLY. I knew the book was worth a great deal of money. I knew that it was really a fine book, and I worked five years on it. And I knew that I was being gypped. It was the first time in 22 or 23 years that I really realised I was being terribly gypped -- just gang-banged is what it was. And Doubleday was crowing about this great book, and they were going to go to town. They were going to do this and do that with it, and I kept saying, "Well, why don't you give me a little more money? I mean, if you recognise the quality of the work, and you have such plans for it" and that's when they said, "You're mercenary." And so they didn't get a shot at the next book. And they know it.[dcxciv]

This money situation was a sore point for Dick and he refers to Doubleday and A SCANNER DARKLY again:

Doubleday went up to three thousand dollars advance for my new book, A SCANNER DARKLY. They said that that was the most they could go for a "science fiction" novel. So after they had acquired it for three thousand dollars, they turned it over to the trade department, which has no limit on what it can offer, and then they told me that the real limit was four thousand dollars. But I was too dumb to know the difference. They acquired it for three thousand dollars, which is just chicken feed, let's face it--three thousand bucks, and it took me like three years to write the book. Now that's a thousand dollars a year. Somebody sits down to write science fiction, and then the publisher markets it as a mainstream novel and gets to sit on both stools. They get to eat the porridge out of one pot, and then they get to eat the porridge out of the other pot, and I got no porridge in mine at all. They're going to make a bundle on it, but Ballantine deserves to make a bundle on it because Judy-Lynn Del Rey at Ballantine went over the manuscript page by page with me and told me what it needed in order to be a truly competent book. This is the first time that any editor has ever done that with me since THE MAN IN THE HIGH CASTLE.[dcxcv]

This argument with Doubleday, then, occurring after April 1973, resulted in the rough draft manuscript being sent to Ballantine Books where Judy-Lyn Del Rey looked it over and made suggestions.[dcxcvi]

At this point it is worth the time to look at the SCANNER documents that Paul Williams offered for auction in 1986. In his description we find a thorough history for A SCANNER DARKLY and as PKD himself said therein, "the only written evidence in existence of all the stages through which A SCANNER DARKLY went.":

AUCTION: A SCANNER DARKLY manuscript and correspondence package. Minimum bid $750. Paul Williams.

Description:

1. Doubleday 1st .ed. A SCANNER DARKLY, signed and dated by PKD, book in mint condition, dw torn on spine.

2. Original letter from PKD dated 3-7-77 describing all materials in this package except items 1 and 2. Typed; signed in pen. Letter concludes: "This collection of MSS is the only written evidence in existence of all the stages through which A SCANNER DARKLY went."

3. Xerox of a letter from Judy-Lynn Del Rey at Ballantine, 2pp. detailing revisions she would like to see in ASD; PKD has made notes in pen on the Xerox, indicating his initial reactions.

4. PKD's carbon of his 4-page letter replying to Del Rey, responding in detail on every point. "Well maybe I've found my Maxwell Perkins at last." Signed in pen.

5. Original letter from Del Rey, with copies of ms pages.

6. 29 carbons of ms pages, described by PKD as the new pages written at Judy Lynn's request.

7. PKD's handwritten list of pages of ASD on which German words appear.

8. PKD's personal carbon-copy of MS of SCANNER as submitted to Doubleday (prior to the 1976 correspondence with Del Rey). Very good condition. 297pp. Signed in pen on title page.

Xerox copy of the original rough draft of ASD written in 1973 and never submitted to Doubleday. This Xerox circulated to other publishers when Phil was trying to get out of the Doubleday contract. "This rough draft differs enormously from later versions" -- PKD. 298pp plus 6pp insertions. First page very ragged, others in good condition...

The total package allows one to follow the path of the novel, from first completed draft to the fully revised draft submitted for publication, and then to the third state after Del Rey's editorial input.[dcxcvii]

For Del Rey's input, Dick was grateful, saying

The person who came along and saved the book was Judy-Lynn Del Rey... she had me completely revise the book. She showed me how to develop the characters, and when she got through working with me on that book... I'd written a great novel.[dcxcviii]

And again,

I remember when Ballantine acquired the manuscript. Judy-Lynn Del Rey wanted me to revise it. She said, "Well, it's set in the future, and they're talking slang from the 60s. I want you to abolish" -- as if by a wave of the hand -- "*all* of the slang, throughout the *entire book*, and *manufacture*, from your own brain, an *entirely new slang*. I decree that you will do this.

And I wrote back and I says, "Judy, you know *damn well* the book is about the 60s. it says so in the author's Afterword." ({...}) "First of all, I'm not able to make up a whole new slang." And she says, "Well, they did it in *Clockwork Orange*. And if he can do it, why can't you do it?" And I says, "The book is *not* about the future. The book is about the *past*, as a matter of fact. You know it because it says so." Not that I'm lazy... It's just that I'm trying to capture a milieu which is already perishing, and I'm setting it ahead, since this is a convention of my writing.[dcxcix]

But on reflection Dick got over his first reaction to this criticism:

Pete Israel, who was the editor for Putnam then, went over THE MAN IN THE HIGH CASTLE page by page, and now Judy-Lynn has done that with A SCANNER DARKLY. So now I've got two good novels under my belt because I've had two good editors. Judy-Lynn Del Rey is probably the greatest editor since Maxwell Perkins: she showed me how to create a character. I've been selling novels for twenty-two years, and she showed me how to develop a character. My first reaction was, "Dear Judy-Lynn, how would you like to take a one-way walk off the Long Beach Pier?" But then I started thinking about what she was saying, and soon as my fuse had burned out--being very short, it didn't take long--I realized that she was teaching me how to write. It's too bad that nobody did that twenty-five years ago, because then maybe my books would have made more sense. But A SCANNER DARKLY? A master craftsman came into that book--Judy-Lynn Del Rey. Now I know what to do when I write a book. You don't just write whatever comes into your head while you're sitting there in front of the typewriter.[dcc]

So then, despite the contractual squabble with Doubleday and the editorial work by Ballantine, the first edition of A SCANNER DARKLY was published by Doubleday in January 1977 and they followed it with their SFBC edition six weeks later. The Ballantine paperback edition didn't see publication until Dec 1977 – after the first UK edition from Gollancz in November. [dcci]

In the pages of *The Philip K. Dick Society Newsletter* a reader from Czechoslovakia notes an edition of SCANNER published in that country in 1986 with a printing of 50,000 copies.[dccii]

And K.W. Jeter, PKD's friend and science fiction writer, speaks of the fidelity of the French translation:

Apparently the French editions are very faithful, to the point where the French edition of A SCANNER DARKLY is so faithful that it has to have footnotes explaining some Americanisms. Like, what are M&Ms. {...} And product or brand names that wouldn't be familiar to a French person. Instead of translating it into some kind of French equivalent to some kind of candy, they actually kept it. The footnotes are on just about every other page.[dcciii]

The French edition from Denoel in 1978 enabled Dick to win the 1979 Graouilly d'Or Award for Best Novel presented at the Festival de Metz in France.

Some of the editions of A SCANNER DARKLY are quite valuable. The first Doubleday edition commands prices of $150 and up depending on condition. The Gollancz edition from England is worth $50 or more while the most common, the SFBC edition from Doubleday, can be had for about $30. The Ballantine paperback is fairly cheap at about $15. But perhaps the ultimate SCANNER package, besides the one offered for auction by Paul Williams, is that put up for sale by bookseller Ken Lopez in 1997:

A SCANNER DARKLY. (Published by Doubleday, 1977). Two complete manuscripts. The original ribbon copy typescript, with pages numbered 1-128 and 3 pages that appeared in the book as the "Author's Note." The text has been extensively reworked in ink by the author, with revisions on a majority of pages and at least two scenes that do not appear in the final book. Together with a second copy, this a complete re-typing consisting of 300 ribbon copy pages, with a few small ink notes and changes by the author, and a number of pencil copy editor's marks. $16,500.[dcciv]

Inevitably with A SCANNER DARKLY the subject of drugs comes up – and above we've noted a few of Dick's comments on this -- but as to suggestions, once again, that Dick wrote the novel while 'on drugs' we find a quick dismissal:

It's about an undercover agent who must take dope to conceal his cover and the dope damages his brain progressively, as well as making him an addict. The book follows him along to the end until his brain is damaged to such an extent that he can no longer wash pots and pans in the kitchen of a rehabilitation center. I hope the reader won't say, "Boy! I bet he did that!" This is the verisimilitude the author is trying to create, the sense that the novel actually is real. Now I was at a heroin rehab center in Canada, and I did draw from it, and I've had friends who dropped acid and became permanently psychotic. And a number who killed themselves too. But I wouldn't say that if affected my writing directly, that the acid wrote the book.[dccv]

As to whether drugs had actually affected PKD's brain around the time of the SCANNER writing, his friend and collaborator, Roger Zelazny, recalls a funny incident:

Then Phil, in a profound moment afterwards, said, "Roger, a strange thing happened to me." Which is not really unusual, because strange things always happen to Phil. I nodded. "I have this book, A SCANNER DARKLY. I have these characters who have been on hard drugs for a long time, and they're burnt-out cases. I wanted to choose a scene which exemplified the extent of their mental deterioration. I had them attempting to figure out the functioning of the gear-shift on a ten-speed bicycle." (Phil always chooses good examples for things)
So he had written this up and indicated that they were wrong, because this is how the gear-shift on a ten-speed bicycle really works. His editor called him: "Phil... A funny thing in this manuscript of yours. I happen to own a ten-speed bicycle. I went out and looked at the gear-shift, and -- um -- you've got it wrong yourself."
Phil said, "My God, you know what that means? Roger, how do you know when you're a burnt-out case?" [dccvi]

But burnt-out or not, for Philip K. Dick A SCANNER DARKLY was an important book:

There more than any other book I was recording what actual people did and said which would have vanished into the ether otherwise. I was in a position that no one else was in. I was in a position to remember it and recapture it. These were, for the most part, illiterate people, so they'll never know. The one thing that really means something to me is little braveries, little displays of strength and courage, and something more than competence.[dccvii]

And, while complaining again about Doubleday's advance payment rates, Dick calls SCANNER a masterpiece:

I felt I had written a novel equal to *ALL QUIET ON THE WESTERN FRONT*. I felt that what *ALL QUIET ON THE WESTERN FRONT* was to war -- that anybody that read it would never pick up a rifle as long as they lived -- that anybody who ever read A SCANNER DARKLY would never drop dope as long as they lived. In it I had all my friends who are now dead or crazy from dope, sitting around laughing and talking, you know, and then they all go crazy and die. It broke my heart to read it, it broke my heart to do the galleys. I did the galleys two weeks ago, and I cried for two days after I did the galleys. Every time I read it I cry. And I believe that it is a masterpiece. I believe it is the only masterpiece I will <u>ever</u> write. Not that it's the only masterpiece I have ever written, but the only one I will <u>ever</u> write, because it is a book that is unique. And when I got $2500 for all this work, I <u>knew</u> I was being burned. Because there were human beings in that book who have never been put down on paper before.

{...} They're all taking dope, and they're all happy, and they're all wonderful people. Then the terrible destruction of their brains begins, and they begin to lose contact with reality, and they begin to gyrate around, and they no longer can function. And by the time the book ends, the protagonist is lucky if he can clean out a bathroom -- clean out a toilet. Every time I read it, it has the same effect on me. The funny parts are the funniest parts ever written, and the sad parts are the saddest parts ever written, and they're both in the same book.[dccviii]

Many fans, too, consider A SCANNER DARKLY to be a masterpiece. David Keller selects the novel as his favorite in the *FDO* Fan Poll: A SCANNER DARKLY.

His best... the local settings add to my interest but SCANNER is simply his best novel in my opinion. Needs at least four readings to pick up on a lot of connections and symbols and whatnot. Much more complex than it first appears to be and is unusually coherent without sacrificing deep questioning/ambiguity about the nature of reality.[dccix]

The critics, too, were favorable and PKD took the opportunity to respond to a scholarly article on A SCANNER DARKLY to further explain his novel:

SCANNER deals not with schizophrenia and not with neurosis but with organic brain damage producing split-brain dysfunction and a tragic parody of bilateral hemispheric parity, inasmuch as damage to the normally dominant left hemisphere (Bob Arctor) allows a secondary personality to form in the right hemisphere (Fred), but the two brain hemispheres simply war on each other until at last they collapse into the deteriorated third personality Bruce. See, I said it all in a few sentences; there is no more to say. Here is an instance where that which we are as a species striving for -- bilateral hemispheric parity -- misfires; when at last a unitary self is formed it is not a metaself, but, and this is so terribly evident toward the conclusion of the novel, a mere reflex thing that only repeats back what it has heard; biological life continues, but the soul is dead.[dccx]

Which pretty much sums up the main plot of the novel. But to read of Bob Arctor's spying on himself, his deterioration, and that of his friends, is both hilarious and horrifying. For one who has lived through the times that Dick wrote about in A SCANNER DARKLY, the novel strikes a numbing chord. In the *FDO* Fan Poll I chose this as my second favorite PKD novel with the response:

Such an intense book. So funny and sad and bitterly truthful. I didn't see it as an anti-drug novel, as has sometimes been mentioned. It really had nothing to do with drugs except as an example. Dick could have written the same novel using any of commodity-capitalism's snares. An indictment of the System so biting that it's no wonder PKD's safe was blown open ... In my opinion there has not been a better novel than A SCANNER DARKLY written in English since George Orwell's *1984.*[dccxi]

And with that said I can only rate the novel ✶ ✶ ✶ ✶ ✶.

In 2006 A SCANNER DARKLY was turned into a movie that was directed by Richard Linklater and starring Keanu Reeves, Rory Cochrane, Robert Downey Jr., Woody Harrelson and Winona Ryder. The film was shown at the Cannes Film Festival and went into general release in June. Using the rotoscoping technique that Linklater used in his earlier movie "Waking Life', the film of A SCANNER DARKLY is likely the most true of any of the PKD movies to Dick's novel.

For Dick, then, 1973 was an up and down year. He'd found some sort of stability with Tessa and was able to return to writing, finishing FLOW MY TEARS, THE POLICEMAN SAID and completing a first draft of A SCANNER DARKLY as well as writing two short stories: "A Little Something For us Tempunauts" and "The Pre-Persons."
And now we come to 1974, one of the most important years in Philip K. Dick's life.

1974

The first good news of the year 1974 was publication by Doubleday of the first edition of FLOW MY TEARS, THE POLICEMAN SAID in February – PKD got an advance copy in January. And while he was looking over his novel, noting the juxtaposition of the words KING and FELIX in the text, he was likely anticipating payment for his short story "The Pre-Persons" from *F & SF*. With that out of the way in February, Philip K. Dick was hanging around the house playing with baby Christopher (born July 25, 1973) and worrying about his taxes when one of his wisdom teeth became infected. This would scarcely deserve comment except that it was the beginning of a train of strange occurrences in Phil and Tessa's life.

After surgery on his tooth in which PKD was given sodium pentathol he was sent home. But he was still in great pain and Tessa called the pharmacy to have some pain medicine delivered (Darvon). We'll let PKD continue the story:

I was in such great pain that I went out to meet the girl when she came. She was wearing a golden fish in profile on a necklace. The sun struck it and it shone, and I was dazed by it.

For some reason I was hypnotized by the gleaming golden fish. I forgot my pain, forgot the medication, forgot why the girl was there. I just kept staring at the fish sign.

"What does that mean?" I asked her. The girl touched the glimmering golden fish with her hand and said, ""This is a sign worn by the early Christians." She then gave me the package of medication.

In that instant as I stared at the gleaming fish sign and heard her words, I suddenly experienced what I later learned is called *anamnesis* – a Greek word meaning, literally, 'loss of forgetfulness.'

I remembered who I was and where I was. In an instant, in the twinkling of an eye, it all came back to me. And not only could I remember it but I could see it. The girl was a secret Christian and so was I. We lived in fear of detection by the Romans. We had to communicate in cryptic signs. She had just told me all this, and it was true.

I saw the world as the world of the apostolic Christian times of ancient Rome, when the fish sign was in use. It only lasted a few seconds. I went in and took the pain medication. I was hemorrhaging. I was bleeding badly, in great discomfort. [dccxii]

This passage is taken from "The Religious Experience of Philip K. Dick" by the renowned comics artist R. Crumb and which appeared in *Weirdo* magazine in 1985. In this illustrated article Crumb takes his text from the transcription of interviews PKD had with Gregg Rickman and which were published in Rickman's *IN HIS OWN WORDS* in 1984. [dccxiii]

The story of these 2-3/74 experiences – also known as the 'pink beam' experiences and PKD's theophany – has been told in several places. Philip K. Dick himself described and fictionalized his theophany in his novel VALIS and continued his speculation and theorizing on the 2-3/74 events in THE DIVINE INVASION. They also sparked another of his novels, RADIO FREE ALBEMUTH, which is an earlier version of VALIS. And, of course, in his *EXEGESIS* – begun in 1974 after the events and continuing on to his death in 1982 -- he spent much of his time wondering, worrying and explaining his experiences. Although the *EXEGESIS* has yet to be published in full, there are excerpts scattered around various books and articles, most of them to be found in Lawrence Sutin's *IN PURSUIT OF VALIS* and throughout *The Philip K. Dick Society Newsletter*. More excerpts are found in Sutin's *THE SHIFTING REALITIES OF PHILIP K. DICK: Selected Literary and Philosophical Writings*.

We will look at these three novels – and a fourth, THE TRANSMIGRATION OF TIMOTHY ARCHER – and the *EXEGESIS* shortly. These novels are collectively called the 'Valis Trilogy' even though there are four books (most PKD scholars exclude RADIO FREE ALBEMUTH for some reason[dccxiv]). But, now, we'll continue on with R. Crumb and his selections from *IHOW* as this article succinctly describes what happened in March 1974.

And then a month later, it all began to seep through. There wasn't any way I could hold it back. The transformation occurred and it stayed for a year... I saw the world under the aspect of the Christian apocalypse.
{...} it invaded my mind and assumed control of my motor centers and did my acting and thinking for me. I was a spectator to it... This mind, whose identity was totally obscured to me, was equipped with tremendous technical knowledge. It had memories dating back over two thousand years. It spoke Greek, Hebrew, Sanskrit, there wasn't anything that it didn't seem to know.
It immediately set about putting my affairs in order. It fired my agent and publisher... My wife was impressed by the fact that {...} I made quite a lot of money very rapidly. We began to get checks for thousands of dollars – money that was owed me.[dccxv]

But PKD didn't actually fire his agent and publisher (Doubleday). The contretemps was induced by what Dick thought were inconsistent sales figures for FLOW MY TEARS, THE POLICEMAN SAID. PKD asked in May for an audit of all the sales for all of his books published by Doubleday. At about the same time in May he fired his agent, Scott Meredith, because he didn't think the Agency was supporting him in his quarrel with Doubleday. But the audit showed that PKD was wrong in his analysis of the number of copies of FLOW MY TEARS sold and also wrong in his other dispute with Doubleday concerning the paperback rights sale of FLOW MY TEARS to DAW books. PKD had thought the $2500 sale was too low. But, as Sutin points out, the $2500 bid from DAW books was the highest Doubleday had received and, therefore, there could be no argument with Doubleday on this.

So Dick reinstated his agent in a letter on May 12, 1974. But a condition of this was that the Agency go after Ace Books for what Dick – and the writer's organization, The Science Fiction Writers of America, thought were inconsistent royalty statements from Ace. The result of this thrust was that Dick received a check for over $3000 in back royalties from Ace Books by the end of May.[dccxvi]

Dick's strange experiences continued:

I didn't want to involve my wife in this. She was a witness on one crucial matter. She was there when all that information about our little boy's birth defect was transferred to me. {...} I was sitting there listening to 'Strawberry Fields Forever'; with my eyes shut, when all of a sudden this tremendous light hit me.
Literally, in the sense I saw the light. I was blinded... I thought, Jesus Christ! What's happening? I'm blind, my head hurts, can't see nothing. All I can see is pink... A phosphene after image, like you see when a flashbulb fires off. All I could see was a pink haze, and the words of the Beatles song got all changed around: 'Your eyes are closed to your son's birth defect... Your son is in danger... He has a right inguinal hernia that's popped the hydroseal, and gone into the scrotal sac... You must get him to the doctor immediately...'
I leaped up... Tess was in the other room changing Christopher – I walked in and said, 'Tess, he's got a birth defect, and its going to kill him. We've got to get him to a doctor.
{...} She came back an hour later and she was absolutely ashen. She said '{...} The doctor said he should have surgery immediately.'[dccxvii]

One may think what one will of the weird experiences PKD underwent in the spring and summer of 1974 but the fact remains that his son *did* need immediate surgery to save his life. And Phil's finances did improve; not only with the dealings with his agent and publishers mentioned above but also later in the year when French film producer J.P. Gorin visited PKD in September. Gorin paid $1500 down-payment for a screenplay of UBIK which Dick was to write before the end of the next year, 1975.[dccxviii] Two other would-be movie makers visited PKD in November: Robert Jaffe who had written a screenplay for DO ANDROIDS DREAM OF ELECTRIC SHEEP? and Hampton Fancher who was also interested in turning ANDROIDS into a movie. It helped that Fancher brought along on one of his visits the actress Barbara Hershey. This suitably impressed Phil (he probably fell immediately in love with her) and he began to think enthusiastically about the filming of his novel.[dccxix]

We'll take a look at UBIK: THE SCREENPLAY momentarily but, first, the strange events continued:

One of my experiences – it was '74 – I bought one of those fish signs with the Greek letters on it, and pasted it up on my window. I was sitting there one day and the upsilon, which looks like a capital 'Y', suddenly turned into a palm tree, and then opened up into the entire Mesopotamian world, the Middle-eastern world.[dccxx]

This transformation occurred in Feb 1975. On the symbology of the palm tree PKD wrote in his *EXEGESIS*

Palm trees are a Christian symbol of the Holy land; what I saw in 2-75, then, is a vision of the Holy Land. I did not go (journey) to it; it came to me. I was already seeing a palm tree (like the Afrika Korps palm tree emblem) in the FISH sign, months before...[dccxxi]

Beyond seeing this vision of the Holy Land in his fish sign, Dick also began to see the world of apostolic times superimposed over the real world of Orange county in 1974. He also felt himself to be a secret Christian living in that time whose name was Thomas. For a month thereafter PKD felt himself being taken over by the personality of Thomas and he gradually became Thomas over the next year:

I used to be able to pick up his thoughts while I was falling asleep... And I picked up his thoughts one night, and he was thinking, 'There's somebody else inside my head, and he's living in another century' ... Meaning me. I thought, 'Tell me about it!' I can say the same thing!' At first he thought he was still back in Rome.

{...} He had the sense of a regime that was murderous, not just oppressive, but murderous! He thought Christianity was an illegal religion. He was afraid of being killed for being a Christian, that's what he was afraid of ... Damnedest thing... [dccxxii]

Perhaps Thomas' fears were real. Dick continues his explication, sometimes thinking he was possessed by the spirit of Elijah and at other times by John the Baptist:

I just know that some kind of spirit took me over... Through its help I was able to solve problems and concerns, the things I couldn't do... It seemed able to discern anything it looked at.

I *did* have grandiose illusions that the spirit of Elijah entered me and I uttered prophesies... and for what? Because the prophecies had to be fulfilled, that Elijah comes first, and second, that the news be revealed, and that is what John the Baptist did for

Jesus... having done so he faded away. In fact they cut off his head, and by the way I dreamed about that... I was in a dungeon, a Roman dungeon, and they came and cut off my head, took a wire and garroted me... I remember them coming to that cell and taking and slicing my head off... It was horrible.

The voice that I heard, that I call the A.I. voice {artificial intelligence}, is the voice that Elijah heard... The still small voice, the little murmuring voice... it spoke in a feminine voice... I heard it say: 'The time you've waited for is come... your work is complete... the final world is here... he has been transplanted and he is alive!'

I asked the *I Ching* if indeed the 'Parousia' (the Second Coming) was here, Christ had returned. I got 'Darkening of the Light' and the following line, the only time I ever got this line: 'Darkening of the Light injures him in the left thigh. He gives aid with the strength of a horse. Good fortune.'

Here the Lord of Light is in a subordinate place and is wounded by the Lord of Darkness, but the injury is not fatal. It is only a hindrance... Therefore he tries with all his strength to save all that can be saved... There is good fortune. I interpret these words as saying that indeed Christ has returned... The Lord of Light is the Christ who has come here and subordinated himself... the Saviour, you see?[dccxxiii]

A year later, in 1976, the voice faded away from PKD's mind. This was a painful parting and he keenly felt the loss, attempting suicide that year. But PKD realised that:

In essence, I had served my purpose in FLOW MY TEARS (...) I even rallied back from the suicide attempt but if I hadn't rallied it would all have gone on without me.[dccxxiv]

This truncated description of the events of 2-3/74 (which continued on into 1975) tells the main line but there are other strange happenings not included in it. For instance, Dick's experiencing 8 hours of 'whirling lights' while lying awake in mid-March 1974 that a few days later turned into a night of modern abstract paintings clipping through his mind one after the other at a great rate, paintings similar to those of Klee and Kandinsky. Or, the strange case of the 'Xerox missive' a few weeks later. This was a letter that the A.I. voice had forewarned Dick was coming. He fearfully awaited its arrival and when it came in a bundle of letters in the mail one day, he quickly singled it out. But he didn't read it. Instead, he had Tessa open it and tell him of its contents. As Dick describes the incident in VALIS:

Beth opened it. Instead of a letter per se she found a Xerox sheet on which two book reviews from the left-wing New York newspaper *The Daily World* had been juxtaposed. The reviewer described the author of the book as a Soviet national living in the United States. From the reviews it was obvious that the author was a Party member...[dccxxv]

Tessa recalls Phil having her summarize it for him:

Certain words in the article [book review] were underlined, some in red and some in blue. All were what Phil called "die messages"...[dccxxvi]

Sutin says that PKD believed that the Xerox missive was somehow connected to his two-week amnesia period in Vancouver in March 1972 and that Phil feared that the missive was supposed to trigger something in him. He was afraid and took prompt action, sending the missive off to the FBI. He also called the FBI and wrote more letters to them in an attempt to forestall any doubts as to his loyalty to the United States. But the FBI didn't seem too interested, sending him a form-letter response. But, at least, Dick's attempts to communicate with the FBI did have the benefit of lifting the sense of dread that had hung over him since the break-in of his apartment in 1971.[dccxxvii]

And then there was the radio that played obscenities to Phil at night, even though it was turned off. This just prior to the pink beam zapping information into his brain, telling him, for one, to surreptitiously administer the Christian Eucharist to his son Christopher; this PKD did, using a hot dog and cup of hot chocolate as the sacraments to baptize him.

Tessa recalls the radio incidents in conversation with J.B. Reynolds. Sadassa Ulna is a character in RADIO FREE ALBEMUTH:

(TD:) The thing about Sadassa Ulna came from a different source. For a while there, we used to sleep with the radio on. One night the radio was playing, Helen Reddy singing "You're So Vain."...

(JB:) You mean Carly Simon.

(TD:) Carly Simon, yeah. Only Phil kept getting it mixed up in his mind with Linda Ronstadt: "You're No Good." But it was "You're So Vain" that was playing. I was a little more awake than Phil was; he was kind of half awake, and all of a sudden he jumped up and -- well, he yelled at me to turn the radio off, and I didn't do it fast enough so he turned it off himself. And he unplugged it and took it out to the kitchen. See, he thought he'd heard the radio saying his name, and telling him that he was no good, no good, and he should crawl into a corner and die.

(JB:) Huh. In RADIO FREE ALBEMUTH, the character Nicholas is sitting in the living room, and hears the radio saying, "Nick is a prick!", obscenities. Was that based on that incident?

(TD:) Well, yeah. It was saying "Phil is a pill", and stuff like that.

(CD:) Laughs.

(JB:) That was one of the items on my list, the "obscenities over the radio."

(TD:) Oh yeah, it was saying all kinds of horrible things to him. Well, the thing is, the radio stayed in the kitchen unplugged, for about a week, and we kept hearing the radio at night anyway. We did have one wall in common with the apartment next door. So we checked with the girls there to see if they were playing the radio at night, but the wall in our bedroom connected with their kitchen, and they didn't even have a radio in the kitchen. The thing about that was that we both heard the music, and it was always between 2 and 6 ayem, and the radio wasn't even plugged in.

(JB:) Was it the same kind of music that you'd had before?

(TD:) Yeah, sounded like the same station, so Phil even went out and un-tuned the unplugged radio to something else. But we still got easy-listening music, only Phil kept hearing it tell him that he was no good, that he should die. And I didn't hear that. We gave up and plugged the radio back in again, because it was easier to sleep with music on.[dccxxviii]

One of the names PKD gave to whatever he thought was communicating with him was Valis – Vast Active Living Intelligence System. Valis, by means of a series of tutelary dreams starting in March and continuing on into the summer, transmitted information to him:

{...} almost each night, during sleep I was receiving information in the form of print-outs, words and sentences, letters and names and numbers – sometimes whole pages, sometimes in the form of writing paper and holographic writing, sometimes, oddly, in the form of a baby's cereal box on which all sorts of quite meaningful information was written and typed, and finally galley proofs held up for me to read which I was told in my dream "contained prophecies about the future," and during the last two weeks a huge book, again and again, with page after page of printed lines.[dccxxix]

One can easily become skeptical about all this: strange dreams, whirling lights, A.I. voices and all the rest. But to make sense of it doesn't really matter. For Dick himself these experiences were very important and he spent the rest of his life trying to attach some sort of explanation to them, writing in his *EXEGESIS* night after night in search of true meaning. All this has been covered by PKD himself in his novels VALIS, RADIO FREE ALBEMUTH and THE DIVINE INVASION. It remains for us only to look at these novels – in due time – in light of PKD's pink-beam experiences at the same time as we take them on their own merits.

But, weird experiences aside, the year 1974 continued. In April Berkley printed a paperback edition of THE MAN IN THE HIGH CASTLE and in May Berkley Medallion reissued two of PKD's novels in paperback: COUNTER-CLOCK WORLD and GALACTIC POT-HEALER. Also in May Manor Books published their paperback edition of NOW WAIT FOR LAST YEAR. In June White Lion publishers in the UK issued the first hardcover of THE GAME-PLAYERS OF TITAN. For collectors this would be the most valuable edition of THE GAME-PLAYERS OF TITAN.[dccxxx]

Other reprints continued throughout the year with editions of THE CRACK IN SPACE from Ace Books and, in October, Gollancz in the UK published the first hardback edition of FLOW MY TEARS, THE POLICEMAN SAID to appear in that conglomeration of countries. Finally, "A Little Something For Us Tempunauts" was first published in *FINAL STAGE* from Charterhouse publishers in hardback. A paperback edition of *FINAL STAGE* also came from Penguin in the UK towards the end of the year.

From this roster of publications we can see that PKD's list of books continued to grow in 1974. The bandwagon would roll on in 1975.

UBIK: The Screenplay

As we've seen above, in September 1974 French film producer J.P. Gorin visited Dick in his home and after an enthusiastic conversation between the two Gorin paid PKD $1500 to write a screenplay for his novel UBIK. The screenplay to be finished by the end of the next year, 1975. But, to Gorin's consternation, Dick finished the screenplay in a month instead of the allotted year; completing the screenplay by the middle of Oct 1974.

Part of the agreement between Dick and Gorin was that Gorin would pay $2500 on completion of the screenplay but, having finished it so quickly, Gorin found himself unable to get this money immediately although he did eventually pay PKD the sum. However, despite great effort Gorin was unable to interest a producer in the project. PKD talks of his screenplay in an interview with Mike Hodel of radio station KPFK-FM which was broadcast on June 26, 1976:

Mike: You wrote a screenplay of one of your own things.
Phil: Yeah, I wrote a good screenplay. I wrote a really good one of Ubik. And it seems to be the fate that the better the screenplay - boy, there's Gresham's Law. I don't know how it applies to science fiction writing in general but it sure applies to screenplays, you know, that the bad screenplays force the good out. If given a choice they will make a movie out of a bad screenplay and they'll throw the good screenplay back at the author.
Mike: If I remember, The *Rolling Stone* piece, that screenplay you did of Ubik is currently bouncing around Europe trying to get finances. Is that still the case or is that –
Phil: Yeah, it's still optioned and they're still trying to get financing for it. It's not the director's fault. He spent all the money he had, Jean-Pierre Gorin, and he couldn't get the financial backing. He couldn't get the millions of dollars that it would cost. And he got really sick. He got sick with liver trouble and he had to give up being a director and go teach down in San Diego. He just about died trying to get a movie made out of that. But I wrote a really great - I must say, I wish you'd - I'd like to read it over the air sometime. There's the funniest scenes in that screenplay that aren't in the book that I added that I went back to the old silent film days where these - you know, it's a tragedy. That's the one thing I am bitter about. If I had written a novel with that stuff in it I wouldn't have any trouble selling it. But I can't sell that screenplay. It's too bad.[dccxxxi]

The *Rolling Stone* article that Mike Hodel refers to was the pivotal one for Dick's popularity written by Paul Williams and published in the November 1975 issue of that magazine. In it PKD and Williams talk about UBIK: The Screenplay:

PKD: I've got a little screen in my head, and the people walk around on it.
PW: They're real.
PKD: They're *little*, Paul, they're about that big. [laughter] I didn't realise it until I did the screenplay [for UBIK – Phil's first screenplay, completed in three weeks last year], where I had to visualize, and I realised I didn't have to 'cause I was, I didn't know any other way to do it. I got to where I was literally looking up, type type type and look up. They move around, y'know, and I was going like this, looking up, typing, and saying, 'And there goes Joe out the door, slam!' With one character I deduced he had a child 'cause I could see a tricycle in the driveway.[dccxxxii]

UBIK: The Screenplay was eventually published by Corroboree Press in 1985. This is a beautiful edition with many colored plates by Ron Lindahn, Val Lakey-Lindahn and Doug Rice illustrating the text. There is also a deluxe edition of 50 signed by the artists, Tim Powers, Paul

Williams and with signatures cut from PKD's old checks tipped-in. Both of these editions are quite valuable to collectors. [dccxxxiii]

After completing his screenplay for UBIK, Dick wrote nothing new in 1974.

1975

The miraculous events continued into 1975. In January and February PKD had his vision of the Palm Tree Garden. He included a description of this in his novel DEUS IRAE.

PKD's first fictional attempt of the New Year was a short story called "The Eye of the Sibyl". Dick's friend the cartoonist Art Spiegelman visited PKD in the Spring of 1975 and the two conjured up a collaboration with, presumably, Dick to write the story and Spiegelman to do the illustrations. Spiegelman was at the time editor at the magazine *Arcade* and the story was to appear there. But the story PKD wrote, "The Eye of the Sibyl," was too complicated to be easily transferred to the cartoon medium and when he sent it off to the SMLA where it arrived on May 15, 1975, it never made the transformation.[dccxxxiv]

Instead "The Eye of the Sibyl" actually saw first publication in D. Scot Apel's *PHILIP K. DICK: THE DREAM CONNECTION* in March 1987. The first edition of this book was limited to a print run of 500 copies and it is now a valuable collector's item. *THE DREAM CONNECTION* was reprinted in a larger edition in 1999 though still quite valuable.[dccxxxv]

On this story, Charles Coulombe notes:

He could not, however, write for publication without some reference to his {Valis} experience. His first post-being piece was a short story called "The Eye Of The Sibyl". Eventually rejected by the venue it was written for, it eventually saw the light in *Gnosis Magazine* (#5 Fall 1987). In it, the major points of Dick's 1975 worldview are set forth, in a style reminiscent of his earlier work.[dccxxxvi]

The *Gnosis* magazine printing actually came after the story's appearance in *THE DREAM CONNECTION* in 1987. Gregg Rickman refers to "The Eye of the Sibyl" in connection with the young Philip K. Dick's deciding to become a writer in 1945:

It was right at the time that Dick was contributing to the YAC {Aunt Flo's *Young Author's Club*}that he seems to have decided to become a writer. In his autobiographical short story "Eye Of The Sibyl", his protagonist reports that one night, while he was in junior high and "getting ready to go to Berkeley High next year" he had a vivid dream of seeing a "man from another universe... he couldn't talk; he just looked at me with funny eyes."

The story's hero was thus disposed, responding to a question about his future, to reply "I AM GOING TO BE A SCIENCE FICTION WRITER."

That made my family mad, but then, see, when they got mad I got stubborn... (I was told) science fiction was dumb and only people with pimples read it. So I decided for sure to write it, because people with pimples should have someone writing for them. It's unfair otherwise, just to write for people with fair complexions.[dccxxxvii]

All in all, including its inclusion in THE COLLECTED STORIES OF PHILIP K. DICK, Vol. 5, "The Eye of the Sibyl" was published three times in 1987. The only year in which it was ever published.

The story itself is autobiographical with PKD weaving in elements of his 'pink beam' inspirations into a story that spans the period from ancient Rome to the present day.

Philos Diktos of Tyana, a priest at the temple in Cumae where the Cumaean sibyl was located, writes of seeing the sibyl in conversation with two slit-eyed 'gods' and hearing of a projected period of decline for the Roman Republic that will span 2000 years. Philos Diktos finds himself transferred to the future where he is now a schoolboy named Philip Dick who is having strange dreams about a repressive police state and conspiracies at the highest levels. He experiences anamnesis - the loss of forgetfulness - and remembers that he is from ancient times and before that came from the star Albemuth. The two slit-eyed gods visit him and explain about the tyranny and their effort to wake the people up.

At the end of the story with Diktos/Dick back in Roman times he quotes a verse from Virgil:

At last the Final Time announced by the Sibyl will arrive:
The procession of ages turns to its origin.
The Virgin returns and Saturn reigns as before;
A new race from heaven on high descends.
Goddess of Birth, smile on the new-born baby,
In whose time the Iron Prison will fall to ruin
And a golden race arises everywhere.
Apollo, the rightful king, is restored! [dccxxxviii]

This is an important story for understanding PKD's 'pink beam' experiences and as a story in light of that "The Eye of the Sibyl" rates ✳ ✳ ✳ ✳

In 1975 PKD had many editions of his books published both domestically and abroad. We'll list only a few of them here: In the UK, the first edition of THE ZAP GUN came out from Panther in Feb and in May Gollancz published the first UK hardback edition of THE MAN IN THE HIGH CASTLE. Other UK editions of his novels, CLANS OF THE ALPHANE MOON and NOW WAIT FOR LAST YEAR appeared from Panther in paperback.[dccxxxix]

In the USA Entwhistle Books published the first edition of CONFESSIONS OF A CRAP ARTIST – the only one of his mainstream novels that PKD was to see published in his lifetime.[dccxl] Many other reprints of his novels came out in 1975, particularly the first paperback edition of FLOW MY TEARS, THE POLICEMAN SAID from DAW Books and, notably, his short story "The Golden Man" made two anthology appearances, one in the UK and one in the USA.[dccxli]

All in all, 1974 and 1975 were good years for PKD's publications. As Sutin notes, in 1974 Dick had had an income of about $19,000 and $30,000 in 1975, most of this income from foreign sales (A quick and incomplete survey of foreign editions in 1975 shows nineteen editions of PKD's books published that year; three from J'ai Lu publishers in France and three from Goldmann in Germany alone).[dccxlii]

With his improved financial circumstances, PKD, Tessa and Christopher moved to a better rented house in Fullerton in March and PKD indulged himself with the purchase of the new 3rd edition of *The Encyclopedia Britannica*; Tessa got a new guitar and a horse while the couple shared a red Fiat Spyder sports car.[dccxliii]

And, at last, Roger Zelazny had finished his part of the novel DEUS IRAE. This was done by Aug 17, 1975.[dccxliv]

When Zelazny sent the manuscript back to PKD, Dick added a final chapter and sent the manuscript to Doubleday.[dccxlv]

We will take one final look at DEUS IRAE when we reach the year 1976 in this chronology; the year the novel was actually published.

Another essay PKD wrote in 1975 was "Man, Android and Machine".

"Man, Android and Machine" was first published in the anthology *Science Fiction At Large*, edited by Peter Nicholls and published by Gollancz in the UK in 1976. Later it would be reprinted in THE DARK-HAIRED GIRL. Perhaps the most convenient place to find it now is in Sutin's THE SHIFTING REALITIES OF PHILIP K. DICK (1995).[dccxlvi]

The essay is perhaps the earliest deeply considered writing that PKD wrote to try to explain his pink-beam experiences. It deals not so much with the difference between man, android and machine although in it PKD writes:

The greatest change growing across our world these days is probably the momentum of the living toward reification, and at the same time a reciprocal entry into animation by the mechanical. We hold now no pure categories of the living versus the non-living... [dccxlvii]

But the essay is more concerned with the meaning of 'time.' Here PKD writes of a Gnostic view of the universe wherein we are living in a world veiled by our experience of time. Time, PKD, explains:

"To see the universe backward?" What would that mean? Well, let me give you one possibility: that we experience time backward; or more precisely, that our inner, subjective category of experience of time (in the sense that Kant spoke of, a way by which we arrange experience), our time experience, is orthogonal to the flow of time itself – at right angles. There are two times: the time that is our experience or perception or construct of ontological matrix, an extensiveness along with space as an inseparable extensiveness into another area – this is real, but the outer time flow of the universe moves in a different direction. Both are real, but by experiencing time, orthogonally to its actual direction, we get a totally wrong idea of the sequence of events, of causality, of what is past and what is future, where the universe is going.
I hope you realise the importance of this... [dccxlviii]

This essay is indeed an important one for the idea of orthogonal time, or sideways time, is something that runs through the published excerpts of PKD's extended *EXEGESIS*.

Above when we looked at UBIK we included another short selection from "Man, Android and Machine."

1975 continues on then, with Dick finishing his revisions for A SCANNER DARKLY. In November the *Rolling Stone* article by Paul Williams came out. This interesting if outré conversation between PKD and Williams was expanded on in Williams' book, *ONLY APPARENTLY REAL*.

Generally, in his life, times were hard for Philip K. Dick in 1975. Sutin writes of bottomed-out finances in the summer, having to borrow money from old friend Robert Heinlein, and growing discord between Phil and Tessa that dragged on into the new year. And, yes, another woman was involved.

So, then, the hapless Phil having weird visions, broke, fighting with his wife and scribbling in his *EXEGESIS* night after night…

As far as his career though 1975 was a good year for publications but not such a good one for writing. DEUS IRAE was finished at last, the SCANNER revisions were done, he'd written one short story, "The Eye of the Sibyl" and written his first real insights for publication of his mystical experiences, the essay "Man, Androids and Machine."

1976

The Bicentennial Year had an unhappy beginning for Phil and his family. In February Tessa left with little Christopher. This was all too much for PKD. Again he tried to commit suicide, employing multiple methods at once. Fortunately the attempt failed due to sheer luck more than anything else and the next day after feeding his cat, he called the doctors. After a rapid trip to the hospital where a depleted Phil was patched up, he was carted off to the mental hospital. This is all covered in chapter four of VALIS and it was indeed a sad time for Phil.

But he got better, as they say, and in the summer of 1976 moved into a new apartment in Santa Ana, California. His new love Doris moved in with him for, as Sutin notes, a summer of happiness.

Publications for the year were again high with at least seventeen editions of his stories and collections published in the United Kingdom and the United States. Notable among these were the first UK editions of OUR FRIENDS FROM FROLIX 8 from Panther in Jan; MARTIAN TIME-SLIP from NEL in June; and THE UNTELEPORTED MAN from Methuen in August. As for THE MAN IN THE HIGH CASTLE, it had its UK Book Club edition released in March and this was followed by a paperback from Penguin in April. In the USA the first edition of DEUS IRAE made it to the stands from Doubleday in July and the first hardcover edition of SOLAR LOTTERY came from Gregg Press in June. FLOW MY TEARS, THE POLICEMAN SAID had its second DAW edition and THE PRESERVING MACHINE was reprinted by Ace.

Of the editions published in 1976 the one by Gregg Press of SOLAR LOTTERY would be the most valuable, fetching up to $200 while the first edition of DEUS IRAE can be found for around $100. Of the rest, Ace's THE PRESERVING MACHINE collection is difficult to find in anything but beat-up, read-several-times condition so a fine example might run you $20. The UKSFBC edition from Reader's Union though can be had for about $10.

As the year progressed so did the editing on A SCANNER DARKLY. As we've noted above, PKD was working with Judy-Lyn Del Rey on extensive changes to the manuscript this year. The first edition was ready to go from Doubleday at the end of 1976.

Dick had returned to writing again, too, working on his novel RADIO FREE ALEMUTH in the summer. We'll return to RADIO FREE ALBEMUTH ourselves shortly but first let's take one last look at DEUS IRAE.

DEUS IRAE (Part 5)

As we've seen, Zelazny finished writing his part of DEUS IRAE by August 1975. To this PKD had added a final chapter and dispatched the novel to Doubleday who published it in July 1976.[dccxlix]

Daniel DePrez of *Science Fiction Review* covers the whole saga:

SFR: Then what about the collaboration between you and Roger Zelazny? How did that come about?

DICK: Well, that came about because I started DEUS IRAE, and I couldn't finish it because of my lack of knowledge of theology. And I met Roger in '68, and asked him if he would help me with the book, and he said he would, and he did, and his knowledge was adequate, and we were able to finish it, but it still took twelve years for the two of us to write the book, and it was very arduous for us to write. And we just sold that in England for a very large sum of money, so we finally will get some money out of it. I don't think we will get much in this country, but we will get something on the English sale.

SFR: The bookstores in Portland are selling out of the book.

DICK: Well, it's sold pretty well in this country. It's sold over 5,000 copies in the United States, so we will make some money. But the English sale was good, it was between 8,000 and 9,000 dollars, and we hope for other good foreign sales.

{...}

The only exception, say, would be the collaboration with Roger Zelazny, where I'd do a part, and Roger would do a part, and I'd do a part, and years would go by between our parts. And we lost a lot of money from having to spend so many years writing it. But, as I say, I was in difficulty, and simply didn't have the background for the book, and needed his assistance.

SFR: Had he been thinking of something along those lines himself?

DICK: I think he just -- his broad knowledge of things permitted him to pick it up. He's a very educated person, and a very skillful writer, and he was just an ideal person for those two reasons. I like the parts that Roger wrote. I think he wrote some very funny parts. The pogo stick part that he wrote was the funniest part of the book. I was very pleased with what he did.[dccl]

As to the amount Dick and Zelazny got for DEUS IRAE, PKD in another conversation said:

...then eight years went by, and I didn't hear from Roger until I got a postcard one time from him from the East Coast. Roger's in over his head just like me, but he's doing research. We each got four hundred dollars apiece or something like that. We'll never be able to earn back what we put into that book in the way of research and work. Now I, too, spend my time doing research before I do a book; I'm not going to get burned like that again.[dccli]

In 1977 Dick would meet Zelazny again at the science fiction convention held in Metz, France that year.

For collectors of PKD editions, the first Doubleday edition of 1976 can be found for $75 to $100 in Fine condition although with a little searching you might get a very good copy for about $25. Surprisingly, the UK SFBC edition from Reader's Union in 1978 can be bought for as low as $20. I've a feeling this one will be going up though.

Some lucky collector is the proud owner of the ultimate DEUS IRAE package; Ken Lopez Bookseller offered in 1997 the following item:

Deus Irae. (Published by Doubleday, 1976). Co-written with Roger Zelazny (author of Lord of Light, etc.). Ribbon copy typescript, 240 pages, typed on three typewriters (two of them Zelazny's), with small holograph corrections in both authors' hands, and a brief note explaining which typewriter represents which writer.
{...} Very good condition. $7500.[dcclii]

For a synopsis of DEUS IRAE we turn to Andrew Butler:

In the 1980's Carleton Lufteufel set off the bombs that half-destroyed the world; some say he was the God of Wrath. Phocomelus Tibor McMasters has been commissioned to paint his likeness on an altar and cannot work from the Polaroid provided. Tibor sets out on his cow-drawn cart to find Carleton, and encounters a homicidal computer, the Great C, and intelligent lizards, along the way. Pete Sands, who has had mystical visions, is sent along to try and sabotage the mission. They meet Jack Schuld, who promises Tibor that he will help him find Carleton, and reveals to Pete that he *is* in fact Carleton. Tibor kills him, and believes Pete when he locates someone willing to say he is Carleton. The completed altar is declared authentic, and Tibor is canonized after his death.

A drawn-out novel that shows the difficulty of its creation DEUS IRAE is worth ✷ ✷ ✷.

RADIO FREE ALBEMUTH

RADIO FREE ALBEMUTH had its genesis in 1974. In April of that year PKD received a call from fellow sf writer Philip Jose Farmer asking him to contribute a story to an anthology of stories written supposedly by fictional authors.[dccliii] Paul Williams explains:

Dick liked the idea, and agreed to come up with a story by Hawthorne Abendsen, author of *The Grasshopper Lies Heavy*, a character in Dick's novel, THE MAN IN THE HIGH CASTLE.
The story had a working title, "A Man For No Countries," and Dick noted that it would be about "'our' world (not quite) and what happened to me 11/17/71" (the date of the mysterious break-in at Dick's house in San Rafael, California), but it was never written, or rather, it evolved into a novel, RADIO FREE ALBEMUTH (written in 1976, published in 1985). RADIO FREE ALBEMUTH, originally called VALISYSTEM A, was the first Philip K. Dick novel in which Philip K. Dick was a fictional character, under his own name. The second was VALIS (written in '78, published in '81). The third was *THE SECRET ASCENSION* (*PHILIP K. DICK IS DEAD, ALAS*), written after Dick's death by Michael Bishop (published in 1987).[dccliv]

Williams continues the story:

VALISYSTEM A was written in the Summer of 1976, Mark Hurst, then an editor at Bantam Books, purchased the book on the understanding that it would be revised. Apparently Hurst and Dick discussed these revisions, on the phone or in person, and Dick agreed in principle to rather extensive changes. There followed several years in which Dick wrote Hurst long letters suggesting totally new plots that he would layer over the existing novel. He never actually drafted any of this material. Dick did refer often to the research he was doing for his Bantam novel; this research, the thousands of pages of notes, formed part of what he later called his *EXEGESIS*.
My guess is that Phil gave up fairly quickly on the idea of revising VALISYSTEM A to satisfy what he and Mark had discussed, and turned instead to planning a new novel based on the earlier material. This in turn left him feeling blocked on the project, and so he did no novel writing until October/November of 1978, when he broke through and in a rush of creativity wrote VALIS.
The point is that VALISYSTEM A was the rough draft of VALIS only in a technical sense. The two novels are very different in plot, theme and style...
The name RADIO FREE ALBEMUTH was chosen because it was felt that the titles VALIS and VALISYSTEM A are too similar and would cause confusion. {...}
David Hartwell is the editor at Arbor House responsible for acquiring RFA...[dcclv]

VALISYSTEM A was completed by Aug 19, 1976.[dcclvi] The manuscript that was published by Arbor House in 1985 as RADIO FREE ALBEMUTH was likely the one that Tim Powers provided to PKD's estate. Dick had given Powers a manuscript for VALISYSTEM A with pencilled corrections by Dick for Powers' collection.[dcclvii]

Philip K. Dick talks of VALISYSTEM A to Daniel DePrez. In this interview conducted in Aug 1976 Dick has already mentioned that he has sold VALISYSTEM A to Bantam Books who, although they didn't publish RADIO FREE ALBEMUTH, did publish VALIS in 1978:

SFR: How can you describe the novel?

DICK: Well, that's the most difficult question of all to answer, I've found. I would actually prefer not to describe the novel. For one thing, they purchased it from the rough draft, and there'll be many changes in the final draft, and I wouldn't want to have it freeze in the rough draft form. I know it seems strange not to be able to answer a question like that, "What is the novel about?", I always say, well, if somebody asked Shakespeare, "I understand you're writing a play called ROMEO AND JULIET, what's it about?" If he were to give an oral description of it, it'd probably sound like a terrible bomb. And after he got halfway through describing it, he'd begin to realize it sounded like a terrible bomb, and he would probably not write it. So, short oral synopses do not give adequate account of books. Let's say it's the story of an alternate universe, and of a tyrant named Ferris F. Fremont, who's President of the United States, and in 1968, after having shot the Kennedys, Dr. King, Jim Pike, Malcolm X, everybody - George Wallace - so that he is elected by a very large vote, there not being any real contenders, and sets out to destroy the two-party system. And it's the story of a group of people who manage to overthrow him.

SFR: Is this going to be marketed as a science fiction novel?

DICK: Oh yes, it's definitely science fiction, because the people who overthrow him are picked at random by an extraterrestrial satellite communications system which informs them what to do, and what information will bring down the tyrant, Ferris Fremont. And coordinates their efforts through direct radio communications with the satellite, which has been in orbit around the Earth for several thousand years, and periodically intervenes when tyrannical governments become too tyrannical. There seems to be no other way to depose them.

{...}

SFR: So whenever the next novel comes up depends on when you get the next handle?

DICK: Exactly. I could go for a year, I could go two years, I could go two weeks. This one, I was beginning to think I'd never get the handle. I had done almost 300,000 words of notes, and I was really beginning to think I would never get a novel out of it. And one day I was just thinking -- just sitting there thinking -- and all of a sudden the handle came to me. And the next morning I sat down and began to write. And within twelve days I had a complete rough draft, which I sold to Bantam. After 25 years of writing, I've learned one way of doing it, and I just don't know of any other way of doing it.

The initials of Ferris F. Fremont – FFF – are equivalent to 666 and the name itself, of course, is a substitute for Richard M. Nixon the US president who was deposed in 1974 after the Watergate scandal.

In April 1985 it was announced in the *PKD Society Newsletter* that Arbor House publishers had purchased North American rights to VALISYTSTEM A and would be publishing the novel as RADIO FREE ALBEMUTH in Dec 1985.[dcclviii]

By June at the American Booksellers Association (ABA) meeting in San Francisco, Arbor House had a large blowup of the cover for RADIO FREE ALBEMUTH, and included it in a flyer containing their top books for promotion for the next six months (they claim a $25,000 advertising and promotion budget, which would certainly be a first for a PKD book)...[dcclix]

By the Spring of 1986 the book had sold well with 8,000 copies sent to booksellers. As Williams notes, this would be PKD's most successful hardcover. The reviews were also coming in, positive ones including those in *The New York Times* and *Saturday Review*.[dcclx]

The first edition of RADIO FREE ALBEMUTH from Arbor House was published in Dec 1985. The SFBC edition followed in Jun 1986 and the first UK edition was the paperback from Grafton in May 1987. The first paperback in the USA was from Avon in Jun 1987. A hardback from Severn House in England also came out in Oct 1987.[dcclxi]

Of these editions I suspect the Severn House one would be the most scarce. The first edition from Arbor House currently fetches $25 or so while the SFBC edition goes for less than $20. Ken Lopez, again, has the best RADIO FREE ALBEMUTH manuscript package for sale:

VALISYSTEM A. (Published in 1985 as RADIO FREE ALBEMUTH). Written in 1976, prior to VALIS, but not published until after Dick's death. This is a ribbon copy typescript, 292 pages, with many ink changes and additions in Dick's hand, many of which do not appear in the published book. Inscribed and signed by the author. Together with a six page fake manuscript excerpt, numbered "85" through "90" and beginning and ending in mid-sentence, which Dick wrote solely to photocopy and send to his publisher to prove that this book, not yet begun, was well underway. Although the scene does involve the book's characters, it does not appear in the final book.
{...} For the novel and fake excerpt manuscripts: $12,500.[dcclxii]

RADIO FREE ALBEMUTH transforms PKD's pink-beam experiences into a Nixonian world of repression wherein the character Philip K. Dick and his friend Nicholas Brady are contacted by what may be an alien satellite from the star Albemuth. PKD's mystical experiences are now ascribed to Brady and the two, spurred on by Valis, become part of a conspiracy to overthrow the regime of President Ferris F. Fremont.

But the satellite Valis is shot down and Phil and Nick are arrested. Nick is executed and Phil thrown in a concentration camp. As a last ray of hope, though, he hears the words of a popular song with lyrics which he knows are subversive.

As a precursor to VALIS this novel is very dissimilar and stands up well on its own. RADIO FREE ALBEMUTH is worth all of ✳ ✳ ✳ ✳.

With the leverage provided by the popular and widely-read *Rolling Stone* article at the end of 1975 and Dick's continuing good sales, Mark Hurst, then an editor at Bantam Books struck a deal with the SMLA in May 1976 to buy reprint rights for three of PKD's novels: THE THREE STIGMATA OF PALMER ELDRITCH, UBIK, and A MAZE OF DEATH. This sale grossed $20,000 for the Agency and Dick. Hurst also negotiated a deal to publish PKD's next novel -- then titled VALISYSTEM A as we've seen above – for a $12,000 advance. This novel was, of course, published as VALIS in 1981.[dcclxiii]

After completing VALISYSTEM A and rewriting parts of A SCANNER DARKLY, other than his *EXEGESIS* Dick wrote nothing new in 1976. Late in the year he was, once again, having trouble with his girlfriend Doris and by the end of the year he was living alone, although Doris had moved into the apartment next door.

To 1977, then, and publication of A SCANNER DARKLY.

1977

Doubleday published A SCANNER DARKLY in January 1977, the SFBC edition followed in March with the paperback from Ballantine coming out in December. UK publication came from Gollancz in November.

PKD's new Ballantine collection of short stories was published in March. This was THE BEST OF PHILIP K. DICK, a paperback tome (450pp) that contains many of Dick's stories from his very first "Roog" to one of his last "A Little Something For Us Tempunauts". All in all there are nineteen short stories in this collection as well as an Introduction by John Brunner and Afterthoughts by Dick himself.[dcclxiv]

We've seen above in connection with Ace Books' THE BOOK OF PHILIP K. DICK (1973) how PKD says Don Wollheim howled at the leftovers of Dick's stories after Ballantine had made their selection; although the 5-year hiatus between Ballantine's inferred contract for the collection in 1973 and final publication in 1978, is curious.

For collectors, THE BEST OF PHILIP K. DICK presents some problems: finding a copy in anything but complete beat-up shape is difficult. Even mere reading copies can fetch about $10. I imagine a fine edition would demand around $40. The collection was never reissued until the hardback edition from Garland in 1982. This edition would be a prize but I have never seen one offered for sale.[dcclxv]

Of course, bookseller Ken Lopez has the top offering of THE BEST OF PHILIP K. DICK:

The Best of Philip K. Dick. (Published by Ballantine, 1977). The ribbon copy typescript of the 10-page "Afterthoughts by the Author" provided by Dick to this collection of stories, which he helped select and which contains therefore many of his very best short works, including the story Lawrence Sutin, his biographer, calls "the best of all his stories, `The Electric Ant.'" On a scale of 1 to 10, this is one of the very few books that Sutin gives a rating of 10. The last five pages consist of paragraphs of typescript cut apart and glued on to sheets of typing paper. There is one change in Dick's hand. Together with the setting copy of the book, consisting of a typed contents page and photocopied tearsheets of the book's contents from various magazines (lacking the 14 page John Brunner introduction). While there was no "original manuscript," per se, for this book, it is an important element of the Dick canon, and this is a unique copy, and the best possible copy. Good. $6000. [dcclxvi]

As a collection THE BEST OF PHILIP K. DICK deserves its ✮✮✮✮✮.

In August 1977 the Gregg Press published its second edition of PKD's novels in hardback. This was DR. BLOODMONEY.[dcclxvii] This fine edition can be found for around $200.

The UK hardback edition of DEUS IRAE was published in June 1977 by Gollancz. The first paperback came from Dell in September. And in November the first UK edition of A SCANNER DARKLY was published by Gollancz. The Del Rey paperback followed in December.

With his relationship with Doris breaking up at the beginning of the year (the two retained good relations), PKD cast about for another woman. According to Sutin, a friend of the woman PKD was destined to meet asked Joan Simpson who she would like most to meet. Philip K. Dick topped her list. So, unbeknownst to Joan, the friend, Ray Torrance, wrote a letter of introduction to PKD who called her up and invited her over. In April 1977 she made the visit and stayed for a week. Thus the beginning of a new love for Phil with the foxy Joan Simpson. They would establish house together in Sonoma in May. In the Summer PKD wrote the short story "The Day Mr. Computer Fell Out Of Its Tree" for Joan.[dcclxviii]

"The Day Mr. Computer Fell Out Of Its Tree" is another of PKD's weird late short stories. It was written in the summer of 1977 and saw publication only once and that in Volume 5 of THE COLLECTED STORIES in 1987.

In a future world governed by a central computer that micro-manages everything something has gone wrong with the computer and it is doing silly things like pouring soapy water instead of coffee. The problem is traced, with the help of Joan Simpson; the head of World Mental Health who has been buried at the center of the earth for just such occasions, to one Joe Contemptible who's anomie and discontent are causing the computer to fuck up. In the end Joe must move in with the wonderfully beautiful Joan Simpson and his expected happiness will cure the computer of its ills.

A silly story, obviously written for the real-world Joan Simpson, "The Day Mr. Computer Fell Out Of Its Tree" rates ✷ ✷ ✷.

Apart from a new love the highlight for the year though must've been Phil and Joan's trip to France for the Second International Festival of Science Fiction held in Metz in September. Philip K. Dick was to be Guest of Honor at this convention. Despite his agoraphobia, PKD actually made the trip and to commemorate the occasion PKD's short story "Explorers We" was reprinted in a special booklet.[dcclxix]

On this visit to France, we've already noted that at one point PKD was sequestered in a back room with Roger Zelazny, probably signing copies of the 1977 Denoel edition of DEUS IRAE.

While in Metz PKD discovered that he was a highly regarded writer; even the best sf writer in the world. To the French his novel UBIK was considered a worthy successor to Alfred Jarry's *PERE UBU.* Phil's Guest of Honor Speech, "If You Find This World Bad, You Should See Some Of The Others" had a strange reception in the mostly French audience. As Sutin relates, Dick had given a copy to a French translator but at the last minute he was required to make twenty minutes worth of cuts. This he did but while giving the speech itself he changed his cuts on the fly and was saying one thing while the translator speaking along simultaneously was saying something else. The aftermath of this was many weird looks and remarks. Roger Zelazny writes that after the speech people came up to him, one in particular asking

"Monsieur Zelazny, you have written a book with Monsieur Dick. You know his mind. I have just come from his talk. Is it true he wishes to found a new religion, with himself as Pope?"[dcclxx]

To this Zelazny responded that he didn't think so. Then:

The fellow who was behind me said, "*Non*, I think you are wrong. I rode back to the hotel in a taxi, and Monsieur Dick gave me the power to remit sins and to kill fleas."[dcclxxi]

Zelazny had to fend off several strange questions from the audience. As to the Metz Speech itself, as it is sometimes called, it delivers more of PKD's *EXEGESIS*-like speculation positing a series of universes which God treats like a rack of cheap suits, trying on one then another until He is satisfied for a time.

PKD refers again to the concept of orthogonal time:

> We are accustomed to supposing that all change takes place along the linear time axis: from past to present to future. The present is an accrual of the past and is different from it. The future will accrue from the present on and be different yet. That an orthogonal or right-angle time axis could exist, a lateral domain in which change takes place – processes occurring sideways in reality, so to speak – this is almost impossible to imagine.[dcclxxii]

He goes on to expand on this lateral domain theme:

> ... if they do indeed exist, and if they do indeed overlap, then we may in some literal, very real sense inhabit several of them to various degrees at any given time. And although we all see one another as living humans walking about and talking and acting, some of us may inhabit relatively greater amounts of, say, Universe One than the other people do; and some of us may inhabit relatively greater amounts of Universe Two, Track Two, instead, and so on. It may not merely be that our subjective impressions of the world differ, but there may be an overlapping, a superimposition, of a number of worlds so that objectively, not subjectively, our worlds may differ. Our perceptions differ as a *result* of this. And I want to add this statement at this point, which I find to be a fascinating concept: It may be that some of these superimposed worlds are passing out of existence, along the lateral time line I spoke of, and some are in the process of moving toward greater, rather than lesser, actualization. These processes would occur simultaneously and not at all in linear time. The kind of process we are talking about here is a *transformation*, a kind of metamorphosis, invisibly achieved. But very real. And very important.[dcclxxiii]

One can sense in this mode of being postulated here by PKD that he was thinking of his own experiences as Thomas, the secret Christian who seemed to live in two worlds at once: Rome circa AD 50 and Orange County, California in 1975. It certainly serves as an explanation for the fading in and out of the personality of Thomas.

Dick goes on to equate one of these parallel worlds with the Christian heaven and poses the notion that the essential task of Jesus was to teach his disciples the secret of traversing between these many universes. Although lost, thanks to the Romans, PKD believes this secret can be refound now that we are once again aware of it.

It is also in this speech that PKD makes his remarks equating one or more of these parallel worlds – worse ones than our current consensual one – with the alternate worlds arising for Mr. Tagomi and Hawthorne Abendsen in THE MAN IN THE HIGH CASTLE and the one into which Felix Buckman drifted at the end of FLOW MY TEARS, THE POLICEMAN SAID.[dcclxxiv]

He then goes into a description of his pink-beam experiences to the by now totally bewildered French audience.

In the Metz Speech PKD talks of the downfall of Richard Nixon as an event triggered in lineal time by God who, operating in orthogonal time, has determined that it should happen just so. But Dick remembers a previous time-track in which Nixon did not fall and an oppressive police state was the actuality. After describing the fall of Nixon, PKD goes on to recall an alternate reality, describing the world of FLOW MY TEARS:

In the alternate world that I remembered, the civil rights movement, the antiwar movement of the sixties, had failed. And, evidently, in the midseventies Nixon was not removed from power. That which opposed him (if indeed anything existed that did or could) was inadequate. Therefore one or more factors tending toward that destruction of the entrenched tyrannical power had retroactively, to us, come to be introduced.

{...}

... Examine the text of FLOW MY TEARS ... One small but critical theme is alluded to twice (I believe) in FLOW MY TEARS. It has to do with Nixon. In the future world of FLOW MY TEARS, in the dreadful slave state that exists and evidently has existed for decades, Richard Nixon is remembered as an exalted, heroic leader – referred to, in fact, as the "Second Only Begotten Son of God." It is evident from this and many other clues that FLOW MY TEARS deals not with *our* future but the future of a present world *alternate* to our own.[dcclxxv]

This is a pretty fascinating idea. Here we have a science fiction writer whose job it is to write about the future of *our* world but instead he's writing about the future of an alternate world! An amazing fictional concept. In FLOW MY TEARS Dick adds the extra twist in having Felix Buckman slip over from his fictional future alternate world to *our* world at the end when he hugs the black man. PKD if not God is writing in orthogonal time.

Returning home to Santa Ana after the Metz Festival PKD attended the Octocon science fiction convention in Santa Rosa in October. But he and Joan were about to split up, he not wanting to move to Northern California and she not wanting to move to Santa Ana. Despite the breakup, which saddened them both, Phil was doing okay financially for possibly the first time in his life. Sutin states that in 1977 PKD grossed about $55,000 and in 1978 his income was over $90,000.

In 1977 PKD became part of a circle of friends in the Santa Ana area. These included Tim Powers, K.W. Jeter and Jim Blaylock who, all three, would go on to become popular science fiction writers. These and other friends used to meet on Thursday nights at Powers' place. After the breakup with Joan late in the year these meetings continued. Some of the circle, particularly Powers, Jeter and Blaylock, were thinly-disguised characters in the novel he would begin in 1978: VALIS.[dcclxxvi]

1978 VALIS

At the start of 1978, Philip K. Dick had still not worked out a plot for his overdue Bantam novel. Trying to get a handle on his ideas in January 1978 he wrote what would become "Cosmogony and Cosmology."[dcclxxvii]

"Cosmogony and Cosmology" is a summary of what Dick had written in his *EXEGESIS* to that time. It was first published in a limited edition by Kerosina Books as part of their 1987 hardback edition of VALIS. The novel and the 'essay' were slipcased together in this valuable edition.[dcclxxviii]

In this piece PKD posits a universe that would explain the infinitude of God and at the same time explain the reason for suffering on this world that we all live in. He's obviously been doing some heavy reading in his new *Encyclopedia Britannica*, referring to such religious and philosophical thinkers as Plato, Bohme, Bruno and Hans Driesch and incorporating ideas from several religions including Gnosticism, Hinduism and Christianity.

Basically, PKD takes Bohme's notion of God as an 'Urgrund' which seeks self-knowledge, but as it is infinite and knows no boundaries the Urgrund cannot comprehend, because it cannot get outside itself, its own nature. So it has spun off an artifact, a sort of cosmic mirror, the task of which is to attempt to show God to Himself. Our universe is the result (or one of the results). As the artifact proceeds in its task, creating lineal time as a necessary tool to perfect its mirror, it comes closer and closer to a perfect image of the Urgrund until when perfection is reached the Urgrund and our reality become one and the same and the artifact's task is done. Suffering and any other imperfections are seen in Dick's model as the results of this imperfection in the universe and us.

The artifact is not then necessarily evil. Just doing its job.

This union with the Urgrund can happen to individuals separate from the forthcoming complete union of the Urgrund with everything. Philip K. Dick believed this individual union happened to him in 1974 with his pink-beam experiences.

Then, as God is superior to the artifact, He can interfere at any time with the artifact's construction to make it go where he wants it to go (for God is learning of Himself as lineal time progresses and can see imperfection developing in the mirror and can step in and change it in positive directions).

Note the word 'positive.' Dick explains:

… The world is moving toward some kind of end state or goal, the nature of which is obscure, but the evolutionary aspect of the change states suggests a good and purposeful end state that has been designed by a sentient and benign proto-entity.

A further point. It appears that there is a feedback circuit between the Urgrund and the artifact in which the Urgrund can exert pressure on the artifact under certain exceptional circumstances, these being instances in which the artifact has strayed from the correct sequences moving the projected world toward an analog state vis-a-vis the Urgrund. Either the Urgrund directly modifies the activity of the artifact by pressure directly on the artifact, or the Urgrund goes to the projected world and modulates it, bypassing the artifact, or both. In any case, the artifact is as occluded as to the nature and existence of the Urgrund as we are to the artifact. A full circle of unawareness is achieved in which the primal source (Urgrund) and the final reality (our world) are moving toward fusion, and the intermediary entity (the artifact) is moving toward elimination. Thus the total schema moves toward perfection and simplification, and away from complexity and imperfection.[dcclxxix]

What makes this model attractive to PKD is that it eliminates the problem of the source of evil. Mankind cannot accept the notion of original sin wherein evil is our own fault and nor can we accept the notion of God, the Creator, as evil because in that case we are all doomed. So Dick's model poses evil as an unwitting byproduct of universal progress.

But, at times, Dick does impute intelligence to the artifact , or if not intelligence, a blind reaction toward stasis when faced with outside interference by the Urgrund. For the artifact any changes in its mirror other than those it makes itself are seen as imperfections to be eliminated. Like our blindness to the artifact, the artifact itself is blind to the Urgrund.

This explains Dick's idea, experienced in 1974 by him and written into VALIS, of 'the Empire never ended' and we are still living in Roman times. The Urgrund – God – with the birth of Christ has broken into the mirror and introduced an element of Himself into the world. This being such a powerful change in the mirror's structure has aroused a consequent powerful reaction in the artifact. While the artifact continues on in lineal time with its task it must deal with this major breakthrough by the Urgrund. It must deal with Christ and the ideas that He brought to the world. It has been unable to do this effectively and can only continue blindly in its job of constructing God's mirror. But to itself the artifact is always and only dealing with the perfections introduced by God which it sees as imperfections. Unfortunately for us, because we are constructions of the artifact, we are caught up in lineal time too and dragged into a spurious reality. But the true situation is that we are still in Roman times awaiting the return of our Saviour.

The thing that distinguishes these ideas of Dick's is that God by bringing Himself directly into the world as Christ, has done something that He likes. He has created a union between Himself and His image. The task he set the artifact is done but the artifact doesn't realise it and continues on. He occludes us from true knowledge of union with God – which is always inside us – by wrapping us up in time.

God now finds Himself in opposition to the artifact. He has made union of himself with Man but the artifact, as we are its creations, has used time to make us forget. We must somehow awake to the true state of things and be at one with the Urgrund inside ourselves.

While an interesting construction these religious ideas of Dick's are full of logical holes but they certainly illustrate PKD's far-ranging imagination and for students of his writing they form the basis of VALIS which he was preparing to write.

Before tracing out the history of VALIS further we'll glance at what else was going on for PKD in 1978.

In June the Gregg Press published the first USA hardback edition of the short story collection A HANDFUL OF DARKNESS.[dcclxxx]

The first paperback edition of DEUS IRAE came from Dell in February and in the UK the UKSFBC edition of DEUS IRAE came out in March followed by the paperback from Sphere in July.

THE MAN WHO JAPED saw its first hardback and paperback editions from Eyre Methuen and Magnum in October. Several other editions of PKD's novels and collections appeared in the USA and UK in 1978, at least sixteen in all.

The really bad news for the year was the death in August of his mother Dorothy. Phil's reaction to this has been described as mixed.[dcclxxxi]

Dick wrote one more speech/essay in 1978. This is titled "How To Build A Universe That Doesn't Fall Apart Three Days Later". It was published first in THE DARK-HAIRED GIRL (1985) and is now most available in Sutin's THE SHIFTING REALITIES OF PHILIP K. DICK.

The structure and delivery of this speech are much looser and genial than the Metz Speech of 1977.

PKD starts out with him in the whirling tea-cups at Disneyland being interviewed for French TV then goes on to the main themes in his fiction, what is real? and what is human? He speaks of our false media-created reality and wonders what effect it will have on our children since they watch so much TV. Soon he's off into *EXEGESIS*-inspired neo-gnosticism and writes of the false in reality and the true in fiction.

FLOW MY TEARS, THE POLICEMAN SAID is singled out as showing the truth in fiction. As a mundane example he relates how in the novel he created a character named Kathy who was a drug dealer and possible nark for a particular policeman. Then, after he'd completed the novel, he actually met this character named Kathy. For more esoteric support he singles out the section in FLOW MY TEARS where Felix Buckman meets the black man stranger at the all-night gas station and they talk. Phil recalls telling the story to his priest:

> As I described the scene in more and more detail, my priest became progressively more agitated. At last he said, "That is a scene from the Book of Acts, from the Bible! In Acts, the person who meets the black man on the road is named Philip – your name." Father Rasch was so upset by the resemblance that he could not even locate the scene in his Bible. "Read Acts," he instructed me. "And you'll agree. It's the same down to specific details."[dcclxxxii]

Phil goes on to single out a few similarities between the scene in FLOW MY TEARS and the Book of Acts; the name of Felix for the Roman official who arrests St. Paul and PKD's own police official Felix Buckman. The name Jason, PKD notes, is found in only one place in the Bible and that is in the Book of Acts. The situation for the Biblical Jason is similar to that of Jason Taverner in the novel. PKD concludes:

> A careful study of my novel shows that for reasons I cannot even begin to explain, I had managed to retell several of the basic incidents from a particular book of the Bible, and even had the right names. What could explain this? That was four years ago that I discovered all this. For four years I have tried to come up with a theory and I have not. I doubt if I ever will.[dcclxxxiii]

One theory, perhaps not, but several, certainly. This speech which was probably never delivered, is in a sense PKD's justification for seeing FLOW MY TEARS, THE POLICEMAN SAID as in part, at least, a revealed text important for the effects that accompanied its publication, such as Nixon's downfall.

VALIS

The *EXEGESIS* aside, Dick in September was still not able to get a grip on how to write his Bantam novel. This is where a new agent at the SMLA, Russ Galen, stepped in to get the novel going. As a fan of Dick's work Galen had asked that he be assigned to Dick's account at the Agency. This was done and Galen effected the republication of several of Dick's dormant novels and, most importantly, fired Dick up enough for him to begin writing VALIS. The novel was dedicated to Galen on its publication in 1981. In October 1978 then PKD began writing VALIS, interrupting a long session of *EXEGESIS* speculation to abruptly start the novel. On Nov 29th he sent the manuscript off to Galen at the Agency.

As Lawrence Sutin observes, Dick had written two informal pieces, his Introduction to THE GOLDEN MAN collection and a brief piece on his story "Roog." This easy style of writing enabled PKD to find a mode suitable to the writing of VALIS. Instead of heavy-handed and obscure theorizing as found in his *EXEGESIS* Dick would write VALIS with a much lighter tone of informality and humour. [dcclxxxiv]

In an interview with John Boonstra published in *Twilight Zone* magazine in June 1982, PKD covers how he decided to write VALIS:

> I jettisoned the first version of *VALIS*, which was a very conventional book. That version appears in the finished book as the movie. I cast around for a model that would bring something new into science fiction, and it occurred to me to go all the way back to the

picaresque novel and have my characters be *picaroons* -- rogues -- and write it in the first person vernacular, using a rather loose plot. I feel there's tremendous relevance in the picaresque novel at this time. Donleavy's *The Ginger Man* is one; so is *The Adventures of Augie March* by Saul Bellow. I see this as a protest form of the novel, a repudiation of the more structured bourgeois novel that has been so popular. **dcclxxxv**

As to the meaning of VALIS and, perhaps, to address some of his contemporaries who feared Dick had gone insane, PKD in 1980 wrote:

Here is the puzzle of VALIS. In VALIS I say, I know a madman who imagines that he saw Christ; and I am that madman. But if I know that I am a madman I know that in fact I did not see Christ. Therefore I assert nothing about Christ. Or do I? Who can solve this puzzle? I say in fact only that I am mad. But if I say only that, then I have made no mad claim; I do not, then, say that I saw Christ. Therefore I am not mad. And the regress begins again, and continues forever. The reader must know on his own what has really been said, what has actually been asserted, but what is it? Does it have to do with Christ or only with myself? This paradox was known in antiquity; the pre-Socratics propounded it...[dcclxxxvi]

The reception of VALIS at Bantam publishers was a bewildered and uncertain one, Mark Hurst who had arranged the original contract had left and Bantam waited until the very end of the contract time before publishing the novel in Feb 1981. No doubt it took some effort from Russ Galen to prod the Bantam management.[dcclxxxvii]

The first edition paperback from Bantam in 1981 is easily attainable for the PKD collector. In near-fine condition one can be found for about $25 on the internet. In used bookstores it is uncommon but goes for $5 to $8 in variable shape. The Kerosina editions that we've already mentioned above in connection with PKD's essay "Cosmogony and Cosmology" would be the most valuable to collectors. In searching the internet in 1997 one might have found Bookseller Ken Lopez' online catalog. We've already seen some of the PKD materials he had for sale and now this is his VALIS offering:

VALIS. (Published by Bantam, 1981). The original manuscript of a book that is widely considered to be one of his two greatest works the other being THE THREE STIGMATA OF PALMER ELDRITCH. 311 pages of ribbon-copy typescript, inscribed by the author on the top page "with love" to Tim Powers, and additionally inscribed to "the best friend I ever had" on the verso of a proof of the novel's paperback cover. With a letter from the publisher laid in returning this to Dick for his files, and a photocopy of a letter from Dick to the publisher requesting that the book's dedication be changed [it was].
{...} The manuscripts from the first two-thirds of Dick's career have been institutionalized; other writings by Dick in manuscript form have shown up on the market only very occasionally, a recent catalogue by a leading science fiction specialist dealer had a four-page short story typescript (with a letter of transmittal and tear-sheet of the story) for $2200, or roughly $500 per page of Dick manuscript. This manuscript 311 pages of his most important novel, warmly inscribed (twice) to a close friend represents the pinnacle of Dick's achievement, and the best possible association. A unique item that is a landmark in the career of one of science fiction's greatest authors ever. Top sheet a bit wrinkled, otherwise fine in a literary agency box. $22,000.[dcclxxxviii]

Another internet dealer, Lame Duck Books, offered the following package in 2000:

Two Typed Letters, Signed accompanied by Galley Proofs of Dick's Novel VALIS and of the Anthology *Perpetual Light*, Edited by Alan Ryan, 1980-1982. Two excellent typed letters, signed, addressed from Dick to fellow science fiction writer and editor Alan Ryan, both dates 13 March 1980. The letters concern Ryan's projected anthology on the subject of Science Fiction and Religion to which he has asked that Dick contribute. Naturally, Dick is quite warm to the idea, as most of his later work treats of exactly that subject in some fashion. The letters possess superb content and enthusiastically support the project. The second letter is primarily a thank-you to Ryan for his intelligent review of Dick's THE GOLDEN MAN. Included is a proof copy of THE GOLDEN MAN; rare long galleys of the Bantam first edition of VALIS and a bound proof of *Perpetual Light*, to which, however, Dick did not end up contributing, apparently due to a financial maneuver by his agent, who required that whatever work might be contributed would have to be accepted sight-unseen -- a condition he realized could not be accepted by a conscientious editor, and which permitted him to sell the promised story to *Playboy* instead. Further description of the letters will be provided to interested parties. $6500. [dcclxxxix]

This story that was sold to *Playboy* was "Frozen Journey" also titled "I Hope I Shall Arrive Soon."

With VALIS essentially finished at the end of 1978. Philip K. Dick once more took up his *EXEGESIS* writing, continuing into 1979.

The novel VALIS itself, given its soul-searching start in PKD's pink-beam experiences and his efforts to understand them as scribbled in his *EXEGESIS*, is a wonderfully entertaining story that leads the reader into a world of madness and then out again into the light of a newly-defined reality. Here's what a contemporary reviewer had to say:

And speaking of superstitions and theology, there's Philip K. Dick's new novel, VALIS. Now if there's one thing I dislike more than people telling me their dreams, it's people telling me their drug experiences, particularly the religious ones. I disliked VALIS a whole lot.

It's written in the first person by a narrator who editorializes a great deal and tells us a lot more than we (or at least I) want to know about a character named Horselover Fat. Early on, we are informed that the narrator and Horselover Fat are one and the same, and it is being written in this way to give "much needed objectivity." Later the narrator refers to several of his (the narrator's) books, such as THE MAN IN THE HIGH CASTLE and A SCANNER DARKLY. Make of this what you will.

Horselover Fat has an encounter with God a la St. Paul about which he is writing an endless exegesis, of which we are told all too much. God may, in fact, be an alien or may be Horselover Fat from the far future (as opposed to the near past; Horselover comes across as one of those embarrassing hippies left over from two decades ago). Her (they?) encounter a child, daughter of a jet-set rock singer, who may be a computer terminal, or God, or the Wisdom of the World, or … There are lots of quotes from Schopenhauer, Xenophanes, Wordsworth, et al., not to mention an eight-page appendix of yet more quotes. Need I go on?

This all may be one big boring joke or it may be meant seriously; it doesn't matter much. VALIS is embarrassingly, datedly hip, cute, and infinitely tedious, so far as I'm concerned. A major danger to science fiction these days is in its becoming the new mysticism, what with flying saucers, god's chariots, Bermuda Triangle and all. Writers such as Mr. Dick are not helping matters.[dccxc]

At the time of its publication VALIS must have been disturbing indeed to Dick's fellow writers and fans of his science fiction. As in RADIO FREE ALBEMUTH, there is a character named Philip K. Dick. He has an alter ego named Horselover Fat (Philip Dick ontonomologically in Greek and German) who has a series of mystical experiences – PKD's own pink-beam visions – with which he involves his friends in a search for the Saviour. They **see** a film called *VALIS* and seek out its authors, finding a little girl who appears to be the Saviour but then she is accidentally killed. In the end Fat roams the Earth still looking for his Saviour and sending cryptic messages back to his friends.

The novel is accompanied by an appendix *The Tractates Cryptica Scriptura* which succinctly if not cryptically sets forth the essence of the messages Horselover Fat received from Valis. These *Tractates* have been the cause for much speculation among readers of this quantum leap of a novel.

VALIS is worth ✳ ✳ ✳ ✳ ✳

1979

1979 is notable for the whole-hearted effort accomplished by the Gregg Press to publish a large slice of PKD's novels in attractive hardcover form. Over the year, starting in April, the Gregg Press published ten novels: COUNTER-CLOCK WORLD, THE GAME-PLAYERS OF TITAN, THE ZAP GUN, TIME OUT OF JOINT, UBIK, EYE IN THE SKY, CLANS OF THE ALPHANE MOON, THE 3 STIGMATA OF PALMER ELDRITCH, THE WORLD JONES MADE, and VULCAN'S HAMMER.

These Gregg Press editions are all sought-after collector's items but cost up to $200 each or more from dealers over the internet.

Other notable publications over the year were the short story "The Exit Door Leads In" in the debut issue of *Rolling Stone's College Papers*, a short-lived companion to *Rolling Stone* aimed at college students. And "We Can Remember it For you Wholesale" was reprinted in the 30th anniversary issue of *F & SF*. Many other editions of Dick's stories appeared in the United States, Britain and other countries in 1979. Enough so that his income for the year was about $75,000 (for 1978 it had been $101,000).[dccxci]

The year started out right in January with the Russ Galen engineered sale of three of PKD's novels to Berkley Books for $14,000. These were THE COSMIC PUPPETS, DR. FUTURITY and THE UNTELEPORTED MAN. In 1983 and 1984 Berkley would issue their editions of these books. In May PKD learned that A SCANNER DARKLY, in its French translation, had won the Grand Prize at the Metz Science Fiction Festival he'd attended in 1977. In June he began another short story, "The Exit Door Leads In."

The manuscript for "The Exit Door Leads In" arrived at the SMLA on Jun 21, 1979. The story was requested by the editors of *Rolling Stone College Papers*, a new and short-lived publication. The story was published in the first issue of *Rolling Stone College Papers* later in Fall1979. Terry Carr selected the story for his anthology *THE BEST SF OF THE YEAR #9* in 1980 and it was included in the Philip K. Dick collection I HOPE I SHALL ARRIVE SOON in 1980.[dccxcii]

On reading "The Exit Door Leads In" one can see that it was obviously written for the attention and edification of college students. Bob Bibleman, the protagonist, is singled out by a robot fast-food vendor and tricked into mandatory enrollment in the College. Once enrolled Bob is warned by his instructor that knowledge of the Panther Engine – a construct based on PKD's vision of a futuristic machine described in ? – is top secret. Then in his studies Bob lucks into the schematics for the Panther Engine and prints them out. But when confronted by his instructor Bob meekly hands over his schematics and is then expelled from the College. What he *should* have done is attempt to publish the schematics for the benefit of the world and to hell with the College. But it's all a setup; the Panther Engine is worthless, it's just been a test for Bob to see if he can exhibit independent thought instead of merely kowtowing to Authority and he is expelled for that reason.

PKD seems with this story to be trying to foster a questioning attitude and independent thought in his student readers. As a story, though, "The Exit Door Leads In" rates ✴ ✴ ✴.

Soon after completing "The Exit Door Leads In" Dick wrote another short story, "Chains of Air, Web of Aethyr."

With the manuscript title "The Man Who Knew How To Lose" this story reached the SMLA on July 9, 1979, a month after receipt of "The Exit Door Leads In." How it found a home at *Stellar #5* as "Chains Of Air, Web Of Aethyr" in 1980 I'm not sure. PKD had established good relations with Judy-Lyn Del Rey, editor at Ballantine, and perhaps the Agency sent it directly to her.[dccxciii]

This story was used by PKD as the first part of his novel to follow VALIS. Originally called VALIS REGAINED, this novel was eventually titled THE DIVINE INVASION on publication by Simon & Schuster in 1981. Soon we will look at THE DIVINE INVASION.[dccxciv]

This story tells of isolated communications technicians living in domes on the planets of far-flung stars. Leo McVane's job is to transmit weather reports and the music of Linda Fox to other galactic outposts. He likes being alone. But his nearest neighbor, Rybus Rommey, is sick and wasting away in her dome. McVane reluctantly visits her out of a minimum of human compassion and helps her get well. But, once involved with Rybus, McVane is stuck with her -- and her destructive personality.

Linda Fox is based on one of PKD's favorite singers: Linda Ronstadt. The character of Rybus Rommey, in slightly altered form as Rybus Romney, is reprised by Dick in THE DIVINE INVASION, the novel that he would write in 1980.

A difficult story "Chains of Air, Web of Aethyr" receives ✴ ✴ ✴.

One more short story was written in 1979, although it's not really a short story but an autobiographical essay.

"Strange Memories Of Death", written in late 1979, reached the SMLA on Mar 27, 1980 and was published in *Interzone #8* in the Summer of 1984.

The title was PKD's although, in an unusual turnabout, his agent tried to market the story, unsuccessfully under the title "Blessing In Disguise". Usually it was the other way around with PKD's original titles being changed.[dccxcv]

"Strange Memories Of Death" was selected for the PKD collection I HOPE I SHALL ARRIVE SOON in 1985 and then included in THE COLLECTED STORIES in 1987. Today it can be conveniently found in *THE SHIFTING REALITIES OF PHILIP K. DICK* edited by Lawrence Sutin.[dccxcvi]

What occasioned the story was the conversion of PKD's apartment building in Santa Ana into condominiums. Dick was able to afford to make the change but some of his neighbors were not so fortunate. The "Lysol Lady" in the story was one such of these.[dccxcvii]

The story is a popular one with readers. Biographer Gregg Rickman selected it as his favorite story:

A haunting tale. Phil's writing just got better and better. Let no one tell you that he wouldn't still be writing great stuff today if he hadn't died in 1982; this story proves it. Phil's early death was a catastrophe for world literature. No one has remarked on this enough.[dccxcviii]

And another fan, Karl-Heinz Wiedemann wrote:

I am spellbound time and again by "Strange Memories of Death," one of the greatest short stories I know. It seems that Dick's narrative voice inevitably gives you the feeling of being personally addressed by an intimate yet anonymous acquaintance, which would account for that special joy you feel if now and again the originator of that voice sheds the distancing guise of third person narrative and speaks for himself a while.[dccxcix]

"Strange Memories of Death" is written in the first person narrative and is definitely autobiographical. It tells of the narrator (PKD) sitting in his newly converted condo worrying about one of his neighbors, the crazy Lysol Lady, who is being evicted. He knows no way to help and in the end discovers that two weeks previously she had been moved by the Housing Authority who are paying her new rent. The narrator wishes someone would pay his rent but is informed by the landlord that he's not paying rent, he's buying his apartment.

In the tale PKD mentions the 1979 school shooting in which two children were killed by a fellow female student. Asked why she did it she replied, "I don't like Mondays." This sad story was recorded in musical form by the Boomtown Rats with the same title, "I don't like Mondays" in 1980.

Considered as a short story, "Strange Memories of Death" is very different from any of PKD's other stories. I repeat, it's really not a story but as a story it rates ✶ ✶ ✶ ✶.

After his apartment building went condo in October, his love and neighbor Doris Sauter moved away for good, not being able to afford the new condo payments. Despite PKD's offering to help she left. In "Strange Memories of Death" Dick mentions this too.

That's about it for 1979 and accordingly we move on to 1980 and THE DIVINE INVASION.

1980 THE DIVINE INVASION

In the first two months of 1980 PKD was writing away in his *EXEGESIS* and thinking over his short story "Chains of Air, Web of Aethyr", thinking perhaps that it would make a good beginning to his follow-up novel to VALIS which he'd tentatively titled VALIS REGAINED. After taking some time in January to write a synopsis for a novel idea called THE ACTS OF PAUL that came to nothing, he was ready to go by March.

In two weeks in March ending on the 22nd, Philip K. Dick wrote VALIS REGAINED.[dccc] Although it is possible that the outline was done by March 14th and the novel completed in May and June 1980.[dccci]

VALIS REGAINED was published as THE DIVINE INVASION by Simon & Schuster in June 1981.[dcccii]

PKD's editor on the novel was David G. Hartwell at Simon & Schuster.[dccciii]

This two-week period to write THE DIVINE INVASION might seem awfully short since PKD had taken so long to write VALIS and had, since 1970 and FLOW MY TEARS, taken years to write his next book A SCANNER DARKLY. Dick himself said of that time that he was "no longer able to dash off stuff at the rate that I had before."[dccciv]

So is he back again to doing it the old way? Not really; his work habits had changed but mostly in the area of preparation. K.W. Jeter explains to Andy Watson:

(KWJ): I think there were about three different periods. There was that period where he wrote very fast without revision, simply because of economic pressure, when he was up in the Bay Area. That accounted for that period. Then there was a later period in the 70s which would include FLOW MY TEARS and A SCANNER DARKLY, books like that, where he was no longer under that economic pressure, and he did go through drafts and drafts of his books. I can't say for sure, but I would have been very much surprised if there were more than one or two drafts of VALIS, and, uh –

(AW:) THE DIVINE INVASION.

(KWJ:) Yeah, *Son Of VALIS*, or *VALIS Regained*, which was Phil's original title for it. I would be surprised because when Phil got around to the point of writing those books, he wrote them in a period of a few days. That is not taking into account the years and years of *thinking* about the material that's in the books. But when it came to actually physically sitting down at a typewriter and typing a book that started out with a title page saying VALIS and going straight through to the end, he did that very quickly. When he did it, he reverted to his old work habits, when he did work under a time and economic pressure. Also I think its somewhat internally consistent, just looking at the books. They weren't done on a draft by draft basis. Structurally the books are very poor.

(AW:) They ramble.

(KWJ:) They ramble, and they go from one thing to another, and its just one idea after another popping into Phil's head. That doesn't say anything about the quality of the ideas. But just in terms of a structure, this may be something that I think about the books that nobody else thinks about the books because I tend to be a structuralist in my approach to writing. To me, I think its internally consistent to look at the books as just being a straight through unrevised draft of ideas Phil has been working on in another form for a long time. In terms of the actual dramatic content of the book, characters and so forth, I can't believe that those last couple of books were done draft by draft.[dcccv]

In 1981 to the sf fanzine *Venom*, Dick wrote an odd letter:

That curious wasp Charles Platt says that you will print book reviews in which the author pans his own work. Can I do that please? I have no motive except, well, I'd like to see if I can do it. So enclosed you will find my attack on THE DIVINE INVASION, my most recent novel. If, as Platt says, you are secretly financed by David Hartwell, this may prove embarrassing, since Hartwell published this novel. Anyhow, as a challenge it fascinates me.

Be sure to let me know if the enclosed review is satisfactory and will see publication.[dcccvi]

To which *Venom* replied:

Chipdip K. Kill's review of THE DIVINE INVASION will be in *Venom #3*. Meanwhile here is a copy of *Venom #2* for your amusement. By the way, we agree that the review is one of the funniest we've ever read. Best. Venom.[dcccvii]

Paul Williams notes that *Venom #3* was never published and that David Hartwell did not finance the zine although he encouraged the anonymous editors. Chipdip K. Kill's review of THE DIVINE INVASION can be found in *PKDS-29*.

For another review we go to the pages of *Analog* and Tom Easton in 1981:

In the end Philip K. Dick's THE DIVINE INVASION affirms the role of free will in a universe dictated by God. But on the way to that end! Dick repeated many of the themes of his last book, VALIS, even to the knowledgeable beam of pink light, as he tells us of a God who, exiled, must return to Earth doubly enwombed, woman-borne, spaceship borne, to fight the devil who has ruled our planet for two millennia.

{...} A brain-damaged, imperfect God Who must learn compassion. The Torah as heroine. Humanity as battleground. The primordial nature of the split personality. Dick is vitally concerned with making sense of the human condition. In this he resembles the greats of classical literature. Like them, he uses metaphor and personifications to turn abstractions into highly readable and provocative stories. But like them again, he borrows his points – he says nothing we cannot recognize in the weaker of more academic arguments of predecessors and contemporaries, and we do wish for more philosophical originality.

Or perhaps we can say that Dick's philosophical originality lies in his contrast to the depressing stories I mentioned before. He is optimistic. He has faith in a future worth living. And where other sf writers play their games in the head – even Ellison does this, really – he plays in the soul, the heart of hearts. He must be horribly shocking to True believers, though I doubt they read him.[dcccviii]

Certainly a more sympathetic review than the one by Baird Searles on VALIS! Still, not everyone was pleased with THE DIVINE INVASION; in the *FDO* fan poll Erik Davis writes:

At some point in *FDO* you asked what the most boring PKD novel is. THE DIVINE INVASION wins that contest for me hands down. I would prefer reading VULCAN'S HAMMER or another minor work any day. VALIS is as far as I go.[dcccix]

As THE DIVINE INVASION was, really, more of PKD's *EXEGESIS* explorations turned into a novel, it is not surprising that the novel fed back into the *EXEGESIS* after its publication. Here's PKD deeply into it all:

I just now looked over DIVINE INVASION. As I recently realised about VALIS, the dialectic that is the inner life of God -- as revealed to Boehme & explicated later by Schelling -- & commented on by e.g. Tillich -- is presented as the very bases of the book. In VALIS it is expressed dramatically as world-order in which the irrational confronts the "bright" or rational, designated (properly) *Logos*. In DI this same dialectic reappears & this time is *stated* to be the two sides of God (rather than world order; that is, in DI it is now correctly seen to be *within* God himself!): it is now (in DI) between Emmanuel who is the terrible, destroying "solar heat" warring side -- & Zina who is loving, playful, tender, associated with bells & flowers; & what unifies the two at last (by the way; it is *she* who takes the lead in restoring memory & hence unification: Emmanuel is the side that has forgotten -- i.e., is impaired; she has not & is not impaired) is *play*. She plays, & Emmanuel has a secret desire to play.

So both novels basically deal with the dialectic that I experienced as the nature of Valis & which I construe to be the dynamic inner life of God.

{...}

Really, then DI simply continues the fundamental theme of VALIS -- but does not *seem* to do so -- not unless one perceives this theme & what it is (the dialectic that is the

242

dynamic inner life of God). DI is not so *loose* a sequel to VALIS as it might seem (by in the shift from Gnosticism, the present, realism, to Kabbala, the future, that which would not and could not come with POT... [dcccx]

In 1990 after nearly a decade of work, Russ Galen at the Agency, arranged a publishing deal with Vintage Books that would bring PKD's novels to the American public in a form not directly associated with science fiction. THE DIVINE INVASION was one of the first to be published. Paul Williams makes the proud announcement:

Eight years of effort on the part of Russell Galen at the Scott Meredith Literary Agency have come to fruition with the announcement that Vintage Books, probably the most prestigious literary paperback publisher in the U.S., will be reissuing six Dick novels, with the possibility of more to follow if these do well.

The first books to be released will be the so-called Valis Trilogy, VALIS, THE DIVINE INVASION and THE TRANSMIGRATION OF TIMOTHY ARCHER, in separate trade paperback volumes ($10 each), tentatively scheduled for publication in July 1991. The other three Dick novels covered by this agreement are still to be named. I believe that this is the first time Vintage has published any science fiction (with the possible exception of non-genre works like Zamyatin's *We*).

What is hoped for is that the books will attract new readers beyond the SF genre and the existing Dick coterie, and that they will be kept in print (mass market paperbacks, as Dick readers well know, tend to come and go like the tide).

"The idea was to accumulate a large number of major Dick works," Galen told *Locus*, "so that a publisher could buy them as a group. With the reversion two months ago of a large cache of former Doubleday titles, we finally made our move. Vintage was the only publisher we approached." [dcccxi]

The Vintage trade paperback editions of the Valis Trilogy accordingly came out in July 1991. They have had several printings since from Vintage.

For collectors, though, the major edition is the first from Simon & Schuster. At the turn of the century this edition was still easy to find for about $50. In the bookstores though, if not on the internet, it is becoming more scarce. For the ultimate package on THE DIVINE INVASION we once more peruse Ken Lopez' online catalog:

VALIS REGAINED. (Published by Simon & Schuster in 1981 as THE DIVINE INVASION). Three manuscripts. Carbon copy typescript, 80 pages, of "VALIS REGAINED/Outline for a science fiction novel." An unpublished outline for the book, with a handwritten note by the author on the first page: "published as `The Divine Invasion'/ Philip K. Dick." And a stray sheet that appears to be a couple of handwritten notes Dick wrote to himself on the subject of Yahweh and his own federal taxes. Together with the ribbon copy typescript, 297 pages, of the full novel, with many typesetter's marks and a few corrections in Dick's hand. Inscribed by the author on the first page: "To Serena & Tim Powers -- my two dearest friends/ Philip K. Dick." Together with a carbon copy typescript, 297 pages, with a handful of minor ink corrections in Dick's hand. Inscribed: "To my best friend/ Tim Powers -/ with thanks &/ appreciation./ Philip K. Dick." The first few pages of the ribbon copy typescript are tattered; otherwise each of the three manuscripts is in very good condition.

{...} For the three manuscripts, which both pertain to Dick's greatest work and also reflect an extraordinary association: $10,000. [dcccxii]

Besides the manuscript package Lopez also offers a signed first edition for sale:

THE DIVINE INVASION, Timescape, hb, 1981. NF/NF. <u>Inscribed by Dick to Tim Powers in the year of publication:</u> "This novel will teach you the <u>True</u> religion." Powers noted that "not more than a dozen copies of this title can ever have been inscribed by Dick, and those in the hands of close friends outside the book world." Near fine in near fine dust jacket. An important book; an excellent association; and an exceptional rarity signed. $1750.[dcccxiii]

Fortunately, the Vintage editions can still be bought for $12...

Here's a description of THE DIVINE INVASION from Martin Skidmore:

THE DIVINE INVASION concerns a much more traditional theological view, with the son of God being born from a human virgin, opposed by the establishment, and battling the devil for human souls...

Dick's style is, however, much more simple, and it is this, combined with his prodigious output at times in the past, which have unjustly given him a reputation as a 'hack' in some circles. Ursula Le Guin states my views beautifully when she says "the fact that what Dick is entertaining us about is reality and madness, time and death, sin and salvation -- this has escaped most critics." The nature of reality and sanity (two closely interlinked concepts) have been the dominant theme through much of his work, and this book is no exception.

Manny, the second son of God, suffers brain damage at a very young age, and much of the book concerns his struggle to understand the nature of the world, and particularly of Zina, a young girl who is his constant companion, but who hides her enigmatic true self from him. Dick leaves the reader in doubt almost to the end as to whether Zina is an agent of God or the devil, or some completely separate entity. He also examines the problems faced by Manny's legal father, an ordinary human, as the war for the soul of mankind progresses. Herb Asher is constantly at or near the center of the action, yet is completely helpless to influence events in the smallest way. He acts as the typical human observer, and many other characters strike a chord in a person living in today's times, thus giving us a stable base from which to view events. Dick is also a master of delightfully humorous interjections...

Neither of these are great books, but they're both good ones, well worth yer 'ard earned cash.[dcccxiv]

One cannot expect THE DIVINE INVASION to be as good as VALIS, but it is. The only thing that it lacked was 'the shock of the new'; VALIS had caused a great stir in science fiction circles with many people thinking PKD had gone crazy while many others thought that he'd 'got religion' and was now unreadable. This made the reception of THE DIVINE INVASION a suspicious one; what would the madman do next? So the novel had a stroke against it before it began. But if it had been written before VALIS it would have had that novel's spectacular debut.

What I'm trying to say is that these two novels are really one; everything about them is similar. It's as if PKD had written his *EXEGESIS* in the form of two long novels instead of page after page of notes.

So, I can do nothing but give THE DIVINE INVASION ✯ ✯ ✯ ✯ ✯

THE DIVINE INVASION, even though its part of what is called the Valis Trilogy (VALIS, THE DIVINE INVASION and THE TRANSMIGRATION OF TIMOTHY ARCHER) was supposed to be part of *another* trilogy which would have also been called the Valis Trilogy.

This trilogy to comprise VALIS, THE DIVINE INVASION and a third book that was never written called THE OWL IN DAYLIGHT.

At this time we will look at what we know of THE OWL IN DAYLIGHT.

THE OWL IN DAYLIGHT

THE TRANSMIGRATION OF TIMOTHY ARCHER completed in June 1981 was part of a two-book contract. The second book PKD was to write was a science fiction novel and it was to be due by the beginning of 1983. Dick speaks of this novel in the *Twilight Zone* interview with John Boonstra:

(PKD): The contract is a two-book contract, and there's a science fiction novel in it. And it pays exactly three times for the science fiction what is being paid for TIMOTHY ARCHER.

(TZ): Have you begun the sf novel?

(PKD): I've done two different outlines. I'll probably wind up laminating them together and making one book out of it, which is what I like to do, develop independent outlines and then laminate them into one book. That's where I got my multiple plot ideas. I really enjoy doing that, a paste-up job. A synthesis, in other words.

This second novel is not due until January 1, 1983, so I've got time. Right now I'm just physically too tired to do the typing. It looks like it's going to be a good book, too. It's called THE OWL IN DAYLIGHT.

{...} I'm now working very closely with the Ladd Company and, I'm on very good terms with them. In fact, that's one of the things that's worn me out. I've been so amped-up over *BLADE RUNNER* I couldn't work on THE OWL IN DAYLIGHT.[dcccxv]

In a letter to his editor at Timescape Books, David Hartwell, PKD makes an 'informal statement' about THE OWL IN DAYLIGHT:

It will be based somewhat (as I have discussed with you and Russell Galen) on Dante's COMMEDIA - and also on Goethe's FAUST Part One, In the future a scientist who is very old supervises the construction of an amusement park (something like the "lands" at Disneyland) of Berkeley, California circa 1949-1952 with all the various groups and subcultures of that time and place represented. In order to impose coherency on the Park he involves one of the planet's leading computers in the operation of it, turning this high-level computer into the mind behind the Park. The computer resents this, since it prefers to solve abstract, theoretical problems of the highest order. The computer pays the scientist back by trapping him in the Park and making him subject to its mind (that is, the computer's mind): the scientist is given the physical body of a high school boy, and he is deprived of his memories of his true identity (you can see the influence of Van Vogt on me, here, and also that of a number of my earlier novels) . Now the scientist, trapped in his own amusement Park and subject to the mind of the misused

(misused and knowing it and keenly resenting it) must solve the maze that the Park represents and find his way out of it by solving problems propounded by the computer and presented to him in sequence. When he fails to solve a problem — they are by and large ethical choice problems — he experiences a dreary transformation of the Park (which to him is world, not Park) into Inferno. He finds this highly perplexing, inasmuch as he does not remember his true identity, nor does he now comprehend that he is in an amusement Park or maze controlled by an artificial intelligence. Needless to say, when he solves a problem correctly, he ascends to Paradiso. Now, this is a high school boy, no longer an aged scientist, but he is very smart; his memories are gone but his intellect remains; he figures out that he is up against some kind of vast mind that is presenting him with subtle problems, and, as a result of his solving — or failing to solve -these sequential problems he is either rewarded or punished. Thus he spends a lot of time trying to figure out the situation (shades of TIME OUT OF JOINT!) . Now, this problem-solving is along what I call a vertical axis; it is one of rising and falling within three coaxial realms, resembling alternate presents (this is the theory he decides on, and it is of course incorrect) . He is aided by a mysterious female who shows up in plural guises and gives him cryptic hints; this is in fact his own daughter who is outside the Park trying to communicate with him and help him (being a high school boy in the Park he is, ironically, younger than his daughter, now). Also, the computer manifests itself as various people he encounters, and in these polyforms propounds the problems that the boy must solve. In addition to the vertical axis, he moves along an ostensible horizontal axis, and this is the one of normal growth and development from high school boy to first job to marriage: the normal axis we all move along. This is the only axis he is consciously aware of: the vertical axis is latent and obscured: it can be known only inferentially, and no one else seems aware of it. {...}[dccccxvi]

In this letter, of which we have quoted a brief section, PKD goes on to develop this plot further.

Of the story itself Andy Watson and K.W. Jeter of the Philip K. Dick Society sketch out an alternative plot:

(Andy Watson:) To me that seems the truly profound and criminal element in there not having been time for him to at least write THE OWL IN DAYLIGHT. I'm suspecting that it would have been a breakaway from that set, the so-called trilogy.

(KW Jeter:) Possibly. the only thing I know about (THE OWL IN DAYLIGHT) was that it was supposedly based on Beethoven's life.

(AW:)Was it going to be science fiction?

(KW:)Supposedly

(AW:)But based on Beethoven's life?

(KW:)In some way. It would have references to Beethoven's life. After Phil died, I was contacted by his daughter's lawyers, asking what I knew about it and if I had any ideas about whether the book could be successfully completed based upon the outline Phil wrote to get the contract. I wrote back to them saying that from my conversations with Phil, it was my understanding that the outline was very incomplete, no more than a few pages long.

(AW:)Perhaps they were concerned with the legal obligation of the contract and whether the money had to be returned?

(KW:)Yeah, something like that. Or whether they could find somebody who'd be able to write the book. And I said no. Seeing as Phil would deviate or diverge so much from his outlines anyway, there wasn't much of a chance.[dccccxvii]

In the last interview PKD conducted in his life with Gwen Lee and which was published in *Starlog* in 1982 shortly after his death, PKD talks more of THE OWL IN DAYLIGHT:

(PKD:) This is the book I'm *allegedly* writing, THE OWL IN DAYLIGHT. Its a folk expression from the South -- an owl being blind in the daylight. It simply means a person whose judgement is clouded over. The book is about the inability to understand. I can't even put it into words.

{...}

(*Starlog*): And you have a new outline for this novel?

(PKD:)Within a short period of time. It has jelled quite a bit. I talked to my agent. He said, "Are you sure you can do it?" Because the novel would be from the viewpoint of an entity that was not human but from presumably another star system. Its view of us and our culture. It would begin on another star system on a planet with a civilization quite different from ours -- a civilization where there's no atmosphere such as we have and as a result, speech is never developed; they're mute and deaf. And because of the failure to utilize sound, they have no art predicated on sound. Now, our art predicated on sound is, of course, music, and we take music for granted. But for them, since they do not employ sound, there is no analog that will correlate in their world for music. And what I want to do is, you know, the way we have in our world mystical visions of heaven, like at the end of Dante's *Divine Comedy*, and these visions are generally that heaven is light -- the concept of light is almost always associated with the next world to us. Now, this planet, not having sound, utilizes *colour* for language. Just as we use different audio frequencies, they use different colour frequencies. Their world is one that employs vision and visual things entirely and no sound whatsoever. Their normal world would be the way we envision the *next* world to be.{...}.[dcccxviii]

In this final interview PKD goes on at length about the plot of THE OWL IN DAYLIGHT. The interested reader is referred to the 1982 issue of *Starlog* for more details.

From these above, somewhat conflicting plot descriptions, we can see that THE OWL IN DAYLIGHT was to be a complex novel but we cannot know for sure what it was to be about. To different people it seems that PKD pitched different ideas and no one of them described a true outline for the proposed novel. It's also possible that PKD actually began writing this novel for in a letter to a young fan, Kris Hummel, at the end of Jan 1982, he writes:

{...} I'd be happy to read a story by you, but you must send me a return manila envelope with postage, because I can never manage to get down to the store to buy manila envelopes, especially now that I've started on my new s-f novel for Simon & Schuster (called THE OWL IN DAYLIGHT).[dcccxix]

So perhaps out there somewhere there is a partial manuscript for THE OWL IN DAYLIGHT?

Although Sutin has the short story "I Hope I Shall Arrive Soon" being written by June 1979, the manuscript for "I Hope I Shall Arrive Soon" reached the SMLA on April 24, 1980. It was sold to *Playboy Magazine* and was first published in the Dec 1980 issue under the title "Frozen Journey." [dcccxx]

The story lent its title to Mark Hurst and Paul Williams' collection I HOPE I SHALL ARRIVE SOON (1985) and also to editions of this collection in the United Kingdom (Gollancz 1986, Grafton 1988). A paperback edition is also available in the USA from St. Martin's Press (1987). In 1999 Harper Collins Publishers printed the story in *THE PLAYBOY BOOK OF SCIENCE FICTION*.

In his introduction to the 1985 Doubleday collection I HOPE I SHALL ARRIVE SOON Paul Williams comments on the story:

"Exit Door" earned Phil a large fee, but "I Hope I Shall Arrive Soon" was really his first sale to a recognized major short story market (*Playboy*), closely followed by "Rautavaara's Case" (*Omni*). "I Hope I Shall Arrive Soon" was Phil's original title; the story appeared in *Playboy* as "Frozen Journey". It later won the *Playboy* Award for best short story of the year by a new contributor, and appeared in Terry Carr's "Best Of The Year" collection. Ray Torrence is a real person, a *PKDS* member. [dcccxxi]

In an October 1981 letter PKD mentions his *Playboy* sale:

All in all, except for burning myself out writing a goddamn literary novel things are just great for me... Did you see my story in the December *Playboy*? I won an award for it, a trophy and a thousand dollars....[dcccxxii]

Here's what the *Playboy* editors wrote about the story in the Dec 1980 issue:

Speaking of captives, imagine yourself locked in a two-by-six-foot box, half awake and bound for a journey through space that will take ten years. That's precisely the horror Philip K. Dick's tragic hero faces in *Frozen journey*, illustrated by Pater Sato. This is the first *Playboy* appearance for Dick, the renowned science-fiction author of more than 30 novels (his best known is THE MAN IN THE HIGH CASTLE).

That was in the 'Playbill' near the Table of Contents page. And on the contents page itself:

It's rough being neurotic, even with plenty of earthly distractions and a good shrink. But when you're going crazy on a spaceship with only a computer to help you, snapping is, well, a snap.[dcccxxiii]

"Frozen Journey" reappeared in 1995 in HarperPrism publishers' anthology: *45 Years Of Science Fiction in Playboy*.

In the story Victor Kemmings is in cryonic suspension while on a ten-year trip to a colony planet and a new life. But, there's a malfunction in the machinery and Victor is conscious. Realizing that after ten years of consciousness with no activity Victor will go insane the spaceship's computer feeds Victor's childhood memories back to him in an attempt to maintain his sanity. But Victor's early memories are bad and once brought to the surface contaminate all the computer's efforts to lull him happily along until the ship lands. To the computer Victor says he only wishes they'd get to the end of the journey. So the computer grants his wish with more false perceptions. But, once brought to his mind Victor's bad early memories continue to suborn the computer's now desperate efforts to keep him sane. In the end when the spaceship does land and his old girlfriend is waiting for him on the colony world, Victor still doesn't believe its real. He's been through it too many times before already.

A somewhat wry story akin to A MAZE OF DEATH, "Frozen Journey" rates ✳ ✳ ✳ ✳

In May 1980 a signal event in the distribution of PKD's short stories occurred. This was publication by Berkley Books of THE GOLDEN MAN collection, edited by Mark Hurst and containing fifteen of PKD's very best short stories from all parts of his career such as "Sales Pitch", The Mold of Yancy" and the title story "The Golden Man."[dcccxxiv]

What marks this collection, other than the stories, is the Introduction and 'story notes' written by PKD specifically for this edition. Sometimes, indeed in many cases, these comments are the only ones made by Dick on the stories.

For collectors the first edition from Berkley is uncommon but can be found on the internet for around $40. A signed copy of the first edition could be had for $110. The SFBC hardback edition from Berkley in 1981 goes for around $30.[dcccxxv]

As a collection of PKD's short stories THE GOLDEN MAN rates ✶ ✶ ✶ ✶

May 1980 also saw PKD sending off another short story to the SMLA. This was "Rautavaara's Case"

"Rautavaara's Case' reached the SMLA on May 13, 1980. It was sold to *Omni* and published in the Oct 1980 issue of that magazine. The story has appeared in some prestigious anthologies and was selected for Mark Hurst and Paul Williams' collection I HOPE I SHALL ARRIVE SOON in 1985. It was PKD's second sale to a major magazine following "Frozen Journey" to *Playboy*.

Very little comment has been made on "Rautavaara's Case". The story itself tells of an accident in space in which three humans are killed. However, the alien Proximations from the Proxima system are on hand to save the brain of Agneta Rautavaara and she, along with her two dead companions, see a vision of Christ. This interests the Proximations greatly as they have their own version of the Saviour. They wonder if, with a slight change, she might have a vision of their Saviour. This she does but, unfortunately, as the Proximations are a plasmatic lifeform – effectively the opposite of humans who are a somatic lifeform – she is horrified when their Saviour starts to eat her companions. To the Proximations this is the highest honor: to be eaten by their God. But to humans this is the reverse of the Christian sacrament and Agneta's brain is shut down and the Proximations censured in the intergalactic courts.

"Rautavaara's Case" rates ✶ ✶ ✶

Not long after sending in "Rautavaara's Case' Philip K. Dick was no doubt looking over his short story "Oh, To Be A Blobel" which appeared in the 30th anniversary issue of *Galaxy* in June. Soon after, in August, he was working on an outline for another unwritten novel.

"Fawn, Look Back" was a novel outline written in Aug 1980. It appeared first (and for the only time) in *Science Fiction Eye #2* in Aug 1987 as part of a special 16-page Philip K. Dick section. The Introduction is by Paul Williams.[dccccxxvi]

In the end this outline came to nothing.

In October 1980 *Omni* published "Rautavaara's Case" and PKD found himself being interviewed over the phone by the *Denver Clarion*.[dccccxxvii]

In this interview Dick talks of VALIS:

It's the theological study of the inbreaking of futuristic technology, established by supernatural intelligence, into the life of an ordinary, present-day man. It basically deals with this invasion from the future into the present and man's attempts to cope with it.[dccccxxviii]

And drops as if in passing mention of big Hollywood deals. Prodded by the interviewer he drops the name of Ridley Scott and a budget of $20,000,000 for the filming of DO ANDROIDS DREAM OF ELECTRIC SHEEP?

Dick did have one gripe though, possibly feeling gypped by the Hollywood moguls:

I thought I was getting an exorbitant sum of money for the films, {...} And I was having a drink with Ray Bradbury, telling him about it, and he had an apoplectic stroke He told me I was a babe in the woods and I wasn't getting nearly enough out of it. I thought it was large amounts of money. I was crushed.[dcccxxix]

An interesting thing about this interview is Dick's response to a question about his religious beliefs. After a slight pause -- one imagines the whole weight of the *EXEGESIS* plopping into PKD's head at that moment – he described himself as a "religious anarchist" and then

I'm totally against organized religion, {...} I believe you have a direct relation with the divine or you have no relation with the divine. It has nothing to do with faith or dogmatic creeds. The initiative comes from the divine side. There is nothing you can do. All you can do is live an honest life, be brutally honest with yourself, and hope to become an object of interest with the divine beings. Using a formula to evoke them is technically called "magic." I guess you could call me a neo-Platonist with Gnostic overtones.[dcccxxx]

With the completion of THE DIVINE INVASION, Dick felt the AI voice that had spoken inside his head since his pink beam experiences depart. But it returned again with a vengeance on Nov 17, 1980. In his *EXEGESIS* he cranked out what happened. This excerpt from the *EXEGESIS* under the title "11-17-80" is published in full in Sutin's *DIVINE INVASIONS*. Briefly, PKD had another visit from God who tried to reassure Phil of a better life to come. God posed a problem, saying:

"I am the infinite. I will show you. Where I am, infinity is; where infinity is, there I am. Construct lines of reasoning by which to understand your experience in 1974. I will enter the field against their shifting nature. You think they are logical but they are not; they are infinitely creative." [dcccxxxi]

For every explanation that Dick could come up with he entered an infinite regress where each explanation degenerated into an infinite progression of thesis and antithesis. To each theory God answered "here is infinity; here am I. Try again."

But at least God, no doubt fed up with PKD's night-after-night theorizing in his *EXEGESIS*, had stepped in with a personal visit and a challenge by which PKD might see the light. And with this final personal visit – and a few more stabs at explanation in his *EXEGESIS* – PKD, a couple of weeks later, decided to end his *EXEGESIS*. On Dec 2, 1980 he wrote "END" on the last page of the *EXEGESIS* and typed up a title page:

3/20/74
12-2-80

THE DIALECTIC: God against Satan, & God's Final Victory foretold & shown
Philip K. Dick
AN EXEGESIS
Apologia Pro Mia Vita [dcccxxxii]

But soon he was at it again, scribbling notes and stuffing them in envelopes…

For 1980, then, it is left for us only to look into the 'big Hollywood deals' that Dick referred to in his *Denver Clarion* interview.

BLADE RUNNER (Part 2)

We've seen how DO ANDROIDS DREAM OF ELECTRIC SHEEP? was optioned for film around the time of the novel's publication in May 1968 and how Robert Jaffe wrote a screenplay in 1973 which Dick detested. And we've glanced in passing at how he battled with the movie producers to re-release DO ANDROIDS DREAM instead of writing an el cheapo novelization of the movie. This at great financial cost to himself. Now we'll go more deeply into all this.

In 1975 Hampton Fancher approached PKD about optioning DO ANDROIDS DREAM for film. But the option was already held by Herb Jaffe. When this option expired in 1978, Fancher and his partner, Brian Kelly, picked it up. Kelly then submitted the option to producer Michael Deeley, who refused it. Fancher then decided to write a screenplay himself. This he did and when he again returned to Deeley the option was accepted. As Fancher noted, after that it was all sales work. Deeley was a famous producer who'd just won an Academy Award for the movie *The Deer Hunter.*

But even with this powerful backing no studio would commit to producing the movie, all having objections of one sort or another. So Fancher kept tinkering with his script and in 1979 Deeley brought it to the attention of Ridley Scott, the director of *Alien*, a blockbuster movie, and famous in his own right. Scott initially passed on it but maintained an interest and during a hiatus in another project he again asked to see the script. This time he decided to go with it and within a week had pitched the idea to Filmways. Soon after the movie that would become *BLADE RUNNER* went into pre-production and Syd Mead was hired as Production Designer. But then in late 1980 Filmways dropped the project due to the expense (*BLADE RUNNER* was budgeted at around $18 or $19 million at the time -- $4 to $5 over Filmways limit). Filmways financial role was immediately taken up by Tandem and soon The Ladd Company hopped on board, assuming some financial responsibility. The final budget was $22 Million.[dcccxxxiii]

More script rewrites followed with a disgruntled Hampton Fancher feeling his role being reduced to that of a contract writer and not liking it. These revisions by the recalcitrant Fancher resulted in another writer being brought in to work over the script which, by this time, had taken on a life of its own. The new writer was David Peoples and he first came to the project in Nov 1980. He completed a script for *BLADE RUNNER* in Feb 1981.

Fancher did not actually work with Peoples on the script; that was between Peoples and Ridley Scott. But of the Peoples' script Fancher said:

... I was surprised because when I got Peoples' script those things that Ridley had wanted that I thought couldn't be integrated into the concept had been rendered by Peoples in ways that were original, tight and admirable.[dcccxxxiv]

Fancher's reduced role as sole screenwriter did not result in bad feelings between the parties and he was called back toward the end of production to help rewrite a few scenes.

Peoples talks of writing the screenplay:

The thing that can be confusing about all this is how enormously collaborative all of this stuff is, especially at the stage that I was involved. I was brought in when there were sets already being constructed. One time I changed a scene and somebody said, 'Jesus, you wrote the ambulance out!' I said so what and they said, 'Well, it's already built.' So this was a source of some aggravation.[dcccxxxv]

As production continued Peoples found himself writing scenes on the fly, sometimes with suggestions and dialogue from Scott and the two principal actors, Harrison Ford and Rutger Hauer. The term 'replicant' occurred to Peoples after he talked to his scientist daughter about some of the scientific background to the movie. She'd spoken of cell replication and he snatched the term to use instead of 'android' which he felt had been overused.

To Peoples, PKD's theme of what is human? was important in his script. But he stresses that the movie is Ridley Scott's; he's the one with the full vision of the movie:

Ridley is sort of the Hieronymus Bosch of our time. He goes way beyond what's on the paper. I mean, you can't imagine it – in the sense of you write down a bunch of things and then you go see what's shot and it just blows your mind.[dcccxxxvi]

As for the actors in *BLADE RUNNER*, Philip K. Dick was greatly pleased. Rutger Hauer, he thought, was definitely appropriate for the part of Roy Batty:

I was looking at the stills of him and I said, 'Oh my God, this is the Nordic superman that Hitler said would come marching out of the laboratory. This is the blond beast that the Nazis were creating. And of course the origin of the book DO ANDROIDS DREAM OF ELECTRIC SHEEP? was my research into the Nazis for THE MAN IN THE HIGH CASTLE.[dcccxxxvii]

And of the choice of Sean Young to play Rachel Rosen, PKD was ecstatic:

Sean Young, who plays Rachel, I have never seen her act. I've seen Harrison Ford act, and I've seen Rutger Hauer act, but when I saw those stills of her I was blown away! I said, that's Rachel! You could have hung pictures of a hundred different women and I would have unerringly picked out that one as Rachel. That's not a simulation of Rachel, that *is* Rachel. They went and found her. It's the *femme fatale belle dame sans merci* that I eternally write about and now I've seen a photograph of her and I know that she exists. I've shown the pictures to several of my friends and they all agree that that's exactly how they imagined her.[dcccxxxviii]

Unfortunately, I have been able to find no remarks by PKD on the choice of Harrison Ford to play the part of Rick Deckard, nor of how he played the part. Leaving the movie for a minute we'll look now at the brouhaha with the *BLADE RUNNER* novelization. In the *Twilight Zone* interview PKD addresses this issue:

(TZ): Your forthcoming novel, THE TRANSMIGRATION OF TIMOTHY ARCHER, is essentially a non-sf literary work based on the mysterious death in the desert of your friend Bishop James Pike, and I've been told that you wrote it in lieu of doing a novelization of the *BLADE RUNNER* screenplay. Why did you choose to write a book with openly religious themes instead of a lucrative, all-but-certain bestseller?
(PKD): The amount of money involved would have been very great, and the film people offered to cut us in on the merchandising rights. But they required a suppression of

the original novel DO ANDROIDS DREAM OF ELECTRIC SHEEP? in favor of the commercialized novelization based on the screenplay. My agency computed that I would accrue, conservatively, $400,000 if I did the novelization. In contrast, if we went the route of rereleasing the original novel, I would make about $12,500.

BLADE RUNNER's people were putting tremendous pressure on us to do the novelization -- or to allow someone else to come in and do it, like Alan Dean Foster. But we felt that the original was a good novel. And also, I did not want to write what I call the "El Cheapo" novelization. I *did* want to do the TIMOTHY ARCHER novel.

So we stuck to our guns, and at one point *BLADE RUNNER* became so cold-blooded they threatened to withdraw the logo rights. We wouldn't be able to say, "The novel on which *BLADE RUNNER* is based." We'd be unable to use any stills from the film.

Finally we came to an agreement with them. We are adamant about rereleasing the original novel. And I have done THE TRANSMIGRATION OF TIMOTHY ARCHER.

{...}

This is something that is extremely important to me in terms of the organic development of my ideas and preoccupations in my writing. So for me to derail myself and do that cheapo novelization of *BLADE RUNNER* -- a completely commercialized thing aimed at twelve-year-olds -- would have probably been disastrous to me artistically. Although financially, as my agent explained it, I would literally be set up for life. I don't think my agent figures I'm going to live much longer.

It's like Dante's *Inferno*. A writer sent to the Inferno is sentenced to rewrite all his novels -- his best ones, at least -- as cheapo, twelve-year-old hack stuff for all eternity. A *terrible* punishment! The fact that it would earn me a lot of money illuminates the grotesqueness of the situation. When it's finally offered to me, I'm more or less apathetic to the megabucks. I live a rather ascetic life. I don't have any material wants and I have no debts. My condominium is paid off, my car is paid off, my stereo is paid off.[dcccxxxix]

PKD refers to the reissue of DO ANDROIDS DREAM OF ELECTRIC SHEEP? in conjunction with the release of the movie:

As to my novel DO ANDROIDS DREAM OF ELECTRIC SHEEP? it has been pulled from the stores deliberately, kept out of circulation, and will be rereleased next May in conjunction with the film; it'll have Harrison Ford's picture on the cover, and, inside, stills from the film. I've been told that a used paperback copy has sold for as much as $65, because of the film. The original hardcover is so rare that Ballantine had to obtain my copy for their printing from me directly; they could not obtain a hardcover copy anywhere at any price, because it is now such a sought-after collector's item.[dcccxl]

Perhaps beginning with Herb Jaffe's lousy script in 1973, Dick had felt an antipathy toward the would-be producers of his movie. But his attitude changed after he saw a section on the *BLADE RUNNER* special effects on the TV news: "I recognized it immediately. It was my own interior world. They caught it perfectly." So pleased was Dick that he wrote a letter to the TV station who sent it along to the Ladd Company who, in turn, mailed a copy of the new screenplay to PKD. This screenplay was still Fancher's but had been worked over by David Peoples, unknown to Dick. On reading it he now thought it sensational:

I couldn't believe what I was reading! It was simply sensational -- still Hampton Fancher's screenplay, but miraculously transfigured, as it were. The whole thing had simply been rejuvenated in a very fundamental way.

After I finished reading the screenplay, I got the novel out and looked through it. The two reinforce each other, so that someone who started with the novel would enjoy the movie and someone who started with the movie would enjoy the novel. I was amazed that Peoples could get some of those scenes to work. It taught me things about writing that I didn't know.[dccccxli]

Peoples' script turned PKD around. He had not wanted to meet Ridley Scott and go up to Hollywood to be wined and dined. But now he was on good terms with Hollywood and got involved in the production – the reason as we've seen that he was too tired to write THE OWL IN DAYLIGHT.

PKD did see part of the movie in early 1982, writing to Kris Hummel:

Kris, I haven't yet seen the film in complete form, but I did see about twenty minutes of it, and it is super; I'm not kidding. The opening scene is simply beyond belief. It is likely that in late February we'll be shown a rough cut of the total film... but they're running behind schedule, I understand. *BLADE RUNNER* is truly a dynamite film {...}[dcccxlii]

But although amicable relations existed, Dick soon got himself in trouble with Hollywood again by referring to 'androids' in an interview for *Select TV Guide*

Shit, *BLADE RUNNER* started yelling at me because, in an article that I wrote in the *Select TV Guide*, I mentioned androids. They said, "That's very dangerous talk, mentioning androids in connection with this film. We're not using the word *android*." Well, it seems hard to avoid a word that's in the title of your own book. And they wanted to know how I'd gotten hold of a copy of the screenplay. "How did *you* get hold of it?" they said, with the emphasis on the word "you," you know? [dcccxliii]

PKD also commented on the transformation of his novel into movie terms:

"The sets, I'm sure, are marvelous. Russell (Russell Galen, Dick's representative at the Scott Meredith agency) called me up and said, "You've *got* to go up there." Well, in a way it's a Chinese finger-trap. If the sets are that good, maybe I'll go up there and fall into the mode that exists now in science fiction, where the special effects and the sets are everything. And as an author I can't afford, as a practical matter, to adopt that ideology, because it reduces the author to merely setting up a simple plot-outline in which special effects can be brought in. His job is very much a means to an end, rather than an end in itself.

"Ridley Scott is a director who has a visual sense rather than a narrative sense. This is not a matter of insulting Ridley Scott. He thinks visually, and of course this is why he's in movies. It is perhaps the way it should be. But I am an author, and I think in narrative terms, in terms of a story line."[dcccxliv]

BLADE RUNNER, the movie, was released to an indifferent public in the Summer of 1982 but its status has risen since and by the turn of the century *BLADE RUNNER* is considered a cult classic. Norman Spinrad reviewed the movie soon after it came out. Initially he had a bad attitude, brought on by the fact that he could not find the name Philip K. Dick anywhere in the ads and posters proclaiming the movie, but his attitude changed on actually seeing the movie:

... far from being a turkey, a case could be made for *BLADE RUNNER* as the best science fiction film of the past decade, and certainly of the post-*Star Wars* crop.
{...}

The plot itself is extremely simple. Rick Deckard is a cop of sorts in a future megalopolis. His job is to hunt down four escaped "replicants," that is, androids with deliberately shortened lifespans manufactured for off-world use. He succeeds in slaying ("retiring") three of them, more or less falling in love with a fifth replicant, Rachel, in the process. Roy Batty, the fourth and most dangerous replicant, has Deckard at his mercy as he, Batty, is about to die, but decides to let Deckard live. Deckard runs off with Rachel. Fade out.[dcccxlv]

As a science fiction writer himself Spinrad is concerned with the fidelity of the movie to the book. In the course of his review he sees *BLADE RUNNER* as a fair transformation of the novel to movie form:

... the core of the novel, the essential story, is the core of the film. The intellectual level of the screenplay and its perceived audience are both much closer to the intent of Dick than to "action-adventure" and the theme and its mode of expression are intellectually and spiritually true to the novel to an impressive degree...
{...}
In addition to being true in essence to the novel despite public statements to the contrary, *BLADE RUNNER*, despite more public statements to the contrary, is truer to what science fiction is all about than just about any "SF film" yet made. Scott (and here we are definitely dealing with the creative contribution of the director) has created the most dense, detailed, and fully realized future world ever put on film.[dcccxlvi]

However, Spinrad does find a few things to complain about in the movie, particularly "the ponderous pace of the editing" and the director's lingering over some scenes for too long. And, of course, the horrible voice-over by Harrison Ford that runs throughout the movie is criticized. He also wonders where the title came from and assumes it was something someone came up with because it sounded snappy; even though it has nothing to do with the film or the novel. But despite these quibbles, if such they are, Spinrad concludes his review with:

BLADE RUNNER is an essentially true translation of DO ANDROID DREAM OF ELECTRIC SHEEP?, it is a serious film for adults, and it is more of a real science fiction film than just about anything else has been. Flaws and all, it is a minor masterpiece at the least, and anyone looking for a *real* science fiction film of truly serious intent should go see it.[dcccxlvii]

In 1990 The Ladd Company released a 'Director's Cut' of *BLADE RUNNER* in which the voice-over was removed and some other scenes expanded and a few new ones put in. This version too was released to the public but seems to have aroused only the attentions of die-hard Dick fans and *BLADE RUNNER* cultists. This version mostly ended up on video-tape and on laser discs and DVD's for the affluent fan.

As for the reissue of DO ANDROIDS DREAM OF ELECTRIC SHEEP? that accompanied the movie under the title *BLADE RUNNER*, this was done by Del Rey Books in May 1982. The cover features a copy of the movie poster and has the distinctive *BLADE RUNNER* logo for its title. The original title of the novel is in parentheses beneath the logo.[dcccxlviii]

The British edition followed from Granada in August 1982.[dcccxlix]

As for *BLADE RUNNER* collectibles, an original movie poster may cost you $500 and up. But of the books, the first edition paperbacks from the USA and UK are not particularly valuable – there were so many printed – and they can be had for about $10. Valuable items do exist though; for instance, the *BLADE RUNNER* Souvenir Magazine, published by Friedman, Inc. in 1982 commands a price from $350 to $500 while *THE BLADE RUNNER SKETCH BOOK* from Blue Dolphin Press, also in 1982, which features original production artwork illustrations is a heady $750.[dcccl]

There is also a comic book version of *BLADE RUNNER* that was published in two parts by Marvel Comics in 1982.

The first paperback edition of *BLADE RUNNER* from Del Rey became PKD's best selling edition to its time (and probably forever) with over 325,000 copies sold. Many additional printings of *BLADE RUNNER* have followed this first one both in the USA and UK – and in many other countries as well. By now one imagines the worldwide royalties from *BLADE RUNNER* editions must be a tremendous amount of money.[dcccli]

With this short section on *BLADE RUNNER* we end the year 1980 and turn to 1981 even though *BLADE RUNNER* has dragged us on into 1981 already.

1981

1981, Philip K. Dick's last full year on Earth, began with him writing one more short story: "The Alien Mind." According to Paul Williams this was the last short story that PKD ever wrote. It also has a strange genesis with Williams declaring that it was

done at the request of a high school student Phil met while buying cat food at the grocery store.[dccclii]

This statement has proven to be false, as we shall see in a moment.

"The Alien Mind" did indeed make its first appearance in a high school periodical: *The Yuba City High Times* in Feb 1981. It was then sold to *F & SF* where it was accepted on April 23, 1981 and published in the Oct 1981 edition of *F & SF*.

In 1982 "The Alien Mind" was reprinted in Edward L. Ferman's *THE BEST FROM FANTASY & SCIENCE FICTION*, 24TH Series and was selected by Mark Hurst and Paul Williams for the Doubleday PKD collection, I HOPE I SHALL ARRIVE SOON in 1985.

In 2002 PKD collector and scholar Frank Hollander published an article in *PKD Otaku* in which he decides to track down the truth of the 'cat food' origin of "The Alien Mind". With much diligence Hollander sought out a copy of *The Yuba City High Times*, discovering in passing that the origin of the 'cat food' statement was not Paul Williams but whoever wrote the blurb for the story when it appeared in *F & SF*. Here's the blurb in full:

This short and surprising tale grew from an encounter at a Santa Ana, CA grocery store, where the author was buying cat food and encountered a teenager who was editor of the Yuba City High School student paper and who was enterprising enough to ask Mr. Dick to write a story for the paper. Phil agreed, and here is the happy result (which will also appear in the *Yuba City High School Times*).[dcccliii]

By following clues on the internet Hollander found an Alumni group from Yuba City high school to whom he emailed his request for information. With this and good luck he got a reply from someone who actually had a stack of old *Yuba City High Times* newspapers in a box. The first one his correspondent pulled from the box was the issue in question dated Feb 20, 1981!

Hollander also found out that the student who supposedly asked PKD for a short story in the grocery store was named Ben Adams, a freshman at the high school at the time.

With more effort Hollander actually located Ben Adams on the internet and learned the real story. Adams also sent Hollander a copy of a letter PKD had written to Adams which referred to the short story:

> Enclosed you will find a short-short story that I wrote for you. Needless to say, I expect no monetary remuneration; go ahead and print it.[dcccliv]

Hollander asked Adams to write a brief description of his encounter with PKD. Adams consequently wrote of that in an article published in *PKD Otaku* directly after Hollander's piece. In his article Adams takes us back to when he first met PKD as a boy in the 70s. his father, an Episcopal priest living in Santa Ana, knew Doris Sauter. As we've noted Doris Sauter was PKD's girlfriend in the late 70s. She also knew that the young Benjamin Adams was a science fiction fan and she herself knew several science fiction writers: Ray Bradbury, Norman Spinrad, and Philip K. Dick.

Adams had never heard of Philip K. Dick until his father left a first edition of DEUS IRAE laying around in his house. Adams read it and notes, now, that his father is the person who forms the basis for the character 'Father Larry' in VALIS.

The 11-year old Adams actually met PKD at Thanksgiving in 1978 when the writer visited his house as Doris' date. After dinner, to keep the boy quiet, PKD gave him paperback editions of his novels THE THREE STIGMATA OF PALMER ELDRITCH and CONFESSIONS OF A CRAP ARTIST which he signed.

After the Adams family moved to Yuba City, Benjamin corresponded with Philip Dick, sending him his own short stories which PKD would critique. Adams ended up on the staff of the high school paper and without really thinking about it wrote to PKD asking him for a short story for the paper. PKD sent him the manuscript for "The Alien Mind."

As for the 'cat food' anecdote Adams dismisses it as a fabrication of Ed Ferman, then the editor of *F & SF*.

One more item concerns Adams and Dick, this was the dedication in THE TRANSMIGRATION OF TIMOTHY ARCHER which is from the poem "An Ode To Him" by the 17th century poet Robert Herrick which begins, "Ah Ben!" Adams believes this was meant for him.[dccclv]

We certainly thank Hollander and Adams for clearing up the 'cat food' mystery. As for the story "The Alien Mind" it tells of an arrogant spaceman on his way to the alien planet Meknos III to deliver needed medical supplies. Aroused from his deep-sleep by his ship he discovers he is off course due to his pet cat having pushed some buttons as it floated around the cabin. Incensed that he has been belittled in the eyes of the alien Meknosians the man strangles his cat.

On arrival at Meknos III the aliens ask to see his pet cat but the man blows them off and takes to his spaceship for the return trip home. Unfortunately for him, though, the Meknosians have disabled his deep-sleep chamber and it will take him two years of normal consciousness to get home. His problems are compounded when his plan to entertain himself with video tapes proves useless as the contents of the tape locker now contain only a squeaky toy for his ex-pet cat. Desperately he plans to maintain his sanity by building his trip around the preparation and enjoyment of his food supply. But... a two-year supply of kibble holds little promise of enjoyment.

This story is similar to PKD's 1981 short story "I Hope I Shall Arrive Soon" though one can tell that it was written more quickly. Still, once again Dick shows his caritas for cats and "The Alien Mind" gets ✳ ✳ ✳

As well as "The Alien Mind" in February, PKD also had published that month the first edition of VALIS from Bantam Books. The first edition of THE DIVINE INVASION followed in June together with the second edition of VALIS from Bantam.

July saw the SFBC edition of THE GOLEN MAN available to the sf fans.

In September the SFBC edition of THE DIVINE INVASION came out and in October his short story "Return Match" saw publication in *Starlog #52*. As well, "The Alien Mind" saw its second publication in *F & SF* as we've just seen.

The last item of prime interest published in 1981 was PKD's official bibliography from the Underwood Press. Compiled by Daniel J. H. Levack and annotated by Steven Owen Godersky, *'PKD: A Philip K. Dick Bibliography'* is now twenty years later a main source of bibliographic information as well as a treasured PKD collectible. In this present work I have relied much on Levack's earlier volume.[dccclvi]

In this his last year PKD wrote his last novel, THE TRANSMIGRATION OF TIMOTHY ARCHER.

THE TRANSMIGRATION OF TIMOTHY ARCHER

In April and May of 1981 PKD wrote THE TRANSMIGRATION OF TIMOTHY ARCHER. The novel was complete by May 13th. Dick's editor, David Hartwell at Timescape Books published the novel in April 1982.[dccclvii]

The UK edition from Gollancz followed in Oct 1982.[dccclviii]

With THE TRANSMIGRATION OF TIMOTHY ARCHER Philip K. Dick returned to writing a mainstream novel. Although Dick had considered THE DIVINE INVASION a mainstream novel; or, at least, he tried to convince his editor David Hartwell at Timescape to publish it as such, it was not until THE TRANSMIGRATION OF TIMOTHY ARCHER that he had a successful mainstream novel published. Unhappily, he didn't live to see it.[dccclix] But THE TRANSMIGRATION OF TIMOTHY ARCHER could well have ended up as a science-fiction novel. Norman Spinrad explains:

Phil had come to know Pike {...} and wanted to write a novel about Pike's spiritual odyssey. Somehow, perhaps because he felt he was irrevocably typed as an SF writer, Phil had gotten it into his head that the only way he could get such a novel published was to tart it up with a lot of thriller-cum-SF paraphernalia involving CIA plots, alien invasions, and the usual razzmatazz.

"Jeez, Phil," I told him, "you've got a great story here, you don't need all that crap. Why don't you just tell it straight?"

"You think I could get it published?"

I told him I thought he could, and he decided to discuss the matter with Russell Galen, his agent and friend, whom he really trusted. Galen concurred, encouraged Phil to go ahead, and the result was THE TRANSMIGRATION OF TIMOTHY ARCHER, which I believe is one of Phil's three or four best novels, and a return to the level of THE MAN IN THE HIGH CASTLE, THE THREE STIGMATA OF PALMER ELDRITHC, and UBIK, after too many years of floundering around with lesser works. Certainly it is far superior to VALIS or THE DIVINE INVASION, utterly coherent, totally controlled, spiritually lucid, and filled with loving clarity.[dccclx]

Above we've seen how PKD refused to do a 'cheapo novelization' of *BLADE RUNNER* and chose instead to write TIMOTHY ARCHER. By doing this he stood to lose a lot of money. PKD comments on this:

Now, the payment on that novel is very small. It's only $7,500, which is just about minimum these days. It's because in the mainstream field I am essentially a novice writer. I'm not known. And I'm being paid on the scale that a new writer coming into the field would be paid on. The contract is a two-book contract, and there's a science fiction novel in it. And it pays exactly three times for the science fiction what is being paid for TIMOTHY ARCHER.

{...} Simon and Schuster wanted ARCHER first, and I wanted to do it first. Of course, I may find that I made a very great error, because it may not turn out to be a successful book. It may be that I've lost the ability to write a literary novel, if indeed I ever had the ability to do so. It's been over twenty years since I've written a non-science-fiction novel, and it's very problematical whether I can write mainstream, literary-quality-type fiction. This is definitely an unproven thing, an X factor. I may find that I've turned down $400,000 and wound up with nothing.[dccclxi]

The science fiction novel PKD refers to in this contract was for THE OWL IN DAYLIGHT which he never wrote.

In June 1981 PKD was waiting to hear from his agent on acceptance of TIMOTHY ARCHER. Russ Galen had read the novel and commented:

You know, in your science fiction they drive things called flobbles and quibbles, and in this one they drive Hondas -- but it's still essentially a science fiction novel. Although I can't explain exactly *how*.[dccclxii]

To this PKD responds in the *Twilight Zone* interview:

TIMOTHY ARCHER is in no way science fiction; it starts out the day John Lennon is shot and then goes into flashbacks. And yet the three do form a trilogy constellating around a basic theme. This is something that is extremely important to me in terms of the organic development of my ideas and preoccupations in my writing. So for me to derail myself and do that cheapo novelization of *BLADE RUNNER* -- a completely commercialized thing aimed at twelve-year-olds -- would have probably been disastrous to me artistically.[dccclxiii]

The trilogy PKD talks about is the 'Valis trilogy': VALIS, THE DIVINE INVASION and THE TRANSMIGRATION OF TIMOTHY ARCHER. He speaks about this trilogy again with John Boonstra, and at the same time gets another dig in at the *BLADE RUNNER* people:

TIMOTHY ARCHER is essentially the third novel in a trilogy of which VALIS is the first and THE DIVINE INVASION is the second; which is sort of interesting because each book is unique. It really was necessary for me to do the novel, as a projection of thematic material going back years and years and years in my writing, in stuff even as early as EYE IN THE

SKY and TIME OUT OF JOINT. Those themes are constant preoccupations with me, they unfold by their own inner, organic drive, and I don't really have the option of aborting that process and just suddenly going into a completely commercialized thing aimed at twelve-year-olds.[dccclxiv]

Of his characters in TIMOTHY ARCHER Dick sez:

I've managed to put into TIMOTHY ARCHER two very good characters, the Bishop himself and the protagonist, a young woman, a lot more educated than I am, a lot smarter than I am, a lot more rational than I am. I was very much into a post-partum depression after I finished writing it, because I was so happy enjoying her company, listening to her dialogues. I really fell in love with her. She's entirely fictional, as far as I know. An ad-hoc creation, like Pallas Athena from the brow of Zeus. Out of nothing.

To present the Bishop, I needed a protagonist who was smart enough to understand him, and loving enough to forgive him. That's a tall order, because the Bishop is a very mercurial, complex person, who does many things which are dubious, ethically. She intellectually understands what he's doing, and she's able to love him; in a sense she is more profoundly a wise person than the Bishop himself.

The climax of the book is the effect on her of his death. She says that it turned her into a machine; when she heard that he was dead in Israel, she devolved to the level of a machine and lost her own human nature, in a period where she is just tragically reified, and knows it. But at the end of the book, a Sufi scholar who is giving seminars in Sausalito is able to restore her to the state of a human being. So it is not a bummer ending; it is a very positive ending.[dccclxv]

The character of Angel Archer has been hailed by those who would defend PKD's female characterizations in his earlier novels. Accusations of misogynism in PKD's early portrayals of women run like a sullen thread through the pages of PKD commentary. Both of Dick's main biographers remark on this. Ursula Le Guin, for one, took Dick to task for this. In a letter from science fiction writer Michael Bishop to PKD in Feb 1981 which PKD himself quotes from in a letter he in turn wrote to *Science Fiction Review,* we find one expression of this reaction to Dick's female characters:

I'm looking at a recent letter to me from Michael Bishop. Michael likes my new novel VALIS, but learned that Ursula Le Guin had been tremendously upset by it, "not only for its examination of perhaps unresolvable metaphysical matters (into which she seems to fear you are plunging at the risk of never emerging again) but for its treatment of female characters – every one of which, she argued, was at bottom (I cannot remember her exact phrase) a hateful and not to be trusted death figure [...] she had the utmost admiration for the work of Philip K. Dick, who had been shamefully ignored in this country and who appeared to be spiraling into himself and going slowly crazy in Santa Ana, California." Her dismay, Michael says, "Results solely from a genuine human concern about you intellectual and emotional well-being."[dccclxvi]

Well, someone had to say it in the post-publication time of VALIS and Ursula stepped in… Later she would send a letter of apology to *Science Fiction Review,* this being published in the same issue as PKD's first letter. In a talk with Lawrence Sutin in 1986 Le Guin stood by her stance re the females in PKD's stories:

The women were symbols – whether goddess, bitch, hag, witch – but there weren't any women left, and there used to be women in his books.[dccclxvii]

Dick himself grudgingly acquiesced to this evaluation. After offering the weak explanation that the women in VALIS were, like the men, picaresque rogues, he wrote to his agent, Russ Galen, and admitted that prior to THE DIVINE INVASION:

My depiction of females has been inadequate and even somewhat vicious.[dccclxviii]

As the original contretemps with Le Guin began in January or February 1981 and PKD didn't begin writing THE TRANSMIGRATION OF TIMOTHY ARCHER until April and May, perhaps he kept Ursula Le Guin's remarks in mind when he created the character of Angel Archer. When he had completed the novel in May one of the first things he did was write to Le Guin:

This is the happiest moment of my life, Ursula, to meet face-to-face this bright, scrappy, witty, educated, tender woman, […] and had it not been for your analysis of my writing I probably never would have discovered her.[dccclxix]

As for editions of THE TRANSMIGRATION OF TIMOTHY ARCHER of interest to the PKD collector, the first edition hardcover from Timescape (Simon & Schuster) varies in price and quality, a Fine edition you can buy for around $50. The 1982 edition from Gollancz goes for $40 on up.

Ken Lopez, again, has a fine offering of TIMOTHY ARCHER related items for sale:

THE TRANSMIGRATION OF TIMOTHY ARCHER. (Published by Simon & Schuster, 1982). Carbon copy typescript, 286 pages, with corrections and changes by the author on 39 pages, plus author notes on two other pages. Together with the one-page (21 line) ribbon copy typescript for the "Author's Note," with several minor changes in Dick's hand. Together with ten discarded manuscript pages: pages 1-4 ribbon copy with the title handwritten by Dick: "Bishop Timothy Archer" and more than 50 words added or changed by Dick; pages 5-10 carbon copy with one handwritten correction. And also together with four pieces of correspondence: a carbon copy of a letter from Dick to his editor, with a copy of the text used to epigraph the novel; a carbon copy of a letter from Dick to his agent, 2 pages, reflecting on and analyzing his own novel after rereading the first third of it; a 5 page letter from Dick's agent to Dick, along with one leaf with a six-line poem in Dick's handwriting; and a carbon copy, two pages, of Dick's response to the above. All fine.
For the set of manuscripts: $9500.[dccclxx]

The question remains to be answered of whether TIMOTHY ARCHER is science fiction or not, as suggested by Russ Galen and despite PKD's remarks.

The answer depends on how you define science fiction and fantasy. The main distinction between the two is that science fiction, to be defined as such, proceeds from a basis of consensual possibility. For example, it *is* possible that mankind will develop a gravity drive and go on to the stars. It's also possible that we will develop a time-machine or attain immortality. But it is not possible according to the consensus of Western thought that fairies will sprinkle one's St. Bernard with magic dust and the dog will rise into the air and fly. Or, more to the point, that ancient Zoroastrian deities will take over a town and conduct a cosmic battle in and above it. That's why THE COSMIC PUPPETS is fantasy.

It's the old distinction between religion and science reoccurring in the field of literature. It's also the reason why sf traditionalists like Don Wollheim become apoplectic when something like a disappearing soft-drink stand is replaced by a scrap of paper in TIME OUT OF JOINT.

So, then, is the premise of THE TRANSMIGRATION OF TIMOTHY ARCHER science fiction or fantasy; or is it neither and instead straight realist fiction?

This third category of realism doesn't complicate matters too much if we define realism strictly as literature that deals with 'what is'; the consensual world with no fantasy or science fiction elements included.

To simplify the whole thing we can say that realism deals with the actual and *probable* whereas science fiction is about the *possible* and fantasy concerns the *impossible*.

The premise of THE TRANSMIGRATION OF TIMOTHY ARCHER is that ancient documents supposedly recently discovered in the Judean desert throw doubt upon the origins of Christianity. Is this actual, possible or impossible? Well, obviously the answer is that it *is* possible, ancient scrolls can be discovered at any time. Therefore TIMOTHY ARCHER is science fiction.

If the Zadokite scrolls in the novel had actually already been discovered then TIMOTHY ARCHER would be a straight mainstream realist novel. If the premise had been that the Zadokite scrolls were guarded by a giant dragon then it would be fantasy.

But what if they hadn't been discovered, which they *haven't* – the Zadokite scrolls are a fiction made up by Dick -- but the novel is written *as if they had*? What do we hold in our hands then as far as literary classifications? Do we have fake realism!?

I think that Philip K. Dick, perhaps unconsciously but at least with some idea of what he was trying to do, was attempting to blur these categories into one. He said, as quoted above, about THE TRANSMIGRATION OF TIMOTHY ARCHER:

It really was necessary for me to do the novel, as a projection of thematic material going back years and years and years in my writing, in stuff even as early as EYE IN THE SKY and TIME OUT OF JOINT. [dccclxxi]

And, talking about TIME OUT OF JOINT he says:

What I was trying to do in that book was account for the diversity of worlds that people live in. I had not read Heraclitus then, I didn't know his concept of *idios kosmos*, the private world, versus *koinos kosmos*, which we all share. I didn't know that the pre-Socratics had begun to discern these things. {...} It reminded me of the idea that Van Vogt had dealt with, of artificial memory, as occurs in *THE WORLD OF NULL-A* where a person has false memories implanted. [dccclxxii]

And, talking further on TIME OUT OF JOINT: It was really a risky thing to do. But there again we are dealing with fake reality and I had become obsessed with the idea of fake reality. I was just fascinated with the idea. So that's a pivotal book in terms of my career. It was my first hardcover sale, and it was the first novel in which the entire world is fake. You find yourself in it when you pick up the book and turn to page one. The world that you are reading about does not exist. And this was to be essentially the premise of my entire corpus of writing, really. [dccclxxiii]

If we put this all together then we arrive at PKD's notion of 'fake reality.' And to this we apply our category test. Is a fake reality real, possible or impossible? To which PKD forces us to answer – as no doubt he nebulously intended – we don't know, we don't know, and no.

The idea is not fantasy, that we can decide. It's not impossible. As to actuality or possibility PKD in the extended body of his work writes in such a way that the line blurring science fiction and realism is dissolved.

The key to all this is, of course, Dick's pink beam experiences.

According to Dick these actually happened, were *real*. Which is fine except that now he writes a novel based on these experiences: VALIS. So is VALIS science fiction, fantasy or realism?

Dick, with the veracity of his pink beam experiences affirmed, does in VALIS something that pretty much abolishes these categories. Despite the accidents in VALIS which are science fictional, the essence of the novel is that VALIS is true, it is real, hence VALIS is a realist novel. But in fact it is the *opposite* of a realist novel, it is an anti-realist novel because it doesn't take the consensual world as real for its basis but affirms the normal world as false.

To Dick VALIS is real but to the real world it is fantasy but since it is possible that a man may be visited by God; whole religions are based on this, then VALIS becomes science fiction.

Fake reality… a notion that has shaken up the literary world. The academics call it post-modernism. For Western literature it means abolishment of categories and a literature in which fantasy, science fiction and realism are all blurred together.[dcclxxiv]

All his life PKD wanted to write mainstream or realist novels. He indeed wrote several but he doubted the truth of reality itself, its realism, and came to understand that a fake reality cannot be expressed as if it were real. Perhaps this is why his mainstream novels are unconvincing. But the obverse of this: that a true reality can be expressed as if it was fake is exactly where PKD ended up in novels like THE MAN IN THE HIGH CASTLE; FLOW MY TEARS, THE POLICEMAN SAID and VALIS.

Which brings us full circle to the categorization of THE TRANSMIGRATION OF TIMOTHY ARCHER. Is it science fiction, fantasy or realism?

And now we have our answer: it is all of them at once because with the advent of VALIS all subsequent literature is post-modernist in nature. And a main tenet of post-modernism is that reality itself is brought into question and the literary category of realism is abolished. In a sense with VALIS Philip K. Dick, continuing on from A. E. Van Vogt, is doing a scientific task: the advancement of human knowledge. For with VALIS he brings out into the open that which he has only hinted at before; the recognition that accepted literary categories are redundant. Such artificialities as fantasy, science fiction and realism are meaningless in other than superficial ways when the nature of reality itself *is not known*.

Now if that accomplishment isn't a landmark in Western literature what is? As has been noted by his biographers, THE TRANSMIGRATION OF TIMOTHY ARCHER is a sort of *roman a clef* with Bishop Archer himself based on PKD's friend and former Bishop of California, James A. Pike. The character of Edgar Barefoot is supposedly Alan Watts, the British mystic who brought Zen to the hippie masses of California in the 60s and 70s, and Kirsten Lundborg is a loose portrait of Maren Hackett, his ex-wife Nancy's mother.[dcclxxv]

Discounting all theoretical consideration of post-modernism, THE TRANSMIGRATION OF TIMOTHY ARCHER is the story of Angel Archer and how she copes with death in her life.

The death of her husband, Jeff, by suicide, the death of her friend Kirsten by suicide, and the death of Bishop Pike himself from stupidity.

Unlike VALIS and THE DIVINE INVASION, it is not full of *EXEGESIS*-like speculation but religion and philosophy figure heavily into it. Underlying the plot, as we've seen, is the premise that ancient pre-Christian documents have been discovered in a Zadokite temple in the Middle-East. These documents, pre-dating Jesus by two hundred years, are full of the very ideas even down to the language used that have been ascribed to Jesus himself. This causes a massive doubt in the mind of Bishop Archer about whether Jesus was the Saviour or not; was the actual Son of God manifesting on Earth.. Bishop Archer's quandary is succinctly described:

> "My point," Tim said, "is that if the Logia predate Jesus by two hundred years, then the Gospels are suspect, we have no evidence that Jesus was God, very God, God incarnate, and therefore the basis of our religion is gone. Jesus simply becomes a teacher representing a particular Jewish sect that ate and drank some kind of – well, whatever it was, the *anokhi*, and it made them immortal."[dccclxxvi]

What makes matters worse for the good Bishop is that even the mystery of transubstantiation is brought into doubt when he finds out that the *anokhi* is a psychedelic mushroom out of which the Zadokites made a broth and a bread: they drank the broth and ate the bread. An actual authority on the Qumran scrolls (the Dead Sea scrolls), John Allegro, is referred to as having written a book about this in which he discovered that the early Christians were a secret mushroom cult. In his bibliography at the end of the novel PKD neglects, however, to mention which book of Allegro's he is talking about. Perhaps, as I think is much of PKD's religious speculation in this novel, his source is his *Encyclopedia Britannica*.[dccclxxvii]

Of course, given this about the *anokhi* mushroom, Jesus in the novel becomes a dope dealer and the Disciples nothing more than smugglers who get busted at the border while trying to run a supply of *anokhi* into a Roman city.

With his foundations falling apart, then, Bishop Archer and his girlfriend claim to experience ghostly visits from his dead son, Jeff. Both he and Kirsten believe that Jeff is trying to contact them from the 'other side.' The Bishop is going to write a book about it. This doesn't sit happily with Kirsten who sees his career as a powerful Bishop going down the tubes and her reflected status along with it.

Eventually, Bishop Archer, Kirsten and Angel Archer visit a medium who, despite Angel's skepticism (she sees the whole thing with the incorporeal Jeff as a *folie a deux* between the Bishop and Kirsten by which they assuage their guilty feelings) seems to be genuine in some respects. She predicts Kirsten's death and later Bishop Archer's death.

And Kirsten does kill herself after believing that her cancer had returned. Bishop Archer, in his quest for the *anoki* mushroom, visits the Judean desert and searches for the Zadokite wadi in a Datsun with a gas-station map and two bottles of Coca Cola. Without a guide or any aid he dies in the desert.

These deaths of her friends cause Angel to become numb, a machine without feelings. But in the end we flash backward to the day John Lennon was shot and Angel's visit to the mystic Edgar Barefoot.

Barefoot singles her out and tries to give her something to live by and, somewhat comforted, she goes on with her life.

After writing THE TRANSMIGRATION OF TIMOTHY ARCHER, Dick began thinking of his next contracted-for novel, THE OWL IN DAYLIGHT. And on TV he saw clips from *BLADE RUNNER* showing the special effects. In September the movie was done shooting and into the editing stage. It was also in September that PKD had one last visit from the AI voice. As he was falling asleep on Sep 17, 1981 he was startled into wakefulness by a vision of the Saviour, now named Tagore and living in Ceylon. This was more than a verbal contact, PKD actually saw Tagore if only vaguely. It was a vision that he said would remain with him as long as he lived and he believed it was his duty to tell it to the world. So, then, on Sep 23rd he wrote a letter to the sf fanzine *Niekas* and some other 85 people in which he described Tagore and his teachings.[dccclxxviii]

A new girlfriend came along in October but the relationship lasted only a month and toward the end of the year Phil was sort of getting back together with Tessa. One highlight in November was PKD being given the Hollywood star treatment when he was taken by limousine to a private showing of some special effects from *BLADE RUNNER*. With him he took his long-time friend Mary Wilson, who, being an actress, was familiar with the ways of Hollywood.[dccclxxix]

And for the new year 1982 he had been invited to return to Metz, France to be guest of honor at that year's Festival of Science Fiction. He and Ms. Wilson planned to go to the festival and then travel around Europe for a bit. But it wouldn't happen. For in 1982, a year that started out promisingly for PKD, it would all come to a sudden end.

1982

On Feb 17, 1982 after a final interview with biographer Gregg Rickman, Philip K. Dick called his psychiatrist complaining of failing eyesight and muddled thinking he'd experienced during the interview. His psychiatrist told him to go straight to the hospital but Dick didn't go.

The next day he was found unconscious in his apartment by his neighbors and an ambulance came and took him to the hospital. He was diagnosed as having had a stroke and although conscious he could not speak. There came more strokes and then heart failure. Philip K. Dick died on March 2, 1982. He is buried in the quiet heart of Ft. Morgan, Colorado next to his twin sister Jane. On the headstone there is an engraving of the face of a cat.[dccclxxx]

But even though PKD was dead new publications continued to come. The first hardback edition of THE TRANSMIGRATION OF TIMOTHY ARCHER came from Timescape in April. A reissue of CONFESSIONS OF A CRAP ARTIST also from Timescape appeared in May and the first edition of *BLADE RUNNER* as such the same month. The movie itself coming out in June. July had the first paperback edition of THE DIVINE INVASION and the first UK edition of THE TRANSMIGRATION OF TIMOTHY ARCHER was published by Gollancz in October.[dccclxxxi]

In the next few years and, indeed, into the 21st Century, editions of Philip K. Dick's novels and story collections continued to be published in the United States, Great Britain, and many more countries around the world. His popularity and respect have risen such that he is now considered the foremost American fiction writer – not just science fiction – of the last half of the 20th century. After his death PKD accomplished one of his main goals, that of becoming a mainstream writer. That he did it by abolishing the category altogether would probably have amused him.

APPENDICES

Apendix 1: A Question of Chronology: 1955 – 1958. By Lord RC, Dec 2003. This essay first appeared in PKD OTAKU, 2003.

In a letter to Anthony Boucher, editor at F&SF, in June 1957 Philip K. Dick states that he has "stopped writing short stuff for magazine publication back in May of '55..." The reception at the Scott Meredith Literary Agency of his short story "The Unreconstructed M" on June 2, 1955 seems to confirm this.[dccclxxxii]

But in 1958 we note the reception of three more short stories by the SMLA. These were: "Recall Mechanism", "Explorers We" and "War Game." On the face of it there is nothing wrong with this accepted chronology but when we look more closely at what is known about the publishing history of these three stories we note a couple of anomalies that cast doubt on the origin of two of them and by inference doubt on the third.

To me it is necessary to sort out the chronology of four stories: "The Unreconstructed M", "Recall Mechanism", "Explorers We" and "War Game." I see this as important because there is a gap of some five years uncertainty involved in the dating of these stories. These stories could have been written as early as 1953 or as late as 1958.

To figure out the likely actual composition dates we must take the evidence of these stories singly and then all together and put them in the context of what PKD was writing in this period.

We start with "The Unreconstructed M" and note that the manuscript for this story arrived at the SMLA on June 2, 1955. To support this date we have the above-mentioned letter he sent to Tony Boucher on June 3, 1957 in which he states "I have ceased to write either s.f. or fantasy, Tony; I stopped writing short stuff for magazine publication back in May of '55." This then would solidify the composition date for "The Unreconstructed M" as no later than May 1955.

The next story, "Recall Mechanism" reached the SMLA on May 2, 1958. But was it actually written shortly before that date as one might assume? Or was it written much earlier in 1955?

We have two reasons for saying that the story was probably written in the earlier time frame. First is a letter from PKD to Bill Hamlin, editor at Imagination, dated Sep 2, 1955 in which PKD refuses to do a rewrite of "Recall Mechanism". The second reason is more subjective and relies on another of our stories assigned to 1958 -- "Explorers We" -- and the uncertainty around its dating.[dccclxxxiii]

"Explorers We" reached the SMLA on May 6, 1958. However, there is evidence that it was written much earlier. In a letter to Tony Boucher, editor at F&SF dated April 8, 1954 PKD explicitly refers to this story "late in September of last year..." {1953}.[dccclxxxiv]

Taking these two cases together: "Recall Mechanism" and "Explorers We" and the doubt thrown on their 1958 ascription by these letters, then we find that if we assign their composition back to 1955 or earlier we have a stark anomaly in the chronology.

The short story "War Game" now stands out singly and sharply as the only remaining short story assigned to 1958. It nestles in its singularity amidst manuscripts of several novels including NICHOLAS AND THE HIGS, TIME OUT OF JOINT and IN MILT LUMKY TERRITORY. Now although the SMLA records delivery of "War Game' on Oct 31, 1958 would PKD drop his straight novel aspirations to suddenly revert to an earlier time and crank out a short science fiction story?

I think not. And when "War Game" is shorn of its 1958 bolster of "Recall Mechanism" and "Explorers We" and we take in PKD's statement that he stopped writing short fiction in May 1955 we can reasonably assign "War Game" to 1955 or earlier.

But, why then, if these three stories were written earlier, is their reception dates at the SMLA recorded in 1958?

The answer to this perhaps lies in the two letters mentioned above: "Recall Mechanism" due to Bill Hamlin wanting a rewrite and PKD not wanting to do it probably laid around the Agency or Dick's abode and just sort of got forgotten. And "Explorers We", also needing a rewrite, seems to have got lost in the shuffle between the Agency, Dick and *F&SF*.

With no earlier reference to "War Game" than 1958 we assume that sometime in early 1958 PKD went through his files or instructed the Agency to go through theirs to search for any unsold short stories. The four that showed up were "The Unreconstructed M", "Recall Mechanism", "Explorers We" and "War Game."

So, then, in light of this analysis we'll put these stories into our composition chronology at different dates than the accepted ones. Thus:

65. "Null-O", received at the SMLA on Aug 31, 1953
66. "Explorers We", referred in letter to Sep 1953
67. "To Serve The Master", received at the SMLA on Oct 21, 1953
...   Five novels, many short stories
85. "War Game", indeterminate, received at SMLA Oct 31, 1958
86. "Recall Mechanism", before Sep 1955 {before May 1955?}
87. "The Unreconstructed M", received at the SMLA on June 2, 1955

This ordering leaves the year 1958 with no short stories written and PKD working on his straight novels with a sporadic effort to get his old short stories published. It is then not until 1963 that PKD returned to writing short stories. "If There Were No Benny Cemoli" was the first of this series.

NOTES

[1] **SL-38 35:** {...}Tiresome as all this is, there's worse to come. I have ceased to write either s.f. or fantasy, Tony; I stopped writing short stuff for magazine publication back in May of '55; since then I've done only novels, both s.f. and what I call straight contemporary serious quality fiction about non-myth type people, and in the last year its been just the latter, the non-s.f. I have five of these novels in circulation (...){**PKD to A. Boucher, June 3, 1957**}

[1] **SL:38 34:** Dear Bill: My agent Scott Meredith has relayed to me your request for a rewrite on my story RECALL MECHANISM.
The story is a good one, and I am proud of it. When a rewrite improves the story I'm glad to perform it. I welcome suggestions that help a story. In this case, however, the rewrite would turn a good yarn into a cornball nothing.

With great pride, and a sense of my responsibility to writers in general, to my own ethics, and to science-fiction readers, I refuse.

I have informed Scott, and I assume he'll be looking for the MS back.

Cordially, Philip K. Dick {**PKD to Bill Hamling, Editor** *Imagination*, **Sep 2, 1955**}

[1] **SL:38 ?:** Dear Mr. Boucher, I'm sorry to keep bothering you with phone call and letter, but I understand that Scott Meredith is going to write to you about "Explorers We" and I wanted to get hold of you first.

As you recall, late in September of last year you wrote to me, expressing an interest in that story, and suggesting changes. I made changes and mailed them back within the week; during the first part of October. Since then I haven't heard hide nor hair from you, but I understand that you are officially away, these days, so I have been happy to wait. However, now I'm getting worried. Maybe there was a slip-up and you didn't receive my rewrite. Or something.

In any case, if you want another rewrite, etc, etc. let me know and I will produce. It may be that the time travel angle didn't convince you, in which case I'm sure another resolution can be found. Okay? Thanks a lot ... and maybe we could get together one of these days, as both of us repeatedly suggest.

Very truly yours, Phil Dick {**PKD>Tony Boucher, Apr 8, 1954**}

Appendix 2: PKD Research Survey

Many books and aricles have been written on the life and career of Philip K. Dick, the late, great Californian master of the science fiction novel. But how useful are these various efforts to explain PKD to the semi-serious student of the Master's work? To which should one turn for details of PKD's life, his philosophy, his novels and short stories?

Perhaps a survey of the surveyors is needed? As publisher of *For Dickheads Only*, a fanzine dedicated to the study of Philip K. Dick's work, I find the following materials most often stacked around me as I do my research.

The first of these is Gregg Rickman's *To The high Castle, Philip K. Dick: A Life 1925-1962*. (1989). I turn to this volume when I wish to find information on the publishing circumstances of PKD's early novels and short stories. For instance, one can look in the index under SOLAR LOTTERY and find nineteen citations, many of which are useful toward gaining an idea of why, when, and how PKD's first science fiction novel came to be published by Ace Books in 1955 (and as WORLD OF CHANCE by Rich & Cowan in 1956 in the U.K.). Most of PKD's early novels and many short stories are covered in similar depth. Of course, *To The High Castle* (TTHC) is primarily a biography and as such has details of PKD's life from birth until 1962 when he wrote his Hugo Award-winning novel THE MAN IN THE HIGH CASTLE. The only fault to this study of Rickman's to my mind is that Rickman appears to have certain *idee fixes* concerning PKD's childhood -- for example, it is here that we find mention and detailed exposition of PKD's supposed child molestation at the hands of one of his family. Also, there is too much reference to various psychological authorities to bolster Rickman's ideas. Well, perhaps the fault is mine; I have little time for psychological 'theorizing.'

Fortunately, there is another biography to complement Rickman's. This is Lawrence Sutin's *Divine Invasions*: *A Life of Philip K. Dick* (1989). To a researcher more interested in the history of PKD's novels themselves, this book lacks the concentration of Rickman's *To The High Castle* -- it covers PKD's complete career in slightly less pages than Rickman spends on the first 34 years. But it is useful, nevertheless, in that, between the two studies, one can build a more complete picture of how each of PKD's novels came to fruition. And as biography it of course lacks Rickman's psychological emphasis and is, thus, a more sympathetic portrait of the Master.

To these two indispensible biographical works one must add, in book form, Paul William's *Only Apparently Real* (1986). this slim volume of mostly interview material between Williams and PKD covers the events that surround the mysterious break-in of PKD's apartment in 1971 and touch on his 2/3-74 'Valis' experiences. As a friend of PKD's as well as his literary executor, Paul Williams perhaps comes closest to a feel for PKD as he was in real life. *Only Apparently Real* also includes in an appendix the definitive chronological ordering of PKD's work by order of composition -- a matter that has been somewhat shrouded in confusion.

There are two interviews available in book form: Gregg Rickman's *In His Own Words* (1984) and *The Last Testament* (1985). The first of these I find most useful as in it PKD discusses each of his novels with much digression into his life, his influences and the art of writing. The second volume delves more into PKD's philosophy and visions.

Some interview material is also available on audiocassette. Notable is Gregg Rickman's *Piper In The Woods* (1987) and John Boonstra's interviews of 1981. There may be more.

But now we're getting into the realm of the hard-to-come-by: the cassettes, the 'zines, the scholarly works, the obscure publications. There are many of these, one needs only to turn to the listings in Levack's *PKD: A Philip K. Dick Bibliography* (1981) -- if you can find a copy of this rare book -- or the more accessible Galactic Central bibliography, *PKD:Metaphysical Conjurer, A Working Bibliography* (1990) to find a feast of PhilDickiana large enough to satisfy any fans appetite.

Before taking a look at some of these more obscure items we must mention a few other important works without which a study of PKD cannot begin to be complete. The first of these is *In Pursuit Of VALIS: Selections From The Exegesis* (1991), compiled by Lawrence Sutin. This, apart from a few excerpts, is the lengthiest extraction of material from PKD's obsessive, mostly hand-written, notes that he wrote from 1974 till his death in 1982. Much is related here by PKD himself on his 2/3-74 mystical experiences and on many of his novels including VALIS, THE DIVINE INVASION, A MAZE OF DEATH, EYE IN THE SKY, A SCANNER DARKLY, FLOW MY TEARS, THE POLICEMAN SAID, and others. Mostly it is interpretation and theorizing as PKD tried to sort out the meaning of his visions and how his books tied into it all somehow. Until a complete edition of 'The Exegesis' is published (not planned at this time), this volume will have to serve to give us some idea of what it's all about. As a selection from a million-word project, *In Pursuit Of VALIS* has its faults, mainly in that a particularly fascinating excerpt will be unceremoniously cut off in mid-flight, as it were, leaving the reader grasping futilely at a glimmer of understanding only to see it wink out with the abrupt editing. Still, another indispensible volume for the comitted Dickophile.

In the academic world, quite a few books have been written and compiled on PKD. Most recent of these is *On PKD: 40 Articles From Science Fiction Studies* (1993). this volume of scholarly essays cannot be easily summarized. Suffice it to say that on every page there is much to think about: some of it startling, suggestive and illuminating, and some of it boring, idiotic and impenetrable. However, the book includes an interesting Introduction and a listing of all the PKD material housed in the California State University at Fullerton archives as well as a controversial Letters section, PKD's Foreward to his short-story collection, THE PRESERVING MACHINE, and Stanislaw Lem's "A Visionary Among The Charletans." This is a book no student of Philip K. Dick can afford to be without.

There are other academic-type books available, some serving as introductions to PKD's work and others which focus more on specific works. Of the former, I will mention Douglas Mackey's *Philip K. Dick (1988),* Hazel Pierce's *Philip K. Dick* (1983) and Kim Stanley Robinson's *The Novels Of Philip K. Dick* (1984). Of the latter, these bear mention: *Philip K. Dick* (1983) edited by Greenberg and Olander, and *Mind In Motion: The Fiction Of Philip K. Dick* (1987) by Patricia S. Warrick. There are many more.

Perhaps the single greatest resource for the Dickophile is the complete, 30-edition collection of *The Philip K. Dick Society Newsletter* (1982-92), edited by Paul Williams. This publication ceased after ten years in 1992 but is still available from the publisher. Each issue of PKDS, as it is known, contains a wealth of information on Philip K. Dick-related matters, including letters from fans, writers, critics and essays from same. Occasional interviews can also be found and much material on the stories and novels of PKD, even including some of Dick's correspondence with his publishers, excerpts from the Exegesis, photographs, theories, reviews, important essays, new editions, upcoming events such as movies, plays and musical works based on PKD's works. And a whole lot more. Now I've used the word 'indispensible' a lot in this survey but if there is one set of items that are truly so it is the collection of the *The Philip K. Dick Society Newsletter.*

Luckily for PKD fans the *The Philip K. Dick Society Newsletter* was replaced in 1992 by *Radio Free PKD*, edited by Greg Lee, and our own more occasional effort, *For Dickheads Only.*

Radio Free PKD has access to much of the material left over from the PKD Society files and is an ongoing forum for the discussionand dissemination of PKD's work and life. This is the zine to keep us up to date on the life after life of Philip K. Dick.

For Dickheads Only focuses in each issue on one of PKD's science fiction novels and includes letters from fans, reader want lists, xeroxed covers of ancient editions and essays on the novel at hand. A popular feature is the 'fave PKD story horse-race where readers vote for their favorite PKD story. The most recent issue concerned itself with SOLAR LOTTERY.

Now we must turn to the many and varied articles and interviews available (or not: much of this material seems to exist only in xerox form) in small press publications and science fiction magazines of various quality. A mere listing of the most prominent will have to do here.

An interesting and lengthy interview with PKD, conducted by Gwen Lee and Doris E. Sauter can be found in *Starlog #165*, April 1991, and another by Gregg Rickman in *Argosy* Nov 1990. And *Twilight Zone Magazine*, June 1982, has an interview with John Boonstra, while in *Science Fiction Eye, Vol.1, #2*, August 1987 we find another interview conducted with PKD by Richard Lupoff. Perhaps the oldest interview available is the one in *Science Fiction Review, #19*, August 1976, conducted by Daniel DePrez. And maybe the best of the lot is that by Charles Platt found in Platt's book *Dream Makers: The Uncommon People Who Write Science Fiction.* (1980). This book can still be found in libraries and occasionally in the used-book stores. And there are more interviews scattered about here and there. For the interested reader, acquiring one of the Philip K. Dick bibliographies mentioned above will be the best bet to find them.

In the world of 'other media' we must, of course, mention the two versions of the film BLADERUNNER (1982) based on PKD's novel DO ANDROIDS DREAM OF ELECTRIC SHEEP? The first videocassette version of this movie is the standard pan-and-scan version dating, perhaps, to 1983. This was recently superseded by the 'Director's Cut,' letter-boxed version of 1993. Also, Carolco has produced a version of TOTAL RECALL (1991) which was based on PKD's short story "We Can Remember It For You Wholesale." This videocassette came out in 1992.

In audiocassette form -- though I don't know where you'll be able to get them from -- can be found tapes of PKD's radio versions of his short stories, "The Defenders" and "Colony". The originals I have to hand are copyrighted 1986 by a company called 'Radio Showcase', address unknown. And a recent reading of PKD's short story, "The Short, happy Life Of The Brown Oxford" by Ed Begley Jr. is also out there somewhere. There are a few other items in this form but are just too obscure to mention here.

So, that should be enough for any fan of Philip K. Dick and his work who is willing and ready to take the next step into obsession! But be warned! Once in the world of PKD you may find, like Barney Mayerson of THE THREE STIGMATA OF PALMER ELDRITCH, that you can never be sure if you'll ever get out again.

-- Dave Hyde Jan 1994. {This article appeared in *Slipstream* in 1994}

A PHILIP K. DICK CHRONOLOGY, 1943-1982
Including his Novels and Short Stories Ordered by Composition

In this chronology I have modified the standard one compiled by Paul Williams and published in his book *ONLY APPARENTLY REAL* (see 'References') and reflected for the most part by the ordering of the short stories in the five volumes of THE COLLECTED STORIES OF PHILIP K. DICK.

While doing research for my manuscript *PINK BEAM: A Philip K. Dick Companion* I didn't hesitate to jump to conclusions on the slimmest of evidence that some story was incorrectly placed in the standard chronology. For example, the short story "Of Withered Apples" is now dated to a much earlier time than that given in the standard chronology.

There is still a lot of uncertainty involved in compiling a true chronology of Philip K. Dick stories. No doubt I have made mistakes. For these I apologise. But with this new compilation I'm proud to present the New Standard PKD Chronology -- Lord RC, Dec 2003.

Novels are in Bold Capital Letters, Short Stories are in Small Letters: Novels and Collections, because these are actual 'books', are in the same chronology (N) while short stories are in the (S) chronology.

Num	N	S	Title	Writing Date	SMLA Date	Pub. Date	Notes
1	1		**RETURN TO LILIPUT**	1943	Not completed	Not published	Lost ms
2		1	Stratosphere Betty	1943		Aug 30, 1943	Mimeo sheet, self-published
3		2	Stability	1947		1987	
4	2		**THE EARTH SHAKER**	1948-49			Outline and a few chapters remain
5		3	Of Withered Apples	1950c	Jan 1953	July 1954	
6	3		**GATHER YOURSELVES TOGETHER**	1951	May 1952	1994	
7		4	Roog	<Oct 1951		Feb 1953	Accepted at *F & SF* on Nov 15, 1951
8		5	Beyond Lies The Wub	<Dec 1951		July 1952	
9		6	The Little Movement	Feb 1952 <> Mar 1952		Nov 1952	Accepted at *F & SF* Feb 15, 1952
10		7	The Skull	<Mar 1952		Sep 1952	
11		8	Project: Earth	<Mar 1952		Dec 1953	
12		9	Expendable	<Mar 1952		July 1953	Accepted at *F & SF* Apr 7, 1952
13		10	The Short, Happy Life Of The Brown Oxford	Feb 1952 <> Apr1952		Jan 1954	Accepted at *F & SF May 7, 1952*
14		11	The Preserving Machine	Feb 1952 <> May1952		June 1953	Accepted at *F & SF May 15, 1952*

15		12	The Gun	<May 1952		Sep 1952	
16		13	Mr. Spaceship	Early 1952		Jan 1953	
17		14	Piper In The Woods	<May 1952		Feb 1953	
18		15	The Infinites	<May 1952		May 1953	
19		16	The Indefatigable Frog	<May 1952		July 1953	
20		17	The Variable Man	<May 1952		Sep 1953	
21		18	The Crystal Crypt	<May 1952		Jan 1954	
22		19	The Defenders	<May 1952		Jan 1953	
23	**4**		**VOICES FROM THE STREET**	< Jun 1952	June 1952	na	To be published in 2007
24		20	The Builder		July 23, 1952	Dec 1953	PKD's first short story sent to the SMLA?
25		21	Meddler		July 24, 1952	Oct 1954	
26		22	Paycheck		July 31, 1952	Jun 1953	
27		23	Out In The Garden		July 31, 1952	Aug 1953	
28		24	The Great C		July 31, 1952	Sep 1953	
29		25	The King of The Elves		Aug 4, 1952	Sep 1953	
30		26	Colony		Aug 11, 1952	Jun 1953	
31		27	Prize Ship		Aug 14, 1952	Winter 1954	
32		28	Nanny		Aug 26, 1952	Spring 1955	
33		29	The Cookie Lady		Aug 27, 1952	Jun 1953	
34		30	Beyond The Door		Aug 29, 1952	Jan 1954	
35		31	Second Variety		Oct 3, 1952	May 1953	
36		32	Jon's World		Oct 21, 1952	1954	
37		33	The Cosmic Poachers		Oct 22, 1952	Jul 1953	
38		34	Some Kinds Of Life		Nov 3, 1952	Oct 1953	
39		35	Progeny		Nov 3, 1952	Nov 1954	
40		36	Martians Come In Clouds		Nov 5, 1952	Jun 1953	
41		37	The Commuter		Nov 19, 1952	Aug 1953	
42		38	The World She Wanted		Nov 24, 1952	May 1953	
43		39	A Surface Raid		Dec 2, 1952	Jul 1955	
44		40	The Trouble With Bubbles		Jan 13, 1953	Sep 1953	
45		41	A Present For Pat		Jan 17, 1953	Jan 1954	
46		42	Breakfast At Twilight		Jan 17,	Jan 1954	

					1953	
47		43	The Hood Maker		Jan 26, 1953	Jul 1954	
48		44	Human Is		Feb 2, 1953	Winter 1955	
49		45	The Impossible Planet		Feb 11, 1953	Oct 1953	
50		46	Adjustment Team		Feb 11, 1953	Oct 1954	
51		47	Impostor		Feb 24, 1953	Jun 1953	
52		48	James P. Crow		Mar 17, 1953	May 1954	
53		49	Planet For Transients		Mar 23, 1953	Oct 1953	
54		50	Small Town		Mar 23, 1953	May 1954	
55		51	Souvenir		Mar 26, 1953	Oct 1954	
56		52	Survey Team		Apr 3, 1953	May 1954	
57		53	Vulcan's Hammer		Apr 16, 1953	1956	
58		54	Prominent Author		Apr 20, 1953	May 1954	
59		55	Fair Game		Apr 21, 1953	Sep 1959	
60		56	The Hanging Stranger		May 4, 1953	Dec 1953	
61		57	The Eyes Have It		May 13, 1953	Late 1953	
62		58	Time Pawn		Jun 5, 1953	Summer 1954	
63		59	The Golden Man		Jun 24, 1953	Apr 1954	
64		60	The Turning Wheel		Jul 8, 1953	1954	
65		61	The Last of The Masters		Jul 15, 1953	Nov 1954	
66		62	The Father-Thing		Jul 21, 1953	Dec 1954	
67		63	Strange Eden		Aug 4, 1953	Dec 1954	
68		64	A Glass of Darkness		Aug 19, 1953	Dec 1956	
69		65	Tony And The Beetles		Aug 31, 1953	Dec 1953	Also as "Retreat From Rigel"
70		66	Null-O		Aug 31, 1953	Dec 1958	
71		67	Explorers We	<Sep 1953	May 6, 1958	Jan 1959	See: **A Question Of Chronology**
72		68	To Serve The Master		Oct 21, 1953	Feb 1956	
73		69	Exhibit Piece		Oct 21, 1953	Aug 1954	
74		70	The Crawlers		Oct 29, 1953	Jul 1954	

75		71	Sales Pitch		Nov 19, 1953	Jan 1954	
76		72	Shell Game		Dec 22, 1953	Sep 1954	
77		73	Upon The Dull Earth		Dec 30, 1953	1954	
78		74	Foster, You're Dead!		Dec 31, 1953	1955	
79		75	Pay For The Printer		Jan 28, 1954	Oct 1956	
80		76	War Veteran		Feb 17, 1954	Mar 1955	
81	5		**SOLAR LOTTERY**		Mar 23, 1954	May 1955	
82	6		**WORLD OF CHANCE**		Mar 23, 1954	Jun 1956	A UK version of SOLAR LOTTERY
83		77	The Chromium Fence		Apr 19, 1954	Jul 1955	
84		78	Misadjustment		May 14, 1954	Feb 1957	
85		79	A World Of Talent		Jun 4, 1954	Oct 1954	
86		80	Psi-Man, heal My Child!		Jun 8, 1954	Nov 1955	
87		81	Service Call		Oct 11, 1954	Jul 1955	
88		82	Autofac		Oct 11, 1954	Nov 1955	
89		83	Captive Market		Oct 18, 1954	Apr 1955	
90		84	The Mold Of Yancy		Oct 18, 1954	Aug 1955	
91		85	The Minority Report		Dec 22, 1954	Jan 1956	
92	7		**THE WORLD JONES MADE**		Dec 28, 1954	Mar 1956	
93	8		**EYE IN THE SKY**		Feb 15, 1955	1957	
94	9		**MARY AND THE GIANT**	1953<> Jun 1955		Apr 1987	
95		86	War Game		Oct 31, 1958		See: **A Question Of Chronology**
96		87	Recall Mechanism	<Sep 1955	May 2, 1958		See: **A Question Of Chronology**
97		88	The Unreconstructed M		Jun 2, 1955		See: **A Question Of Chronology**
98	10		**A HANDFUL OF DARKNES (Col.)**			Aug 1955	
99	11		**THE MAN WHO JAPED**		Oct 17, 1955	Dec 1956	
100	12		**A TIME FOR GEORGE STAVROS**	Late 1955 - Early 1956		na	Lost ms
101	13		**PILGRIM ON THE HILL**		Nov 8, 1956	na	Lost ms
102	14		**THE BROKEN BUBBLE**		Nov 13, 1956	1988	

103	15		**THE COSMIC PUPPETS**		May 1, 1957	Oct 1957	Exp. "A Glass Of Darkness"
104	16		**PUTTERING ABOUT IN A SMALL LAND**		May 15, 1957	Oct 1985	
105	17		**THE VARIABLE MAN (Col.)**			Jun 1957	
106	18		**NICHOLAS AND THE HIGS**	Late 1957 - Early 1958		na	Lost ms
107	19		**TIME OUT OF JOINT**	Jan 1958	Apr 7, 1958		
108	20		**IN MILT LUMKY TERRITORY**		Oct 8, 1958	Jun 1985	
109	21		**DR. FUTURITY**		Jul 28, 1959	Feb 1960	Exp. "Time Pawn"
110	22		**CONFESSIONS OF A CRAP ARTIST**	mid-1959		1975	
111	23		**THE MAN WHOSE TEETH WERE ALL EXACTLY ALIKE**	Early 1960		Jun 1984	
112	24		**VULCAN'S HAMMER**	Exp. Mar-Apr 1960		Sep 1960	Exp. "Vulcan's Hammer"
113	25		**HUMPTY DUMPTY IN OAKLAND**		Oct 1960	Oct 1986	
114	26		**THE MAN IN THE HIGH CASTLE**	Fall 1961	Nov 1961	Oct 1962	
115	27		**WE CAN BUILD YOU**		Oct 4, 1962	Jul 1972	
116		89	All We Marsmen		Oct 31, 1962		Serialization of MARTIAN TIME-SLIP
117	28		**MARTIAN TIME-SLIP**		Oct 31, 1962	Apr 1964	
118	29		**DR. BLOODMONEY**		Feb 11, 1963	Jun 1965	
119		90	If There Were No Benny Cemoli		Feb 27, 1963	Dec 1963	
120		91	Novelty Act		Mar 23, 1963	Feb 1964	
121		92	Waterspider		Apr 10, 1963	Jan 1964	
122		93	What The Dead Men Say		Apr 15, 1963	Jun 1964	
123		94	Orpheus With Clay Feet		Apr 16, 1963	1964	
124		95	Stand-By		Apr 18, 1963	Oct 1963	
125		96	The Days Of Perky Pat		Apr 18, 1963	Dec 1963	
126		97	What'll We Do With Ragland Park?		Apr 29, 1963	Nov 1963	
127		98	Oh To Be A Blobel!		May 6, 1963	Feb 1964	
128		99	The Little Black Box		May 6, 1963	Aug 1964	
129		100	The War With The Fnools			Spring 1964	
130	30		**THE GAME-PLAYERS OF TITAN**		Jun 4, 1963	Dec 1963	

131	31		**THE SIMULACRA**	Mar 1963 <> Aug 1963	Aug 28, 1963	Aug 1964	
132		101	Cantata 140		Sep 9, 1963	Jul 1964	Accepted at ***F&SF*** on Jan 13, 1964
133	32		**NOW WAIT FOR LAST YEAR**		Dec 4, 1963	May 1966	
134	33		**THE ZAP GUN**	Oct-Dec 1963	Dec 5, 1963	1967	
135		102	Precious Artifact		Dec 9, 1963	Oct 1964	
136		103	A Game of Unchance		Dec 9, 1963	Jul 1964	
137		104	Retreat Syndrome		Dec 23, 1963	Jan 1965	
138	34		**CLANS OF THE ALPHANE MOON**	Dec 1963 - Jan 1964	Jan 16, 1964	Nov 1964	
139	35		**THE CRACK IN SPACE**	Sep 1963 - Mar 1964	Mar 17, 1964	Feb 1966	
140	36		**THE THREE STIGMATA OF PALMER ELDRITCH**	Early 1964	Mar 18, 1964	Nov 1964	
141	37		**THE PENULTIMATE TRUTH**	Mar 1964 - May 1964	May 12, 1964	Sep 1964	
142		105	The Unteleported Man	Mid 1964	Aug 26, 1964	Dec 1964	
143	38		**THE UNTELEPORTED MAN**	Exp. Nov 1964 - Mar 1965		Nov 1966	Exp. of "The Unteleported Man"
144		106	Your Appointment Will Be Yesterday		Aug 27, 1965	Aug 1966	
145		107	We Can Remember It For You Wholesale		Sep 13, 1965	Apr 1966	
146		108	Holy Quarrel		Sep 13, 1965	May 1966	
147		109	Not By Its Cover		Sep 21, 1965	Summer 1968	
148		110	Return Match		Oct 14, 1965	Feb 1967	
149	39		**COUNTERCLOCK WORLD**	1965 - 1966		Feb 1967	
150	40		**THE GANYMEDE TAKEOVER**	1964 - 1966		Jun 1967	idea in 1964
151		111	Faith Of Our Fathers		Jan 17, 1966	1967	
152	41		**DO ANDROIDS DREAM OF ELECTRIC SHEEP?**		Jun 20, 1966	Mar 1968	
153	42		**UBIK**		Dec 7, 1966		
154	43		**NICK AND THE GLIMMUNG**		Dec 7, 1966	Jun 1988	
155	44		**GALACTIC POT-HEALER**	Nov 1967 <> Feb 1968		Jun 1969	
156	45		**THE PRESERVING MACHINE (Col.)**			Apr 1969	Collection began in 1965
157		112	The Story To End All Stories For Harlan Ellison's	Fall 1968		Fall 1968	in ***Niekas #20***

			DANGEROUS VISIONS				
158	46		**A MAZE OF DEATH**	Mid-1968	Oct 1968	Jul 1970	
159	47		**OUR FRIENDS FROM FROLIX 8**	Oct 1968 <> Jun 1969	Outline Nov 6, 1968	Jun 1970	
160		113	The Electric Ant	Nov 1968	Jan 4, 1969	Oct 1969	accepted at *F&SF* Dec 4, 1968
161	48		**FLOW MY TEARS, THE POLICEMAN SAID**	May 1970 <> Jan 1973	Feb 7, 1973	1974	
162		114	Cadbury, The Beaver That lacked	1970	Dec 1971?	1987	
163	49		**A SCANNER DARKLY**	1972- 1976		Jan 1977	Began in 1972
164		115	A Little Something For Us Tempunauts	Dec 1972?	Feb 13, 1973	1974	
165	50		**THE BOOK OF PHILIP K. DICK**			Feb 1973	Collection
166		116	The Pre-Persons		Dec 20, 1973?	Oct 1974	
167	51		**UBIK: The Screenplay**	Sep - Oct 1974		1985	
168		117	The Eye Of The Sibyl		May 15, 1975	Mar 1987	
169	52		**DEUS IRAE**	1964 - 1976		Jul 1976	Began in 1964
170	53		**RADIO FREE ALBEMUTH**	1976	Aug 19, 1976	Dec 1985	
171	54		**THE BEST OF PHILIP K. DICK**			Mar 1977	Collection
172		118	The Day Mr. Computer Fell Out Of its Tree	Summer 1977		1987	
173	55		**VALIS**	Oct - Nov 1978	Nov 29, 1978	Feb 1981	
174		119	The Exit Door Leads In	Jun 1979	Jun 21, 1979	Fall 1979	
175		120	Chains Of Air, Web Of Aethyr		Jul 9, 1979	1980	
176		121	Strange Memories Of Death	Late 1979	Mar 27, 1980	1984	
177	56		**THE DIVINE INVASION**	Mar 1980		Jun 1981	
178		122	I Hope I Shall Arrive Soon	1979 - 1980	Apr 24, 1980	Dec 1980	
179	57		**THE GOLDEN MAN**			Feb 1980	Collection
180		123	Rautavaara's Case		May 13, 1980	Oct 1980	
181		124	Fawn, Look Back	Aug 1980		Aug 1987	outline
182		125	The Alien Mind	Early 1981		Feb 1981	
183	58		**THE TRANSMIGRATION OF TIMOTHY ARCHER**	Apr - May 1981	May 13, 1981	Apr 1982	
184	59		**THE OWL IN DAYLIGHT**	Outline 1981		na	outline only and interview notes

REFERENCES

Aquarian The Aquarian, Oct 11, 1978 interview by Joe Vitale

The PKD Materials at the Bowling Green State University Popular Culture Library, Bowling Green, Ohio (Aug 1997). Brief prepared by Patrick Clark.

brg #1, Oct 1990. A talk written by Bruce Gillespie for the Oct 1990 meeting of the Nova Mob; for ANZAPA (Australia and New Zealand Amateur Publishing Association)

Denver Clarion, Oct 23, 1980 'Philip K. Dick: Confessions of an SF Artist' an interview by George Cain and Dana Longo.

THE DARK-HAIRED GIRL, Mark Ziesing Publisher, hb, 1988, ISBN: 0-929480-03-1

DIVINE INVASIONS:A Life of Philip K. Dick. By Lawrence Sutin, Harmony Books, hb, 1989. ISBN: 0-517-57204-4

For Dickheads Only, Ed. David Hyde, 1992-1997. Kokomo, Indiana.

PHILIP K. DICK: Metaphysical Conjuror, Phil Stephenson-Payne and Gordon Benson Jr., Galactic Central Press,1991.'Imladris', 25a Copgrove Rd., Leeds, W. Yorks, LS8 2SP, England OR POBox 40494, Albuquerque, NM 87196. ISBN: 1-871133-20-3 (3rd revised edition)

HOUR 25: A Talk With Philip K. Dick, hosted by Mike Hodel, KPFK-FM, North Hollywood, California, June 26, 1976. Transcribed by Frank C. Bertrand on www.philipkdick.com

IN HIS OWN WORDS by Gregg Rickman, Fragments West /The Valentine Press, 2705 E. 7th St., Long Beach, CA 90804. 1984/1988.ISBN: 0-916063-01-1 (1988 edition)

IN PURSUIT OF VALIS: Selections From The Exegesis, Ed. Lawrence Sutin,:Underwood-Miller Press, 708 Westover Drive, Lancaster, PA 17601, hb, 1991, ISBN: 0-88733-093-2

PKD: A Philip K. Dick Bibliography, by Daniel J. H. Levack, Underwood-Miller Press, tp, 1981. ISBN: 0-934438-33-1

Niekas #11, Mar 1965. "Schizophrenia & The Book Of Changes"

Niekas # 34, 1986. "Bumbejimas: PKD And Me" by Ed Meskys

ONLY APPARENTLY REAL, by Paul Williams, Arbor House, New York, tp, 1986. ISBN: 0-87795-800-9

ON PHILIP K. DICK: 40 Articles from *Science Fiction Studies*. Editors: R.D.Mullen, Istvan Csicsery-Ronay Jr,. A.B.Evans, Veronica Hollinger. SF-TH Inc., East College, DePauw University, Greencastle, IN 46135-0037. 1992. ISBN: 0-9633169-1-5

POCKET ESSENTIALS PHILIP K. DICK by Andrew M. Butler, Pocket Essentials Press (UK), pb, 2000. ISBN: 1-903047-29-3

PKD: Electric Shepherd by Bruce Gillespie, Norstrillia Press (Australia), 1975

PKD OTAKU #1, Patrick Clark Publisher, MN 2001. Also subsequent issues of this zine.

THE PHILIP K. DICK SOCIETY NEWSLETTER, Ed. Paul Williams, POBox 611, Glen Ellen, CA (not current) 1982-1992

Playboy Dec 1980 (The story "Frozen Journey")

RADIO FREE PKD, Greg Lee Publisher, Noel Productions, 27068 S. La Paz, #430, Aliso Viejo, CA 92656, 1992-1997.

Rolling Stone, Nov 6, 1975. 'The True Stories Of Philip K. Dick' by Paul Williams.

Rouzleweave #1, Perry Kinman Publisher, Japan, March 2002 (and subsequent issues of this zine).

SF Commentary #9, Feb 1970. Also #54.

SF Commentary, July-Sep 1973. 'Philip K. Dick: Breakthroughs And Break-ins' an open letter from Philip K. Dick to John Sladek, Apr 23, 1973.

Science Fiction Eye magazine, Vol.1 #2, Aug 1987. 'A Conversation With Philip K. Dick' by Richard Lupoff

Science Fiction Review #19, *Vol.5, #3*, Aug 1976. 'An Interview With Philip K. Dick' by Daniel DePrez

Simulacrum Meltdown #3, Ed. Patrick Clark, Oct 2001.

THE SELECTED LETTERS OF PKD: 1938 - 71, Underwood-Miller Books, hb, 1996. ISBN: 1-887424-21-0.

THE SELECTED LETTERS OF PKD: 1974, Underwood-Miller Books, hb, 1991. ISBN: 0-99733-104-1

Starlog Feb 1982, May 1982, Aug 1982.Nov 1982.

Starmont Reader's Guide 12, by Hazel Pierce, Starmont House, Mercer Island, WA, 1982. ISBN: 0-916732-34-7.

THE COLLECTED STORIES OF PHILIP K. DICK, Vols 1-5, Citadel-Twilight Press, tp, 1990-1991. ISBN: 0-8065-1153-2; 0-8065-1226-1; 0-8065-1276-8 etc.

PHILIP K. DICK: The Dream Connection by D.S. Apel, The Permanent Press, San Jose, California, 1987. LCCCN: 87-60689.

THE DREAM MAKERS:The Uncommon People Who Write Science Fiction by Charles Platt, Berkley Books, pb, New York, 1980. ISBN: 0-425-04668-0.

The Patchin Review #5, Oct-Dec 1982. PKD interview with John Boonstra.

THE GOLDEN MAN, Ed. Mark Hurst, Berkley, hb, SFBC, 1980. "Story Notes"

THE NOVELS OF PKD by Kim Stanley Robinson, ?

THE SHIFTING REALITIES OF PHILIP K. DICK: Selected Literary And Philosophical Writings, Ed. Lawrence Sutin, Vintage Press, tp, 1995. ISBN: 0-679-74787-7

TO THE HIGH CASTLE: Philip K. Dick, A Life: 1928-1962, by Gregg Rickman, Fragments-West/The Valentine Press, pb, 1989. ISBN: 0-916063-24-0

The Twilight Zone magazine Vol.2 #3, June 1982. John Boonstra interviewer.

Vertex, Vol.1 #6, Feb 1974. Interviewer Arthur Byron Cover

Weirdo #?, 'The Religious Experience of Philip K. Dick' by R. Crumb

Welcome To Reality: The Nightmares of Philip K. Dick, Ed. Uwe Anton, Broken Mirrors Press, tp, 1991, ISBN: 0-9623824-5-0

INDEX

FOOTNOTES

[i] See **TO THE HIGH CASTLE: Philip K. Dick, A Life: 1928-1962, Gregg Rickman, Fragments West/The Valentine Press, pb, 1989. ISBN: 0-916063-24-0** (Hereinafter referenced as **TTHC**) and **DIVINE INVASIONS: A Life Of Philip K. Dick, Lawrence Sutin, Harmony Books, hb, 1989, ISBN: 0-517-57204-4** (Herein after referenced as **DI**)

[ii] **ONLY APPARENTLY REAL, Paul Williams, Arbor House, New York, tp, 1986. ISBN: 0-87795-800-9.** Hereinafter **OAR**.

[iii] **THE COLLECTED STORIES OF PHILIP K. DICK, Volumes 1 to 5, Citadel Twilight, tp, 1990. ISBN: 0-8065-1153-2** (Hereinafter **CSVol1-5**)

[iv] The Scott Meredith Literary Agency will be abbreviated henceforth as SMLA, sometimes as the Agency. The Agency starts listing submissions in July but Rickman dates PKD's signing with the SMLA in May 1952.

[v] These records are extensively referenced in the biographies mentioned above as well as in the pages of *The Philip K. Dick Society Newsletter* (1982-1992) edited by Paul Williams. Throughout my own study these books and the PKDS Newsletter (hereinafter **PKDS**) are the ones I've most relied on. A reading of the books in particular would be suggested before one even reads this present study.

[vi] TTHC 149. See also the Appendix B in TTHC p386 for a list of this early work.

[vii] TTHC 151. To my mind 18,000 words does not constitute a novel but to the schoolboy Phil it may have. I don't know if he worked further on the story after Oct 1943.

[viii] **Hour 25: A Talk With Philip K. Dick, hosted by Mike Hodel, KPFK-FM, North Hollywood, California. June 26, 1976.** Transcribed by Frank C. Bertrand on WWW.Philipkdick.com. Hereinafter **Hour 25**.

[ix] TTHC 151

[x] TTHC 152. One of these stories, "Santa's Return" is published in Appendix C of TTHC.

[xi] TTHC 156. I've included these short poems here, just as Rickman presented them, so that the reader without access to Rickman's biography can get a sense of how the poems read and decide whether or not they 'read like' early work of PKD.

[xii] DI 317-318 footnotes

[xiii] DI 41. Although Sutin discusses the "Teddy" poems in the above footnote (DI 317-318), he did not stress the connection between the present quote on p41 of DI and his belief that the "Teddy" poems were done by PKD – perhaps as he wrote his book Sutin didn't make the connection as the two passages are so far apart (p41 to p317). To me, though, it is most likely that this was the point that PKD actually stopped sending anything to Aunt Flo. PKD directly says here: "last contribution, I think. Have gotten to the point where she doesn't understand my pieces. No point in sending in any more." This would certainly negate the "Teddy" poems and the whole "Teddy" contention – that is, if the young PKD kept to his written word.

[xiv] TTHC 154. For a detailed look at this early work of PKD I suggest a reading of Chapter 15. The Young Author's Club in TTHC and the Appendix B: Literary Chronology, 1940-1961.

[xv] DI 46. And TTHC 216. Rickman ascribes the date to Paul Williams.

[xvi] DI 63-64. See also GC, 3rd Rev. Ed., p91.

[xvii] For details of the plot of THE EARTHSHAKER, see DI and TTHC.

[xviii] TTHC 254.

[xix] **Rouzleweave #3, Ed. Perry Kinman, zine, Japan, Aug 2002, p4.** Kleo was married to Phil on Jun 14 1950; they were divorced in Feb 1959.

[xx] TTHC 283-4. 'S.M.' would be PKD's literary agent, Scott Meredith, who he contacted first in May 1952. In Paul Williams' *ONLY APPARENTLY REAL*, VOICES IN THE STREET is given chronological priority. Lawrence Sutin in the 'Chronological Survey and Guide' (DI 290ff) dates GATHER YOURSELVES TOGETHER to 1949-50.

[xxi] See SL-38 41. PKD in a letter to James Blish, February 10th, 1958.

[xxii] GATHER YOURSELVES TOGETHER, WCS Books, hb, 05-7, June **1994**, 291pp, $40 (James Kibo Perry) ISBN: 1-878914-05-7.

[xxiii] GSM's PKD Xerox collection.

[xxiv] **THE SELECTED LETTERS OF PHILIP K. DICK: 1938 – 1971, Underwood Books, hb, 1996. ISBN: 1-887424-21-0.** (Hereinafter **SL-38**). PKD to Francis McComas, Oct 29, 1951

[xxv] DI 71. Sutin says PKD was paid $75 for "Roog" – a generous and encouraging sum for the day.

[xxvi] SL-38 19. PKD to Anthony Boucher and J. Francis McComas, Nov 8, 1951. The new title PKD refers to in this letter is "Roog," the editors at *F & SF* changed it from PKD's original "Friday Morning." Gordon Van Gelder in communication with the author states that "Roog" was accepted at *F & SF* on Nov 15, 1951.

[xxvii] CSVol1, p401.

[xxviii] Ibid. The 'anthologer' PKD writes about is Judith Merrill.

[xxix] **Science Fiction Eye, Vol. 1, No. 2, August 1987**, pp. 45-54. Richard Lupoff interviewer. (Hereinafter **SF EYE**)

[xxx] TTHC 254

[xxxi] DI 69

[xxxii] CSVol1 p403. Also THE BEST OF PHILIP K. DICK, Ballantine, 1977, p446

[xxxiii] **THE SHIFTING REALITIES OF PHILIP K. DICK: Selected Literary and Philosophical Writings, Ed. Lawrence Sutin, Vintage Press, tp, 1995, ISBN: 0-679-74787-7, p.14.** Hereinafter **TSR**.

[xxxiv] *Radio Free PKD,* **Newsletter (Ed. Greg Lee), 1992-1997,** (Hereinafter **RFPKD**). RFPKD #3, p1. Also in the Introduction to "Beyond Lies The Wub" in FIRST VOYAGES, Avon, pb, 1981

[xxxv] CS Vol1 p403

[xxxvi] SL-38 42, PKD to The Editors of *F & SF*, Mar 19, 1952

[xxxvii] SL-38 42. PKD to Tony Boucher, Oct 29, 1958.

[xxxviii] (1982): THE EUREKA YEARS {Ed.: McComas} Bantam; (1984:): ROBOTS, ANDROIDS AND MECHANICAL ODDITIES

[xxxix] PKDS-22/23 12

[xl] **THE PHILIP K. DICK SOCIETY NEWSLETTER** (Hereinafter **PKDS**) **#22/23**, p12. Underwood-Miller published the five volume set of THE SELECTED LETTERS OF PHILIP K. DICK as well as the first editions of THE COLLECTED STORIES OF PHILIP K. DICK.

[xli] TSR 14

[xlii] In his 1968 'Self Portrait', PKD mentions *Astounding* and *Galaxy*. These two magazines were the most prestigious of the time and writing of selling stories to each of them in 1968 would be more impressive than recalling *Imagination*, which was considered by science fiction fans in the 1950s as of lesser quality than *Astounding* and *Galaxy*.

[xliii] TTHC 253

[xliv] PKDS-22/23 12

[xlv] SL-38 21. PKD to Anthony Boucher, Mar 5, 1952. See also SL-38 19. PKD to Anthony Boucher and J. Francis McComas, Nov 8, 1951.

[xlvi] SL-38 29. "Left Shoe, My Foot" is an early title for "The Short, Happy Life Of The Brown Oxford." The author has email from ??? that the foreign rights sold were to the French magazine *Fiction*.

[xlvii] Gordon van Gelder to Lord RC, email, Feb 2003.

[xlviii] CSVol1 403. PKD in 1976. Also in THE BEST OF PKD, Ballantine, 1977, p447.

[xlix] SL-38 20. PKD to The Editors of *F & SF*, Feb 11, 1952. "Left Shoe, My Foot" was later retitled "The Short, Happy Life Of The Brown Oxford."

[l] Sl-38 21. PKD to Boucher Mar 5, 1952.

[li] SL-38 23. PKD to Boucher Apr 13, 1952.

[lii] SL-38 23. PKD to The Editors of *F & SF*, May 7, 1952.

[liii] SL-38 22. PKD to Anthony Boucher, April 12, 1952.

[liv] SL-38 29. PKD to Boucher, May 18, 1953. Although this issue of *F & SF* is dated June, it was – and still is – the practice of magazine publishers to issue their publications a month before the cover date, thus PKD responds to the printing of his story in May.

[lv] Found in TTHC 263. Clareson's essay titled "Planet Stories" is in SCIENCE FICTION, FANTASY, AND WEIRD FICTION MAGAZINES, ?, ? pp479-80.

[lvi] TTHC 261.

[lvii] TTHC 429 fn. 25. Also see GC, 3rd Rev. Ed, Part 2, p50. Air date given as May 22, 1956. Reading issued on audiocassette in 1961 by Living Literature, inc.

[lviii] PKD's short story *Waterspider*, in THE COLLECTED STORIES OF PHILIP K. DICK, Vol. 4, p. 230-231. 'Anderson' here is sf writer Poul Anderson. See "Waterspider."

[lix] We can date this initial contact between Dick and the SMLA to shortly before May 6, 1952 when Scott Meredith wrote to Dick insisting that he handle all of PKD's writing and not just the "off trail pieces that are difficult to sell." (See TTHC 258)

[lx] Rickman sets the figure at 15 short stories sold before PKD joined the SMLA. (TTHC 256) and my own count reaches the same number.

[lxi] TTHC 283: "Dick joined the Scott Meredith Agency so that they could circulate the manuscripts of his harder to sell items, it will be recalled; GATHER was probably what Dick had on hand, in mid-1952, for Meredith to sell.

There's no doubt in my mind that Dick was writing what I believe to be his second book, VOICES FROM THE STREET, in June 1952; the book is set right at that time, and is dedicated "To S.M.'"

lxii VOICES FROM THE STREET is unpublished but is about people working in a TV store and likely draws on Phil's years of experience as a sales clerk at Art Music.

lxiii TTHC 284. Rickman sees VOICES as being superior to GATHER.

lxiv TTHC 264.

lxv **THE GOLDEN MAN {Ed. Mark Hurst}, Berkley, hb, SFBC, 1980, "Story Notes", p323. (Hereinafter TGM.)**

lxvi CSVol1, p404. End Notes. Also in THE BEST OF PKD, Ballantine, 1977, p446.

lxvii TGM 321. Story Notes

lxviii TTHC 429: fn25. See also GC, 3rd Rev. Ed, Part 2, p49. Air date given as Oct 10, 1956.

lxix **Hour 25**: A Talk With Philip K. Dick hosted by Mike Hodel, KPFK-FM, North Hollywood, California. June 26, 1976. Transcribed by Frank C. Bertrand. Hereinafter **HOUR 25**.

lxx THE BEST OF PKD, Ballantine, 1977, p447.

lxxi GC, 3rd Rev. Ed., Part 2 – Non-fiction, p49.

lxxii TTHC 263

lxxiii Levack 123. Also in THE BEST OF PKD, Ballantine, 1977, p446.

lxxiv *The Patchin Review*, **No. 5. Oct-Dec 1982**, pp2-6. Interviewer John Boonstra. See DO ANDROIDS DREAM OF ELECTRIC SHEEP? For more from this interview.

lxxv TTHC 263

lxxvi TTHC 265

lxxvii See my essay on "Beyond Lies The Wub" in *For Dickheads Only* **#5, Ed. Dave Hyde, Ganymedean Slime Mold Prods, zine, Kokomo, Indiana, 1995.** Hereinafter **FDO**.

lxxviii TTHC 263

lxxix In FDO #5, The 'Wub' issue, I expand on this notion.

lxxx TTHC 237

1953

lxxxi TTHC 263

lxxxii Levack 84. Also in THE BEST OF PKD, Ballantine, 1977, p448.

lxxxiii TTHC 254

lxxxiv SL-38 129. PKD to Terry Carr, Nov 20, 1964. I'm not sure what collection PKD is referring to here in this 1964 letter. The nearest one in time published by Ace Books is THE PRESERVING MACHINE in 1969. This collection only has nine stories in it, none of which is "Human Is." Surely it didn't take five years to assemble this collection?

lxxxv Levack 99. Also in THE BEST OF PKD, Ballantine, 1977, p449.

lxxxvi Levack 81. THE SANDS OF MARS AND OTHER STORIES (Australian), Jubilee Publications Pty Ltd., Sydney, undated (No 213, March 1958). This is the third issue of the "Satellite Series", whose numbering started with No 211.

lxxxvii In *Galaktika 52*, ?, tp, 1983, ?, ? (?) Tr. Into **Hungarian** as "Helyreigazito Csoport."

lxxxviii **The PKD Materials at the Bowling Green State University Popular Culture Library, Bowling Green, Ohio (Aug 1997) Brief prepared by Patrick Clark.** (Hereinafter BGSU Papers) {PKD > Sidney Meredith, SMLA, 5-26-1968}

lxxxix GREAT SCIENCE FICTION OF THE 20TH CENTURY {Ed. Silverberg and Greenburg}, Crown-Avenal, hb, 1987. Introduction

xc Levack 101. Also in THE BEST OF PKD, Ballantine, p447.

xci Found in TTHC 263. Clareson's essay titled "Planet Stories" is in SCIENCE FICTION, FANTASY, AND WEIRD FICTION MAGAZINES, "?, ? pp479-80. See above, fn. xlix. "The Infinites."

xcii THE GOLDEN MAN story notes by PKD

xciii TTHC 389

xciv Levack 132. At 28,000-plus words it's quite a long story but whether it fits in better with what PKD was writing in 1953 or 1954 I cannot really tell.

xcv SL-38 51. PKD in a letter to Scott Meredith, 1-4-60.

1954

[xcvi] "The Eyes have It" was selected for: *101 SCIENCE FICTION STORIES*, (ed. Greenberg, Waugh), Crown-Avenal, hb, 1986 and *THE GIANT BOOK OF SCIENCE FICTION STORIES,* Magpie, hb, 1992.

[xcvii] Patrick Clark notes that "Cantata 140" was also omitted from THE COLLECTED STORIES; because it was included wholesale as the first part of THE CRACK IN SPACE. See Sim Melt#2, Ed. P. Clark, zine, 2000.

[xcviii] See SIM MELT#2, p6ff 'The Doctor Will See You Now: The Evolution Of DR. FUTURITY, Part One: Time Pawn' by Patrick Clark

[xcix] TTHC 263

[c] Between 1952 and 1964 PKD had thirteen stories published in *If*. As far as I can determine PKD had only one story ever published in John W. Campbell, Jr.'s magazines and that was "Impostor" in *Astounding*.

[ci] THE COLLECTED STORIES OF PHILIP K. DICK, Vol.3, Citadel Twilight, tp, 1991. ISBN: 0-8065-1226-1, p411-412. (Hereinafter CSVol3)

[cii] TTHC 244

[ciii] TGM 'Story Notes'

[civ] **Starmont Reader's Guide 12, by Hazel Pierce, Starmont House, Mercer Island, WA, 1982. ISBN: 0-916732-34-7. Hereinafter SRG.**

[cv] SL-38 30. PKD to A. Boucher and A. McComas, Sep 2 1953

[cvi] SL-38 31. PKD to A. Boucher and A. McComas, Sep 6 1953

[cvii] TCSVol3, p413. Also in THE BEST OF PKD, Ballantine, 1977, p448.

[cviii] TTHC 22. PKD to Ann, Oct 14 1975.

[cix] Ivan Linderman to the author, Jan 2003: The 1956 film "Invasion of the Body Snatchers" was based on Jack Finney's 1955 novelization of his 1954 three-part serial, "The Body Snatchers." All the essential features of Finney's story were published in the November 26, December 10, and December 24, 1954 editions of *Collier's* magazine, predating Dick's December 1954 publication of "The Father Thing" in *Fantasy and Science Fiction* by at least two weeks. Don Siegel, director of "Invasion of the Body Snatchers," visited Finney in January 1955 to discuss adapting the *Collier's* story for film, just as Finney was finishing his novelization, published in February 1955 by Dell; no more than two months after Dick's story appear in *Fantasy and Science Fiction*, and hardly enough time for it to be influenced by Dick's story. At best, Jack Finney and Philip K. Dick were working on their stories simultaneously, and very probably, independently.

[cx] TTHC 299

[cxi] PKDS#17 6 Tony Boucher in a letter to PKD, Jun 5 1957

[cxii] SL-38 33. PKD > Mr. Haas, Sep 16, 1954.

[cxiii] IHOW 125/116 fn.22

[cxiv] TTHC 263

[cxv] TTHC 274

[cxvi] SL-38 ? PKD>Anthony Boucher, Apr 8 1954.

[cxvii] TTHC 263

[cxviii] TGM. 'Story Notes.'

[cxix] TTHC 266

[cxx] Levack 96

[cxxi] TTHC 266

[cxxii] SL-38 48. PKD>Walt Lanferman, Dec 30, 1958

[cxxiii] SL-38 42. PKD>A.Boucher, Oct 29, 1958

[cxxiv] CSVol3 p.413 'Notes'. Also in THE BEST OF PKD, Ballantine, 1977, p448.

[cxxv] This essay appeared originally in *For Dickheads Only* #4, 1994. It has been adapted for inclusion here.

[cxxvi] PKDS#21 4

[cxxvii] TTHC 286ff

[cxxviii] TTHC 289

[cxxix] TTHC 289

[cxxx] TTHC 290

[cxxxi] PKDS#2 6 *The Oakland Tribune,* Jan 10, 1955: "... he has a pocket book novel QUIZMASTER TAKE ALL readied for Fall, US publication."

[cxxxii] TTHC 290

[cxxxiii] TTHC 291

[cxxxiv] TTHC 291

[cxxxv] TTHC 289

[cxxxvi] PKDS#21 5, TTHC 191, SL-38 34. "For the chicken-feed sum of $184, Rich & Cowan expects me to perform a major overhaul on the novel. There'd have to be another decimal to that figure to make it worth it." …

[cxxxvii] PKDS-21 5

[cxxxviii] SF EYE 48

[cxxxix] PKDS#2 12

[cxl] Vertex, Vol. 1, no. 6, February 1974. Interviewer Arthur Byron Cover.

[cxli] **PHILIP K. DICK: In His Own Words, Gregg Rickman, Fragments West/The Valentine press, Long Beach, California, 1984/1988, ISBN: 0-916063-01-1 (1988 edition), p112. Hereinafter IHOW.**

[cxlii] **THE DREAM MAKERS, ed. Charles Platt, Berkley Books, New York, pb, 1980, ISBN: 0-425-04668-0, p147. Hereinafter TDM.**

[cxliii] **On Philip K. Dick: 40 Articles from *Science Fiction Studies*, Ed. Mullen, Csicsery-Ronay Jr., Evans, Hollinger, SF-TH Inc., DePauw University, Greencastle, Indiana, tp, 1992. ISBN: 0-9633169-1-5, p170 ff.** Hereinafter **OnPKD**. "Philip K. Dick: Authenticity and Insincerity" by John Huntington.

[cxliv] TDM 134

[cxlv] PKDS#5 6 PKD-APEL & BRIGGS 1977

[cxlvi] IHOW 84

[cxlvii] PKDS#2 12

[cxlviii] PKD: 'Notes Made Late At Night By A Weary SF Writer.'

[cxlix] TTHC 297

[cl] Gregg Press, hb, 2330-4, Jun 1976, 188pp, $9.50 (?) Introduction. 'Toward The Transcendent' by Thomas M. Disch.

[cli] TTHC 297, IHOW 128

[clii] IPOV 175

[cliii] IHOW 121

[cliv] See 'Solar Lottery' by Barb Morningchild at www.philipkdickfans.com/pkdweb/'Solar%20Lottery'%20by%20Barb.htm

[clv] PKDS#4 8

[clvi] *Twilight Zone Magazine*, **Vol. 2, No. 3, June 1982, p51: John Boonstra, interviewer.** Hereinafter **TZ**.

[clvii] *F & SF*, Aug 1955, p.94. I'd like to thank Patrick Clark for collecting together many short contemporary reviews of PKD's stories and publishing them in his fanzine *PKD OTAKU*, beginning with the 6th issue in Nov 2002. All the short reviews within the body of this work are taken from the issues of *PKD OTAKU*.

[clviii] *Galaxy*, Nov 1955, p105. *PKD OTAKU* #7, Nov 2002

[clix] As a final footnote to this section on SOLAR LOTTERY, in a letter to Terry and Carol Carr in 1964, PKD credited Marty Greenburg with suggesting to him that he write an sf novel, and also mentions the sales figures of SOLAR LOTTERY at 149,000. See: SL-38 122.

[clx] TTHC 263

[clxi] SL-38 ? PKD>Anthony Boucher, Apr 8 1954.

[clxii] TTHC 262. . {fn18: IHOW 66/62; DC 75-6}

[clxiii] CSVol4 375. PKD in 1976. Also in THE BEST OF PKD, Ballantine, 1977, p448.

[clxiv] TTHC 262. {fn16: Dick, "Memoir," 232. Dick's secession from *Galaxy* is confirmed by a letter from Meredith, 1-17-56 (published in PKDS-17 5). "I refused to sell any more stories to *Galaxy*," he told Kandy Smith in 1973. "They kept making changes that I hadn't written, and my name appeared on it too... If he didn't like the kind of girl you had in your stories, he'd take her out and make her a pumpkin." The story that seems to have done it for Phil was "Autofac."}

[clxv] SRG 43

[clxvi] CSVol4 375. Also in THE BEST OF PKD, Ballantine, 1977, p449.

[clxvii] THE PENULTIMATE TRUTH Afterword, Carroll & Graf, 1989, p210

[clxviii] TTHC 264

[clxix] TGM 'Story Notes' Also CSVol4 376. PKD In 1978.

[clxx] PEPKD 20. Andrew M. Butler sets the date for completion of THE WORLD JONES MADE as Dec 13 1954.

[clxxi] TTHC 294

[clxxii] ACE, pb, D-150, March 1956, 192pp, $0.35, (Shulz)//AGENT OF THE UNKNOWN by Margaret St.Clair

clxxiii RADIO FREE ALBEMUTH p.2

clxxiv See: TSR 181, TDC 88 and also SL-38 40: PKD in a letter to James Blish, 10-2-58

clxxv SL-38 40: PKD in a letter to James Blish, 10-2-58. For an excellent essay that explores the meaning of the mutants see "The World Jones Made" by Barb Morning Child. This essay, with others, can be found in FDO#2, 1992 and on www.philipkdickfans.com/pkdweb

clxxvi SL-38 40: PKD in a letter to James Blish, 10-2-58

1955

clxxvii TTHC 296

clxxviii SL-38 35. PKD to Tony Boucher, June 3, 1957.

clxxix TTHC 295ff

clxxx DI 90

clxxxi TTHC 295ff

clxxxii SL-38 35. PKD to Tony Boucher, June 3, 1957.

clxxxiii PKDS 2-13 and PKDS 6-12 Apel & Briggs).

clxxxiv PKDS 2-12

clxxxv PKDS 17-6 Wollheim > PKD, March 29, 1957.

clxxxvi PKDS 6-12 Apel & Briggs

clxxxvii TTHC 295 PKD > Sandra Meisal, August 27, 1970

clxxxviii OAR 122

clxxxix IHOW 120. Gregg Rickman had the wit to ask PKD about fan mail and he replied that after EYE was published he got his first fan letter from an author whose book on numismatics he had read, Murray Teigh Boom (see: IHOW 72)

cxc DI 90

cxci IPOV 165. Selection from THE EXEGESIS. In other places, too, EYE IN THE SKY is mentioned. See also DI 90.

cxcii See my "A Question Of Chronology" in the appendix and also found in PKD OTAKU # , 2003.

cxciii DI 294

cxciv TTHC 308. Edwin Fadiman Jr. to PKD, Jun 2 1955

cxcv SL-38 35. PKD to Anthony Boucher, Jun 3 1957

cxcvi TTHC 308. Millen Brand to SMLA, Jan 3 1956. Brand, the editor at Crown publishers, was, PKD said later, the editor he worked best with: "He once wrote me that he felt I had worked better in response to him than any other writer he could remember…" (See: PKDS-28 6. PKD in a letter to Diane Cleaver, 9 Apr 1973)

cxcvii TTHC 304

cxcviii MARY AND THE GIANT, Arbor House, hb, 850-5, 1987 Apr, 224pp, $16.95 (Richard Powers) 0-87795-850-5

cxcix TGM 'Story Notes'

cc Here's the editions taken from the bibliography on the CD: Rich & Cowan, hb, , Aug 1955, 216pp, 10/6d (Rudland); Rich & Cowan, hb, ?, Jun 1957, ?, 6/6d (?);Gregg Press, hb, 2413-0, Jun 1978, 223pp, $11.00 (no dj) The Gregg Press edition, also, usually cost collector's today about $100.

cci SF EYE, Vol.1, #2, Aug 1987, p48. PKD in interview with Richard Lupoff.

ccii The contents of A HANDFUL OF DARKNESS are: "Colony," "Impostor," "Expendable," "Planet For Transients," "Prominent Author," "The Builder," "Impossible Planet," "The Indefatigable Frog," "The Turning Wheel," "Progeny," "Upon The Dull Earth," "The Cookie Lady," and "Exhibit Piece."

cciii F & SF, April 1956, p79. PKD OTAKU #7, Nov 2002, p12

cciv PKDS-22 13.

ccv DI 90

ccvi SL: 38 35 PKD in a letter to Tony Boucher, June 3rd, 1957

ccvii SL: 38 41 PKD in a letter to James Blish, February 10th, 1958. In a letter to The Philip K. Dick Society Newsletter, Nick Pratt notes that this letter to Blish was the first time Dick ever wrote to a critic (see PKDS-6 10).

ccviii TTHC 297/431. Fn. 14. Thomas M. Disch 'Toward The Transcendent.'

ccix See DI 295 and TTHC 287.

ccx SL: 38 41 PKD in a letter to James Blish, February 10th, 1958.

ccxi SL-38 35. PKD to Anthony Boucher, June 3, 1957

[ccxii] These novels are probably: GATHER YOURSLEVES TOGETHER, MARY AND THE GIANT, A TIME FOR GEORGE STAVROS, THE BROKEN BUBBLE OF THISBE HOLT, PUTTERING ABOUT IN A SMALL LAND and, after Jan 1958, NICHOLAS AND THE HIGS. We've noted above that VOICES FROM THE STREET was withdrawn from circulation in 1955.

[ccxiii] TTHC 363 The SMLA card for GEORE STAVROS, in 1956, read (implying one rewrite of it already): Didn't like this before, & still don't. Long, rambling, glum novel about 65 yr old Greek immigrant who has a weakling son, a second son about whom he's indifferent, a wife who doesn't love him (she's being unfaithful to him). Nothing much happens. Guy, selling garage and retiring, tires{sic} to buy another garage in new development, has a couple of falls, dies at end. Point is murky but seems to be that world is disintegrating, Stavros is supposed to be symbol of vigorous individuality, now a lost commodity.

[ccxiv] TTHC 308. Don Wickenden to SMLA, 2-21-56.
[ccxv] PKDS Pamphlet #1 3 {PKD>Eleanor Dimoff, 01 Feb 1960}. In many cases, this letter contains the only information we have on many of PKD's early mainstream novels.
[ccxvi] Ibid. {PKD>Eleanor Dimoff, 01 Feb 1960}
[ccxvii] TTHC 363
[ccxviii] PKDS Pamphlet #1 3 {PKD>Eleanor Dimoff, 01 Feb 1960}

1956

[ccxix] ACE, pb, D-150, March 1956, 192pp, $0.35, (Shulz)//AGENT OF THE UNKNOWN by Margaret St.Clair
[ccxx] DI 296, TTHC 309-310
[ccxxi] TTHC 304
[ccxxii] THE BROKEN BUBBLE, Arbor House, hb, 012-8, 1988, 246pp, $16.95, (Powers) {1-55710-012-8} and Gollancz, hb, 04434-9, 1989 Jul, 246pp, L12.95 (Richard Jones) {0-575-04434-9}
[ccxxiii] TTHC 309
[ccxxiv] TTHC 310
[ccxxv] FDO#4, 1994
[ccxxvi] PKDS#20 19 and PKDS#26 17.
[ccxxvii] **THE POCKET ESSENTIAL PHILIP K. DICK by Andrew M. Butler, Pocket Essentials (UK), pb, 2000, ISBN: 1-903047-29-3, p.25. Hereinafter PEPKD.**
[ccxxviii] PKDS Pamphlet #1 3 {PKD>Eleanor Dimoff, 01 Feb 1960}
[ccxxix] THE MAN WHO JAPED, ACE, pb, D-193, Dec 1956, 160pp, 40.35, (emsh) // THE SPACE BORN by E.C. Tubb

1957

[ccxxx] ACE, pb, D-211, 1957, 255pp, $0.35, (Valigursky)
[ccxxxi] PKDS-17 6. Don Wollheim > PKD, 3-29-57
[ccxxxii] PKDS#17 3 [Wollheim's March 29, 1957 letter did cause the Agency to submit to ACE the novel from *Satellite*, which was quickly accepted and published by ACE as THE COSMIC PUPPETS...] Julian Messner, Inc. Publishers, New York to PKDS

[ccxxxiii] PKDS#17 6 ...& why, I wonder, haven't I seen any of the long Dicks in MS? If I'd liked A GLASS OF DARKNESS we'd've paid exactly twice *Satellite's* $400. I'd certainly have bought EYE & probably SOLAR LOTTERY – either (depending on our publishers variable policy at the moment) as a serial or to be condensed into a one-shot – wh wd've meant anywhere fr $600 to $1600 according to the length used. -- Tony Boucher in a letter to PKD, 6-5-57

[ccxxxiv] ACE, pb, D-249, Oct 1957, 127pp, $0.35, (Valigursky) // SARGASSO OF SPACE by Andrew North (Andre Norton)
[ccxxxv] SL-38 35. PKD > Anthony Boucher, Jun 3 1957

[ccxxxvi] PKDS#12 12

[ccxxxvii] See FDO#3, 1992. 'Through A Magnifying Glass Idly' by Dave Hyde.

[ccxxxviii] FDO#3, 1992

[ccxxxix] Ibid. 'The Cosmic Puppets" by Barb Morning Child.

[ccxl] TTHC 309

[ccxli] TTHC 304 and 311

[ccxlii] PKDS-26 4

[ccxliii] PKDS-3 5

[ccxliv] PUTTERING ABOUT IN A SMALL LAND, Academy Chicago, hb, 149-4, Oct 1985, 291pp, $16.95, (Armen Kojoyian) 0-89733-149-4

[ccxlv] PKDS-24 11

[ccxlvi] ACE, pb, D-261, , 1957, 255pp, $0.35 (Emsh). Contents: "The Variable Man", "Second Variety", "The Minority Report", "Autofac" and "A World Of Talent."

[ccxlvii] Tony Boucher in *F & SF*, Feb 1958, p109. *PKD OTAKU* #7, Nov 2002, p13

[ccxlviii] PEPKD 27

[ccxlix] TTHC 297

[ccl] DI 297. SMLA review by one "hm"

[ccli] PKDS Pamphlet #1 3 {PKD>Eleanor Dimoff, 01 Feb 1960}

[cclii] TTHC 301

1958

[ccliii] TTHC 302: Don Wollheim in communication with critic Greg Rickman.

[ccliv] Vertex Interviews with Philip K. Dick" By Arthur Byron Cover. In *Vertex*, vol. 1, no. 6 February 1974), p. 34-37 & 96-98. {Thanks to Eric A. Johnson}: "My first hard-cover novel, TIME OUT OF JOINT sold for $750. And my agent was so excited that he sent me a telegram to announce this joyous news."

[cclv] **Simulacrum Meltdown #3,** ed. Patrick Clark, Oct 2001, p.4-5. 'Joints Out Of Time: PKD Comments on his novel TIME OUT OF JOINT – in chronological order…' Compiled by Frank C. Bertrand. Hereinafter **SIM MELT#3**

[cclvi] PKDS Pamphlet #1 3 {PKD>Eleanor Dimoff, 01 Feb 1960}

[cclvii] TDM 150

[cclviii] SIM MELT#3, p.4-5

[cclix] Ibid, p.7. Originally found in IHOW.

[cclx] PKDS-26 7. Bruce Gillespie "The Non-Science Fiction Novels Of Philip K. Dick". Delivered as a speech to the Melbourne (Australia) Science Fiction Club.

[cclxi] *Astounding*, Jan 1960, p174. *PKD OTAKU* #3, Nov 2002, p14.

[cclxii] SL-38 34. PKD>Bill Hamlin, *Imagination*, Sep 2, 1955.

[cclxiii] SL-38 ? PKD>Anthony Boucher, Apr 8 1954.

[cclxiv] In an email from Gordon van Gelder, the current editor at *F & SF*, to the author in Feb 2003, the acceptance date for "Explorer's We" is stated as Jun 2, 1958.

[cclxv] PKDS-8 9. Paul Williams states that the story was written in 1958.

[cclxvi] TTHC 304/311

[cclxvii] TTHC 311. Arthur C. Fields > SMLA, Apr 16 1959.

[cclxviii] SL-38 59. PKD > Eleanor Dimoff, Feb 1, 1960.

[cclxix] TTHC 263

[cclxx] "Tony And The Beetles" was published as "Retreat From Rigel" in *PLANET OF DOOM And Other Stories*, Jubilee, pb, 212, 1958.

[cclxxi] TTHC 266

[cclxxii] See Rickman's and Sutin's biographies for more details of PKD's life at this time.

1959

[cclxxiii] SF EYE, Vol. 1, No. 2, August 1987, pp. 45-54. 'A Conversation With Philip K. Dick' by Richard Lupoff.

[cclxxiv] SIM MELT#3, 2001, p11. 'The Doctor Will See You Now: The Evolution Of DR. FUTURITY, Part Two: Dr. Futurity' by Patrick Clark.

[cclxxv] SL-38 51. PKD> Scott Meredith, Jan 5 1960.

[cclxxvi] SF EYE, Vol.1, #2, Aug 1987, p53. Interviewer Richard Lupoff.

[cclxxvii] PKDS-12 7. From Mark Hurst's Chronology of his relationship with PKD.

[cclxxviii] Patrick Clark notes that a condition of this 1979 deal with Berkley Books was that PKD rewrite the three novels (THE COSMIC PUPPETS, DR. FUTURITY and THE UNTELEPORTED MAN). He selected first – and only – THE UNTELEPORTED MAN for a rewrite which he began in 1979. See SIM MELT#3

[cclxxix] DI 105

[cclxxx] DI 107. See also TTHC 351 and PKDS Pamphlet #1. PKD>Eleanor Dimoff, Feb 1 1960: "I am free to write all day… Most of the work, for me, lies in the pre-typing stage, in the note taking. I generally spend five to six months doing no typing, but simply outlining. At best, I can now bring forth no more than two novels a year…" ALSO: In TTHC Rickman notes (p352) "By 1958 Philip K. Dick had established a system for writing novels… The ideas for his novels came, he told Anne, "in one intuitive flash: but he couldn't tell me what the idea was, he said, 'in under 60,000 words.'"

[cclxxxi] TTHC 358. Don Wickenden > SMLA, Oct 29, 1959

[cclxxxii] TTHC 359. Don Wickenden > SMLA, Oct 29, 1959

[cclxxxiii] DI 104

[cclxxxiv] TTHC 358

[cclxxxv] *Denver Clarion*, October 23, 1980. 'Philip K. Dick: Confessions Of A SF Artist' An interview with Philip K. Dick by George Cain and Dana Longo.

1960

[cclxxxvi] TTHC 359. Eleanor Dimoff > SMLA, July 14 1960.

[cclxxxvii] TTHC 359.

[cclxxxviii] SL-38 51: PKD in a letter to Scott Meredith, Jan 4 1960.

[cclxxxix] Probably THE MAN WHOSE TEETH WERE ALL EXACTLY ALIKE

[ccxc] SL-38 51ff. PKD in a letter to Scott Meredith, Jan 4 1960

[ccxci] VULCAN'S HAMMER, Ace, pb, D-457, Sep 1960, 139pp, $0.35 (Emsh) // *THE SKYNAPPERS* by John Brunner

[ccxcii] TTHC 363

[ccxciii] Ibid.

[ccxciv] Ibid. Don Wickenden > SMLA, 1-30-61

[ccxcv] Ibid. fn20: Russ Galen doesn't believe that Dick had to return the money, as "it was an option and not returnable. I'm quite sure it wasn't repaid."

[ccxcvi] HUMPTY DUMPTY IN OAKLAND, Gollancz, hb, 03875-6, Oct 1986, 199pp, L9.95 (Mark Foreman ISBN: 0-575-03875-6

[ccxcvii] DI 299

1961

[ccxcviii] TTHC 370. Fn.11: PKD > Sandra Meisel, Sep 9 1970

[ccxcix] TZ pp47-52. Interview by John Boonstra. Anne Dick is a successful jewelry maker today. In 2001 I bought a pair of her earrings in Muncie, Indiana and gave them to my girlfriend.

[ccc] TTHC 366. PKD > Joseph Sirak, Jr. Nov 8 1970

[ccci] DI 109

[cccii] *Science Fiction Review*, **No. 19, Vol. 5, no. 3, August 1976.** Interview with Daniel DePrez, Sep 10 1976. Hereinafter **SF Review**.

[ccciii] DI 111

[ccciv] See DI 111-113

[cccv] Hour 25. Interview with Mike Hodel.

[cccvi] TZ Magazine pp47-52. Interview by John Boonstra.

[cccvii] Vertex, Vol. 1, no. 6, February 1974. Interviewer: Arthur Byron Cover

[cccviii] **Philip K. Dick: The Dream Connection by D. Scott Apel, The Permanent Press, San Jose, CA, hb, 1987, LCCCN: 87-60689, p.70**. Hereinafter **TDC**.

[cccix] Vertex, Vol. 1, no. 6, February 1974. Interviewer: Arthur Byron Cover

[cccx] TSR 19. "Notes Made Late At night By A Weary SF Writer." (1968) First published in *Eternity Science Fiction*, July 1972.

[cccxi] PEPKD 35

[cccxii] TZ Magazine

[cccxiii] SL-38 63. PKD > Tony Boucher, 25 Apr 1962. Final legal acceptance of HIGH CASTLE came on March 1 1962.

[cccxiv] SL-38 63. PKD > Tony Boucher, 25 Apr 1962

[cccxv] THE MAN IN THE HIGH CASTLE, Putnams, hb, 62-18262, Oct 1962, 239pp, $3.95 (Robert Galster) {Levack: "Bound in black cloth with red lettering on the front cover and spine. Date code 'D36' [36th week 1962] on lower left margin of page 239. Yop edges stained yellow. No date on the title page. [Putnam normally does not mark first printings, but explicitly marks later printings]"}

[cccxvi] Levack 42. Levack notes that the SFBC edition from Doubleday has a "date code 'D45' on lower left margin of page 239." This date code would indicate the 45th week (1st week of November) of 1962 for printing of the SFBC edition. The edition was most likely published – available to the public – by early December 1962. By the way, the date code for the Putnam's first edition is 'D36' on the lower left margin of page 239. This would indicate that the Putnam's edition was printed in the first week of September 1962. It was published in Oct 1962.

[cccxvii] TZ Magazine

[cccxviii] As to the differences in the two editions, See Levack 42.. See above fn.ccxcv for distinguishing date codes.

[cccxix] *The Patchin Review*, No. 5. Oct-Dec 1982, pp2-6. Interviewer John Boonstra.

[cccxx] PKD OTAKU #11, Sep 2003, p10. Donald A. Wollheim [Phil's editor at Ace Books] responding to "Naziism and the High Castle". Source: *Niekas#10*, Dec 1964, p5.

[cccxxi] *NIEKAS*, **No. 34, 1986, pp. 3-4. 'Bumbejimas : PKD And Me' by Ed Meskys**. Hereinafter **Niekas**.

[cccxxii] TSR 16. PKD 'Self Portrait', 1968.

[cccxxiii] BGSU Papers

[cccxxiv] OAR 181

[cccxxv] Ibid.

[cccxxvi] BGSU Papers. PKD > Shokichi Kawaguchi (Tokyo), Dec 8 1968.

[cccxxvii] PKD: "The Mainstream That Through The Ghetto Flows." Strangely this essay is not found in TSR.

[cccxxviii] Ibid. The German edition that PKD refers to is probably that published by Konig Verlag in 1973 as DAS ORAKEL VOM BERGE. There have been several German editions since, notably those published by Bastei Lubbe. Whether HIGH CASTLE has been retranslated or not I do not know.

[cccxxix] OnPKD 87. Patricia S. Warrick "The Encounter of Taoism and Fascism in THE MAN IN THE HIGH CASTLE."

[cccxxx] TSR 237. "If You Find This World Bad, You Should See Some Of The Others" (1977)

[cccxxxi] TSR 245. The Metz Speech

[cccxxxii] TSR 119ff. Sutin reprints these two chapters in full here. However, in the 'Introduction' to TSR, Sutin dates these two chapters to 1974 but in the section dealing with HIGH CASTLE itself, he dates the chapters as 1964 (TSR 111). Almost certainly they were written in 1974.

[cccxxxiii] Hour 25. Interview with Mike Hodel.

[cccxxxiv] TDC 71

1962

[cccxxxv] It is possible that PKD worked on MARTIAN TIME-SLIP before WE CAN BUILD YOU but the calendar of submissions at the SMLA definitely records the reception of WE CAN BUILD YOU before that of MARTIAN TIME-SLIP, even though these dates both fall in the month of Oct 1962.

[cccxxxvi] See OAR 181. WE CAN BUILD YOU, DAW, pb, UQ 1014 (#14), Jul 1972, 206pp, $0.95 (John Schoenherr)

[cccxxxvii] TDC 43. The magazine PKD refers to is *Amazing Stories*, then edited by Ted White.

[cccxxxviii] PKDS-6 8. Ted White > PKDS, nd {c.1984}

[cccxxxix] TDC 42

[cccxl] OAR 181

[cccxli] *Galaxy*, Jan 1973, pp173-74. *PKD OTAKU* #8, Jan 2003, p7.

[cccxlii] MARTIAN TIME-SLIP, Ballantine, pb, U2191, Apr 1964, 220pp, $0.50, (Brillhart) See OAR 92

[cccxliii] DI 118

[cccxliv] PKDS-2 13. PKD in 1968

[cccxlv] PKDS-6 12. PKD in interview with Apel & Briggs, 1977

[cccxlvi] FDO-4

[cccxlvii] OAR 92

[cccxlviii] SL-38 79. PKD in a letter to James Blish, Jun 7 1964

[cccxlix] DI 299. PKD to Dorothy Hudner, Oct 1976

[cccl] TTHC 411, note 7. Rickman goes on to note "Autism was at the time Dick wrote TIME SLIP largely blamed on inadequate parenting, as it is in Bettelheim's work. More recent studies of autism do not follow Bettelheim on this."

[cccli] DI 82

[ccclii] DI 299

[cccliii] DI 103

[cccliv] See TTHC 64 and IPOV 143 fn

[ccclv] **SF Commentary #9**, Feb 1970, pp8-10, Letter of Comment by PKD written 8 Jun 1969. Or found in *PKD: Electric Shepherd* by Bruce Gillespie, Norstrilia Press (Australia), 1975, p32.

[ccclvi] PKDS-28 10

[ccclvii] PKDS-12 7. The Mark Hurst Chronology.

[ccclviii] IPOV 81

[ccclix] DHG 212

[ccclx] DHG 209 "Man, Android & Machine." (1976) Also in TSR 216 "Man, Android & Machine."

[ccclxi] DHG 220 and also TSR 224 "Man, Android & Machine." (1976)

[ccclxii] Levack 46

1963

[ccclxiii] DR. BLOODMONEY, Ace, pb, F-337, Jun 1965, 222pp, $0.40 (Gaughan). See DI 300. It's possible that PKD had titled his manuscript IN EARTH'S DIURNAL COURSE *or* A TERRAN ODYSSEY.

[ccclxiv] CSVol5 390.

[ccclxv] SL-38 189. PKD to Scott Meredith, May 22 1965.

[ccclxvi] PKDS-6 9. Terry Carr>PKDS, 1985. See THE UNTELEPORTED MAN for more from this letter.

[ccclxvii] PKDS-2 13

[ccclxviii] TDC ?

[ccclxix] SL-38 285. PKD>Sandra Miesal, Sep 8, 1970.

[ccclxx] SF EYE, #14, Spring 1996, pp. 37-46. Interview by Uwe Anton & Werner Fuchs, transcribed by Frank C. Bertrand. Interview conducted at Metz in 1977. The edition of DR. BLOODMONEY referred to here is probably the Gregg Press edition of June 1977. And the metaphysical novel Dick mentions is most likely VALIS.

[ccclxxi] TSR 80. Also to be found in the 1985 Bluejay edition and the Carroll & Graf editions of DR. BLOODMONEY.

[ccclxxii] Levack 100. Also CSVol4 376. Also in THE BEST OF PKD, Ballantine, 1977, p449.

[ccclxxiii] SL-38 71. PKD>Fred Pohl, Jun 23 1963

[ccclxxiv] Those mentioned are: Jonathon Swift, H.G. Wells, Poul Anderson, Karen Anderson, Astrid Anderson (Poul's wife and daughter), A. E. Van Vogt, Howard Browne (editor of *Amazing*), Isaac Asimov, Jack Vance, Murray Leinster, Ray Bradbury, Jack Williamson, Margaret St. Clair, Evelyn Paige, Robert Bloch, Tony Boucher, Robert Heinlein, Kris Neville, Mildred Clingerman, James Gunn, Virgil Finlay (sf artist) and Scott Meredith (agent). The stories mentioned in "Waterspider" in addition to the three PKD stories listed above, are: "Night Flight" by Poul Anderson, "The Fisher Of Men" by Poul Anderson, "The World Of Null-A" by A. E. Van Vogt, "Legion Of Time" by Jack Williamson, "The Scarlet Hexapod" by Margaret St. Clair.

[ccclxxv] See PKDS-20 20. Marc Landau to PKDS, 1989.

[ccclxxvi] RADIO FREE ALBEMUTH, Ch.4.

[ccclxxvii] Levack 89. Also in THE BEST OF PKD, Ballantine, p447.

[ccclxxviii] CSVol4 377. PKD 1979

[ccclxxix] SL-38 88. PKD>Terry Carr, Aug 13, 1964

ccclxxx SL-38 186. PKD>Scott Meredith, undated 1965 {note: From reading it this letter was probably written after March 25, 1965 and before April 6, 1965 -- Lord RC}

ccclxxxi Levack 113. PKD 1976. Also in THE BEST OF PKD, Ballantine, 1977, p449.

ccclxxxii CSVol4   379. PKD 1979

ccclxxxiii DI 309.

ccclxxxiv Levack 106 also TGM 'Story Notes.'

ccclxxxv TGM Afterword by PKD.

ccclxxxvi SRG 52. Written by Hazel Pierce.

ccclxxxvii THE GOLDEN MAN Story Notes By PKD

ccclxxxviii THE GAME-PLAYERS OF TITAN, Ace, pb, F-251, Dec 1963, 191pp, $0.40 (Jack Gaughan)

ccclxxxix SL-38 190. PKD to Scott Meredith, May 22, 1965. Copy to Don Wollheim, Ace Books Inc.

cccxc THE SIMULACRA, Ace, pb, F-301, 1964, 192pp, $0.40 (Ed Emshwiller)

cccxci SL-38 71. PKD to Terry Carr, Aug 8 1964.

cccxcii SL-38 89. PKD to Terry Carr, Aug 19, 1964.

cccxciii SL-38 115. PKD to Terry and Carol Carr, Oct 16 1964.

cccxciv TDC 78

cccxcv SF EYE #14 Spring 1996 p.39-43. Interview by Uwe Anton and Werner Fuchs, tr. Frank C. Bertrand. 1977 Metz

cccxcvi PKD OTAKU #1, Pub. Patrick Clark, 2001. Gilles Goullet: 'Le ParaDick': unreleased interview, Metz 1977

cccxcvii FDO#6, 1996. 'PKD Horserace'. Peter Fenelon via Paul Rydeen.

cccxcviii See: PEPKD ? and Rouzleweave # 1, Pub. By Perry Kinman, Japan, March 2002, p3. Also: Levack 24: "Cantata 140" … forms the first half of this title " {THE CRACK IN SPACE} and Levack 85: "First half of THE CRACK IN SPACE."

cccxcix SL-38 79. PKD> James Blish, Jun 7, 1964

cd Levack 85

cdi PKDS-16 1: Records at the Scott Meredith Literary Agency in New York indicate that the outline {for THE ZAP GUN} {...} was received by the Agency December 5, 1963 (one day after the recorded receipt of the manuscript of NOW WAIT FOR LAST YEAR.)

cdii Doubleday, hb, 66-017393, May 1966, 214pp, $3.95 (Lawrence Ratzkin) {Levack: "Bound in charcoal black cloth with gold lettering on the spine. '1966' on the title page. 'First Edition' on the copyright page. Date code H9 [9th week of 1966] at the lower right margin of page 214."} This date code would indicate the first week of Feb or so.

cdiii BGSU Papers. Marcia M. Howell > PKD, Aug 29, 1968

cdiv PKDS-24 11. {This would be the edition from Ediciones Jucar translated into Spanish as AGUARDANDO EL ANO PASADO}

cdv SF EYE #14, Spring 1996, p.38 Interviewer Uwe Anton and Werner Fuchs, transcribed by Frank C. Bertrand.

cdvi TSR 19

cdvii SF Commentary 9 February 1970, pp. 11–25, Bruce Gillespie on NOW WAIT FOR LAST YEAR,

cdviii PKDS-16 1. Scott Meredith to PKD, Oct 31 ? (probably 1963)

cdix THE ZAP GUN, Pyramid, pb, R1569, Jan 1967, 176pp, $0.50 (Gaughan). See PKDS-16 1.

cdx CS Vol5 390.

cdxi THE GOLDEN MAN Story Notes By PKD

cdxii CS Vol5 390 and DI 309.

cdxiii TGM 'Story Notes' by PKD.

cdxiv CS Vol5 390.

cdxv CSVol4 377

1964

cdxvi DI 133. {Without going into PKD's love affairs too deeply, he'd had at least one other girlfriend between the time he left Anne and met Nancy Hackett. This was Grania Davidson, ex-wife of sf writer Avram Davidson. She moved in with Phil in Oakland in June 1964. By Halloween it was over.}

cdxvii PEPKD 43. Sutin in DI has the novel written in 1963-64." And Perry Kinman in Rouzleweave #1 has it written on 16 Jan 1964.

cdxviii CLANS OF THE ALPHANE MOON, Ace, pb, F-309, Nov 1964, 189pp, $0.40 (Va;igursky). See PKDS-2 10 [cdxix] TDC ? PKD in conversation with Kevin Briggs and D.S. Apel, 1977.

[cdxx] Ibid. PKD mentions CLANS OF THE ALPHANE MOON and implies an edition from the French publisher Editions Opta. But Editions Opta never published an edition of CLANS as far as I can tell. The first French edition was from Albin Michel in 1973 (Albin Michel, pb, SF 18, 1973, 249pp, ?, ? (?) {tr. Into French by Francois Truchaud as LES CLANS DE LA LUNE ALPHANE}

[cdxxi] PKDS-8 5. J.B.Reynolds, Tim Powers, Serena Powers, Andy Watson, Jim Blaylock in conversation.

[cdxxii] THE CRACK IN SPACE, Ace, pb, F-377, Feb 1966, 190pp, $0.40 (Jerome Podwill).

[cdxxiii] SL-38 79. PKD> James Blish, Jun 7, 1964

[cdxxiv] PKD OTAKU #11, Sep 2003, p9. (Source: from an interview with Terry Carr in *Speaking of Science Fiction: The Paul Walker Interviews*; Luna Publications: 1978, p207)

[cdxxv] FDO#6. 1996 'PKD Horserace.'

[cdxxvi] Rickman in TTHC mentions 1963 parenthetically in passing and Sutin in DI has that it was written in 1964 and notes that PKD mailed it to the SMLA in Mar 1964 (DI 128). Perry Kinman in *Rouzleweave #1* accords with Butler that the ms was received at the SMLA on 18 Mar 1964.

[cdxxvii] THE THREE STIGMATA OF PALMER ELDRITCH, Doubleday, hb, 65-011537, Nov 1964, 278pp, $3.30, (Tom Chibbaro) {Levack: "... 1965 ... $4.95 ...." "Bound in light grey cloth with black lettering on the spine. '1965' on the title page. 'First Edition' on the copyright page. ... no date code in this book. Also unusual for Doubleday, in this time frame, is the fact that the book is 'perfect bound' (this is somewhat hidden by a headband). This first edition contains a page not found in the Book Club edition, which lists current and forthcoming titles by Dick.; some of these titles, such as THE FIRST LADY OF EARTH and IN THE MOLD OF YANCY, were apparently discarded before the books in question saw publication. The price printed on the dustjacket is $4.59 which, in all copies seen, has had a sticker placed over it stating "$4.95 D & CO.INC.""} /// SFBC, hb, ?, Jan **1965**, 230pp, $1.20 (Chibbaro) {Levack: "Bound in gray paper boards with black lettering on the spine. Top edges stained blue. '1965' on title page. Perfect binding. No date code."}

[cdxxviii] Cape, hb, ?, 1966, 278pp, 21/- (Jan Pienkowski){Levack: " Bound in light grey paper boards with gold lettering on the spine. No date on the title page. 'First published in Great Britain 1966' on the copyright page."} These early editions are now valuable. Paul Williams notes that the May 1990 issue of *Book Collector* magazine from Britain lists several of PKD's early works. THE THREE STIGMATA, for instance, is listed at 300 pounds.

[cdxxix] DI 132.

[cdxxx] PKDS-12 7. Oddly enough there is no Bantam edition of THE THREE STIGMATA. The nearest to 1976 in date is the Manor Books paperback from 1977.

[cdxxxi] SL-38 186. PKD>Scott Meredith, undated 1965. note: Probably written between March 22 and April 6, 1965. See also OH TO BE A BLOBEL for more from this letter. This letter almost certainly refers to THE 3 STIGMATA, Cape, hb, , 1966, 278pp, 21/-

[cdxxxii] CSVol4 377

[cdxxxiii] *SF Commentary #9*, Feb 1970, pp8-10, Letter of Comment by PKD written 8 Jun 1969. Or found in *PKD: Electric Shepherd* by Bruce Gillespie, Norstrillia Press (Australia), 1975, p32.

[cdxxxiv] Vertex, Vol. 1, no. 6, February 1974. Interview by Arthur Byron Cover

[cdxxxv] **Aquarian**, 10-11-78. Joe Vitale interviewer

[cdxxxvi] SF EYE #14 Spring, 1996 p46.

[cdxxxvii] TSR 206. "The Android And The Human" 1972

[cdxxxviii] SF EYE #14 Spring, 1996 p46. Interview with Anton & Fuchs.

[cdxxxix] SF EYE, Vol. 1, No. 2, August 1987, pp. 45-54 interview by Richard Lupoff

[cdxl] TDC 79. PKD interview with Apel & Briggs, 1977.

[cdxli] TSR 58

[cdxlii] CSVol4 377. PKD in 1979.

[cdxliii] PKDS-2 13. 'Self Portrait' 1968.

[cdxliv] PKDS-22 1. Lawrence Sutin: 'Confessions of a PKD biographer.'

[cdxlv] IPOV 20. Fn. *: "Terrible Separation" is a reference to PKD's own sense of the gulf that existed in the 1960s between his own limited human existence and a genuine encounter with the divine as a positive, redeeming force in the universe.

[cdxlvi] IPOV 20.

[cdxlvii] IPOV 136.

[cdxlviii] *F & SF*, June 1965, p74-75. *PKD OTAKU # 8*, Jan 2003.

[cdxlix] SL-38 237. PKD > Andy, May 21, 1968

[cdl] Hour 25

[cdli] PEPKD 83. I don't know where Butler found this date.

[cdlii] GSM Xerox Collection. Patrick Clark to Perry Kinman, Oct 7, 2002. Clark dates the letter to Blish as May 22, 1964.

[cdliii] PKDS-16 2. 'Musings From Melbourne' by Roger Zelazny. This article is condensed from a transcript of a speech given by Zelazny at Unicon, Melbourne, Australia, Easter 1978; the complete transcript was published in *Science Fiction Commentary* #54, under the title "A Burnt-out Case."

[cdliv] Levack 25. Here Levack gives the ms title as "THE KNEELING, LEGLESS MAN. Also, repeated in PEPKD 83

[cdlv] PKDS-2 13

[cdlvi] THE PENULTIMATE TRUTH 'Afterword' by Thomas M. Disch. Found in the Bluejay and Carroll & Graf editions.

[cdlvii] SL-38 285. PKD to Sandra Miesel, Sep 8 1970.

[cdlviii] PKDS-6 12. PKD interview with Apel & Briggs, 1977

[cdlix] THE ZAP GUN 'Afterword' by Maxim Jakubowski, found in THE ZAP GUN, Carroll & Graf, 1989, p.253. Also in the Bluejay edition which I don't have handy. This is PKD in April 1981.

[cdlx] See PKDS-6 4 and other places.

[cdlxi] PKDS-2 13

[cdlxii] THE PENULTIMATE TRUTH, Belmont, pb, 92-603, Sep 1964, 174pp, $0.50 (?). In his 'Afterword' to the Bluejay edition of THE PENULTIMATE TRUTH, Thomas Disch says that the Outline for this novel was completed by March 1964. Butler and Kinman have the finished manuscript at the SMLA on 12 May 1964,

[cdlxiii] ibid

[cdlxiv] TGM 'Story Notes'. Also in CSVol4 376. PKD in 1978

[cdlxv] PKDS-2 13

[cdlxvi] *The Aquarian*, Oct 11 1978 interview by Joe Vitale.

[cdlxvii] THE 3 STIGMATA OF PALMER ELDRITCH, Doubleday, hb, 65-011537, Nov 1964, 278pp, $3.30, (Tom Chibbaro) {Levack: "... 1965 ... $4.95 ...." "Bound in light grey cloth with black lettering on the spine. '1965' on the title page. 'First Edition' on the copyright page. ... no date code in this book. Also unusual for Doubleday, in this time frame, is the fact that the book is 'perfect bound' (this is somewhat hidden by a headband). This first edition contains a page not found in the Book Club edition, which lists current and forthcoming titles by Dick.; some of these titles, such as THE FIRST LADY OF EARTH and IN THE MOLD OF YANCY, were apparently discarded before the books in question saw publication. The price printed on the dustjacket is $4.59 which, in all copies seen, has had a sticker placed over it stating "$4.95 D & CO.INC.""}

[cdlxviii] See DI 135ff for biographical material mentioned here.

[cdlxix] PKDS-8 2: From 'The Missing Pages Of THE UNTELEPORTED MAN.' {The name of Dr. Bloode's book within TUM is *The True and Complete Economic and Political History of Newcolonizedland*, By Dr. Bloode. }

[cdlxx] PKDS-6 9. Terry Carr to PKDS, 1985.

[cdlxxi] DI 136

[cdlxxii] SL-38 190. PKD > Terry and Carol Carr, Nov 11, 1964.

[cdlxxiii] SL-38 172. PKD > Carol Carr, Jan 10, 1965. East Gakville refers to Oakland.

[cdlxxiv] PKDS-6 9. Terry Carr to PKDS, 1985.

[cdlxxv] SL-38 190. PKD > Scott Meredith, May 22, 1965. Cc: Don Wollheim, Ace Books, Inc.

[cdlxxvi] PKDS-6 9. Terry Carr to PKDS, 1985.

[cdlxxvii] FDO #2

[cdlxxviii] THE UNTELEPORTED MAN, ACE, pb, G-602, Nov 1966, 100pp, $0.50, (Kelly Freas) // THE MIND MONSTERS by Howard Cory.

[cdlxxix] In A PKD OMNIBUS, Sidgwick & Jackson, hb, 48450-0, Oct 1970, 424pp, L1.95 (?) {Levack: ...Bound in blue paper boards with silver lettering on the spine. No date on the title page. "This omnibus edition copyright © 1970 by // Sidgwick and Jackson Limited" on the copyright page.}

[cdlxxx] DI 305: "In 1984, after the discovery of further 1979 revisions by Phil, Gollancz published a third version as LIES, INC. (with two brief gap-filling passages by John Sladek). A summary of the whole: The part-one tale of overpopulation and migration to an alternate world is transformed into a part-two horror story of invasive irreality like PALMER ELDRITCH and then back again, with some 2-3-74 reflections (by way of the 1979 revisions) for good measure..."

[cdlxxxi] PKDS-8 2. 'The Missing Pages Of THE UNTELEPORTEFD MAN.'

cdlxxxii http://www.kruse.demon.co.uk/philip.htm

cdlxxxiii DI 304

cdlxxxiv FDO #6. 'PKD Horserace'; fan fave by Lord RC {pseudonym of the present writer...}

cdlxxxv This essay is most conveniently found in TSR 167ff

1965

cdlxxxvi PKDS-6 8. Ted White to PKDS.

cdlxxxvii SL-38 237. PKD to Andy, May 21 1968.

cdlxxxviii *Niekas #11*, Mar 1965. "Schizophrenia & The book Of Changes" was later published in pamphlet form as *PKDSN#14* in June 1987. Then, in TSR in 1995 – the most convenient place to find it.

cdlxxxix DI 305 for COUNTER-CLOCK WORLD date and DI 151 for THE GANYMEDE TAKEOVER date.

cdxc TSR 176. "Schizophrenia And The Book Of Changes."

cdxci DI 305. Also, Andrew Butler has the novel written in 'late 1965'(see PEPKD 51)

cdxcii COUNTER-CLOCK WORLD, Berkley, pb, X1372, Feb 1967, 160pp, $0.60 (Hoot).

cdxciii SL-38 201. PKD > Cynthia, Feb 27, 1967

cdxciv DI 305

cdxcv TDC ?. PKD in 1977. {note: PKD is probably talking about the Club de Livre d'Anticipation hardback edition of COUNTER-CLOCK WORLD backed with NOW WAIT FOR LAST YEAR (1968) Or, alternatively, the Club de Livre d'Anticipation hardback edition of THE MAN IN THE HIGH CASTLE // Dr. BLOODMONEY (1970).

cdxcvi IPOV 216. PKD circa 1974-75

cdxcvii TDC 135

cdxcviii TDC 138

cdxcix PKKD had met Ray Nelson in late 1962 or early 1963. See: Ed Meskys in *Bumbejimas.*

d SL-38 229. PKD > Scott Meredith Feb 28, 1968

di PKDS-6 9. Terry Carr > PKDS, 1985. See THE UNTELEPORTED MAN for more from this letter.

1966

dii THE GANYMEDE TAKEOVER (with Ray Nelson), ACE, pb, G-627, Jun 1967, 157pp, $0.50, (Jack Gaughan)

diii PKDS-8 9

div Levack 98. Description by Steven Owen Godersky.

dv TGM 'Story Notes' by PKD.

dvi TGM 'Story Notes' by PKD.

dvii DI 161. Also see the different editions of DV.

dviii DV 214. This is in the 1972 Berkley paperback edition, D2274.

dix Vertex, Vol. 1, no. 6, February 1974. Interviewer, Arthur Byron Cover.

dx Levack 94.. Also in THE BEST OF PKD, Ballantine, 1977, p449.

dxi DV 243. The 1972 Berkley edition of DV.

dxii PKD OTAKU #11, Sep 2003, p8. (Letter to Olga Vezeris [at Signet Books] Nov 13, 1974).

dxiii IPOV 20.

dxiv PKDS-29 12. "Faith Of Our Fathers": A Comparison of the Original Manuscript with the Published Text by Sam Umland. (Note: The remainder of this article delves into minute differences between the ms. and published versions of this story. See PKDS-29)

dxv SRG ?

dxvi Doubleday, hb, 68-11779, Mar 1968, 210pp, $3.95, (Harry Sehring){Levack: "Bound in grey cloth with gold lettering on the spine. '1968' on the title page. 'FIRST EDITION' on the copyright page. Date code J5 [5th week of 1968] at lower right margin of page 210"}

dxvii TDC 79. Interview by D.S. Apel and Kevin Briggs

dxviii BGSU Papers. Sidney Meredith > PKD, May 23, 1968

dxix Ibid.. PKD > Sidney Meredith, SMLA, 5-26-1968

dxx Ibid. Marcia M. Howell > PKD, Aug 29, 1968

dxxi Ibid. PKD > Roger Zelazny, 11-13-1968

dxxii PKDS-4 8.

[dxxiii] PKDS-11 6. The first *BLADE RUNNER*: Del Rey, pb, 30129-3, May 1982, 216pp, $2.75 (Movie poster by Alvin) On the cover under the large *BLADE RUNNER* title logo is found, in parentheses, DO ANDROIDS DREAM OF ELECTRIC SHEEP?

[dxxiv] PKDS-2 13. PKD's 'Self Portrait', 1968

[dxxv] FDO 'PKD Horserace' comment by David Anonymous, CA.

[dxxvi] Doubleday, hb, 69-15205, May 1969, 202pp, $4.50, (Peter Rauch) {Levack: "Bound in gray cloth with silver lettering on the spine. '1969' on the title page. 'First Edition' on the copyright page. Date code 'K10' [10th week of 1969] on page 202."}

[dxxvii] BGSU Papers. Lawrence P. Ashmead > PKD, Jan 17, 1968

[dxxviii] Ibid. Lawrence P. Ashmead > PKD, Mar 10, 1968

[dxxix] Ibid. Lawrence P. Ashmead > PKD, May 29, 1968

[dxxx] SL-38 246. PKD>Peter Fitting, before May 1969

[dxxxi] Dell, pb, 9200, May 1970, 208pp, $0.95 (Jones)

[dxxxii] Hour 25

[dxxxiii] Bantam, pb, 10402-0, Jan 1977, 212pp, $!.75 (Szafran)

[dxxxiv] TDC 79

[dxxxv] Hour 25

[dxxxvi] TDC 108

[dxxxvii] TSR 216

[dxxxviii] IPOV 63

[dxxxix] TSR 243

[dxl] TSR 224

[dxli] **21C** #4 1995 p78ff. Article by George Melrod

[dxlii] PKDS-16 5.

[dxliii] SL-38 199. PKD to A. Boucher, undated, circa Christmas 1966. If the dating of this letter is correct then UBIK must've sold to Doubleday shortly after its reception at the SMLA on Dec 7, 1966. I cannot confirm this though.

[dxliv] PKDS-16 5.

[dxlv] PKDS-18 7. Capsule review by Andy Watson. First edition: Gollancz, hb, 04307-5, Jun 1988, 141pp, L7.95 (Paul Demeyer) 0-575-04307-5. Illustrated.

[dxlvi] PKDS-22/23 12.

[dxlvii] NICK AND THE GLIMMUNG, Piper, pb, 31374-2, Jul 1990, 141pp, L2.50 (Demeyer) 0-330-31474-2

1967

[dxlviii] DI 158ff

[dxlix] See DI 156 and TSR 149ff

[dl] *New Worlds #2*, 'Joe Protagoras Is Alive and Living On Earth' *and* 'The Name Of The Game Is Death' by Philip K. Dick, Introduction by Paul Williams, illustrated by Jim Burns. This quote is from Williams' Introduction.

[dli] Ibid.

[dlii] Ibid.

[dliii] On all this Patrick Clark in a letter to Perry Kinman, Oct 7 2002 says: "{…}Presumably Zelazny nixed the 'Joe Protagoras' plot and went with DEUS IRAE instead. But if White did not send him the manuscript until 1968 then why did Zelazny contact Phil in October 1967 with the idea of collaborating? The assumption has been he read the DEUS IRAE outline ms., presumably sent to him by White, and approached Phil as a result. The simplest solution is that White has the year wrong, that he sent Zelazny the ms. in 1967, not 1968. But if so, why did Phil suggest a totally unrelated plot? And Phil's letter of October 26th is curious in that he does not mention DEUS IRAE at all. He also seems genuinely surprised, though delighted, to have heard from Zelazny in the first place. As if it was unexpected." – from the GSM Xerox Collection.

My solution to this, as stated in the body of this text, is that Zelazny contacted PKD with the idea of a collaboration before he knew about the DEUS IRAE sample pages. What inspired Zelazny to talk of collaboration is not known. Then, through correspondence, PKD mentioned the DEUS IRAE contract and the two decided to work on that. So, then, it was after October 1967 that one or the other contacted Ted White asking for the sample pages to be sent to Zelazny. This White did most probably in late 1967 or early 1968.

[dliv] DI 162-3

[dlv] SL-38 227. PKD > Scott Meredith, Nov 3, 1967

[dlvi] SL-38 229. PKD > S. Meredith, Feb 28 1968

[dlvii] GALACTIC POT-HEALER, Berkley, pb, X1705, Jun 1969, 144pp, $0.60 (Kossut) and SFBC, hb, 2239, Apr 1970, ?, $1.49 (Kossut) {Levack: "Bound in black paper boards with grey lettering on the spine. Date code 'O81' at lower left margin of page 145. No date on the title page."}

[dlviii] Gollancz, hb, 00596-3, Jul **1971**, 191pp, L1.60 (?) {Levack: "Bound in maroon paper boards with gold lettering on the spine. '1971' on the title page"}

[dlix] GALACTIC POT-HEALER, Blackstone Audio Books, cassette, 3499, 1989.

[dlx] TDC 79

[dlxi] SL-38 285. PKD>Sandra Miesel, Sep 8, 1970

[dlxii] PKDS-8 4. Tim Powers and Jim Blaylock in conversation, 1985.

[dlxiii] PKDS-15 8. James Tiptree Jr. was the pseudonym of Alice Sheldon (d. 1989). In 1969-70 she corresponded with PKD while she was starting her own science fiction writing career.

[dlxiv] *Analog*, Mar 1970, p105. *PKD OTAKU # 6*, Sep 2002, p10.

1968

[dlxv] Doubleday, hb, 65-011537, Nov 1964, 278pp, $3.30, (Tom Chibbaro) {Levack: "... 1965 ... $4.95 ...." "Bound in light grey cloth with black lettering on the spine. '1965' on the title page. 'First Edition' on the copyright page. ... no date code in this book. Also unusual for Doubleday, in this time frame, is the fact that the book is 'perfect bound' (this is somewhat hidden by a headband). This first edition contains a page not found in the Book Club edition, which lists current and forthcoming titles by Dick.; some of these titles, such as THE FIRST LADY OF EARTH and IN THE MOLD OF YANCY, were apparently discarded before the books in question saw publication. The price printed on the dustjacket is $4.59 which, in all copies seen, has had a sticker placed over it stating "$4.95 D & CO.INC.""}

[dlxvi] DI 160

[dlxvii] BGSU Papers. Sidney Meredith to PKD, Jan 20, 1968. The Dutch edition of SOLAR LOTTERY mentioned here is probably: DE AARDE ALS HOOFDPRIJS, Born Pockets, pb, ?, 1969, ?, ? (?)

[dlxviii] Doubleday, hb, 68-11779, Mar 1968, 210pp, $3.95, (Harry Sehring){Levack: "Bound in grey cloth with gold lettering on the spine. '1968' on the title page. 'FIRST EDITION' on the copyright page. Date code J5 [5th week of 1968] at lower right margin of page 210"}

[dlxix] SL-38 238. PKD > Lawrence Ashmead, Editor, Doubleday & Co., Sep 7, 1968

[dlxx] SL-38 238. PKD > Lawrence Ashmead, Editor, Doubleday & Co., Sep 7, 1968

[dlxxi] Hour 25

[dlxxii] GSM Xerox collection, Scott Meredith to PKD, Sep 30, 1968. From the BGSU Papers. THE NAME OF THE GAME IS DEATH was the title for an outline, it's possible the title alone was transformed into A MAZE OF DEATH. The outline and the story have nothing to do with one another. Collier Books never did a PKD collection as far as I can tell. As for Essex House, I can find no editions from them. What the $1350 check was for I don't know either.

[dlxxiii] BGSU Papers. PKD to Roger Zelazny, Nov 13, 1968.

[dlxxiv] SL-38 190. PKD > Scott Meredith, May 22, 1965. Cc: Don Wollheim, Ace Books, Inc.

[dlxxv] BGSU Papers. Terry Carr to PKD, Feb 4, 1968.

[dlxxvi] Ibid. Marcia M. Howell to PKD, Oct 22, 1968

[dlxxvii] Ibid. Terry Carr to PKD, Nov 6, 1968

[dlxxviii] Ibid. Terry Carr to PKD, Nov 12, 1968.

[dlxxix] Ibid. PKD to Terry Carr, Nov 13, 1968.

[dlxxx] Ibid. PKD to John Brunner, Dec 7, 1968

[dlxxxi] Ibid. Terry Carr to PKD, Dec 19, 1968.

[dlxxxii] SL-38 246. PKD to Peter Fitting, April 29, 1969.

[dlxxxiii] SL-38 262. PKD to John Jakes, June 8, 1969

[dlxxxiv] THE PRESERVING MACHINE, ACE, pb, 67800, Apr 1969, 317pp, $0.95, (Leo and Diane Dillon); SFBC, hb, 2134, Jan 1970, ?, $1.69 (Leo & Diane Dillon) {Levack: "Bound in grey paper boards with green lettering on the spine. Ace Books logo on the spine. Top edges stained green. Date code 48K [48th week of 1969] at lower left

margin of page 309."}; Gollancz, hb, 00562-9, Feb 1971, 256pp, L1.80 (?) {**GC:** -A146 "What The Dead Men Say"}{Levack: "Bound in maroon paper boards with gold lettering on the spine. '1971' on the title page."}

      The Contents for the Ace editions is: *Upon The Dull Earth (1954),The Preserving Machine(1953),War Game(1959),Roog(1952),War Veteran(1955),Beyond Lies The Wub(1952),We Can Remember It For You Wholesale(1966),Captive Market(1955),If There Were No Benny Cemoli(1953), Retreat Syndrome(1964), The Crawlers(1954), Oh, To Be A Blobel!(1964), What The Dead Men Say(1964), Pay For The Printer(1956)*

^{dlxxxv} *PKD OTAKU* #7, Nov 2002, p1ff. Clark also refers the interested reader to RFPKD #7, Aug 1998, for a description of the collection at BGSU from which the Tench notes came.

^{dlxxxvi} RFPKD #7, Aug 1998. 'Phil Dick in 1968: From the Collection at Bowling Green' by Patrick Clark.

^{dlxxxvii} RFPKD #7, p2.

^{dlxxxviii} BGSU Papers. PKD to Don Wollheim, Oct 22, 1968.

^{dlxxxix} Patrick Clark too sees THE HOUR OF THE T.E.N.C.H. as being written before Oct 22, 1968.

^{dxc} Ibid. PKD to Scott Meredith, Oct 22, 1968. Note: The second novel PKD mentions here is most likely OUR FRIENDS FROM FROLIX 8, published by Ace in 1970.

^{dxci} Ibid. PKD to Terry Carr, Nov 13, 1968.

^{dxcii} GSM Xerox Collection. 'The Game Of "THE NAME OF THE GAME IS DEATH"' by Patrick Clark. The quote is from a letter from PKD to Judith M. Glushanok, Jan 13, 1970.

^{dxciii} Doubleday, hb, 70-111158, Jul 1970, 216pp, $4.95, (Michelle Moschella) {Levack: "Bound in royal blue cloth with silver lettering on the spine, '1970' on the title page. 'First Edition' on the copyright page. Date code 'L21' at the lower right margin of page 216. According to David Hartwell this book was accidentally pulped, leaving only library and review copies actually distributed."}

^{dxciv} Gollancz, hb, 00694-3, Jan 1972, 216pp, L1.80 (?) {Levack: "Bound in maroon paper boards with gold lettering stamped on the spine. '1972' on the title page. States nothing about printing or edition on the copyright page.[normal practice for Gollancz, however, they generally mark later printings."]}

^{dxcv} A MAZE OF DEATH. Bantam, pb, 10740-2, Sep 1977, 182pp, $1.75 (Szafran).

^{dxcvi} TDC 79.

^{dxcvii} IPOV 20

^{dxcviii} TSR 218

^{dxcix} BGSU Papers. PKD to Scott Meredith, Oct 22, 1968.

^{dc} Ibid. Description prepared by Patrick Clark.

^{dci} PKDS-19 1. This issue of PKDS is a special pamphlet devoted to OUR FRIENDS FROM FROLIX 8. It contains the text of the complete outline.

^{dcii} PKDS-19. Pamphlet devoted to OUR FRIENDS FROM FROLIX 8, 1989. For continuation of this Outline read it in the Pamphlet.

^{dciii} BGSU Papers. PKD > Don Wollheim, editor, Ace Books, Apr 14, 1969

^{dciv} SL-38 260. PKD to Don Wollheim, Jun 6, 1969.

^{dcv} OUR FRIENDS FROM FROLIX 8, ACE, pb, 64400, Jun 1970, 189pp, $0.60 (Schoenherr)

^{dcvi} SFBC, hb, ?, Feb 1971, ?, $1.49 (Kim Whitesides) {Levack: "Bound in rust brown paper boards with black lettering on the spine. 'Ace Books' on spine. Date code B3 [3rd week of 1971] at lower right margin on page 184."}

^{dcvii} Panther, pb, 04295-4, Oct 1976, ?, 60p (Jim Burns)

^{dcviii} OUR FRIENDS FROM FROLIX 8, Kinnell, hb, 08-2, Jun 1989, 211pp, L11.95 (Keith Roberts) 1-870532-08-2

^{dcix} BGSU Papers. {This letter}Requests a short story to be published in the 20th anniversary issue (Oct 1969) of *The Magazine of Fantasy and Science Fiction.* Edward L. Ferman > PKD, 2 Nov 1968

^{dcx} Ibid. PKD > Marcia M. Howell, SMLA, 11-15-1968

^{dcxi} Levack 91. Also in THE BEST OF PKD, Ballantine, 1977, p449.

^{dcxii} BGSU Papers. Lawrence P. Ashmead > PKD, May 29, 1968.

^{dcxiii} TSR 11. PKD 'Self Portrait', 1968.

^{dcxiv} TSR 137.

^{dcxv} **Starlog** #55, p20. PKD on *BLADE RUNNER* by James Van Hise.

^{dcxvi} Hour 25.

1969

^{dcxvii}DO ANDROIDS DREAM OF ELECTRIC SHEEP? Signet, pb, T3800, Mar 1969, 159pp, $0.75 (Graham).

dcxviii DO ANDROIDS DREAM OF ELECTRIC SHEEP? Rapp & Whiting, hb, 081-2, Mar 1969, 192pp, 21/- (Lawrence Edwards)

dcxix THE PRESERVING MACHINE, ACE, pb, 67800, Apr 1969, 317pp, $0.95, (Leo and Diane Dillon)

dcxx THE GAME-PLAYERS OF TITAN, Sphere, pb, 2957-2, May 1969, 157pp, 5/- (?)

dcxxi UBIK, Doubleday, hb, 69-15205, May 1969, 202pp, $4.50, (Peter Rauch) {Levack: "Bound in gray cloth with silver lettering on the spine. '1969' on the title page. 'First Edition' on the copyright page. Date code 'K10' [10th week of 1969] on page 202."}

dcxxii GALACTIC POT-HEALER, Berkley, pb, X1705, Jun 1969, 144pp, $0.60 (Kossut)

dcxxiii UBIK, SFBC, hb, 1909, 1969, 202pp, ? (?) {Levack: "Bound in grey paper boards with pink lettering on the spine. No date on the title page. Date code '28K' on lower left margin of unnumbered page 203."

dcxxiv *Amazing*, Nov 1969 and Jan 1970 {GC 4th : "with 3,000 word ending written by Ted White"}

dcxxv DI 163 and DI 330. PKD to Lynne Cecil, Mar 21, 1969.

dcxxvi DI 163ff

dcxxvii Ibid.

1970

dcxxviii OUR FRIENDS FROM FROLIX 8, ACE, pb, 64400, Jun 1970, 189pp, $0.60 (Schoenherr)

dcxxix UBIK, Rapp & Whiting, hb, 164-9, Jun 1970, 202pp, 28/- (?) {Levack: Bound in black paper boards with silver lettering on the spine. No date on the title page. "First Published in Great Britain 1970" on the copyright page.}

dcxxx A PKD OMNIBUS, Sidgwick & Jackson, hb, 48450-0, Oct 1970. 424pp, L1.95 (?)

dcxxxi Hour 25

dcxxxii PKDS-28 6ff. PKD to Sandra Meisal, Aug 27, 1970

dcxxxiii DI 165 and DI 330. PKD to Jim, Sep 17, 1970.

dcxxxiv TDC 35. PKD interview with D. Scot Apel & Kevin Briggs, 1977.

dcxxxv SL-38 271. PKD to Scott Meredith, Aug 2, 1970.

dcxxxvi SL-38 304. PKD to Valerie McMillan, Oct 2, 1970.

dcxxxvii Biographical material for this period comes mostly from DI and PKDS.

dcxxxviii DI 168 and in OAR. PKD in interview with Paul Williams.

dcxxxix DI 179

dcxl GSM Xerox Collection. PKD to Hans Alpers, July 29, 1975. {His stamp collection was also stolen. See: PKD to Kris Hummel, Feb 2, 1982. GSM Xerox collection. Also found on philipkdick.com.

dcxli Philip K. Dick married Tessa Busby in April 1973.

dcxlii PKDS-28 6ff. This issue of PKDS contains much bibliographic material for FLOW MY TEARS, THE POLICEMAN SAID as well as an excerpt (The Different Stages Of Love) from an early draft of the novel.

dcxliii PKDS-28 6ff.

dcxliv GSM Xerox Collection. PKD to Charles Brown, *Locus Magazine*, Apr 6, 1973. Also found on philipkdick.com.

dcxlv Ibid. PKD to Goran Bengtson, May 4, 1973.

dcxlvi Ibid.

dcxlvii ibid. PKD to Patrice Duvic, Nov 20, 1973. Sutin notes (DI 199) that Duvic visited PKD sometime in late 1973 and brought up the subject of a screenplay for Dick's novel UBIK.

dcxlviii Ibid. PKD to Lawrence Ashmead, Jan 23, 1974.

dcxlix FLOW MY TEARS, THE POLICEMAN SAID, Doubleday, hb, 00887-2, 1974, 231pp, $6.95, (One Plus One)

dcl FLOW MY TEARS, THE POLICEMAN SAID, Gollancz, hb, 01880-1, Oct 1974, 231pp, L2.20, (?) {Levack: "Bound in maroon paper boards with gold lettering on the spine. '1974' on the title page."}

dcli PKDS-28

dclii PKDS-28 1. CONCERNING PAGES ARISING FROM NOTHINGNESS by Gerard Klein. A preface to the second French edition of FLOW MY TEARS, THE POLICEMAN SAID (Editions Robert Laffont, 1985) translated by Paul Williams.

dcliii Ibid.

dcliv ibid.

dclv Ibid.

dclvi Laffont, pb, ?, 1985, ?, ?, (?) {tr. into French by Michel Deutsch as COULEZ MES LARMES, DIT LE POLICIER}ISBN: 2-221-04246-8

dclvii PKDS-4 1. PKD to Joan, May 20, 1977. The 'same forces' would be those who broke into his house and stole his files.

dclviii TDC 89.

dclix SF EYE, #14, Spring 1996. Anton & Fuchs interview, 1977 Metz, translated by. F.C. Bertrand

dclx TSR 250.

dclxi PKDS-4 5.

dclxii PKDS-3 13.

dclxiii TDC 90. Apel & Briggs interview, 1977.

dclxiv Peter Fenelon, NY. FDO. 'PKD Horserace.'

dclxv Deborah Eley, LA. FDO. 'PKD Horserace.'

dclxvi Phildickian.com: FLOW MY TEARS, THE POLICEMAN SAID by Linda Hartinian, Dramatic Publishing Company -- Woodstock, IL, wraps, 1990. NF. This is the screenplay based on the novel. A clean unread copy with just a hint of shelfwear. $100. The author has a copy of this video, directed by Dan Sutherland, and had it shown on public access TV several times in 1995 in Ft. Wayne, Indiana.

dclxvii TSR 247.

1971

dclxviii NOW WAIT FOR LAST YEAR, SOLAR LOTTERY, SOLAR LOTTERY, THE PENULTIMATE TRUTH, THE WORLD JONES MADE, THE ZAP GUN.

dclxix TTHC 415: fn9. Although Rickman ascribes the story to 1970 in Vol. 5 of THE COLLECTED STORIES "Cadbury The Beaver That Lacked" is dated to Dec 1971.

1972

dclxx Philip K. Dick expands on his time spent in X-Kalay in the *Vertex* interview, Vertex, Vol. 1, no. 6, February 1974, interviewer Arthur Byron Cover.

dclxxi DI 190ff. Lawrence Sutin goes into much more detail on this period of Dick's life than I have in this brief summary. I recommend the interested reader acquire Sutin's biography.

dclxxii See PKDS-13 5. Tessa Dick and J.B. Reynolds in conversation.

dclxxiii DAW, pb, UQ 1014 (#14), Jul 1972, 206pp, $0.95 (Schoenherr)

dclxxiv UBIK, Wydawnictwa Literackie, Krakow, ?, ?, 1975, ?, ?, (?) {tr. Into Polish by Michal Ronikier as UBIK}

dclxxv *Vertex*, Vol. 1, no. 6, February 1974. Arthur Byron Cover interviewer.

1973

dclxxvi PKDS-13 5. Tessa Dick in conversation with J.B. Reynolds, 1986.

dclxxvii Philip K. Dick: Breakthroughs & Breakins, *SF Commentary,* July-Sep 1973. An open letter from Philip K. Dick to John Sladek, Apr 23, 1973.

dclxxviii A Little Something For Us Tempunauts" in FINAL STAGE {Ed. Ferman, Malzberg}, Charterhouse, hb, ?, 1974, ?, ? (?).

dclxxix GSM Xerox Collection. PKD to Charles Brown, *Locus Magazine*, Apr 6, 1973. Also found on philipkdick.com

dclxxx Levack 107. Also in THE BEST OF PKD, Ballantine, 1977, p450.

dclxxxi THE TURNING WHEEL AND OTHER STORIES, Coronet, pb, 21829-0, Jul 1977, 189pp, 80p (?)

dclxxxii TDC 41.

dclxxxiii THE BOOK OF PHILIP K. DICK, DAW, pb, #44, Feb 1973, 187pp, $0.95 (Karel Thole) {Levack: The U.S. 1st printing is marked: FIRST PRINTING, FEBRUARY 1973 on the copyright page. However, it is also marked with a vertical string "FIRST PRINTING", SECOND PRINTING" and so on through "TENTH PRINTING". The Canadian edition, which is marked "Printed in Canada" contains only the first printing statement. Contents: Nanny, The Turning Wheel, The Defenders, Adjustment Team, Psi-Man, The Commuter, A Present For Pat, Breakfast At Twilight, Shell Game.

dclxxxiv TGM 'Story Notes' by PKD

dclxxxv TGM 'Afterword' by PKD, 1979

dclxxxvi SRG 53.

dclxxxvii TDC ?. PKD interview with Apel & Briggs, 1977.

dclxxxviii DI 205. PKD to Nancy and Isa, Apr 8, 1973. Dick refers to A SCANNER DARKLY as having gone to Doubleday before Apr 6, 1973: "The editors at Doubleday have also received first-look at a 62-page outline and sample chapters for my novel following TEARS; they are considering it now, called, A SCANNER DARKLY, this new s-f novel, which will run really long (for me anyhow), is anti-dope and based on much first-hand experience. It's a downer, even though I am putting as much humor into it as I can. Ultimately I found very little that was amusing in the dope world and much that was heart breaking." – GSM Xerox Collection: PKD to Charles Brown, *Locus*, Apr 6, 1973. Also found at philipkdick.com.

dclxxxix *SF Commentary*, July-Sep 1973. 'Philip K. Dick: Breakthroughs & Breakins'. An open letter to John T. Sladek, Apr 23, 1973. The other novel PKD refers to is FLOW MY TEARS, THE POLIEMAN SAID.

dcxc PKDS ?. PKD>Goran Bengston, his Swedish translator, 4 May 1973

dcxci SF EYE, #14, Spring 1996, pp. 37-46. Conducted by Uwe Anton & Werner Fuchs. Transcribed by Frank C. Bertrand.

dcxcii *SF Commentary,* July-'Sep 1973. 'Philip K. Dick: Breakthroughs & Breakins'. An open letter to John T. Sladek, Apr 23, 1973.

dcxciii PKDS-8 13: Auction: A SCANNER DARKLY manuscript and correspondence package. Minimum bid $750.

dcxciv *Science Fiction Review*, No. 19, Vol. 5, no. 3, August 1976, 'An Interview with Philip K. Dick' by Daniel DePrez.

dcxcv Hour 25

dcxcvi *NIEKAS*, No. 34, 1986, pp. 3-4. Bumbejimas: PKD And Me' by Ed Meskys: {PKD didn't only complain about Doubleday but also Ace Books when it came to royalties, as Ed Meskys says}:

"He said that Don Wollheim kept writing him complaining now that he had a major success with CASTLE he would be abandoning Don and Ace. Phil also complained of strange quirks in the royalty reports from Ace. Back then Ace was publishing its "Ace Doubles", two books back to back. Usually one book was longer than the other and they were by different authors and unrelated in any way. Occasionally both sides were by the same author. One such pair was by Phil, and the royalty statement in question gave totally different sales figures for the two halves of the same book. Obviously this made Phil very suspicious of the veracity of other royalty statements from Ace."

dcxcvii PKDS-8 13: Auction: A SCANNER DARKLY manuscript and correspondence package. Minimum bid $750.

dcxcviii PKDS-11 6.

dcxcix TDC 77.

dcc Hour 25

dcci A SCANNER DARKLY, Doubleday, hb, 01613-1, 1977, 220pp, $6.95, (The Quay Brothers) {Levack: "Bound in beige paper boards with black lettering on the spine. Date code 'G51' [51st week of 1976] appears on the lower right margin of page 216. '1977' on the title page. States 'First Edition' on the copyright page."}. A SCANNER DARKLY, SFBC, hb, 15503, 1977, 220pp, $2.98 (Quay Brothers) {Levack: "Date code H05 on page 216."} A SCANNER DARKLY, Gollancz, hb, 02381-3 Nov **1977**, 220pp, L3.50 (?) {Levack: "Bound in blue paper boards with gold lettering on the spine. '1977' on the title page."} A SCANNER DARKLY, Ballantine (Del Rey), pb, 26064, Dec 1977, 288pp, $1.95 (Ochagavia).

dccii PKDS-13 16. Vaclav Kriz sent two items from Czechoslovakia... a copy of the 1986 hardcover TEMNY OBRAZ (A SCANNER DARKLY), translated by Jan Kamenisty and published by Smena Publishing in a first edition of 50,000 copies!

dcciii PKDS-5 11. K.W. Jeter in conversation with Andy Watson. The French edition Jeter refers to is probably the one from Denoel published in 1978; A SCANNER DARKLY, Denoel – Presence de Futur, pb, 252, 1978, 304pp, ? (?) {tr. Into French by Robert Louit as SUBSTANCE MORT}

dcciv Ken Lopez, Bookseller, Online catalog May 1997.

dccv Vertex, Vol. 1, no. 6, February 1974. Interviewer: Arthur Byron Cover

dccvi PKDS-16 4. Roger Zelazny, 1978.

dccvii PKDS-6 14. PKD in 1977.

dccviii *Science Fiction Review*, No. 19, Vol. 5, no. 3, August 1976, Daniel DePrez, interviewer

dccix FDO 4. 'PKD Horserace'. David Keller, Santa Ana, CA. to *FDO*.

dccx GSM Xerox Collection. PKD in a letter to Erwin Bush, Burning Bush Publications, 16 Sep 1981. In response to the article "Kant's 'Noumenal Self' and Doppelganger in P.K.Dick's A SCANNER DARKLY." {This essay can be found in OnPKD} dccxi FDO 5. 'PKD Horserace'. Lord RC to FDO.

1974

dccxii *Weirdo # 17*, 'The Religious Experience of Philip K. Dick' by R. Crumb. This is an illustrated article by R. Crumb, the distinctive comics artist.

dccxiii PHILIP K. DICK: IN HIS OWN WORDS, (IHOW), by Gregg Rickman, Fragments West, tp, 01-1, Aug 1984, 250pp, $9.95 (?). Also a revised edition in 1988.

dccxiv The reason for not including RADIO FREE ALBEMUTH in the 'VALIS Trilogy' seems to be that RADIO FREE ALBEMUTH was a draft of VALIS that PKD himself had rejected as unsatisfactory. The manuscript was revealed by Tim Powers after PKD's death.

dccxv *Weirdo #17*

dccxvi DI 222

dccxvii *Weirdo #17*

dccxviii DI 226. Sutin notes that PKD finished the screenplay in a *month* not a year.

dccxix DI 227-228

dccxx *Weirdo*

dccxxi TSR 324

dccxxii *Weirdo*

dccxxiii Ibid. The *I Ching* hexagram 'Darkening of the Light' is number 36.

dccxxiv Ibid.

dccxxv DI 214. Also in VALIS

dccxxvi DI 215ff

dccxxvii Ibid.

dccxxviii PKDS-13 6, Feb 1987

dccxxix DI 219

dccxxx THE GAME-PLYERS OF TITAN, White Lion, hb, 577-3, Jun 1974, 188pp, L1.80 (?) {Levack: "Bound in dark blue paper boards with gold lettering stamped on the spine. States 'White Lion edition, 1974' on copyright page and otherwise makes no indication of edition or printing. Name on spine is 'R.A.Dick' (the author of *THE GHOST AND MRS. MUIR*). No date on the title page."}

dccxxxi Hour 25: A Talk With Philip K. Dick hosted by Mike Hodel. KPFK-FM, North Hollywood, California. June 26, 1976. Transcribed and edited by Frank C. Bertrand.

dccxxxii *Rolling Stone* Nov 6, 1975. 'The True Stories Of Philip K. Dick' by Paul Williams.

dccxxxiii UBIK: The Screenplay, Corroboree, hb, ?, 1985, 154pp, $23.00 (Ron Lindahn, Val Lakey-Lindahn and Doug Rice) 0-911169-06-7 {*Locus:* There is also a 50-copy deluxe edition signed by the artists, Powers, Williams, and Dick (signatures from checks), for $180.00}. The ordinary edition can fetch prices from $150 on up depending on condition. The deluxe edition, I imagine, would fetch over $500.

1975

dccxxxiv See DI 235-6. The SMLA reception date is taken from THE COLLECTED STORIES, Vol. 5, p303.

dccxxxv *PHILIP K. DICK: THE DREAM CONNECTION* {Ed. D. Scot Apel}, The Permanent Press, hb, Mar 1987, 269pp, $19.95 (?) {limited to 500 copies}. See the Galactic Central bibliography, part 2 – non-fiction, 3rd revised edition, p88. PHILIP K. DICK: THE DREAM CONNECTION {Ed. D.S. Apel} Impermanent Press, pb, 1999 (2nd).

dccxxxvi GSM Xerox Collection. Charles A. Coulombe, "The Ghost In The Android" (nd)

dccxxxvii TTHC 158

dccxxxviii TCSVol5 305

dccxxxix THE ZAP GUN, Panther, pb, 04112-5, Feb 1975, 190pp, 40p (Peter Jones); THE MAN IN THE HIGH CASTLE, Gollancz, hb, 01958-1, May 1975, 222pp, L3.20 (?) {Levack: "Bound in blue paper boards with gold lettering on the spine. '1975' on the title page.

dccxl CONFESSIONS OF A CRAP ARTIST, Entwhistle, hb, 2-7, 1975, 171pp, $5.95 (Richard Powers) Also: 90 numbered copies, signed by Dick ($25.00) and an edition of 410 copies ($10.00) dccxli FLOW MY TEARS, THE POLICEMAN SAID, DAW, pb, UW 1166 (#146), Apr 1975, 208pp, $1.50 (Osterwalder); "The Golden Man" in *EVIL EARTHS*, {Ed. Aldiss}, Weidenfield & Nicholson, hb, ?, 1975, ?, L4.25 (?); in *STRANGE GIFTS* {Ed. Silverberg}, Thomas Nelson, hb, ?, 1975, ?, $6.95 (?).

dccxlii DI 235.

dccxliii Ibid.

dccxliv PEPKD 83.

dccxlv PKDS-2 7, Dec 1983

dccxlvi TSROPKD 165 and 211ff.

dccxlvii TSROPKD 212.

dccxlviii TSROPKD 215.

1976

dccxlix DEUS IRAE, Doubleday, hb, 04527-1, Jul 1976, 182pp, $5.95 (John Cayea) {Levack: "Bound in black paper boards with red lettering on the spine. Date code 'G 27' (27th week of 1976) appears at the lower left margin of page 181. States 'First Edition' on the copyright page. '1976' on the title page."}

dccl *Science Fiction Review*, No. 19, Vol. 5, no. 3, August 1976. AN INTERVIEW WITH PHILIP K. DICK conducted Sep 10, 1976, by Daniel DePrez

dccli Hour 25: A Talk With Philip K. Dick hosted by Mike Hodel. KPFK-FM, North Hollywood, California. June 26, 1976. Transcribed and edited by Frank C. Bertrand.

dcclii Ken Lopez, Bookseller online catalog, May 1997

dccliii PKDS-29 10, Patrick Clark to PKDS, Oct 1991. Clark dates a letter from PKD to Farmer dated Apr 15, 1974 that mentions PKD as about to send "A Man For No Countries" to Farmer.

dccliv Paul Williams in the Introduction to *Welcome To Reality: The Nightmares of Philip K. Dick*, Broken Mirrors Press, tp, ISBN 0-9623824-5-0, Feb 1991, 208pp, $12.95 (D. Wilson) Edited by Uwe Anton.} {Welcome To Reality is a collection of short stories by various authors in which Philip K. Dick is a character or figures largely in some way}. See also OAR 75-84 and OAR 147.

dcclv PKDS-6 3, Apr 1985

dcclvi PEPKD 63

dcclvii PKDS-6 3, Apr 1985

dcclviii Ibid.

dcclix PKDS-8 10, Sep 1985

dcclx PKDS-11 5, May 1986

dcclxi RADIO FREE ALBEMUTH, Arbor House, hb, 762-2, Dec 1985, 214pp, $14.95, (Ron Walotsky) 0-87795-762-2; RADIO FREE ALBEMUTH, Grafton, pb, 06936-4, May 1987, 286pp, L2.95 (Tony Roberts) 0-586-06936-4.

dcclxii Ken Lopez Bookseller, online catalog 1997.

dcclxiii DI 241

1977

dcclxiv THE BEST OF PHILIP K. DICK, Ballantine, pb, 25359-0, Mar 1977, 450pp, $1.95 (DiFate).
Contents: Introduction, "The Reality of Philip K. Dick" by John Brunner; Beyond Lies The Wub; Roog ; Second Variety; Paycheck; Impostor; Colony; Expendable; The Days Of Perky Pat; Breakfast At Twilight; Foster, You're Dead; The Father Thing; Service Call; Autofac; Human is; If There Were No Benny Cemoli; Oh, To Be A Blobel!; Faith Of Our Fathers; The Electric Ant; A Little Something For Us Tempunauts; Afterthoughts by PKD.

dcclxv THE BEST OF PHILIP K. DICK. Garland, hb, 4208-5, 1982, 450pp, $19.95 (?)

dcclxvi Ken Lopez Bookseller, online catalog 1997.

dcclxvii DR. BLOODMONEY, Gregg Press, hb, 2365-7, Jun 1977, 222pp, $11 (no cover pic) {Levack: "Bound in dark green cloth with gold lettering on the spine. Title and author's name are on bright red background on the spine. 'First Printing, June 1977' on the copyright page. Issued without dustjacket. Text is photoreproduced from the 1965 Ace edition.'}

dcclxviii DI 246ff

dcclxix PKDS-8 9, Aug 1985.

dcclxx DI 251

dcclxxi Ibid. Also in PKDS-16, Jan 1988. 'Musings From Melbourne' by Roger Zelazny.

dcclxxii TSR 235. "If You Find This World Bad, You Should See Some Of The others"; the Metz Speech, 1977.

dcclxxiii TSR 237-8.

dcclxxiv See TSR 246. {In the section on THE MAN IN THE HIGH CASTLE we have included a brief quote from this part of the Metz Speech.}

dcclxxv TSR 247

dcclxxvi These biographical details are taken from Lawrence Sutin's DIVINE INVASIONS (DI) biography.

1978

dcclxxvii DI 253.

dcclxxviii VALIS, Kerosina, hb, 15-X, Nov 1987. In three versions: **One**. Kerosina, hb, 15-X, Nov 1987, 256pp, L75 (Keith Roberts), limited to 25 copies, signed by Kim Stanley Robinson and with a 'tipped-in' Dick signature. Packaged in slipcase with "Cosmogony and Cosmology", Kerosina, hb, 0-948893-17-6, Nov 1987, 37pp, ? (?). **Two**. VALIS, Kerosina, hb, 15-X, Nov 1987, 256pp, L37.50 (Keith Roberts), limited to 275 copies, signed by Kim Stanley Robinson, 0-948893-15-X {*Locus*: Cloth-bound version of VALIS plus a hardcover edition of "Cosmogony and Cosmology". There is a **third** Kerosina edition of VALIS that omits "Cosmogony and Cosmology." VALIS, Kerosina, hb, 16-8, Nov **1987**, 256pp, L13.95 (Keith Roberts) limited to 2200 copies, 0-948893-16-8.

The Galactic Central bibliography lists two versions of "Cosmogony and Cosmology": Kerosina, hb, 17-6, Nov 1987, 45pp (325 copies distributed with the collector's edition of VALIS) and Kerosina, tp, 18-4, Nov 1987, 45pp, L4.50 (Keith Roberts) {500 copies}.

dcclxxix TSR 281ff. "Cosmogony and Cosmology."

dcclxxx A HANDFUL OF DARKNESS, Gregg Press, hb, 2413-0, Jun 1978, 223pp, $11 (?) {Levack: Introduction by Richard Lupoff. Frontispiece by Hannah Shapero. Bound in dark-green cloth with gold lettering on the spine. "First Printing, June 1978" on the copyright page. Issued without dust-jacket. Text is photo-reproduced from the 1955 Rich & Cowan edition.

dcclxxxi See DI 254.

dcclxxxii TSR 267.

dcclxxxiii TSR 268.

dcclxxxiv DI 255ff

dcclxxxv Twilight Zone Magazine, Vol. 2, No. 3, June 1982, p5ff1: John Boonstra, interviewer.

dcclxxxvi IPOV 103. PKD in 1980.

dcclxxxvii See DI. VALIS, Bantam, pb, 14156-2, Feb 1981, 227pp, $2.25 (Berkey)

dcclxxxviii Ken Lopex bookseller, online catalog 1997.

dcclxxxix Lame Duck Books, online catalog 2000. As part of its PKD offerings, lame Duck also has the following: THE 3 STIGMATA OF PALMER ELDRITCH, Gregg Press, 1979. FINE. Inscribed by Dick to fellow sci-fi author and editor Alan Ryan, one of the most intelligent and literate of the fraternity, 'To Alan -- a good friend.' $950.

dccxc *Asimov's Science Fiction Magazine*, March 1981, p16. Found in *PKD OTAKU* #6, Sep 2002, p11.

1979

dccxci DI 261

dccxcii PKDS-8 9. Paul Williams notes that "The Exit Door leads In" was PKD's first short story, other than occasional pieces, since 1974.

dccxciii PKDS-8 9.

dccxciv DI 266

dccxcv PKDS-8 9.

dccxcvi THE SHIFTING REALITIES OF PHILIP K. DICK: Selected Literary and Philosophical Writings, Ed. Lawrence Sutin, Vintage Press, tp, 1995, ISBN: 0-679-74787-7. (TSR)

dccxcvii DI 265.

dccxcviii FDO 4. 'PKD Horserace.'

dccxcix PKDS-29 11. Karl-Heinz Wiedemann to PKDS, Jul 1991.

1980

[dccc] DI 266

[dccci] PEPKD 68 and *Rouzleweave #1*, March 2002, p4.

[dcccii] THE DIVINE INVASION, Timescape, hb, 41776-2, Jun 1981, 239pp, $12.95 (Rowena Morrill) {Levack: "Simon & Schuster, New York ... Three-piece binding, with royal blue cloth spine and light blue paper boards with gold lettering on the spine. No date on the title page. Printing code '10 9 8 7 6 5 4 3 2 1' on copyright page. A Timescape book"}

[dccciii] PKDS-13 14.

[dccciv] TDC ?. PKD interview with Apel & Briggs, 1977.

[dcccv] PKDS-5 13, Dec 1984. The PKDS Interview with K.W. Jeter conducted by Andy Watson

[dcccvi] PKDS-29 5, "Three By PKD: VENOM", Sept 29, 1981, *Venom* Magazine, POBox 11626, San Francisco. CA 94101.

[dcccvii] PKDS-29ff

[dcccviii] *Analog*, Dec 7, 1981, pp96-97. Review by Tom Easton. Found in *PKD OTAKU* #8, Jan 2003, pp7-8.

[dcccix] FDO ? Eric Johnson, Wash D.C.

[dcccx] IPOV 194. PKD refers not to marijuana here but to his novel GALACTIC POT-HEALER.

[dcccxi] PKDS-25 19.

[dcccxii] Ken Lopez Bookseller, online catalog May 1997.

[dcccxiii] Ken Lopez Bookseller, online catalog May 1997.

[dcccxiv] Unknown source. GSM Xerox Collection. Martin Skidmore on PKD. The other book Skidmore refers to is Ian Watson's *GOD'S WORLD*; 1982.

[dcccxv] TZ, Vol. 2, No. 3, June 1982, pp. 47-52. Interviewer, John Boonstra

[dcccxvi] PKD to David Hartwell, May 21, 1981.

[dcccxvii] PKDS-5 14.

[dcccxviii] *Starlog* #165, p53. See same for continuation. Interview with PKD conducted in 1982 by Gwen Lee and Doris E. Sauter.

[dcccxix] GSM Xerox Collection. PKD to Kris Hummel, Jan 27, 1982.

[dcccxx] DI 261.

[dcccxxi] PKDS-8 9. The 'Best of the Year' anthology Williams refers to is: *THE BEST SF OF THE YEAR #10*, ed. Terry Carr, Timescape, pb, 42262-6, Jul 1981, 434pp, $3.50 (?) ISBN: 0-671-42262-6. PKD's story "Frozen Journey" starts on p97.

[dcccxxii] *PKD OTAKU* #8, Jan 2003, p5 – 6. PKD to Cathy, Oct 1, 1981.

[dcccxxiii] *Playboy*, Dec 1980, 'Playbill', p5; Contents, p8.

[dcccxxiv] THE GOLDEN MAN, Berkley, pb, 04288-X, Feb 1980, 337pp, $3.35 (Walter Velez). Contents: The Golden Man, Return Match, The King of the Elves, The Mold of Yancy, Not By Its Cover, The Little Black Box, The Unreconstructed M, The War With The Fnools, The Last of the Masters, Meddler, A Game Of Unchance, Sales Pitch, Precious Artifact, Small Town, The pre-Persons.

[dcccxxv] Internet bookseller Monroe Bethea Books had the following offering in 2001: THE GOLDEN MAN, Berkley, pb, 04288, 1980 (1st). VG-. Signed by Author. This paperback book is in very good minus condition. It has glossy covers, with a light crease to the upper right front cover, a crease and small 1/8 inch piece missing to lower left back cover, a remainder mark on bottom page edges, a store stamp on inside rear cover and a spine crease. The condition reads way worse than the book looks. It is bright and square and has Phil's signature on the title page. $110.

[dcccxxvi] PKDS-15 8. See also DI 269.

[dcccxxvii] *Denver Clarion*, October 23, 1980. 'Philip K. Dick: Confessions Of A SF Artist', An interview with Philip K. Dick by George Cain and Dana Longo.

[dcccxxviii] *Denver Clarion*, October 23, 1980. 'Philip K. Dick: Confessions Of A SF Artist' Interview by George Cain and Dana Longo

[dcccxxix] ibid.

[dcccxxx] ibid.

[dcccxxxi] DI 269. "11-17-80"

[dcccxxxii] DI 272-73.

[dcccxxxiii] *Fantastic Films Magazine*, Aug 1982.'BLADE RUNNER: Ridley Scott Interviewed' by Blake Mitchell and Jim Ferguson, p12 ff.

dcccxxxiv *Starlog*, May 1982, p22ff, 'Interview with the *BLADE RUNNER* Screenwriters: Hampton Fancher & David Peoples' by James Van Hise.

dcccxxxv Ibid.

dcccxxxvi Ibid.

dcccxxxvii *Starlog*, Feb 1982. 'Philip K. Dick on *BLADE RUNNER*' by James Van Hise. In a letter to Kris Hummel dated Jan 27, 1982 PKD refers to this interview and comments on Fancher, Peoples and Scott.

dcccxxxviii *Starlog*, Aug 1982. '*BLADE RUNNER*'s Sean Young' interview by James Van Hise. PKD quote from Sep 1981.

dcccxxxix *Twilight Zone*, Vol. 2, No. 3, June 1982, pp. 47-52. Interview by John Boonstra.

dcccxl GSM Xerox Collection. PKD to Kris Hummel, Jan 19, 1982.

dcccxli Ibid. See also DI.

dcccxlii GSM Xerox Collection. PKD to Kris Hummel, Jan 12, 1982. Also on philipkdick.com

dcccxliii *The Patchin Review*, No. 5. Oct-Dec 1982, pp2-6. Interviewer John Boonstra

dcccxliv Ibid.

dcccxlv *Starlog*, Nov 1982, p55ff. '*BLADE RUNNER*' reviewed by Norman Spinrad.

dcccxlvi Ibid.

dcccxlvii Ibid.

dcccxlviii *BLADE RUNNER* (DO ANDROIDS DREAM OF ELECTRIC SHEEP?), Del Rey, pb, 30129-3, May 1982, 216pp, $2.75 (Movie poster by Alvin)

dcccxlix *BLADE RUNNER* (DO ANDROIDS DREAM OF ELECTRIC SHEEP?), Granada, pb, 03605-9, Aug 1982, 183pp, L1.50 (Movie poster)

dcccl *BLADE RUNNER* OFFICIAL SOUVENIR MAGAZINE, Friedman, Inc, 1982, $2.95, 68pp, 140 photos and illustrations. And *BLADE RUNNER* SKETCHBOOK, Blue Dolphin, 11 X 8 3/8, 1982, $6.95, 96pp. A profusely illustrated collection featuring original artwork by Syd Mead, Mentour Huebner, Charles Knode, Michael Kaplan and Ridley Scott from the motion picture.

Blue Dolphin issued two other publications in conjunction with the movie: *THE ILLUSTRATED BLADE RUNNER*, 8 ½ X 11, 1982, $6.95,128 pp, illustrated. And: *BLADE RUNNER PORTFOLIO*, 9 ¼ X 12 ¼, 1982, $9.95, twelve hi-gloss action photos of Harrison Ford and cast in prime moments from the film. Full-color sharp images ready for instant display. Produced on high-quality stock, all twelve reproductions cover the action and suspense of *BLADE RUNNER*. Each plate I approx. 9 ¼ by 12 ¼ and is packaged in a handsome illustrated folder…

dcccli PKDS-4 8.

1981

dccclii PKDS-8 9.

dcccliii *PKD OTAKU* # 7, Nov 2002, p3ff, 'Stalking the PKD Fiction oddities: Part 1 (*Yuba City High Times*)' by Frank Hollander. See also the Oct 1981 *F & SF*.

dcccliv Ibid.

dccclv Ibid. p5ff, 'Nobly Wild, Not Mad: Memories of Philip K. Dick' by Benjamin Adams. Adams is now a writer and editor of horror stories, appearing in such anthologies as *BLOOD MUSE, DARK THEATRES* and *HORRORS! 365 SCARY STORIES*. He was also co-editor of *THE CHILDREN OF CTHULHU* which was published by Del Rey in 2002.

dccclvi PKD: A PHILIP K. DICK BIBLIOGRAPHY, Daniel J. H. Levack, Underwood/Miller Press, tp, 1981. ISBN: 0-934438-33-1.

dccclvii THE TRANSMIGRATION OF TIMOTHY ARCHER, Timescape, hb, 44066-7, Apr 1982, 240pp, $15.50 (Powers)

dccclviii THE TRANSMIGRATION OF TIMOTHY ARCHER, Gollancz, hb, 03220-0, Oct 1982, 254pp, L6.95 (?)

dccclix **brg**, No. 1, October 1990. A talk written by Bruce Gillespie for the October 1990 meeting of the Nova Mob; for ANZAPA (Australia and New Zealand Amateur Publishing Association)

dccclx PKD OTAKU #11, Sep 2003, p11. (Source: Norman Spinrad, "The Transmogrification of Philip K. Dick" in *Science Fiction in the Real World*; Southern Illinois University Press, 1990, p200)

dccclxi *Twilight Zone*, Vol. 2, No. 3, June 1982, John Boonstra, interviewer.

dccclxii Ibid.

dccclxiii Ibid. The 'three' PKD talks about are VALIS, THE DIVINE INASION and THE TRANSMIGRATION OF TIMOTHY ARCHER – the 'Valis Trilogy.'

dccclxiv *The Patchin Review*, No. 5, Oct/Dec 1982, pp. 2-6. Interview by John Boonstra

dccclxv Ibid.

dccclxvi DI 275-76. (DI 341: PKD on Le Guin comments: Letter, PKD to editor, Feb 20, 1981, published in *Science Fiction Review*, Summer 1981).

dccclxvii DI 276.

dccclxviii DI 277.(DI 341: Inadequate depiction of women: Letter, PKD to Russell Galen, June 29 1981).

dccclxix DI 277. PKD to Ursula Le Guin, May 13, 1981.

dccclxx Ken Lopez Bookseller, Online catalog May 1997. Lopez also had the following item: THE TRANSMIGRATION OF TIMOTHY ARCHER, Timescape, hb, 066-7, 1982 (1st). FINE. The uncorrected proof copy of the final book in the Valis trilogy. Fine in wrappers. $300.

dccclxxi *The Patchin Review*, No. 5, Oct/Dec 1982, pp. 2-6. Interview by John Boonstra

dccclxxii TDM 150 PKD interview with Charles Platt.

dccclxxiii In His Own Words, by Gregg Rickman, 9-30-81

dccclxxiv The example of Tim Powers pops into mind on this. His novels, as befitting a friend and student of PKD, effectively blur literary distinctions.

dccclxxv DI 279.

dccclxxvi THE TRANSMIGRATION OF TIMOTHY ARCHER, Timescape, pb, 46751, Apr 1983, p82.

dccclxxvii In *THE DEAD SEA SCROLLS: A New Translation*, by Michael Wise, Martin Abegg, Jr., & Edward Cook, Harper Collins, hb, 0-06-069200-6, 1996, the bibliography lists the following of Allegro's books:

Allegro, J. M. *The Treasure of the Copper Scroll*, London: Routledge and Kegan Paul, 1960.

■ -- *The Treasure of the Copper Scroll*, 2d. rev. ed. Garden City, NY: Doubleday, 1964.

■ -- "An Unpublished Fragment of Essene Halakah (4Q ordinances)." *Journal of Semitic Studies* 6 (1961): 71-73.

Of these the most likely to cross PKD's path is the Doubleday book of 1964. I have not found any of these books (though I didn't really look…)

dccclxxviii DI 283.

dccclxxix DI 286-87

1982

dccclxxx DI 288-89.

dccclxxxi THE TRANSMIGRATION OF TIMOTHY ARCHER, Timescape, hb, 44066-7, Apr 1982, 240pp, $15.50 (Powers) and THE TRANSMIGRATION OF TIMOTHY ARCHER, Gollancz, hb, 03220-0, Oct 1982, 254pp, L6.95 (?)

NOTES

dccclxxxii **SL-38 35:** {...}Tiresome as all this is, there's worse to come. I have ceased to write either s.f. or fantasy, Tony; I stopped writing short stuff for magazine publication back in May of '55; since then I've done only novels, both s.f. and what I call straight contemporary serious quality fiction about non-myth type people, and in the last year its been just the latter, the non-s.f. I have five of these novels in circulation (...){**PKD to A. Boucher, June 3, 1957**}

dccclxxxiii **SL:38 34:** Dear Bill: My agent Scott Meredith has relayed to me your request for a rewrite on my story RECALL MECHANISM.

The story is a good one, and I am proud of it. When a rewrite improves the story I'm glad to perform it. I welcome suggestions that help a story. In this case, however, the rewrite would turn a good yarn into a cornball nothing.

With great pride, and a sense of my responsibility to writers in general, to my own ethics, and to science-fiction readers, I refuse.

I have informed Scott, and I assume he'll be looking for the MS back.

Cordially, Philip K. Dick {**PKD to Bill Hamling, Editor** *Imagination*, **Sep 2, 1955**}

^{dccclxxxiv} **SL:38 ?:** Dear Mr. Boucher, I'm sorry to keep bothering you with phone call and letter, but I understand that Scott Meredith is going to write to you about "Explorers We" and I wanted to get hold of you first.

As you recall, late in September of last year you wrote to me, expressing an interest in that story, and suggesting

changes. I made changes and mailed them back within the week; during the first part of October. Since then I

haven't heard hide nor hair from you, but I understand that you are officially away, these days, so I have been happy

to wait. However, now I'm getting worried. Maybe there was a slip-up and you didn't receive my rewrite. Or

something.

In any case, if you want another rewrite, etc, etc. let me know and I will produce. It may be that the time travel angle didn't convince you, in which case I'm sure another resolution can be found. Okay? Thanks a lot ... and maybe we could get together one of these days, as both of us repeatedly suggest.

Very truly yours, Phil Dick {**PKD>Tony Boucher, Apr 8, 1954**}

PINK BEAM AFTERWORD

Looking back later on what I've written here I see that I have not completed what I set out to do, that is, provide an explanation for Philip K. Dick's "pink beam" experiences. What I have done instead is provide a context for understanding these events. Let's face it, my initial intention was overly ambitious: if Philip K. Dick himself could make little (or too much) sense of his own experiences, how could I, a stranger, working from incomplete and secondary material expect to explain it all? But I wrote here in the faith that if I could order what was known of PKD's literary work into a chronology then it would inevitably reveal avenues for further research. And this, I think, has happened. For the researcher into PKD's writing and it's place in modern literature there are many roads – too many perhaps – branching out from this present study. I would go so far as to say that it forms an essential hub, a foundation for any research into the life and work of Philip K. Dick. Any student of Dick's writing has read essays, treatises, articles, opinions, and on and on wherein it seems the writer doesn't know what he or she is talking about. They haven't done sufficient research. With this book I intended to at least proffer a basic text so that students of literature can better prepare themselves before committing their own thoughts to print.

I began writing this book in 2002. It took me a year to complete it. A year in which I retired to the mountains and lived in a small cabin with my brother. I refused to take a job or do any but casual work until I had got this done. I immersed myself in Philip K. Dick's writing and the writings about him. I lived on coffee and hand-rolled cigarettes, my fingers froze, my computer blew up, I got drunk much too often -- but I got the job done. Then I tried to find a publisher but even though I knew a lot about how Philip K. Dick came and continued to be published I had little clue about how to do it for myself. My attempts led me to the conclusion that Publishing in the United States is some sort of elitist process open only to the select few insiders; one has to know somebody or be rich or something, there's no room for the earnest amateur… So I set the manuscript aside and made only sporadic attempts to contact publishers. It wasn't until 2006 that my friend Mark Ivins – he did the great cover design for PINK BEAM -- took matters into his own hands and helped me get the manuscript online at lulu.com. This is a print-on-demand website where you can buy one or as many copies of your book as you want at any time. So this spurred me into rereading the manuscript and adding this Afterword and the appendices and index. I did not revise the text as such, a few minor corrections only, preferring to leave it as it is, a document from 2003.

So, then, can I wrap up this Afterword now? Or would I be remiss by not mentioning some of the areas worth looking into for a better understanding of Dick's work? Hmmm, I'm writing this three years later and although I occasionally read one of PKD's novels or some short stories, I'm no longer immersed in his work and life. It's a blur but I will write, inevitably incoherently, about some of the main 'themes' that remain in my memory and which have been prodded by my recent reading of this manuscript.

A main intent of PINK BEAM is to place the strange events of 1974 – 1975 into some context. I looked for the threads that wove through PKD's stories and comments to see if there were any with a continuous connection to Dick's "pink beam" experiences. There are many. Without going into it deeply here we can say that Dick's "pink beam" experiences did not come out of the blue, as it were. Ahem. We need only read his THE COSMIC PUPPETS and then VALIS to see the beginning and ending of a way-of-writing.

Remember, Philip K. Dick at the start of his career liked to write fantasies and he always wanted to write fantasies but market conditions and the lack of editorial response mostly squashed this ambition. But not entirely. Philip K. Dick was what they called a genre writer. He wrote science fiction and was constrained by the sf market to accord with the conventions of that market. Throughout his career PKD struggled to meld his fantastic urges into science fiction. "A Glass Of Darkness" (THE COSMIC PUPPETS) is straight fantasy and probably the only novel-length fantasy he had published. By the time of EYE IN THE SKY a few years later PKD shows his early method to overcome the split between fantasy and science fiction: he sets up a science fiction premise – the Bevatron accident – and then switches directly to fantasy.

We can follow this line through PKD's career. His first short story sale, "Roog", is a fantasy. And although his next few short stories are science fiction they have, as I've noted in the main text, fantastic results. "Beyond Lies The Wub", for example, has an sf premise – the space explorers – but turns pretty much to fantasy with the telepathic talking pig. But we note that this typifies PKD's early method of melding fantasy and science fiction together and as exemplified in EYE IN THE SKY. This early method reached its peak in the Doc Labyrinth stories from 1952 ("The Short, Happy Life Of The Brown Oxford" and "The Preserving Machine"). A facile science fiction premise then a jump into fantasy. "The Indefatigable Frog" is another example of this. Recall that PKD thought that he was into something good with this style, urging the prospect of a Doc Labyrinth series on the editors of *F & SF*. This met with a lukewarm response from the editors probably because the method was so crude: just zap an item with a strange ray and fantasies follow. It was a lame excuse for science fiction. Even EYE IN THE SKY, arguably the apex of this method, is only saved by its bravado.

But in between these early stories and EYE IN THE SKY (1955) Dick wrote "A Glass Of Darkness" (1953). Here there is no science-fictional setup, just an immediate step into a fantasy world. To me this novelette (and it's expansion into THE COSMIC PUPPETS (1957)) is an important one for an understanding of PKD's style. It's a long way from this story to VALIS but I can see the line clearly. Let's see if we can't briefly here walk that line.

Most of what PKD wrote was science fiction, every now and then he snuck a straight fantasy into the mix. Or a mainstream novel. In his early writing days Dick, when he wrote at novel length, wrote straight mainstream realist fiction (GATHER YOURSELVES TOGETHER, VOICES FROM THE STREET). He always wanted to be a serious mainstream writer. And, yes, he wanted to write fantasies and science fiction. This present volume is littered with details of the struggle he had trying to achieve all these goals. As I've just written, we can see an early method he used to meld his fantasies into science fiction. He used a similar method to meld his mainstream into his science fiction. TIME OUT OF JOINT (1958) is the first real attempt at this but note that in this novel the method is reversed: instead of a quick sf introduction and then switch to fantasy here we have a long mainstream introduction with a brief switch to sf at the end. Note too that TIME OUT OF JOINT was preceded by a long string of failed mainstream novels (failed in that they could not find a publisher) and was followed by a similar string. This was the dark days of PKD's career and it wasn't until 1961 and THE MAN IN THE HIGH CASTLE that he returned to his initial method of a brief sf introduction followed by a switch to another genre to write a successful novel. In this case, he combined his fantasy method with the way he wrote TIME OUT OF JOINT into a more sophisticated style that can be characterized as an unstated science fiction premise – the Allies lost World War 2 and the Axis won – followed by a realistic exposition.

With the success of THE MAN IN THE HIGH CASTLE Philip K. Dick was excited because he thought he'd found a new way of writing that would satisfy the readers and editors of science fiction and at the same time allow him full reign for his mainstream writing. But his next novel WE CAN BUILD YOU, which PKD saw as an advance on the method he used to write THE MAN IN THE HIGH CASTLE, took a different approach. Here the science fictional is mixed in with the realistic in a way that leaves the reader with no choice but to classify the novel as science fiction. He wasn't able to pull off the novel and it remains an awkward hybrid.

MARTIAN TIME SLIP, the manuscript of which reached the SMLA only one month after they got the ms for WE CAN BUILD YOU, is problematical. It's science fiction alright, but is it also mainstream? There is no obvious split, this is not a two-genre novel. Whatever it is MARTIAN TIME-SLIP is a good novel, even a great one, and deserves a fuller study in light of what I'm writing here. Perhaps it's a retreat into the safe haven of science fiction for PKD?

The novel that followed MARTIAN TIME-SLIP was DR. BLOODMONEY: Or How We Got Along After The Bomb. This reverts to the method PKD used in writing THE MAN IN THE HIGH CASTLE – a universal sf premise followed by mainstream exposition in a sf context.

With his career rejuvenated by the Hugo Award for THE MAN IN THE HIGH CASTLE, Philip K. Dick quickly wrote a series of science fiction short stories with a few novels mixed in (THE GAME-PLAYERS OF TITAN, THE SIMULACRA, NOW WAIT FOR LAST YEAR). It wasn't until 1964 and THE THREE STIGMATA OF PALMER ELDRITCH that he tried something new. But what was it?

If there was any stylistic change with PALMER ELDRITCH we know, at least, what sparked it: PKD's vision of a metallic, slot-eyed face in the sky above his walking path near Pt. Reyes Station, California. In PALMER ELDRITCH PKD recaps the technique that made EYE IN THE SKY such a success. He detaches the novel from reality itself in such a way that at the end the reader is left questioning What is Reality? This is something that PKD's stories have done all along, of course, but I think for the most part unconsciously. EYE IN THE SKY with its reduction of realities leaves the reader looking up from the book and staring at his own four walls and wondering if these also are some psychotic's imagination. But THE THREE STIGMATA OF PALMER ELDRITCH shakes one's foundations more pointedly. Not only are you perhaps in some psychotic's imagination but you're never gonna get out!

What this means to my gloss is that PKD attempted to cut loose from the conventions of the realistic novel. He uses science fiction to undermine consensus reality with the aim and result of undermining the literary conventions of realistic fiction. His struggle with categories had found an answer here in THREE STIGMATA. They would not yet be abolished only questioned and ignored.

It's interesting that THE THREE STIGMATA OF PALMER ELDRITCH was followed by THE PENULTIMATE TRUTH and "The Unteleported Man." These two tales tell of a sinister reality underlying that of the consensus and both are straight science fiction, a field in which Dick was comfortable writing. Thinking about it, it's as if PKD himself never really left the world of the THREE STIGMATA. I see this novel as a crossroads in PKD's career. He's unhinged himself from consensus reality and is left with nothing much to hold onto except the gloomy prognosis of the THREE STIGMATA. He turned to the dark side, seeing reality as an evil plot against mankind that, as had been indicated in the THREE STIGMATA, was opposed by the strength of the common man. In THE PENULTIMATE TRUTH and "The Unteleported

Man" he sees the evil imposed reality as somehow political. This line would find it's end with THE GANYMEDE TAKEOVER.

With the dismissal of reality accomplished by THREE STIGMATA Dick was free of stylistic worries and able to explore nasty possible alternatives to reality unconcerned with literary classification. THREE STIGMATA is the first novel wherein PKD grabbed reality and made it his own. One might even go so far as to say – it's a bit of a stretch – that henceforth from THREE STIGMATA OF PALMER ELDRITCH PKD would be *creating* reality. It took him a while to realize it, though, as he next studied reality from a solipsistic point of view with "Holy Quarrel" and turned to the problem of Time with "We Can Remember It For You Wholesale" and "Your Appointment Will Be Yesterday". These are interesting stories and continue PKD's thoughts on the nature of time from his beginning. The most ambitious of these mid-Sixties stories was COUNTER-CLOCK WORLD. With this story time goes backwards and, I think, too, PKD's progressive understanding of reality.

Soon he was writing of another nasty possible reality in which a drug-saturated population is kept from the truth. This was "Faith Of Our Fathers", and is a direct descendent of THE THREE STIGMATA OF PALMER ELDRITCH. One thing about Philip K. Dick, when he decided that consensus reality had no more meaning than anything he could make up, he really went to town. One can see him almost, writing merrily away, making it up as he goes along, creating reality with the best of them. It's quite an amazing feat to write this way free of any restraints. Most of us write within the consensus reality, we don't even think about it we just do it naturally. It hasn't occurred to us that we are proscribed by this unconscious acceptance, limited in what we can say by the hidden conventions of the common reality, or *koinos kosmos* as PKD would call it. But after THREE STIGMATA we can see PKD slowly distrusting the common world and looking for its faults and, basically, providing answers to the question Why is Reality so bad? These answers usually exposed something worse than the *koinos kosmos* and the *koinos kosmos* was in place to occlude us to the harsher reality below Reality.

DO ANDROIDS DREAM OF ELECTRIC SHEEP? and UBIK, his major novels of 1966, fit my notions in different ways. ANDROIDS on the surface of it is a realization of one of PKD's gloomy realities. One tries to hold on to truth and beauty, fooling oneself into belief that religion or possessions somehow contain the essence of these concepts. The novel holds metaphysics to the dim light of a bad reality and finds it to be a fraud and it posits the notion that where we can find no truth or beauty in the real then we must find it in the fake even knowing that the fake is fake. Here PKD begins his adventures into the meaning of a 'fake fake.'

UBIK, on the other pseudopodium, presents a reality where time itself is the enemy. Stylistically these two novels deepen PKD's grasp of reality by removing more layers that cover up its bones, so to speak. In UBIK, as in THE UNTELEPORTED MAN, he introduces cut-and-paste techniques as he questions the reality of the written page, the very meaning of linear narration itself. Another attraction of UBIK to the literary student is that with UBIK Philip K. Dick is saying that, well, if reality itself has no foundation then literary categories are also bunk. So UBIK is a sly novel that attacks literary conventions by undermining our understanding of reality itself with the purpose of making his fiction acceptable as 'mainstream'! Which is an amusing idea. It's as if Dick is reminding us of something we all know but have forgotten: reality is a convention and conventions are based only on agreements amongst ourselves. Further ramifications of this process obscure the fact that this is what we do. We forget we're doing it and take our conventions as reality. Conventions, categories, it's the same thing. PKD in UBIK merely states that the category of Science Fiction is equivalent to the category of Mainstream. A novel we've skipped over, CLANS OF THE ALPHANE MOON, is a blatant example of this challenge with its attack on the category of 'Psychology.'

After UBIK Dick wrote mostly science fiction. A MAZE OF DEATH looks at Time again, positing reality as, again, based on a real time that is occluded by us because the real time is too awful to contemplate. We can see that all through his writing career PKD was bothered by the nature of time. He saw linear time as a component of a trans-dimensional whole that included his notion of orthogonal time – a time dimension at right angles to linear time – as part of that whole. It's a difficult thing to visualize. I sometimes try to look at time from PKD's perspective and visualize a fuzzy cube made up of a pile of blankets each being woven on a loom. Linear time is the continuous thread going back and forth that constructs the blankets as it progresses. The cube itself cannot be seen by us as we cannot transcend our own blanket of linear time.

But I think PKD enjoyed bouncing up and down on these blankets of time within the cube, landing in a different spot each time to pick up once again the linear track. FLOW MY TEARS, THE POLICEMAN SAID is an example of this. The novel begins on an initial bounce of the protagonist having just landed in a reality where he doesn't exist. Later other bounces occur.

This is similar to what happened to Mr. Tagomi in THE MAN IN THE HIGH CASTLE when he sat gazing at the piece of jewelry.

A couple of short-stories can be read in this regard: "The Electric Ant" and "A Little Something For Us Tempunauts."

Which brings us to A SCANNER DARKLY.

By the time of this novel Philip K. Dick was a master of the changes; he'd internalized all this reality business and after making his point with FLOW MY TEARS, THE POLICEMAN SAID he simply sat down and wrote a mainstream masterpiece. Sure, it's passed off as science fiction but A SCANNER DARKLY is also, and as stated by PKD, a mainstream novel. He argued with Judy-Lynn Del Rey about this very thing. But I think that what he learned from Judy-Lynn Del Rey – and as he acknowledges – is that to write a good mainstream novel you have to know how to create good mainstream characters. The cartoon-cutouts of genre sf just won't do anymore. It's a long way from GATHER YOURSELVES TOGETHER to A SCANNER DARKLY. One wishes to say more about this novel. It's a creature of its time as is the somewhat similar RADIO FREE ALBEMUTH. Literary considerations aside I see it as a political novel. I remember how it was back in the Sixties, there was a war going on not only in Vietnam but also in the streets of America. All of us who opposed back then Richard Nixon and all he stood for were fighting in this war. Some died. Philip K. Dick wrote about it in A SCANNER DARKLY.

RADIO FREE ALBEMUTH, also, was a weapon in this war as well as a forerunner of VALIS. I think its funny that in response to a question about RADIO FREE ALBEMUTH Dick describes a straightforward novel of political intrigue, assassinations, shenanigans in high places, unrest and overthrow but when the questioner follows up with, "Is it science fiction?" Dick replies Of course! The people who overthrow the tyrant are selected by an extraterrestrial alien satellite! Doesn't this show PKD's grasp of the whole categorical thing?

And what do we have with VALIS? Is it RADIO FREE ALBEMUTH with an added dimension of the transreal? We've got Pink Beams, alien satellites, an oppressive political regime that is now reified into a religious archetype and all kinds of things. It's fun to read but… is PKD serious? Does he *believe* all this? Let's look at it in light of what I've developed here so far.

Philip K. Dick had just written a mainstream masterpiece: A SCANNER DARKLY. He must now write a science fiction masterpiece because if even something vaguely like my thesis is true then PKD knew what he was doing by the time he came to write VALIS. Given that, then his purpose with VALIS was to create a worthwhile alternative to mainstream reality that was *more real than reality itself.* By this I mean that he points out to the arbiters of Literature that the standard by which they judge value are based on a premise that is insufficiently inclusionary. The thing with VALIS that caught everyone's attention was that it took our consensual world and extended it into orthogonal time, though, of course, few people realized it at the time. He gave us a portrayal of reality that was larger than life, indeed one that *included* life.

VALIS and THE DIVINE INVASION are novels that challenge our notions of conventional reality. Whether Philip K. Dick truly experienced the 'pink beam' events of 1974-75 is of interest to those of us who hope for some revelatory writing from this Master who has given us such outstanding sceince fiction stories all along, but to one who is interested in how he challenged and changed literary conventions it's all irrelevant. What matters are the novels that came from his experiences – and how he prepared VALIS, in particular, to shock the literary establishment.

Let's look at how this was done.

Philip K. Dick experienced strange events in 1974-75. To his friends and other writers he was not shy in describing what happened to him and he spent much of the rest of his life in trying to understand these events. And he wrote a novel, VALIS, that included these events as an integral part of the plot.

The publication of VALIS caused quite a stir in the science fiction field. Many of his fans, friends and fellow writers thought that Dick had either gone mad, seen God, or was tweaking the sf field in a self-destructive way. But, even though all three of these things may be true, as far as the definition of the novel itself is concerned he blurred all distinctions between the genres of Fantasy, Science Fiction and Mainstream. It is my contention that he did this on purpose. As I've already indicated above, Dick over his writing career had trouble according to these classifications – he wanted to write them all, and did. And with VALIS he finally did what he nebulously intended from the start: write a novel that defied literary boundaries and forced the publishers, readers and critics to accept the fact that henceforth these distinctions did not apply to a serious modern writer.

To accomplish this PKD, as I've indicated, had to establish a reality that was more inclusive than what was conventionally accepted as such. He had to do this to have the novel VALIS accepted as a masterpiece of *Mainstream* fiction. By his openness about his Pink Beam experiences, followed by the novel and subsequent speculation amongst his readers as to the meaning of it all, PKD thrust his apprehension of Reality into the discussion of modern literature. Critics in the science fiction genre may well have granted VALIS status as a sf masterpiece but for PKD that wasn't enough. He wanted VALIS to be seen as a mainstream masterpiece too. By all this blurring of categories, the sense of expanded reality, his speculations on the Pink Beam events outside of the novel, Dick did indeed accomplish his goal.

Mainstream, Science Fiction, Fantasy? After VALIS they become one and the same thing. PKD had spent too long fighting these categorical wars and was done with it all by the time he wrote VALIS and THE DIVINE INVASION. He wrote what he wanted to write and by so doing dissolved any idea of categorical genres other than the simplest into one single category: fiction. One might even go so far as to say that he turned the categories on their head relegating mainstream fiction to a genre enclosed in the larger genre of Science Fiction. One thing for sure, though, these facile literary distinctions are shown by Dick to be no more than the left-over ideas of a Publishing juggernaut that at one time decided on categorization to better sell its products. Dick showed that marketing strategies do not define literature. And with VALIS he demolished this hidebound way of thinking and operating. Henceforth, from the date of its publication, VALIS marked the beginning of a literary movement known as Post-modernism, a movement distinguished by the very characteristics of VALIS: categorical blurring, equating of fantasy, science fiction and mainstream into a larger defintion of literature, and subversion of comventional reality itself.

As to the question of whether Philip K. Dick himself believed any of what he wrote in VALIS that is for others to decide, here I can only say that he believed in what he wrote, he knew what he was doing and, most importantly as a writer, he wanted us, his readers to believe it!

And with that I'll end this Afterword. Thanks for your patience in reading all this.

Dave Hyde (Lord RC) December 2006.

Printed in Great Britain
by Amazon